Henri

Henri

Dave Delony

To order additional copies of this book, contact:
Xlibris Corporation
1-888-795-4274
www.Xlibris.com
Orders@Xlibris.com
50270

Contents

Dedication

This book is dedicated to the Henris of this world, of past worlds, and of fact and fiction. One cannot fathom or surmise their sacrifices, contributions, and loyalties to their leaders and countries. This is also dedicated to the loves of their lives.

They alone know who they may be.

Author's Note

During genealogical research into family history, it was discovered that my fifth-generation grandfather, a professional soldier, had served in the Grande Armée of France with Napoleon. From all accounts, he was a child of peasant farmers and rose through the ranks to officer. The story, a careful mix of fiction and historical fact, is what one might imagine occurred in the era.

An epoch love story, it follows the loves of Henri Devreney—his loves of life, adventure, knowledge, country, military, and, above all, the true love of his life. What began as a hobby has developed into a story of the age and wars of Napoleon. It is my hope that you will enjoy the journey.

Special Thanks

A very special *merci* is due Glenda Cain Behm for her professional editing, diligence to detail, and the multitude of headaches, keeping the author on the straight and narrow. Glenda, a high school classmate and a friend of many years, has made a contribution to this work that is without equal. Another special merci is offered to Don Behm, Glenda's husband, for the professional and enhancing artwork. Finally and certainly not least, *merci beaucoup* to my wife and family for the support, patience through hours of writing, honest criticism, and ideas offered during the time of research and creation of Henri.

Prologue

Henri lay quiet and motionless, segmenting the sights, sounds, and scents of the early dawn. He had been awake for some time now, and as realized many years ago, he had required less sleep as he aged. The eastern sky was filling with a soft-glowing rose color accented with wisps of clouds. A lovely sight so familiar to his old eyes. A new day. Another in a life, which now had spanned some ninety-eight years. As much as he loved the sights and sounds, perhaps he loved the exuding odors even more. The damp musky odor of the earth warming to an inevitable sun brought forth the other scents of the plants and flowers in the beds surrounding the house. The magnolia blossoms, jasmine, zinnias, roses, the old herb plot, and the grasses and weeds of the surrounding yards and fields permeated odors and fragrances that were individual and unique and yet, when combined, were an entirely different almost-overwhelming aroma. Probably his favorite fragrance wouldn't be present until late afternoon. The four-o'clocks would be blooming under the windows, and he would savor the sweet fragrances until he drifted into a fitful and uneasy sleep.

As the darkness and shadows slowly surrendered to light, Henri observed the first awakenings of life in his immediate world. Several sparrows, with nests in the magnolia tree, were flitting and hopping around in the grass surrounding the tree, hunting in efforts to satisfy hungry cheeping mouths. One could barely see the yellow beaks on scrawny necks protruding over the edge of the nests. Blue jays and mockingbirds were squawking and jumping from branch to branch to search for food or just to annoy each other. Squirrels in the huge old pecan tree were making their presence known by chasing one another around and around the main trunk and into the smaller branches. He could hear the nervous chatter and tiny paws tearing at the bark as they raced. The cooing of doves sitting on top of the outhouse added to the prattle, and as if not to be left out, the shrill calls of the bobwhites came from the field behind the barn. A hapless crow ventured too near and was immediately assailed by the mockingbirds, whose loud squawking was certain to awaken the rest of life in the general area.

Henri's bed had been moved from the small converted downstairs bedroom at the rear of the house to the much larger dining room. It was probably his favorite room in the entire house other than the upstairs bedroom shared for many years with his wife. The entire upstairs was devoid of life now, and the furniture was covered with protective cloths. It had been several years since anyone had even been up there except to quickly check the windows and to confirm there were no leaks in the roof. This dining room, adjacent kitchen, and living room had always been so full of life with the chatter and noise of children and the many activities of household life. He could almost close his eyes and hear the sounds again. These rooms had been the center of their family life and held many precious memories. He had requested the move, mainly because the bedroom that had been converted was too small, too lonely, and did not afford the views as did the dining room and living room windows. All he could see from the small bedroom windows were the fields, the outhouse, and the now-empty chicken-and-duck yard, barn, and sheds. It often made him sad to look out on the emptiness where once life had been so prevalent. He could almost feel the presence of his wife and children as they went about the thousand and one routines of chores and play that had gone on here for what seemed like eons. Oh *oui*, the dining room was much better.

The last window in the dining room just next to the door leading to the kitchen had been Henri and his wife's, Angelette, special window. Hundreds, nay, probably thousands of evenings had been spent there, watching the sunset, sharing news, or just chattering idly. It was often mentioned that a special window had always been in their lives. Many fond and vivid memories of the bedroom window in Paris so many years ago were brought to mind. The sharing was so precious to both. This was a part of their very personal and private world. A world that only they could know and cherish.

From the large French doors leading to the living room, he could see down the street almost to Swakart's large mercantile store, the livery stable, and Matt's blacksmith shop. At least here he could pass the day with ongoing life. He loved to watch people, wagons, horses, and events of a busy street scene in between fitful naps.

He felt an urge to relieve himself and fumbled for the small gray granite pot on the table at his bedside. *Mon dieu*, he was glad his other function was still not calling. His granddaughter, Ginny, who lived two houses away, would always fuss in her sweet, caring way when he used the little pot for such. He was always very kindly reminded that he was supposed to wait for her to help him to the larger slop jar in the bath closet. Sometimes, however, he just could not wait; and yes, sometimes he would do it just to make her fuss. Even at his very tender age of ninety-eight, he was not about to lose his keen sense of humor, a trait for which he had been noted in his much younger years. Ninety-eight short years and a lifetime like no other. He had seen and done so much in the short years before this year of the Lord 1893. Who would ever have believed he would be on this earth this long. Ginny would soon be here after getting her family off to work and school. Her nickname of Ginny was often confused as short for Jennifer, but in reality, her name was Ginger. Why her mother had named her Ginger, heaven only knew. But Ginger certainly did fit her sweet and loving personality.

Ah! The welcome relief of his bladder emptying. Careful not to spill any of the smelly stuff, he replaced the pot on the table. Sometime back, he had been careless or just plain clumsy and spilled some on his bed. His vain efforts at cleaning had only made matters worse. Times like those were so frustrating for a man who had been so self-sufficient all of his life. He had never had to depend on anyone for his personal matters, not even his wife and love of his life, who would have been only too willing to do whatever may have been required.

As the light of the dawning day increased, he could see his image becoming more vivid in the large oval mirror over the buffet. A total stranger stared back at him out of the mirror. The old man framed in the mirror continued to stare at him with pale brown eyes. He could see a weathered, deeply lined face, sparse white hair, and, as he had teased his daughters, ears that stuck out like buggy hubs. The most predominate feature, however, was a stark white mark under the nose where only a few days ago had been a mustache. The old man in the mirror had worn that proud symbol of his masculinity for most of his adult life. It had been shaved off once before when a horse had kicked him in the face and mouth. He had lost a tooth and split his lip, and his loving had suffered for a month or so, but the mustache had grown back to its original splendor. He had reluctantly agreed to let Ginny help shave it off a few days ago, but only on a trial basis. His great-granddaughter, Kayla, whom he absolutely worshipped, had refused to give Pepaw his usual hug and kiss because she saw boogers in Pepaw's mustache. Ginny had agreed that maybe it should come off to make him more comfortable with his being in the bed so much and with the hot, dry Texas summer at its full zenith. He argued that no one coming to his funeral would recognize the stranger in the box, but he knew she was right. His nose did leak frequently these days, and he would give it a try. He could always grow it back. But oh, hell, everything else had gone from him, so why not the damn mustache too?

The stranger in the mirror continued staring at him for a long time. Merde! This could not be the once-trim, active, and full-of-life person in the mirror. Ah! Perhaps God will call for him today and end this trouble for everyone and especially the stranger in the mirror. He wondered what it would be like to pass from this life as so many he had known had done. Would those whom he had loved and befriended be there waiting for him as he had heard in old tales? Ha, there were some he had known that he hoped would not be waiting. This might indicate a journey he may not want. He would know soon enough.

As the light increased, he could see an array of framed documents and adornments neatly hung in rows on the wall. His son-in-law, Samuel, Ginny's husband, had moved them from the upstairs study when he was moved here. The testimonials to his life. It seemed these were all that was left of a legacy equal to few others. There was his graduation diploma from Saint-Cyr, the famous military academy of France; Officer's Commission; citations; and various awards of battles and campaigns all signed by Napoleon Bonaparte. There were several medals awarded for bravery and, in particular, one earned as just a young drummer. Baby Tiger indeed. Perhaps among his most proud and recent was his official commission to the Texas Rangers and the discharge from the Texas Army of 1836 signed by Sam Houston himself.

The hot Texas sun was rising higher now and, as he had teasingly told his wife in years past, appeared to be rising up out of the outhouse. Later in the year, the sun would seem to rise out of the barn, then the chicken coops, and so on as the year progressed. Just another of the many private and very personal things they had shared over a lifetime. Another hot, dry, dusty day was evidently due, and another boring one as well. There was nothing to do but laze here, watch the ever-repetitive street scene, and an occasional doze.

Boredom led to daydreams and reflections on a life more full than most men can even dream of. The daydreams and reflections were more often of the good things rather than stewing about what should have been. Hell, whatever will be, will be. Worrying gave one stomach pains, loss of hair, and God only knows what other ailments. Worrying was not one of his traits anyway, and he had often been accused of being too blasé about things. Blasé, no, but not to worry either. He cared in his own way, deep inside. He could never remember crying as a man or giving way to what he considered unmasculine things. That was a lot of the trouble now with him being so dependent on others. Ginny told him repeatedly and laughing that he was probably the worst patient in the whole world. Worry, ha! *Si jeunesse savait, si vieillesse pouvait*; if youth only knew, if age only could.

Besides, he had never had to worry that much with his Angelette, or Ange, as her short name was, he often told her, worried enough for both of them. His wife, his precious wife, his Angelette. Her name had the meaning of "little angel" in their native French, and she certainly had been the angel in his life. He thought of her often these days. She had passed on sometime ago. He couldn't remember the date exactly, but he did recall the pain and the terrible emptiness that haunted him still. This emptiness was not like the times he had left home for war, business, with the Rangers, and such. This emptiness was complete and total.

He always knew that Ange would be there on his return, fussing about the house, tending the children, and the million and one things wives do in managing the affairs of a household. The hollow emptiness was with him and would be until he too passed on and would be with Ange forever as they had promised many years ago.

He felt his finger for the small gold wedding band ring Ange had given him so long, long ago. Yes, it was still there; and it had been his request that it never leave his finger, not even at his passing. There on his pinkie finger next to his "Ange" ring was another small gold ring that had been moved from finger to finger as he had grown. It had rarely left his hand since he was a small boy. That small ring with the nearly worn off crest was to be passed on to his great-grandson along with the stories that went with it. As the ancients often do, Henri began to reflect on his memories, his precious, beautiful, and wondrous memories. All that he had left in this world. The recollections brought forth to mind another hot, dry, and dusty day so long ago, so very, very long ago.

1

The Boy

"Henri, Henri, please come sit with me. I do need for us to talk," his mother, Helene, called in a weak and urgent voice.

"I am coming, Mère. What is wrong? You sound so different today."

"Oui, possibly I do, my son, I am very weak today and fear we must talk soon. There is much I need for you to know. I know this is a burdensome thing because you are so young, but I must speak to you of these things."

Henri sat in the chair next to his mother's bed. Thus began the rapid events in his young life that he would never forget.

The ninety-eight-year-old Henri's thoughts drifted back to a time when a small boy sat next to his mother's bed that hot, dry, and dusty morning in a rural French village, trying to comprehend what was happening to his world. Some of the events of that time were distant, and he had to think deeply to recall them to place them in proper perspective. Others were so very vivid as if all happened only yesterday. *Yesterday*, he thought. Yesterday, today, tomorrow. Words, only words, but words of a lifetime. Words like pages of a book of history or a gypsy fortune-teller's glass ball. How did his thoughts really begin? Too much, too much, too much.

He remembered his mother, Helene, speaking to him, trying to convey her love, and adding apologies for the illness that kept her from being the mother that she so wanted to be. She was a small, frail, and delicate woman now who had grown ever so much more withered in recent months. Her hair was still the natural light brown, and her face retained the features of her youthful beauty. Her large hazel eyes were still bright and alert, yet at times reflecting the twinges of pain she constantly felt these days. Looking at her now, Henri could not envision such a frail body replacing the one that he remembered just a short time ago. She was the robust one who danced so gracefully at the harvest festival, the one that moved about the house and garden with such vigor and determination, constantly moving, seemingly never to stop. Helene moaned ever so slightly, trying to hide the pain and explain more to Henri.

"Mère, what is wrong? Why can't you get up with me?" asked Henri.

"Oh, my child, I do not know really what it is. The village midwife tells me I have a malady of something. She does not know what it is. I only know the pain seems to get worse every day. It is my every wish that I could get up and be with you. I will get better. You shall see. Then we can do things together once more."

The midwife had thought, perhaps, her blood may have been tainted and had bled her often. All efforts seemed to no avail as she grew weaker and weaker until finally she realized the truth. She accepted her fate as those with little hope often do, but she felt a great sadness for Henri. She felt that she had failed him by departing this world so suddenly with Henri so young. What would he do? Where would he go? How would he fend for himself? They would have to rely on relations for help, but most of these poor peasant village people lived in poverty just as they. The landowner of the farmland would be certain to take the farm and all stock at her passing, leaving Henri and Marcel, Henri's uncle and his father's brother, without livelihood. She must prepare Henri and the family for whatever may lie ahead.

It was a cruel life in rural France these days. The revolution and ensuing rise of Napoleon and his wars had taken so many men and boys for the military. Henri's own father had been taken for the military. His mother had told him the stories over and over, but he never tired of them. As if to change the subject of his immediate future, which he did not really understand, he mentioned his father. His mother loved to recant the stories of his father and their lives in the days they were all together. Her mood immediately changed as she began, once again, to tell Henri the stories. Henri did remember his father, but only as a distant shadowy figure. During storytelling sessions, Henri could almost replace himself with his father. As little men-children often do, he loved the thought of adventure and could almost be immersed in the faraway places and battles.

Arsene had left when Henri was barely four years old, but the repeated stories had created memories of a father he had never actually known. The visions were firmly implanted in Henri's mind. As she spoke, he could picture the figure his mother described.

They were both from this same farming village and planned to stay here forever. It was the only life they had ever known. The stories related to the good times of their courtship, marriage, and her capturing the heart of the most handsome man in the area. The stories of the festivals, events at the church, fishing trips, hard work in the fields, and about relatives and friends captivated Henri. Arsene was a man of medium height and muscular stature with wavy dark hair and bright dark eyes. He had a very pleasant nature and an acute sense of humor. He was always ready for a prank or joke and remembered as a very loving and caring husband and father. A very hardworking man of peasant farm class, he had lived for his farm and family.

She began to wince more with the pain and could not seem to go on, but she asked him to lean closer. She asked, "Henri, take the small gold ring with the pretty little crest from my finger and place it on yours. This ring had belonged to your father and his father. It is now yours. Promise never to lose it or remove it from your finger unless necessary." He promised, leaned over, and kissed her cheek to seal the vow. She seemed to grow a little better at that and started a story again. She fumbled with her frail hand for Henri's as she spoke in a soft and raspy voice.

On the one day in 1799 his mother would never forget, and could never forgive or understand, a group of military men came to the village square and announced that all men and boys over the age of twelve must report at once. If they were found to be fit physically, could at least conduct themselves with some logic, and could not present proper reasons for not serving in the Armée, they were to be conscripted immediately. All of this in the name of loyalty to the new empire and order, political things most in the village knew nothing about and couldn't care less.

One dared not refuse, for disloyalty often brought disastrous consequences for the man and his family. Rumors of entire families vanishing were often heard. Arsene Devreney had been chosen along with fifteen other men and boys of the village and surrounding area. With a heavy and sorrowful heart, Henri's father kissed his wife and small son goodbye. The group ambled off down the road to the training camps under the guard of the military men. Henri barely remembered the shouting and cursing of the military men in charge of the group and the fear and confusion showing in the eyes of those leaving. Several of the boys cried openly but were shouted down or whipped into submission by the military men. They were told that a two-year period in the Armée would be required. Henri's father had no idea what a two-year period was and only related time to the rising and setting of the sun and the seasons of the year.

Arsene and several others from the village came home for a very brief period after his training of two months in nearby Blois. The men had been trained and given uniforms at regional camps before sending them to the main Armée near Paris. His father was indeed most handsome in his uniform of the Grande Armée of France, shiny black boots, and his new musket and bayonet. He took Henri and Marcel in the fields behind the house and showed them how he had been taught to fire the musket. Henri would never forget the roar, smoke, and sparks as the gun fired and the small tree breaking when struck by the ball. And all in a time before Henri could even blink an eye. Arsene told Helene during his brief stay that their lives would now change forever. He would do things that he never had dreamed of. But all to end in the time when he would be released, and he could return home to his love and farm. They made passionate love the night before his leaving. Helene knew by her every female instinct that she would be with child at this union.

In the very brief time before his father's departure to Paris, he had charged his brother Marcel with the care of his family and farm duties. Henri's mother, even though a strong and determined woman, could not handle the heavy farm chores of plowing and tending the stock plus the household cooking, baking, and cleaning as well. Marcel might have been chosen for the Armée also, but for a crippled leg that had been badly broken when a hay cart had turned over on it. Henri's family had cared for Marcel during the bad times of his recovery, and Marcel was forever attempting to show his gratitude. This was to be his big chance in life, to care for the family he never had and probably never would. Truthfully, everyone knew that Marcel would not be of much help other than to just have a man around the place for emergencies. Henri's mother would have to treat Marcel as she would a child and constantly follow up on her instructions. However, all felt that the crisis would soon pass, and Henri's father would soon return in two years, however long that was.

Marcel was a slovenly individual who used his lame leg to his advantage at every opportunity. He had long matted hair, rarely bathed, and as Henri's father was heard to say, one could tell what Marcel had had to eat last week by the remains on his clothing. His large beak of a nose and a constant tic of his left eye further worsened any remote chance Marcel may have had at courtship. The local girls of eligible age refused to have anything to do with him and regarded him as the village outcast as far as romance was concerned. Marcel resigned himself to a permanent bachelor life and actually preferred being alone and not having to bother with the responsibility of a permanent family or nagging woman. This temporary family arrangement would do just fine. He could almost be head of a family and not have any of the problems and responsibilities. It soon became evident to Henri that Marcel would try to put most of the work on him. He began with just the suggestions that Henri do this chore or that chore. Then the suggestions became orders and warnings not to tell Helene or there would be hell to pay. A few slaps across the face, and Henri knew if he was to get along, he had better do as he was told. He talked back to Marcel one day and was hit with the end of a hoe handle on the leg. Henri jumped back crying and told Marcel if he ever hurt him again, he had better stay awake all night because he would get him. This frightened Marcel, and he knew he had gone too far this time. The boy really meant this. He would need to be more cautious in the future.

Henri's aunt, or Mags as she was affectionately known, was his father's only sister and a nun in the convent at Orléans, nearer to Paris than their home village. The city was much nicer than this small, dirty, dusty, and smelly village, she often bragged to whoever would listen. She had been so homely that suitors had been extremely rare, and her contrary nature had discouraged the one or two that had happened by. Mags had finally left for the convent to make her own way in the world and not further burden her already poor peasant family. Even though Mags was considered the family busybody and grouch, she adored Henri and spoiled him as if he were the child she had always desired.

Henri loved his aunt Mags but did hate it when she gave him hugs and nearly smothered him in her enormous bosom. Her forever-foul breath and scratchy starched nun's habit made the ordeal even more trying. He would often hide in the barn or behind the chicken-and-duck pen when she came for visits and only appear for short "ordeals" and, hopefully, run out again, giving any number of excuses to avoid further smothering.

One of Henri's most vivid memories of his early family life was a trip to the market at Blois. The family farm was on a small stream that flowed into the much larger river Loire. The small village that was the center of their local world was about a half day's journey to the nearest larger city of the region. Blois was an ancient city with huge buildings and castles. Henri had only been there once with his father, mother, and several other villagers to deliver sheep, goats, and other things to the large market. They had to leave very early in the morning and travel steadily during the day to arrive in the early afternoon. Henri and the other small children had the good fortune to ride the goats, but his parents and other people in the small group walked. They camped for the night under trees on the banks of the largest river Henri had ever seen.

His father said, "This is the Loire that has very good fishing, but there will not be time for such pleasures on this journey. Besides, the small stream near the farm yielded some very good fish." And it was always a great adventure to accompany his father there on fishing trips. On the high hill was a very large castle called a château. His father continued, "The ruler of the region, a very rich and powerful man, lives there."

The next morning, they entered the main city and slowly made their way to the market. There were more people than Henri had ever seen before. His mother warned, "Henri, stay close or you will get lost forever and fed to the rich man's dogs." That did it! Henri clung to his mother's skirts the remainder of the day and didn't let the group out of his sight. He marveled at the huge buildings, enormous church, throngs of people, cobblestone streets, and interesting array of shops and things for sale or barter in the huge central market. The group conducted their business early and made their way to the road out of Blois and back to their village. No goats or sheep to ride this time, and they arrived totally exhausted. Henri had ridden the last miles on his father's back sound asleep. He did not even remember being flopped into his bed.

Several months after Arsene's departure, it was evident that Helene was pregnant. She was elated and knew Arsene would be too. She took Henri aside one evening and explained that he was going to have a little brother or sister.

This was a gift from God, Helene explained, and the love of the parents had spilled over into a child. This was all he needed to know at this point. He was satisfied as she held his hand to her stomach to see if he could feel any movement. A month later, he could feel slight movement and was surprised. He had seen some of the stock having babies but never dreamed that fathers and mothers could be involved that way.

Near Christmas 1801, one of the returning villagers from the Armée brought word that Henri's father had been killed in battle. He had died along with hundreds of others in a foreboding place called the Black Forest in Austria. The returning villager said he was one of the lucky ones, only losing an arm in the battles. Henri's mother was devastated and cried uncontrollably for days. The weather was cold and misty, and she just could not seem to keep warm even under several layers of blankets and close to the fire. She had little appetite and slowly grew weaker and weaker. Henri was sent running for the village midwife one day. Henri was told later that his baby brother or sister had gone to heaven. The only will for her to live now was Henri, but no one could console or comfort her for the loss of her husband and infant child. She just existed during the months ahead until she just could not seem to go on any longer. Even though she appeared to get better during the spring and early summer months, still, something was wrong. Her winter months had been spent nearly entirely in bed. Now in the better weather, she could not seem to get back to normal no matter how she tried. She still told many stories to Henri; but now they were filled with bitterness and distrust of the military, Armée, and France in general for the ruination of her life. Marcel and Henri were doing the major work in the house and fields. Marcel had complete control now and watched as Henri did most of the chores. A few repairs to the house and barn and some of the spring planting and gardens were accomplished with the help of neighbors and relatives. During later spring and as summer approached, Helene grew much worse. Her will to live had been destroyed. Now Henri too could blame the Armée for their problems. He didn't know much about it, but his mother hated it, and so should he.

After she had the final talk with Henri, Helene passed on to join the saints, Arsene, and her unborn child a few days later. Women from the village came to the farm and took his mother for burial in the cemetery alongside the small church. The old priest uttered a few brief words, and his mother was buried in a large hole and covered with dirt. No casket or wooden box, just simply wrapped and bound in blankets from her bed. A few relatives of both Arsene and Helene were there. Helene's mother wanted Henri to come home with them, but he would have to sleep in the barn. All of the relatives were so overcrowded in their tiny shanties. Henri decided to stay with Marcel for the time being and warned Marcel to leave him alone. The slovenly Marcel knew better than to confront Henri now. There would not be anyone to stop Henri. Henri could not fully comprehend much of what had happened and realized only that his mother was gone as was his father. A plain wooden marker, with her name and dates of her birth and death, was the only sign of her passing. Henri only knew the loneliness and cried himself to sleep many nights. Marcel was no help at all in his loss and only thought of what might happen to him now that Arsene and Helene were gone. *What could he do?*

This was the early summer of 1803; and Henri, now an orphan, was nearing his eighth birthday. Aunt Mags arrived within the week and told Marcel that she had received permission for Henri to stay with her at the convent in Orléans until something permanent could be worked out. She arrived in a carriage from the convent, hastily gathered Henri's few clothes and items, and put them in an old leather bag. Marcel stuck out one grimy hand to Henri and wished him Godspeed. Henri never saw Marcel again and would wonder what had happened to him in years to come.

"Henri, do you understand what I am trying to tell you?" asked Aunt Mags. "This part of your life will possibly be gone forever. With the grace of a merciful and just god, you must go forward with courage. Always believe in yourself. Try to remember these times and your family, my young son. Those memories will be with you forever. But do not dwell on these memories, for certain unpleasant memories could be your undoing. Remember the happy times and love that you have been given."

They continued to talk as the carriage lumbered on. Try as he may, he could never fully comprehend what Aunt Mags was trying to tell him. That would come much later in his life. Tired and very frightened, he soon fell asleep snuggled in the safety of Aunt Mags's lap. They arrived at the convent early the next morning. It was still dark on arrival, and he remembered always approaching the high walls and turret of the convent. It was frightening in the very early morning darkness with the sliver of a moon hanging over the scene like a scythe.

After he awoke and had a meal of mush and tea, he was introduced to the other nuns and to Mother Superior, Sister Catherine, head of the order here. She was a slim, frail, slightly stooped, and kindly person but let him know firmly at this first meeting that his stay here must be completely trouble free. He would be assigned duties in the gardens and kitchen, and he must attend vigil prayers with the others of the convent. Aunt Mags taught him prayers and started him in reading and counting. Life in the convent was one of mostly serenity and quiet. There was a sense of peaceful safety here away from harm and the cruel world outside these walls. It was totally different than his first impression in the darkness.

The convent was very large and old, and Mother Superior told Henri he could explore as long as he didn't go into certain forbidden areas and not cause problems. The nuns and others here were not used to children and especially inquisitive young boys. Those areas forbidden were either marked or locked.

The walls were very high, and one could walk completely around the convent on the upper reaches. The huge wooden gates were locked at all times, and visitors had to ring a bell to announce their presence in order to gain permission to enter. There were parts of the towers that appeared very high; and he could see, for what seemed like, all the way back to the farm. A large river flowed adjacent to the convent walls, and Henri liked to throw stones to see if he could hit the water. Whether he did or not, he could never tell. The forbidden areas contained things of great and ancient mysteries. Aunt Mags took him to some of the places. Small, dark, and gloomy rooms with very old furniture, pictures, and many things of no apparent interest to small boys were all he saw. These visits were to satisfy his curiosity because she suspected he might be prone to prowl on his own. Little boys are always subject to curiosity and will always be, as God intended, just little boys.

Aunt Mags told him many stories about the old convent and the area around Orléans. Orléans was a very old settlement of Celtic tribes that was later, in ancient times, torched by the Romans. It was rebuilt with beautiful castles and châteaus along the river Loire. Aunt Mags told him this very same river was the one that flowed close to his village and farm. Henri wondered if a stick could be thrown into the river and sent as a present to his home. He tried it one day and never did know what happened to the stick. This entire region was steeped in history since before the birth of Christ. Aunt Mags was well read and a student of history. She loved to relate stories and events. Of course, the ever curious, Henri was all ears and very attentive.

One of her favorite stories was of Joan of Arc. "Joan had been a very devout girl who heard voices from saints, giving her instructions to fight for France. Joan and her followers had won a very famous battle right here in Orléans. She was later known as the Maid of Orléans. She had entered martyrdom, burned at the stake by the English in 1431."

Aunt Mags insisted on his studies of reading and told him repeatedly reading would unlock many gates to the worlds of knowledge and culture. Indeed, the more he practiced and read, the more he understood, and the more his thirst for knowledge increased. The lessons in numbers were less desirable, but Aunt Mags insisted he must learn.

"Henri, how can one not be cheated in business or in life if he does not know numbers and counting?" she often insisted.

One morning, Henri was up especially early; remembering his introduction to the convent, and Aunt Mags's warning about the dark areas, his curiosity got the best of him. One of the most interesting places was a forbidden place Henri named the cave. It was a large room in the upper reaches of the turret. Even though it was forbidden, Henri had opened the door and peeked in the gloom several times. The large pile of old furniture and trunks was just too much to just look at through the door. It was a drab day with drizzling rain, and his outside duties were suspended.

He crept up the flights of stairs, making certain that no one was watching. As he approached the door, he remembered to push it open very slowly to avoid any creaking of the old hinges. The only light was emitted through several high windows. He could see a little better after waiting a moment or two, letting his eyes became accustomed to the dim light. Even though his first steps into the gloom resulted in bumping into a pile of old trunks. The noise, even though slight, sounded even louder. He froze for an instant and heard nothing except his own small heart.

Opening one of the trunks, he found nun's habits, shoes, a rosary, prayer books, and other personal things. The other trunks revealed the same things. He was very careful not to dig too much and replace the things in exact order. Even though the dust, which he never considered, was disturbed. The trunks and small footprints left glaring evidence of his curiosity. The old furniture was not really interesting to him. After nearly half an hour, he was satisfied that nothing more of interest was there. He left, closing the door.

The next morning, Mother Catherine came into the kitchen as he was peeling vegetables. She said, "Henri, please come with me. I need to have a chat with you."

They went to her office. Aunt Mags came in as he stood before the desk. Mother Catherine accused, "I see you have been in one of our forbidden areas. You were told about these places. You can't deny it as the small footprints in the dust marked the crime. What do you have to say for yourself?"

"I am sorry," Henri stammered. "I did know better, but I wanted to see the things in there. I didn't take anything."

Aunt Mags said, "Henri, I showed you these places before to satisfy your curiosity, but still you persisted in going there. We are disappointed. And especially that particular room. That room contains personal things of nuns who have gone to another world from here. These things are considered almost sacred. Someday all of the nuns you know here, including me, will have a trunk there. We know you didn't take anything, but you did break the rules. What are we going to do with you?"

"I am sorry, Aunt Mags. I promise not to go in any of the places again."

"On your honor and before God?" demanded Mother Catherine.

"Oui, Mother."

"Repeat it then, on my honor and before God," she said sternly.

"On my honor and before God, I will not go in the forbidden areas."

Aunt Mags said, "As punishment, we will expect you say ten Our Fathers and ten Hail Marys this evening at chapel. All right, Henri. Remember this. Now go back to the kitchen."

Henri scooted to the kitchen, grateful to be getting off so easy. But he did have to admit to himself that he enjoyed the cave very much if he could dig more extensively.

Henri's duties in the kitchen were to assist with peeling and preparation of vegetables and various other things, always under the dutiful eyes of the nun in charge. Sister Celine was a robust person who wore thick glasses. She took her kitchen duties very seriously and expected all others to do the same. She was a kind, almost-patient person and took great pains to teach Henri the fine art of peeling vegetables without a great deal of loss. Seeming to have the energy of several people, she bustled around the kitchen stirring pots, stoking fires, adding seasonings, and doing the hundreds of things one must do to prepare meals for large groups.

The morning meal consisted of freshly baked rolls or the long loaves of bread, freshly churned butter, fruit, and milk. A light lunch, usually served around midday, was again of bread, churned butter, vegetables, and milk.

One could always snack during the day before the main meal that was usually in the late evening before dark. This meal would have much more and was, by far, Henri's favorite meal of the day. The usual fare served was meat or chicken with the usual vegetables, bread, and milk. Often for dessert, Sister Celine had prepared sweet bread rolls, pudding, or some other sweet treat.

Concluding the main meal, dishes, pots, pans, and utensils used during the day were washed, put away, and the kitchen cleaned for the next day. This task was always shared by a group of nuns who made the cleaning much faster. The nuns always sang and teased with each other, which always made the work enjoyable and fun.

The one kitchen duty he most disliked was churning butter. One had to sit on a high stool and push and pull the plunger up and down in the churn at just the right pace. Too fast or too slow and the butter would not turn out well. Sister Celine showed him just the right pace of up and down and still had to remind him many times he was going too fast or too slow.

"Henri, you are daydreaming again. How many times must I tell you? Here, try saying the rosary as you churn. That always seemed to help me," she said.

Prayers were observed before every meal, and an hour prayer service was held each night after the kitchen was cleaned. It was mandatory to attend evening prayer, and Aunt Mags jokingly told Henri that he could be excused only by death and that it would have to be his own. Henri had to sit in the back of the small chapel and be very quiet while the nuns were at prayer. He was to learn from the prayer service. He was given a rosary and shown to follow the prayers by counting on the beads as Aunt Mags had taught him. His counting and numbers improved dramatically with this exercise. Aunt Mags and the others taught him other prayers, and with his reading ability improving every day, he could also follow in the prayer books.

Of all his duties, he enjoyed the work in the yards the most. There was the vegetable garden, the chicken-and-duck pens, and the area on the far side, away from the central courtyard where the stables were located. In the stables were three cows and several goats. It was part of his duties to help Sister Agnes milk the cows and goats and carry the heavy wooden pails back to the kitchen. It didn't always end there because Sister Celine often made him help with the churning. It wasn't all bad, however, as a special treat of a sweet roll may be offered as a reward.

Sister Agnes was also in charge of the chicken-and-duck yard. She collected the eggs each day in a large basket with a cloth in the bottom, taking special care that each egg was wiped clean and not cracked. Henri assisted her in the collecting and final preparation for Sister Elaine. He would never forget the day he had reached high in a nest and felt a chicken snake coiled there. He had screamed and fallen, tumbling back over the row of lower nests. Only once had this happened before on the farm, and he should have known better than to reach high without being able to see in the nest. Sister Agnes came running and laughed at the sight of him, lying there with wide, frightened eyes.

Sister Elaine was the marketing nun of sorts. She went to the market each day with fresh butter and eggs, delivering them to merchants, regular customers, and local supporters of the convent. Occasionally, she took special orders for vegetables or other things the nuns may be able to supply. Some of the nuns were very good at sewing and embroidery, making lovely table linens, scarves, small blankets, as well as taking special orders for ladies' apparel. She always brought back things donated either by the customers or by other well-wishers to the convent. Henri accompanied her often and was thrilled to see the sights of Orléans. He silently observed the counting skills of Sister Agnes and tried to remember the methods.

Being outside of the convent walls made him feel reminiscent of a bird out of a cage. The streets were lined with shops filled with all sorts of wondrous things. People of the town always seemed in a rush, scurrying around like ants, or so he thought.

Watching ants had become one of his favorite pastimes, and he could lie for hours watching them. Being alone and not having other children about, he could almost go into other worlds of thought just by watching ants hastily running to and fro in a trail. He would often drop bread crumbs or small bits of food just to watch them carry it back to their nest. He was always amazed at the size of the things they could manage to lift and carry.

The large cathedral on the main town square with the tall steeples and colored glass windows was a sight to behold. They went inside on every occasion, and Henri was fascinated by the huge domed ceiling with its magnificent interior sparkling with a myriad of colors. The huge main altar was a magnificent sight with the greens, reds, and golds. The stained glass windows depicting biblical scenes were beautiful in the reflecting light. Sister Elaine told him this was the Sainte-Croix Cathedral, the pride of the town. They often saw several of the priests who would inquire about general conditions and news from the convent.

Henri especially liked the bridge over the large river in the center of town. The sometimes fast-swirling, muddy current seemed so far beneath them. At times he could almost think he saw fish. He loved to drop small stones and try to hit branches and other debris floating by. Several times he was able to send sticks "home." He saw other children near his age playing in groups, and he would silently go by, hoping perhaps they hadn't seen him. How he longed to play and be like the others. On the trip back, he was usually quiet and silently wishing the trip would never end.

Life went on day by day in the convent, and Henri was the darling of the nuns. He tried very hard to be quiet and polite and to perform his duties as best he could. He was quiet and just a bit shy by nature, and being alone so much, he did not cause problems. Aunt Mags had told him initially and several times after that this was just a temporary arrangement for him to live here, and she was trying to arrange for something more permanent.

One day, several months later, a lady from town made a visit to Aunt Mags. Henri was called in from his duties in the garden and told that special arrangements had been made for him with the lady's relatives in Paris. Henri could stay with them and attend formal school with their two children. To help pay for his keep, he would have assigned duties just as he did here. Henri found this news was very disturbing and did not sleep well that night or the others that followed. He bombarded Aunt Mags with many questions that she said she could not answer and was told he would mostly just have to wait and see for himself. She assured Henri that everything would be all right, and this move would be in his best interest. What would happen now? So many moves and changes in his young life often caused him to flee to his room and cry himself to sleep. His losses, the changes, and moves in such rapid succession were very unsettling and confusing to him.

And so just eight years of age in the late fall of 1803, with a very heavy heart, fighting back tears, and yet anticipating, just a little, the future ahead, Henri hugged his aunt Mags and the other kindly nuns and mounted a carriage for the trip to Paris. The lady from town, Madame Dijoin, was to accompany Henri and would introduce him to her relatives. She said she needed a visit anyway, and this was an opportune time.

Aunt Mags and Henri had a long talk the night before his departure. "Henri, my brave young man. Please be brave, as brave as you can in the days to come, and try to never forget the lessons in grace and humility you have learned here. God is with you always. You can trust in Him when no other can seem to comfort you. When a situation seems very bad, try to seek a quiet place and talk to Him. He will always answer. Maybe not at that moment, and maybe not with the answer you want, but He will answer you. Always try to be honest and polite with others, and all things will follow. I hope you heed this advice, my Henri. Go with God, my precious boy, and please do write to me."

"I promise, Aunt Mags. I will try to be brave and make you proud of me."

Looking back as the carriage gained speed, he watched as the nuns stood in a neat black-and-white row waving and disappeared in a light mist of rain. Some were openly crying, and he was fighting hard to hold back his tears. Aunt Mags had tried to be brave, but she was crying too. In her heart, she probably knew her Henri may be gone forever. He had promised to write letters, and he would. Everything he knew as familiar disappeared in the swirling mist. He covered his head and shoulders with his blanket, thinking to himself, *How brave can I be?* and cried hot, wet tears until he fell into a fitful sleep.

The weather was terrible with a misting rain and harder showers part of the way. It wasn't that cold, but the dampness did give a chill to everything. Madame Dijoin and he snuggled in light blankets, and after a while, he was cozy and warm. He could hear the patter of rain on the carriage roof, the drivers urging the horses on, and the mud splashing under the carriage. To pass the time as they journeyed, Madame Dijoin talked to him for a long time and told him many things about the family he was about to meet.

"The two children of the household are a boy very near your age and a girl a year younger. Their names are Jean and Angelette. They live with their mother, Madame de Chabot, my younger sister, and her husband. The gentleman of the household is an officer in the Grande Armée of France and is off at wars somewhere in Europe with Napoleon.

"Henri, you will find Jean a bit spoiled and abrupt, but he is nice and loves to play with toy soldiers. He said he wants to be like his father and a soldier himself. Angelette is a pretty young thing and spoiled. But she is nice, although a bit shy. So do not be surprised if they may appear unfriendly at first. All of this will seem so new to you. It will be a completely different life than the one you know now. Please try to understand and cope with these changes. Above all, please be brave and try hard to understand. They are a fine and respected family, and you are very fortunate to have this opportunity."

Once again he was asked to be brave. He would try his best, but in his private times, he could cry all he wanted. It would be best that way, if no one could see or hear just how brave he really was. He lay there and pondered all of these things. *Most of all, what will become of me now?*

The carriage groaned, creaked, squeaked, and splashed on through the mud; and late that evening, just after dark, they stopped at an inn. The driver took the carriage and horses to the stable as Henri and Madame Dijoin went into the inn. She had, evidently, been here before because the innkeeper and his wife greeted her as an old acquaintance.

The large main room of the inn was comfortable and warmed by a moderate fire in a huge stone fireplace. Tables and benches of rough-hewn wood were placed at strategic intervals around the warming fire. Shedding their coats, they hung them on the pegs for such near the door and sat at one of the empty tables. Several other groups and patrons were quietly eating and talking among themselves. Several bursts of laughter came from a group of men, all apparently drinking wine.

They were served a filling meal of roast meat, vegetables, coarse dark bread, and a delightful sweet wine. He was to share a room with the madame, but not the bed. He was given a bed of folded blankets on the floor, but he couldn't have cared less. Henri was so tired from the bouncing and swaying of the carriage, he could have slept standing up or leaning against the wall. Besides, he was stuffed with the fine and filling meal.

The food served at the convent was certainly very sufficient and tasty, but this food had a robust, seasoned flavor. *The several mugs of the good, sweet wine would make sleep almost next to heaven*, he thought to himself. Madame Dijoin was not really tipsy, but one could certainly tell she had consumed three mugs. They were awakened just before dawn the next morning. After a short meal of sweet bread and hot tea and coffee, they mounted the dreaded bouncing and swaying carriage for the final part of the journey to Paris.

2

Paris

Paris suddenly loomed out of the mist and forests along the narrow winding mud road about midafternoon. For some time, the villages had become closer together, indicating they were nearing a larger place. As they rounded a bend and the view of the fields flattened out, Henri could barely see a faint outline of tall buildings. Certain skeptical and uneasy previous apprehension turned to feelings of excitement. Fears of the unknown turned to anticipation. As the carriage approached the outskirts of the city, one building, much taller than the rest, dominated the skyline. Madame Dijoin said that was Notre Dame Cathedral, and Henri would be living close to it. She was excited now and talking faster, telling Henri that she could not wait to see her sister and the family. It had been over a year since she had done so.

The mud roads turned to paved cobblestone streets with people hurrying along with their early daily business. The splish-splash of the slinging mud took on a different tone as the carriage wheels rumbled over the paving stones. At times, it was almost a roar. They crossed a beautiful ornate bridge over a large river and turned down several more rues. At long last, they stopped in front of a large black iron gate set in an ivy-covered white stone wall. One of the drivers dismounted to open the gate, revealing a large stone house surrounded by trees and colorful, fragrant gardens. This could not be the place where he would be living. *It was one the nicest places he had ever seen,* he thought. They drove up a circular paved drive leading to large stone steps. The front entrance of the large two-story stone house was massive. A large front porch with white columns and plants and furniture for sitting in better weather dominated the entire front of the house. Madame Dijoin, very excited, was the first out of the carriage. She took several steps at a time and was turning the doorbell handle before he got out of the carriage. A pretty lady opened the door. The two hugged and cried.

They entered the largest foyer Henri had ever seen other than at the convent. The huge room held statues, fine furniture, and a large red carpet with dazzling designs of gold and blue. They went into another room with equally fine furniture and furnishings. A large white marble fireplace with a warming fire was in the far wall. Henri stood warming himself by the fireplace while the ladies chattered away, seeming to forget him. "How was the trip? Are you hungry? We expected you tomorrow." And the chattering went on and on.

After several minutes, the lady noticed Henri standing near the fireplace and introduced herself, "I am so sorry. We were so busy catching up on old news, I failed to notice you. Please forgive me. You must be the lad we have been expecting? My name is Madame de Chabot, and I am very happy to greet you into our home. I hope you will feel comfortable and welcome here. I want you to meet my children, Jean and Angelette."

She went to the spiral staircase in the foyer and called for the children to come down. After a time, they came bouncing down the stairs. Jean was slim, almost skinny, with brown hair, bright dark eyes, and a little taller than Henri. Angelette had dark brown hair and equally bright dark eyes as Jean. She was very petite and pretty for her young years. Henri could see a slight sprinkling of tiny freckles across her nose. Both children and Madame de Chabot were dressed in some of the finest clothes Henri had seen. This couldn't be their daily dress. They must have dressed for the special occasion of company coming. Henri looked down at his clothes and felt very much out of place with his shabby clothes. Angelette shyly smiled at him. The two boys shook hands at a distance, and Angelette gave a slight courtesy as they were introduced.

Jean and Angelette were asked to take Henri upstairs and show him his room. They went up three large flights of stairs to the third floor. Jean opened a door to a neat large room completely furnished with bed, dressing table with mirror, stuffed chair, and other small tables. Best of all was a window with a lovely view, through the treetops, of the river. It was the most beautiful room Henri had ever seen and far better than his tiny windowless closet affair at the convent.

Jean told him in a haughty manner, "We were told you do not have any parents, and you are coming here to share ours. Well, you just better not if you know what is good for you."

Henri replied, "I didn't ask to come here. I won't steal your parents. Don't worry. I thought we could be friends, but if you don't want to, that is all right with me."

Angelette didn't say anything. She just turned and walked away with a blank expression. Jean turned and walked out, leaving the door open as he left. Henri closed the door, sat in the chair next to the window, and stared out at the scenes below. He wondered what life would happen now. Jean had made it clear he was not welcome.

Henri's small cloth bag of clothes and personal things was brought to him by one of the servants. He was shown to the washroom by the servant.

"You might want to wash and prepare for the evening meal. You will be called at the appropriate time. It will not be too long," she informed him.

Henri opened his bag to reveal his worldly treasures, which consisted of one pair of extra stockings with the heels and toes mended by Aunt Mags, an old sweater with mending in various places, one pair of extra pants, and two shirts, all with patches of mending. There were two wooden figures, a horse and a goose, carved by one of the caretakers at the convent, a small polished rock he had found in the stream at the farm, and the rosary given to him at the convent. On his right index finger was the ring given to him by his mother. This was not much to show for nearly nine years of life. He put the things in a drawer and returned, looking out of the window at the river.

Opening the window, he found if he looked down the side of the house, he could see the twin spires of Notre Dame. A biting wind blew in, taking what little heat there was in the room, causing him to shiver. He hurriedly closed the window. A rude loud knock sounded on the door, jerking him out of his reverie. It was Jean.

"Hurry and come to the evening meal. Don't be late," he said in an abrupt tone, as if ordering a servant.

The evening meal was in the large dining room with the huge buffet loaded with urns and dishes emitting very tantalizing odors. The table was set with exquisite china and silver utensils and surrounded by chairs with red-and-blue embroidered seats, and candles burning in large candelabras. Henri felt so out of place and nervously hoped he would not spill anything or embarrass himself. Madame de Chabot asked Henri if he knew a prayer for the meal. He recited the prayer the nuns said before each meal. Madame de Chabot was impressed and said in front of all of the others that she seemed pleased so far with Henri, his manners, and now this lovely prayer. She officially welcomed him to the family and asked the others to please try to make him feel as family. Henri looked at Jean and saw a blank stare with no emotion. *Oh, well*, thought Henri. Ange shyly smiled.

When they were seated, the cook served a sumptuous meal of leek soup, roast duck, cabbage, carrots, and, for dessert, a wonderful cake with a berry sauce poured over it. Henri thought, again, that *this could not possibly be the normal fare.* He tried to watch the others and copy the proper uses of the utensils, napkins, and such. He thought he did fairly well, but after the meal, he was informed by Madame de Chabot that he would be given formal instructions in all sorts of manners including proper table etiquette.

With the meal and light conversation finished, after a short visit in the parlor next to the huge fireplace, the children were sent to their rooms and to bed for the night. Henri was given a candle in a little holder and told to blow it out when he was in bed for the night. He spied a small chamber pot partially under his bed for nighttime urges, but he doubted he would need it. The room was cold, but he loved to sleep in the cold, snuggled warmly under the bedcovers. A nice feather down coverlet was on his bed. Staying warm would not be a problem.

He did feel an urge to pee and used the larger chamber pot in the water closet down the hall. On the way back to his room, he saw Angelette peering at him from a very slightly opened door. He pretended not to see her and hurried on to his room.

Madame de Chabot had been ill during the earlier winter months, and Madame Dijoin had made this journey to help her sister for a month or so. To escort Henri was just another excuse for the visit. The two sisters were very close and had been since childhood here in Paris. Madame Dijoin's husband was a wealthy owner of a river transport company based in Orléans. They had married a few years before her sister. The move to Orléans had been difficult for both women. Madame Dijoin made it explicitly clear to her husband prior to their marriage that she would be making somewhat frequent trips back to Paris. The visits would be required for maintaining a household peace. Madame Dijoin, thus far, was childless; and the two children of Madame de Chabot were her idols especially Angelette, or Ange as was her short name.

Henri awoke with a start early the next morning. He was in a strange place and had a very fierce urge to pee. He got out of his warm bed, put on his trousers, and ran down the hall to the water closet. He could have gone in the little chamber pot in his room but was too embarrassed to do so. Relieved at last, he went back to his room to finish dressing. Donning his tattered shirt and jacket, stockings, and nearly worn out high-top shoes, he went downstairs in search of something to eat. He was used to rising very early at the convent. Following the tantalizing odors led him to the kitchen where he introduced himself to the cook who was just getting the fires started and heating water for morning tea and brewing coffee.

"Bonjour, madame. I am Henri. I came last evening. I hope I won't bother you."

"Hello back to you. My name is Mimi. I did see you at the evening meal last night. I have been with the de Chabot family for a long time. Welcome to you. Madame de Chabot told me that you would be helping in the kitchen and around the house."

Henri replied, "Oui, I do know about kitchen things. I helped in the kitchen at the convent."

Mimi was a heavyset woman with a black dress, a white apron, and a floppy white hat. The floppy white hat and slim squinty glasses gave her slight resemblance of Chinese, or so Henri thought. She shuffled around the kitchen in nearly worn out old slippers much as Sister Celine had done. Henri wondered if all cooks were supposed to be this way. She fixed him a mug of good, hot, strong coffee. The coffee ran quickly to his tummy and started to bring him back to life. And at last, Mimi asked, "Are you hungry?"

"Oui, like a wolf," replied Henri.

Mimi laughed and gave him some sweet rolls and another cup of coffee. The formal morning meal wouldn't be served until later when the others awakened.

Henri, being an early riser and not feeling like part of the family, asked, "Is it all right if I come early to the kitchen and help you get things for the morning meal? Do you think it will be all right if I have my meal here in the kitchen?"

Mimi replied, "I guess so with me, but I will have to make certain with Madame. I would enjoy the company. I think you are supposed to be in here helping anyway. There is wood for the stove stacked on the back porch through that door. You can start by filling the wood box here."

After finishing his coffee and sweet rolls, Henri hopped up and hurried to the task.

Mimi was not married; and her live-in lover of many years, Jules Perrodin, was off at war somewhere with the master of the house. She had longed to have children, but now as it was so late in life, she probably would never have the opportunity. And so for the second time in several months, Henri was semiadopted by a kindly cook.

The rest of the household began to stir after nearly an hour. When Madame de Chabot came into the kitchen, to her surprise and delight, she found Henri busy helping Mimi.

"Well, good for you, Henri. I see you are earning your morning meal." She thought to herself, *I do wish I could get Jean to do more than just tease Ange. All he delights in is trying to make her unhappy and cry.*

The others were gathered in the dining room, and the two sisters were chattering away about everything. Jean was sitting quietly, dunking his sweet roll in his tea. Ange was very quiet, nibbling on her roll, listening intently to the ladies chatter. Henri had already eaten earlier and did not join them, but Madame de Chabot called for him to join them anyway. She casually mentioned his volunteer efforts of the early morning. Madame Dijoin said it was probably habit from his days on the farm and at the convent. They all rose early and had a day's work completed when others were just waking.

Jean continued to glower at him at every opportunity while Ange seemed complacent about the whole affair of his being here. Henri knew he wasn't trying to earn merit. He was just doing what he had always done. He had to grow into his own person and was always made to work hard. There was no shame or reason to defend the fact that he could and would carry his share of the load. His manners, taught by Aunt Mags, were particularly to everyone's liking. Aunt Mags taught him to always try to consider the sensitivities of others, never to show weakness, and always stand your ground if you believe you are right. Well, so far, so good.

After the morning meal, Madame C or Madame, as Madame de Chabot told him to address her, called Henri aside. "Henri, I am taking you shopping for appropriate clothes today. Please be ready in a short time."

He was already as ready as he could get, so he decided to look around. Opening a large set of double doors, he discovered the library. It was like heaven as Henri had come to love books and reading. Prowling the shelves, he discovered extensive volumes of wonderful books on seemingly every subject. He selected a book of old fables from times long ago and seated himself in one of the large stuffed chairs.

As he sat reading, Ange, seeing the open doors, slipped into the room. Curious about what he was doing, she asked, "What are you doing with that book?"

"I am reading, Ange. I love to read."

"I do not believe you. Jean told me you are stupid and do not know your lessons from school."

"Well, I am not stupid, and I do know how to read," he defended. "My aunt Mags and the nuns at the convent showed me how. Come sit over here, and I will prove it to you."

Ange hopped up in the chair next to him, and Henri started to read some of the stories from the book. That is how Madame C found them when she was ready to go shopping. She silently listened for a time and thought about this young lad reading aloud with such clarity. She really hated to intervene. Ange was listening so intently. It was a beautiful and touching moment. Finally, as they realized Madame was behind them, Henri stopped reading and stood up as if almost embarrassed.

Ange asked, "Henri, will you read more to me later and teach me about reading?"

"I will. You can teach me more about manners."

"I am not that good in all of my manners, but I will show you what I do know."

Madame C, Madame D, Henri, and Ange were going to walk to the shops that were on the huge main square near Notre Dame Cathedral. Jean said he did not want to go and would rather stay home and play with his toy soldiers. He was almost obsessed with being a soldier like his father. With Henri, remembering back, there was still a distrust of military things. The morning was crisp and cool, but a beautiful day was pending. A warming sun was climbing higher in the sky.

Henri reading to Ange

Henri noticed that most houses they walked past were almost or the same size and grandeur as the de Chabot's. All of the houses had neat, trimmed gardens and bushes surrounding the walls and walkways. The paved streets were mostly void of trash, unlike Orléans and other places he had been. There were, however, the usual horse droppings on the streets. One had to be careful where one stepped.

The two ladies were walking ahead, and the two children were following and talking. Ange was pointing out things and places to Henri and trying to answer his many questions. She was impressed with Henri's knowledge of farm and garden things and asked many questions herself. It was almost like they were all by themselves.

As they approached the large central market square, there were people rushing about, hurrying on their many errands. A gentleman recognized the two ladies, tipped his hat, and inquired about General de Chabot. General de Chabot? Henri had not realized he was of such rank in the military. It was little wonder they lived in such luxury. He would have to ask Mimi about all this. Another shot of fear raced through him.

As they continued from shop to shop, the two ladies began to choose clothing items for Henri. There were real underpants that he was embarrassed for Ange to see, stockings, and several pants and shirts for around the house and work. The next shop was the cobbler, and Henri was fitted with several pair of the funny-looking shoes like Jean wore. A pair of short-top work boots and slippers, for the house only, were added to the bags.

The tailor was an entirely new experience for Henri. He was fitted for several suits of clothes, dress shirts, and pants. Madame C chose for the suits material of bottle green, crimson, and dark blue. The shirts were white and shades of pastel yellow, pink, and blue. The odd pants were matching and contrasting colors to the suits and the shirts. The tailor informed them the clothes would be ready in about two weeks but that they would need to return in five days for the final fittings. Henri couldn't believe the clothes. Never in his life did he dare to dream of wearing such clothes.

Embarrassed, he whispered to Madame C, "Madame, I can't possibly pay for these clothes."

She just smiled and laughed, "Henri, never you mind the cost. Our arrangement will be for you to help Mimi in the kitchen and the gardeners. We will keep a register, and you can work off the cost of the clothes. We are not offering you charity, but if you are going to live with us, you must dress the part."

Henri nodded his agreement as he pondered the phrase "live with us." Did that mean as one of the family?

On the return home, they went into Notre Dame. The enormity and magnificence of the building left Henri awestruck with serenity of the atmosphere and of feelings flowing through and around him. Being much larger and ornate than the church in Orléans, the twin spires seemed to touch the clouds when he looked straight up near them.

The décor of the interior was especially beautiful, and in the sanctuary was almost total silence. Now and then, a cough, sneeze, scuff of a foot, or some other sound could be heard. The slightest sound seemed to reverberate off the walls through the silence. The lighted offering candles in neat rows and banks of little crimson flickering lights seemed to extend the entire length of the far wall. The main altar was draped with cloths of white and purple, the gold of the candlesticks and adornments glittering in splendor amid another myriad of candles, and the huge colored glass windows in the background made the entire scene almost indescribable.

A priest came up to them and hugged both ladies and Ange. "I saw you come into the church, and I am so glad to see you, Dolace. I knew you were coming for a visit, but I did not know it would be this soon. Vivien, are you feeling better? You look much better."

"Oui, I am feeling much better. Merci, Father. Will you join us for dinner? I will have Mimi prepare something special."

"Merci, I will be most happy to get a good meal. The food here cannot compare with Mimi's." He was introduced to Henri as Father Etty, a cousin of the ladies.

They entered a pew near the main altar and knelt down in prayer. As Ange knelt next to him, her arm touched his. He didn't move his arm, and neither did she. The quiet touch of her warm arm let him know they would be friends. They both desperately needed a friend. He never wanted to leave. The silence was broken only by the two ladies softly reciting their rosary. After a time, the spell was broken as they left one of the most peaceful places and times Henri had known in some time. Only the small chapel at the convent might come close in comparison.

3

de Chabot Household

That afternoon, Henri was in the kitchen peeling vegetables when the priest he had met at church came through the door, held his finger over his lips in a signal for Henri to be silent, and sneaked up behind Mimi. He smacked her on the back and yelled at her. She screamed and jumped back. The priest was laughing as he backed away, holding up his hands in mock fright.

"Father Etty! You scared me out of two years' growth. I might have known it was you. Let me catch my breath."

"Mimi, my favorite cook. How have you been?"

"I am fine if I can catch my breath. Does Madame know you are here? Dolace is here visiting from Orléans."

"Oui, I know. That is why I came over. I haven't really talked to Dolace in nearly a year."

"Henri, I want you to meet Father Etty. His real name is Etienne Guillot. He is Madame's cousin and has been hanging around the house forever, stealing my cookies. He is a priest at Notre Dame, and I am surprised he hasn't been here before now."

"I know, Mimi, I met him this morning at church when we were shopping."

Father Etty was a tall man of nearly thirty years with wavy dark hair and the piercing eyes of the family. He wore the black frock of his order and had in his hand a wide-brim hat. He wore sandals, and the unkempt toes on his large feet stuck out of the front.

"I would have been here before now, Mimi, but I have been on retreat for the last two weeks in Marseille. We have to go once a year, you know. Cleanse our souls and so forth. It is so good to be back. The food was awful and not like yours at all." He walked over to Henri and shook hands with him. "I know you are to be part of the permanent family here, and welcome again. I know you will be happy here."

"Oui, Father. Merci."

"Oh, please, Henri, call me Father Etty or Father, but never late for a meal of Mimi's." He asked Mimi, "Have you been behaving lately, or are you still indulging in your old sinful ways?"

"Why, of course I have been behaving. Jules is still with the general off at war somewhere."

"But I know you have been thinking sinful things anyway. You know, Mimi, for a loaf of sweet bread to take with me, I could arrange absolution."

Mimi laughed, "You old charlatan. Never mind the absolution, but you will have your sweet bread."

"This is holding me captive, you know? That must be some sort of sin on you." He left the kitchen, calling for Vivien and Dolace in a loud voice.

He did stay for the evening meal, and once again, Madame asked Henri to say the blessing. She just wanted to see what Father Etty would say. When Henri had finished, Father Etty sat silent for a minute then exclaimed the prayer was excellent and very well done. He rose and offered his hand to Henri. Ange kicked his leg under the table and smiled at him. The rest, with the exception of Jean, offered their congratulations.

The days that followed were full and happy for Henri. Mimi introduced him to the head of the yard services, Louis, making it clear that Henri would be helping in the outside only if he did not have anything to do for her. Louis was a kindly rather tall thin individual. Standing in the kitchen door with his floppy hat in his hands, he waited for Mimi to invite him inside. He wore scruffy pants and a heavy shirt of some type of rough brown material. His heavy leather boots were scraped off to assure mud did not get on Mimi's floor. Henri thought to himself that this man could be a likely substitute for the garden false man to ward off the pesky birds.

"Come in, Louis, I want you to meet Henri. He will be helping you and the others outside at times."

Louis, coming into the kitchen, held out his hand. "Welcome, Henri. I need all of the help I can get. Mostly the work is in the early spring though. We will need a little help in the stables and barn. When you finish in here, come find me, and I will show you around. This is a pleasant surprise to get more help. Are you sure you can carry your share of the work though?"

"I think so. I have lived on a farm and helped with many duties at the convent with my aunt Mags."

Mimi said, "He can go now, Louis. I won't need him for a while."

As they went outside, Louis said, "Lad, I want to give you a bit of friendly advice. Never, but never track mud on Mimi's floors or the porches. Always scrape it off on the scraper blades over there by the steps. And God help you twice if you track manure inside. That is a certain notice of death."

Louis showed him the garden area, now mostly devoid of things. There were long rows of cabbages still there and other green things now starting to turn yellowish. There was a small house of glass panes at the rear of the barn. Louis opened the small door and explained that special delicate things were kept in here. The special things were mostly for the master who brought them home from his travels. A small chicken-and-duck yard was at the rear of the barn next to the glass house, and a special covered lean-to affair with nests for eggs was attached to the back of the barn. Inside the barn was a maze of garden tools and work and repair areas. Owing to the amount of things in the barn, it looked well organized and neat. A little walled-off area at the rear was, evidently, the workers' rest area with a small bench and several chairs around a small table. A solitary grimy window was the only light for the area, which provided slight illumination for a small separate room on the side that had beds for all of the men as they lived on the premises.

Henri knew now why Mimi cooked such large amounts of food. There were two fellows sitting at the table playing cards whom Louis introduced as Gussie and Leon. These were the regular help with not much to do these days, Louis explained. He also made it clear that things going on in his areas stayed in that area. Henri assured him that he did not carry tales. All it did was cause trouble. Louis patted him on the back at that.

The stable area was quite impressive. It consisted of a large wooden building with large doors at the front. Louis said one could find it blind due to the smell. Henri thought it typical of all stables and actually liked the smell as it gave him a sense of his past and belonging somewhere. It housed four horses; two carriages, one covered and one uncovered; a smaller wagon; two cows; and several goats. The place, although smelling like a stable, was clean and orderly. Bridles and implements were hung neatly along the walls. Louis said one could never tell when Madame might come around just to look, and she was worse than the general regarding neatness.

Henri was kept busy learning the manners he must know not to cause embarrassment. The manners a gentleman should and must know: table etiquette, proper greetings to peers, proper dress, a proper stance during conversation, and on and on. The manners should have included passing gas. Louis and the others did it all of the time but always outdoors. Mimi laughed when he told her about it. Even though some of it was mind boggling and didn't make much sense, he never grew weary of learning these new things. Thankfully, Madame and Ange were patient, explaining the details fully and completely. For her young years, Ange was very knowledgeable of manners.

The two grew closer and spent many happy hours with Henri, reading to her or telling stories of his earlier childhood. Jean, at first, appeared very aloof and distant from the two. But a jealousy was silently brewing. Henri tried several times to include Jean in things of mutual interest, but the efforts were always brushed aside. Jean kept much to himself, was selfish and unfriendly, and always appeared better than everyone else in his surroundings. Madame observed this, watched, waited, and prayed for changes to, hopefully, come about with maturity. Ange was the complete opposite of her brother and knew no strangers. She was friendly and polite to everyone in her surroundings, even the servants. Being quite lively, she seemed to positively bubble with life. She was a delight, and often Henri couldn't wait to finish his duties and spend time with her.

One day the next week, Henri came into the house after finishing his duties in the barn and stable and found Ange by herself in the sitting room crying. "Ange, what is wrong? Why are you crying?"

She explained between sobs, "Jean hit me so hard that I fell back against a table. It really hurt, Henri. I will have a bad bruise on my arm."

Henri took her by the hand and said, "Come with me. Let's go find Jean."

"What are you going to do?"

"You will see. Enough is enough."

They found Jean playing with his soldiers under the table in the large dining room. Henri asked Jean, "Did you hit Ange?"

Jean replied, "Oui, I did hit the little brat. It is none of your business. She is my sister."

Henri replied, "She is my sister now too, and I am not going to see her hurt. Don't ever do this again."

"Or what?"

"Or you will find out. I am not scared of you."

"So now you are a big dog, huh? I am not scared of you either. This is my house, and I will do what I want."

"It is her house too, and I mean it, if you ever hurt her again, we are going to have bad trouble."

Henri and Ange turned to leave, and Jean flew at their backs in a rage, hitting and shoving. Henri and Ange fell in a tangle on the floor with Jean standing over them, screaming and shaking his fists. Henri jumped up, pushed Jean back, and ended the entire affair with a strong blow to Jean's nose. A surprised Jean immediately found himself on the floor with a bleeding nose. Henri helped an equally surprised and wide-eyed Ange to her feet and led her out of the room. They heard Jean crying as they left.

Ange held tightly to Henri's arm as they left. "Oh, Henri, I don't know what to say. Merci beaucoup. No one has ever fought for me before. He usually just pushes everyone around and gets away with it."

Mimi heard the shouting and commotion from the kitchen and went to the dining room door. She saw a crying Jean sitting on the floor with a table napkin over his nose. She didn't say anything but did tell Madame later.

"Madame, I heard the shouting from the kitchen and knew it was trouble. When I went in the dining room, Jean was sitting under the table, holding his nose. Henri must have really thumped him. I'll bet Jean doesn't tangle with Henri again. From what I heard, Henri was right to do it."

The die was now cast for long years of cat and mouse between the three. Jean's hate continued to grow. However, Jean did know now that to tease or hurt Ange would bring Henri's wrath. It never happened again.

After the conversation with Mimi, Madame confronted Ange to get the truth of what had happened. After the explanation by Ange, she did not say anything further but did continue to watch more closely and worry with anxiety.

Henri asked Mimi about General de Chabot and was informed the master of the house was indeed a general on the staff of Napoleon. He had been a close confidant and trusted friend of Napoleon since their early days in the military together. The general had been gone for long months this time, and Mimi had heard he might return just prior to Christmas. The campaigns to the north were slower due to the winter months, and troops were being granted leave for home. Henri thought to himself of the master of the house being a general. How would this work with his strong distrust of the military? He would just have to wait until the general came home, and he could meet him.

The weather was mostly dreary and cold this time of year. Most of Henri's outside duties were put aside for better weather. He still had to help Mimi in the kitchen, bringing in the firewood and water from the well just off the big porch, peeling vegetables, and whatever Mimi might need. He had been here for several months and had become so comfortable it seemed to him that he had been here forever. These days, his very early life on the farm and at the convent was an increasingly distant memory. He still thought, at times, about Aunt Mags and the other nuns, but now with increasing rarity. Marcel and the farm were very distant in his memory. Now and then, he would look at his ring and think of his mother and the wonderful stories of his father, but the bitterness he felt at the many cruelties of war remained with him. He kept these very personal things to himself and, as Aunt Mags had told him one time, tucked away in a small corner of his heart. He thought about sharing them with Ange and thought he would with time. They had become extremely close now and could talk about most things.

Madame had the servants begin to unpack the decorations for the Christmas season. The house was suddenly transformed almost overnight from a peaceful one to scenes of hurried confusion. Boxes and cases containing everything imaginable for the Christmas season were brought down from the large attic storage room into the sitting room. Madame told everyone the general would be home in a few days, and she virtually glowed with anticipation. The ever-so-clean house was cleaned again, and special preparations for the general's favorite foods kept Mimi busy into the evenings.

Two days later, in the late afternoon, General de Chabot did arrive with all of the flourish and grandeur of his station. A military carriage with a mounted escort of six lancers entered the circular drive. The general jumped out almost before the carriage stopped. He ran up the steps to the large front porch and smothered Madame in a huge bear hug. Madame was crying, as was Mimi and the other two servants. Jean and Ange entered the fray, hugging the general's legs. Henri stood to one side against the wall behind one of the large porch chairs and just observed. The general dismissed his carriage and escort, and they all went into the house. Henri noticed Madame held the general's arm tightly, and he had his other arm around her waist.

Henri followed Mimi into the kitchen, and she inquired, "Why didn't you introduce yourself? You are not usually so shy."

"I don't know. He just looked so huge and scary in that uniform. I will meet him later, Mimi. It looked like a special time, and I guess I was shy about butting in." Mimi didn't say anything but understood Henri was right in not barging in.

Believe it or not, one of the general's favorite foods was a hash of sorts consisting of roast meat cut into smaller pieces with potatoes, onions, and vegetables of the season and smothered into a sauce. It certainly wasn't the usual French fare, and Mimi wondered how it came to be one of his favorites. Mimi said he had told her about this dish upon returning from one of his war adventures in other places in Northern Europe. She had prepared a large dish for his return. Mimi was busy and really didn't have much time to talk, so Henri decided to go to his room and hide out for a while before dinner.

On the way up the stairs, he came across Ange coming down. She asked where had he been and insisted he meet her father. She wouldn't take no for an answer and, grabbing him by the hand, turned him around and marched him back down the stairs. The general, Madame, and Jean were in the large sitting room, enjoying a warming fire and listening to all of the news of Napoleon and the recent battles in upper Europe. He loved to talk about such.

Henri and Ange entered the room, and Ange said, "Poppa, this is Henri. He has come to stay with us."

Turning his attention to Henri, the general said, "So this is the young man I have been hearing so much about. Come closer, lad. Don't be shy. I promise not to bite."

Henri went a little closer and took the offered hand, saying, "I am honored, monsieur. I have heard a lot about you. I have looked forward to meeting you."

Ange said, "See, I told you he was nice and would not bite you." They all laughed except Jean who stared at Henri and waited for Andre to continue the war stories.

General Andre de Chabot was a tall man and struck an imposing and impressive figure. He had wavy dark hair with just a slight presence of gray at the temples. He often commented it was in his genes to gray early, and it was his every right to have the mature look of a gentleman. His eyes were dark and piercing at times, almost appearing to flash as he spoke. His mustache enhanced his eyes framed with large bushy dark eyebrows. However, fierce as he may appear, he had the gentleness of a lamb when he was with Madame. He may be a general in the Grande Armée of France, but the home was her domain. He had always respected the territorial rights to her sphere of influence. Others in the household followed his lead for the sake of peace. He spoke with authority and firmness, his meanings very adamant in any conversation. One hardly heard him raise his voice or get excited to any great extent. He had others doing his bidding to become excited as necessary. He carried his heavy frame very erect, and when he walked, he seemed to glide. Seeing him here, in the privacy of his home with his shirttail out and in his stockinged feet was a sight seen by few in his command. Napoleon had mentioned to him in their early days together that the boss should always look like a boss. It challenged subordinates to cower and to follow orders. He had never forgotten the advice of his friend and through the years did see it work that way. He always tried to be precise and immaculately dressed in his finest uniforms and with his medals, sword, and boots polished to a glasslike shine. Being of his rank, others could do the polishing and grooming anyway.

Mimi rang the little tinkly silver bell to signal the evening meal was ready. They all filed into the dining room led by the general and Madame, holding hands like two lovebirds. He held her chair and very properly seated her at the table. Usually they sat at opposite ends of the table, but tonight she sat at his side so they could converse more quietly and privately. Not to mention touch each other. Lovebirds indeed! Madame Dijoin was seated across from Madame, and the children next to the adults. Ange sat next to her mother, Henri at her side, and Jean on the other side of the table. Father Etty, a late arrival, was seated next to Jean. Mimi served the general his dish of hash stuff, as Madame called it, and the others had their choice of roast mutton, leek soup, and vegetables, or they could try the hash stuff if they wanted.

Henri was the only one who opted to try the hash. The others had evidently tried it before and found it was not to their liking. Mimi served Henri a small portion, and all eyes would be on him at first taste. Mimi poured the general the first wine, and he tasted it with approval. She then moved to each of the others and filled their glasses.

"Mimi, you have been a member of this family for as long as I can remember. Would you care to join us at the table this evening as our guest?" inquired the general.

"Oh, Andre, merci. I would be so honored. I appreciate this more than you can know." She sat next to Henri, saying she would probably have to be up and down anyway.

The general was about to say the blessing when Madame pulled at his arm, whispering something to him. He looked directly at Henri and said, "Would the guest in our home please honor us with a blessing for this fine meal and those in attendance?" Normally this would have been a duty of Father Etty, but he understood Madame's wish this evening.

Henri blushed and replied it would be his pleasure and recited the prayer taught by Aunt Mags and the nuns. His voice was clear, and he did not hesitate or stutter.

"Bless us, Oh Lord, and these thy gifts which we are about to receive from Thy bounty, through Christ our Lord. Bless all at this gathering and those who have prepared this fine meal." And having been previously coached by Madame, he added, "And, Lord, we give you special grateful thanks this evening for the safe return journey of the head of our family and father."

When he finished, the general looked at him, saying, "Amen, bravo, bravo. Well done, lad."

Madame glanced at him and smiled, looking pleased. Ange kicked his leg under the table. Jean just unsmilingly looked away. Mimi sat back with a wide grin. Father Etty again stood and smiling silently offered his hand to Henri.

Henri, being used to a variety of foods from the farm, convent, and other places, tasted the hash. It was not bad, and he ate his entire portion. As the serving dishes were passed around the table, he took a larger amount of the hash stuff along with the other items. During the meal, Henri noticed the general taking greenish "something" from a small porcelain urn and adding it to his hash. Henri asked Ange what it was, and she replied she did not know the name of it. She had seen him add it to many other things. No one else would touch it, and Madame had cautioned her never to. She asked her father, "Poppa, what is that in the little bottle you put on your food?"

He replied, "My girl, the fires of the underworld would be cool compared to this. It is a special concoction of peppers and oils that comes from Egypt. Mimi can tell you. She helped me mix it up until it was just right. I acquired a taste for it when in Egypt with Napoleon. I brought some of the pepper seeds back home. Now the gardeners grow them behind the barn."

Mimi added, "It is so hot that it could cause blisters on the tongue and probably does. I could never understand why people eat such hot things. I tried just a small taste one time, and it burned for all afternoon."

Henri asked, "Monsieur, could I try just a small taste? I have eaten spicy things before." The general didn't say a word and, with a smug look on his face, passed the little urn to Henri. Henri put just a very small amount on his hash with a small spoon and stirred it around with his fork.

I hope it kills him, thought Jean.

Henri took a taste with all eyes on him, and the general had been more than right. If he had not been accustomed to spicy foods at times, it would have been like eating glowing coals from Mimi's stove.

"This is the hottest I have ever tried. You are right, monsieur." Henri did his best not to show watering eyes. "But it does add tremendous flavor to the dish." He continued to eat and finished the smoldering portion.

The general remarked that Henri was the only one in the household able to stand his private stock and jokingly said he would have to keep an eye on it from now on. Mimi asked him if he would like more, as there was plenty.

When he received his second and then third portions, the general again jokingly said he must be an Austrian spy in disguise. "It pleases me to see a young lad with a healthful appetite and for the hash, a soldier's food. This is what we had for weeks during one of my campaigns, and I learned to truly love it. The rest of my aristocratic family finds it the food of peasants and do not care for it."

Henri replied, "It is very good and filling. I have eaten a lot worse."

"So have I and the men of my command," said the general. "When the Armée is in the field, we eat whatever can be found. Why, at times, we even eat horses, cats, dogs, snakes, and even rats. Chickens and cows are a rare plus and mostly reserved by the foragers for the officers."

"Now that is a big spoof, Andre. You shouldn't tell these innocent children such things. You must go to confession before the Christmas Mass."

"Ah, woman, but we do eat some of those things, and besides, what a dull life it would be without a bit of spoof and humor. I can be serious when I am at my Armée things, but here at home, I can take my boots off and joke with those I love. Moments like these are rare treasures for me."

"Oui, I suppose they are, you old ruffian, but please try not talk of eating strange things while we are dining. Some of it is revolting and so unmannerly. Why, one might think you are a common lancer and not a general."

"Your ever-so-wise words of correction are duly noted, as usual, *mon amour*."

During the course of the dinner conversations, Jean had remained mostly quiet and to himself. When asked certain things, he replied with short and curt answers. Madame asked him if anything was bothering him, and he replied he had a headache and really didn't feel well. The truth of the matter was Henri was getting attention that Jean thought he should have been given as the son of the house. He was smoldering with a jealous rage and trying his best to maintain his poise.

He eventually excused himself and asked to take leave to go to his room. The fires of hatred were steadily being fanned. This country peasant was gaining the favor of his parents. He felt he must do everything in his power to discredit this most unwanted menace and get rid of him. Actually, Madame and Andre had long conversations when the two were together in private concerning Jean and his overall attitude and hostility toward most in his general vicinity. He was considered spoiled, sullen, and jealous and did have an underlying cruelty about him. They were very concerned about all of this as it seemed to increase and not decrease during his maturing years. All the parents could do was watch, wait, and hope for changes. They had tried most everything, including whippings by the father, but everything seemed to just make Jean go farther back into a shell.

A few days later, it was the eve of Christmas and almost time for the celebration of the holy season. Mimi was making considerable preparations and kept Henri and the upstairs maid, Juliette, busy with the many peeling, pouring, stirring, sifting, and lifting duties for the second day in a row. Small colored pastries, tarts, candies, several types of bread, and things Henri had never seen before were being prepared.

With everything completed late that evening, the entire family took naps in preparation of the ordeal to come. The children were awakened late evening and instructed to start getting dressed for Midnight Mass. This very special mass was a ritual in the family and others of prominence and had not been missed in many years. Just before leaving for mass, Jean, Ange, and Henri put their shoes on the hearth of the fireplace in the sitting room in hope that Père Noël would leave fruits, candies, and gifts. Care must be taken to have the shoes clean; otherwise, Père Noël would take offense and pass them by.

The general was dressed in his finest uniform complete with medals and other adornments of woven gold. He was without his sword and said he felt a bit naked in uniform without it as Madame didn't like him taking it into the church. She said this was the house of God and others, and the priests didn't have weapons. He retorted by saying, "Ah, woman, but they have the best weapons of all. Their tongues. They are the true robbers among us."

"Andre, for shame, for shame. Please do not repeat that."

Madame had a lovely gown of dark blue with white lace at the collar and sleeves. Ange wore a dark blue satin gown of similar design to Madame's. Her bright dark eyes peering from the hood of her cloak had the appearance of two glowing coals. Henri had on his suit of hunter green and Jean a similarly designed suit of burgundy with white lace at the sleeves. Both boys had their new black shoes with higher heels than normal and a silver buckle on the front. Henri was not used to these shoes, and his toes felt pinched.

The night was cold, foggy, and with a heavier swirling mist at times. Indeed, a very dreary night for going out. Wrapped in their heavy cloaks, they walked the short distance to Notre Dame and entered the already crowded church. They weren't worried about seating as their places were perpetually reserved as honored patrons of the church.

As the pageantry began, Henri was again awed by the sheer size of the church and the spectacle before him. The priests and assistants, indeed, the entire church was adorned with the finest ceremonial garments, cloths, candles, and adornments of the season. The church was ablaze with candles and hanging chandeliers of other candles. The ceremony began with the priests blessing everything as they went down every aisle, sprinkling holy water and shaking the incense braziers. Father Etty splashed the family pew with what seemed like an especially heavy dose, and it made little watermarks in the powder on Ange's cheeks. Madame had insisted they all wear powder for this and special occasions.

Henri whispered to Ange, "You look like you have the pox. Here, take my handkerchief, or do you want me to fix it?"

"Oui, please, if you dare to with everyone watching." He handed her the hanky.

Ange, as usual, was sitting next to Henri and, after fixing her powder, fumbled for his hand under the cloaks. They clutched hands and played fingers seemingly in their own little world. If the adults would have seen them, there would have been a spectacle after Mass. One just did not play at Mass as this was a very serious time, but try to explain that to two young people who cared very much for each other. Even in their very young years, the two had formed a bond of deep caring and respect.

Madame, who never missed anything, had noticed the eyes and movements of the two over the past several weeks and watched with increasing interest. They were always respectful to each other and were never out of line with anything, but Madame would always watch to see that intimacy and private moments be avoided if possible. Mimi, sitting next to Henri, did see slight movement under the cloaks and silently smiled to herself. She had done the same in her younger years with her "friends."

The pageantry continued and was much more than the routine Mass they usually attended. After nearly two hours, Ange leaned her head on Henri's shoulder and closed her eyes. In fact, everyone in the church was starting to show signs of restlessness, and several people around them were actively dozing. Madame nudged Andre several times, and now it was his turn to nudge Madame.

Andre whispered to Madame that this was not natural. "If God intended me to stay awake all night, He would have mounted a candle on my head."

Madame noticed Ange starting to doze on Henri's shoulder and motioned for him to awaken her. Henri nudged Ange. She awoke with a start and smiled up at him. The Christmas hymns were a welcome relief, and almost everyone sang with vigor. The men surrounding them seemed to try to outdo the others. The general was no exception and boomed out the songs in his rich baritone voice. Finally the ordeal was over. Henri had never been to such a long ceremony, not even at the convent. Everyone seemed relieved to finally leave the pews after such a long time of sitting, standing, kneeling, and then repeating them all over again for countless times all the while listening to the priests chanting in Latin.

It took them, perhaps, another half hour to finally gain the main entrance to the church. Many well-wishers and admirers of the general and of the victories of Napoleon stopped them for congratulations and the greetings that seemed to go on forever. Madame seemed to glow as her husband was praised over and over again by some of the leading dignitaries of France and the city. Finally, and at long last, they walked down the large front steps of Notre Dame.

Father Etty met them on the large porch and promised, "I will be over as soon as I can get away. Keep Andre away from the food, Mimi. Save some for me."

And they made their way through the fog and mist toward home.

"What a wretched night," remarked the general. "It is only fitting for an attack on poor unsuspecting enemy troops. Napoleon has used that tactic several times, and I have suspected myself of sticking my own troops with my sword in the darkness. In combat, it is everyone for himself. Please hurry, all, I will surely pee in my pants."

Henri too was about to burst and received approval from Madame to visit a tree in a dark spot. Jean followed suit, and the two watered the tree with vigor.

Madame said, "This is not fair. Ladies can do no such thing, even at this dark hour."

The general laughed, "As God intended, mon amour. If I had ladies among my troops, we would surely lose every battle with them having to squat during battle. Men, at least, can stand and pause and often run while doing it. Most just forget the whole thing."

Madame said, "Oh, Andre, you are just impossible. Whoever would have thought such things?"

He laughed as he replied, "Well, it is all so very true, mon amour. Think of it in reality."

They arrived home in the wee hours of the morning tired and hungry. The réveillon was a very special mealtime and only served once a year. Mimi told Henri she gave special thanks for the "just once a year" part as it was a real pain in the rump to fix all of this. It was a meal said to restore the faithful, and indeed, it was a relief. They were all exhausted from the long ceremony and with throats hoarse from singing the many praises to the Lord. Mimi had outdone herself, as was usual, and served the first dish.

The *poularde*, a capon of rice, was the obligatory dish for this nocturnal meal taking the place of soup, which is never served. It was attended by four hors d'oeuvres consisting of piping hot sausages, fat well-stuffed andouilles, boudins blanc au crème, and properly defatted black puddings. This was followed by pickled ox tongue dressed in a beautiful setting of the season. Pig's trotters or feet stuffed with truffles and pistachio nuts were a special treat, and the dish of fresh pork cutlets was especially good. Mimi placed at each corner of the table a silver plate heaped with the petit fours of tarts, tartlets, and other sweet desserts. Large apple pies with cream rounded out the desserts; and the faithful, thus fortified and their devotions restored, could retire or await the dawn, which was very near now.

Everyone decided to just retire and sleep the sleep of the very satisfied. Henri lit his small candle from a splint of wood in the fireplace and went upstairs to his room. On the way up, he met Ange and wished her the peace and blessings of Christmas. She, being a step ahead, turned, leaned over, and kissed him very lightly on the cheek then slightly brushed his lips with hers. He moved slightly back and looked at her with surprise. Then he laughed when he saw the white powder on her lips. She started to get angry until he explained and gently brushed the powder away.

He told her, "Ange, you look funny with the white powder on your lips. Don't you know that your pretty lips are supposed to be red like wine and not white like snow?"

She laughed, "Right now, I would rather have the snow." She blushed, turned quickly, and ran up the rest of the stairs. He heard her door close as she reached her room.

Henri went to his room, blew out the candle, and jumped into the cold bed sure to warm up soon, but seemingly never as fast as one wanted. He thought a long time about the kiss, and he shouldn't have jumped back so startled. But it did startle him. They shouldn't even be thinking about big people stuff, but they were both above their years in maturity. Because of the war, many young people their age were already working and serving in the roles of adults. She was his closest and dearest friend in all of this world. He drifted off to sleep without care or worries. The entire family, including the servants, slept late the next morning. Surprisingly, after such a foul night, it was the beginning of a beautiful day, clear and cold. The rising sun held promise for warming during the day.

Mimi knocked on Henri's door and opened it slightly. "Henri, it is time to stir your worthless bones. The day is wasting away while you laze in the bed. It is not your birthday, and I need some wood brought in. *Allon*! Get up!"

He raised up and slid to the floor. "I am coming, Mimi."

"My lord, just look at those skinny legs. We need to work on this and get some meat on your bones."

Henri looked down, and she was right. His legs were skinny and thin. Surely his legs would gain more "meat," as Mimi said, as he got older. Henri quickly dressed and went to the kitchen. As he entered the kitchen, he could see that

Mimi really didn't have much for him to do. He ate a little of the leftover food from the feast of the night before. Mimi sat down across the table.

"Henri, I need to talk to you very privately. Please don't tell anyone we are having this talk."

"I won't, Mimi. What is it? Am I in trouble?"

"Lord, no. You haven't done anything. It is really none of my business, and I do not usually meddle in affairs of others, but you are one of my favorites here. I feel I need to warn you about Jean. He is a spiteful and mean boy, but you know that already. He feels that you are a threat to his existence here and are getting the attention that he should be getting. I don't know what he will do, but just be very careful in any dealings with him."

Henri replied, "Oui, I know he doesn't like me. I am sorry about that. I didn't do anything. We are the same age, and we could share a lot like Ange and I do. He told me one time that I was not here to steal his parents. Well, I am not. He was mean to Ange a few weeks ago, and I hit him. If I didn't, he would have hurt her again."

"Oh oui, the entire household knows about that even Madame now, but you were right. We are all proud of you. Just be very careful in the future, and if we hear anything or any mean plans, we will inform you."

"Merci, Mimi, I will."

Mimi went back to preparing the traditional French pain d'épices or spice bread that Henri dearly loved. She gave him a small taste of the doughy substance from her mixing bowl; and the flavors of ginger, cloves, aniseed, and honey had been mixed with perfection. The result would be a dense, dark, and rich spice bread.

The other members of the household started to stir, and Henri heard Ange bouncing down the stairs.

"Oh look. Père Noël did come last night," she exclaimed as she ran to find her treasures.

Henri had forgotten about Père Noël and ran into the room with Ange. All of the children's shoes were filled with fruits, candies, and small gifts. Ange had combs and ribbons for her hair, a small doll, and a lovely gold ring with her initials engraved on the crest.

Jean had a smug look on his face as he entered the room, but that look soon turned to fury. He knew he had sneaked in during the night and put mud on Henri's shoes so Père Noël would pass him by, and he was at a loss to explain the sparkling clean shoes that were there for Henri. Even though Jean had more toy soldiers, a small red wagon, and a ring similar to Ange's with his initials on it, he virtually ignored all of it.

Henri, oblivious to Jean, had nearly same amount of toy soldiers, a pair of new black boots, and an envelope. Opening the envelope, he found a personal note penned in the fine script of Madame's handwriting.

Our Dear Henri,

A very Holy and Happy first Holiday Season with us. Please accept as our gift to you, this note of cancellation of your debts for clothes and other necessary items when you first came to us. We have enjoyed your presence with us as a family member. We hope you have enjoyed your stay here and will continue as our second son for as long as you may want.

Sincerely and With Much Love,
Your de Chabot Family

Henri looked around, stunned. This was more than he had ever expected and meant that now he was truly accepted. He felt tears welling up just as Madame was coming into the room with the general. Fighting back the tears as he approached her, he extended his hand. "Madame C, merci. I don't know what else to say, but I am so happy here."

She leaned over, giving him a hug, and said, "Henri, we are happy to have you here. You have made a very welcome addition to our family."

It was the first time Madame had shown any signs of physical affection toward him. He didn't really know how to react. Madame turned her attention to the others, and the moment ended. Henri quickly left the room and went into the small closet on the back porch where Mimi kept some of her kitchen things. He did cry then with tears of relief and gratitude. This wonderful and gracious family had made him a member.

The next week, the general came back from the Armée offices and announced they were invited to dine with Napoleon and the rest of his personal staff at the palace. For once, entire families were to attend. Napoleon wanted to meet the entire families of those in his command staff. The dinner was to be tomorrow evening. Another scurry of activity unfolded the next morning as boots and shoes were cleaned and polished, hair trimmed, the finest clothes laid out, and, worst of all, baths, perfume, and sweet scents.

The general was dressed in his finest uniform and this time complete with sword and gleaming medals. Madame was dressed in a beautiful pale blue gown with lace at the cuffs. The dress revealed her ample cleavage which was further enhanced by a gleaming diamond necklace. Diamond dangling earrings and a tiara to match the necklace completed her ensemble. The cloak of darker blue contrasted her dress to perfection. Ange wore a full-length gown of white with small pink rosebuds in trails down the length of the train. The white gown with her dark hair and sparkling dark eyes made her look every bit the essence of her name, Little Angel. Jean wore his finest suit of dark burgundy with the usual lace at the cuffs and around the collar. Henri wore his suit of dark blue and, as Jean, had white lace around the cuffs and neck. His only jewelry was his small gold ring given to him by his mother.

The children all stood inspection by Madame in the main entrance room just before leaving. She inspected them much as the general may have done with his troops, leaving nothing undone. At the appointed hour, the carriage drove up to the front entrance. They all climbed in the carriage for the trip to the palace.

The general warned each child, "Positively behave and do not speak unless spoken to first. Stand up straight and tall, do not slouch." And on and on. With all of the inspection and firm orders, the children were nervous. That is all except the general and Madame who were used to such and knew the manner of such events.

The carriage arrived at the huge entrance to the palace and was admitted with a flurry of salutes from the detachment of guards on duty. This was Napoleon's personal imperial guard and the elite of the troops at his command. All of their movements were precise, sharp, and very brisk. Their uniforms were white pants and jacket accented with red and blue sleeves and epaulets. Crossed belts of white covered their chests, and the tall hats were of matching red and blue with white-plumed feathers. The boots were like polished glass, and rifles and swords gleamed in the torchlight.

They emerged from the carriage and made their way up the many stairs to the main palace entrance. The building was enormous, and Henri remarked to himself that his was much more magnificent than even Notre Dame. The palace was alight with chandeliers, candles, and lamps everywhere. A soft music drifted down from the string orchestra on the balcony above the main stairway. The main entranceway was enormous with the main curved stairway appearing to go into heaven itself. Others had already started to gather and, like the general and his family, were dressed in their finest array. This gathering was the elite of the command of the Grande Armée. The music suddenly changed tempo and started a ringing march. All eyes turned to the stairway, and Emperor Napoleon and Empress Josephine made their grand entrance.

Napoleon was dressed in the uniform of the commander of the Grande Armée. The uniform was similar to the general's and others, but the shoulder epaulets and other accessories were gold and red. His high boots were, as the others, polished and gleaming. His very stature and composure radiated an air of leadership and command, leaving little doubt he was a person of great importance.

Empress Josephine was stunning, gliding down the stairs on Napoleon's arm. She too had the air of aristocracy about her. Her white gown was a long and flowing fine silk covered with lace in the image of small flowers. Covering her gown was a scarlet cloak with a high collar of the same fine lace as was on her dress. Her light brown hair was piled high on her head and complemented by combs glittering with diamonds. A large necklace and hanging earrings were diamonds matching all of her other accessories to perfection.

As they descended the stairs to the music of the stirring march, Henri stood in total awe. It resembled a scene from a fairy tale one only reads about. Yet here he was, a poor child of peasant farmers in the presence of the emperor of France and the commander of the Grande Armée.

Napoleon and Josephine made their way to the entrance of the main ballroom and waited to be presented to the guests. The guests lined up according to station, and as they approached the royal couple, an attendant announced their names.

The general stated to the attendant, "General de Chabot, Madame de Chabot, and children Jean and Angelette. Accompanied by houseguest Henri Devreney of Blois."

They were presented, and Napoleon inquired, "A houseguest, Andre, he must be honored indeed, being a guest of your home."

"Your Excellency, he has been orphaned. His mother passed on last year, and his father was killed while in my command at the Battle of Marengo. He is proving to be a fine lad and will no doubt be a candidate for our fine Grande Armée in the future."

"Indeed," replied Napoleon, "he will bear watching. Please keep me informed, Andre."

Napoleon held out his hand, and Henri bowed and shook the offered hand with firmness and respect. He looked at the empress, and she was smiling at him with kindness. He smiled back as she too offered her hand. He very lightly kissed the back of her hand while bowing with courtesy and respect. Thank the heavens for Ange and her manners classes. The moment was his and would be remembered always. Heaven could not have been nearly this close.

As they walked away, Ange slightly poked him in the ribs with her elbow, Madame leaned over and hugged him, the general patted his shoulder, and Jean glowered more than ever. *Well, to hell with Jean*, thought Henri. He was not about to agitate matters.

Ange whispered, "Henri, I didn't know about your father and my father knowing him. That was a surprise."

"It was to me too. I will ask him about it. My mother told me about him, but never anything like this," replied a startled Henri.

He knew who he was and where he came from but was shocked at the words of the general. He did not know until now that his father had served in the general's command. Did the general have plans for him to enter the military?

He would have to question the general about this at a later time. The Battle of Marengo. Where and what was that? There was so much he wanted to know. This started to bring back the memories his mother had shared and may complete the stories. The bitterness he felt all those years returned, but he discovered it had been tempered by time and the de Chabot family.

The group entered the enormous main dining hall. The room, as the others in the palace, was ablaze with light. Everything in sight was gleaming and sparkling. The huge and very lengthy table was set with magnificent tableware, crystal, and silver utensils. Large centerpieces of flowers and greenery were placed at intervals along the table. Placards with names of the guests were arranged in order of importance and rank.

The general and his group were very near the head of the table reserved for Napoleon and Josephine. Henri, as was his usual station, was seated next to Ange. He had teased her about being always seated next to him, saying she planned it just so she could kick him under the table. The guests found their places and stood behind their chairs, waiting for the royal couple to enter and be seated. As soon as they entered and were seated, the signal was given for the guests to seat. The wine servants made their way around the table and filled each crystal glass.

Napoleon rose to offer a toast, and everyone followed suit. "May the Lord our God bless this gathering of the elite of French military and their fine families. We pray our proud country continues until the end of time and our successes know no end." He continued, "I am very honored to know and to be associated with such a fine company of leaders. Vive le France!"

Everyone responded in unison, "Vive le France!" Each took a sip of their wine, and Napoleon again was seated.

A small army of servants came out with the first course of soup and ladled it into waiting soup dishes. No one touched anything until Napoleon had taken his first taste. Henri made very certain to watch the others and not embarrass himself or the general. This evening must be very proper and correct. Again, the signal of Napoleon taking his spoon and the first taste was the response everyone had been waiting for, and the meal began. With the first course over, the other courses followed in quick succession. There were dishes of duck, mutton, and some of the most delicious vegetables with cream sauce Henri had ever tasted. Actually, it was better than Mimi's, but he would never mention it to her. So this was how royalty dined.

To Henri, this would have been boring at every meal. He thought about the hash stuff and special peppers and softly chuckled to himself. It would probably kill this elite group. The people were chatting quietly, and it was evident the men and most of the ladies knew each other. All seemed very comfortable in the company of each other. With the main dinner courses complete, dessert was served, a delicious spice cake of the season complete with a pile of heavy sweet cream. The serving was ample, but Henri could have eaten another. During the meal, Henri had noticed Napoleon eyeing him from time to time with curiosity. He hoped he had not done any embarrassing thing, thus causing the emperor to take notice. The two made direct eye contact several times, and Henri felt uneasy.

Henri leaned over to Ange and whispered, "Ange, do you notice the emperor watching us or me especially?"

"Oui, I did, but don't pay any attention. He is just curious."

"You don't think I am silly looking or anything, do you?"

"Oui, I do, but don't worry about it." She giggled and again kicked him under the table, and he kicked her back.

With the formal meal over, Napoleon once again arose and announced that gentlemen could retire to the main conference room for drink and cigars, and the ladies and children could go into the other conference room for social visits and refreshments. He further announced there would be a staff meeting tomorrow morning for the purpose of planning the spring campaign. Northern Europe was much under control, but the Spanish were starting to be restless.

Henri went into the conference room with the rest of the children and ladies. There was the usual small talk of domestic things, and some of the smaller children played quietly under the huge table in the center of the room. Henri met two other boys near his own age, and as usual, the talk led to military and war things. One of the boys was nearing twelve years of age and told the other two that he was going into the Armée as a drummer in the next few months. One had to be at least twelve years of age and be accepted mentally and physically. Henri wasn't doing all that well in school, and maybe this could be what the general had meant in his conversation with Napoleon. The boy's father had agreed to let him join, much to the dismay of his mother.

Henri thought to himself, twelve years of age and he could certainly pass the tests. He was fairly large and strong for his age, and while he had done well enough in school, it wasn't to his liking to be a scholar or storekeeper. Still, this would be quite an undertaking living the life of a soldier. He wondered if he could put his bitterness for the Armée behind him and also wondered what Ange and Madame would think if he made such a decision.

After a time, the general and some of the other men came into the room to gather their brood for the trip back home. This had been a very memorable evening for Henri. Meeting Napoleon and the empress had been an inspiration as no other in his short life.

The next morning, Henri made a point of asking the general if he could have a private moment with him. They went into his private library and closed the door. The room was filled with shelves of books and a massive desk with leather covering on the top.

"Well, to what do I owe this honor, lad?" inquired the general.

"Monsieur, it is about my father. Last night you said that he had been in your command. And he was killed at some battle somewhere. Could you tell me anything about him? My mother told me stories about him, but I was a little boy when all that happened. I don't remember much about him."

"Henri, your father distinguished himself before my very eyes. It was early summer during 1800 at the Battle of Marengo. That is in Austria to the north of France. The Austrians were in, what we thought, full retreat. Our troops were chasing them faster than our main body could catch up. Suddenly out of the forest came a regiment of Austrians direct at our left flank. Your father saw them first and tried to organize an outer defense. There were perhaps ten men in his group and about one hundred of the enemy. The main body, given the alarm, wheeled to meet the threat; but it was too late to assist the men with your father. Your father and three others were killed almost at once. As I said, it happened right in front of me, and I will never forget the bravery shown that day.

"Your father was in their midst shouting and whirling this way, using his bayonet, and then his musket as a club, never giving ground. Finally a lancer hit him from behind, but he still wouldn't go down or give up. He personally accounted for eight of the enemy. We arrived about that time, and I went over to him to inquire his name and origin. He told me and died with your mother's name on his lips.

"I made note of it in my personal dispatch to Napoleon and in my diary. Your mother's name was Helene. When Madame's sister made inquiry if an orphaned lad could stay with us for a while, and gave the name and origin, there was little doubt in my mind who you might be. This is the very least I can do for one of my own, and it is a pleasure to have you here. It is evident to me now you are your father's son."

"Monsieur, do you mean for me to join the military? You did say to Napoleon that I would."

"That will strictly be your option, my boy. It is a good life and has been for me. Think on it."

"Merci, monsieur. I do have to tell you that I have some bad feelings about the military. When my father was taken, it ruined our lives at home. Things were very hard for us. When news came that he was killed, it killed my mother too. She lost a baby and never got over it until she died. We knew it wasn't the Armée's fault, but it was too for making him go. Isn't there a lot of danger?"

"Merci for confiding your thoughts to me. I can certainly respect your feelings. Henri, there is always danger no matter what you do. I always thrived on the adventure and seeing the many new places. Think about all of that too. It is a man's world out there."

The general left the following week to rejoin his troops and prepare for the next campaign against the Spanish. The following April, Henri reached the magic age of twelve years. On the next trip home for the general, he would think more about the Armée. Until then, no one must know his secret, especially Jean who so desperately wanted to be a soldier but did not have the physical or mental capabilities now that were required. He just was not physically robust and was more of a spoiled "mommy's baby."

The days droned on, and he settled into his humdrum life of duties in the kitchen, gardens, and stable. School had started again. His duties plus school kept him busy, and he did not have much time to devote to dreaming of the soldier's life. As his other memories, the dreaming of a soldier's life was put in a small corner of his heart to be drawn out from time to time and returned.

School had been not difficult and yet not very easy either. The master at the academy was Monsieur Elave Gustave, and a meaner and uglier individual never graced the earth. Goosey, as the children called him in private, was a very thin individual with a large long thin nose. A pair of spectacles was forever perched on nearly the end of his nose, and to further disgust one, hair grew out of it as well as his ears. He was sparsely balding at the back of his head, and the rest of his hair hung over his face in long strings of dark brown and gray. His large brown-and-gray eyebrows had a nervous twitch and seemed to jump up and down, with an Adam's apple that bobbed up and down seemingly in rhythm with his eyebrows. Most of the time he had a wild look in his eyes. They darted from every angle, and he never looked anyone directly in the eyes. His appearance alone struck terror in the hearts of his charges. Henri had never seen such an individual and made it his business to do whatever it may take to do well and stay out of this monster's line of vision.

One day, as the students were filing out for exercise, Jean was last in line. As he passed Henri's desk, he quickly spilled ink from the inkwell all over Henri's desk and papers. When they returned, Henri was appalled at the mess.

Goosey was livid! "Monsieur Devreney, you are an impossible dolt. Go at once to the storeroom and get cleaning towels. Clean this horrible mess. *Alon*! *Alon*! Hurry, hurry!"

Henri replied, "Oui, Monsieur Gustave, but I do not how this happened. I did not do it."

The master accused, "You are a little liar, and I will deal with you after you clean up this mess."

"Please, Monsieur Gustave, I do not lie. It is the truth. This was here when we came back inside."

"Well, I say you do lie. Has anyone here seen anyone else making this mess?"

"I saw him," said Jean. "He spilled it just before we left for exercise."

"You lie, Jean," accused Henri.

"Enough of this," said the master. "Any more and I will beat both of you."

Jean realized now that he had gone too far, but it was too late to back down. Henri left to get the cleaning towels, and the master followed him into the storeroom. He took his stick and began to hit Henri, demanding the truth.

Henri pleaded with him, "I did tell the truth. I don't how that happened. Jean lied."

"I will beat you half to death unless you admit to this."

"I can't ever when I didn't do it."

The master beat him all the more, and as much as it hurt, Henri refused to cry out. This made the master all the more angry, and he ordered Henri, "Gather your things and leave this school." He knew he would have to bring Madame back with him to sort things out now that Jean was involved.

Henri trudged the several blocks home. As he crossed the bridge over the Seine near Notre Dame, he stopped to stare into the water and think of what had happened. He stared down for a long time. It seemed to help him think by doing so. He remembered Mimi's warning, but Jean could not possibly hate him this much. As he thought about things, possibly Jean could too hate him this much. Henri, just being himself, had gained much favor with Ange, the family, and the servants. Henri was becoming everything Jean could not. He realized he was a menace to Jean who would probably do most anything to get rid of him. Henri entered the main gate and went straight for Mimi's kitchen.

"Well, bonjour, you are very early. What is the matter, lad?" she inquired. "You have a lost look on your face."

"Nothing, Mimi. Nothing is really wrong. I'll bet a piece of sweet bread and tea could fix it."

He was given a piece of sweet bread and tea, and he quietly ate while Mimi still tried to pry the problem out of him. He just told her that he was waiting for Jean to come home so both of them could talk with Madame.

Later in the early afternoon, Jean came home with Ange following and yelling at him. He was yelling back at her. Madame heard the noise as they came into the house and came to investigate. Henri came out of the kitchen as Jean was telling Madame what had happened.

"Tell her the truth, if you dare, and on your honor," dared Henri.

"That is the truth, so help me God," Jean said.

"Now you are in trouble with God too. You had better go to confession."

Ange interjected, "Jean, I know you lied to the master. One of the other girls told me that you were the last one out of the room. Henri was one of the first and was laughing and talking to the other boys. She said she will swear to it to the master."

Jean was trapped, and he knew it. He started to cry, saying he was sick and wanted to go to bed. Madame told him to go and turned to Henri and Ange and hugged them, and she too began to cry.

"I really don't know what to do or how to approach this. He is growing angrier with the entire world with each passing day, and nothing seems to help. Perhaps when his father returns, we can get a resolution. Henri, I can see you were caught in a situation beyond your control, and I will go with you tomorrow and speak with the master."

That evening after dinner, Henri was in his bedroom, examining his back in the mirror. The door was partially ajar; and Ange, seeing the light, peeked in.

"Henri," she exclaimed, "your back is covered with marks and bruises! Does it hurt?"

"Oui, like little fires. Please don't look at my bare back and chest."

"Oh, don't worry. I have seen your bare chest before, but you didn't know I was watching."

"Ha, if I did that to you, you would scream."

"Girls are different. Don't you dare try to see my bare chest."

"I won't embarrass you, but now I can spy on you."

Later after the evening meal, Ange went to her mother's room and told her about Henri's back. Madame went to the kitchen where Henri was sitting and talking with Mimi.

"Henri, I need to speak to you in private," she said. They went into the main room near the fire, and Madame informed him she would like to see his back.

Oh, Ange, I'll get even with you for this, thought Henri. She helped him pull his shirt up and gasped at the sight. She went in the kitchen and asked Mimi for some of the healing salve she always kept on the pantry shelf. Madame and Mimi went into the room with Henri and started to apply the salve. Mimi stated she would like to give that horrid man a taste of his own doing. Madame said not to worry, she would handle things tomorrow.

The next morning at breakfast, Madame asked where Jean might be.

Ange responded, "He told me he was sick and not going to school today."

"Oh oui, he is, sick or not," said Madame. "I will sort this out."

They all trudged the several blocks to school in silence. Henri and Ange were side by side as usual, and Jean was walking very close to Madame. They entered the school and met the master in his office. Madame stated what she had learned and said there would be no more about this. What was done was done. Then she asked the children to leave the room.

"Monsieur Gustave, I am appalled at what has taken place here. Have you seen that boy's back? If the general were here, he would deal with this much more severely and just may on his return. We pay you well to educate our children, and while you may be the master here, you do not have the right to beat them so severely. This matter will be over, but if ever I hear of your brutality toward any child in this school, I will immediately withdraw my children and advise others to do as well. I am not without influence, Monsieur Gustave, and I promise this."

The master mumbled an apology, Madame left in a huff, and the matter was over except for the smoldering hate of Jean and now the master.

4

The Teacher is the Devil

The following weeks at school were probably the closest to a hell Henri had experienced thus far in his young life. Monsieur Gustave or Goosey made every effort to criticize him and scrutinized his work and papers in the most minute detail. Henri hoped things might get better as time progressed, but he probably knew better.

In frustration, he cornered Jean on the way home one afternoon and asked, "Are you behind all of this devilment?"

"No, but I am glad to see Old Goosey is not after me. You are getting it now."

Henri just walked away, telling Jean, "And you will get yours too. You can go to hell."

We will see about that, thought Jean to himself. Actually he was adding fuel to the fire at every opportunity and telling the master lies about Henri. Ange heard the entire conversation between the two and, as usual, reported the matter to her mother.

Madame called Henri aside that night and inquired, "Henri, is there still a problem with school?"

Henri knew Ange had probably said something and replied, "There is a little thing with the master, but I will talk to him."

Madame told him, "Be sure to see me if you need any assistance."

But she knew better. Henri was only a twelve-year-old boy and could not possibly fight this elusive monster alone. Now she would keep a very close eye on the situation. She could sense somehow that Jean was behind the problem, and this would bear watching. Entering Henri's room the next morning, she found some of the very strictly corrected papers. There was no reasoning to this, only spiteful actions by the master. The papers had been corrected properly, but overly so and not in the realm of a twelve-year-old boy. This was more to the university level.

Henri's marks continued to fall and were now to the point of failing. With his papers being very severely corrected and the slightest thing resulting in point reduction, Henri approached the master and asked, "Monsieur Gustave, is there anything I can do to improve my marks? Could I do extra work to bring my marks back up?"

"Things are working out exactly as I wish, and you can do nothing." Goosey leered over the glasses perched on the end of his nose. "Now get out and leave me alone."

Henri felt it was now evident that he and his talents were wasted with formal education with this taskmaster. He went home that evening and talked to Mimi, telling her the entire affair and swearing her, upon her mother's grave, to absolute secrecy. Mimi told him to talk to Madame, but Henri told her it would just cause more problems with the already bad relationship with Jean. Henri was sure Jean was behind most of this. After all, he was their blood son, and he didn't want any more trouble. Mimi put all of this into her heart just as she had put the rest of the family and now had added Henri.

Henri did speak to Madame the following week. "Madame, I believe it would be best if I withdraw from school. I could have more time on my other duties around the house, yard, garden, and stable. My marks have dropped so much. I can't really do anything right in school any more."

Madame replied, "I will take the matter into consideration."

In the next several days, she had talks with Jean and Ange. Jean told her he was having the usual problems with the master, but nothing unusual. He told her about the conversation Henri had with him on the way home one afternoon. Things began to fit in her mind now. The master was making Henri an example over what had happened during her last visit. To confirm her suspicions, she had a very pointed conversation with Ange.

"Ange, do you know anything of the master being overly critical of Henri?"

"I have seen some of it, but only after your last visit. He is a mean man and does pick on Henri. All of the others are afraid of him." Ange sat in the same single room with the other students, but in a grade below. The classes were slightly separated but only in specific studies.

Madame confided in a friend down the street with children nearly the same age as hers. She was told about the school the others attended. That afternoon, Madame visited the other school, which was a little closer to their house. She was surprised she had not known of it. The school had a much younger master who seemed very energetic. He was very polite and proper and said he would be honored to have her children in his school. He had only been at the school for about two years, having inherited the job from his father who had been the master for many years and had retired. She could certainly speak with some of the other parents for recommendations. In complete secrecy from her household, she did speak to two other ladies about the new school. One of the ladies had similar problems with the same master at the old school and gave Madame a very precise explanation why she took her children away from what she said was an "evil situation."

Madame's mind was made up now, and the very next day, she told the children, "Do not to go to school today. Stay home and wait for my return." She went into the school and found the master in his office. Closing the door behind her, she informed him, "My children will not be coming today or any other day to your school. During our last conversation, I warned you that any further evildoings would be reported to other parents along with the reasons I will be taking my children out of your care."

He fumbled with apologies and even at one point begged her to reconsider. He would surely be ruined if she took this action.

She further told him, "You have no business dealing with the education of children and would better serve humanity in another profession." She abruptly left, leaving him to his thoughts of "what if and what now." He would be ruined now, no doubt of that. His easy life could be over for the sake of foolhardy spite.

The new school was much better. The children there were much happier. The new master explained points of study in better detail. Henri's test scores rose to almost the top of the class. Jean watched and simmered with rage as the new master seemed to like Henri more than him. He knew he could not possibly do anything further with devilment at this school, but he would watch and wait for an opportunity.

That April, Henri was twelve years of age. Mimi made him a special cake of chocolate with the cream filling he dearly loved. He didn't realize it was his birthday until the evening meal and Mimi brought in the cake. Madame presented him with a toast and a fine new suit of clothes. It was a rich color of dark blue and a shirt with white lace at the collar and sleeves. He was surprised and was very uncomfortable being the center of attraction. Madame asked him to say a few words on this, his special day.

He rose and, blushing deeply, stammered, "Merci beaucoup. I don't know what to say, but thank all of you very much." As he sat back down, he thought to himself, *Why didn't I say I was so thankful for being accepted as one of the family and that I will always try to uphold the honor of the de Chabot name as long as I live?* He wasn't really one for fancy speeches. Well, too late now. Ange kicked his leg under the table and smiled at him in her pretty coy little way. *She was getting better with her kicks, he thought, that one did hurt.* Jean showed no emotion, as was his usual nowadays.

In the days that followed, Henri assumed the stable duties. Upon entering the house one day, Madame called to him and handed him an envelope. "Henri, you have a letter from your aunt Mags at the convent."

Henri, My Dearest Little Man,

I hope this writing finds you well and happy. I haven't heard from you since your leaving and think possibly your fingers are broken. It just is not the same at the convent without you. We all think of you often and how we miss your friendly smile. You are mentioned every night at prayer. Nothing here really has changed and probably never will. As Sisters of Saint Joseph that is the way it should be for our lives of charitable work. We are all happy and our days are full of the Lord and His work. Sister Celine especially misses you as she has had to take on most of the dreaded duties with the churn. She fusses and, as usual, says her rosary as she churns. The river next to the convent rose very high last week and very nearly went into houses along the banks. One would suppose the upstream rains lately were the cause. All seems well now.

Have not heard news of Marcel or from the village since you left there. One can only assume nothing has changed there either. It probably never will, just as here.

The workers in the yard ask about you and how you are. Are you continuing with your writings and numbers? Try to remember the great importance and study often.

We are sending a small medal blessed by all of the nuns. It is the medal of Saint Jeanne d'Arc who you already know so much about. She is my favorite Saint and was actually here in these buildings before the English burned her at the stake in Rouen. It should protect you and help keep you from harm.

Always remember the love of the Lord our God and that He is with you always. Please do take pen to paper and let us know how you are faring.

We all love you very much,
Your Aunt Magdalene

Henri let Madame read the letter and went to find Ange to share it with her. He must remember to write a return letter as soon as he could. There was so much to tell Aunt Mags.

In the following week, the general came home with the usual fanfare of mounted escort. They clopped into the main drive, and the general limped up the main steps assisted by a soldier who had arrived with him. It was evident something was wrong, and Madame rushed to him to assist him up the steps.

He scolded her, "Woman, don't fuss over me so much right here in front of my men. I will be teased if word of this ever gets out." One just did not tease a general. "I'm not a baby. Besides, we will get to the 'fussing' over each other later in more private quarters."

The soldier dismissed the guard unit and came back to the general. "Here, *mon général*. The guard is gone. I can help him, madame. It really isn't that bad."

"Merci, Jules," Madame said. "Take him into the sitting room where he will be comfortable."

Jules Perrodin was a short medium-framed individual with the usual slender mustache of the day and dark eyes. He was dressed in the uniform of a plain soldier with the blue-and-red fourragère of personal aide to the general staff looped across his shoulder. His uniform was filthy, and his boots looked as if they had not been polished in a month. Maybe they had not. By the appearance of Jules and the general, it was evident they had left the war zone in a rush. Jules deposited the general in one of the large chairs in the sitting room and propped his leg on the footstool. The general sat slumped down, evidently near exhaustion.

"Begging your pardon, mon général. May I take leave? Madame can take over if you desire. I have need to see someone in the kitchen," said Jules.

"Oui, I know, you old sex maniac. Tell her hello for me," said the general. They heard a squeal of happy surprise as Jules went into the kitchen.

Henri was in the stable when the general arrived. This was a surprise. The general had not given much notice of his coming. Madame had only had a message the day before, stating he would be home soon, but it did not state when. She had no time to properly prepare her all-day procedure of bathing, powdering, and primping before he arrived. They went into the sitting room, and the general slumped down exhausted in one of the large chairs. Madame helped him remove his boots and stepped back at the odor.

"Mon dieu! Andre, don't you soldiers ever bathe?"

"We do what we have to do. I didn't really have much time if I was going to get here when the next troop from Spain was leaving."

She noticed his stocking had been soaked with blood and was now dried. She cried out, "Andre, you are injured!"

"A mere scratch, mon amour, a mere scratch. A small group of Spaniards got through near our headquarters late in the evening, and we had some sword practice with them. This was the day before I left. I was cut with a sabre on the back of the leg just the day before I left. I didn't dare report this to the butchers and bound the wound myself. They would have reported this to Napoleon, and he would have insisted on my staying in that meat market."

He removed his stocking and bindings, causing her to gasp in horror. "Andre, it is a very deep cut. Come with me at once. Mimi and I will tend this wound. You are terrible, you old bear. Don't you know that your well-being is my life?" She started to cry.

"Oui, mon amour, but I just could not miss this trip back home. I only have a short time here and only got the trip home to do a special mission for His Excellency. I must return in a week or so."

They went to the privacy of their room; and Mimi came in with a wide grin, pan of water, her special healing salve, and clean bindings.

"Ha, I can see your happiness at Jules's arrival. I'll bet you didn't even notice me!" said the general.

"Oui, I did notice you, and double oui, I am happy to see him. You two have fun. I will try too." As Mimi left, Andre pulled Madame over to him, and they enjoyed a long and loving kiss.

"Before things can go further," Madame said, "I must attend to your wound. Besides, in your weakened state, you could not possibly 'perform' and, indeed, may cause further harm."

"Indeed, woman, I could perform on my deathbed if need be."

"Well, I don't want your deathbed to be here and now. You just behave and let me tend this horrible wound and wash you back to a civilized presentation."

"Ah, woman, you are so demanding of me. How could you possibly resist this passionate moment?"

"Andre, resistance will be much less when I have taken proper care of you and especially after you bathe. You smell like a barnyard on a warm day."

He laughed and said, "As you wish, mon amour, as always. I could never resist your charms or your wishes."

Henri came into the kitchen later, and Mimi informed him, "The general is home, and Madame is tending a wound he managed to come home with."

"Mimi, why are you smiling that way? I have never seen you this way."

"My Jules came home with him. I haven't seen him in a long time. I am so happy."

"Who is Jules? Do I know him?"

"He is my special soldier and makes me happy all over. He has gone to the Armée barracks and will be back later. I will introduce him to you when he returns." She giggled.

"Is it a bad wound?" inquired Henri.

"No, it appears to be only a cut on the leg. He was growling, so I guess he will be all right. Go get cleaned up, Henri, dinner will be soon, and you smell like the stable. Mind you, wash well so the rest of the family does not take offense. I am preparing some of his special hash and will have enough for you too. I even had the gardener pick some of those hellish pepper things that both of you like. It is good to be back to seminormal if one can ever be so with all of these wars going on all of the time." She was still talking and giggling to her pots and pans about everything in general and nothing in particular as he quietly slipped out of the kitchen.

Henri went to the water trough in back of the stable, took off his shirt, and began to wash. Ange had noticed him leave the house and followed him. She was peering around the corner of the building watching him when he heard her giggle. "Ange, are you spying on me again? That isn't nice."

"No, not spying, just looking. Henri, your skin is all brown."

"Oui, I know. I have been working in the garden without a shirt. It is hot and much cooler without a shirt. We worked without shirts a lot on the farm. Aunt Mags wouldn't let me at the convent. She said it wasn't nice, even for boys."

Ange asked, "Why, Henri? Are you embarrassed that I am seeing you without your shirt again?"

"No, you have spied on me before. Don't stare though. I thought we talked about all of this before."

"Well, I can see your muscles and your brown skin."

"Well, I would still tease you if I saw you without your top."

"Henri! You know better than that! Gentlemen do not look at ladies without tops. Not until they are married anyway."

"Well, when we get married, I'll stare at you all the time."

She suddenly became very serious. "What did you just say? Get married? Why did you say that?"

"I don't know," said Henri, "don't be mad."

"I won't get mad! Please don't ever tell my secret, but I would be glad." She blushed a dark beet red, turned, and walked back toward the house.

Henri was stunned at Ange saying that. He was just teasing her, and she seemed to have taken it seriously. She was a very outspoken girl, but this was a very young age for both of them to even be thinking of such things. Still there was something so adult, honest, deep, and mysterious about their relationship. There was a sincere respect, and one could always call upon the other for nearly anything at any time. Their talks were very often lengthy and covered every possible subject with the exception of things proper young gentlemen and ladies just do not talk about. Henri was the brother she had always wanted; and she was the sister, soul mate, and companion he needed. They were in complete comfort and complement to each other.

Madame, Mimi, and the others, even Jean, had noticed this and were watching with interest. A match made in heaven perhaps? Why, Henri was only twelve and Ange eleven. They were so young and then again possibly not. The young grew to adults so rapidly in these days.

The evening meal was served to the starving general while he growled to Mimi, "Please hurry, Mimi. I will waste away to bones before you are finished. You are worse than Madame with all of your fussing about."

"Patience, monsieur, I haven't let you famish in all of the years I have worked, first with Madame's mother, and now with you."

This was something new to Henri. He knew Mimi was a very solid part of this family, but this related to her complete authority.

Father Etty came to the house just in time for the evening meal. He always said he couldn't be late for Mimi's fine cooking. "Andre, what is this? You are hobbling around like a lame horse. I'll bet you had too much wine and fell down the stairs."

"Nonsense, Priest. You know better. It would be you, in any case, that fell down the stairs. This is just a small setback. The Spaniards fared much worse."

"No doubt, Andre, no doubt."

"Ah, Mimi, my favorite hash stuff. Bless you. Well done, well done. Henri, where have you been hiding? Will you join me in a fine dish of hash?"

"Oui, monsieur, and even some of the peppers if you have enough."

"Father Etty, will you join us with the hash and peppers?"

"Not on my oath," he laughed. "That is revolting and not to my liking. The peppers make me sick."

The general passed the small urn of peppers to Henri. "Here, lad, if you care to roast your tongue and innards."

Ange turned her nose up in disgust. "How can you eat that stuff? It smells hot even from here and makes my eyes water. I did take a small taste one time and almost died."

Henri laughed and said, "It takes real men to eat this stuff." He said it without thinking and quickly looked at Jean. He was glowering as usual but said nothing and went back to eating his meal.

The next day, as Jean was passing his parents' room, he noticed his father's prized watch on the bureau. That watch had been given to the general by Jean's grandfather on the occasion of his father being accepted into the officer corps, and it was one of his father's prized possessions. Jean quickly slipped the watch into his pocket and went straight to Henri's room. No one was around. They were all downstairs listening to the general telling war stories about the Spanish campaign. Jean slipped the watch under Henri's bedcovers and quickly left. That afternoon, everyone heard shouting from upstairs.

"Has anyone seen my watch?" roared the general.

Madame, Ange, Mimi, and the other two maids went scurrying up the stairs and started looking for the watch. Henri was in the garden and did not hear the commotion. After searching the immediate vicinity for the watch, it was evident it was not in the room.

"We need to search the entire house, and until it is found, no one will stop looking."

They searched the room again and then started going from room to room. Over two hours passed before one of the maids discovered the watch in Henri's bed.

"So what is it doing there?" asked the general. "There must be an explanation." Henri was called in from the garden and into the presence of the general and Madame. "Henri, my watch has been missing from my room and has been found under your mattress. Do you know about this?"

"No, monsieur, I have never been in your room."

"Well, do you suppose it walked into your room and hid under your mattress?"

"No, monsieur, I didn't take it. I swear on my honor."

"Henri, Madame and I have discussed this before we called you. We believe you. Not to worry on your part. There is another culprit here unless my watch has grown feet. I think everyone in the household knows the truth and who this culprit may be. Unfortunately, without proof, there is nothing to do except just drop the matter. The more one stirs a pot merde, the more it smells. If I had not made such a fuss at first, it would now not be such a mess."

"Andre, that is your nature to growl like an angry old bear, but we all know you are a tenderhearted pussycat."

"Hush, woman, not here in front of the lad. I'll be the point of jokes."

"No, monsieur, not by me."

"Merci, lad, do you have anything else to discuss? You look like you have something bothering you."

"Monsieur, I have been thinking for a while about joining the Armée. I am now twelve years old. I heard that you have to be twelve to become a drummer."

"Henri, are you certain you are ready to leave this easy life for one of a soldier in the field? Times can be harsh with the heat, cold, rain, and not to mention the dangers of battle. You need to be absolutely sure."

"Oh, Andre, he is a mere boy. You couldn't possibly consider such a thing."

"But, madame, I have thought about this for a while. I don't think it would be that bad. I want to try it if I can. My father did it, and maybe I can too. I like the outside, and there is the adventure. Besides, I would be out of Jean's way."

Uh, oh! Henri thought maybe he had gone too far. The general had only mentioned a culprit, but then everyone knew anyway.

"Oui, you may have a point," said the general. "We just don't know what else to do or what Jean may do as he grows more jealous of your presence here every day. I will talk to him as a general this time and not a father. We will discuss this before I leave and let you know."

"Merci, monsieur. I hope I can try." Henri left the room, and Madame started to cry.

"Andre, he is right, you know, but we all have come to love him as our own, and he is so young."

"Ah oui, mon amour, I know, but he has had to grow up quickly and will do well. I can see that he gets into my command. My men would watch for his safety. A boy may leave here, but a man will return."

"Andre, no matter what the outcome, I shall always consider him one of my own."

"I know, mon amour, I know. Leave this to me in the world of men things. Besides, I feel responsible for the loss of his father, and if this in any way can repay some of that debt, I will accept him. There shall be no harm," assured the general as he affectionately patted her hand.

The next few days were ones of extreme anxiety and worry for Henri. Had he done the right thing, and would the military be as he thought? He could not tell anyone about this and certainly not Ange. He was sure she would cry, beg him to stay, and be very sad. He finally broke down and told Mimi, and to his surprise, she encouraged him to go if he had the opportunity. "This was a man's world and a man's war. If I were a man, I would be there." She never ceased to amaze Henri with her very honest approach to life.

"Besides," she said, "there is this difficulty with the young master. It will not go away and only continues to get worse. He knows now he can get away with most anything and can do no wrong. It would be best that you go if you can and avoid any problems in the future."

Henri tried to go about his chores as usual but could not get his mind off this turning point in his life. The more he thought about the adventure of Armée life and going to different places, the more he talked himself into it. Still there was the distrust of the military instilled by his mother. He just could not forget it and her words to him. With all this inner conflict, his head felt like it was literally spinning on his shoulders.

Finally the general summoned him. He was working in the back garden when Ange came out and said her father would like to speak to him.

"What is this about, Henri?"

"I think I know, and I will tell you all about it later."

"You aren't still in trouble about that stupid watch, are you? Everyone knows what happened, and Father can't be that dumb."

"I really don't know for sure, Ange, but I promise to tell you later." He pulled his shirt off to wash in the water trough, and she giggled.

"I see you, but you can't see me," and then she ran off to the house.

Henri's heart was pounding like the beat of a fast-running horse by the time he got into the house and went into the general's library. Madame was there with him and appeared anxious and nervous. Might this be a no or an oui? He couldn't tell by the expression on their faces.

"Lad," the general said after almost an eternity, "I have considered your request and have taken the wise counsel of my best friend sitting here with me. I leave in two more days, but you will need proper Armée training here in Paris at the drummer school."

Henri couldn't believe his ears. He would be given a chance.

The general went on to explain, "Henri, my boy, you will have to pass many tests of physical and mental capabilities, and life will not be easy. You will be indoctrinated into the military way. I will take you to the school tomorrow and give my recommendation for you to enter. The rest will be up to you."

"Oh, monsieur," said Henri, "merci. I will do my very best."

"Oui, I am sure you will, lad, or I would have never considered this. You realize, of course, what you do will be a reflection on my recommendation and me."

"Oui, monsieur."

"Go and get your things ready. We will leave by midmorning tomorrow."

As Henri left the room, he knew he was walking, but his feet were not touching the floor. He went in the kitchen and told Mimi. She continued stirring something in a pot for a minute or two and was slow to answer. When she did turn to him, he saw the tears running down her cheeks.

"Henri," she said, "I will miss you more than you know. You have become like the son I never had. Be very careful and please don't get hurt. I will pound you with my wooden spoon if you do. Now please go and fetch a few more sticks of firewood for my stove."

Henri hurriedly left, not even noticing her wood box was full. As he went down the back steps, Ange was waiting for him.

"Well, smartie, what have you done now? I hope it wasn't that stupid watch thing again."

"Ange, please go with me to the back garden. I have something very important to tell you."

"Henri, you look so serious. What is it?" On the way to the back garden, he told her he was leaving for the Armée tomorrow. She was shocked at first and then turned to him and grabbed him by the shoulders.

"Henri, you can't leave me," she said, starting to cry. "What will I do? I will have no one like you to be my friend and to share everything with."

"Ange, you know you mean more to me than probably anyone. I don't want to leave you, but the Armée is something I have got to do. Please don't think I will ever forget you. I will be home from time to time. I will write you as often as I can. Do you remember our secret?"

"Oui, I do."

"Well, keep it. Ange, I want you to do me the biggest favor eve. can."

"I will try."

"My ring is the most important thing I have, and I sure don't want to lose i I don't know what they are going to make me do, but my ring will be safe with you here. Please keep it for me. I have thought about this for some time. Hide it with the rest of your secret things. If Jean knew you had it, I'm sure he would do something, like maybe throw it to the bottom of the river."

"Oh oui, Henri, I will keep it safe. Do you know what it means when a gentleman gives a lady a ring?"

"Oui, I do, Ange. Keep our secret." He slipped the ring off and gave it to her.

She leaned up and softly kissed him on the lips. "I love you, Henri." And then she blushed, turned, and ran to the house crying. He stood there for some time with all sorts of wild thoughts running through his head. She did love him and had kissed him on the lips. As usual, it had caught him by total surprise, and he did not react and kiss her back.

Just as well, he thought, *I have never kissed a girl in my life. I don't know how. I'll bet I would have been clumsy and made a fool of both of us.*

That night at dinner, the general made the announcement that Henri would be leaving in the morning for Armée drummer school here in Paris; and then if all went well, he would join the general's troops wherever they may be. Henri looked at Jean who had a shocked look on his face.

So the menace was leaving, but not like this. He was being given a chance to be what Jean had dreamed of. Jean, being more frail, realized deep down that he may never get the chance. He was deeply, deeply envious. He felt a mad rage building in him but decided to keep his calm. Good riddance.

The general rose to give a toast and wish Henri luck in his new endeavor. Jean went through the motions, and it all went well through the remainder of the meal. Father Etty rose after the general's toast and gave Henri a special blessing, wishing him health and safety.

After dinner, Jean caught Henri at a private moment and said, "So you are leaving. Well, good riddance."

"Jean, I don't know why you don't like me. I really don't give a damn any longer."

Jean started to say something, and Henri pushed him back, saying, "Just shut up and listen if you know what is good for you. I know you have made stupid problems for me while I have been here. God only knows why. I did want to be your friend. But I will tell you now that if you hurt any member of the family, and especially Ange, while I am gone, I will come back and stick my drum so far up your ass it will never be found. To prove my promise, here is the first of it."

Henri slapped Jean hard across the face, and Jean just stood there in bewilderment as Henri turned and walked away. Neither boy knew the general was just around the corner and had heard every word. The general thought to himself, *If only the two lads could be interchanged. That lad will go far in this man's world, but what of my Jean?* He felt tears starting to form in his eyes.

Henri asked Madame if he could use the study to write a letter to his aunt Mags before he had to leave.

"Why, of course, you can. You didn't even have to ask. There are writing things in the left top drawer, and the pen and ink are right there on top. I have never met her, but she must be a fine person."

Ange went into the study to be with Henri on his last night there. "Henri, you can't escape me for even one minute. I won't read your old letter, but I do want to be with you as much as I can."

"I know, and I want you with me too. I have to write Aunt Mags before I leave. I don't know when I will get the chance again."

Dear Aunt Mags,

I am sorry for not writing you before this. Don't worry about my fingers being broken. I am just too lazy. Ha ha. Merci beaucoup for the medal. Madame gave me a chain to wear with it and I will take it to the Armee with me. I think about you and the other nuns a lot. Please thank them for me. Tell Sister Celine not to go too fast with the churn. I was very happy at the convent with you, and as you promised, it is very nice here, and I have been happy. Their names are General de Chabot, Madame de Chabot, Jean, and Ange. Ange is near my age and like my sister. We talk a lot. She is very nice. Our cook is Mimi and she is very nice like Sister Celine. We were in a school and the master was very mean. Now we go to another school. I have been doing my writing and numbers like you said. I work in the gardens, stable, and help Mimi. I really do like it here.

Tomorrow I will leave to go to the Armee and be a drummer. Don't worry. The General said I would not get hurt. My medal will help. I will write later and tell you about the Armee.

I have not forgotten God like you told me. We go to church a lot. It is a big church called Notre Dame. It is very beautiful. I will say prayers for you and the others there.

I love you.
Henri Devreney

Henri read the letter to Ange to ask if it sounded all right.

"Oui, it does, Henri, and merci for saying nice things about me."

"I was telling the truth, Ange. You mean a lot to me."

They hugged and walked arm in arm upstairs to their rooms. Henri tried and tried to go to sleep but could not until very late. He sat in thought looking out of his window and listening to the night sounds of Paris. He prayed he had done the right thing with this military venture. *Ha, I will know soon enough,* he thought to himself.

The next morning, Henri rose early as was his usual schedule and went into the kitchen to see Mimi. She was cheerfully talking to Jules. He would be going back to duty with the general. It was obvious she was hiding her true emotions. Henri poured some coffee, took a slice of sweet cake, and sat on the tall stool near her stove. Jules got up and left to get his things together.

Henri said, "Mimi, please don't worry. I will be all right."

"Oh, I know, Henri, but all of us will miss you very much."

"And I will miss all of you too. I am going out to see Louis, Gussie, and Leon. I need to tell them goodbye." He gobbled the sweet cake and hurriedly gulped his coffee. "I'll be right back. Please tell the general if he comes looking for me."

He returned a short time later and told Mimi that Louis, Leon, and Gussie had hugged him and wished him Godspeed. Louis had told him to be careful not to cut his feet on any piles of horse shit, and Leon had given him a small bit of earth from the garden carefully sewed in a tiny cloth sack with a string to wear it around his neck. He said it would make certain of his return. Something about the earth-of-home superstition.

The rest of the household was waking by then, and Mimi was hurrying around with the morning meal. The general inquired if Henri was ready, and he replied with enthusiasm, "Oh oui, monsieur."

Henri saw Ange for only a very brief private moment and asked her to add the small bag of earth to their secret treasures. She leaned up and kissed him again. This time he responded, and the childish kiss lingered for a moment. The general had told him not to take anything but the clothes on his body. He would be given all that he needed at the school. With breakfast over, and the carriage being brought to the front of the house, Henri hugged a tearful Madame, Ange, and Mimi and got into the carriage with the general. The general, leaning back in the seat, said, "Remember this day, Henri. It will prove to be a memorable first day for the rest of your life."

It was to be a memorable first day for the rest of his life, and truer words were never uttered even by the most famous of philosophers.

5

Military Introduction

During the journey to the military school this morning, the general was unusually quiet. He only entered into a brief conversation with Henri and inquired if he was absolutely certain this is what he really wanted to do.

"Henri, before we get there, I want to confirm that this is absolutely what you want. Once your foot is in that door, there can be no turning back, and you will have to deal with any bitterness that still lingers in your heart from the loss of your mother and father. A loss which started with the Armée. This is very big step for a twelve-year-old boy. If you have any reservations, please let me know now and save us both any heartache."

"Monsieur, I know this is right for me. I know I can do it."

"I think I understand, lad, I think I can. This whole thing takes me back a few years when I entered the officer corps. But I was much older then than you are now and a lot less confused. I knew this was what I wanted and must do. I pray both of us have made the proper choices."

The school was a large white building with an impressive black-and-gold iron gate. Sentries were just inside the gates in a little wooden guardhouse. The general opened the carriage door, and the sentries jumped to attention as they were granted permission to pass. Henri and the general dismounted the carriage and entered the main front doors. The general inquired of the attendant sitting behind the desk where the person in charge may be and were escorted into a larger waiting room with several more people sitting in chairs. The sentry asked them to please wait a moment, and he would announce their presence to the commanding officer. Immediately, a captain came out and ushered them into his office.

"Greetings to our humble school, mon général, how may I be of service? Your wish is my command." They all sat down.

"Captain, I wish to introduce Monsieur Henri Devreney who has a strong desire to serve His Excellency as a member of the Grande Armée drummer corps. I highly recommend his character and would not do so if I had the slightest doubt as to his abilities. How do we proceed from here? Are there any documents that may require my signature?"

"Only one, monsieur, and only to verify to my commander that we have indeed accepted this fine young man into our care. Might there be any further instructions, monsieur?"

"No, Capitaine, I will take my leave now. I return to the Spanish front with His Excellency tomorrow. May I see you in private?"

"Of course, mon général."

"Recruit candidate Devreney, will you please wait for me in the outer room?"

"Oui, monsieur." Henri left the room, closing the door behind him.

"I am recommending this fine lad to your care, Captain, but no special privileges. He must be just like all of the others and make his own way. I sincerely do not think he would want it otherwise. When his training is complete, I do wish him to be posted to my command. I will be in touch with the school and advise my location at that time. As commander of this institution, I shall hold you personally responsible to see that he is adequately and properly trained. How long is the training here?"

"Eight weeks, General. The training is intense to prepare the lads for military life and to take what may be of the mother element out of them. Then they must learn the proper drum signals. I can assure you that he will be properly trained."

The general laughed, "I don't think there will be a problem with the aspect of mother coddling. He is an orphan and the son of a dead hero of my command. I hope you will see and bring about his best qualities."

"We always do our very best, monsieur."

As the general walked with Henri toward the main entrance to leave, he turned to Henri, offered his hand, and said, "*Bonne chance*, Henri, and God bless."

The captain took Henri into another room, gave the signed authorization form to a clerk, and told him to take all of Henri's personal information. The clerk was a very brief, soft-spoken, and mousy man with glasses and balding dark hair. He told Henri to speak only when spoken to and to reply in a loud and distinct voice. He wrote all information of name, birthplace, birth date, and home address. When the clerk came to next of kin and the address, Henri gave the name of the general and his address in Paris.

"This is most unusual, Cadet. Does the general know you are claiming him as your next of kin?"

"Oui, monsieur."

"Please explain this. I need to make notation in your records."

"Monsieur, my father was killed serving with the general. I am an orphan and have been living in his house for over four years. Madame is like my mother."

"I see, all right. I will note this in your records."

At this, the clerk could certainly see political clout, and one dared not offend people in such high places. The clerk became more human after this part of the interview and could see that Henri did have some of the qualities they needed at the school. With the records session over, Henri was given to another member of the clerk's office and told to report to the incoming recruit office. He was handed a report to give to the next in command. They went down long and dark passageways and finally arrived at the desk of a sweating heavyset man with a large bushy mustache and thick glasses. The man did not look up as they approached. They stood there for a few minutes while the man noisily went through some papers. Finally, he looked up and, without facial expression or emotion, took Henri's papers.

"Ah, what do we have here, fresh meat? I guess we will have to see about getting you properly attired so you can meet the 'evil one.'"

"Evil one." Who the devil is that? I hope the name doesn't mean what I think it does, thought Henri. He didn't say anything but did begin to have second thoughts about all of this. So far everyone had been fairly civilized. The "evil one" must be something else again. They were sent into the next room with shelves stacked high with uniforms, other clothing, blankets, and an array of things Henri would soon be learning about. He was given his issue of things and told to stuff them in a large bag at the end of a long counter. He signed a form of acceptance of His Excellency's property. More dragging than carrying the heavy bag, he was shown into a large barracks room. There were several other boys sitting on bunks about his age. The corporal in charge told him to take an empty bed, put his things on it, sit down, be quiet, and wait for further orders. Henri noticed there were not many smiles here. Everyone was so serious and seemingly unfriendly. *This must be the military way*, he thought.

The lad sitting on the next bed said, "Hello, my name is Michael, Michael Pasar. I am from Cherbourg near the ocean coast. What's your name, and where are you from?"

"Is it all right to speak? I thought that other fellow said to be quiet."

"It's all right, just so we don't make any loud noise. I have been here since yesterday, and I have been told we are waiting until we get a full class of ten before we begin training. There are eight of us now including you, so we need two more."

"I am Henri Devreney from here in Paris. Before that, I lived in Orléans and Blois. Who is this 'evil one' I was told about?"

"He is supposed to be our instructor, and they told me he eats little boys for the fun of it. I think they are full of merde. Hey, so many places you have been," said Michael, "I have never been anywhere except home and here. Maybe now I can see other places."

"And I'll bet we will."

That afternoon, the class was filled with the addition of two more boys.

Later that evening, a tall muscular man entered the room. Immaculately dressed with a large leather belt and highly polished boots, he was, as most everyone else here, unsmiling. His large face was made even more fierce by his mustache and bushy eyebrows.

He yelled at them, "Get off your asses, stand at attention, and do not move."

They jumped up and stood at attention near their beds. So this must be the "evil one." They would see, and he responded, "I can't hear you, girls. Speak up! Do you understand me?"

"Oui, monsieur," they responded nearly in unison and much louder this time.

"Well, maybe we are getting somewhere. It's time for the evening meal. Follow me in single file and no foolishness or grabass. Everything from now is very serious business, even sleep. Dammit! Get in a straight line, girls, where I can see what miserable creatures I have been given this time. My name is Corporal Perrilliat, and I will be addressed at all times as monsieur. Do you understand?" He received some muttering.

They filed down the passageways and into a large kitchen area with wooden tables and benches. They were served large heaping portions of mutton and vegetables in a metal bowl. Spoons were in a box on the end of the serving table.

A metal cup of bitter red wine was given to each one and two cups to the corporal. They ate in silence. Only a slight chewing and smacking could be heard. Every now and then, Henri would look up from his meal and find the corporal staring at them, not as a group but as individuals. They finished their meal and were herded through the back door of the kitchen where they washed their bowls, spoons, and cups in a large tub of water. Then they dried their utensils and returned them to their proper places in the kitchen. All at the firm step-by-step instructions of the corporal.

Returning to their room with beds and wooden boxes at the foot of each, they were told to sit at attention and were given an hour-long lecture on what to expect in the next few weeks. Tomorrow they would be given a physical examination and instructions on the military uniform, how to wear it and how to care for it. They would be given about an hour of free time now, and the lamps would go out then until morning. The corporal suggested getting their racks (beds) in order for the night before the lamps went out unless they wanted to sleep on the bare straps. Any personal things of the toilet should be addressed. If any boy here had a problem wetting the bed, let him know now. Henri thought about that, but had never wet the bed from the time of a small boy. One of the other boys spoke up and said he had in the past on rare occasion, but not in recent months.

"Damn good thing, Recruit, because if and when you do, out you go. No one pisses in my racks. You best tie a string around it to make certain."

Michael and Henri sat for a while, quietly talking about their past lives and getting to know one another. They were joined by another of the boys, and before long all were sitting in a group, talking and sharing. This was Henri's first taste of camaraderie here.

The corporal came in the room. "Lamps out and no foolishness. I will be in the room next to you, and if I hear one sound from here, you will all be sorry. And not just the culprit, but the whole damn lot of you."

They jumped in the racks as the lamps were blown out.

The next morning, they were rudely awakened by the sound of drums in the hall and people yelling to get up, get dressed, or the morning meal would go without them. The corporal entered the room and yelled the same thing. Henri ran for the water closet at the end of the long hall for blessed relief. He ran back to his room and hastily got dressed for the formation to the kitchen. The morning meal was a heaping bowl of mush with bits of fruit, and a cup of milk. After the same routine of washing up after the meal, they returned to their area.

They were to be given a physical examination this morning. "Remove all clothes except your underpants and follow me," instructed their corporal.

Thank God it wasn't cold or they would have frozen to death in this damp old building. They trooped down the hall single file with nothing on except underpants. All felt very uncomfortable unclothed in this manner. They saw others around in the building pointing and laughing. Well, someday it would be their turn to point and laugh, but for now, he could do nothing except accept the shame. They were lined up as a group and told to remove their underpants.

Most hesitated until the corporal yelled, "Get them off, girls! We don't care about little boys' naked peckers. We just need to make sure you have one and a girl hasn't slipped in here."

Michael quietly giggled at Henri. "Mine is bigger than yours."

And it was, but what difference should that make? The doctor entered the room. He was a heavyset man with balding gray hair and wearing the usual glasses. Henri thought to himself, *Everyone here must wear glasses except the "evil one."* The doctor had a long white coat of his trade. The pockets were bulging with little instruments of his trade.

The doctor stopped in front of each boy, made each one touch his toes, squat as low as he could, looked him direct and close in the eyes, and as a final insult fondled each boy's private parts with cold fingers. Henri winced and grunted as the doctor fondled him.

The doctor said, "All right, Corporal, each new recruit seems to have all God gave him, although a few seem more endowed than others." He laughed,

"I hope they grow some more and not be a disappointment to the ladies when they find out what to do with it. Now they are all yours. You had better give them a cleaning and teach them to wipe clean after a shit though. Some of them stink like whores."

What an insult, thought Henri. He had never been around people who spoke to others like this. Should he learn to talk this way too? They replaced their underpants and stood for a moment.

"All right, girls, as the kind doctor has advised, we need to get you more sanitary before you put on your nice new uniforms."

They were taken to an area behind the stables with large wooden tubs and instructed to get water from the large pond nearby and fill one of the tubs. Five boys to a tub and then the next five was the rule. It saved time and God's good water. Henri, Michael, and the others made several trips to the pond and filled the tub to nearly half and stood waiting for the next command from the corporal. Each tubful was given a small piece of white soap cake and told to get with it. They leaped into the cold water, and then one and the other used the soap to get the majority of the dirt off.

"I said everything is to be washed!" shouted the corporal. "Get those heads under the water and soap everything, hair, balls, peckers, and especially that crusty ass!"

Michael laughed, and the corporal asked him what was funny. "Nothing, monsieur. Sorry."

"Well, I'll be watching you, Recruit. Shape up there."

"Oui, monsieur."

They stood in the tub until the corporal inspected each tub load. Some he made start over and scrub this or that until he was satisfied. "Remember, girls, you must wash everything when I say wash. Don't be afraid to touch it. It is yours for life, and I have never heard of one hurting the owner."

Finally satisfied, each tub load was given a cloth with which to dry. They were instructed to turn their underpants back to front and inside out and put them back on. The corporal explained the clean side was now to the clean part, and they must remember this in case they could not readily wash their underpants.

"Well, I see some of you have mud marks on your underpants. Must we have a special class in cleaning of the ass? You girls must wipe clean from now on as it will be you and not your mother doing your laundry and washing muddy underpants."

They were then sent back to their area at a quick march.

When they arrived, they were told to change into regulation underpants and to put all of their nonmilitary clothes into a special cloth sack for this purpose. This would be taken back home with them as they left at the end of their stay here. The corporal told each boy to stand by his new pile of uniform clothing, and they would be given instructions on each piece, and they had better pay attention. The corporal did not like to give numerous instructions on the same things. He described each piece of clothing and told each boy to put it on. Stockings, pants, shirt, waistcoat, boots, and a special belt looped over the shoulders.

"This is your drum belt," he said, "and you had better take good care of this if you don't want to carry your drum in your hands. I saw a stupid bastard one time that didn't take care of his belt, and he had to roll his drum in front of him like a dog playing with a ball. He had a helluva time trying to beat it."

He laughed at his own joke. One just didn't know if the corporal was serious, joking, or crazy. *Maybe a bit of all of it*, thought Henri. Well, they were dressed in the uniform of a Grande Armée drummer, but each unit in the field had their own colors, and Henri would have to change as he was assigned to his permanent unit. For now, his uniform was white stockings, white pants and shirt, and a blue waistcoat with gold buttons. A double white belt crossed the chest. A flat cap with a shining black visor and chinstrap completed the uniform. The corporal took great care to make the boys see that everything was right and all clothing seams were straight. He said they made a sorry-looking bunch of goats, but by the heavens, he would get them right or they would receive a swift kick in the ass. He seemed a most unhappy man.

"You girls do not get the idea that you are members of His Excellency's fine Grande Armée. You are recruits and will remain so until I say otherwise. As of now, you recruits are lower than whale shit on the bottom of the ocean beneath a rock, and one just does not get much lower than that. Your initial training period here will be for four weeks. After that, you will be allowed one week at home, and then the fun will really commence. I will have boys entering my class and, by god, military drummers leaving. Nothing less than perfect will be accepted. Do I make myself perfectly understood?"

They answered in loud unison, "Oui, monsieur."

"Well, you are learning something at least. Now come outside on the parade field, girls, and we will go for a little stroll together." They filed out of the large wooden doors leading to the parade field and were taught the fine art of the military marching drill.

"Left, right, left, right. Halt! Recruit LeBlanc, do you not know your left from your right? Do you have two left feet? Pick up that rock there and hold it in your right hand. Keep it there for the remainder of this day including the evening meal and sleep tonight. Perhaps the dumb rock can teach you left from right. And what is so damn funny, Recruit Pasar? Must you laugh at everything? Do you think I am funny or a court jester? You too pick up a rock. Maybe the memory of this rock will curb your urge to giggle like a girl. I am deadly serious about what goes on here, and you will be also or by god, I will tear out your giggle box from your puny little body."

Thus the days passed, and the classes of military life, proper uniform dress and care, shining boots, physical exercise, and all of those things they would need to emerge from here as military people.

"You are no longer little mother's babies," the corporal would roar at every chance, and indeed, they were kept so busy that they didn't have time to think of home very much. On Sunday, they were marched out of the school and to a nearby church. "You must attend Mass on Sunday. His Excellency will not have heathens in his Armée."

Sunday afternoons were given to controlled games and running races. They could tell they were starting to be more as the corporal wished, and it gave them an air of confidence. Slowly the corporal began to get a bit more human and even friendly as he joked some with them. After the third week, while standing at inspection, the corporal announced that Henri would now be considered class leader. He would be responsible for the others and assist as he could. He was to be like an officer and could give commands. He was to report any misdoings or problems to the corporal. Henri was shocked and really didn't want this responsibility. He was given no choice, and the corporal asked the class if they understood Henri was to be their leader.

"Oui, monsieur!" they shouted back.

Michael asked Henri later if he should call him monsieur or just kiss his ass. Henri retorted, "I have not asked for this 'honor,' but now it is up to me to help the others as best I can. If you are a true friend, you will try to help me."

"Oh, I'm sorry, Henri. You know I didn't mean it. Of course, I will do anything to help you and the others. We are all in this together."

That night after the evening meal and they were all preparing for bed, Henri called a meeting. Michael went to his side for support.

"I have been appointed class leader, as you know. I didn't ask for this, and I am not going to be a snitch to the corporal, but it will be up to all of you to let me help you. I need to know if any of you are having any problems that we can help with, and maybe we can get through this thing together in one piece. I will do all I can to help in any way I can."

They were shy at first, and then Michael said, "Maybe we could have a lesson in cleaning the behind. The corporal said that had been a problem."

"Good idea. Recruit Pasar, drop your pants and give us a demonstration."

The others howled with laughter, and the shyness disappeared. The others, as they all were, were having problems with drill and asked Henri if they could have some extra instructions. He had caught on better than the most of them, and certainly some extra lessons would help.

"Sure, and we can start right now. We have a few more minutes before the lamps go out."

They all lined up, and Henri gave some special instructions on left turn, right turn, to the rear, and on and on. Michael was right there with Henri and assisting. Little did they know the corporal was just outside the door listening and smiling. This is exactly what he wanted. The boy did have some leadership qualities as he suspected. He was more serious than most of the others and made fewer mistakes.

The corporal called Henri into his room the next day and asked him if he had anything to report.

"No, monsieur. Some of the others asked for a little extra help with drill. I was giving a little help if that is all right."

"Correct, young monsieur. I did notice a little change at drill today. They seemed to be paying more attention. They can do it. Keep at it. If any others have problems that you cannot sort out, please let me know. I am not asking you to wag a tail, but some things you may need my help with. I hope you understand and will assist me."

"Oui, monsieur, I do understand."

This was Henri's first taste of leadership. The corporal gave Henri a stripe for his sleeve and told him to go to the outfitting room and have it sewed on. They would know where and how it was to be done. His first military promotion. The corporal made a visit to the clerk's desk and asked that this be noted in Henri's records. Even though he had been recommended by very high authority, to his credit, he was making his own way in this man's Armée.

During the following week, their drill improved greatly to the satisfaction of the corporal. It appeared everyone was taking more pride and patience with their drill and duties. They seemed to form a team and helped each other with problems. Henri and, now, Michael were right there with them. This was probably one of the better classes the corporal had instructed, and it was now a matter of his pride to have others in the school look on while they were at drill. Indeed, most of the time they moved as one through the maneuvers. The corporal told them that starting the next Saturday at noon, they could go home for a weeklong break. They would have to report back the next Sunday afternoon before the evening meal.

He warned them to leave all of the cheap civilian merde at home so as not to sour their military ways up to now. Upon their return, they would be issued their drums, and special instructions would begin in earnest. They couldn't wait for the trip home and especially to get back to get their drums.

On Saturday, as the group arose, the corporal told them to get busy, clean the area, put their things away, and lock their footlockers. He would keep the keys and give them back on Sunday afternoon on their arrival. They cleaned and scrubbed everything to the corporal's satisfaction and put their uniforms on for inspection. Nothing was ever correct, and several had to brush their boots again and straighten coats and belts. They were very correct now and proud of themselves.

"Girls, do not forget to take your old civilian clothes out of this place. They are contaminating."

As they were leaving, the corporal pulled Henri to one side. "Recruit, your achievements have been noted and recorded in your personnel records. You should be proud of yourself, but not too damn proud to have a big head. I have prepared a note for General de Chabot and ask that you give it to his wife for forwarding. She may want to see your progress also. Hurry back and don't let any civilian merde rub off on you."

"Oui, monsieur. Merci. I can't wait to start with the drum."

They mounted the carriage that was to take them home. Most of them resided in Paris or had relatives and homes to go to. Two others were going be houseguests, and Henri had received permission to have Michael stay with him as Michael's home was on the ocean coast. His father had been in the French Navy and had wanted him to be a sailor too. Michael would have no part of shipboard life. He had been deathly seasick several times even in a small fishing boat with his father. It was a life on dry land for him, much to his father's disappointment. They arrived at the general's home, and as the carriage made its way up the drive, Ange flew out of the door and came running down the drive. Madame and Mimi were now on the porch waving. The carriage stopped, and the boys dismounted. Ange hugged Henri's neck, and he could see she was starting to cry.

"What's the matter, sweetie, are you all right?"

"I am now that you are back. I have missed you terribly."

Henri introduced Ange as his favorite little sister, and they all went up on the porch for more hugs and tears. It was good to be home, and it all seemed so strange. He had only been gone four weeks, but it all seemed like four years.

"Please come inside, Henri, and bring your friend with you," said Madame. "We all have much news to share. Do you know Mimi has prepared some of that horrid hash stuff that you and Andre like so much? How you can eat it, I shall never know. Maybe your friend, Michael, would like to try some and think you are insane like the rest of us do."

Henri handed her the envelope with the note from the corporal and said it was his progress report for the general, and she could read it too.

"Oh, merci, and I will."

Jean came in the room and didn't say anything.

Henri said, "Jean, I can tell you about the military if you want."

Jean was stunned at this and mumbled, "Oui, maybe later."

Madame, Mimi, and Ange were surprised too.

Everyone went to wash for the meal, and Henri and Michael went to the area in back of the barn. They took their shirts off and began to wash when Henri noticed Ange's lovely dark brown hair hanging around the corner of the barn.

"Ange, I forgot you love to spy on me, and why I shall never know."

"Oh, Henri, I am not spying, and if you invite me, I will come there, and we can talk."

"Of course, please come closer. Michael, this is my very special friend, and we have shared so much since I have been here."

"Well, does that mean you two are in love or some sissy stuff like that?"

"No, we are just very special friends." Ange blushed.

Henri asked, "Did you hide my ring?"

"Oui, I did, and I am very careful to take it out only when my room door is locked. There is a special hiding place in my closet where a board can be pulled back. The space is just large enough for my little jewelry box. No one will ever find it there."

"I trust you."

"Hurry and wash so we can have dinner."

"Good," said both boys. They were starving as most boys are at that age.

Ange whispered to Henri, "I still like to look at your bare chest." Then she blushed again.

"Ha, Henri has a sweetheart," said Michael. "But don't worry. I won't tell. You can trust me."

"Michael, I told you we are just very special friends."

"Well, maybe in your eyes, my friend, but that girl has special eyes for you. I can see."

"Maybe, but I have my own things to worry about right now. Let's go. I am starving."

The meal was splendid, and Mimi brought out the hash stuff. Henri dared Michael to try some, and Mimi passed him the bowl.

Michael took a small taste and remarked, "That isn't too bad. You should have tasted some of the fish stew we had at home. Some of it is good when Momma makes it, but when Poppa makes it, whew. We have teased him that even the cats wouldn't eat it because it smells so bad. Now what is that stuff you are putting on your hash stuff? Am I to try that too?"

"Michael, this stuff is hot. Very hot. It could take all of the skin from your tongue."

"I am used to spicy foods. Let me try some."

"Well, take only a tiny bit at first and see how it goes. I am not fooling, it is hot."

Michael took a very small portion and tasted it. All eyes were on him for his reaction. His face turned as scarlet as Madame's dress, and one could swear smoke was going to erupt from his ears. He mumbled something about it being unexpectedly hot, and he would be more careful next time. Ange laughed and said she wouldn't taste it again ever. Her tongue got hot just looking at the stuff. She kicked Henri under the table. Jean mentioned it was the hottest stuff he had ever put to his mouth, and he would never do it again. They finished their meal, and Henri and Ange started helping Mimi gather the dishes from the table.

"You don't have to do this any longer. You have paid your dues," said Mimi.

"But I want to help you, Mimi. We are friends."

"All right, but the mam'selle shouldn't be doing this."

"Well, I want to, Mimi. I have to learn someday if I am to manage my own house."

"Will miracles never cease?" exclaimed Madame as she left the room.

After the kitchen duties were finished, Ange went to her room to change for the night; and Henri was sitting on the back porch, enjoying the cool evening with the sounds of the birds roosting in the trees and the night insects. The sweet smell of flowers planted around the back porch were particularly nice this evening.

Jean came outside and asked, "What did you want to tell me? What are you doing out here all by yourself?"

"Oh, if you are interested, I could tell you a few things you can expect if you go into the Armée."

"Well, today I was confused when you spoke to me. I really didn't expect it."

"Jean, we need to put whatever is between us behind us. I will be leaving for God only knows how long and maybe forever. I won't ever be a threat to you with your family."

Jean said, "Oui, I know, Momma and I have had long talks. Poppa told me that if I didn't change, he would send me off to a special school. Maybe I was mean and selfish. I don't know. If I am ever to get a chance to be a soldier, I have got to change. I will try."

"Let's stop all of this stupid merde, Jean, it is stupid."

"We'll see. What things do you want to tell me?"

"If you are going to get back with your father, maybe if you knew military things, it would get better."

"What type of things?"

"We could start with marching and swords. I know he could relate to that."

"Swords, huh? You just want an excuse to stick me."

"No, I don't. There you go again. Maybe we had better forget the whole thing."

"I will give it a try, Henri. Don't get your guts in a knot."

The next morning, Jean and Henri went behind the barn, and Henri showed him the movements of marching.

"Henri, I didn't know it was this way. Are you sure this is right?"

"Oui, it is. I won't do anything to make you look foolish. You can show Father when he comes home. You know, maybe when he sees you doing Armée things, maybe he will think more of you."

"Maybe you are right. It is worth a try. Show me some sword stuff."

"I haven't been at the swords yet, but maybe we can play at it together. I have seen swords in the reading room. If we are quiet, maybe we can learn."

They did try the swords, but it was soon evident both of them would need considerable more instruction. After Henri received a small cut on the back of his hand, they decided to quit the exercise and stick to marching. The rest of the week until Friday, the two boys met behind the barn for an hour or so; and in that short span of time, Jean actually did become fairly well coordinated with his movements.

On the Friday, Jean said, "Henri, thanks for this. Maybe I trust you a little more now. I wish you could stay a little longer and show me more."

"I wish I could stay longer too, but I have got to return on Sunday evening."

"Well, Henri, we will see. Maybe until then, I can put this childish merde behind us."

"All right. We will see. Madame will be very happy if we can. They do love you very much."

"Oui, I know. I think maybe I was just too jealous of you or too pigheaded to admit it. I will try, and I mean it. I sure do not want Poppa to send me away to school somewhere. I know he meant it this time."

Jean still harbored a distrust of Henri. Having hated and mistrusted Henri for so long, he couldn't help it. He was trying to change, but it could not be overnight. Was this just all an act to make himself look better to Madame? What was the reasoning behind all of this? He knew he had better play along for the time being anyway and see what happened. He certainly did not want to be sent away and knew his father was not fooling around this time.

Henri felt the same way. He wanted all of this hate and mistrust behind them. It just did not make sense to go on this way. But somehow he knew that he could never completely trust Jean, no matter what he said. He had always tried to feather his own selfish nest and would probably continue to do so.

Jean said, "You know, you have done what I have wanted all of my life. Do you think I can get a chance too?"

"Jean, you will be probably become an officer like your father and not just a drummer like me. Exercise to get more fit. By the time you finish your education, you will be fit. You are only a couple more years away."

"Henri, maybe you are right. If I ever start to slide back, punch me, but not as hard as you did before."

"Gladly, but only as a brother and not hard."

Jean thought to himself, *Oui, and if he does, I will probably beat him to death.* Jean left for his room, and Henri was going to look for Ange.

Madame was in the main sitting room and watched the two walking toward the stairs and chatting away as it was meant to be. She couldn't believe it, and when realization struck, she noticed a tear or two starting to streak the powder on her cheeks. She remembered the note from the corporal on the table and opened the envelope. It was a glowing report of a young lad who was considered to be a potential leader and having a very good future in the Armée. He had proven to be mature and well organized and, above all, helped his comrades. The corporal stated that Henri was given no special privileges but had earned everything on his own merit. This note would be very good to forward to the general, wherever he was.

The days seemed to fly by; and Henri was showing Michael, Jean, and Ange all over the gardens, stable, and secret places along the banks of the river Seine a block over.

"You know, I have lived here all of my life and never knew these things existed," said Jean.

"He showed me some of this, but not all," said Ange. "I love to look around and see new things."

Henri took the time to explain about the plants, trees, and stable; and when they caught a fish at the river, that was the most enchanting of all.

"Henri, just one fish?" teased Michael. "Why, near my home on the coast, they bring in huge nets full for the market."

"Maybe so, but we caught this fish. Let's take it home to see if Mimi can cook it for us."

Ange said in her usual practical manner, "There is not enough for all of us. Why don't you just throw the poor thing back in the river? Look how he is gasping for air. He may have a mother back in the river crying for her baby. How could you think of eating him?"

"Ah, Ange," said Jean. "You are my sister I am just now beginning to know. Oui, let's throw the poor thing back."

Henri put the fish gently back in the water, and they all saw him rest a moment and then with a swish of his tail was gone into the depths of the river.

The next day, Henri was alone washing up from work in the garden. He didn't have to do the work, but loved it. He had begged the gardener to let him help. It was enjoyable work in the sun, and the outdoors was one of his loves. Michael and Jean were with each other in the house. Since Jean had become so much friendlier, he found himself being readily accepted. Even Mimi was taken aback when Jean now teased with her. What a difference in only a few days; and Jean was enjoying the change, the acceptance, and sharing with others. He came to realize that he had been lonely with just his toy soldiers for friends. While Henri was washing and thinking about this, Ange came around the corner of the stable.

"So I see you have your shirt off again, and you are becoming even more brown."

"Well, you should try to get brown yourself."

"Henri! You are always so rude about this. You know I can't take my dress off here in the garden, and you wouldn't like me brown anyway. Why, you might think I was a slave for sale in the market."

"Well, if you were for sale, I would buy you in a minute, dark or not."

Her mood changed to very serious, and she said, "Henri, please, before you leave this time, let's not tease about you and me. Don't laugh, but I know I love you, and there will never be anyone else. I will wait for you for as long as it takes, but I need words from you. I missed you more than I have ever missed anyone. I actually ached sometimes."

"Ange, you know I love you too. You know words do not come easily to me. I do owe you so much. We are so young, and yet all of this seems so right. Do you realize I am only twelve years and you are only eleven? Do you think this is a childish thing? I do have feelings for you I can't explain. Sometimes it sort of scares me. I can't explain what it does to me when we are close and holding hands. I get this tingling feeling all over and especially in certain places. I shouldn't be telling you this, but you have got to know what you do to me and what it means to me to have you close."

Ange said, "I know what you mean. I get the tingling feeling too and can't explain it either. When you touch me or hold my hand, it is like I am in heaven and don't want it to go away."

They were standing close and looking into the depths of the other's eyes, savoring the moment.

"Ange, come into the stable with me for just a minute. This isn't like me. Please let me know if you want to stop."

"Why, Henri? Is this something I should be scared of?"

"No, I could never hurt you. I think maybe we should try a real kiss. I don't really know how to do it, but if you are willing . . ."

She grabbed him by the hand and practically dragged him to the stable. She said, "Oh, Henri, I do want to kiss you. We can learn together."

They looked around to make sure no one was around and went into the stable just inside the door and out of eyesight.

She came into his arms and looked up at him, closed her eyes, and puckered up her lips. Henri put his puckered lips to hers, and they stayed that way for a few seconds.

"Ange, I really do love you, but I don't see what kissing does for you."

"Well, I have seen Poppa and Momma kissing before. They thought they were in private, but I did see them pretty close. They didn't pooch out their lips like we just did. They opened their mouths and sorta rubbed lips."

"All right, let's try it again if you want."

She raised her slightly open mouth to his, and when he pressed his open mouth to hers, the lights and sounds of heaven went off in his brain.

"Mon dieu!" he exclaimed.

She was breathless.

"So that is a kiss? Ange, I will never get enough of this, and it does such strange things to me. I am weak all over and wobbly in the knees."

"Oui, I know, and I am too. I have never had such feelings."

They kissed again and felt the closeness of each other's body, rubbing and caressing.

"Oh, Henri, I know we must stop, but I am not strong enough. I am tingling and weak all over. I never want to stop."

"I know. I don't think I can stop either."

Just then, Mimi called from the back porch to one of the garden workers to bring in some firewood. The spell was broken, and they hurried out of the stable, looking at each other not in embarrassment but somewhat in bewilderment.

"Ange," Henri said as he continued to clean up, "I will never forget this. You mean more to me than anyone. Please wait for me."

"I guess this means we are officially engaged or something. Are you asking me to wait to be your wife?" she teased.

"You know it does, and we have got to do the kissing again before I leave."

"I know, and I want to too. We need to find a very private place. I think Momma is watching about these things."

"All right, you choose where, but please make sure it is safe. If we get caught kissing, they might make me leave forever and send you to a convent."

Saturday night before Henri was to return to the school on Sunday, Ange caught him by the hand going up the stairs. "Don't go sound sleep tonight, and I will come visit you in your room."

"Ange, that's insane! If we are caught, it will be very bad."

"Don't worry, I have thought it all out. This is Saturday night. The servants have the night and tomorrow off. Mimi sleeps downstairs near the kitchen. Momma has had several glasses of wine and sleeps very soundly like the others. Don't worry, if we are very quiet, no one will ever know."

"Well, if you are sure, Ange. This is taking a big chance."

She said, "Oh, I know it, but I have to kiss you before you leave."

"All right then, but we have to be very quiet and careful. Wait about an hour after they have gone to their rooms."

"I will, Henri, and I can't wait."

Henri was sitting in a chair watching the full moon looming up over the river and surrounding buildings. He could see the spires of Notre Dame framed in the trees and wondered if the priests were asleep too. It was a peaceful and pastoral scene, and the glow of the full moon gave an iridescent and almost unreal feature to the entire scene. He was fully clothed except for his shoes and stockings and did not want to undress until after Ange had left. He still worried that this was just too much of a chance, but he had to kiss her that way just one more time. He could scarcely hear her approach on her slim bare feet or silently push open the door. He heard a very slight creak as the door opened and saw her standing in the shadows. She closed the door and silently turned the key in the lock. He went over to her and kissed her slightly.

She took him by the hand and led him to the window where they could look at each other. She was in her nightgown with a ribbon in her hair and barefoot. Her oval and pretty face glowed in the moonlight. *Mon dieu, she is so beautiful*, thought Henri.

She whispered, "Henri, you are still dressed except for your shoes. Do you sleep in your clothes?"

"Only for this night, Ange, I am terrified that someone will catch us."

"Oh, don't worry. We won't be that long, and besides, I heard Momma snoring as I went past her room. The other two had their doors partially open and were breathing very heavy. I know they are sound asleep. Everything is going to be all right. Please kiss me like you did in the stable."

He did, and she clung to him with her thin nightgown, making every presence of her slim young body known to him. They kissed for a long time, and during the process, the tips of their tongues touched several times. They were completely lost in another world of inner joy and peace. They hugged tightly for a long time.

"Ange, this is for all time. I love you so much."

"And I love you and promise to wait for you no matter how long it takes."

They looked at each other in the moonlight.

"I must go. We have been here too long now, but I will never forget. Hold me close and kiss me one more time."

They did for what seemed like an eternity. Two young people very much in love and not knowing why. She quietly pushed back, kissed him lightly again, unlocked the door, and peeked out. No one was there or down the dark hall, and she was gone. Henri lay on the bed for a long time and thought about Ange, this time in his life, and the many things of previous times. He had a purpose to his life now, and Ange would be his Angelette and Little Angel forever.

He rose early, as usual, the next morning; and the events of the night before were like a dream. Had this really happened, or was it the figment of a wishing imagination? *It was real, all right*, he thought. He could vividly remember every minute detail. He hurriedly dressed and went downstairs to see Mimi. She was up and had coffee prepared. The hot liquid made his senses jump, and he was now wide awake in the world of reality.

"Henri, you look different this morning. Are you all right?"

"I don't know what you mean, Mimi. How do you mean different?"

"Well, I can't put a finger on it, but there is a sort of glow about you that I haven't seen before. Are you certain you are all right?"

"Of course I am. There is nothing any different, Mimi. I think you are imagining things."

"Oh no, I am not, Monsieur Smartie, there is something different."

Henri blushed and thought, *How can they know about last night? I didn't know it did that to people. What if everyone else noticed that something was different?* They could get into trouble, and then what? He sat there in silence for a time, watching Mimi fussing about her stove and pantry. Finally he asked her if she knew anything about boys and girls liking each other.

Mimi chuckled. "Well now, so that is it. The love bug has bitten you, eh? Who is the lucky girl, as if everyone doesn't already know?"

"Mimi, what do you mean?" exclaimed the horrified Henri. "Everyone knows what?"

"Henri, do you think we are blind? When you and Ange look at each other, there is a special something there. It's all right to like each other and especially you two fine young people. My, how fast people grow up these days with the war and all. And now you at just twelve are going to war. Ange is only eleven, but already she is thinking like a grown lady."

Henri thought to himself, *If you only knew, Mimi, if you only knew.*

Soon the rest came down for breakfast, and Madame announced they could all go to Mass and then come back for a nice Sunday noon meal.

During breakfast, Ange rubbed her bare foot along Henri's leg, and he began to get that tingling sensation again. Oh, how he would hate to leave this evening. The walk to Notre Dame was enjoyable during this time of the year.

There were many well-dressed people going to the church and just generally going for a walk along the river. Ange grabbed Henri's hand, and Madame noticed. The two were very close, she knew; but this was something new, openly holding hands in public. She decided to leave the situation alone and have a talk with Ange later. They were so young to know anything except very close friendship, but then again, she wondered what the future would be.

The Mass at Notre Dame was the usual awe-inspiring event with all of the rituals of High Mass. The candles never failed to inspire Henri. There seemed to be thousands of them flickering in their corners and special places in the old church. Ange was next to him, as usual, and clutching his hand as if to never let it go. The walk back home seemed very long, and they all walked slowly as if to prolong the afternoon. Mimi had prepared a special goose dish with the sauce they all loved so well. After the noon meal, Madame asked Henri if she could have just a minute in privacy with him.

Oh no! thought Henri. *She knows about Ange and me kissing. She will surely tell me never to come back.*

"Henri, you have proven to be quite a young man for only being twelve years of age, but then you young people are asked to grow up so much faster these days with the war and all going on. I would like to tell you that you will always have a home here with us. Jean and Ange can have you as a brother. I have watched you over the several years you have been with us, and I am very proud of you and what you have meant to the entire family and household. I also know that you and Ange are very fond of each other. I have seen you holding hands and playing fingers. This is all right, but please be more cautious in public as most adults we know would not favor such behavior. Am I sensing more attachment than just brother and sister, or is the attraction something more?"

"Madame, I am not sure about anything anymore. Ange is my closest friend, and I would never hurt her. We will be careful about holding hands if it is all right."

"All right, Henri, you may hold hands discreetly. This is enough on the subject. I wish you well, and always remember this is always your home. When your schooling is complete, Andre has asked for you to be assigned to his command. Do not think it will be easy as he will probably expect much more of you than any of the others."

"Merci, madame."

6

Drummer Boy

The carriage came to collect Henri and Michael all too soon. Ange clung to Henri's arm, openly cried, and whispered, "I love you." They kissed just very lightly on the cheek and hugged. Then Henri hugged Jean, Madame, and Mimi; and they climbed aboard the carriage.

Henri and Michael were unusually quiet on the return to the school. Upon arrival, however, they were soon caught up in so much activity, they forgot everything of the past week. The corporal, after meeting them at the entrance, told them to go into their area. Some had already arrived, and others would be there soon.

When the class was all present and accounted for, the corporal stood before them and said, "Well, I hope you have remembered to leave all of that cheap civilian shit with the civilians. We have work to do before the evening meal. Come with me, girls, and we shall see if you can remember anything about marching drill."

They filed into the courtyard and completed a few maneuvers to the orders of the corporal.

"Girls, I can't believe this. Try this again. I think all of you have grown two left feet."

They drilled until time for the evening meal. After they were told they could visit for a short time before getting ready for bed. The lamps would be going out earlier tonight because it appeared they needed more rest. In truth, the corporal didn't want to be bothered and had a lady scheduled for the evening. After lamps were out, they gathered near Henri's rack and shared the experiences of the week. Henri was feeling lonely, as were they all, and this extra time and conversation helped bring them back to reality. They eventually drifted off to sleep with the memories of their first military leave dancing in their heads. Tomorrow would be here soon enough, and the promised drums were anticipated.

The next morning, they were awakened to the usual loud drums in the hall. At first, Henri didn't realize where he was, but the corporal shouting for them to get up and get ready for the morning meal rudely made him realize his surroundings. They leaped out of bed, hastily made their beds, and hurried down to wash and dress for the day. During the morning meal, the corporal announced they would be getting their drums today. Formal training would commence at once. After eating a filling meal of porridge and coffee, they hurried out of the dining hall. They lined up at the supply room and one by one received a drum, a leather drum belt, two sets of drumsticks, and a practice drum pad. The corporal took them with their equipment into the classroom. He held up one of the drums.

"This, girls, is a drum. The purpose of the drum in military drill is a signaling device and can be heard over the noise of battle and across the entire camp. Your task as drummers for His Excellency is one of utmost importance. Your orders for the different beats will be given upon direct orders from the commanding officer of the order of battle. The troops will heed certain commands to the tune of your drums. If you do not do your job well, the entire outcome of the battle may be in jeopardy. If that happens, the commander will have your gizzards extracted usually through your ass. So from this time forward, pay strictest attention and learn. This drum has a wooden shell over which the head is stretched. The head is made of calf skin and stretched tight by lacing the skin through the hoops of the drum with these little pieces of rope. Excess rope is tied at the bottom of the drum by the drag rope."

As he explained each component, he took great patience to explain the names, uses, and what could happen if the drum were not properly cared for. "Keep it clean, dammit, keep the head stretched tight, in the protective cover when not in use. Protect it with your life or, again, your gizzard may be pulled out."

What the hell was a gizzard anyway? Henri would have to find out. Well, whatever it was, they were not about to mess up and find out the hard way. The corporal explained the importance of their responsibilities to their commander, to their units, and to themselves.

"Always be proud of who and what you are," he stressed.

He was being more human now and going to great lengths to explain everything. He even encouraged them to ask questions. Was he human after all? After all, this was the "evil one." The explanations went on most of that day, and the boys were all ears and eager to learn. They were being instilled with the sense of inner pride that would follow most of them the rest of their lives.

Finally, an hour of drill before the evening meal, but this time, they marched to the cadence of a drum played by one of the staff. "Face to the right, right turn, face to the left, left turn," ordered the corporal. It was much easier to march with the drum cadence, making the importance of the drum ever so much clearer.

At last to the wash area and the inevitable evening meal of mutton stew. Henri sure wished he had some peppers to spice it up a bit. They went into their area, and soon the lamps went out.

The next morning, they were told to bring only their drum pad and one set of sticks to the classroom after the morning meal. The corporal showed them how to hold the sticks.

"Hold them firmly, but don't squeeze the poor things to death. Think of these damn sticks as a girl's breast. Would you hold and fondle it, or would you squeeze it and make her cry and hate you? These sticks can be your best friends and will never complain. Much better than a wife, girls, you can beat on them, and they will never argue back. Now, girls, take your drum pad and place it before you like this. Listen to my cadence first, and then we shall practice it."

Ratta-tat-tat, ratta-tat-tat, and on and on.

The corporal was very careful to give as much instruction as needed to each one. Several caught on rapidly with the others not far behind. *They aren't too bad,* thought the corporal. *With practice, this could be one of my better classes.* He had had several before them that were good, and it always gave him a sense of pride of knowing he was doing his job. They became so accomplished on their drum pads by late that afternoon, he allowed them to hook their drums to their belts and go into the drill yard.

"Let's see what you can do with the drum. We will start very slow and try to keep in formation and step to the drum. Halt! You girls look like a goose yard at feeding time. Pay attention to the cadence, dammit, and step to the beat. Look at each other and maintain your distance. Lively now and pay attention."

And so on it went day by day, with the only partial day off on Sunday so the "heathens" could attend Mass. No playday here. They were too involved in their training on the drum. Special skills were shown in care of the drum. How to properly clean it, how to stretch the head just to perfection and maintain the quality sound, care of the drumsticks, and what may happen if they were suddenly inspected and faults were found. The old gizzard thing again.

After the third week, the corporal announced they were doing so well that if they maintained their present pace, they "may" be given another week leave before reporting to a duty post. Henri thought of all of the memories of his last leave and was more eager about this leave than anything ever before in his life. The thoughts of home, Ange, and the rest captivated his every spare moment.

What is this with Ange? he pondered at night in his rack. He liked her more than anyone in his young life. He tried to remember every word they had ever spoken to each other. He could picture her pretty face and, at times, could almost feel her hand in his playing fingers. He could nearly smell the fragrance of her and hear her tinkly little giggle. During this intensive phase of training, he had forgotten her most of the time. Perhaps they had been so busy, he had not had time to think of civilian things. Was this the true way of a soldier? To leave home at home and the Armée for the Armée? He thought about these and many other things lying awake in his rack at night. There was so much he would have to share with Ange. She was the only one in his life with whom he could share such things.

Finally, the day of completion at the drum school. The corporal said there was to be a short ceremony with school officials and certain other dignitaries in the morning, and then they would be given leave and their orders for posting to their units. Henri, as the class leader, would give the drill commands. The corporal would be with the school leaders and only be an observer.

Henri pondered, *Now it comes to today. I certainly know how, but this time, no one will be there to help me. I know I can do it. I have been well trained. I will show them and make them all proud of me.*

He talked to Michael and the rest of them, and all assured him they would be on their very best drill and try to be faultless. "This is for all of us," he said. "I think we are the best class ever at drum school. Our drum cadences are good and sound like we are one. Our marching movements are almost perfect. Let's do ourselves proud."

And indeed, they would try to do their very best.

On graduation morning, they checked each other's uniforms and equipment for perfection. Everything was gleaming and bright. They assembled in the anteroom of the drill yard.

The corporal said, "Troopers, you have come very far from the first time we met. You are troopers now and not girls any longer. I am very proud of each and every one of you. I know you will make your mark out there today as probably one of the best classes. I will be on the reviewing stand, and if any one of you screws up, I will have your gizzard, and you know how it comes out." With that he laughed, and they all started to laugh. The tension was gone, and they were relaxed as professionals.

"Troopers, you may commence when I give the signal from the reviewing stand. Bonne chance and Godspeed." He marched very sharply to the review stand, saluted the commanding officer, and gave the signal.

To the advance, quick march. Forward!

Henri barked, "Class, attention. Slow cadence march."

They stepped out of the anteroom into the drill yard beaming with pride. Their drums were beating in perfection, and there was hardly a flaw in their drill steps. They marched along the back side of the drill yard.

"Face to the left, turn to the left," barked Henri, and they turned in complete unison. They had it all now. There would be nothing to hold them back from a near-perfect drill.

"Face to the left, turn to the left." They were coming on to the final leg to the review stand.

"Face to the right. Pass in review."

It was perfect, and not one of them saw anyone on the stand. There was just a blur of faces. Just as well, for there on the front row was Madame, Ange, and Jean. After all, they were family members and the family of a general. The class made several more maneuvers to Henri's commands and finally marched in a line to face the review stand.

"Class, halt! Present!"

There was a smattering of polite handclaps, and the commander said, "Very well done, Troopers. That was probably one of the premier performances of this school so far. It is with pride I send each of you to our emperor's Grande Armée. May each of you perform with honor. Godspeed, Troopers, Godspeed. You are dismissed."

"Class dismissed," barked Henri, and then he saw his family on the stand.

He was bursting with pride as they rushed up to him, and all started talking at once and hugging him. Ange held his arm so tight, he thought it would break. She was beaming, and he could see a trace of tears in her pretty dark eyes.

Madame told him, "I am so proud other general of mine. The carriage is waiting, and as soon as you collect your things, we can leave. Jean, go with Henri and help him with his bags," which had been packed since the night before.

As they were going down the hall, the corporal stopped them and said, "The commander would like a private word with you, Trooper." The corporal put his hand on Henri's shoulder and said, "Very well done, my young general, very well done. Who is this young man assisting you with your bags?"

"Monsieur, this is my brother, Jean de Chabot."

"Is he coming to our school too?" inquired the corporal.

"I do not know, monsieur. He will probably go into the officer corps when he finishes his education."

They went into the commander's office, and the commander rose and offered his hand. "Trooper Devreney, I just wanted you to know you have excelled as a leader. I will have the clerical staff prepare a special report for the commander of your next assignment. I think it is with General de Chabot, and you will be given his location during the next week and instructions on travel to his location. Bonne chance, Trooper."

"Merci, monsieur, merci."

They left and met Madame and Ange in the carriage. Ange had saved him a place next to her and, as the carriage started, grabbed his hand and put it to her cheek.

"Henri," Madame said, "I thought we would all just burst with pride seeing you in command of the troop and giving orders so smartly. I really am at a loss for words, and you know I am not usually like that." All laughed, including Madame.

Jean promised, "Henri, I will try even harder now at my studies, especially to gain entrance into Armée classes."

They arrived home, and Mimi grabbed him with one of her monstrous bear hugs. "We all missed you, and I hope it all went well."

Jean said, "Mimi, you should have seen Henri. He was the commander and giving all of the orders just like an officer. That is what I will do someday."

"And I'll bet you will," observed Henri, wondering at this change in Jean's attitude. He decided he might make another attempt at trying to settle the differences between them. "Mimi, what's for the evening meal? I am starving."

"A nice roast goose with the special sauce you like so much and, of course, some of that hash stuff with the hellish peppers."

Henri went to his usual spot to wash, knowing Ange wouldn't be far behind. She came around the corner of the stable and said, "I was so proud of you. You looked so smart in your uniform, and why didn't you tell me you were the commander of your troop?"

"I didn't get the chance, and besides, it was not a big thing. They made me do it."

"Well, you were just perfect, and I'll bet you are the best ever." He laughed and was drying off when she grabbed him by the hand and pulled him toward the stable.

"Oh, Henri, please kiss me before I just die."

"I can't wait either, Ange. I live for these kisses."

They clung to each other and kissed. They were lost in another world when they heard someone coming into the back of the stable. They hastily stepped out, and Henri admonished, "We must be careful. It would be just too bad if we were caught at this."

"Henri, sometimes I just do not care. I love you, and that is all that matters. Don't you dare go to sleep early tonight."

"Only for a short time, Ange, and please make sure it is safe."

"Oh, of course I will, silly. Don't be such a scaredy-cat."

The evening meal was the best Henri had had in weeks. Mimi even prepared a special spiced apple pie, and Jean remarked that Henri needed to come home more often so he could have pie. Madame was pleased beyond words at the changes in Jean. She was certain that Henri had more to do with it than she could know, but some things are best unsaid. After the meal, they went into the sitting room for the tales and report of Henri and the training. Even Mimi was there. He explained everything they had learned and the importance of the drum cadence and the signals to the troops. They talked for an hour or so, and they all had a glass of red wine. Madame had three glasses and was getting sleepy. The conversation started to dwindle some. Mimi went back to her kitchen, Jean went upstairs to his room, and Ange stayed until the last.

"Don't forget and don't you dare to go to sleep early. I will be there as soon as it is safe." They went up the stairs holding hands and then to their rooms.

Henri was sitting in a chair with his shirt, pants, and stockings on. His elbows were propped on the windowsill as he looked out at the dark scene below. This was a lovely time of the year. The night air was cool, relieving the warmth of the day. Through the open window came a slight breeze from the river. The curtains danced to a silent melody. He could smell the fragrant scents of trees, plants, and flowers. There was a half-moon that looked like maybe God had taken a huge bite from one side. The remainder of the moon cast a slight glow to the scene below and slightly into the room. He was very anxious about Ange coming to visit and hoped she wouldn't be very much longer. He heard the door creak slightly as it opened and stood up as Ange ran over to him. He was nearly smothered with one of her best kisses yet. The tingling started again and seemed to intensify with each second.

"Oh, Henri, how am I going to live when you have gone away to war? I missed you so much. Not just for kisses but for our very special friendship. I have no one to talk with who truly understands all of the things we share."

"I know, Ange. I am busy with my military things, and my mind is kept very busy, but you are here at home and have more time to think about things. Try to stay busy and read as much as you can."

"Silly goose! Do you expect me to hug and kiss books?"

Both of them quietly laughed, and then he held her close for a long time. She had her head snuggled against his shoulder, and time seemed to stand still. She tilted her head and lips to him, and they kissed again for a long time. Her lips were so soft. The tingling seemed to be more intense than ever the longer they kissed. Ange said she would have to sit down before her legs gave away completely, and he agreed. Nothing in his life had ever made him this weak. Henri pulled another chair next to his at the window so they could look out and talk. They didn't hear the door open behind them, and that is the way Madame found them, sitting side by side framed in the moonlit window and quietly talking. They were both startled and jumped up.

"Angelette, what are you doing in Henri's room in the middle of the night? Have you no decency? Young ladies just do not do such things."

"Oh, Momma, we weren't doing anything bad. It is just that I have missed Henri so much, I wanted to have a long private talk with him. He is my closest brother."

"I understand, child, but you do not have to sneak about. If you two must have such private talks, please do so in the sitting room or place other than bedrooms. I think both of you know much better than this. Why, there could be a scandal if the servants or someone found this out."

If only you knew, if only you knew, thought Henri.

"Momma, may we go to the sitting room and talk if we are quiet?"

"Oui, child, but please be more cautious in the future."

Henri had been very quiet during the entire confrontation and felt like a rat caught in a trap. It was a good thing it was dark so Madame could not see the looks of guilt and blushing.

"Madame, I apologize. I promise to always be a gentleman with Ange."

"Oh, Henri, I wasn't worried about you or Ange misbehaving. It is just the implication of ladies and gentlemen visiting in bedrooms. I hope you both learn and are wiser about these things." She left; and they went down to the sitting room, lit the lamp, and continued their talk.

"Ange, that was too close. I was scared we wouldn't be able to be together anymore. We won't do that again."

"I agree. I was scared too. Not of getting into trouble but of not being able to see you again. I would just die if I couldn't see you. Do you ever think Momma and Poppa will understand how we feel for each other?"

"I am not sure I understand all that is going on with us. I only know that I want to be with you all the time, and your kisses make me crazy. I have to leave in a few days, and I will carry you and your kisses with me. Could I please have a small hanky or something to take with me? I will feel you are close."

"Oui, of course, I will choose something very special."

"Please, not something too girlish I can be teased about."

"All right, silly, nothing that would make the other soldiers think you are a girl. I will be right back."

She ran up the stairs and soon returned with a small white lace handkerchief. "Here, I hope this will be all right. This began as my first attempt at embroidery with the small lace corner and my initials in the next corner. Then as we became closer, I put your initials in the corner opposite of mine. When I realized how much I love you, I embroidered the hearts at the corners between our initials to show the linking of our hearts in a never-ending love. It is sort of girly, but I am sure some of the others will have such things from their lovers. Don't show it to anyone if you will be embarrassed."

"Ange, this is perfect. Just what I wanted. I will put it in the pocket over my heart. Merci, merci beaucoup. Do you think others have noticed anything different about us and the way we act?"

"I don't know, but I have been trying very hard not to be obvious. I used to get all nervous sometimes when you touched me. I do have strange feelings. When I say I love you, I mean it with things I can't explain. Do you know what I am trying to say, and do you have the same feelings?"

"Oui, I do, and I can't explain it either. I know I love you and always will and not just as a sister either."

"Well, we said we would be married someday, and maybe that is what this means."

They soon went back upstairs to their bedrooms. Henri lay there for a long time thinking of Ange, what she meant in his young life. There was a certain inner peace and security knowing how she felt about him. The entire world was perfect and correct when she was with him. The promise of adventures to come crossed his mind. *What of the future now?* he wondered. The few days passed too quickly. Henri and Ange secretly kissed at every opportunity, very careful not to be noticed by anyone.

"Henri, when we kiss for so long, my lips get a little red and sore. Do you think anyone will notice?"

"Mine do too. I hope no one notices. Do you want to stop?"

"Never! Not even if my lips fall off."

A messenger came to the door two days later with word a carriage would be leaving the next morning for the general's command in Spain. Henri's kit was already packed, and the last night was spent with Ange and one of their famous talks. He had spent time with Madame, Jean, Mimi, the gardeners, and the stable workers; but he just could not be with Ange enough. On the morning of departure, Mimi packed him a small basket of cheese, bread, cookies, and a flask to sustain him on his journey. He was thin, she said, but his muscular frame made him look so. The family all hugged him, and then Ange kissed him right on the lips with an adult kiss.

Madame got a peculiar look on her face and smiled slightly, thinking to herself, *They have grown so and are being deprived of their childhood years. First my Andre is gone and now Henri. Where will it end? This damn war, this damn war.*

Henri mounted the carriage. The driver slapped the reins on the back of the horses. Henri looked back for as long as he could at Ange and his family as the carriage eased down the drive and turned onto the street. And then she was gone, and Paris would be too in a short time. He felt for her hanky folded neatly in his breast pocket. This would be Henri's first real essence of military life.

7

La Musique Corps

The carriage stopped at the main barracks in Paris to pick up two more passengers traveling to the command area of General de Chabot. Henri was all ears as to their destination and what he might expect. One of the passengers, a wounded sergeant, was returning from leave to his troop. He was very talkative and knew most of the latest gossip and news. They were going to Bayonne, a coastal city on the ocean near the border of Spain.

Spain had been under French control for some time, and now the Spanish had given rise to throwing them out. The Spaniards had defeated the French at the Battle of Baylen, and the French were now evacuating Madrid. Napoleon was livid and starting to mass troops for dealing with the Spanish. They were certain to see action in the near future.

The sergeant thought the weather would be right and much better than the colder climates of Northern Europe. He had served in campaigns in several places where it was said one could freeze his balls off and do nothing about it. Even fires did not help no matter how close one stood. He had even burned holes in the crotch of his pants standing straddle over a fire. Nothing did much good, and no amount of blankets or cognac worked either. This would be a much better place to fight if they must.

This was a fast-moving dispatch coach with two drivers. The only stops would be to change horses, eat, pee, and rest a bit. The roads were not very good, and even though rain had not occurred in some time, there were hard ruts and deep spots. This made the ride very rough and dusty at times. The damn dust, even though much of it boiled behind them, did, on most occasions, enter the open windows. They left Paris and went through Versailles in the late afternoon. Horses were changed at a small military post just out of town. They ate a meal of mutton stew, bread, and wine. The sergeant advised them to try to down several cups of wine to aid sleep during the night. Henri did just that and soon after departure was fast asleep to the steady rocking of the carriage, dreaming of Ange's pretty face and kisses. They stopped during the night to change drivers and relieve themselves along the dark roadside. The other driver got into the carriage and was soon snoring with the rest.

Just after dawn, they approached Orléans. Henri could see the tall spires of the cathedral and the familiar turret of the convent. He wondered about Aunt Mags and the nuns. Had any more trunks been added to the forbidden room? He hoped not. He would give anything to stop and see them. Had it really been several years? They stopped at another military post to change horses and a morning meal. The meal of good hot tea and warm fresh bread with butter and honey was a welcome relief. They were soon on their way again.

Henri spent long hours watching the countryside and listening to the sergeant, who was a wealth of knowledge on just about every subject. His knowledge seemed vast, and he loved to talk. Henri napped as much as possible to stave off the boredom of just the older soldiers talking. Although he was very interested, at times he did want his private thoughts. At midday, they crossed the river Loire and arrived at Blois.

There were so many vague memories of long ago at this place. The military post was very close to the area Henri's family had camped on their trip to the market. He could see the large château on top of the hill. He remembered his mother telling him the master of the château would capture him and feed him to his dogs if he didn't stay close with them. Remembering his mother as a distant figure in a deep past, he was ashamed that he hadn't thought of her in a long time and could only vaguely picture her face, but he could not forget her pain.

This recall of memories brought about other thoughts and vague memories. He wondered what had ever become of Marcel and the farm, the villagers, and others he had known. So much had happened, so much.

Another meal of mutton stew, bread, and wine was filling, but boring. Mutton stew! The French army must have a vast supply of sheep for such a supply of mutton stew. A quick change of horses, and they were on their way again. Henri's entire body and especially his butt ached by this time. He tried to sit on one buttock and then the other, but short of standing on his head, there seemed to be no relief. The stops, every several hours to rest and relieve themselves, were the only welcome sort of relief. Henri thought he would rather walk a thousand miles than ride another one mile in this damn thing. The roads were a bit better in this region, and the ruts were not nearly as bad as they were closer to Orléans and Paris. There wasn't as much traffic here. They rarely saw anything along the main road and only hay wagons and smaller carts nearer the villages. The sergeant said the rains are not as bad in this region. The ruts were not as deep, but the dust was much worse. Henri and his aching body gave thanks for the ruts anyway.

Henri began to notice vast fields of grape vineyards and made some remark about it.

"Hell, lad, this is wine country. The wines from here are supplied to the royalty of the world."

They rolled through Cognac or La Ville de Cognac. The sergeant commented this was one of the most famous places of all regarding famous wines. The cognac or brandy as it was called in other places of the world originated from here in an ancient process that was said to have been developed during Roman times.

"Romans!" exclaimed Henri. "Were they here at one time?"

"Why, oui, of course. They ruled this entire place for a long time. When we go through the old parts of towns, you can still some of their old forts."

The sergeant, as well as being well informed, had also traveled extensively and knew a lot of the history of various regions of France and other places. One could tell he was an educated man and was also a ladies' man of sorts. He loved to relate his conquests in great detail and said the score of the ladies probably ran into the hundreds. Henri couldn't imagine such. The other passenger, when he wasn't asleep, laughed knowingly. He told Henri at one of the stops that the sergeant was probably lying to boost his ego, which was sizable.

The next larger town was Bordeaux. They could see the tall spires of a church in the fading light of dusk. It seemed every town of any size had a large church. Another stop for a change of horses; and another meal of the ever-famous mutton stew, bread, and wine. This stew had large amounts of onions and carrots and was much more palatable than some of the others. Henri again drank several cups of wine to partially put him to sleep. He was soon dozing and trying to ignore the bouncing coach and his aching body. His butt hurt all the way to his neck and in the other direction all the way to his feet. *How in the hell did these drivers do this all of the time?* he thought. He guessed one gets used to anything in time. Never this! Dawn brought Mont-de-Marsan, and the sergeant said they would probably arrive in Bayonne late in the afternoon. *Thank God*, thought Henri. He would surely go mad if much more of this bouncing, rocking, and constant jabbering was to be endured. True, some of the talk was interesting and informative, but mostly just prattle. As the general had stated, more like diarrhea of the vocal chords.

Henri could see large mountains in the distance and asked the sergeant about them.

"Those are the Pyrenees," he said, "and that is Spain just over them. These mountains are the border of France and Spain and have probably kept the damn Spanish on their side over the centuries."

Another change of horses for the final dash to Bayonne. Henri was starving this morning. He had long ago eaten all of Mimi's things in the little basket, having shared some with the others. Surprise! A very gratifying change of carte du jour of roast chicken, cabbage, bread, and wine, a welcome change from the damn mutton. *What a hell of a morning meal*, thought Henri, but at this stage, he could have gnawed on the leather seats of the carriage. The chicken could have been raw and still with feathers and Henri would not have cared.

True to the sergeant's words, they reached Bayonne late evening. The military encampment was just out of town on a large flat plain with just sprinkling patches of trees. Several small creeks ran through the maze of tents and merged in a larger one. Henri could smell the clean, fresh salt air of the ocean and made a promise to try to see it as soon as he could.

They poured themselves out of the hated coach, gathered their kit, and made their way to the troop receiving area. Henri just wanted any old place to flop for the night where he could stretch out and not be bounced to death. He was sure to sleep standing up if need be and not in that damn coach.

Henri awoke with a start at the sound of the bugle and drums. Where was he? In a daze, he wondered, were all of the events of the past days real? It was still dark outside, and he fumbled for his jacket. It all seemed like a dream or possibly a nightmare. He was still fully clothed except for his jacket and boots. He had indeed slept the sleep of the dead last night after being shown to a large tent with about ten others. He was stiff and sore all over as he tried to stretch out the kinks. The pallets were on the ground, but at least there was a cover over their heads to ward off the damp night chill and dew. He jumped up, put on his jacket, pulled on his boots, and glanced around at the others. Several seemed nearly his age. No one said anything and didn't look up much as if each was lost in his own thoughts. They rolled up their pallets and tidied up the immediate area.

A man stuck his head in the tent to tell them the morning meal would be served in a few minutes, and if they wanted to eat, they needed to hurry and get their asses to the kitchen area. They went to the kitchen area, which was just more tents, benches, and tables set up under trees. The cooks were serving mush, fresh bread, and tea. Luckily, there were sufficient amounts, and one could eat his fill.

Henri looked around, and there were hundreds if not thousands of tents all set in neat rows. He could smell the musky odor of animals and smoke of many fires. There appeared to be a cloud hovering over the entire area. The morning sun was just starting to appear over the hills to the east. On the way back to the tent area, he paused for several minutes to watch the water in one of the streams rushing by. He threw a small stick in the water and watched it until it ran on out of sight. *Where would it finally go?* he thought.

A few of the other fellows spoke to Henri and inquired where he was from. They were all members of the music detachment, and most were drummers. One was Anton from near Paris, and another was Gerard from Orléans. Henri told Gerard he had lived in Orléans at the convent with his aunt Mags. Gerard said he knew exactly where it was and asked what was he doing living in a convent. Another had his back turned. He suddenly turned and rushed at Henri, nearly knocking him down. Henri knew in an instant and by the laughter it was Michael Pasar from the Musique Academy. Henri grabbed him, and they hugged and pounded on each other.

"Henri, I am so glad to see you. I didn't know you were going to be with this troop."

"Well, neither did I, and it is good to see you too, *mon ami.*"

They were all talking now and getting acquainted when the sergeant came in the tent. "Who the hell is a Henri Devreney?" he shouted.

Henri replied, "I am, monsieur."

"I am not a monsieur, Trooper, if you don't mind. I am a sergeant, and you may call me sergeant or a piece of merde, but do not ever call me monsieur. I am not an officer. The enemy always shoots the sons of bitches first. Is that understood?"

"Oui . . . uh, uh, Sergeant."

"What did you do to have our general request you as soon as possible? Are you some kind of spy for the officers or something?"

Henri replied, "I don't know. I just got here last night."

"Oui, I know that, but whatever it is, stir your ass and get over there fast, and you are requested to bring any letter from home. Damn, you must be a spy for the officers. Next, you may be requested by le Petit Tondu himself, and that could be the end for of us all private soldiers. Just what is this all about with the general?"

"I have been living with the general's family for several years. He was my sponsor for the la Musique Corps. I am not a spy."

"Well, just make sure you are properly dressed. Come on, we need to hurry."

Henri hurried off with the sergeant to the area where the general and his staff were camped. The sergeant saluted and said something to an officer sitting at a table in front of a large tent. The officer told Henri to go right in as he was expected. The general, sitting at a small table studying a map, looked up as Henri came in.

"Well, Henri, I see you made it through the drum school. I am told you did very well. Are you well, and have you had something to eat?"

"Oui, monsieur, I have been treated very well, but the long coach ride makes me feel like a bag of sore bones. It is so good to stretch and walk again."

"Ha, I know just what you mean, but carriages do have their advantages. At least those in the carriage can ride out of the weather. Do you have a letter from home for me?"

"Oui, monsieur." Henri handed him the sealed letter.

"Sit down, my boy, you will get enough of standing later." The general read the letter from the school commander and the one from Madame. "Do you know what is in this letter from your school?"

"No, monsieur."

"Well, it is a strong letter of commendation from the commander of the school. He states you have shown leadership abilities. Did you know that your class was noted as one of the best recently at the school? He said you were a strong contributor to the class."

"Merci, monsieur." Henri blushed.

"Here, you may read the letter, but return it. It will go in your personnel file. I don't know what to say about this except very well done, my boy. And the letter from my wife tells me that my Jean is doing much better with growing up. His general attitude is much better. She said you talked with him. Is this true, or what did happen? Did you make good your promise and stick your drum up his ass? Oh, don't look so surprised. I couldn't help but overhear the night you told Jean that, and to be quite frank, I had to bite my lip to keep from laughing. But whatever made this change in him, I am grateful. I will tell you that you have become quite close to my Vivien and I. Although I haven't been home that much since you arrived, I see admirable qualities already instilled in you. Do you have any questions of me, or can I be of any personal assistance to you?"

"No, monsieur, I am concerned, though, how I will do in combat. I hope I stand like a man."

"All you can do, Henri, is your best. Things will work out. If you ever need me for anything or have any concerns, just come directly to me."

"Merci, monsieur."

"You are dismissed then, Trooper, and please let me know how you are from time to time. My wife would have my balls nailed to the front door if anything happened to you."

When Henri returned to his area, the captain in charge of the Musique Corps for the regiment called him in his tent. "Well now, I hear we have a celebrity among us. The corps sergeant thought you may have been a spy for the officers." The captain laughed. "We are not in the habit of giving any special privileges in this unit, so do not even think of getting anything easy."

"*Mon capitaine*, I don't expect anything special. I only want to be one of the fellows."

"Well, all right, young drummer, we shall see in time. You are dismissed, but bear in mind we will be watching."

"Oui, monsieur, merci."

Time in the camp was typical of the military way. Hurry over here, and hurry there, and then wait until someone in charge of nothing tries to make a decision. Usually the decision is soundless and makes no sense at all to those waiting. Orders are orders, however, and one must never question orders. Because Henri sees things in a different light, he does not question the orders but always keeps in mind a better or more efficient method to do things. An example came one day when a detail was formed to distribute firewood to the different sites for cooking.

Six members of the detail were given a cart and told to go to the wood-chopping area, load the cart, and distribute the wood in even portions.

Henri had been on this detail before and noticed only enough wood was portioned out to last approximately two days. He envisioned that if they made two trips and doubled the portions of wood, the detail would only have to work every four days rather than two. He told the others about this, and they were only too glad to work two hours longer and save the two extra days. This was a despised detail anyway. No one said anything about any changes to the sergeant, and when he found out, he was livid.

"Who the hell made this decision to double the portions of wood?" he raged at the entire detail.

"No one, Sergeant, but the idea was mine," said Henri. "By working just two extra hours, we will not have to distribute wood again for four days."

"So now you are promoted to general, are you? Any orders or decisions will come from those in charge and not a drummer. Do I make myself clear?"

"Oui, Sergeant." *Stupid merde*, thought Henri, but orders were orders and only to be blindly carried out.

Later that day, the sergeant came to Henri in private and told him that his idea was good and would be used in the future, but if he had any more bright ideas, to please come to him with suggestions. "We don't want to look stupid and turn the entire Armée over to drummers."

Laughing, the sergeant walked away. That was the way it was and always will be. If the change of orders come from the right place, the decision is always right. Henri had learned a valuable lesson of the military way. Think for yourself, but play dumb.

Endless days of marching drill and details seemingly devised by the devil himself were always present. The sergeant told them, "Troops must be kept busy to keep their minds on military things. Idle hands are the devil's workshop. The next thing would be you young clowns pulling on your peckers."

Michael, being of a very mischievous nature, particularly had to be kept busy. He was full of pranks and practical jokes. Any poor unsuspecting bug or stray piece of horse shit was sure to find its way into someone's pallet roll or private things. Anton, being more overweight than the others, was always hungry. He was often the brunt of Michael's schemes. One afternoon as Anton was sleeping with his head propped against a tree, Michael put one of his endless supply of horse turds under Anton's back. As luck would have it, Anton turned over and rolled in the mess. The laughter woke Anton. He promptly grabbed the smaller Michael and threw him down in the mess. Michael was so startled he didn't have a chance to react as the fuming Anton told him if ever this or anything else happened again, he would tear Michael's head off and shit down his neck. Michael took him at his word and forevermore left Anton out of his jokes. They were all friends, but respect for getting one's head torn off was another thing.

Henri and Michael would sneak rides on the horses from the grooms in the livery area. Both boys had always loved to ride. Henri was quite adept at riding during his farm life and mostly in Paris working at the stables. Michael had been riding for years too. Some of the grooms were excellent horsemen and would practice various tricks of riding standing in the saddle and hanging underneath the horse's neck and belly while at full gallop. The sergeant caught them one day and asked them what the hell they were doing in this area. Henri told him the truth and that he loved to ride. He assured the sergeant that he didn't shirk any of his duties with this but did it on rest periods and off-duty times.

The grooms were only too glad to have help in exercising the horses. The sergeant told them it would be all right as long as no one objected. The next day, the sergeant went to the area and watched with amazement as Henri, Michael, and two of the grooms went through their paces of tricks. Henri was quite a horseman for his age and size. Michael was good too, but not as quick and agile as Henri. The sergeant kept all of this in mind.

Then in late August, le Patron (the Boss) himself made his appearance and set up his headquarters near a small stream on the other side of camp. The entire encampment was bristling with excitement, and everyone was certain the invasion of Spain was imminent. Drills became more serious. The supply wagons were being loaded. Observation patrols were seen leaving and returning. The grooms told of horsemen leaving and not returning, and other tales of horses returning with no rider, and blood on the horse's sides and saddles.

Henri was summoned by the general one day in late October. "Well, lad, I haven't seen you in some time and had a letter from my wife asking about you. I have been so busy with le Patron here that I let you slip my mind. I guess you know it's no secret that we are planning an advance into Spain in the very near future. This will be your first taste of combat, and I need to know if you have had any other thoughts about it. Are there any things you might want to share with me?"

"No, monsieur, I guess I will be scared and confused though."

"Henri, your unit will be among the first to go in. Just follow the rest, and I am sure you will do well. Remember your training, and listen to your commanders. Most are veterans and will know what to do. By the way, you have a note here from my daughter. It is triple wax sealed, so I can only assume it is very private. It makes a father wonder what a daughter and a handsome young soldier are up to."

Henri blushed a deep purple and replied, "Oh, nothing, monsieur. Ange is like my sister. We aren't up to anything except that."

The general laughed and clapped Henri on the shoulder with his huge hand. "Oh hell, lad, I didn't mean to presume anything improper. It's just that a pretty young girl and a soldier are the brunt of many jokes here. If you haven't heard any of them yet, you most certainly will. Just cope with it, and whatever you do, do not tell my Vivien any of the jokes or Armée slang. I think she knows, but we never discuss such." He laughed again and gave Henri the note from

Ange. "We men have our own world, and the ladies would never understand. Please come again, Henri, and let me know how you are faring in this Armée life of ours. I hope the best to both of us in our future combat."

"Oui, monsieur, I will, and merci for the letter."

He left and couldn't wait to get into private and read Ange's words from home. It was penned in the tiny fine script she always used.

Dearest Henri,

> *I really do not know what to write. There is so much I want to say to you. I miss you so much. I cannot wait for you to come home. Everyone here can't wait either. I am helping Mimi in the kitchen to learn cooking. She said I might learn to cook someday and maybe not poison my future husband and family. I go to your room sometimes and open the windows for fresh air and watch the moon. Your ring is still in the safe place. I take it out every day and make sure it is all right. Momma and Jean are fine. Jean is kind to me now and knows I am lonesome. He went with me to the river and our special place, but we did not try to catch a fish. We just sat and watched the ducks. Please come home soon and think of me.*

> *Love to my special brother,*
> *Ange*

Ha, what a sly one, thought Henri. *She is telling me about her future husband and going to my room in the night. Then she says she loves her brother.* Well, that might be to anyone else reading the letter, but to him, it was an entire other world. He could picture her pretty face and smile in the moonlight. He suddenly felt very sad and lonely.

"What have I done? Why am I here anyway?" He looked up at the moon again and smiled secretly to himself. From now on, he would think Ange may be looking at the same moon at this very time. Henri told no one about the letter especially Michael. He had met Ange, and no amount of teasing might result.

Word came that the French had been driven out of Madrid. Napoleon was determined to have his revenge. In the two weeks that followed, the Grande Armée mobilized for war. Training, especially marching, was particularly stressed. The old-timers said this was to get the legs in shape, but in reality, it was to take their minds off the coming events. They knew this was typical of le Petite Tondu just before the la Fête. If nothing else, he had said, the fine marching and grandeur of the Armée would scare hell out of the enemy. Only small personal items were allowed other than regulation things in their kit to be carried. All were advised to make certain their water flasks were filled. Henri

118 | Dave Delony

had the note from Ange and her hanky folded in a small piece of oilcloth in his breast pocket.

Early in the morning just before dawn, the order was given to assemble in ranks after a hasty grabbing of bread rolls and coffee, "Route step forward in columns of four." The Musique Corps was second after the advance party of about fifty men. The drums sounded the initial steps to thousands of marching feet. After about five minutes, the order was given to stop the drumbeat. The columns were under way and generally lined out. After a rest period and meal of bread and water during midday, they resumed the march. At each rest, usually an hour apart, the overweight Anton flopped on the side of the road, panting like an old dog. The sergeant laughed and told him a few more marches like this would soon get him slim as a worm.

Late in the afternoon nearing dark, they approached a pass between the mountains. They were halted for the night. Tomorrow they would do battle with the Spanish for control of the pass and then on to Madrid. They were fed a hasty meal of the ever-present bread rolls and tea. There was as much as they wanted. They watched as Anton stuffed as much down his shirt as he could. The sergeant just shook his head. This time, the bread was some of the best Henri had ever tasted. To his surprise, there were jars of honey to dip the bread in. The tea was hot, and as it slid down, one seemed to come to life again.

Henri and his group took cover under the trees and covered up with blankets for the night. Fires were permitted as the Spanish knew exactly where they were, but everyone was just too tired to bother. Although it was late fall, the night chill wasn't that bad if one completely covered up, head and all. Their bone-weary bodies slept soundly. Henri was amazed at the different sounds of the men sleeping. Some made little cheeping sounds like birds, some whistled, and others snored like raging bulls. He fell asleep to these tunes, the memory of Ange's letter, and peeking out of his covers at the "Ange" moon.

Nearing the first light of day, the Armée was awakened by bugle calls. They went to an adjacent cook area and were given more bread rolls and coffee. Anton again filled his shirt. A short time later, officers started shouting and running about in great excitement. The captain of the Musique Corps shouted for immediate assembly and to sound ranks assembly with their drums. Bugles signaled the final assembly. Officers were aligning the ranks in battle formation, and Henri barely had time to think about what was going on.

Henri looked to the far left of the assembled ranks and saw Napoleon himself and his officer corps on a high hill overlooking the scene. Henri thought he could see the general, but he was not certain. Cannons from the artillery units began to fire from the right and the left; and huge plumes of dirt, dust, and smoke could be seen rising from the Spanish positions. The cannon roar was deafening, and they were not even that close. Little wonder the artillery men were all deaf and always screamed at each other rather than talk in normal tones.

The order was given to beat the drums at a slower pace now, almost anticipating the quick march yet to come. After some minutes of cannonade, the firing stopped. The officers gave the order to move forward, and rank after rank of smart stepping men lowered their bayoneted muskets and moved toward the Spanish lines. Gerard, next to Henri, said he knew he was going to piss his pants. Michael, on the other side, said he thought he just did. Anton looked as though he was going to cry and indeed had already pissed his pants. This was nothing to be ashamed of, and no one said anything. Henri didn't say anything but wondered if he would do likewise. His knees were weak, and it took all he had to force himself to move forward.

Surely there must not be any Spanish left alive after that tremendous cannon bombardment, Henri thought. The ranks of French troops approached the narrower pass. The first ranks were just inside the pass when the Spanish fired volley after volley. Henri's group was just behind the main first ranks. With eyes wide and mouth open, he watched as soldier after soldier fell. He could see the white puffs of smoke from the Spanish muskets and the

Les Canon
Old smoke and thunder—one of thousands

sounds of *thack, thack, thud,* and the cries of the soldiers as musket balls found their mark.

His group marched right over the fallen men. As if by magic, another large rank of men stepped in front of the *musique* group.

The volleys from the Spanish muskets and now cannons never let up, and man after man fell in bloody heaps. Henri saw one poor fellow's head completely vanish in the blink of an eye. He took a dozen steps before he fell. Others were seen lying on the ground, trying to hold entrails inside or to stop gushing blood. Finally the signal was given to the bugler to sound the retreat. This had been an initial probing action to see the strength of the enemy. Henri couldn't wait to get away from the roar of battle and screams of the wounded. It was to be an orderly fall back to the rear, but some ran in retreat. The officers around them kept yelling to hold fast and be steady.

This was Henri's and the others' baptism of fire in combat, and they had made it. They were terrified, but they didn't run. Henri had managed not to piss in his pants as a few others had. The officers were now waving their swords and shouting for reassembly. The drums sounded rank assembly again. These Spanish bastards were not going to get away with this and would be taught a lesson.

As the troops were assembling for another mass charge, this time at the Spanish, bugles were heard from the rear. Officers shouted for the troops to part. A huge cavalry troop swept through the lines of infantry. Huge mounted men with tall fur hats, swinging sabres, and screaming in a strange language charged through the ranks. In almost an instant, they disappeared in a cloud of dust toward the Spanish lines. He heard later these were Polish cavalry units on special assignment from Napoleon himself to break through the Spanish lines.

As the dust subsided a bit, Henri could see the white puffs of smoke erupt from the Spanish lines, and the mounted men began to fall. Horses and men went down in the carnage, but the greater majority swept through the Spanish lines, and the chaos was on. The infantry was given orders to advance on the double time. Henri and the others were so engrossed in the scene, they forgot to beat the drums.

The sergeant shouted, "What the hell are you people gawking at? Pound those drums and stir your asses forward. On the double! Get after it!"

Soon they were among the broken Spanish lines. The sight of so many dead, dying, and wounded men and horses was overwhelming. The remnants of the Spanish Army were seen in the distance in full chaotic retreat. The advance halted near a small stream. The order was given to stand down and rest in ranks. This battle was over.

Henri stared at the stream and couldn't wait to at least soak his head and wash the dust from his dry throat. After a few minutes, the order was given to take rest. Henri and the others ran over to the stream. Henri started to put his head in the water. He jumped back with a start as a severed head bobbed up and down in the reeds, staring at him with lifeless wide-open eyes. Michael screamed and fell over himself getting back. Was it Spanish or French? Henri would never know as he rapidly backed away. Well, so much for this spot. He, Anton, Michael, and Gerard went upstream and, after looking carefully around this time, stuck their heads in the refreshing water. The others laughed at Michael for screaming and falling all over himself at just a little old head. The joke was certainly on him this time, or was it? Henri might have screamed too if Michael had not done it first. They filled their canteens, found a spot nearby under some bushes, and fell into an exhaustive and fitful lull.

So this was war. Henri thought it wasn't really that bad if he wasn't the one getting shot, bayoneted, or run over by wild horses.

For the next several days, the main group of the Armée stopped to lick its wounds. The cavalry units would keep a constant pressure on the remainder of the Spaniards and would move right to Madrid. Part of the Musique Corp's duties the next day was to assist the medical corps. The three drummers worked together with a medical orderly picking up the less wounded, placing them on stretchers, and carrying them to the hospital area. Many badly wounded were left in the field. Some very near death, some more alert than others, knowing their fate.

A young soldier of around sixteen had a badly mangled leg and was crying for help and his mother. The orderly stopped and saw there was not much he could do, but the pleading of the soldier was too much. They put him on a stretcher and carried him to the rear. When they arrived, the doctor asked them what they were doing carrying dead people. They were supposed to be tending the wounded only. The boy had died on the way to the back.

They worked well into the night by lantern light. Henri figured they must have carried hundreds to the rear. Vultures and large black birds coming out of nowhere circled the scene and were landing among the dead and dying. Often it was a race to get to the wounded before the birds. Some troops fired muskets to ward off the pestilence, but they kept coming back, growing bolder by the hour.

Henri would have this scene emblazoned in his mind and hate those damned black birds forever. He made a silent vow never to be at their mercy.

The second day, the stench became overpowering. Another pestilence, flies, was everywhere. Where did they all come from so far back in the wilderness? The ones gathering wounded and stacking the dead tried to cover their faces with cloth masks, but nothing seemed to help. Finally with the wounded sorted out and the dead piled for burial, life returned to seminormal in the camp. They were told they were to have several days of total rest and then prepare for the final push to Madrid.

After tending to the burials, the Armée did rest for several days. They could see mounted troops leave the area early in the morning and return later in the day. The sergeant said these were patrols sent out to confirm there were not any Spanish troops in the area and to secure a safe route to Madrid. Although the cavalry had chased the majority far back, one could not be too careful. Early in the morning on the third day, the order was given to sound the drums for assembly. No drums or music on this march. Only an assembly call. This was to be a forced march with the entire Armée hastening to Madrid.

They marched at route step each man at a steady pace but always keeping up with the remainder of the troops. They marched in columns of four men abreast. Henri was glad they were near the front of the thousands of men. He looked back as they crested a large hill to see the long column stretched as far as the eye could see. A large cloud of dust stirred by the thousands of shuffling feet hovered over the column and gave the entire scene an almost illusory appearance of a gigantic snake writhing through the clouds.

Word passed at midmorning for a rest. The Armée flopped as one on both sides of the dusty road. Henri and his group were fortunate to have small trees in their area. After a brief rest, the Armée pushed on and toward midday once again stopped for a rest and a brief meal of bread and water from their flasks.

Midafternoon brought the same events, and they wondered if this monotonous marching on into oblivion would ever end. Just as they thought all was lost and before dusk, the order was given to rest and camp for the night. Anton said he thought he would surely die during the night and if he did just leave him under a tree for the vultures to eat. Michael said he would be happy to oblige his request and told Anton he would be sure to take his spare water flask.

"What a true friend you are," said Anton. "I hope something terrible comes up out of the ground and eats you."

They were all becoming inseparable friends and made so by the common bond of survival. The night was cold but not damp. They built fires with wood hastily gathered. Henri looked back and saw literally thousands of fires glowing along a long line stretching in the distance. Another meal of bread and this time a cup of wine. Henri drank his wine and asked for a second cup. The bitter wine went down all too easy, and soon Henri was curled up in his blanket under a small bush fast asleep. Sometime during the night, it must have rained because he woke up with a corner of his blanket wet. He had never been so tired as last night, but today he felt much stronger. Maybe he was getting used to long marches.

The cook tents had been set up; but there was nothing except more bread, coffee, and tea. They were soon on the march again, and as the previous day, the marching seemed endless. They were getting out of the higher hills now and more to the plains, much to the delight of all. They passed through several small villages, and Anton caught a chicken. He tied the squawking bird in the strap of his drum, and during the afternoon rest, they killed the poor unfortunate thing. During the night rest, they roasted the chicken over the fire, and chicken had never tasted so good. Henri's portion, a wing, and with the bread and wine, made a fine meal.

Late in the evening on the third day of March, they were told they were approaching Madrid. In the distance, as dusk was approaching, one could indeed see the spires of churches and tall buildings against the dim sky. Again, a rest for the night, but the anxious troops were anticipating the march into Madrid.

Early the next morning, they got their wish. The officers called for assembly and the Musique Corps to sound the march. The long line of troops in the column of fours marched into the city of Madrid. Citizens peered out from behind shutters and walls as they entered the outskirts of the city. Finally they were in full parade and went to the center of the town into a large plaza. The drums called the troops to order and to final assembly.

Napoleon and his officer corps rode up on fine horses. Napoleon dismounted in front of a large building, mounted the steps, and confronted a Spanish officer in full military dress. The officer, evidently one of outstanding rank, drew his sword, bowed, and offered the sword to Napoleon. Henri noticed the general accompanied Napoleon during all of this ceremony. Napoleon gave the sword to the general who, in turn, gave it back to the Spanish officer as a token of recognition and yet friendship.

The surrender was complete, and the Spanish Army was at the command of the French. The drums sounded and signaled the French to withdraw. Officers gave the order to march to the camp area on the edge of town. They wheeled sharply and left the plaza.

The next morning, the sergeant came to Henri and told him the general would like to see him as soon as he could get away from his duties. Of course everyone knew this meant to stop everything and go at once. A general is not to be kept waiting. Henri hurried to the general's area and presented himself to the orderly.

"Henri, do come in. I have wanted to talk to you after the battle at the pass and see how you fared. We lost a lot of men, and I worried you may have been injured."

"Oh no, monsieur. I was not even scratched, but I did see a lot for my first time in battle."

"Were you scared, Henri?"

"Oui, monsieur, I was scared, but I didn't piss my pants like a few of the others."

The general laughed. "I'm scared every time we go into battle. Only a fool would not be afraid. But you know, I too have never pissed my pants. Please do not tell anyone what I am about to tell you or I will have to cut your tongue off." The general laughed again and said, "A certain amount of this command will be returning to Paris soon for reassignment. Napoleon himself has made me personally aware of this. So if you want to see anything of Madrid, do it now as you can because you will be going back to Paris with my detachment."

"My sacred oath I will not tell, monsieur, but please, can another go back with us? He is my special friend I have known since the Musique Academy."

"Don't worry, my little ami, the entire Musique Corps of this command is going. The Spanish Army is now under the control of Napoleon and his brother, Joseph. All we need here is a detachment of several thousand security troops. The British are on the run too, and that bastard Wellington is leaving for his beloved England. Just do not tell anyone we are going. I am just giving you an advance warning."

"Oui, monsieur, and merci beaucoup." Henri was delighted. He was going home and would see Ange and the family maybe within a month or so.

Madrid was a charming and wonderful city. The weather was warm and pleasant during the day and a little cooler at night. This was the winter in Spain, and it was a welcome relief to have warm weather without the usual dreary cold rain of Paris and the upper regions of France. The Armée was camped on the north side of Madrid along the Manzanares River, which coursed its way through the center of the city and onward. Henri and the others couldn't wait to get into the city and see the sights he heard the other soldiers talking about.

Finally after a few days and after begging the sergeant, the four boys were given leave to enter the city. They could be gone from the unit for two days and would have to find their own lodging and meals. That would be easy enough. There were ample parks to sleep in just like the other soldiers, and there were small shops and restaurants in every plaza and side street. Between the four of them, they had little money, but they would survive. There was just too much to see and do. Anton worried that maybe they wouldn't have enough money to eat, and the others laughed at him.

"Always thinking of your belly, Anton. Look at you these days. The march with only bread and marching food has made you thinner than you have ever been. Why not just stay that way?"

But old habits of food were hard to break. They each had some money taken from pockets of dead soldiers, both French and Spanish. Carrying the wounded had its benefits after all. They wandered along the river and marveled at the beautiful bridges. There was an old castle on a high hill where they heard the Moors and Christians had fought a terrific battle before the Spanish had driven the Arabs out for good. At the end of almost each street, there were lovely plazas, and most plazas had fountains. This was where the people came to collect water.

Girls and women could be seen dipping large water jars in the fountains and carrying the jars on their heads back to their homes. Henri and his buddies were not really into the soldier ways of preying on the girls yet but were getting the general idea. The boys watched and wondered what they would do with a willing girl if they found one. Henri had a fairly good idea because of his feelings for Ange, but these men were older and making fools of themselves.

"Henri, what do you think we would do if a girl was willing?" Michael asked.

"I don't know, Michael. Have you ever done it with one?"

"No. I wonder how you start to do it. I have seen animals do it, but that makes babies."

"Yeah, I know, Michael. I sure wouldn't want to make a baby and have to get married. I have heard that is what happens. They say it is fun and feels good, but I can't imagine how. It looks awful, and I'll bet it hurts."

"It would be my luck to make a baby with an ugly girl and have to marry her," complained Michael.

There were special detachments of soldiers with orders to arrest any of the men trying to misbehave with the local citizenry. Toward midday, they were getting hungry and came to a small café with tables set up outside under a tree. They sat down, and soon the proprietor came out and asked what they might want. He was speaking Spanish, but the boys understand bits of the language. They ordered tapas, which are bits of fried fish served with cheese, mussels, sausage, and bread. The usual *botella* of red wine and the meal was perfect. They tried to pay for the meal with French coins. The owner accepted them, saying maybe the French were here to stay. After lunch, they went into the plaza at the end of the street and slept the afternoon away to the tune of birds singing and water gurgling from the fountain. This was the most restful time they had had for many weeks.

They awoke in the early afternoon and, once again, began their sightseeing tour. There was a very peaceful park along the river that they decided would be their place for the night, but it was much too early. They came to a very large plaza with huge ornate buildings and an immense church that covered one entire side. This was surely a place of great importance. There were French troops guarding one of the larger buildings. Officers hurried from building to building. There was a huge central fountain with statues of, evidently, important Spanish dignitaries covered with birds of all sizes and type drinking and causing a fuss. Henri wondered if possibly some of the larger black ones were not from the battle area. They went into the church and were amazed at the ornate artwork and statues. The candles gave a dim glow to the interior, and slight noises could be heard on the gloom. After they knelt to pray, they left through a side door.

An officer stopped them and asked what they were doing in this area. They told him they were from the detachment camped out of town and were given permission to enter the city for sightseeing purposes. "Well then, it is all right to enter the city, but this area is where the royal palace and government offices are located. It would be a good idea to keep away from here."

Hurriedly thanking the officer, they left by way of a side street leading back to the park where they would spend the night. It was nearing dark now anyway, and they didn't want to be wandering around after dark in a strange place.

They came to a quaint little café just across from the park, and the odor of cooking food wafting in the breeze was just too tempting. They sat outside, and a lovely young girl came out to take their orders. She was about their age and very slim with dark eyes and dark hair covered by a bright red kerchief. They ordered *pollo* or chicken fried in oil and garlic served with a delightful sauce of onion, pimentos, tomatoes, and bits of ham. There was plenty of very tasty dark bread and a special dish of very hot pepper sauce. Anton took a huge bite, jumped up, and ran for the fountain in the park. They laughed and said it served him right for trying to eat it all. Someday Anton would learn. The meal was delicious. Michael asked the girl to join them for a glass of wine. She would have to ask her father. He came out to meet the boys.

In Spanish, he asked, "What do you want of my daughter? She is a nice girl and only works here for the family business."

"Oh, senor," Henri replied, "we only wanted company and didn't mean anything bad. We wanted to know if she knows about Madrid and could tell us things."

"I guess it will be all right then, but remember I will be watching, and your word is accepted as gentlemen that no dishonor will be involved. I was a young man before I was old, you know."

The girl was delighted at the permission to join them. She was bored and wanted to hear new things too. Her name was Tierra, and she was twelve years of age. She did not speak much French, but as before, the boys did not have much of a problem understanding. She seemed to understand the questions they asked.

Tierra's sweet even girl's voice and laugh was a welcome change to the harsh voices of soldiers shouting and giving commands. Michael said her laughter had the sound of tiny silver bells. Her eyes were the most striking part of her appearance and were like endless deep pools of black liquid. She had a way of looking not at a person but through them. They had talked perhaps an hour when Tierra asked if her sister could also join them.

The sister was fourteen and could probably answer much more of their questions than she could. Tierra rushed off to ask her father's permission and to go get her sister. Soon she returned with a striking girl, a little taller than Tierra, and with the same dark hair and lovely dark eyes. Her name was Patia, and her voice and laughter was every bit as delightful as Tierra's.

Patia loved to study names and their meaning. Her name meant leaf, and Tierra's meant earth. She asked each boy his name to see if she could decipher the meaning. Henri had the meaning of ruler, Anton was worthy, Gerard was brave, and Michael was godlike. They all had a good laugh at Michael's explaining to the girl that Michael was certainly not like a god at all.

They talked well after dark, sharing many tales of battle, their homeland, what had transpired in their short lifetimes, and how sometimes like this they did get extremely homesick. The girls were asked many questions about Spanish life, customs, and life in general in Madrid. Surprisingly, life here was much like life in Paris and the homes of the boys. Henri shared with them his love and caring for Ange and said he thought of her as much more than a sister. Michael said he had met Ange, and she was indeed the lady Henri described. They were all too young to understand the meaning of real adult love as adults knew. Patia said Angelette had the meaning of little angel and Henri thought to himself *no truer words were ever spoken*.

The girls' father came over to the table and informed the group that he was closing for the evening, and the girls needed to go home. The boys bought loaves of bread for a morning meal. A large bottle of the sweet Spanish wine would be for tonight in the park. The boys thanked him and the girls for a lovely evening and said they would never forget the wonderful hospitality shown to them today. The girls thanked them for inviting them to an equally lovely time. The boys went across to the park and picked a spot with low bushes and thick grass near the river. After the wine was gone and conversation dwindling, they were soon fast asleep.

Michael felt something tapping him on the shoulder and glanced up. It was Patia leaning over close. She put her finger to her lips in the signal to be quiet. Michael got up. They went behind a tree, and he whispered, "Patia, what is up?"

"I sneaked out for just a minute. I just had to see you one more time. You are the first French soldier I have ever met. You seem so nice. I can't stay long. If Poppa finds out, he will kill me."

"Yeah, and me too."

"I know, I will never see you again, and I have never kissed a boy. Could you kiss me? I want to see what it is like."

"I have never kissed a girl, Patia. I couldn't show you much, but we can try if you really want to."

She came up closer to him. He could barely see her lovely face in the darkness. She tilted her head and pressed her lips to his. They stayed that way for several seconds. They parted, and then he pulled her back to him and pressed his lips to hers once more. She began to move her lips against his, and he responded. *So this was kissing,* he thought. There is something to this after all. She moved in closer. Her body was pressing as close as she could. Michael had a funny tingling sensation in his crotch. The more they kissed and rubbed lips, the more tingling the sensation became. At times their tongues touched, and the tingling grew worse. Finally they parted, panting and breathing heavily.

"Mon dieu! This is kissing. I love it," he said.

"I love it too, Michael. I think I could do this forever. I think I love you. I am scared and must get back home. I have been gone too long now. Don't forget me."

"How could I? I will always remember you and this."

She kissed him one more time and hurried off into the darkness. Michael was astounded and could not believe his luck. This experience was earthshaking and very unexpected.

The next morning as they were slowly waking, the night before had seemed like a dream. The pleasant company and nice, quiet, peaceful conversation certainly had a direct effect and made them think of other times and home. Michael thought his entire episode may have been wishful thinking and a dream. He pulled Henri to one side and told him the whole thing.

"Last night Patia woke me up, and we went off behind that tree over there. She said she had never kissed anyone and wanted to try it with me. We did, and god, Henri, I have never felt anything like that. We touched tongues several times. I was tingling all over and more and more around my dick. I could feel it getting hard. After we kissed for several minutes, she had to go home. What do you think?"

Henri put his hand on his friend's shoulder. "Michael, I know just what you mean. Ange and I have done that, and the tingling gets so bad, I think I am going to explode. Please don't tell anyone."

"I won't, Henri. You keep my secret, and I will keep yours."

While they were eating their bread, they heard the bells of the church at the end of the plaza and noticed people hurrying down the street. Having almost lost track of the days of the week, the bells reminded them that today was the Sabbath and felt the need to go to Mass too. They entered the church and sat near the back. This church wasn't nearly as ornate as the huge cathedral on the main plaza, but they certainly didn't want to go back there and maybe have a problem.

Just then, they saw Tierra, Patia, and the rest of their family enter the church. Patia, blushing deeply, shyly and knowingly smiled at Michael. Michael blushed back and was afraid someone would notice. After Mass, the boys greeted the girls and started to leave when their father asked them to join them for a meal.

There would be a bullfight that afternoon, and if they hurried and ate, they could just make it to the arena near the other side of town. They had a fine meal of roast chicken, rice, and a wonderful sauce with the onions, pimentos, and tomatoes as they had last night. There was the hot sauce too, but only Henri took some. The girls' father, two neighbors, the two girls, and the boys were all going to the bullfights. The women were going to stay home with the smaller children and do whatever women do on a leisurely Sunday afternoon. They would certainly enjoy the peace and quiet with the rest of the family being gone.

The weather was beautiful with scarcely a cloud in the bright blue sky. Even though it was midwinter in Spain, the sun warmed the earthly regions to almost hot. While walking to the arena, the boys removed their jackets, rolled them up in military fashion, and stowed them in their backpacks. After a lengthy walk and joining the crowds, they arrived at the Plaza de Toros.

The arena was set in circular fashion with high stone steps on the inside and a high straight wall on the outside. After paying their admittance fee, they entered through the massive wooden gate. It was nearing midafternoon. The sun was still high in the heavens, plus their exertion from the long walk made them overly warm. One of the neighbors and Anton were out of breath and huffing and puffing like one of the bulls to perform. They mounted the stone steps and made their way to an area where they normally sat.

"These are the best places," said Patia. "You can see everything from here."

They were all comfortable sitting on their coats and backpacks and drinking water from their flasks. The boys were constantly asking the girls questions about the event to come. Patia was sitting next to Michael, and Henri noticed they discreetly touched at every opportunity. Tierra was sitting next to Henri and did the same. He looked at her several times as they touched arms, legs, or feet. She shyly smiled and did not move away. Several times she moved closer until they were touching more. Finally she whispered in Henri's ear, "Did Michael talk to you?"

"About what, Tierra?"

"Patia told me she went to him last night, and they kissed a lot. He didn't tell you?"

"Oui, he did, why?"

"Patia told me that she had never felt anything like that and I would have to try it."

"You mean you want to kiss me?"

"If you want to. Do you think I am pretty?"

"Oui, you are very pretty. I would like to kiss you. When though and where?"

"After the bullfight. We can find a place."

"All right."

"I can't wait, Henri. Do you think I am bad?"

"No. I can't wait either."

They had never seen fighting with bulls. It just wasn't done in France. Everyone seemed to get so excited about it. They were told this corrida would last for quite some time this afternoon. Probably several hours. Henri wondered when he would get the chance to kiss Tierra.

Finally the trumpets sounded, and the pageant began. The performers trooped out of a gate on the far side of the arena floor and marched the entire way around to the sound of the blaring trumpets and drums. The crowd was cheering and yelling to the brightly dressed men on the floor below. Most of the performers were dressed in very bright cloaks and jackets of red, green, black, and purple. Others were dressed in jackets of bright gold braid.

Tierra, sitting next to Henri, explained these were the matadors and were the brave ones to fight the bulls. Their bright clothes were called *traje de luces* or a suit of lights. In addition, each matador had a sword and a bright red cloak. Surely these foolish men were not going to fight raging bulls with just a sword? As soon as the procession ended, a hushed quiet fell over the crowd. A gate banged open on the side of the arena, and a huge black bull ran out, bellowing and throwing large amounts of earth into the air with his hooves. Tierra said the bull was already very angry as he had been teased and cut with knives before he was let into the arena.

A man mounted on a horse with huge heavy blankets on his sides came into the arena. The man was also dressed in a brightly colored jacket and carried a long lance. When the bull saw the mounted rider, he made a dash for him. The bull hit the horse on the side, and as he did so, the rider buried the lance deep in the bull's back. He bellowed in pain and came at the rider again in a fury. Again the lance went deep into the back of the bull. After several more sessions of this, the bull seemed to understand the lance would always follow his charge at the horse, and he became more reluctant to charge again.

Blood was pouring freely down the bull's back and sides. Tierra explained this was getting the bull weak so the matador could fight him. This didn't seem fair to Henri.

Another man entered the arena on foot. He carried a shorter barbed lance with brightly colored ribbons in each hand. He approached the bull head-on; and the bull, sensing this other tormenter may be easier prey, made a charge at the man. This man was known as a banderillero, Henri was told, and it was his job to further weaken the bull.

This is still not fair, thought Henri. *Soon there will not be a live bull for the matador to fight.* As the bull charged the banderillero, he deftly stepped to the side and implanted the barbed lances in the bull's back. The man ran back to the gate and was handed another set of lances by an assistant.

Four more rounds of this, and the bull's back was covered with lances and the bright colored ribbons shaking and glimmering against the pouring red blood. The crowd was wildly cheering and yelling.

The hero of the event, the matador, came out of the gate. He marched straight for the bull and yelled at him to attract his attention.

"Hey, hey, Toro, hey, hey," taunted the matador all the while holding his bright red cape before the bull. The bull made a mad charge as the matador stepped to the side with the bull's horns barely missing him.

"Ole!" shouted the crowd, and again and again as the bull charged the red cape. Finally the exhausted bull just stood glaring at the matador. He was snorting and pawing the earth, again throwing large amounts of dust in the air. The matador drew his sword, placed it in the fold of his cape, and walked directly up to the bull.

He waved the cape and yelled, "Toro, Toro, Toro, hey, hey!"

The bull made one last attempt to rid himself of his tormenter, but this time, a sword was planted deep in his back as he rushed by. He went a very short distance and fell in a heap of blood and bright colored ribbons. The crowd was now frenzied and yelling and waving white handkerchiefs. A shower of flowers went into the arena around the matador.

Two mounted riders entered the arena and dismounted at the bull. One of them plunged a knife deep in the back of the bull's neck and cut off both ears. One ear he kept, and the other he gave to the matador. Then the riders tied ropes on the bull and dragged him out of the arena.

This entire performance was repeated six times that afternoon, and Henri was secretly hoping at least one of the bulls would catch someone and even the score. It was a gory and bloody sport, and Henri didn't see much sense in it at all. He didn't say anything to his hosts, but he was glad when they left and started back to the camp area. The boys bowed and shook hands with the girls.

Tierra whispered to Henri, "Stay in the park as long as you can. I'll be there."

Henri could see Patia whispering something to Michael and knew what was up.

Michael whispered to Henri, "The girls want to come over. Can you wait?"

"All right, but we need to get rid of Anton and Gerard. We can tell them to go ahead and we will catch up. Say you don't feel good and want to rest a bit. I will say I will stay with you."

"Good idea. Let's do it." Michael, feigning some sort of illness or another, lay down; and the act was on. Anton and Gerard packed up and left soon after.

Henri said they would catch up as soon as things got better. Little did the other two know just how much better.

Just at dark, the two girls came to the park. Not a word was said as Patia took Michael by the hand and went farther back in the trees. Henri shyly stood there, and Tierra took his hand and pulled him in the other direction. She stood in the shadows and moved a little closer.

"Henri, are you sure you want to kiss me?"

"We can try if you want to."

She moved closer and moved her head and lips closer to his. He touched his lips to hers. They stood there for several seconds with just lips touching. Then Henri moved, pulling her body completely to his. He moved his lips in the rubbing motion taught by Ange. Tierra immediately responded and started rubbing her lips to his. They touched tongues several times. Henri felt the tingling starting as it had with Ange. He hugged Tierra closer. She pressed to him and put her arms around his waist, pulling him closer until they were almost as one. The kisses intensified; and the tingling was as Michael's was, as Michael had said, mostly in his nether regions. They finally parted. Henri looked deeply in her eyes. They were partially glazed.

"Henri, I have never felt anything like this. Patia was right. I could do this forever."

"Me too, Tierra. I have this funny feeling."

"I know, me too. I feel funny all over."

At that, Patia called to them. They would have to get back before they were found out. Henri kissed Tierra one more time. She responded with fire. Her tongue danced on his lips. His head was spinning as they parted again. They agreed that they would never forget this as long as they lived. Henri and Michael picked up their packs, slung them over their backs, and trudged off. The girls stood there for a time and went to their home. Neither one said anything. They would compare notes later when their thoughts were more sane.

Neither the girls nor the boys would ever forget this. Comrades, friends, and lovers for a short time and probably never to see each other again. What would ever happen to each of them? Henri would think of this over and over again with wonder. *Oh well, c'est la vie,* thought Henri. He would never tell any of this. Michael and Henri swore the other to secrecy after comparing their every feeling, actions, and reactions.

The next several days were a frenzy of activity as word spread through the camp they would be leaving for France in the near future. Home, home, home, Ange, Ange, Ange captured Henri's every thought. À bientôt, Spain.

8

Austria Campaign 1809,

The march back to France during January 1809 took nearly three weeks; and the fair weather of Spain turned to the mud, rain, and cold the farther north they went. This was not a forced march going into battle, but Napoleon would not let his Armée become slack. Once they got out of the low mountains and into the more flat plains of France, the going was better. Henri was glad they were, once again, more toward the front of the column because of the roads.

First it was the choking dust and now the damn mud. The thousands of marching feet, horses, carriages, wagons, cannons, and caissons stirred the dust into clouds that constantly hovered over the column. Now with the wetness, it had churned the mud into a morass of dark ooze. Slosh, slip, and slide was the order of march now; but whatever, stay on your feet. It was miserable enough from the knees down, but to be wet and muddy all over would be beyond endurance. Rest stops were frequent, and at day's end, the men slept in whatever shelter they could find. Very often, it was a tree or low bush at the side of the road near a fire.

The four inseparable drummers always slept in a huddle with tree limbs or any other cover over their cloaks. The rain and mist persisted during most of the march, and only the hardiest did not have a malady of some sort. Henri and the rest of the four had head colds and were running a fever by the time the outskirts of Paris were reached.

Excitement grew with every step as the outline of the city could be seen in the dusk. Only a short time now, and they could rest forever. Henri had his drum slung across his back with the rest of his gear. This made the carrying much easier than a front carry. It really wasn't regulation, but no one seemed to pay attention as long as they kept up. This damn drum was a pain in the backside literally, but it was his instrument of war. Maybe someday he could trade it in for a musket or at best be with the mounted troops and ride on top of the ankle-deep goo.

The march had been very monotonous, and it was one step after another for days never ending without even thinking of the march. One foot forward and the next foot behind that one. Plod and plod. Slip and slide in the goo.

His mind wandered a lot during these times; and he recalled memories of the farm, Aunt Mags, life in Paris, but, most of all, Ange. He thought of Tierra too. Should he ever tell Ange? Nothing really had happened except kisses. He finally decided that this would be his secret. Telling any of it would only bring misunderstanding and hurt. Tierra would vanish forever. Most of his thoughts were of Ange. He could picture every feature of her face, trim figure, and delicate hands and even imagine her in some of her favorite dresses. Her tinkly little giggle and laugh jerked him back to reality at odd times, and he would turn and look for her. No one had ever captivated him like this before, nor did he think would ever again. He would often just feel for the letter and hanky in the oilskin wrapping just to make certain it was still there in his breast pocket. How often he had read it over and over again he could not count. How many years old was she now? The only way he could remember was that he now was nearing fourteen years, and she was one year less. She would be almost thirteen now, nearly a woman.

And one could say he was a man now with the battle and war experiences. He wished the march would go faster. At times, the pace seemed like snails he had watched in the garden at home.

"This damn drum," complained Henri, "it keeps bumping my already numb shoulder and seems to be getting heavier with every step." Michael, marching next to him, was faring no better and grumbled with each step. Anton was complaining about being hungry. Only Gerard was quiet and just sloshed along step by squishy step.

The first sections of the column wound its way into Paris and to the troop encampment area. It would be near morning before the long snake of the column finally arrived. The weather was still damp and cold, and a chilling wind was making the situation all the more miserable. They had been wet and muddy for days. Henri's uniform was a mass of mud, and his boots were about to fall apart. He was none the worse than the rest of the Armée though. Some were dragging along like walking dead men, sick and lame. At least he had his youth and health.

Finally, and at last, the encampment area with real buildings and tents. The first order here was to get fires going as soon as possible. Henri saw Napoleon's personal detachment and carriage leave the area and proceed toward the main part of the city. *Lucky people,* he thought. *They will be in warm quarters tonight, and we will be here in this damn mud with only a small fire for warmth.* True, they would be in drafty tents, and still the cold would persist, but at least it was a cover. The damp cold seemed like it penetrated to one's very bones. The four boys went into their assigned tent, stripped their gear, and set their pallets. Even though there was a clamor all night with the arriving troops, the four were beyond hearing and slept like logs.

Henri was awakened with a start very early the next morning.

The sergeant was yelling at him, "Trooper Devreney, stir your ass! The general has been asking for you. We have been looking all over for you."

Henri hastily pulled on his cold wet boots and followed the sergeant to the general's area. He was shown in by an aide, saying they had been looking all over for him and the general was in a lather.

"Henri, where in the hell have you been, and look at you. My god, it will take days to get that crust of mud off, and you smell like the north end of a horse traveling south. And you have a cold. Well, we don't have time now to clean you up for the trip home. My wife is going to have both our heads, but it certainly won't be the first time she has seen weary and dirty soldiers home from the wars. Actually this may be a blessing and gain you more sympathy than you can imagine. Stir your ass, lad, and run get your gear. My carriage will leave as soon as you can get back here. Move now, I would like to get home within the hour."

"Oui, monsieur." And Henri departed on the run to retrieve his gear.

The carriage ride home was faster than anticipated, and they soon entered the massive iron gates and dismounted in front of the familiar house. There was no one to greet them this time. They took off their muddy boots and entered the house with the general booming, "Bonjour! Bonjour! Where is everyone? Vivien, Mimi! Your men are home from the war."

The bedlam that followed was truly that, a bedlam. Everyone rushed from the other parts of the house and completely enveloped them. Madame, Jean, Mimi, and the two maids with hugs and pats all the while chattering away like chickens at feeding time. Ange came running from the kitchen squealing and grabbed Henri with a hug so tight it almost hurt. Then she backed away with her nose wrinkled.

"Henri, you smell awful. I don't think you bathed since you left. But it is still so good to see you, smell and all." She giggled as she pointed to his feet. "And look at your stockings! They are full of holes. How can you wear such awful things?"

He looked at his feet and saw that the stockings were almost mere threads. He just as well may not have had stockings at all. Embarrassed, he tried to cover the worst muddy foot with the other, but nothing could hide his unkempt feet with toes sticking out like muddy stubs.

True to the general's word and knowledge of previous homecomings, as soon as the excitement died down a bit, Madame took charge.

"This is disgraceful to come home in such a state. Both of you are filthy and smell terribly. Off with both of you to the back of the barn to wash the majority of this off, and then you can have a proper bath in the house. Henri, we will need to tend to that cold too."

The general was in much better condition than Henri, but he had to suffer the fate of a cold-water rinse too. He laughed, "See what you have done to us, lad. Let this be a lesson. Next time we come home prepare a bit better."

"But, monsieur, I had no time. You told me to run."

The general laughed and said, "Oui, true, I know. I was in a hurry to get home, and I take the blame. A general has to complain about something though. Keep the troops grumbling and they are happy is one of the theories of Napoleon."

It was still misting rain, and the cold wind made them hurry as fast as they could. As soon as they had basically rinsed off the majority of the mud, they went back into the house to find the servants preparing hot baths.

Mimi came in with large mugs of hot tea with wine and honey. "Here, drink this. It should take away some of the chill and make you feel better."

Henri drank his down almost in one gulp.

"That was supposed to be sipped slowly and not gulped like a hungry hound. I will fix you another. Drink it slowly this time, or would you like two?"

"Oh, two please, Mimi. That was so good, and I am still cold."

The general went in the main bath in the master bedroom area, and Henri was in the bath area down the hall. Madame was going to give the general a bath, but Henri would have no such luxury. Fresh clothes had been laid out. Henri stripped the muddy uniform off and eased himself into the hot water. Ah, the closest thing to heaven since he had left. Baths in cold streams could never compare with this. The hot water, refreshing scented oil, and the mug of Mimi's stuff gave new life to him. He was soaking in luxury when a soft persistent knock on the door brought him back to reality.

"Henri, it's me, Ange. Are you going to stay in there all day? Or is a better-smelling you going to come out and properly greet me? I know, I'll just come in there and do what Momma and Poppa are doing and give you a scrub myself. You should hear the laughing, splashing, and noise coming from their room."

"Ange! Don't you dare! You know the trouble it would cause." There was a lot of giggling behind the door as she teased him by rattling the doorknob. "All right, all right, I'm hurrying."

He did hurry, dried off with a nice, sweet-smelling cloth, and put on fresh clothes. Oh, they were tight, and the arms and legs were a bit short. Had he grown that much in just a few short months? Well, he must have. He opened the door, and Ange rushed into his arms. She squeezed him again so tight he gasped a tiny bit.

"You are strong for such a little thing. Someday you will squeeze me to death."

"Be quiet and kiss me quick before someone comes. I have been desperate to get my hands on you since you came home. You looked so pitiful covered with mud and nearly barefoot. I love you, Henri." She raised her mouth to his, and the wonderful tingling so entrenched in his memory returned as their lips touched. The moment left both of them breathless.

"I love you, Ange. You will never know just how much." He kissed her again, and they hastily pushed away when they heard noises down the hall.

"Oh, wait, Ange, let me get something from my uniform before I forget. I have the hanky and letter from you in my breast pocket. Please put the letter with my other treasures. That letter has kept you with me these many months. I have read it over and over. The hanky I want to keep with me." He found the letter and hanky wrapped in a small piece of oilcloth and started to put it in his breast pocket out of habit.

"Henri, I thought you were going to give that letter to me to put in your treasure box."

"Oh, I'm sorry. Here, please take care of it. I wasn't thinking."

She grabbed his hand and said, "Let's go downstairs and see Mimi and Jean. They are anxious to hear your stories. I can hear them again later in privacy, and I can't wait."

Jean was waiting at the bottom of the stairs. They went to the kitchen by way of the dining room. "Well, Monsieur War Hero, you certainly do smell better," he observed. Ange laughed.

"I feel better too after washing at least ten kilos of mud off and getting clean clothes. But look at me. My good clothes are tight and short. I couldn't have grown that much."

Ange said maybe it was the Armée food and exercise that agreed with him making him grow so fast. Standing next to Ange and Jean, they looked at themselves in the large mirror over the buffet.

"We have all grown," Jean remarked, "and especially Ange. Look at her. She is no longer a little sister, but a young lady."

It was true. She was becoming a strikingly beautiful girl. Her dark eyes were like pools that Henri had said seemed bottomless. Her dark hair was hanging over her shoulder and had a bright blue ribbon to match her dress. Her slim, petite figure had all of the appearances of budding into adulthood. Her face was losing childlike features and taking on the resemblance of womanhood. She still had the slightly oval face with the ever-present pleasant smile and those twinkling eyes. It was her eyes that always seemed to be her most vivid feature. When she was angry, they burned like lit coals and at other times had the passive appearance of dark liquid pools. Her eyes were always alive and seemed to reflect her very soul and moods. She was so petite and feminine, and yet there was a quality about her as a lady and one who would be able to bear most hardships. She barely reached his shoulder, and Jean was a little taller than Henri. He had never really noticed them standing together like this and was pleasantly surprised at the nice couple they made. Jean was there too, but Henri had eyes only for Ange. He moved away before Jean might be able to detect any secret feelings. However, anyone with the sense of a yard goose could see what was happening.

They went into the kitchen, and Mimi grabbed him with another hard, tight hug. Surely someone would break his back before the day was over.

Mimi rattled on, "It is so good to have you home, Henri. My, you do smell so much better. You were foul. Is everything all right? Did they feed you well? By the looks of you and the way you have grown, I would say something must have been good. I will have to trim your long locks before long or you will be mistaken for a girl. Is it true the Armée eats a lot of horse? We do here sometimes; but it is not as good as beef, mutton, or goat."

"Mimi, we were hungry all the time. It seemed like we could never get enough to eat. We did eat a lot of things that we didn't know what it was and hoped the cooks did. Every time we were near villages, we ate chicken if we could steal them. Eggs were a rare thing, and mostly the officers got them first or were traded for special favors. My friends and I did small favors and ran errands for the cooks. We got extra things to eat. Most of the time, it was just a larger bowl of stew or whatever, but we did get special things. It is called survival, and we did all right."

Ange said, "I'll bet he had to eat all the weird things that Poppa has to when he is gone."

Henri told stories about his other friends and the experiences in battle and Madrid. He was very careful not to go into detail about Patia and Tierra. When he told the story about the head and Michael screaming, they all laughed. They remembered Michael from his visit.

"Mimi, what is that you are cooking for the evening meal? It smells wonderful."

She said, "You know very well what that is, Monsieur Smartie Pants. It is that special hash stuff you and the general love with those terrible peppers. It will be ready in a short time. While it is cooking, please sit with me and tell me all about what happened if it isn't too bad."

They sat at the kitchen table for nearly half an hour while Henri related to life in the camps, the marches, the battles, and most of all Spain and the people there. He did mention the girls but only that they were very nice to the four boys, and their father was with them the entire time. He explained about the bullfights and how cruel and bloody it was. He actually had secretly hoped the bull might somehow catch the matador with his horn. He had heard that, on occasion, they did get caught by the bull; but he hadn't seen any of it. Standing, he demonstrated how the matador swished about making a total fool of the bull. Then he showed how they plunged a sword in the poor thing's neck. He heard they sometimes prepared a special soup with the tail of the bull, but he had not eaten any.

"Just as well," observed Mimi, "the tail was probably all broken and ruined after all that fighting. The soup would probably be bitter."

The meal was served, and Henri ate like a starving man. The hash stuff with the peppers was totally unlike the "stuff" from the Armée.

Jean asked, "Henri, I still say, how can you eat that terrible stuff? I have tried, but it is too greasy. Those peppers from hell burn my mouth for hours. I even held my burning tongue to the icy window glass, but nothing would put out the fire."

Henri laughed. "That is what we ate in the Armée almost the entire time. If you are going to join, you had better learn to eat it and like it."

"Well, I will just starve or have to survive on bread, rats, and wine," he said.

During the meal, the general told events of their victory in Spain and said he had good word about Henri's conduct and baptism into combat. He had performed well and had done his duty. Henri didn't say anything but did bask in the pride of having done well. Ange rubbed her stockinged foot on his leg and smiled at him. She had a look of pride too.

Jean did say, "Someday I will do it too. When my education is complete and I can be accepted in the officer corps." This was only a year or so away.

The general replied, "I am pleased to hear this. I will certainly do all I can to see to it if that is what you really want. Jean, you have done a lot to change and improve. I believe that you will make a fine officer someday and help carry on our family tradition."

Jean nodded. "I hope there will still be a war for me to fight."

The general said, "As long as there is Napoleon as emperor of France, there will be wars to fight. There is a lot left in this world to conquer. It appears that this next war with Austria is imminent. That is the major reason Napoleon left Spain in such a rush. Serious preparations for dealing with the Austrians will begin as soon as the Armée is rested and reequipped."

After a time of talking, drinking several bottles of wine, and watching the fire slowly die, the family made preparations to retire for the night. All were exhausted from the hurried events of the day, and a good night's rest was needed. The general and Madame seemed particularly interested in retiring but really didn't seem all that tired. They all left the main dining room, and the general and Madame went upstairs to their room.

Henri, Ange, and Jean went into the sitting room with the other dying fire and drank another bottle of wine. They chatted for a time, and Ange asked Henri to help her to her room. They were all tipsy and tired by then. They excused themselves to Jean, but he said he was going up too. He was just too sleepy and had too much wine to stay down here by himself. They went up the stairs, and Jean went into his room and closed the door.

Ange said, "Henri, don't you dare go to sleep. If you can't stay awake just a while longer, at least leave the door unlocked, and I will wake you. I will wait a short time and come visit you." Then she turned and went down to her room.

Henri climbed the stairs to the third floor to his room, being careful to leave the door unlocked. As he closed the door and blew out his candle, he realized his heart was pounding like a carpenter's hammer. He had been sleepy up to this moment, but now he was wide awake. It was still raining, and he could hear the drops plinking against the windowpanes. Even though it was a dark, rainy night, there was a faint glow of light coming from the large windows. It gave the room an almost eerie glimmering.

Where is she? I hope she didn't fall asleep. She told me not to. Would she really come? Oh, he knew she would. She always did. At that moment, he heard the doorknob softly turn. He had pulled two chairs next to the window as they had done before. Ange felt her way into his arms, and they gently hugged for a long time. He could feel her heart pounding and knew his was doing the same. They kissed with a tenderness and passion only they could know. The tips of their tongues touched, and the tingling sensation nearly drove him crazy with thoughts he had had before. He became numb all over and thought he would fall to his knees. To him, Tierra could never compare with this.

"Mon dieu, Ange! What are you doing to me? I am so weak all over. I almost can't stand."

"Oh, I know. Me too, mon amour. Let's sit down before we fall."

They kissed again and did the tongue-touch thing again. Ange told him again she had seen Momma do that with Poppa when they didn't know anyone was around. Now she would know what it was like. Henri said it made him go mad, and Ange agreed and that the madness was so nice.

Henri went back to the door and checked to make certain the door was open, in case someone might be prowling around. They returned to their chairs and sat and quietly chatted, all the while holding hands. If they were caught, this wouldn't be as bad. Madame had already warned Ange, but they both knew she and the general were too busy to bother with them. Holding hands was promiscuous enough, but kissing was another thing, and they must not get caught at that, especially the tongue-touch thing.

They talked and shared many private things. How they had missed one another, how Ange was learning ways of the kitchen and general household managing, events at school, and things in her world with Jean and around the house. He related his world of the Armée again, his friends, the battles, and once again the events of Spain and the people there. She asked him several times about the girls in Spain. He reassured her that he had not even looked at or thought of another girl in the way that he did her. There was only one girl for him, and Ange was stuck with him as long as she would have him. She didn't say anything and just rubbed and squeezed his hands.

"I do believe you, Henri. I want you to believe there can never be anyone else with me either. Please take care of yourself in the wars. I worry so about you and that you will not come home to me."

She leaned over and met him halfway for another kiss. This one was a long and gentle kiss with much of the tongue touching. Henri thought he would fall out of his chair. He could never get enough of this. He told her so, and she responded that there would be a lot more kisses and probably enough to last his entire lifetime. After several hours of talking and just enjoying one another, they decided it may be best if they went to bed.

Ange stood up, and Henri walked her to the door. She again leaned into his arms, and their bodies pressed against each other. They stayed that way for a long time in a tight embrace; and finally Ange kissed him again, turned, and went out of the door without a word.

Henri lay across the bed, listening to the rain against the glass. He thought for a long time of just how confusing this world and life really was. He was completely and entirely captivated by this beautiful and delicate creature. Things were so simple in his man's world of the Armée. One just followed orders, and things were generally all right, but this was something else again where no orders were given. Only the laws of the most primitive nature prevailed. All very confusing.

The next morning, he slept a little late as was not his habit and went downstairs to see Mimi and maybe "borrow" something to eat. He was starving. The events of last night with Ange seemed unreal and like a foggy dream. Mimi was fussing about the kitchen in her usual huffy manner. There was the aroma of fresh brewed coffee and baked bread. He sat next to the warm stove, and Mimi brought him a mug of hot coffee. It burned his tongue, but it was oh so good. He could feel the heat gliding down his throat and spreading all over his entire body.

Mimi said again, "It was so good to have you home where you belong. You should never have left. Why did you do such a thing? Oh, I know what I said before, but that was before you really left and were in these things."

Finally she gave up, quit fussing, and said, "I thought I understood why men should make war, but now it just doesn't make good sense. Women don't do these things." *She was right in a way*, he thought.

He had seen so much waste of men, boys, horses, and many thousands of kilos of equipment. Not to mention the damage inflicted to the enemy lands, cities, and villages. But there were other things to consider, and from the accounts in books he had read, men had made war from the beginning of time. As long as there were two men, there would be a fight.

Mimi told him all of the household gossip about the maids, about the workers in the garden, about the stable, and about Ange taking so much interest in cooking and affairs of the house. She said Ange would make a fine wife and homemaker someday for some lucky man. As she said this, she watched very closely for any reactions by Henri. He was wise to her watching and tried not to show any telltale emotion. Still Mimi mentioned Ange several times, and now he wondered if Ange may have told her something. *Surely she wouldn't,* thought Henri. After a second mug of coffee, he felt almost totally revived and ready for the world. The other members of the house were starting to stir, and Mimi was bustling around, preparing the morning meal.

After the morning meal, Henri went outside to visit the workers in the stable and garden. It was still misting rain and cloudy this morning, so everyone was working inside. Each person quizzed him with the same questions of how it had been in the war and in Spain. He was polite, understood their interest, and had to tell the same stories over and over. Finally Jean searched him out and rescued him temporarily. Madame had been asking for him and wanted to take him to the tailor and get some decent-fitting clothes. Jean slipped up and said Madame had said he looked like an orphan.

He caught himself as soon as he said it and said, "I'm sorry, Henri. I didn't mean it that way. It is just an expression."

Henri laughed and playfully poked at Jean. "Oh, Jean, that's all right. I am not sensitive about it. I know you didn't mean anything. Come on, let's go and get this orphan some decent-fitting clothes."

Madame and Ange were waiting to walk to the tailor shop. Jean said he really didn't want to go. They looked in the cloak closet in the entranceway and retrieved their heavy cloaks and parasols. They went down the large steps and into the main street for the walk to the main square and the tailor shop.

Ange and Henri shared a parasol and used the excuse to snuggle close to each other. Madame, with her ever-watchful eye, took careful note. She had watched this budding romance for some time and approved as long as emotions were controlled. They seemed to be until now anyway.

The tailor took new measurements but said he could alter certain seams and cuffs for a temporary fit if Henri promised not to grow any more during the next several weeks. The general had said this was to be a short vacation and rest, and then it would probably be on to Austria. Henri had wondered about Austria for a long time. His father had died in the Black Forest of Austria. He couldn't imagine a black forest. It must be a dismal and gloomy place full of ghosts and all manner of terrible things. Why would anyone want to fight over such a place? He had a feeling maybe he would find out.

The general and Henri stayed home for almost a week. Just as they were falling into the relaxing and complacent atmosphere of family life, a courier arrived at the house late in the evening.

"All troops are being recalled to duty the next midday. We have expected this, but this final order makes it more definitive," he explained.

Heavy hearts were at the evening meal, but the general assured them, "Not to worry. All we have to do is to report to the troop encampment area outside of Paris. We can still come home. The troops are to resume their training, and the general staff is to be briefed regarding this pending push into Austria."

Ange was particularly saddened by the news and kept her stockinged foot in Henri's lap during the entire meal. Not much toe wriggling this time. Just to be close. Henri was so afraid that Madame or the general would take note, but neither seemed to pay attention to what was taking place under the tablecloth. Her foot and sometimes wiggling toes in his lap caused a strange stirring sensation from deep within his very soul as it had before. *The little devil,* he thought. She knew what she was doing and having the best time in the world driving him completely mad. Surely the others must sense what was happening under the tablecloth, but if they did, nothing was said or even noted in their expressions.

As soon as the meal was over, and the family once again had retired to the sitting room, Henri made certain Ange would behave. Jean, Ange, and Henri went out on the large back porch and watched the last glow of orange and purple colors of the disappearing sun. Finally it had stopped raining, but the cold still prevailed. The wind was not blowing nearly as hard tonight, and while cool, it was almost pleasant. Each had a mug of Mimi's hot coffee with wine and honey; and they stood for a long time watching the sunset, softly talking, and sipping their coffee. They made attempts at conversation to hide the pending events of tomorrow with Henri and Poppa having to report for duty.

Later that evening after all were in their rooms, Henri was sitting in the chair by the window and thinking about his feelings for Ange. Without a doubt, he loved her beyond anything he had ever imagined possible. He wanted to be with her every waking minute, and it seemed impossible to live without her or her presence. Leaving tomorrow would be one of the most difficult things he would have to do. The entire episode of tomorrow would have been much easier if she had not put her foot in his lap. Mon dieu! Such a sensation. It was marvelous, and yet he knew it was wrong. He was deep in thought and did not hear her come up behind him padding softly in stockinged feet.

A soft hand on his shoulder startled him, and he jumped. She fell into his arms, and they embraced for a long time before he slowly tilted her head and brought his lips to hers. He could feel her soft and maturing body press against him with such urgency, and the strange feeling of earlier returned.

Finally breathless, she said, "Mon amour, I didn't mean to startle you."

"Well, you did, and I am not sorry."

"I am so glad you are here. I want to be with you all the time. I become more frustrated by the minute when you are away."

"I know and I feel the same way. I can't seem to sleep or eat when I am not with you. Ange, this time will not be so bad. I will at least be here in Paris and can come home. You heard your father. We will be training for several months."

"Oui, I heard him, and then what happens when the times comes for more damn war?"

"Ange! You cursed. I have never heard you curse before."

"I only cursed this stupid war that takes you and Poppa away, and I will do it again. Damn war, damn war, damn war. There, Monsieur Henri Devreney, you have heard me curse again. Do you think less of me as a lady?"

"Never, mon amour, but please let us keep our cursing in private between just the two of us. By the way, Ange, did you know what you were doing to me with wriggling your toes in my lap? How would you like it if I wriggled my toes in your lap?"

"We will have to try it sometime and see if I like it." She giggled and said, "I'll bet I would too."

They sat and talked for hours. This time they shared possible future plans. They both agreed marriage would be in their future, but only when a positive future could be. Henri would have to provide a source of income and a means of security for Ange. They talked of children, and if the moon had been brighter, both of them would have seen the other blush. They knew all of the facts of life, but still some of it was embarrassing. Their talk went to more private things to be shared only by two lovers. He told her that during their tight embraces, he could feel her body becoming a woman. She told him that she had felt something too but wouldn't say what. He could feel the heat of the severe blush and found it embarrassing that he could not control himself.

"Oh, Ange, I am sorry and ashamed. I know it happens, but I can't help it. I have tried, and I just can't. I would never do anything bad or hurt you."

She giggled. "C'est la vie, mon amour. I trust you with my life. I know you would never hurt me. That doesn't hurt me. I sort of like it. Must we be so damn serious all the time?" She tickled him in the ribs and jumped back.

The morning meal was a solemn affair as everyone knew what a few hours would bring.

"Why is everyone being so glum?" asked the general. "Why, one would think this was a death watch. We will be back in a few days. This is only a training and preparation. The real thing is months away. Enjoy ourselves while we can."

Ange continued to wiggle her toes in Henri's lap and all the while smiling coyly, knowing what she was doing to him. He stuck his hand under the tablecloth and pinched her toes, wishing the moment would never end. But end it did as they heard horses and a carriage enter the front drive.

The general kissed Madame and turned to leave. Ange reached up and kissed Henri on the lips right in front of everyone. Henri blushed deeply and without a word entered the carriage.

"So," said the general, "my regimental drummer appears to have a lady love, eh?"

"Oh, monsieur, we are only like brother and sister. We do not mean anything."

"I have noticed she doesn't kiss Jean that way. Ha, *c'est la poule qui chante qui a fait l'oeuf* (the guilty dog barks the loudest). Do you think me blind, stupid, or both? As long as nothing immoral develops and Vivien doesn't come after me about it, both of you have my blessing. You are both young, and the future is so full of uncertainties. Vivien and I have been watching the two of you for some time. Everything appears all right. Bear with me, lad. I will only tease you about it."

The training proved very serious and intense. The Musique Corps drilled from the morning meal and camp and personal cleanup to the noon meal. After a short duration of rest, they were back at it until the evening meal. They marched to the sound of drumbeat, and Henri found out just how lax and out of shape he had become. Surprisingly, he found little time to think of personal things and of missing home life. This was the general plan of things before leaving. Keep the troops so busy they will have little time for mischief and to feel sorry for themselves. *This damn drum*, Henri thought. But on the other hand, he should be grateful it wasn't a cannon to lug around. Still he longed for a musket, sword, or other weapon that may be easier managed.

All of the four drummers were not back to duty as yet. Michael had arrived two days late from his home, and Gerard was still not back from Orléans. Anton came into camp several days later with Gerard right behind him. This was understandable and accepted, but after a week, there would be hell to pay for late returnees. If this were under war circumstances, punishment by flogging or worse could be the result.

The standard bearers marched with them, and Henri observed that things could indeed be worse than dragging his drum around. A cold wind was blowing, and the bearers were having a terrible time with their flags and the wind. They had to march with their standards straight. The gusting wind jerked them all around. Finally to prevent the flags from being torn or dropped, the sergeant gave the order to furl flags and march with standards only. Again, not so with these damn drums. The heavy thing hung by his belt like a dead mule. There was no easy way. The week flew by, and those with homes close by were given leave.

Henri and the general were home late Friday afternoon and had to return Sunday. Henri couldn't wait to be home and with Ange. He told Ange what the general had said, and she said her mother had spoken to her about their relationship. She had told Ange essentially the same thing. As long as proper conduct and respect was maintained, it would be all right for them to continue. Henri thought about the wiggling toes and tight embraces and wondered just how long he could continue to maintain himself.

As all soldiers eventually do, the others in the foursome had shared girl experiences with each other. Anton was the only one without a girl. Gerard had a girl at home but was always on the hunt for new grounds. Michael was not serious about much at all but related he had loved several girls. Only Henri knew better and looked at him when he said things. Henri just shared that he had a girl, but nothing was really serious. They were just close as brother and sister. The fellows all knew his girl was the general's daughter and didn't envy having wrath directed his way if the general ever found out. Henri never let on that anything was there except close friendship. Best for everyone to avoid gossip.

Only one person on the face of the earth knew how truly close he was to Ange, and that was Michael. The two were very close and shared most everything. Michael teased him about it several times. When Henri told him, laughingly, that if he didn't stop he would tear Michael's head off and shit down his neck, Henri remembered and echoed what Anton had told Michael at one time. Besides, Henri explained, one does not joke about very private things. Michael understood.

The days rolled into weeks and the weeks into over two months. In early Avril and a lovely, lazy spring around Paris, word came that the Austrians had invaded Bavaria. Napoleon was caught by surprise and had not expected any confrontation this early. One last weekend here and then immediate mobilization for Bavaria.

The weekend home was the scene of sadness and crying as the ladies realized the troops may be gone for some time, and battles were soon to be joined. The last night in Henri's room, Ange cried and held him very close for a long time. She pressed her body into his, and this time there was no control for him. He apologized, and she told him never to apologize for loving her.

"Hold me tight and never let me go, mon amour," she said. She clung to him all the more tightly, and he wished he could hold her forever. They embraced and kissed until the first light of dawn, and then she ran sobbing to her room. Madame saw her run to her room and softly knocked on her door.

"Ange, is there anything I should know about?"

"Oh no, Momma. No. Henri and I were only talking, and we did hold hands. He is a perfect gentleman. Don't worry. I will miss him so much. I know now what you go through with Poppa going off to war." Mother embraced daughter with the first realization that her daughter was now a young woman.

"Merci, Ange. I won't worry. Let's get ready for the morning meal, and then the men must go. We need to try to be brave and put on a happy face. Try to never let them remember us with tears in our eyes and a sad face."

As the carriage came in the front gate, Henri drew Mimi to one side. "Mimi, please help to take care of Ange while I am gone. You were right in guessing that she is very dear to me. I guess by now everyone knows. Watch out for Jean. I still don't trust him. He says a lot of things, but I don't really believe him."

Mimi laughed and said, "Henri, anyone would have to be blind in one eye and not to see out of the other what is going on between you and Ange. I will, on my word, see that no harm comes to her. Go with God and don't worry."

Mimi hugged him as if to seal the pact. Henri went over to Ange, and she made certain the others were preoccupied. She gave him a kiss on the lips and did a very quick tongue-touch thing.

"Something for you to remember me," she whispered in his ear. Then she parted and quickly went inside the house as Henri and the general mounted the carriage.

As soon as they arrived at the encampment, they made ready for the long march from Paris to Austria. They had been issued new uniforms and boots, and thank God, they had drilled in their new boots for several weeks to relieve the stiffness of the leather. Even so after the first day of intense marching, many of the men had sore and blistered feet. Anton had one blister so bad that it was bleeding. At the rest point for the night, Henri washed Anton's blister, rinsed out his bloody sock, and said to let the blister air out for the night. The next morning, Anton put on double socks, and the wound was much better by the next nightfall. They were learning. They had to.

Calm before the storm. Waiting for the advance.

9

Le Bébé du Tigre

After several days' forced march from Paris, the main body of the Armée attacked the Austrians near Ratisbon. Napoleon gave the attack orders just at dawn. It was his usual time and said it gave all day to right any wrongs. French cavalry units, braving a mighty fusillade of cannon fire, hit the center of the Austrian lines and divided them. Napoleon, seizing the opportunity, drove his infantry in the gap.

The two separated groups of Austrians ran in full retreat. One retreating group had to cross several small bridges over the Danube River. The rapid advance gave the French troops no time to even think about what was happening. The Musique Corps with the rest of the troops was almost running to keep up with the fleeing Austrians. There was no time to even think of beating the drums. They were moving too fast.

"Henri, don't run so damn fast! Wait for us! This goddamn drum is beating me to death!" yelled Michael.

Henri did slow down and yelled back, "All right, Michael! Mine is getting heavy as a log! This damn drum strap is cutting me in half!"

Anton had stopped completely and was throwing up his morning meal. Gerard was trying to run past him and dodge the spewing stuff.

"Serves him right," panted Michael. "I saw him stuff maybe eight or ten bread rolls down his gullet this morning. He knows better, but you can't argue with a hog."

As they ran past the fallen Austrians, some of the wounded tried to trip them or give further resistance. Henri hit one with his drumstick. The officers ordered the advancing infantry to bayonet those offering resistance. After seeing the bayoneting of several, all resistance stopped.

The way was now wide open to Vienna. Napoleon and the Armée arrived in Vienna on May 13 and observed the entire remaining Austrian army on the other side of the Danube. They were forming ranks and gathering equipment to fight. Napoleon tried to cross at one point near Nussdorf, down from Vienna, but the Austrians beat them back. There was a river island near Lobau, a very wide place in the Danube that offered a good crossing. The small island could hold several hundred men and be used as a staging point out of range from Austrian fire on the opposite side. From there, it was a short way to the other side by another bridge.

The general's Second Corps crossed to the island and staged for the next crossing over the bridge to the mainland. The cavalry sent a small reconnaissance patrol and reported the way was clear. However, the French patrol did not go far enough. They did not see all they should have and made a critical mistake. The deep woods on the other side contained hundreds of hidden and entrenched enemy troops. The Danube was rising rapidly this time of year from the spring thaws upstream. The one rickety bridge from the island to the mainland broke under the weight of men and horses, not to mention the rapid current. As the bridge started to give way, Austrians suddenly poured out of the woods in attack.

The musique group and several hundred infantry were already on the other side of the Danube. Now they were trapped with no means of retreat. The waters were rushing over the broken bridge, and Henri could see several men swept downstream. "Those may be the lucky ones," said one man. At least they wouldn't be caught by the Austrians. Hasty orders were given to repair the bridge while a rear guard action was staged to hold the Austrians. The bridge was partially stabilized with ropes from the island and mainland sides, and more French troops swarmed across to meet the onslaught.

About midafternoon, startled shouts and men pointing upstream drew everyone's attention. The Austrians had put wagons loaded with logs and hay into the river and set them on fire. Flaming wagons, almost fifty, were floating at the bridge in the fast-moving current. Men started to run for either side and clear the bridge, but many did not make it. Horses and men were screaming as the burning wagons hit the bridge. The bridge broke again, scattering men, horses, and equipment in the swirling current. The bridge did not burn much as it was too wet.

Once again the bridge was hastily repaired as the Austrians attacked the area between the village of Aspern and the Danube. Twice the Austrians were beaten back, and then a much larger main body of Austrians arrived and began to push the exhausted French back. Fighting was savage now and often hand to hand. The drummers were no longer drummers, and now it was a survival of the fittest.

The drummers ran back to the bank of the Danube near the bridge. It was, once again, being hastily repaired by engineers. Troops were still pouring across to meet the attacking Austrians. The drummers crouched down in the reeds and tall grasses on the bank, trying to stay out of the way. *Oh to be visible*, thought Michael. Henri was left behind as he had been partially blocked by an advancing Austrian troop of nearly fifty men. He saw the sergeant go down and then the captain. Still the Austrians came on. Most were fierce-looking huge men with heavy dark beards, screaming, shouting, and waving swords and lances.

Henri was terrified. They would be on him in an instant. He threw down his drum and picked up a musket and fired into the approaching swarm. He saw an Austrian fall, but they did not stop. He grabbed the captain's pistol and sabre, firing point-blank into an Austrian's surprised face. Throwing the empty pistol at another, he began wildly swinging the sabre, screaming at the top of his voice. He hit several, and they quickly drew back but regrouped and came on again in a fury. Just as the Austrians were reaching him with bayonets, a French cavalry troop rode up and chased them back. Henri was still standing over the captain and screaming at the retreating Austrians when several of the cavalry dismounted and threw him to the ground.

"Stop! Stop! It is all over! They are gone! Stop!"

Le Bébé du Tigre

Henri came partially back to his senses as they held him. Then as the numbness started to wear off, he realized he had been cut severely on the right thigh by a bayonet. Another second or two and it could have been all over for him. He had been very close to death, but he had very little recollection of what had happened. Why they had not just shot him was a miracle. He should have run with the rest, but he couldn't get away.

By that time, the French were now amassing and counterattacking in strength, pushing the Austrians farther back. Henri was sitting in the middle of the fallen Austrians staring at his wound when a medical orderly ran up. It was starting to ache more now, and the more he looked at the gaping wound and the gushing blood, the more it seemed to hurt. He lay back as stretcher bearers put him on a stretcher and took him to a nearby area just being organized for a field hospital. As he was lifted, he reached for his drum and put it on his chest. The wound, a deep cut sliced almost to the bone, was really hurting and throbbing now. He was losing quite a lot of blood and soaked the stretcher. He tried not to cry out but did moan loudly. After they arrived at the hospital area, the flow of blood was quickly slowed by tight bindings. He was given a spoonful of a foul-tasting something washed down with a cup of water. The pain started to ease, and he became quieter. The commander of the cavalry troop rode over and inquired of the doctor how the Bébé Tigre was and related what had happened.

"Baby Tiger, eh?" said the surgeon. "An amazing tale." This trooper would certainly get special care after the commander's report.

Word spread about the baby tiger drummer who had single-handedly saved his captain while killing fifteen Austrians. It wasn't really fifteen, maybe only one for sure or possibly two, and several more cut with the sabre, but it made a good story and was a tremendous morale boost for the troops.

By early afternoon, the general and Henri's captamade a personal visit to the hospital area, not realizing who this Bébé Tigre was. A cot was pointed out. As the general approached his bedside, he was astonished at who lay there.

"Henri, lad, mon dieu! You can't be this baby tiger the men are talking about! What happened? Napoleon himself has heard about this and asked me to go see. He will be coming over here. Are you in pain, and is there anything I can do?"

"No, monsieur. They gave me some stuff that helps the pain go away. It doesn't hurt much now."

"Surgeon, this lad is due very special care. Make certain on your life no further harm comes to him."

"Oui, mon général, oui. He is being given all the special care we can give him. He is no longer in danger. It will take time for a full recovery, but then he should be like new in a few weeks. You know, General, he is very lucky though. A bit more to the side of his thigh and his family treasures would be hanging on that Austrian bayonet."

A few weeks, thought Henri. Damn the luck to lie up here in a bed with nothing to do but hurt and listen to birds singing and wounded men moaning.

Later that evening, Napoleon rode up with several of his command staff. He dismounted, saw Andre, and inquired as to who this Bébé Tigre might be and demanded to see him. They went over to Henri's cot.

"Excellency, may I present Trooper Drummer Henri Devreney of my command and household, now known as this Bébé Tigre."

"Ah, oui, I do remember this lad from Paris, Andre. I had a feeling then that he might be worth watching. Wasn't his father also a hero?"

"Oui, Excellency, his father was killed in the Black Forest campaign."

"Well, he has survived this one," Napoleon said. "Are you all right now, lad, and could we do anything for you? I heard you saved the life of one of my officers?"

Saved a life! Henri had not realized until now the captain was still among the living. "I didn't realize it, Excellency. Everything was like in a fog."

"I guess he is still a bit foggy with the medicine. Well, you did, Monsieur Drummer Tigre," said Napoleon. "Damn, if I had several hundred like this, I could probably conquer the world. Surgeon, how long will his recovery time be?"

"Oh, several weeks, Your Excellency," said the surgeon. "We have patched him up as best we can here, but he should have proper hospital care."

"See to it then. As soon as he is able to travel, send him to Paris. Advise my personal physician and staff there to attend him."

"Oui, Excellency. He can travel in a day, maybe two."

Napoleon patted him on the shoulder and said, "Very well done, my boy, I will see that you receive a personal commendation from me. God bless you, and have a safe journey home." He mounted his horse and left the astonished group.

"Now you have done it." The general smiled. "Vivien and my daughter will have my balls nailed to the stable door for allowing you to be injured, but this hero thing just may get me back into their good graces. Your future in this Armée is assured. Now who knows. If I may, I would like to call you son, and I mean it with respect. I will try to come back before they transport you home, but if I cannot, Godspeed and give the family my deepest affection. Oh oui, just one more thing, when you kiss my daughter next time, watch out for her damn tongue. I caught a quick glance on the porch at home. That is exactly what my Vivien used to entrap me, thank God."

He laughed again, patted Henri on the shoulder, mounted his horse, and rode off to join his command. Michael, Anton, and Gerard were standing on the side, taking all of this in.

"The general and the emperor himself," Michael exclaimed, "a real hero! Oh please, Monsieur Shitbird, should we kiss your smelly feet or ass or something?"

They all burst out laughing. Only Michael could think of something like that.

"I'll be back and kick your butt," said Henri. He was growing tired from the medicine, and the guys were about to depart.

Michael came closer and whispered, "Henri, my good friend, please take care. You know how I feel. We will miss you, and congratulations on what you did back there."

Henri said, "You know, Michael, I really don't remember much about it. It happened so fast! I was so scared. Everything was like in a cloud. I am confused by all of this hero talk and from the emperor himself. I didn't know what to say."

"Well, Bébé Tigre," said Michael, "maybe God or the devil was with you. I hope it was God, mon ami."

They all patted his shoulder and tousled his hair, offered congratulations, and left. A very weak and confused Henri went to sleep, thinking about going home.

He awoke in the night with his wound throbbing and pounding. He was so thirsty. He called out to the duty orderly and asked if he could please have his water flask. The orderly could see he was in pain and sweating profusely. In a short time, the surgeon came over and checked his bindings. "I know it hurts, and it will continue to hurt. The bindings must be tight to hold the wound closed. You were awake and didn't whimper much when we did a tailor job on your cut. Blood is still oozing and will for a few days until the healing process starts and the wound closes. We will have to keep a close eye for any changes or the flesh rot that often takes place. You are young and have good health in your favor. I will give you something to ease your pain, but do not get to like it too much. It can make you crave more and more and eventually go mad."

He came back in a short time and gave Henri a mug of hot tea that had a bitter and foul taste. "This is a mixture of cannabis and hot tea," he explained. "Cannabis originally comes from China. Some say it is called the tail of the tiger by the Chinese, so I guess it is fitting for a Bébé Tigre. It should take effect soon and relieve the pain." It did, and soon Henri had the feeling again of too many glasses of wine and drifted off into a fitful yet restful sleep.

He awoke early the next morning ravenously hungry and with the throbbing still in his leg. He was brought a metal bowl with potato stew with strange-looking meat in it, a piece of bread, and a mug of hot coffee. Never mind! It was food, and he was famished. He realized it had been almost two days since he had eaten.

The surgeon came by his bed later and informed him, "Transport will be arranged for the early afternoon to take you to Paris."

True to his word, a medical carriage arrived just after a midday meal of the same stuff served for the morning meal. He was given a final check of his bindings and another mug of the "special tea," and he and six others, all ranking officers, were loaded on the carriage.

The surgeon gave Henri a packet from the general for his wife and family. "The general is sending another packet to the hospital staff containing special orders and instructions from himself and Napoleon regarding your care. The general has sent his apologies for not being able to attend your leaving, but he knew you would understand. His command and the Armée are still at war."

Henri nodded as his stretcher was slid in the stretcher rack next to a cavalry officer, Jean-Claude Ridoux, from a prominent Parisian family.

"So you are the Bébé Tigre I have heard so much about. Is it true you killed over a hundred Austrians and saved the lives of many officers?"

Henri was dumbfounded. "No, monsieur! I think it was only one, maybe two. I did cut several more, but that was all."

Jean-Claude laughed as best he could with the wounds on his shoulder and neck. "Well, we saw the Short Corporal himself come to visit you, so it must be more than you say."

"On my honor, monsieur," said Henri.

"Well, so be it then. Your secret is safe with me. Where did they get you?"

"On the leg with a bayonet. The surgeon said a little more and it would have been my balls."

"I got it in the neck and shoulder. I was riding along minding my own damn business, and the next thing I was on the ground. If it were not for my family's station in Paris, I would not be traveling today."

"What station is that?" asked Henri.

"My father is one of the personal advisors to Napoleon on legal and foreign matters. I was given this commission and told to do well with the promise of special duties and privileges as soon as combat experience was recognized. This is it, and I am certain I will have something. The ladies will be certain to fall all over themselves for a wounded cavalry officer with a creditable war record. Now if I had your record, I could probably have the empress herself. You are one fortunate young man and can probably go far in this Armée."

They chatted for a time, and then both grew weary and sleepy with the "special tea" they had been given for the journey. It would take another entire day to get to Paris, and there was plenty of time for conversation. Even though this carriage had special soft undercarriage, it did bounce some and swayed its way into the late afternoon and night. Paris would be reached by late afternoon the next day. *Another damn carriage ride*, thought Henri, but at least this time he had the "special tea." Henri dreamed of home and Ange. He could almost picture her pretty smiling face and dancing eyes. Couldn't this damn carriage go any faster?

10

Recognition

The hospital carriage stopped during the night at an Armée station almost at the border of France to change horses and give the drivers a brief rest and refreshment. The patients were checked quickly by a medical orderly for any possible endangering symptoms, apply fresh bindings if necessary, and administer another cup of "tea." *Thank God for this stuff*, thought Henri. Even though he was riding in a special medial carriage, the bouncing in the rutty road would have been unbearable without it. Then, after a very short rest onward, once more, to Paris. There was another stop just after the morning sun was appearing through the mist and another near midday.

Bread rolls, water, coffee, or tea was the usual fare for meals; but Henri really didn't care if he ate or not. He just wanted to get out of this damnable thing and in a real bed. The carriage was not moving at any breakneck speed but certainly fast enough to maintain an excellent pace and schedule. When he was awake at times, he would drowsily peep out of the side curtain and watch the countryside flash by. At times the trees were just a blur, so he just forgot the whole thing. They were in France now, and he had asked the orderly during the midday stop how much longer.

"We will dine in Paris tonight, mon ami. We are making excellent time, and the weather is perfect." He laughed and said, "I heard one of the drivers say he was meeting the best lady lover in all of Paris tonight. She told him that if he didn't make it by early evening, she would have a long line of others awaiting her services, and he may be the last in line."

Henri watched the sun start to settle in the west when he heard shouts from the drivers.

"Ah, there is Paris! Just over the next large hill."

Those that could raise themselves on elbows strained to see. He had an excellent view as they crested the hill, and they could see Paris was in the distance. There was the Seine glistening like a bright ribbon in the setting sun, the distinct twin towers of Notre Dame, and domes and spires of other large buildings. A slight haze hovered over the city, giving a slight glow in the early dusk like some sort of a protective cover and beacon guiding them home.

Henri tried to guess where home might be in the maze. Very soon, they entered the outskirts of Paris and passed through small hamlets and then into larger parts of the city. Finally the carriage entered ornate metal gates of a large brown stone building. It stopped at the wooden double doors of the patient receiving area. Jean-Claude said this was the Hospital des Invalides and one of the best for military wounded.

The hospital had originally been founded for use as an old soldier's care facility, but with the flood of wounded coming back from the front, a new wing had been added. Mostly it was reserved for high-ranking officers or persons of preference. Medical orderlies came out, received the passenger list from the carriage orderly, and started to off-load the patients. Jean-Claude told Henri to take care, and he would try to see him later if he could. Henri and three of the others were taken into a ward with about twenty other patients. He was still dressed in the uniform of an ordinary trooper, and the staff wondered why he was traveling with ranking officers and why the special treatment. He was taken to a special room for cleaning and changing his dressings.

He was stripped naked and placed on a cold table where he was bathed by two orderlies with pans of lukewarm water, soap, and clean cloths. They were not gentle especially in the private and tender areas and made jokes about "size." Whether this meant large, small, or medium, he couldn't care less and just wanted this ordeal over quickly. Finally they not so gently dried him. His nasty field bandages and bindings were changed, and more bathing ensued in the wound area. He was given hospital clothes consisting of only a blue gown similar to what ladies might wear. As they carried him back to his bed, he was exhausted and only wanted to sleep.

He was awakened sometime later for an evening meal consisting of a thick soup with potatoes and meat, a large piece of crusty bread, and a very welcome mug of harsh red wine. He asked for a second mug of wine and was tempted to ask for a third but decided it may not be a good idea. Henri could see out of the large window across from his bed, and the sun was gone now. He had the odd sensation of still moving in the carriage, but he knew better. It would go away after a time, as before, after long carriage rides. Until then, he would try to get some rest. He was given another cup of "tea" to ease the throbbing pain in his leg, and that with the two mugs of wine soon let him drift off into a restless sleep.

Something woke him early the next morning, and he was lying partially awake, groggily trying to gather his senses. *Damn, where was he? This strange place! Oh oui,* now he was collecting his thoughts and seemed to remember events of yesterday. The dull throb of his wound was slowly coming back. He tried to think of other things and take his mind off the throbbing. He could see a dim light starting to appear in the courtyard and, every now and then, could see a bird flutter by.

Oh to be a bird, he thought, *and to be so free and fly wherever one wanted. No more pain and bonds of earth.* He heard voices and turned to see a group of men in long white coats entering the ward.

"This is the one," said the duty orderly, pointing to Henri.

"Surely this must be some mistake," said a large portly man reading a paper in his hand. "This is but a mere lad and an ordinary trooper at that."

"No, monsieur," said the orderly, "this is the Henri Devreney mentioned in the dispatches."

There were two dispatches concerning him, one from General de Chabot and another from the emperor himself. Word had not as yet reached the hospital staff about the battle action, and it would be past midday before Jean-Claude could start that rumor circulating. The dispatches only stated that this drummer trooper was very special and required the very best of care. Napoleon requested his personal physician to attend him as soon as possible. This was indeed irregular, but orders from a general and Napoleon were not to be questioned. Who was this trooper, and why was he so special to such men?

He was immediately moved to a private room on the third floor with a wonderful view of Paris, Notre Dame, and the river. *If the windows in this room were a little more to the right,* he thought, *it may be possible to see home.* Even at this height, though, the trees made this impossible. He was served a morning meal of eggs, ham, a soft warm bun, and hot coffee all on a silver tray. There was even a small fresh flower from the garden in a small crystal vase. He was being treated as royalty, and why not? Royalty had requested this. He was in the lap of luxury, but his aching wound and the need to see Ange and the family was his real concern. Midmorning, the family—Madame, Jean, Ange, and even Mimi—rushed into the room and crowded around his bed with hugs and more hugs and kisses.

"Oh, Henri!" exclaimed Madame. "We came as soon as the dispatch came from Andre that you were here and you had been hurt." The general had sent a special dispatch with the carriage to be delivered to his home. She said, "Andre very briefly explained that you had done some heroic thing and have been recognized by the emperor himself."

"How badly are you hurt, and when can you come home?" Mimi was rubbing his good leg and starting to cry.

Then Madame and Mimi started chattering all at once, Jean was standing smiling at him, and Ange had her head on his chest, crying softly. "I thought you said you would be all right," she accused.

"I am, Petite Désordre. Please don't cry." Well, he had tears in his eyes too.

The events of the past several days were overbearing. He did not cry, but was very close. That would come later in a much more private setting. He told of his wound and that it really wasn't that bad and didn't hurt much at all. The hell it didn't! If not for the "tea," he couldn't have made it.

After a short time, a doctor and two orderlies came into the room. The doctor introduced himself as Dr. Lemoine, personal physician to His Excellency. "I have specific instructions from His Excellency to attend and give this patient the best of treatment. I don't have the details, but evidently he has done some remarkable and brave thing."

The family was further astonished.

Jean asked, "Henri, what did you do? What happened?"

"Nothing much. They have made more to it."

"Nothing much, your smelly feet! All of this would not be for nothing much."

Dr. Lemoine asked the family to be excused briefly so he could examine the wound. Ange clung to his hand in near desperation, not wanting to leave. He whispered that he was all right, and she could see him later. She gently kissed his lips in front of everyone, and no one seemed to take note or show embarrassment. No tongue-touch thing now. That would come later.

The doctor and the orderlies removed the bandages and bindings, and the doctor remarked, "Merde, what butchers we have in the field! Whoever did the sewing job on this wound must have been a sailmaker in the English navy. We need to undo all of this and start over again. Have him taken to surgery as soon as possible. We need to do this quickly before the healing process begins in earnest."

Henri was put on a stretcher and taken to the surgical area on the first floor and given a strong dose of laudanum. He was soon very drowsy and vaguely remembered the pushes and pulls on his wound. The family was informed he would be several hours in the surgery and then to recover.

After some time, Dr. Lemoine said at last, "There, that should do fine. I want to leave it partially open for drainage. It needs to heal properly and not from the outside first. I want special instructions that the wound is kept clean and covered to prevent infection. Especially watch for any damn flies. They can cause severe damage to open wounds. If anything goes amiss with his prescribed treatment, someone's head will come off. Madame Guillotine is always hungry."

Henri watched in a daze from his stretcher as the ceilings and doorways went by and then the stairway as he was carried back to his room. He slept fitfully until midafternoon and awoke to find Ange's beautiful dark eyes watching him intently.

"Oh, Henri, I was so scared." She started to cry softly again, and he thought he would too.

"I am all right, Ange. When I just woke up and found you here, I was sure I had died and gone to heaven. It is only a little cut on my leg, and nothing for you to worry about."

"Little cut!" she cried. "Henri! I saw it while you were sleeping. You could have been killed or at least have lost your leg. Does it hurt a lot? Can I get you anything?"

"No, I am all right, I think, but my mouth is dry. Maybe if you could get me a sip of water."

She poured a cup of freshwater from the flask on the table and held it to his lips.

"Ah, merci. I was so dry. Ange, why are you here alone? I would think Madame would be here with you."

"It's all right, mon amour. We didn't know how long you would be with the doctors, and she went home to rest. I think she knew wild horses couldn't drag me away and didn't want to make a scene. She will be back later, and then I will go home with her. Is it all right if I kiss you, or are you too weak or in pain or something?"

"Mon dieu, that would be the best medicine I could get," he said.

She leaned over and softly touched her lips to his. Then the tongue touch and all time became lost in the moment. They were on a cloud of their own and lost in a universe where war or pain did not exist.

"And now, Monsieur Hero, you must tell me really what happened and why all of this fuss from Poppa and His Excellency."

He told her what he had heard he did, and she exclaimed, "Killed people! How many? Weren't you afraid? I could never imagine you killing anyone."

"Well, they say I did," he said, "but I can't remember much about it. I remember I was scared to death. Things happened so fast, and then it was over. I do remember firing a musket and a pistol and then swinging a sabre at the Austrians, but it was almost like in a cloud. It's strange, and I really can't explain it. I really don't like to talk about it that much because I don't understand and can't remember.

"People keep asking me, and I just can't remember. It seems like a bad dream. Michael said it was an act of God or the devil, and maybe he is right. Ange, I just remembered you told me that you had looked at my wound while I was sleeping. When you uncovered me, you didn't peek at anything else, did you?"

She just giggled and blushed deeply. "No, nothing else, Monsieur Hero, nothing at all."

They talked of small things then, and just the sharing and holding her hand made the entire crazy world seem somehow right again. Madame and Jean returned later that afternoon and brought him some of Mimi's small sweet cakes.

"Mimi said these will fix you right up. I talked to Dr. Lemoine just after your surgery. He said if we watched you very carefully and you would promise to behave, you may be able to go home in about a week. The hospital is getting very crowded with returning wounded anyway, and space is becoming an issue. Dr. Lemoine lives just over the river bridge from us and a short walk from our house. He can look in on you every day."

Jean-Claude knocked on the open door frame and said, "Well, bonjour, Trooper Bébé Tigre. I said I would look you up." He came in and introduced himself.

Madame asked, "What is this Bébé Tigre all about? Does it have to do with whatever he did?"

"Madame, you haven't heard of the story then," he said.

"You must hear the tale, and don't you blush, young hero."

"Oh, Jean-Claude, don't embarrass me," said Henri, "and here in front of my family."

"Nonsense, Henri, the truth must be told, and I would rather tell it than have them hear it from rumors."

He recanted the tale of the Bébé Tigre standing in front of the entire charging Austrian army shouting and killing several hundred while saving the lives of many officers.

"That isn't so," said Henri, "and you know it. It was only one maybe two that I know of and one officer, my captain. I did maybe cut several more with a sabre before they were chased away by the cavalry troop."

Jean-Claude laughed, "And there you have it, direct from the mouth of our hero himself. He did this thing and has received a personal recognition from the Short Corporal himself. I saw that myself. The troops will talk about this for a long time. Indeed a single trooper and a drummer at that, chasing the entire Austrian army with his trusty sabre."

"Jean-Claude, you did embarrass me," said Henri, "but merci for telling it to the family."

"Merde, Henri," said Jean, somewhat awed. "You are really a hero then. You will have to tell me more about it."

"And who is this lovely creature?" asked Jean-Claude, looking directly at Ange. "I haven't been formally introduced to your family as yet."

"My apologies, Jean-Claude. This is Angelette de Chabot, my general's daughter, and this is his wife, Madame de Chabot, and his son, Jean. I live with them, and they are my family."

"A pleasure to meet you, and now I have to get back to my ward before the orderlies send out a search party," said Jean-Claude, "but I hope to see you again." He looked straight at Ange again when he said this.

Henri thought, I will have to make it clear that Ange is not the prey of anyone else except me. She is too young for this sly, lady-chasing old fox anyway.

Thanks to Jean-Claude and his ward mates, word of his deed, outrageously exaggerated, did make the rounds in the hospital. He was afforded a wondering respect by the orderlies and others on the staff. A week later, Dr. Lemoine pointedly asked him about it. Henri said the stories had been woefully overproportioned.

"Even so, Monsieur Tigre, they make good listening, and I have another surprise for you. You have made the print and news for the citizenry of Paris to read. This is the *Bulletin de l'Europe*, and this is the *Journal des Debats Politiques et Litteraires*. Both are read extensively here in Paris with special emphasis on the Grande Armée and the followers of His Excellency. Look at this. There is even a drawing of the episode showing a tiger in the uniform of a trooper drummer chasing Austrians with his sabre. The caption of the cartoon reads, 'Vive la France. We will run all the way to Vienna. My sabre is mightier than your pen.'"

The doctor translated this into the previously penned broken treaty now solved with the sabre of Napoleon.

"However, my young hero, your wound appears to be healing very nicely; and in a day or so, you may go home. That is if you really want to leave all of this luxury and notoriety."

"Doctor, you can't imagine how I want to go home. I promise to do what you say."

Even though Madame and Ange visited him each day, he still longed to leave this place of strange smells and moaning people. Ange was allowed to stay from midmorning until late evening; and everyone, including Madame, knew now what they truly meant to each other. Now with these current events, it was accepted more than ever.

"Henri, it is almost as if we were married already," she said.

"Oui, I know, and the more I realize this, the more so I cannot wait. I am at total peace when you are here."

Ange read the news articles and remarked, "You are the talk of all of Paris now, but a Tigre? You will always be my Henri. I want to have this cartoon framed and keep it forever. You look so cute with a tiger's head."

Jean-Claude visited him each day along with others he brought along. One visitor was Jean-Claude's father, and he brought several of his friends, all high-ranking officials in the government. They were very distinguished and dressed impeccably in fine linen suits. They congratulated him and said he must visit the government offices when his wound had healed. They all knew the general well and respected his ability as a leader in the Grande Armée. In a private moment, Jean-Claude made a point of telling him that he had only been teasing about Ange. Everyone with a brain could see that she had eyes only for the hero, so why waste one's time or enrage a ferocious tiger? There were many lovely ladies of the court waiting for his attentions.

Father Etty visited the next day, saying, "I would have been here sooner, but I had heard you had the best nurse in all of Paris." He winked at Ange, laughed, and asked, "Henri, do you need the last rites, or can I hear your confession?" They all laughed.

Then Ange said, "Two weeks ago, Henri may have needed the last rites."

Father Etty, very seriously, said, "I heard what happened, and I can't imagine such. God bless, my son." He gave Henri a special scapular, saying it carried a special blessing for his future safety.

The next morning as Henri was finishing his meal of the usual fare, eggs, ham, bread, and coffee, Dr. Lemoine rushed into the room with several orderlies and told him to hurry with his meal. A very special day was in store for him. The empress had requested her own carriage and personal guard to escort him home. Today was her day of the week to ride through the streets of Paris and be seen by her subjects. Napoleon had said it was very important for persons of station to be seen by the people and not hidden away in some pile of old stones. This was indeed an honor and not one to be taken lightly.

Henri hurriedly gulped his coffee as the orderlies were stripping his gown and putting on a fresh uniform and not the uniform of an ordinary trooper. Henri asked what uniform this was, and Dr. Lemoine said it was the uniform of the special guard borrowed for the occasion. It had a white tunic with ruffled collar, a deep scarlet jacket with gold buttons, and white trousers with a scarlet stripe down each leg. A tall dark fur hat with shiny black visor and bright gold medallion of the guard unit completed the uniform. The leg seam had been let out to compensate for his bindings and could be resewn. He had white stockings and one shiny black boot and looked quite presentable with his hair trimmed military style, face washed, and even his fingernails cleaned and trimmed.

"We can't have you looking like a Paris sewer rat in front of the empress."

What a fuss, thought Henri. *Won't this ever end and I can go home?*

Ange, Madame, and Jean arrived a short time later and were told the empress would be there shortly.

The empress Josephine came into the room with several of her attendants and asked, "Well, would our young hero be up to a short ride through Paris before we take him home?"

Dr. Lemoine bowed and answered, "He is fit, Your Highness. He tires, but getting outdoors may help him."

Josephine greeted the family and was introduced. She went over to him and kissed him lightly on the forehead. "I remember you from an event at the palace. I didn't think we had met before, but now, oui, I do remember." She sat on the bed and asked, "Are you all right? Are the news articles correct? Did you really chase away the entire Austrian army with just a sabre?"

Henri blushed, and she laughed and said, "Oh, I know how these news things are, and pay no mind to them. But enjoy this notoriety for a time. Time and life are so short, and every moment should be lived to the fullest. The people need heroes to bolster morale and gain further confidence in our emperor and the Grande Armée. Come, Monsieur Tigre, your subjects of Paris await. Madame de Chabot, Ange, and Jean can ride in my carriage."

Henri was nearly in shock at all of this treatment. Her Highness, the lovely empress herself! Never in his wildest imagination could he dream of such. As he was carried down the halls on a stretcher, Jean-Claude, standing in the hall with other of the patients who could walk, started to clap his hands. It started a chain reaction, and soon the entire corps of wounded and hospital staff was clapping as he was carried by. When he realized the applause was for him as well as the empress, he was sure he would cry with all of this emotion. He had to bite his lip several times. Ange was walking by his side, holding his hand and with a look of immense pride. He did see tears in her and Madame's eyes. Josephine whispered to Madame de Chabot if this was what she thought it might be between Henri and Ange.

"Oh, I believe so, Your Highness. Those two have been nearly inseparable since they met several years ago. They are so young and yet seem to have such an adult demeanor about them."

"Oh oui, Madame de Chabot, it is the times in which we live. So often these young people are asked to jump from the cradle to the battlefield. There seems to be no time for childhood and play. It all seems so sad in a way."

Henri was propped up and in the open-top carriage with Josephine on one side and Ange on the other. Jean, Madame, and another of the empress's attendants were on the opposite seat that faced each other. A special mounted guard of twelve in front and twelve in the rear made up the entourage. The de Chabot carriage would follow just ahead of the rear guard and carry the other of the empress's attendants. The guards were dressed in the uniform Henri wore and rode magnificent matching black horses. Their sabres and the adornments on the uniforms, saddles, and bridles gleamed and sparkled in the morning sun.

They made their way out of the hospital grounds, through the metal gates, and to the bridge crossing the Seine near the Palais du Louvre. It was a lovely morning, and the sun had not yet risen to the full height and heat of midday. A slight breeze from the east was pleasant and cooling. There were only very high wisps of clouds in the vast blue sky. The troop crossed the bridge and turned left along the river. Josephine and Madame were chattering away about the many things that ladies talk about while Henri and Ange sat holding hands and looking at the river, buildings, trees, and general scenery. They crossed the Place de la Concorde. Jean seemed awestruck and just sat watching the sights.

Madame remembered, "This is the place that I remember when the guillotine and the revolution were so eminent. I came here and watched the execution of King Louis and again when Marie Antoinette was put to death. It was a horrid event, but something one felt compelled to witness as a true French patriot."

She briefly described the screaming of bloodthirsty crowds as the huge blade of the guillotine slammed down and a severed head rolled into a basket. She was sick and had nightmares for weeks. The Place de la Concorde was originally known as Place Louis XV and just after the revolution was renamed Place de la Revolution. All things relating to royalty were renamed or destroyed as the Bastille had been. Now with its third name in a long history, maybe they would leave it alone for a time.

Henri noticed that crowds along the route were pointing and bowing as the troop went by. Some in the larger groups were clapping and cheering. Ange smiled at him and softly patted his hand. Jean was basking in his moment of glory now too and waving at the people.

They turned onto the Avenue des Champs-Élysées and marveled at the huge tree-lined roadway with shops, cafés, and crowds of cheering people. The empress had planned this well and had announced the day before that on her usual parade day she would be escorting the newest hero of the Grande Armée, Bébé Tigre, for all to see. They turned at the uncompleted Arc de Triomphe and went down some narrow cobblestone streets back in the direction of the river.

Josephine informed them, "I usually take a longer tour, but for today and not tire the wounded hero, I am making it a bit shorter. However, if you do not mind, there is just one other place I pass every week where there is usually a large crowd. I do not want to disappoint them as today is special. It isn't that far out of the way and won't take long just to ride by and acknowledge the people."

They followed the river road to the bridge near the Palais du Louvre, crossed the Seine again, and proceeded to the Place du Panthéon. The Panthéon was the old St. Genevieve Church and now renamed Place du Panthéon. The domed structure and tall columns were a masterpiece of architecture.

The old church was now the final resting place of some of the most notable men in recent and ancient French history including Voltaire, Rousseau, Victor Hugo, and others. Some had died of natural causes and others as the result of Madame Guillotine. It was said this is the home of *hommes de l'époque de la liberté française* or great men of the era of French history. As the empress had said, there was a large crowd waiting for her to ride by. The crowd was even larger than along the Avenue des Champs-Élysées and applauded, cheered, and bowed as they went by. The occupants of the carriage waved as they made a short turn in front of the Panthéon and went back the way they had come and through the Place de Invalides where they had started.

The huge golden dome was shining in the morning sun as if a beacon trying to draw Henri back inside. Madame explained the history of this famous hospital and being first commissioned by Louis XIV as a place for sick and homeless soldiers. Being partially built in 1674, it had housed about four thousand men at one time and was now a small town of sorts with small factories manned by the residents. Wonderful handcrafted items could be purchased there; and her parents went there often to buy boots, shoes, tapestries, cloth, and wood items of stools, benches, and small tables.

It wasn't long after leaving the Place de Invalides that they arrived at the de Chabot home and parked the carriages in front of the house. The troops waited outside the main gate as there was not sufficient room inside the small center courtyard and circular drive, beside the fact that this many horses were certain to make many messes.

Madame asked if the empress would care to take refreshments, and the invitation was readily accepted. Mimi had prepared a place in the sitting room for Henri to recline, and he was carried in by two of the guards. The meeting was very gracious and short. Mimi had prepared a special spiced tea, and the empress remarked she must have the blending recipe for use at the palace. It was very tasty, and she was very impressed with it as well as Mimi's special delicate little pastries and sweet cakes.

As the empress left, she leaned over and kissed Henri on the forehead again and said, "Merci for being so gracious today and a hero of the Grande Armée. When my husband returns, we will do you the correct honor as he has promised. Merci all for a lovely time and the special company this morning. We must meet again soon."

She whispered to Ange, "This one is special. Take very good care of him. One can tell you care very much for your 'brother.'"

"I will, Your Highness, I will." Ange bowed, and the empress swept out of the door and mounted the carriage.

At long last, he was home and with family and more at peace than in many weeks. Mimi had a small bed set up for him in the corner of the huge pantry. His room on the third floor was out of the question. There was a small table next to the cot with a candle and a bell. He was instructed to ring the bell when he needed anything. There was another place where he could recline in the sitting room, but the pantry would be more comfortable and private. The smells of the onions, potatoes, spices, and other things Mimi used in her cooking were refreshing and welcome, bringing back kind and warm memories of other times at the farm and convent. There were two windows in the room that overlooked the back spaces of the gardens, stable, and barn.

As he propped up and looked out of the window above his cot, he suddenly was aware that anything going on in the back areas was under the scrutiny of Mimi or whoever else wanted to watch. How many times had he and Ange "visited" at the water trough and just inside the barn? He wondered if they had been observed and just what Mimi or Madame had seen. Oh, there was really nothing out of sorts if they could have been watched, but one did get a guilty complex about kissing and such. He would tell Ange and show her this when she visited.

The noon meal was brought to him on a wooden tray and placed on his table. Mimi had prepared a nice roast chicken and vegetables that tasted nothing like the swill of the Armée kitchens. He teasingly asked Mimi if she would be interested in cooking for his company at the camp. She said there were not enough gold sovereigns in Napoleon's coffers to tempt her of such. The bread was so light and tasty as compared to Armée bread; and the wine, while dark and robust, did not have the sharp bite he was used to having.

Ange came in with a plate for herself and sat on his bed. "Is it all right to sit on the bed? I don't want to bump your wound."

He smiled and said, "If the carriage ride and all of the other events of today didn't bother it, you certainly won't. How could the love of my life sitting next to me ever bother anything? Please come as often as you can and bring a book. Maybe I can read to you like the first times we met. It will help time to pass anyway. I will try to be up and around as soon as I can. I can't stand this lying around."

Mimi brought in the bottle of wine and poured him a second cup. "Ange, you must not bother our Tigre and let him rest so he can gather his strength."

"Mimi, please don't call me a tiger, and Ange is not bothering me. Actually her company is the best medicine I could have."

Mimi mumbled something about puppy love and bustled out of the room, shuffling her slippered feet as she went.

As Mimi left, Ange said, "Pull in your claws, my little Tigre. This is something you will have to live with for a while. We don't call you this for fun, but admiration. This will pass soon enough. I won't tease you anymore because you would probably make up a funny name for me."

"We have, Petite Désordre, already. I like that one."

She said, pulling on his ear, "I am certainly not a little mess, but I will call you Gros Désordre because you are a bigger mess than I will ever be.

"All right, all right, truce." He laughed, reaching for her and pulling her over closer. She leaned over and kissed him, careful not to linger too long. This was Mimi's territory, and one never knew when she might appear. Most of the time, one could hear her shuffling slippers; but other times, she might try to creep up and not be heard.

The days turned into weeks, and Henri was getting around much better now. Dr. Lemoine had brought him crutches from the hospital, and at least he could clump his way around the house and even venture in the back with the help of Ange and Jean. The doctor said he wanted him up and about as soon as possible to prevent the leg from becoming stiff through lack of exercise. Ange stayed with him constantly. The only time she left him was for her personal times of bathing and to sleep in her room. She took her meals with him at the small table in the pantry. She brought him books from the library, and they had spent many hours of him reading to her.

Ange could read, but she said the way he read with such expression made the listening so interesting and a pleasure. Now with the healing wound much better, he was joining the family for meals in the dining room. He and Jean also spent considerable time together. He had to tell the very interested Jean over and over about battle and the noise of the cannon, thunder of hundreds of running horses, musket shots, people shouting and screaming, and the general melee of the confusion. Ange listened to the tales and could not imagine her Henri had been exposed to so much in so short of a time in the Armée. Jean would be eligible for the officer academy later in the year, and he wanted to know all possible about life in the Armée.

Henri jokingly told Jean, "You might be my commanding officer one day."

"Not so, brother, you may be mine. But whatever happens, we need to protect each other."

Ange said, "Oh, I'll bet you both will."

The general came home in late Juillet 1809 and announced that peace had been forced with the Austrians. Napoleon would be home in a couple of weeks with the remainder of the Armée. The Grande Armée would be home until some other problem came up, and they would be compelled to march again. Even now there was growing concern about the Russians trying to make problems. The general had a very private and confidential talk with Henri on the matter of his future with the military. They shared wine in the general's study.

The general told him, "With the record you presently have, any number of things may be possible. Henri, you could now be eligible for the officer academy and after six months become a junior officer. If I were you, that is the route I would suggest. Officers live much better than troopers, and maybe being on a general's staff, one could have a bright future."

"Monsieur, are you thinking I might be able to join your staff of planning and battle orders?" Henri asked.

"As I said, my boy, no promises, but anything may be possible. We must take care of our own. I am still attempting to remove my balls from the stable door for your getting injured. You would be much safer with my staff. You know that."

"Oui, monsieur, I do."

The general added, "We have some time before you report back to duty, so let us see what happens. In the meantime, give some thought on the matter; and by all means, discuss this with my daughter. I know you will anyway, but she will be furious with her Poppa if she is left out of anything to do with you. Maybe this is meant to be, only God knows. Jean will be eligible for the academy later, and anything you can coach him on as to the athletics and academics for graduation will help him. He wants this so much, and I must admit, I do too."

They chatted about the battles after Henri had left Austria, and really, he had not missed that much. Henri had, however, seen some of the Black Forest and had satisfied his curiosity about his father and where he died. Henri did discuss the possibility of becoming an officer with Ange and included Jean as well.

He told Jean, "If I do this, I would learn all I can on the requirements and help you the next year." Jean was very receptive, and the two had long discussions on the matter.

Ange anxiously said, "I'm not really all that excited about you going off to war again, officer or not. You have served and served well. Why not just stay home." She said it with a half heart as she knew it was falling on deaf ears. It was a once-in-a-lifetime opportunity and a true honor to be recommended to be among the elite.

His wound had healed very nicely, and only an angry red scar remained. Henri exercised daily behind the barn and often ran the length of the back garden many times an afternoon. He was soon back in passable shape and starting to lose some of the pudge he had gathered while convalescing.

Henri took Jean into the exercise mode, telling him that he must be more physical and muscular if he was going to the academy next year. It was very important to be fit for military life. It would go much easier for him. Jean struggled at first as he was sorely out of condition, but after a couple of weeks or so, he was keeping up with Henri.

"Come on, fat boy, run harder. You can't let a cripple beat you."

Jean finally did keep up with Henri, and they laughed as they tried to beat the other. Ange watched as they ran back and forth and often would fuss at them for working too hard.

"But I have to," Henri said. "I can't possibly go back to duty in a few weeks out of condition and with all of this belly fat. The sergeants would work me to death. I would much rather do it to myself, and besides, I have such a lovely audience."

"Well, this audience could almost keep up with the two of you if she really wanted," she said.

"Ha! Not so," said Jean. "No little girl can keep up with the likes of us."

With that Ange kicked off her shoes and wiggled her bare toes in the grass, lifted her skirt, and said, "Anytime you are ready."

They lined up, and Ange counted, "One, two, three, go!" She did keep up, and had it not been for the skirt, she would have done much better. "There," she said, huffing and breathing hard, "I am not the weak little girl you may think I am."

"Maybe not," Henri said, "but you do have the prettiest legs and feet of any here."

They all hugged and laughed and pushed and pulled the other down in a heap. Madame watched all of this from the pantry window and remarked to herself, "Oh to be young again. The entire world is theirs at this moment. This is a sight to warm an old woman's soul. Mimi, come see our brood. This moment is forever."

Napoleon returned with the remainder of the Armée in the first week of August. The general had, the week before, been given advance notice and told to prepare the troops for Napoleon's triumphant march down the Champs-Élysées. Henri would ride a horse with the color guard just behind the general. He was issued a new uniform of his regiment complete with new shiny black boots. Madame took Henri to the tailor and had the new uniform fitted to perfection. Early in the morning on the day of the grand entrance, the general and Henri left for the troop encampment.

Henri looked very smart in his new uniform. He was slightly tanned after his workouts in the garden and was slim and muscular again. Ange grabbed his hand as he left and told him that he was so handsome in his uniform that he took her breath away. When they arrived, the general told his aide to see that Henri had a decent horse and not some old nag that would embarrass them in front of the emperor. Henri went with him and picked a fine black horse with a white blaze on his forehead. He was combed, brushed, and fitted with a black military saddle. Henri led the horse back to the general's area and passed the area where Michael and the others were.

"All be quiet and bow. Our Hero approaches," said Michael. They all rushed around him with hugs and backslaps.

"Henri, we have missed you these several months and have wondered how you were. We haven't had any word of you since we saw you put on the dispatch hospital carriage. Is your leg better now? What is the latest news? We have been in for a while but couldn't get away to visit you. We have a new sergeant, and he is something else."

Just then a voice growled behind them, and a sergeant walked up. "And who the hell might you be? Do you belong to this troop, or are you just over here bothering my people?"

"Sergeant, I do belong to this troop. I was wounded in Austria and will rejoin the troop after the grand entrance of the emperor."

"What are you doing with this horse? I'll bet you stole it."

"No, Sergeant, I was ordered to get this horse and ride with the color guard next to the general."

"And just who told you to do that? I suppose it was the general himself, eh?"

"As a matter of fact, it was. Please ask the general or his aide." With that, Henri mounted the horse.

"Just a minute, you young pup. I will go with you and see if this is true."

They went over to the staff area, and the sergeant inquired of the aide, "Is it true that Trooper Henri Devreney is to ride up front with the general?"

"Indeed he will, Sergeant. This soldier is the most decorated hero of the Austrian campaign and will be presented honors by Napoleon himself today. Have you never heard of the Bébé Tigre? Well, here he is balls, claws, and all."

The sergeant drew back and was sorry he had made such a scene and a fool of himself. He should have been more careful and at least found out who this was before the big fuss. Tigre indeed! The ranks were still talking what this soldier had done.

"I apologize, Trooper. I should have had better sense than to make such a noise."

"I understand, Sergeant."

"Merci, Soldier," said the sergeant. "We will meet more formally and talk when you return to the unit."

Henri met the general at the assembly point. Napoleon and his personal guard would lead the parade. The general and the remainder of the troops would immediately follow.

Napoleon was dressed in one of his finest dress uniforms of white trouser, dark blue blazer with gold buttons and matching cloak, and the forever-famous trifold hat. His brilliantly polished knee-high black boots completed his dress. He was mounted on Vizir, his favorite white stallion. He made a splendid spectacle and was the very eminent example of authority and confidence.

The guard and ranking staff officers were dressed essentially the same except with bright red blazers and cloaks and tall brown fur hats with a red pompon on the front. As soon as the signal was given the total troop was ready, the trumpets sounded, and the drums started to sound the cadence. The color guard consisted of almost fifty flags of the various regiments and units of the Grande Armée and an entire line of the tricolor. Henri estimated there must be at least two full divisions complete with artillery and mounted equipment in the parade.

The parade moved forward to the Arc de Triomphe and down the Champs-Élysées. There were enormous crowds of cheering people, and Henri could see the emperor at times remove his hat and wave to the people. The hundreds of marching feet were as one, and the riders were very careful to keep strict alignment. They moved down the broad avenue and over to the Place de la Concorde. The parade came to a momentary halt while Napoleon dismounted to join Josephine on a large viewing stand.

The personal guard made a precise wheel and also dismounted. A group of assembled grooms led the horses away, and the guard formed a solid rank of red facing the viewing stand. They drew sabres, presented a salute to their leader, and brought the sabres to their sides. The color guard and music corps formed on the right of the guard and continued to beat the cadence of standard slow march. The remainder of the troops filed in rank by rank and completely filled the large Place de la Concorde.

The general indicated to Henri to dismount and give his horse to one of the grooms, and he did the same. The two stood by themselves just in front of the color guard.

"And now, son," said the general, "it will be your turn for the most memorable day of your life."

The band struck up the familiar strains of "The Marseillaise," the French national anthem. The huge square filled with troops rang with the singing voices of hundreds. Napoleon mounted a podium in the center of the viewing stand, and a hush came over the crowd. He gave a short speech on the glories of France and the Grande Armée and what the result of these great victories in Austria meant to the people of France.

"Those great victories were at the tremendous sacrifices of those who would never return and others who had given totally of themselves. It is my distinct honor to recognize one of these today."

He gave a very brief explanation of the exploits of Bébé Tigre and asked Henri to come forward. Henri marched very erect to the podium as the emperor came down and was presented a bright blue velvet box by an attendant. Napoleon opened the box and held a gold medal with a ribbon of the tricolors of France, red, white, and blue, up for all to see. The cheering was thunderous as he draped the medal around Henri's neck and kissed both his cheeks. Henri bowed deeply, did a smart about-face, and returned to his place next to the general. The emotion of the moment was paramount. Henri noticed slight moisture had formed around the general's eyes. He supposed his eyes were a bit moist also.

"My son," said the general, "you do not only yourself but me and my family a great honor today. Well done, very well done."

And this was indeed the most memorable day of his young life, one never to be forgotten by himself or his generations.

The groom brought the general his horse, and Henri was told he was relieved of duty and could join the family and dignitaries in the viewing stand. As Henri mounted the viewing stand, he was greeted and hugged by the empress who said to him, "I am honored to know you. This is a proud moment for France."

Suddenly, Madame, Jean, Mimi, and Ange surrounded him. He was hugged and pulled from one to the other. He felt a small hand grip his and pull him around. He found himself staring into the most beautiful dark eyes he would ever know. This time they had the look of wonder and yet relief and puzzlement. He had never before seen such readings in these eyes even though he had done intense study at times.

She hugged him and whispered in his ear, "I do love you so. Not just for this moment but for the Henri you are to me."

The events of this day were much like a tale from the books in the library and not the reality of this world.

The family rode home in the family carriage with all wanting to see his medal. Finally home to the real world of Mimi's hash stuff and the things he treasured most. He felt smothered and wanted quiet time with only Ange, Jean, and his family. He went on to the large back porch, sat in the warm afternoon sun, and was soon dozing with welcome relief and contentment. But not for long.

Ange came out and asked him, "Are you angry? Is anything wrong?"

"No, nothing is wrong, Ange. I just can't believe any of this. It is like a fairy tale or a dream. This can't be happening to me. I want to cry and laugh at the same time. Stay with me, Ange, and we can talk."

"I'll be here, Henri. I always will."

"I know that now, Ange. I will always try to be there for you too."

The general returned home toward evening and at the evening meal announced that Henri would be given a week off duty. On reporting back to duty, he would report directly to the general and be escorted to the officer academy where he would be tested both physically and mentally for acceptance. The general laughed and said that with Henri's recognition of today and the personal recommendation of the emperor, the examining board would be subject to an appointment with Madame Guillotine if they did otherwise than accept him.

The general noticed Henri's medal on the small desk in the large entranceway and picked it up. "Many men would give a right arm for this medal, son, and to think, all you had to give was a 'small scratch' on the leg and a few drops of blood."

"Poppa!" cried Ange. "Did you see his 'scratch'? He could have been killed."

"Oui, Ange, I saw it at the field hospital; and I must admit, I hoped he would make it to Paris and at the very least not lose his leg. Many have died from wounds like this. Be patient with an old soldier who jokes about things. I have seen much worse, and so has he. This is a fine medal, Henri, and one for you to treasure as long as you live."

The medal was of circular solid gold about two inches in diameter and hung on a fine silk ribbon of the tricolors of France, red, white, and blue. A smaller version for wearing on the breast was also in the box. The one worn around the neck was only for formal occasions. On the front was the likeness of Napoleon with the inscription, "Valour, Austria, 1809." On the reverse was the new seal of the republic and the inscription "République Française."

The general remarked this was a simple medal, and yet extreme elegance was shown in its simplicity. The new seal on the reverse side had replaced the old style of the Gallic Rooster used by the kings of old. This seal had a woman holding a pike topped by a cap in the shape of a beehive. The other hand held a lictor's fasces or bundle symbolizing authority. At her feet was a plow, and the entire symbol was said to represent the working simple people of France and the revolution.

"Let's see, Henri, this now gives you three medals to decorate your uniform. The Spanish campaign, the Austrian campaign, and now this one, the best of all."

That night as Henri was lying across the bed trying to fully comprehend the events of the day, the door softly opened.

Ange peered around the door and whispered, "Henri, Henri, are you sleeping?"

"No, Ange, please come in and leave the door open. We can sit by the window and watch the moon and stars."

"All right, but first, I need a hug and kiss."

They held each other tenderly and savored a long kiss.

"Ange, I have never had such feelings as I do these days. Sometimes it scares me."

"I know, I know, but we must wait and be careful. Everyone knows now."

"Ha, I know they do, but they just aren't saying anything."

"Oui, I know. The way everyone looks at us when we are together like we are doing something wrong. Or maybe it is just a guilt feeling for thinking what we really want to do."

"Shhh, we shouldn't talk about such things. Someone could hear us and think we are doing and not just thinking."

"Oh, Henri, sometimes you can be such a merde." He laughed at her soft teasing.

They sat quietly in the chairs facing each other and watching the ever-rising full moon reflecting on the scene below. The river, church, and other large buildings, some with domes and some with spires. They had seen these sights before, many times, but tonight was a bit more special. Henri was now a man and a proven and decorated soldier in the Grande Armée of the republic.

Ange was at the age of womanhood. Both had demonstrated adulthood even now and had somehow gained the respect and knowledge of all around them. The inevitable would be marriage. As they sat, Ange rubbed her bare toes on Henri's feet.

"Petite Désordre, you make it very difficult for me to think when you do that."

"Henri! I am not a little mess, and you know it. You are a bigger one."

"Well, whoever you are, you drive me mad with all of these tongue-touch and toe-rubbing things."

"Well, good! That is the intent, Monsieur Tigre."

And it went on and on into the night. Sharing, slight touching, and words of passion and caring.

Madame came into the room and coughed slightly to let her presence be known. Ange and Henri jumped up, startled.

"You two lovebirds should be in your own beds at this hour. Ange, I thought we had a talk sometime back about late-hour visits to gentlemen's bedrooms. I couldn't sleep and saw your room door open and then Henri's."

"Momma, we are not doing anything wrong. That is why the doors are open. This view of Paris in the full moonlight from these windows is probably the best in the entire house. We couldn't sleep either with all that has happened. We were only sitting and talking."

"Oh, I know, children, but I do wish you would do your talking in places other than a man's bedroom. It just isn't proper for a lady of proper society. Now off to bed both of you. We will discuss this further in the morning."

They did discuss the situation after the morning meal, and Madame finally gave in. "If the doors are open and the chairs are placed such that no doubt 'foolishness' was not going on, you may continue to 'talk.' However, I feel it best that Poppa be made aware of this in case he happens on the scene, and his roaring might awaken the entire near neighborhood. Fathers and especially generals of the Grande Armée just do not understand certain things and are more apt to think of sins of the flesh. With his only daughter involved, heaven help us all."

So the issue was closed, and the meetings could continue, always with dignity and the openness that Madame had mandated.

The week flew by as off-duty times often do. The entire family went to High Mass at Notre Dame on Dimanche knowing that the following day, Lundi, the general and Henri would report back to duty. It would not be bad this time as France was more or less at peace, and the entire Armée would not move. Henri would be going to the officer academy and would be gone for many weeks without leave.

After Mass, a fine dinner of roast goose and delightful vegetables was served. Most all of the family went to their private quarters for an afternoon nap. Ange and Henri went into the back gardens and sat under the fruit trees and talked all afternoon. They were actually making definite plans of their future together. Later that night, they would talk more and hug and kiss their goodbyes.

Henri woke early the next morning, as usual, and realized this was to be another big day in his life. Even though superb recommendations were to be given at the academy, the rest must be up to him. He would do his very best not just to succeed but to excel in his studies and physical tests.

The general had already told him that horsemanship was a quality that would be stressed. Henri wasn't worried about that as his knowledge and skills of riding went back to his very early days on the farm. Maybe he had traded that damn drum for a horse and sabre. The following weeks would tell. He hurriedly dressed and went to meet Mimi in the kitchen for an early coffee and sweet cake.

"We will miss you, Monsieur Gypsy," she said. "It appears you come and go with much more rapidity these days. I wish you could be here more often, but I do understand the times we live in and the military way. The general is the same, and I guess your destiny and Jean's will be the same until there are no wars to fight."

They could hear movement upstairs and the general starting to clump around. Mimi hurriedly started to prepare the morning meal.

"It will be light soon, and you are traveling today," she said.

The rest of the family came down and sat in the quiet silence of dread of departure once more. There was just no easy way for this. Ange sat next to Henri and rubbed her bare toes on his leg. He could sense the anxiety in the movement of her toes and felt anxious himself about leaving again.

With the meal finished and goodbyes said, the carriage rumbled up in the circular drive. On the way to camp, the general said for Henri to report to his duty post and await instructions. He would send for him as soon as he had word.

Henri reported to the area where Michael and the rest were and met the sergeant again.

"Well, Monsieur Tigre, you have returned to us I see," he observed.

"Only for a short time, Sergeant. The general will call for me soon. I will go to officer training today."

"You are very fortunate, Trooper, to have such a tremendous opportunity at such an early age. When you do receive your officer rank, please do not forget the common soldiers that makes the clock of Armée truly tick."

"I promise," said Henri. "I have seen too much of the ordinary soldier to ever forget."

They visited and drank coffee during the early morning, and nearing midmorning, the general's orderly came looking for him. "Come quickly, Henri, the general just received word, and you are to report this afternoon. We haven't much time."

"Where am I going, or did he tell you yet?"

"Oh oui, we received word you will be going to École Spéciale Militaire de Saint-Cyr near Versailles. A very special school indeed and founded by His Excellency. Come we must hurry."

He was wished well with slaps on the back, hugs, and jokes.

Michael said, "I will see you in another lifetime, mon ami. Please don't forget me."

11

École Spéciale Militaire de Saint-Cyr—

"Ils S'instruisent pour Vaincre" (They Study to Vanquish)

Henri followed the general's orderly to the command area and was ushered into the general's office. "Well now, Henri, I guess you are special. The emperor himself has appointed you to the École Spéciale Militaire de Saint-Cyr. I wish I could have gone there instead of the old academy. It is the best of the best now. Napoleon is very proud of it. Both Napoleon and I attended the Collège Militaire de Brienne and the l'École Militaire Royale de Paris both in Paris. We graduated in 1785, becoming friends and junior officers.

"Even then, one could see Napoleon had a destiny. He was so driven by everything. I have served with him since and will do so until one of us quits or dies. He founded the *école* a few years back, and only the very best and most promising are chosen as cadets. Oh, there is the usual class of the rich and aristocrats chosen but only for political favor. Most do not make it anyway. The real heart of our future officer corps will come from ones like yourself. It is no accident that you will attend this school. You have done this on your own. Don't let your head swell so that your hat will not fit. You will have to do a lot of hard work to get you through this. But with what you have already shown, you can do it. Come, let's go for a carriage ride. The école is just past Versailles and a good several-hour carriage ride."

The orderly brought them some sweet cakes and coffee from the kitchens as they boarded the carriage for another special day in Henri's young life. They covered their legs with blankets to ward off the cold. The first few minutes, they sat in silence. They ate their sweet cakes and drank the welcome hot black coffee as the carriage made a slow pace through the troop area. They soon were on the road headed west to Versailles. Henri had never been this way before, and the scenery was one of small villages and farms with picturesque houses, fields, trees, and small streams.

As the general dozed with his head bobbing as the carriage hit ruts in the road, Henri was left mostly to his thoughts of the future, the school, and Ange. It appeared from time to time that his head would be jerked off. He would occasionally awake startled with an exceptionally large jolt. He awoke as they passed a magnificent estate with a huge brick wall and large buildings set back in immense gardens.

"That is the old king's hunting lodge," said the general. "Old King Louis XIII first had a hunting lodge here; and his son, Louis XIV, liked the place so much he had a 'few' additions made. What you see here now in no way resembles the original old hunting lodge. I have been inside several times, and the splendor is beyond belief. There is one main banquet room named the Hall of Mirrors that is exceptional. Mirrors cover every bit of wall space in the entire room. The entire ceiling is of intricate paintings. The chandeliers make a spectacular sight at night with everyone in dress uniform and the ladies in full formal attire. I hope someday you can see inside. Napoleon uses it now as his hideaway palace and comes here to get away from the stress and turmoil of state business. Poor man, he is hounded at every quarter, but he seems to thrive on it and is a person of ceaseless energy."

The village of Saint-Cyr-l'École was just a short ride from Versailles, and soon they stopped at an immense brick entrance way with iron gates. A small guardhouse was just on the inside of the gates. A guard came out, said something to the general's driver, and waved them on.

There was a cluster of white buildings trimmed in blue and topped with blue tile roofs. Most were two and three floors and utilized as barracks and classrooms. The other single-story buildings were offices and the service areas of the school. The stables and riding practice courses were in the rear of the main building complex. The interior grounds and gardens were void of flowers during this time of the year. A light snow had dusted the grounds. No one appeared to be outside. They climbed out of the carriage and shook the stiffness away.

"Damn and hell fire, I am getting too old for these damn carriage rides," said the general. "In my next lifetime, I would like to return as my Vivien's cat. You have seen how she pampers the damn spoiled beast. Sometimes I think she cares more for that cat than she does me. Warm milk and such! I should be so fortunate and get my back rubbed whenever I purr."

A captain met them, and the general stated their names and business. "Oui, monsieur, we have been expecting you. Please come this way." They were escorted into the waiting room of the commanding officer. A very distinguished tall colonel came immediately out of his office.

"Andre! I haven't seen you in several years. I think it was just after the Austrian campaign in the Black Forest that we went our separate ways. What times those were. I have been married since then and am trying to behave myself with a new wife and child. And now you are a general. A shame I was wounded and have this damn stiff leg and back, but I guess someone has to babysit the future officers for le Patron and his next la Fêtes. And I expect this is one Trooper Devreney I have heard so much about?"

"Oui, he is, Emile. Henri, may I present my old mate from my officer academy days. This is Colonel Emile Facet, the commandant of this fine establishment."

Henri shook the colonel's hand, and the colonel remarked, "Oui, I see you have a nice, firm handgrip. Andre must have taught you that. He used to try to squeeze my hand off. Andre, I am going to introduce this young man to his leader, and then we can go for a few drinks and reminisce the good old times unless you have to hurry back, that is."

"No, Emile, I had planned on spending the night here and leaving early in the morning. One can never tell what the damnable weather will do this time of year. There was a light snow just yesterday. I would hate to freeze to death in a disabled carriage on these dark and lonely roads. Henri, carry on the way you have been, and I am certain you will do well."

The general clapped Henri on the back as he was led away by Colonel Facet. They went into the next building and into a small office at the far end. A lieutenant jumped to attention as they entered the room.

"Lieutenant Roussell, this is Cadet Henri Devreney. Please see that he is given proper uniform and supply of the school and show him to his quarters."

"Oui, monsieur. Will there be anything further?"

"No, Lieutenant. He will make the class total of twelve now, and you can commence formal indoctrination tomorrow."

"Oui, monsieur, merci."

The colonel left to rejoin the general, and Lieutenant Roussell asked Henri to accompany him to the supply office. "From now until you quit this école or graduate, you will be addressed as cadet. Officers are addressed by rank and last name. We are more polite here than you have been used to after the regular Armée, but protocol is military, and courtesy is strictly adhered to at all times. Is this clear, Cadet?"

"Oui, monsieur." He was issued a complete supply of new uniforms, clothing, and necessaries of personal kit that filled two large bags.

"I am Supply Sergeant Lemay, Cadet. If you need anything more, come see me. Tomorrow we will fit your uniforms with the tailor and draw your arms and sword. There are no sloppy fit to uniforms here. His Excellency would have our heads."

"Come with me, Cadet," said the lieutenant, "I will show you to your quarters."

Henri struggled to keep up as they went up one flight of stairs and farther down the long hall. Lieutenant Roussell did not offer to assist as it would be beneath his rank. Henri noticed everything was polished and reflections shown as glass. They arrived at a room on the far corner of the building. The lieutenant knocked and opened the door.

A tall slim young man jumped to attention and said, "Monsieur?" as they entered the room.

"Gentleman," said the lieutenant, "I will leave this new cadet, and you can introduce yourselves. The evening meal will be soon. Make sure you are presentable. Things are a bit informal as yet, but starting tomorrow, we will be more military than you might ever imagine."

"Oui, monsieur. Merci."

The lieutenant left and closed the door.

"I am Francis Caudron," said the tall young man, "and who are you?"

"I am Henri Devreney, Francis. I am pleased to meet you. Where can I put all of this stuff?"

"Well, there are two cadets assigned to a room, and it really doesn't matter where I flop," said Francis.

"You were here first, and you should have the first choice."

"All right, I will take this area over here, or we can move things around to both our liking if they will let us."

The corner room offered two walls with outside windows. A small desk and chair for study was at each set of windows, affording plenty of light during daytime hours. A candle was on each desk but indicated they had not been used. Henri doubted they would be put to much use either. A single oil lamp was on one of the desks, but this too did not show any signs of being used. Early to bed and early to rise was the military way. No time to waste candles or lamp oil. As the old sergeant had told the boys at drummer school, you can play with yourselves in the dark, and we will not have to waste candles. Beds were along the opposite walls. There was a wooden footlocker at the foot of each bed for uniforms, clothing, and personal articles. There were no locks anywhere. The code of honor here was very strict. Immediate expulsion and shame would be the result as breakers of the rules were drummed out of the corps either to be returned home or sent back to the ranks as ordinary troopers and cannon silage.

Henri started to sort his new items out when Francis said, "I was told that everything would have to be placed in certain order. We will be given instruction when official training begins."

"That should begin tomorrow," said Henri. "I heard the lieutenant talking about it."

"Excellent!" acknowledged Francis. "I have been just hanging around here with my teeth in my mouth for two days now just waiting, watching, and bored to tears. Henri, I see by your uniform that you were a trooper before coming here. Did you see any combat, and how did you get here?"

"Oui, Francis, I did see combat in Spain and again in Austria. I joined as a drummer and was recommended to come here by General de Chabot. I have lived with his family for several years, and I guess he wouldn't have it any other way than for me to try to be an officer."

Henri was very careful not to mention anything about Ange or his commendation from Napoleon. They would find out soon enough, but until then, he would not have to answer all of those damn questions again. He had several medals he would have to wear at formal dress ceremonies, but these too would be kept under cover until the time.

Francis was from Paris, and his father was on the administrative staff of Napoleon. He had served for a year as a clerk in military headquarters in Paris.

"Do you a know Jean-Claude Ridoux from Paris?" inquired Henri.

"Oui, I do know him, although not very well. We attended the same school in Paris. He is a little older than me. How do you know him?"

"We met in Austria and were in battle together. He mentioned his father was on the staff of Napoleon in Paris. I just thought you might know him."

"Oui, oui, and his father too. Often our two fathers work together. Is Jean-Claude all right?"

"He was the last time I saw him. He had been wounded and was returning to Paris, but he was all right and talking only of ladies he might meet."

"Ha, that's Jean-Claude. He has quite a reputation for the ladies."

Henri quietly thought to himself that *he was glad Ange was too young for Jean-Claude*, but then again, he trusted her completely.

A large brass bell on the back porch of the kitchen sounded the call to the evening meal. Francis said, "Come along and I will show you the mess area." They heard the sounds of running feet on the stairways and the eager shouts of the hungry.

"I don't know why they always run," said Francis. "There is always enough for everyone and then some. Rumors have it that the cooks trade favors with ladies at the village with leftover food. You can guess what those return favors may be."

They entered a long hall with men standing at attention behind chairs at designated places. As yet, their section did not have a designated place, so they stood behind chairs with others of the new arrivals. There was quiet except for muted whispers as the officers entered the hall.

"All be seated," an officer barked. The shuffles of chairs and people being seated were heard. They still sat at attention as no order for rest had been given. Finally, "Troops rest" was the command.

Each place setting had the usual plate, bowl, cup, white napkin, and utensils set in exact order. The assigned kitchen orderlies wheeled out carts with large covered dishes to the head of each table, and the dishes and bowls were passed down from man to man. The meal consisted of a nice thick potato-and-onion soup, roast chicken and potatoes, green beans, and sweet cake for dessert. They would eat a lot of chicken in the days, weeks, and months to come. It was plentiful and cheap and could be prepared in various ways. The usual red wine, tea, and coffee rounded out the liquids of the meal.

Each cadet had to police his own area, scrape the waste in a can, and place the dishes in a large wooden tub filled with water near the kitchen area. There was still an hour or so of daylight during these winter months, and it would give Henri a little more time to sort out his things before dark and bedtime. The general noticed him leaving the kitchen and motioned him over to the staff officer's table.

"Henri, I will be leaving early in the morning and will probably not see you again until Christmas. Bonne chance and study hard."

"Oui, monsieur, I will. I look forward to seeing you and the family at Christmas."

"And especially one, and I'll further think it may not be this old goat," laughed the general. "Remember to beware the sharp tongue, my boy." Henri blushed a deep red. "That is all, Henri, bonne chance."

Henri saluted, turned sharply, and left to join Francis waiting for him by the door.

"What was that all about?" asked Francis. "And why did you seem so embarrassed?"

"The general's daughter and I are very, very close, and everyone knows it. He loves to tease me about it and can get away with it as only a general and father can."

"Well, are you two lovers or what?"

"Oh no, Francis, not lovers, but just very close more as brother and sister." Henri knew he was lying, but no one needed to know any of his personal business. This explanation would suffice for now.

They went up to their room and met several others in the hall. They all chatted for a few minutes and confirmed they were all to be in this class of cadets. Henri did not even know how long the class would run before graduation and was surprised to hear it was for one full year for this special class composed of all having some previous military experience. Others accepted without prior exposure to the military would have to attend two years here.

An entire year! It seemed like a lifetime and prison sentence, but then he would not be in battle or in the elements. Still he would be away from home and Ange. He asked about periodic leaves and was told they would be away for an entire month during Christmas and the New Year. That was only a few weeks away, and he could live with that. The weather was getting colder as the sun was disappearing behind the tall trees. Those who had been here longer knew that the setting sun meant bedtime was close at hand. He was ready. It had been a very long and event-filled day, but still with the excitement, he was wide awake and knew he would have a problem falling asleep.

He asked Francis, "Could you tell me everything you know so far about this école and maybe what to expect?"

Francis told him, "You know, there is a sitting room or lounge with tables, chairs, and a fireplace that students can use for extra study or if we really don't want to go to bed immediately. I have gone there for the two nights I have been here and found out a lot about routines and what to expect. Let's go."

As they went to the study on the first floor, Henri said, "I am not used to all of this politeness and manners in the military. Things were much different where I've been."

Francis laughed and said, "I have been surprised too and have been told this école was to develop the best of the best for the future of France and the Grande Armée."

There were several others in the study and getting explanations of things to come from members of another class scheduled to graduate in the coming spring. They were told there was even a special class for manners and how to conduct oneself in matters of royal court and formal functions. Napoleon wanted nothing less than perfect, knowledgeable gentlemen graduated from this special école. He was given personnel reports on a periodic basis. There were courses in military history, French history, the revolution and its purpose, mathematics, language skills, writing and penmanship, and even astronomy as these future leaders must be able to navigate and lead their commands by the heavenly bodies. There would be a lot of emphasis on physical conditioning, weapons, and horsemanship, if one qualified.

Francis asked Henri, "Are you a skilled horseman? Those who qualify will be considered for the cavalry upon graduation."

Henri decided right then that he would certainly try for this. He had marched too far and too long on foot with that damn drum. At long last, maybe he could ride into battle with a sabre instead of marching, pounding away on a drum. If he was destined to die in battle, this should be the way.

They were enjoying the fire and camaraderie when a lieutenant came in and advised them that tomorrow would be a long day for the new fellows, and maybe it would be a good thought to turn in for the night. How polite! No yelling and telling one to stir his ass. Just the suggestion of a good thought. They took his advice and went to their room. Henri lay awake for a long time watching the crescent moon and clouds drift through the tall trees and wondered what his future and fate would now be with this tremendous advantage. He snuggled deeper in the now-warm bed with the feather blanket and pictured Ange's pretty face and smile. He couldn't wait for the Christmas leave.

The next morning very early, they were awakened by the sound of a bugle from the outside parade ground. Henri got up quickly and put on clothes over his long underwear. Even with the long underwear, it was cold in the rooms. Freshly polished boots and his hat and scarf completed his dress, and the two of them went for morning assembly.

The classes lined up according to seniority and were divided into *pelotons* (platoons). There were twelve plus the lieutenant in Henri's peloton. There was a very quick roll call, attention to colors, and the men were dismissed for the morning meal. After a warming meal of hot porridge, bread, and coffee, the group reported to their first class.

"Gentlemen," said Lieutenant Roussell, "this will be our first official day together. This is a special class composed of those already serving in the military and who have shown leadership and promise as potential officers. The course of this class will be for one year. Other classes here have men who have not had previous military training, and those will course for two years. So you are fortunate already and will save a year. The one thing I will stress most emphatically is that you are all here for one purpose in life. You are here to be officers in the best military organization in the world, and to do so will require a lot of hard work and perseverance. We will always conduct ourselves as gentlemen. The use of proper manners will be upheld at all times, and there will be no excuses for failure to do so. Our Imperial Leader is most emphatic on this; and as he has said, stupidity one can tolerate, slovenliness and rudeness one cannot. As officers, you are the leaders of the future of our great military might. Troops will look to you, leaders.

"Now I will give you a brief history of your present environment and what you will be expected to do. This noble école, École Speciale Militaire de Saint-Cyr, was founded by our emperor on May 1, 1802, and was first located in Fontainebleau near Paris. The present grounds are at the end of the old park of Louis XIV. You have probably already noticed how close we are to the Palace of Versailles. Saint-Cyr was a small village on the Versailles estate, and many of the estate workmen lived there.

"We are housed in the buildings of the Maison Royale de Saint-Louis, a school founded in 1685 by Louis XIV and Madame de Maintenon for the impoverished daughters of noblemen who had died for France. It was a convent of sorts at the time. Madame de Maintenon's vault is in the chapel. Make certain to visit her when we attend Mass. We moved to this location in 1808. I was here for the damn move, and hope I never have to go through anything like that again.

"Our motto was given by Napoleon, and you will be required to memorize it. Write this on your pads, and remember it well. 'Ils s'instruisent pour vaincre'

(They study to vanquish). This école is a brotherhood, and here and forever we will be as one. Always strive to assist your brother in all things. He may, one day, save your life. But enough of the history lesson and camaraderie, we need to draw your sabres and formulate a schedule.

"You will each be required to work at the tasks in the stables and kitchens at times. This is part of your military heritage to do menial labor lest you ever forget the poor bastards in the front ranks getting chewed up by grapeshot. Some of you know exactly what I mean. How many here have seen combat?"

Henri and three others stood up.

"Very good, gentlemen, I will see you later. I was with Napoleon in Egypt and in the Austrian and Spanish campaigns. Combat separates the men from the children. As officers, there can be no children. How many of you are very, and I stress 'very,' proficient with horses and riding?"

The entire class stood up, and the lieutenant said, "This we shall have to see. Gentlemen, remember this is not a training ground for horsemanship, and we cannot all be experts. When the weather clears, we will see who the expert is and who is not.

"I know all of you can probably ride a horse, but I mean expert. Think on this, gentlemen, before you make a fool of yourself. During the course of the next week, I will meet with each of you individually and in private for us to become acquainted and to discuss any potential differences about your lives in the military. Then you will be afforded the same pleasure with the commandant of the école as time progresses."

Lieutenant Roussell dictated the class schedule and important future events almost as fast as they could write. Everything was precisely almost to the minute, and the days to come would be very full. They were in luck due to the fact that the Christmas and New Year holiday period would be from Décembre 15 until Janvier 15. This was mi-Octobre, and the holiday was only some two months away.

"We will go now to draw your sabres from the armory. We will go over the sabre and the importance later this afternoon. Come, gentlemen, follow me."

They went into one of the adjacent buildings and into a large room with muskets lined in racks along the entire inner wall. There were small rooms with locked doors and what appeared to be workbenches along the wall with windows for light. Several men were working on weapons and other things at the benches. Lieutenant Roussell told them to line up facing a desk with an old sergeant sorting through papers and putting on an air of importance.

"Ha, fresh new meat for the cannons," said the sergeant.

"Careful, Sergeant," said Lieutenant Roussell, "one of these may be your future commander."

"In the old days, Lieutenant, we ate new officers for meals. Now I will issue each of you a new sabre, scabbard, and belt. There are benches over there for you to clean the new blades, and I want you to feel free to come here at any time for fresh cleaning cloths or if you have any questions. These units are new and are now your responsibility. The lieutenant will give a formal class on the care of your sabres. First man, please step up to the table in the corner."

There were several large cases on the table filled with new sabres. Each man was given his sabre and then had to stand before the sergeant and sign a release form. "This form will become a part of your permanent records," he said, "and woe be unto the poor bastard who loses his sabre without first losing his own ass."

They each cleaned the new sabres, placed them in the scabbards, and belted them on.

"Gentlemen," said Lieutenant Roussell, "you will wear the sabres at all times for the next week. And of course, this does not include washing, toilet, and bed; but this will accustom you to the presence of your new best friend. It is time for the noon meal, and just after that, we will have class on the history and care of your sabre."

After a filling noon meal and true to his word, the lieutenant called them to order and began his lecture on the sabre.

"Be seated, Cadets, and place your scabbard sabres across your legs, the hilt, or handle for those who do not know the difference, toward your right hand. I assume all of you know the difference. What you have before you, as I stated before, is now your best friend. If you take care of it and learn proper use and care, it will most certainly take care of you in time of need. Mine has never failed me."

Lieutenant Roussell was giving the first lecture of their officer training, and all were listening with rapt attention. "This sabre is named the Light Cavalry Trooper's Sabre and was first issued in 1803 to the *enfants chéries* (cherished children), Napoleon's famous Imperial Guard, Chasseur à Cheval de la Garde. The guard is famous, as some of you may know, in that they are always with our emperor wherever he goes and in every battle. They are considered the very best of all the swords in our weaponry. The sabre proved so good and worthy that it has become adapted for general use. You will note the D-shaped hilt of brass. Please withdraw the blade and take care not to inflict any wounds to yourself or your neighbor. In the days that follow, you will need all of the blood you can muster.

"This blade before you is 85.09 cm. precisely, made of the best grades of steel available. The design has proven to have excellent balance whether on horseback or used by foot troops. I will give you a brief history of your new friend in order for you to more readily identify him in the event you become separated. Notice inscribed on the back of the blade 'Mfture Impale du Klingenthal Coulaux frères.' This signifies your sabre was made at the Manufacture de Klingenthal in the east of France near Strasbourg. This factory is owned by the government and operated by the entrepreneurs, the Coulaux brothers. There is the inspector's stamp on each of your blades. This particular shipment has the 'JC' of Director Julien Coulaux and the little circle star seal of Contrôleur 1re Classes Jean-Jacques Mouton.

"I notice some of you are not taking notes on my talk. Be advised, gentlemen, you will be required to know everything in the manner of information given to you in these classes. I know all of these details not because I am just overly intelligent but because I have noted this information from the factory records that arrived with this particular shipment. Now, note your scabbard. It is lined with wood to prevent a metal-to-metal contact that would dull the blade edge. At your own discretion, at a later date, you may name your friend and have such inscribed on the blade. Many do so. However, nothing may be inscribed until your completion and graduation of this école. There will be a short break now. We will meet in the gymnasium for physical training. As your schedule indicates, there will be an exercise drill every day. Go and return here in one half hour in athletic uniforms. Be prompt, Cadets."

Henri and Francis went to their room to change into the athletic shoes, shorts, and sweater of the uniform. As they were changing, Francis noticed the scar on Henri's leg.

"How did that happen?" he asked. "It looks fresh."

"I was on the wrong end of an Austrian bayonet and very fortunate indeed. The *les carabins* (sawbones) said a bit more to the one side and my balls would have been hanging on the bayonet. I would have preferred death to that."

"Oui, and me too," said Francis. "A man without balls is not a man. Not even a one-ball man would be good for much. I am glad you made it, mon ami. It must have hurt like the fires of hell."

"Oh, it did. Thanks to some special 'tea,' the pain went away. I will have to give you the whole story when we get time. I guess it is quite a story. What happened is part of the reason I am here."

The class met in the gymnasium, and Lieutenant Roussell said, "Now, men, let us see what sort of physical shape you are in and what we need to do for improvement."

A rapid set of exercises and drills left most with red faces and breathing very hard. Henri was one of those in good condition, and he was so glad he had exercised extensively during his rehabilitation. He must remind Jean about this knowing as Jean was lax and would soon gain his large waist back if not driven. Jean wanted this very badly, and that may be the lever to pry him into condition. Lieutenant Roussell separated the class into two sections, one being composed of those who could hold their own and those who would require additional work. He told those requiring additional work that this was not a request but a mandate. If one could not pass the physical requirements, he would be returned to duty at his previous station and rank. He knew of two such cases whereby those failing had just disappeared rather than return to duty in shame.

One had been a high-ranking officer's son, and he had simply disappeared. Whether by suicide or possible venture to a foreign land, no one knew, and they were never heard from again. Others had reckoned they had gone to America and vanished in the wilderness. *What a horrible prospect*, thought Henri. He had heard of the wilderness of America with wild savages and strange beasts. He wanted no part of that place.

Two of the fellows needing special instructions were Julien and Leon. Both were roommates just next to Henri and Francis. Although Francis did not get put in the special group, he said it was close, and he would have to work harder. Henri did fine but would also have to be diligent with his exercise.

Julien was overweight; and the thought of failing was, as he said, maddening and would not be an option. He would do whatever it took to come through this. He had been given his appointment on the recommendation of his uncle, a man of wealth and influence in Paris.

It seemed to Henri that most of the members of his class did come from Paris or nearby. One could see the political influence at work. There were a few here on their own merit, and these would be the backbone of the future officer corps the lieutenant had mentioned. Leon was in fair shape, and the two made a pact to help each other even at night after the lights were out if necessary.

The days were very full, and the first week very regimented with the schedule, meeting their instructors, and mostly getting organized and acclimated into the école and routine. All of the instructors were officers and experts in their specialty. Henri thought one of the most interesting instructors was Lieutenant Marceaux who taught astronomy and history.

He had been an instructor at the Sorbonne in Paris and been given his commission to move here and instruct. The same held true for several other instructors at the école. Napoleon had obtained only the best for his special interest academy and future officer corps.

The next day was reserved for the tailor and fitting of uniforms. The supply sergeant had been correct when he said there would be no slovenliness here. The uniforms were measured to fit in exactness. The heavyset cadets were advised they would lose weight and become fitter. Then they would be measured and fit again.

The uniforms were red trousers with blue stripe, dark blue jacket with high collar, red epaulets, shiny brass buttons, and a wide black leather belt with brass buckle. The crest of the école was on the buckle as well as on all the jacket buttons. The hat was a typical peaked military style with shiny black bill and white feather over the front. It was a very smart uniform and one commanding attention and pride.

Several of the others had mustaches, and Henri thought he might grow one too. It would make him look older and take away some of the little-boy-drummer look. He would have to think about this as some of the others in the drummer unit had tried to grow a mustache and had been teased about peach fuzz and putting cream on it and having the cats lick it off. Still, in such a uniform and with his new sabre, a mustache would set things more mature. There were two uniforms alike and another with a white dress dinner jacket. It was mandatory that white gloves be worn at all official functions including all earned medals. Henri wondered how this display might be accepted and hoped it would not be taken in a manner of flaunting. He was certainly very proud of his medals but was still shy about showing them off.

The following day, Lieutenant Roussell announced the members of his class would be given a personal interview over the next several days and for them to be thinking of any questions or personal matters they wanted to discuss. Henri was the first to be called. He knocked on the lieutenant's door and was given entry. He stood at attention before the desk and was told to be at ease and invited to sit down.

"Cadet, this is a very informal meeting and will serve to better acquaint both of us. We will be together for a year and can dispense with certain formality when in private. You have been on active combat duty and know the routine of military life, but here things are quite different. We want the cadets here to be the leaders of tomorrow, and we strive to instill a pride and confidence not found in the ordinary rank and file. I have your military file before me, and I was quite surprised to read of what you have accomplished in such a short time in your military career. I have the full account of your actions in the Austrian campaign and your citation by our emperor. I am most impressed at all of this considering your youth. Correct me if I am wrong, but I have your age as fifteen years."

"Oui, monsieur, that is correct."

"This is most unusual, but I must say I am impressed with your early maturity and the manner in which you conduct yourself."

"Merci, monsieur. I have been an orphan since an early age and have had to fend for myself a bit."

"Oui, Cadet, I see all of that too and also that your father was also a hero at another time in an Austrian campaign. That makes this all the more remarkable."

"Monsieur, if I could ask a favor please."

"Of course, Cadet, and what might that be?"

"Monsieur, if you could, please not mention this to the others or make example of it. I have had to answer thousands of questions about it, and others look at me with a strange look when they find out."

Lieutenant Roussell laughed lightly and said, "I will keep this in confidence, but it is bound to come out sooner or later, Cadet. We have all heard of the hero of the Austrian campaign and of the tale of the Bébé Tigre, but I never dreamed I would get to meet him face-to-face and especially as a member of my class. As time progresses in our class, we will require certain ones to become the leaders. With what you have already shown and accomplished, and disregarding your youth, you will be considered if you wish."

"Oui, monsieur, I would wish to be considered if I qualify."

"Very well, Cadet. We will have further talks as time progresses. Your next interview is with the commandant. I believe he is waiting for you in his office. Please do not keep him waiting, and return your military file to him. You may read it if you wish. It is yours."

"Oui, monsieur, and merci."

Henri left the lieutenant's office and very quickly glanced through his records. There was nothing in there that he did not know, but he was surprised to see the commendation by Napoleon complete with his personal seal. It was identical to the one given to him during the ceremony. Henri knocked on the commandant's door and was told to enter, be at ease, and sit down in a leather chair in front of his desk.

"So, Cadet, I have been wanting to speak with you since my old friend left. We talked considerably of you, and both agree you have the makings of an officer. Even with your youth, you have the potential of a first-line officer. Andre wants you posted back to his command upon your graduation, and I am certain that is what will occur. I saw in your records your commendation by the emperor, and I am most impressed. Andre told me all about it, and of course, we have all heard previously about the young drummer who so bravely stood in the face of the charging Austrians. Congratulations, my boy, and it is a pleasure to meet you and have you in our école. We will not go on about this, for whatever happens in the future will be on your own merit and not past events."

"Monsieur, merci. I have had millions of questions about this from the beginning. It is almost embarrassing at times."

"Oh, I can understand that, and I can also understand those wanting to meet you and know of what happened by your own words. As I stated, Andre told me about it, and I will not question you further. He said you were shy about telling about it."

In the succeeding weeks, the weather turned milder, and the class was challenged to their expertise at horse riding. Of course, all could ride, but Lieutenant Roussell had stated that only those of expert capability could qualify for the cavalry units. Everyone wanted the cavalry because of the mode of transportation. Riding was far better than walking and eating the dust of those riding. There were several visiting cavalry officers attending to judge and make recommendations. When Henri's turn came, he indeed proved his expertise with a horse. He could ride with only his knees to guide the animal and even stood in the saddle while at full stride This was really nothing new to him, but it certainly impressed those judging the events. He was easily one of the better horsemen in the entire école. The cavalry officers returned to the commandant's office to record their findings in the individual personnel files, and when they were told that Henri was the legend Bébé Tigre, they were amazed.

"But he is so young and has such skill," the leader exclaimed. "He will make a fine officer in any unit of his choosing."

The commandant stated, "He is to be returned to the unit of his sponsor, General de Chabot." He thanked the officers for their time. The commandant wrote a letter that night to Andre telling him of Henri's latest achievement. Andre would be pleased.

That night in the room, Francis asked, "Where on this God's earth did you learn to ride like that? I thought I could ride with skill, but you were easily the best of the lot today. You will be assured of a cavalry posting when we graduate."

"Oh, I hope so, Francis. I carried that damn drum forever. A sabre and horse will be much better."

The weeks that followed were very full, and the time flew by until at last the holiday season was upon them. The next day would be Décembre 15, and the carriages would be rolling to Paris. Most here at the école were from Paris, and the transport home would be well organized in one direction. Those going in other directions were mostly in two other carriages.

They arose early the next morning, and after a final inspection by Lieutenant Roussell, they were set for the journey home. He advised them not to get slovenly and lax into civilian merde but to have a nice holiday season and come back in Janvier ready to study and work harder than ever. The next leave would be over the Easter season and would only last two weeks, not an entire month.

Francis and Henri rode in the same carriage with eight others. They were crowded, but it was warmer and well worth any sacrifice. They would be home within hours. All Henri could think about was home and Ange. He hoped she would be the same, but it seemed every time he left and returned, she had changed a bit more. All for the better though. She had matured so much in the short years since their meeting, and he felt as though he was the most fortunate man alive that she loved him.

The carriage stopped in the street in front of the de Chabot house. There were several more stops to make, and all were anxious to get home. Henri entered the iron gates and started up the circular drive when an anxious cry erupted from the house. The front door flew open, and Ange vaulted down the steps into Henri's arms. A quick kiss, and she grabbed him by the arm and walked as close as she could get to him back up the steps.

"Come, love, let us get inside," she said. "The weather is cold, and Mimi said she feels snow in her old bones."

Henri laughed and said, "Ah, Mimi, always the prophet of things to come. It is so good to be home and you here with me. The école is nice, but not as nice as home and you. Ange, I have only been gone for two months, and I think you have grown more. You are a beautiful lady. Where has my little girl gone?"

Ange said, "I think the girl you knew may be gone forever and will trade places with a lady, wife, and, hopefully, a mother." She blushed as she said this.

"Possibly so, but I shall never forget the girl who captured me and has my heart."

Madame, Jean, and Mimi came rushing out to greet him. As usual, everyone was talking at once. Madame greeted Henri with a hug. "Henri, you are so striking in your new uniform, and you now carry a sabre. All please do come inside. The wind and mist from the river has a biting cold chill."

They went into the sitting room with the nice warming fire. Mimi brought in a serving pot of hot tea of her special blend. Madame said she had heard that Empress Josephine had given the recipe to her cooks at the palace, and they were now using it. It was quite an honor for Mimi. Henri sank back on the large sofa and, with Ange beside him, the radiating fireplace, the tea warming him all the way down to his toes, seemed at complete peace with the entire world.

After much talk and news of the école, news of the general, and the latest from home, Henri finally went up to his room to put away his kit bag and take off his sabre. He lay across the bed and had a few moments of quiet ponder. The general was due in later that afternoon, and the reunion would be complete. This was his family now. It was complete with the love, understanding, and respect that families cherish. Since Jean had grown into maturity and stopped his childish trouble, the circle was complete. Henri still had certain doubts that he could be trusted. He would wait and watch.

Henri felt he had the father, mother, brother, and "sister" he had always yearned for. And there was the always-faithful Mimi whom he truly loved with all of his heart. These were his people to love and protect. He had pledged a long time ago to do just that and hopefully change the sister, God willing, into a wife. Ange was the only one who knew his feelings toward the others, but as she had said, they knew, and actions are more than shouted words. Ange seemed to have an inner sense with him, and it was like the two could communicate without speaking. A slight motion, nod, or look in the eye was often all that was required. He had never been that close to anyone. It still seemed a mystery how this had happened. He often thought about these things. God had truly smiled upon him these past several years, and he hoped God would continue to do so. He had much to live for.

12

Josephine

General Andre de Chabot arrived home in the late evening just at dusk. The usual uproar developed with the general in his usual jovial mood at the expense of several drinks with his staff. He was laughing and joking, and Madame was beside herself at many of his "jokes."

"Andre, please attempt to control yourself. The children are hearing much of this."

"Well, mon femme fatale (hot woman), it is time they knew of life. I am serious all of the time during duty, but at my home, I can be myself and joke with my best friend in this entire world." He groped for her again as she tried to fend him off and push him back.

"You sex fiend, can't you wait for a private time and have more discretion?"

"All right, all right, I will try, but you know you drive me mad with your charms."

Henri and Ange were in the hall near the kitchen door, listening to this exchange and trying to stifle giggles.

"Poppa is so funny at times."

"Oui, I agree and so full of life."

France was at relative peace these days, and the Grande Armée was standing down for the holiday season. There were still the many rumors of political discontent, but it all seemed so distant. Many troops were granted leave for the season but were subject to immediate recall if any situation may warrant.

The evening meal was a jovial affair with Henri telling tales of the officer école and the general interceding with tales of his own days at the academies with Napoleon. The fact that he was a personal and close ally of the emperor had certainly seemed to further his career. But during one's rise, care should always be taken. All were subject to close scrutiny from every quarter. Friendships could end at the bat of an eye. The closer one was, the more he was subject to watch. These days were full of political intrigue and animosity. The emperor surrounded himself with only the most proven loyal. To be in that inner circle left no doubt as to loyalty. They were all in the sitting room after the evening meal enjoying a final glass of wine before retiring when there was a loud knock on the door.

"Merde, now what in the hell?" said the general as he hurried to the door in his stockinged feet.

There were two officers of the Imperial Guard at the door and another twelve or so in a mounted detachment with a carriage on the front circular drive.

"Mon général, a message for your eyes only from the emperor," said the captain as he handed the general an envelope. The readily recognizable personal seal of Napoleon was embossed in a mass of bright red wax. "Mon général, we have orders to wait and escort you and a Cadet Devreney, if he is available, back to the palace with us. We are to leave at once."

"Of course, Captain, we will be with you immediately. Henri, stir your ass. This must be a matter of most urgency. Captain, do you know anything of this?"

"No, mon général, only that it is very urgent, and the emperor appeared very upset."

As the general and Henri were putting on their cloaks, Madame said in a fearful tone, "Andre, what do you think this might be for you to be summoned so late at night? Please get word to me as soon as you can that you are all right."

"Of course, mon amour. Try not to worry. This personal note only states that he is in need of an old friend this night." The general and Henri hurriedly mounted the carriage. This special group rumbled at all haste through the night toward the palace.

"Monsieur, what do you think this might mean?" asked Henri.

"I cannot even speculate, lad, but whatever this is, it is certainly no minor thing. But dammit anyway, just in time to spoil serious loving. That is the only thing a night as this is good for. Don't you ever tell."

"Oui, monsieur."

"You know, I've been thinking about Napoleon including you in this. I am really not that surprised as his personal secretary has a memory of forty men. He keeps extensive journals and notes on everything. I'll bet the idea was his. I will ask the Old Fox when I see him."

As they arrived at the palace, it was ablaze with lights in almost every room. Guards were posted everywhere.

"Something is very, very wrong this evil night," said the general as they got out of the carriage and hurried up the main front steps.

They were escorted down long brightly lit hallways and were admitted into the emperor's private quarters. Napoleon was sitting near the fire and rose as they entered the chamber.

"Merci for coming at such short notice, Andre. Events of this night and past weeks have me greatly in need of an old and loyal friend. Merci for coming too, my boy. I had hoped you might be home for the season. Possibly this may be a lesson in life and learned well from Andre who is an old master at true friendship and loyalty."

"Napoleon, please tell me what this is about and how may I be of service to you. You know you can ask anything of me."

"Oui, I know my friend. The blunt truth is that I am divorcing Josephine, and the marriage is to be annulled immediately. I am heartbroken, and so is she, but this must be done for the succession of the empire. She cannot bear children, and a blood successor to the throne is of utmost importance. I have secretly arranged to wed the daughter of the emperor of Austria. This union will not only assure a creditable peace with Austria, our old adversary, but will give me children. Marie Louise is only eighteen years, but she is ripe for children. One might describe her as a 'walking womb.' I have secretly spoken to all parties involved before this night with Josephine, and all are in agreement. I informed Josephine tonight in a very solemn dinner. And she wishes to leave the palace immediately tonight for her private residence, Malmaison. We have always been known to each other as trusted friends and confidants since our very early days at military école, and you know Josephine well. I want to charge you with the escort of my only love to her new permanent residence."

"Napoleon, I am in total shock. I can fully understand the need of a successor, but can't there be another way? Josephine is a complete complement to you and our beloved France. I remember well when we all first met during the revolutionary years. She was Rose Tascher then, imprisoned and going to the guillotine. She was saved among many others in the prison that day. I remember the fierce battle in the street at the Tuileries. Since then she has eyes for no other than you. I also remember you telling me when we just returned from the Austrian campaign. You said that you win battles and wars, but Josephine wins the hearts."

"Oui, oui, Andre, I know all of that and remember it all very well, but please do not try to argue in her defense. Please believe me when I tell you that this decision was not made in haste. This must be done to preserve what so many have sacrificed to give us."

"Excellency, you know you have my complete loyalty. I will attend to your request at once. Will you be all right here alone, or do you wish me to stay for a time?"

"No, Andre, and merci for asking. I will be all right. I just need to be alone and with my thoughts. Please go to Josephine and see what she may require for immediate travel."

Henri had been standing to the rear of the general and certainly didn't want to be noticed more than absolutely necessary. These were very moving personal matters and yet affairs of a highly political nature. As they turned to leave, the general very gently tugged on Henri's sleeve and motioned for him to follow.

They were escorted to Josephine's personal apartments where her ladies were visibly crying while busily packing her things for the move to Malmaison. Josephine was sitting in a chair near the fireplace and evidently had been weeping too. As they came close, she rose to meet them. Even with her swollen red eyes and makeup in a runny mess, she was beautiful.

"Oh, Andre, it is so good to see a friendly face this dreadful night." She hugged him in a long embrace. "And I see you have brought our hero with you. I think I remember your name as Henri, but correct me if I am wrong."

"Oui, Your Highness, Henri is my name."

The general said, "My dear Josephine, Napoleon summoned me tonight and has told me what this is all about. Is our Corsican losing his mind to even think such a thing?"

"Andre! I am surprised to hear you, of all people, say such things."

"Josephine, I humbly apologize, but we have been known to each other a very long time, and you know I admire you. I have to say what is in my heart. This is a dreadful night for all of us and for France."

"Merci as always, my dear friend, but why did you come to my chambers so late at night. Has Napoleon sent you here?"

"Oui, my friend, he has asked me to personally escort you to Malmaison and to be at your service. How can I help you? Ask anything."

"This journey will be difficult in any manner it occurs, Andre. Napoleon was very wise in having a trusted friend of us both act as personal escort. As soon as my ladies have finished packing, we will leave. I am only taking my personal things this trip and will send for the larger articles later. Malmaison has much already. Will Henri be going with us as well? He is most welcome."

"Merci, my lady, this is his first taste of such political intrigue. One of us will need to return home and let the family know we have been called to duty and should return as soon as possible. We will not speak of this until official word is released, and we must be cautious. As is often said, there are no secrets in Paris, and word travels like the wind. In a very personal meaning, Rose, again, please let me know what I can do. I am heartbroken too."

"I will be all right after this initial shock, Andre, and words cannot express my appreciation of your kindness and friendship. I shall never forget you, and I am sure Napoleon will not either. We will be ready to travel in another hour, and that will give you time to tell your family and relieve any worry."

The general and Henri took their leave and hurried to the waiting carriage. The general was still noticeably upset and said, "That crazy Corsican. Is he mad letting that woman who means so much to us all slip away like this? If he is so enthralled with the Austrian woman, let them be in private. He can arrange such things and has done so many times. I have met this young blonde vixen, and she is a delight to the eyes, but she will never be the empress we take away tonight. He is my emperor and the one to whom I owe my allegiance, but I will certainly fear for his sanity from this day forward. Merde, damn and bedamn it all to hell! What a night."

They arrived at home to find Madame was waiting up for any word. The general told her his secret, what was transpiring, and they would be home as soon as their duty was over.

"Do not worry, mon amour, the problem of this night is the damage to France. Napoleon is certain to be repentant of this night. This is a hell of a way to start our holiday season, and certainly not the way I had planned. I will see that Josephine is safely settled and return as soon as I can."

"Andre, she is my friend too. Please offer her my kindest and warmest regards. Please tell her that if she needs anything at any hour, please do not hesitate to ask."

"I will, mon amour. Come, Henri, let's travel."

Ange held his hand on the way to the carriage and told him to please hurry and return. "I will, Ange. I will be glad when this night is over."

At the palace, lights were still ablaze everywhere. A line of carriages and carts were at the side entrance, and servants were loading large trunks and cases. The general asked Henri to go with him while he conferred with the commander of Josephine's personal guard detachment. No one expected foul play, but during times as these, one cannot be overly cautious. The commander said that everything was nearly ready. They would depart within the next half hour at the latest. Josephine had given explicit instructions she wanted to depart as soon as possible. There was nothing they could do further except wait. Henri and the general returned to their carriage to get out of the cold mist now enveloping the area.

"Merde, a perfect setting for such a night," said the general. "Lad, I have known this great lady for many years; and this is a sad event for Napoleon, France, and us all. I can understand a slight portion of Napoleon's reasoning, but this drastic measure is beyond my comprehension. The fact that they love each other is not in question. He is driven by the urgency of having a blood heir to the empire. I am glad I am not wearing his boots. I could never have done this thing and cannot sanction this. I know I am chattering away like Mimi now, and I will ask that you never repeat my words. There is a great measure of trust between you and me. I know you will hold your tongue."

"Of course, monsieur. You are like my own father."

Henri's head was spinning with the speed of events. As they watched, the empress's ladies started to file out of the palace and enter the waiting carriages.

The general said, "Napoleon has told me on several occasions, 'The wife is made for the husband, the husband for his country, his family, and the glory.' And at what cost is this country and glory if he has no family? My life is my family as well as most men I know. Oh, we all have moments of falling from the wagon from time to time. We are Frenchmen, are we not? But when true fidelity is known, we are complete with our wives. Thank God, they have the wisdom to turn a blind and almost understanding eye from time to time. Henri, I know I am babbling on and on, but please bear with me tonight. I am terribly upset being a close party to all involved. I cannot refuse the request of my emperor and two very dear and old friends. True, as we have climbed the stairs of success together, we have not had adequate time to devote to each other as we once did. However, that is life as you will one day see, my young friend. You must know that I am deeply humbled and honored he did choose to call me tonight. You should be honored also that he mentioned you in his time of need."

The general stood out of the carriage and motioned to Josephine. The empress and one of her ladies entered the carriage without a word. Josephine sat next to Andre, and the lady sat next to Henri. They rode in an awkward silence for a few minutes with only the noise of many horses moving on the darkened streets.

Finally Josephine said to the general, "Andre, my old and dear friend, I think this may be our last meeting. I will probably live a secluded life out of public view. Napoleon has promised my complete safety, and I should want for nothing. I have my own personal fortune, but I will be given an allowance from the state. However, in these evil times and the dangers of politics, who can be certain of anything?"

"Rose, I will call you by that name as was introduced many years ago, or which do you prefer?"

"Either as you prefer, Andre. I am known as Josephine now. Rose is a distant memory."

"Not to me, *chéri*, but I will call you Josephine as you wish and not cause any confusion."

The lady next to Henri spoke to Henri, saying, "I am Helene, the first lady in waiting to the empress."

"Helene," said Josephine, "we must remember from this night forward, I am just Josephine and the empress no longer."

"Oui, my lady, I will try to remember, but this old habit will be most difficult to undo."

Henri introduced himself, saying, "Helene was my mother's name. It seems so long ago, but she has a permanent place in the memories of my heart." Helene asked if he was the general's aide.

The general replied for Henri, "No, he is my adopted son. He is attending officer école at the present after proving leadership."

"Oh oui," said Josephine. "I remember something about Bébé Tigre. I had almost forgotten."

"Oh, and I had forgotten," said Helene. "You rode through Paris with us sometime back. We picked you up at the hospital. I remember now. They did call you something about a *tigre*. We never did hear the full story."

Embarrassed, Henri whispered to her that it would take a long time to explain, and he would later. They all fell back into silence as the procession made its way through the dark and misty streets and then slogged on to the muddy main road. Only an occasional barking dog at obscure villages marked their passage.

On their arrival at a partially darkened Malmaison, lights on the upper floors and outbuildings were just now beginning to pierce the gloom. A rider had been sent ahead to awaken the servants and prepare them for Josephine's arrival. As the main group of troops arrived, the grounds, outbuildings, and main mansion were searched and the servants given specific instructions to assure safety. These troops would remain until the permanent contingent of the personal guard would arrive the next afternoon. Josephine, the general, Henri, and Helene went inside to the main sitting room where a large welcoming fire was roaring in the fireplace. They sat, and Helene excused herself to assist with the placing of the many trunks and crates.

"Helene, please tell the workers to place those things anywhere. It has been a long and trying night, and I know everyone must be very tired. I know I am and should sleep like an infant."

"If you will, then I will too when I return home," said the general. "Are you certain you will be all right? I can't imagine how you must feel."

Servants brought silver trays with refreshments of hot tea, coffee, and sweet cakes. Henri hurriedly gulped down a cup of hot coffee and could feel the warmth spreading in his body. Dawn was just starting to glow through the morning mist, and Henri could see a dim light appearing over the trees. He could almost make out the sprawling and ornate gardens so famous here.

As the general and Henri were preparing to leave, Josephine took the general to one side. "Andre, please do not have any ill thoughts about any of this. This is my ordeal to bear and mine alone. Always remember our friendship and think kindly of Napoleon. His first thoughts were and will always be for the empire and France."

"I understand, Josephine, but certain things I will never be able to understand. I do not have any harsh thoughts for anyone and especially not Napoleon." He gave her one of his famous bear hugs. "I wish you well, chéri. And please, should you ever need anything, please contact me. Your wish will always be my command."

She reached up and held his face in her hands, saying, "Go with God, my special friend." She hugged Henri and whispered to him, "Take care of this old bear, Madame de Chabot, and Ange. These are very special friends. And when you do find the courage to marry that girl, I will be honored to attend the wedding."

They mounted the carriage for the return trip home. Henri looked back at Josephine and etched in his memory how small, frail, and so alone she looked and yet the very epitome of bravery and courage. They rode in silence much of the way. Henri tried to doze a bit, but the recent events made sleep impossible. Each time he was jostled and startled awake, he saw the general chewing on a cigar deep in thought and staring out of the window at some far and distant world.

13

Christmas 1809, New Year 1810

Henri slept until late in the morning and was awakened by Ange. She brought him a tray with a small pot of Mimi's special tea and some sweet cakes. She, carrying the tray, could not turn the knob to open the door; so she kicked it several times calling Henri's name. He drowsily opened the door.

"I was worried," she said. "I thought you were going to sleep all day and ignore me or maybe you had died."

"Chéri, if I did die, I have been met by an angel. It was a long night, Ange. Did you bring this tray all the way up here? Chéri, this is the third floor." She set the tray on the small table and poured tea for both of them.

"I know this is the third floor, but I wanted to see you." Ange took a sip from her cup. "Mmmm! Mimi makes this tea so well. I am trying hard to duplicate her recipe. I almost have it, but something is missing. Mimi says she spits in it, but that is disgusting, and I am sure she wouldn't do that. I am going to write all of it down. Then maybe I can tell what is missing."

Henri laughed and said, "But, Ange, Mimi spits in everything. She says it adds that special taste that can never be duplicated. Most gourmet cooks do that, you know."

"Henri! You are just as disgusting as she is." She quickly kissed him and said, "It is so good that you are home. Please tell me all of what happened last night. Poppa is still very upset about it. He has evidently been awake for hours and just sits and stares out of the windows to the back gardens. He smokes those awful cigars by the handful. Mimi said he has probably had a bathing tub of coffee. I hope you never start with cigars. They stink so much and make everything around stink too."

"Don't worry, Ange. I will not smoke cigars. I tried it one time, and it made me sick and dizzy. I don't know how your father and others do it. But I may try a pipe someday. That does not seem as bad. Some of the pipe stuff smells nice."

"Well, it all smells awful to me. I could never even try it."

They drank their tea and ate the sweet cakes while Henri told Ange about Napoleon and Josephine and last night's events.

"I guess I will never understand," said Henri. "She is such a fine and gracious lady. He said he is going to marry a very young girl who is sure to give him a baby." Henri didn't tell Ange about the description of Napoleon's potential bride as a "walking womb." She would have surely been offended.

The days passed rapidly until the Christmas festivities were upon them again. After the long Christmas Mass at Notre Dame and the ritual of Mimi's wonderful dinner, they all went into the main sitting room for exchange of presents. Father Etty had been made pastor of another smaller church in Paris and would spend part of the time with his new clergy. He said he would be by later and for Andre not to eat it all. The children were too old now for Father Noel, but the tradition was still very much alive. Andre did tease Madame about the possibility of the old gentleman forgetting to stop by this house. He only stopped by the houses with those that believed in him. She assured him she always had believed and always would.

Andre gave Madame a stunning ruby-and-diamond necklace with matching ring and earrings. It was a dazzling ensemble; and Ange asked, as a joke of course, if she could wear it from time to time. Madame gave Andre a box of his favorite cigars and asked if he could possibly smoke them out of the house. Jean received a book on the latest military history involving the time of Napoleon's wars and the revolution. Henri told him to please study it well as they have to learn the same material at the military école. Henri received a warm handmade gray pullover sweater and said it would keep him warm in the field where the Armée was sure to go.

Ange received a gorgeous crimson dress and matching open-front sweater. Henri whispered softly to her that the crimson matched her fiery passion. She blushed a deep red. Andre and Jean laughed.

"Whatever you did tell her, lad, it must have been good to make her blush like that." She blushed again and left the room, saying she was going to try on her dress and sweater.

Madame said, "A thousand shames upon you 'gentlemen' for embarrassing that child like that."

The "gentlemen" laughed, and the general clapped Henri and Jean on the back. "It is time for the older people to retire and leave the fire to the young of the house."

At that time, Ange returned to the room in her new dress and sweater. The crimson dress and sweater with her dark hair falling over her shoulders and sparkling dark dancing eyes made her an object of beauty. Her full, almost-pouting lips curved in a near smile. Just the right hint of rouge on her lips and cheeks accented her dress and sweater. Henri felt his heart pound faster at the sight of her standing there like a goddess in red.

Madame said, "Oh, Ange, the dress is beautiful. Until this moment, I didn't realize what a mature lady you have become. Here, try my ruby necklace and earrings, if Andre doesn't mind. They should go perfectly with the dress."

She went to the mirror over the buffet and slipped them on. When she turned around, it was as if she had aged several years. She was indeed a young lady. A child no longer. Henri could not keep his eyes off her. He thought about a private time later with this gorgeous creature. He almost blushed at the thought.

"Ange, they are perfect," Madame exclaimed. "The rubies enhance everything. Just do not get too attached to my gift."

The general gave Ange a huge bear hug and said, "It will be a very fortunate young man to win your hand and heart, *chaton* (kitten). We will have to watch you much more carefully in the future." He looked directly at Henri, chuckling while saying this. Now it really was Henri's turn to turn scarlet.

The general laughed again and said, "Come, mon chéri, I hope I can make it up the stairs. Mimi's good food has made me feel more like that stuffed Christmas goose she prepared."

Jean said he wanted to retire too and hurried up the stairs after his parents.

Ange was sitting on the sofa and Henri in the chair across from her. The sight of her in the new dress and sweater with the firelight reflecting on her hair and making her eyes sparkle and gleam was a sight Henri would never forget. This lady had completely captivated him, and he had feelings for her that he could not describe. He moved over to the sofa and sat beside her, reaching into his jacket pocket and drawing out a small box wrapped in tissue paper.

"This is a special gift for you, Ange. It isn't really much, but it is all I could seem to find that fit the occasion. I have never seen you with one. I hope you like it."

Ange opened the small box and took out a lovely petite gold locket and chain. She hugged him and said, "Oh Henri, I do love it. Merci, merci, merci!" She kissed him softly on the lips and said, "I do love you so much. There can never be anyone else. I hope you will be with me forever and ever."

"God willing, love," he said, "God willing."

"Henri, wait here, and I will back in a moment." She got up and hurried up the stairs. She returned with a small package and said, "I was going to give you this later, but I guess now should be the time. I am a bit shy about giving it after receiving this lovely locket. I hope you like it. It is from my heart to your heart."

Henri unwrapped the package to reveal a hand-painted likeness of Ange in a small heart-shaped gold frame. The artist had completely captured Ange, and her likeness smiled at him, seeming to jump out of the frame.

"Ange, I could never have wanted anything more perfect than this. It is now my most precious treasure. I can carry you with me."

"Henri, as I said, it is from my heart." She opened the small locket Henri had given her and said, "It is empty, and I know just what to put in it."

She went to Mimi's kitchen and came back with scissors. She cut a tiny curly lock of Henri's hair, opened the second little door of the locket, put the curl inside, and closed it. "Now I shall have a part of you with me all of the time," she said. "Now this will become my most precious treasure." She moved closer, melting into his arms. He could feel a slight dampness as they sat cheek to cheek. Whether it was from her, him, or both, he couldn't tell.

The next days and through the New Year, the time, as holidays and good times often do, seemed to fly as fleet as Mercury, the messenger of the gods. The New Year hurried into the world in the form of a fierce howling winter storm. The family spent most of the days indoors near fires or covered up in their rooms. Mimi kept hot tea and coffee available in the kitchen. Mostly Henri and Ange spent their hours in the sitting room or in the kitchen with Mimi.

Henri, bored to tears, wandered outside and in the stable and barn. But there was little to do there with the weather being so foul except talk with Louis, Gussie, and Leon. None of them had families. This was home and family. All there was to mostly do was sleep.

Louis said this was Leon's favorite thing to do anyway. "I swear the man can sleep all day and night. I have seen him do it. He only gets up to go pee, eat, fart, and go back to bed. He has to be the laziest *chien* (dog) on the face of the earth."

Henri, Jean, and Ange were young adults by the standards of the time. Many such had been killed in battle at this age and younger. Girls were very often married and mothers at this age in the villages and countryside. Henri and Jean had long discussions regarding what Jean could expect when his appointment came about. Jean would be required to spend two years at the école as he had no prior military experience. But that was all right and accepted by Jean. Henri warned him about the physical requirements and that it would be much better for him to start now with a training routine.

All too soon, and much too early to suit all, Janvier 15 approached; and the men must return to their duties. The general would be based in Paris and would be home at night unless summoned by "duty," as he was often known to have to attend. Madame suspected much play may be involved, but never let on. Such was the way of French gentlemen and certain officers of the Grande

Armée. As the general had been known to state, "If you wish to be a success in this world, promise everything, deliver nothing, say nothing."

Madame was not certain what this may have meant to construe, but she certainly wasn't stupid. A French boy will be a French boy forever!

Henri returned to école on the appointed day. Ange did cry just a little and left a soft wetness on his jacket. She had tried to be brave but, at the last moment, hugged him with eyes filled with tears. He vowed to never wash the jacket. He felt for his little heart-shaped gold picture of Ange in his buttoned shirt pocket under his jacket. He carried the picture there over his heart, and there it would remain when he was in the field. At the école, it would be on his study table. The next leave would be during Easter and would last for one week and not the two weeks as he had heard.

Classwork, physical training, and military skills were stressed with more intensity now. Experts in their discipline came to give special instructions and classes. Henri especially liked the class for astronomy. He found the way of the stars and planets fascinating. One could never be lost when navigating by the heavens, unless, of course, the sky was overcast.

Even then, the class was taught other means to tell base direction. The moss always will grow on the north side of a tree. The sun always dawns in the east and sets in the west. The most accurate means of direction was by compass. This class, of all of his others, was the most intense of all. These cadet officers would be the leaders of the future. It had better not be in their destiny to become lost and possibly move troops in the wrong direction. The results could be devastating.

The introduction to maps and map reading was just as intense. They were taught the art of topography reading and the use of the map and compass combined. Many field trips in the surrounding countryside were made for purposes of mapmaking complete with topography. They worked as teams, and often roommates were paired as long as they were compatible. Henri and Francis often studied together and talked of the day's events after lights-out.

Francis, looking at his efforts of mapmaking, said, "Look at this damn mess, Henri. It is supposed to indicate hills and high places. All I see now is *désordre*! I doubt if ants could navigate this."

Henri laughed and said, "It isn't too bad. You should see mine. At least you have the other side of the paper to start all over again."

"Merde on you too."

The two became very close, and Henri swore him to secrecy about the Bébé Tigre story and showed him the medal given to him by Napoleon. Francis was astonished that his roommate was this fabled character. He had heard about it while working at the military offices in Paris. He promised Henri he would not mention it to the others.

Henri's wound was completely healed now. The angry red scar was replaced with one not quite as visible. Several of the class had asked him what had happened, and he simply told them the same story he had first related to Francis. The physical training gave him a firmness and muscles he never knew existed. He especially enjoyed running. Very often, weather permitting, they were ordered to make long cross-country runs. The cool crisp air and the smell of the forest and surrounding fields brought back many memories of his earlier life on the farm and in the barn and stables at home. He would often run for many minutes completely lost in thoughts of Ange, family, and the multitude of things of his past life, his father and mother, Marcel, Aunt Mags, the nuns at the convent, and what may have become of them. Someday, he promised himself, he would try to return and satisfy himself that they were all right or what may have happened to these people. Most of the time while running, however, he was deep in thought of Ange. At times, he could feel her presence running beside him, reaching for his hand. Every night he would stare at her picture in the little heart-shaped frame, blow out the lamp, and fall asleep with her image embossed in his mind.

For those chosen as capable of becoming horsemen, each cadet was issued a horse. This animal would be in their care for the remainder of the école session. They were advised not to become emotionally attached to the animal. They were to learn only the skills of precision military riding and the care of the horse, saddles, and other equipment.

When Henri asked if they should name their steed, the instructor so aptly stated, "Why would you want to befriend this animal when one day you may have to eat it?" Troops in the field very often ate wounded or incapable horses.

"And besides, gentlemen, your best friends are now supposed to be your sabre, pistol, and musket. These weapons can save your lives while a horse is only an animal for transport, pulling carriages, wagons, cannons, and caissons."

They were given instructions on proper feeding, watering, and brushing to bring out the gleam in the coat for parades and inspections. It was true that grooms were assigned to horse troops for the purpose of caring for the animals, but it was the ultimate and final responsibility for the owner to know the complete status of his charge.

Military riding classes were very intense. Cadets were challenged to maintain complete control at all times. Extra disciplinary riding instructions during leisure periods could result if the horse was unruly and the cadet could not maintain control. Most of the cadets did not have difficulty unless the animal was dumb as a box of rocks as the instructors would say. Occasionally that was the way, but for the most part, the cadets maintained sufficient control. Henri's horse did have signs of stubbornness at first until he crawled up on the animal's neck and bit his ear hard several times.

At the first instance, Francis asked, "What in hell are you doing? You just tried to eat your horse's ear!"

Henri replied, "This is the real way to get his attention. I will do that every time this stupid merde does not listen to me. He will soon learn."

The instructors just laughed and said, "Indeed it does work. If a bite on the ear occurs at each stupid act, soon there wouldn't be any more stupid things." Some of the others followed suit.

The first dress inspection was held, and cadets were required to wear complete decorations issued and awarded. Henri had three now, the Spanish campaign, the Austrian campaign, and the special one presented by Napoleon. He told Francis as they were polishing boots again and the thousand and one things to do before inspection, "I dread this inspection because now everyone is going to see this and question me."

Francis said, "Don't worry about it. This is normal, Henri. You should be proud to share your experiences. It could be an inspiration for some of the others."

They dressed in their uniforms and carefully inspected each other before going to the parade field. The uniforms and all accessories must be impeccable and as near to perfection as possible. It was a very clear sunny day with the only clouds high and far to the west. The sun was very bright, making all of their metal accessories gleam and sparkle. This was a time of personal pride for themselves, their école, and their country.

As they stood in lines and groups denoting their class, the officers loudly brought them to attention and sounded to the commandant, "Monsieur, company is ready for inspection."

The commandant and officers of his staff slowly made their way through the ranks, stopping very frequently and personally inspecting a cadet and asking questions of rules, regulations, weapons, tactics, and a number of questions of things they must know. Often a cadet was asked to withdraw and present his sabre for a check of sharpness and cleanliness.

When the officers reached Henri, the commandant saluted and said, "Cadet, it is customary that I salute you and the medal you have been awarded."

Henri sharply returned the salute without a word, knowing that all eyes were on him, and here would come the thousands of questions. He would just have to deal with that over the next several days, but after discussing this with the general several times, it would now be a matter of personal pride. Still he hated the notoriety and answering those damn questions. Bébé Tigre be damned!

As certain as God has made birds of the air, as Mimi would say, the questions did come. "Henri, what happened? What did you do?" In the recreation room that night, Henri explained to the group the tale of the Baby Tiger, how he really didn't recall the exact events, but feeling a certain blind anger and rage at the advancing enemy. He felt the need to do something when he saw his officers and friends falling in the onslaught. With slaps on the back, handshakes, and tousles of the hair, the worst was soon over. The entire école now held him in some sort of respect. Most had heard of the tale of Bébé Tigre but had no idea Henri was the one and among them.

In the weeks that followed, classes of weaponry were intensified and consisted of complete mastering of the sabre, pistol, and musket. Careful detail was made to swordsmanship that required deft moves while on foot and considerable more moves while mounted. Every effort was stressed to protect the mount, for if the animal fell, the rider was at the mercy of the enemy infantry.

Although Henri was a good rider, there was still much to be learned and practiced to be an accomplished cavalry soldier. They spent long hours riding while brandishing sabres and hacking away at dummies and imaginary enemy. The instructors stated that even though cavalry also carried pistols and other weaponry, nothing replaced the sabre as the first-line weapon. A pistol or musket fired but once, and to reload while riding was damn near impossible or at least took longer than it was worth in precious time.

At horse practice in the early evening, Henri and others were practicing a little trick riding. Lieutenant Roussell had warned them to be careful and not to take undue chances. Henri was showing off and standing on the saddle with arms folded when his boot slipped. His broad grin went to mouth wide open as the horse went in one direction and Henri the other. It was a pitiful Henri that flailed and tried to catch anything. All to no avail, though, as he hit the ground hard.

Francis and Lieutenant Roussell were among the small crowd watching and ran to Henri. "I swear he bounced at least three times end over end," said Francis.

Beyond realizing his boot had slipped and the feeling of spinning, Henri never knew what happened next. He was knocked completely senseless and lying in a muddy crumpled heap when the medical orderly arrived. An initial hasty examination revealed only a severely sprained left wrist and various bruises, bumps, and scratches.

Francis was with Henri as he slowly came to. His head was spinning as he came to his senses and realized where he was. "Well, welcome back to the world, shitbird. Glad you can join us. I have never in my life seen such an eloquent tumble from a horse. You get first prize. Are you all right?"

"Damn lucky this is all," said the orderly to Lieutenant Roussell. "And he just missed that fence. The colonel is going to be furious."

About that time, the colonel arrived, and furious he was. Henri had regained his senses and was lying back on a stretcher after taking a drink of water and had tried to wash some of the mud from his face. It had only made a mess and made the matter look much worse.

"Cadet, what or who gave you the right to commit such a dangerous act with property of the emperor? You do not have the sense God gave a goose. Don't you realize that you, your ass, and all that goes with it are the prime property of the military of France and our emperor? You can thank your lucky stars you were not more seriously injured and possibly at risk of expulsion. From what I see out there, you just barely missed the fence. That would have been a tragedy to mangle our nice fence. Dammit! You could at least lie at attention while I am frothing. There is no excuse for this. You will spend the night in the clinic and have your wrist properly tended. We do need to make certain nothing else is wrong with you, perhaps in your head. If all is well, report to your classes and assignments in the morning. There are no slackers here. A full report of this will be entered into your file jacket. No more of this. Do I make myself clear?"

"Oui, monsieur. I am sorry for the trouble."

"I agree you were sorry to do such a damn fool thing with military property in my charge. Dismissed!" The colonel left in a huff. No one saw him smiling *to himself as he left. Fool boy. One of our most promising cadets. Boys will be boys though. We, or at least most of us, Andre included, did the same things.*

The lieutenant said, "Henri, I have never seen the commandant this pissed. It will take a lot of doing to get back in his graces."

"It was a stupid thing to do, but I have done it so many times before. You are right, monsieur, he was red as a rooster and foaming at the mouth. I will never live this one down. He is certain to tell General de Chabot. I will be teased forever."

The weeks seemed to fly with the wind, and soon the Easter holiday of one week was past. Henri had seen the love of his life once more, eaten more than he should have of Mimi's fine cooking, and visited with the general and the rest of the family. There was still the old dread of leaving Ange again, and he had almost started the feelings as soon as he had arrived. He didn't say anything but did sense that maybe Ange felt the same. They were sitting on the back steps talking and watching the black crows fighting over something in the garden.

"Henri, I see your wrist is wrapped up. What happened?"

"Nothing much, Ange. I bumped it."

"Ange, I think it would be easier to have a tooth pulled than to leave you again. No one could ever guess how much I dread it."

"I know, Henri. I dread it each time. It never gets any easier, but please don't lose a tooth over it. Some day you may need it. I promise to keep mine." They laughed and poked each other with elbows.

The general stopped Henri in the hall on the first day of his return. "I guess you know that Emile sent me a note explaining your latest accomplishment.

Congratulations on not being killed or severely maimed. Be more careful in the future. I am still trying to get my balls back off the barn door for the last time you were banged up. Dammit, she always blames me."

"I am sorry, monsieur. I have done that many times before, but I guess it only takes one time."

The family did find out about Henri's mishap at the evening meal. Madame did fuss at both Andre and Henri. Ange waited until a private time and really fussed.

"Henri, what did you mean when you told me nothing much? You *folle singe* (crazy monkey). Don't you know how much I love you and want to share everything? All of the good and the bad. Don't you ever put me off again. This really makes me angry with you."

Henri reached for her, hugged her, and said, "I do apologize, Ange. To me it wasn't as bad as others thought. I will be more careful. Please don't be upset with me."

She smiled at him only in her way and kissed him. All was much better now.

The spring in France that year exploded with bursts of new growth in the trees and wildflowers in the surrounding fields. The gardens seemed to change overnight from the drab of winter to the brightness of a new season. Henri couldn't remember a more beautiful spring, or possibly it was because he was so tired of being cooped up indoors most of the time. With the better weather, outside training of horsemanship and short forced marches of several kilometers increased. Twice each week, a ten-kilometer run was coursed through the countryside. Most of the cadets were in very good condition by this time, but some still continued to lag behind.

The instructors knew that all were not runners and that certain lagging behind was to be expected. However, for the final graduation requirements, all would be expected to measure up to standard. Henri felt he was in the best physical condition of his life, and he enjoyed the runs immensely. He and Francis would jog along side by side and talk, or he would be lost in thoughts of Ange. At the return leg of the run to the école, all would sprint to the finish. Henri did not always win the sprint, but he was always among the leaders.

Henri received a short letter from Michael Pasar. He had visited the de Chabot home and obtained Henri's address from Ange. *Damn him! What else had he tried to get?* Henri thought. He trusted Ange but not the wolves hanging around. Michael stated he just wanted to remain in contact, and this would be a test letter to see if Henri did receive it. He told of the latest news of the others in the unit and that he was still a drummer. He would probably remain so until he was killed in battle or the Armée dispensed with drummers and gave him a musket. Anton and Gerard were still with him in the regimental Musique Corps. Anton was still as hungry as ever. The others were all right, and the new sergeant was much more human now. Henri was elated to receive the letter other than how Michael got his address and answered right away. He included news of the école and what he was learning. He would let Michael know of his next leave, and possibly they could meet. Michael was still based near Paris, and a meeting would be relatively easy to arrange.

The entire école was granted leave for three weeks while some renovations could be made in the kitchens, barracks, and officer quarters during the hot month of Juillet. As the carriages left for Paris, all Henri could think of was home and the blessed relief of complete rest away from study. The curriculum at the école was very intense, and so far Henri had not failed any of his classes, but it was close for two or three of them. Mostly, for several others, the physical standards were not being met. These final months until Octobre and graduation would be crucial.

Henri had decided to ask Lieutenant Roussell what he might think of what had happened at drummer school and how the stronger ones had helped the weaker. Helping the weaker ones after class and in private hours had made a difference there and could possibly help here. He would discuss this with Lieutenant Roussell when they returned from leave, and Henri had written a hasty note to Michael several weeks ago when he found out about this unanticipated leave and hoped Michael had received it. Communications were so very bad these days, and only the dispatches from command staff could be assured of reaching proper destinations.

The carriage dropped him off near the front gate, and as he trudged up the drive, he heard the familiar welcoming squeal of Ange as she came running down the drive path. He held her close for a minute and never wanted to let her go.

Madame came out on the porch and exclaimed, "Angelette! Such a scene in public?"

"Oh, Momma, everyone knows by now that Henri is one of my favorite people on all of the earth."

"Oui, my child, but there are certain things that presentable young ladies just do not do in public. Never display yourself or leave yourself open to controversy."

"Oui, Momma. Come, Henri, let's go inside where I can feel free to hold your hand or touch you."

"Angelette! I am trying to make you a lady, and yet you continue to go your own way. Apologies and hello to you, Henri, it is good to have you home."

"Madame, it is good to be home. It seems as though I have been away for years."

"I have a surprise for you, Henri. My sister, Madame Dijoin, is here for a visit and has news of your aunt Mags and others."

After the evening meal, Madame, her sister, Henri, and Ange retired to the parlor for tea and conversation. Aunt Mags was fine and sent her very best regards and love to Henri along with a special rosary. She had been told of the tale of Bébé Tigre and was astonished. Word of Henri and what had happened spread rapidly through the convent, and the workers further carried the tale throughout the town. All who had known and met him were amazed that one so young could accomplish this feat. Ange patted him on the arm, glowing with pride. Henri was glowing also, but with scarlet blushing.

He was not embarrassed much any longer, but a little by all that had been made of it. All of the nuns sent their love and said he was especially missed in the gardens and kitchen. The old gardener who had taught Henri wood carving had died. There was word of Marcel. He was working and living on a small farm not too far from the old place in his home village. He had taken up fishing with a passion and made a small subsistence wage by selling fish from the river. He would somehow survive. He always did.

After several glasses of wine and a lull in the conversation, Henri asked to be excused as it had been a very long day, and he wanted to get up early and visit the gardens and stable. Ange and the others remained, and stories of Henri and his boyhood were related by Madame Dijoin. As the tales were told, Ange was amazed and yet saddened that he had gone through such hardship so young in life. She had no idea that all of this had occurred. For one who had been so sheltered, she could never relate to such pain. Somehow it made her love him all the more, knowing these very personal things he had never told about. He had never complained or told anyone these things of poverty and death.

Michael came to the house two days later and said he could only get two days' leave and had worked extra duties to get the time off. Henri showed Michael to his room on the second floor next to Jean and was glad he would not be on the third floor near him in case Ange wanted to make one of her midnight visits. Michael remarked how Ange had grown and how beautiful she had become. Henri, in a joking voice, told Michael not to have eyes for his special lady. Michael caught the tone and decided to drop the conversation. After all, Henri was his best friend, and he would never consider betraying a trust. Still Ange was a beautiful young lady.

That afternoon, Michael, Ange, Jean, and Henri went for a walk to the river, stroll along the walkway, and visit the small cafés and shops along the banks. It was very serene and scenic with the ever-present spires of Notre Dame in the background. As they passed a small café, a tall young military officer jumped up and hailed them.

"Henri, Henri, come over and join us." It was Jean-Claude, and Henri had not seen him since his stay at the hospital. Jean-Claude introduced a beautiful blonde girl, Lydie, as his fiancée.

Henri introduced the members of his party, and Jean-Claude remarked, "This cannot be the girl who took care of you at the hospital. Why, she is indeed quite a lady now. Are you two still madly in love?"

Both of them blushed, and Henri said, "Oh, I think so, Jean-Claude, or at least until she gets smarter and finds someone else." Ange hit him on the arm, and they all laughed. They shared a fresh bottle of wine, and Henri told Jean-Claude about events since they last saw each other.

"So you will be an officer too. That is very good, Henri. We need good leaders. Most officers I know just get in the way of the sergeants who really run the Armée."

"Jean-Claude, I notice you have grown a mustache. I almost didn't recognize you. I was thinking of growing one too. Maybe I can hide this little boy face. An officer should command more respect. What do you think, Ange?"

"I think it could be handsome," she said. And she whispered in his ear a few minutes later, "Just so your mustache doesn't feel like I am kissing one of Mimi's brooms."

Jean-Claude told Henri that he and Lydie planned to marry in the coming year and to please keep the date in their plans when the formal invitation arrived. "We will see that invitations are sent to everyone at the de Chabot residence."

Ange and Lydie made friends immediately and found they shared much in likes, dislikes, fashion, dress, and the countless things that young ladies find to discuss. The group talked until well after dark when the lights were beginning to shine across the river. It was one of the best evenings Henri could remember in some time. Henri, Michael, Jean, and Jean-Claude talked extensively about the military and the latest in weaponry and current events.

Henri was surprised at how well informed Jean had become and how much more passionate his interest had become on entering the military. Jean was certainly to be commended on his progress, but he still would have to be prodded a bit on the physical requirements. In the back of Henri's mind, he was still not that sure of Jean's sincerity toward him. After all, Jean had dealt him so much misery earlier on. He did seem sincere, but time would tell the true story.

They departed much later than planned and had consumed a little more wine than normal. As they made their way back home, they were arm in arm and singing "lightly." Ange's clear voice carried well above the tenor and bass of the boys. At times, several stops were made to gather their bearings before venturing on. When they arrived home, Madame and Mimi were sitting in the large white chairs on the front porch waiting for them.

"Well, it is so good of you fine people to grace us with your presence," said Madame. "We could hear you coming some way down the street. What a spectacle! It is a good thing Andre was not here to witness this. Oh, I shouldn't say that. He would be in the middle of such a scene. And, Angelette, you are supposed to be a lady and not a trollop of Pigale."

"Madame, it is all my fault," said Henri. "We met a friend of mine and shared many old times. I guess too much wine too. I apologize for the embarrassment."

"Oh, nonsense, Henri, all of you are to blame; but there is no real harm done. I just wish I was in my youth again and could enjoy those things reserved for the young. Mimi has prepared the evening meal, but it is cold now. All of you must eat something before retiring or the consequences will be worse tomorrow." The party people went into the dining room and ate even though the food was semiwarm.

Ange put her tiny bare foot in Henri's lap and wiggled her toes while smiling at him. She knew he was embarrassed and couldn't do anything about it. The vixen! She knew exactly what she was doing to him. He finally poked her foot with his fork in an effort to make her stop without attracting the attention of the others, but it only enticed her to do it all the more. They would have a very serious talk about this later. After all, she was supposed to be a lady and his special lady at that.

Michael returned to duty the next afternoon and promised to maintain contact. "Henri, you will be an officer one day. If you ever have need of a drummer, don't forget me."

"We shall see, Michael, but I do not believe that I will be in decision making for some time. Junior officers are considered the lowest of the low. I have often heard if junior officers had brains, they would be considered dangerous. I have heard the general and even Napoleon say this. I plan to be a little mouse and not make any stupid remarks and certainly not do any stupid things. I will stay in touch, and please, you do the same."

Michael hugged Ange and said, "Take care of this young fool. He is the luckiest one I know."

She hugged him back and said, "I will try to make him behave, but so far, it has been impossible."

Michael asked Henri if it would be all right for him to visit the de Chabot house from time to time.

Henri said, "Of course, my friend, I know how it is. Your family is so far away, and you can't visit often. Please do. We are brothers anyway."

Henri wondered about this and would certainly have to keep a close eye. Michael, even though very sincere with him, was a very nice-looking fellow and full of fun and life. Ange could very easily become attracted to him. He knew in his heart this would probably never happen. But again, there was always that old word "probably." Henri was almost glad he was gone.

A more peaceful time could not have been planned during the remainder of the time home. Ange, Jean, and Henri would often just go in the back garden and sit or lie under the fruit trees and watch the clouds, birds, and insects and just enjoy the simple things of God's lovely world. They fantasized at the shape of objects in the clouds. They pointed out human faces, animals, demons, and all manner of familiar things. They spent long hours watching ants toiling with enormous burdens toward their nests. Very often, they fell asleep among the peaceful surroundings. Madame didn't say anything about them sleeping because it was always considered brother and sister; and most of the time, there were the three, Jean, Henri, and Ange. The times when it was just Henri and Ange, they were always very careful not to lie too close together or touch. Henri often gazed at a peaceful Ange sleeping and thought what a beautiful sight she was. She was truly a sleeping angel.

The remaining time of the three-week leave went by just as rapidly as the previous times at home. It always seemed to go by too fast. The carriage arrived at the appointed time for the long drive back. There had been the usual farewell hugs, kisses, and tears. They had their farewell kiss in the privacy of the dark hallway between the kitchen and dining room. The long, tantalizing touching of her soft lips and darting tongue had excited him to the point of breathlessness.

"Oh, mon chéri, you will be the death of me with these kisses," Henri stated in gasps.

"Not death, mon amour, life. Just you wait until our wedding night." She blushed and clutched his hand tightly as they went through the large living area and onto the porch.

A final hug from Madame, Mimi, and Ange again, and he climbed in the carriage. He was greeted by the others and teased a bit about Ange waving from the front porch. The carriage jerked into motion; and the steady *clop, clop, clop* of the horse's hooves on the paving stones soon lulled him into deep thought. Not one year had passed since he had entered the école. Yet events of the past months seemed so distant and then again so near. So much had already happened. Octobre, although only three months away, seemed like years. And then what? What would the future bring?

We are stuffed in this carriage like potatoes in a sack, but at least we are not hot and not all that uncomfortable. Someone giggled, and the odor of passing gas made everyone gasp. Merde, there is always one. "Jacques, that had to be you. You giggled first. The chicken that cackled laid the egg."

They opened the windows all the way and drew the curtains back, and the air was soon unpolluted. The carriage continued its swaying bumpy journey and would continue to do so for several more hours. Damn carriage rides anyway. It seemed he was always arriving or departing in one of the damn things.

His thoughts were mostly of Ange and what she meant in his life. That final kiss in the hall had a very disturbing and wonderful effect on him. It wasn't just the kisses but the way she got so close and snuggled to him. It wasn't promiscuous but just so loving and giving, so Ange. Somehow his previous life seemed more vague and somewhat meaningless. Now everything seemed to focus toward goals and a future life of career, love, belonging, and family. Things that had before been missing in his life. Oh, to be sure, there had been others who had tried to make him feel accepted and, for the most part, had done so. Aunt Mags, the nuns, Madame, even poor Marcel, in his own way. But there was always that hollow void and emptiness. Not so now. Ange had completely made him feel so special, so needed, so wanted, so loved. She had become the one special thing in his life that could never be replaced. Nor would he ever consider replacing her. Even the mere thought pained him. *I guess this is the true and everlasting love mentioned in all of the books and word of every mouth*, he thought to himself. He felt for the little gold-framed picture in his shirt pocket and drifted off into a restless slumber.

14

Graduation

As soon as Henri returned to the école, he sought out Lieutenant Roussell. "Monsieur, I have noticed that there are students lacking in certain classes, myself included. In drummer school, it was the same. We helped each other until all passed the courses. The stronger ones in the classes helped the weaker ones after hours. It did work, and possibly it could here too."

Lieutenant Roussell said, "This is a good idea, Cadet. I can't give orders about this, but I can let you talk to the colonel if you wish. Do you want me to speak to him first?"

"If you wish, monsieur, and merci," replied Henri.

"My pleasure. We have four pelotons of nearly fifty cadets we hope to graduate in three months. Most are good candidates, and all have military experience. You are right. Some are in danger of failing."

After the evening meal, Henri approached Francis to share his idea and get his opinion. Francis agreed, "I think it is a very good idea. Others can certainly use the extra help. I know I could. I could offer help with the map reading and direction finding. I know of several who are in danger of failing the course."

Henri volunteered, "I can give assistance in horsemanship, sword skills, and wherever else help may be needed. There are maybe twenty, while not in danger of failing yet, need to acquire considerable more skills before the final tests. The rest of the class seems all right, but I will ask all of them if they want to either instruct or learn more before the final examinations."

The next morning, Lieutenant Roussell told Henri that he had spoken to the colonel. He had been impressed and wanted to see Henri as soon as possible. Henri advised the colonel what had happened at drummer school and how well it had worked. It may work here as well. The colonel told him to start at once and to keep him advised on progress.

The reception among the cadets was unanimous and very well received. Henri told the others, "If you want some extra pointers on horsemanship or any other subject I may be able to help with, meet me at the stables just after the evening meal, and we will organize some classes."

Usually there was a study period at this time anyway, but these instructions would be special and much more specific. The final outcome in the weeks that followed was the stronger helping the weaker in a number of subjects. It seemed that all were both instructors and students. The classes began a camaraderie not seen at the école before. The cadets began to mold as a family unit and gained spirit, confidence, and pride. After a few days, the other peloton leaders duly took note and inquired of Lieutenant Roussell what brought about such a remarkable change. After the first week, all of the four pelotons were molded as one unit. The colonel began to watch the groups with intense interest. A true spirit of a brotherhood had formed, and one could say the old tales of the musketeers might be relived here. "All for one and one for all." The entire one-year class became more proficient in all subject matters, and as graduation approached, it was evident this would be a class without equal in the history of the école.

Henri's class in horsemanship soon included almost the entire group. The movements of wheels, columns, and including some trick riding had the other instructors looking on. Other groups of study followed suit. The entire école took on a new meaning of personal pride and achievement. The colonel was extremely proud as daily improvements began to show. Henri seemed to be everywhere following up on groups and the study. He met with the colonel at least once a week and informed him of progress.

Henri had become the driving force behind the movement to pass the entire class. The other student instructors in other classes recognized the importance and strove for perfection. It was a test of leadership skills for not only Henri but the entire one-year class. These were the future officers of the Grande Armée, and these lessons in leadership and working together would not be forgotten.

With graduation just a few short weeks away, Henri decided to write a personal letter to Josephine and invite her. He had carefully considered the consequences and her position but finally decided to send the letter of invitation anyway. Several weeks went by, and a reply did come. A personal courier of Josephine delivered the letter. Henri was called out of class personally by the colonel to receive the letter with Josephine's private seal.

"Cadet, you never cease to amaze me," said the colonel. "You appear to have very powerful allies."

"Monsieur, I have known and admired Her Majesty for some time and did want to invite her to the graduation if it would be possible."

"She would be most welcome, Henri. I have long been an admirer of her too. She is a lady without equal."

Henri opened the letter and read the reply personally written in her eloquent hand.

Dear Henri,

> *Merci for the invitation to your graduation. It is indeed an honor to be remembered, and to share this momentous event with you. However, please understand, with others of my past political and personal world in attendance, it may be uncomfortable for them, and, as well as, for me to attend. If at all possible, please arrange for Ange and Madame de Chabot to visit me in the future. I have enclosed a small gold medal of my personal religious order that may help to protect you in the years and wars to come. Please give our Andre my regards and love.*

> *God Bless,*
> *Josephine*

Henri let the colonel read the letter. He agreed it was very tactful that she chose not to attend. Napoleon and other high-ranking military would be there. Certain parties may have been uncomfortable. It would be a pity, however. Her presence would have certainly added a charm to the otherwise rigid military presentation.

Graduation week seemed to approach more rapidly by the day, and the thousand and one things for preparation appeared to never be completed. The emperor, a delegation of dignitaries, and high-ranking military would be present; and everything must be the essence of perfection. The cadets spent many hours polishing everything. The walls and floors of the école gleamed as though glass had been applied. Boots, uniforms, sabres, all metal accessories were polished and checked again and again. Most were repolished just to be certain. The horses were curried and combed over and over until their coats gleamed like mirrors. The hoofs were trimmed and polished with equal intensity. As graduation day approached, all seemed in readiness, but final inspections were made until the final hour. Henri and Francis were dressing and inspecting each other for any flaw. Any hair out of place was corrected.

"Hell, Henri, they can't see clearly from the viewing stand. You are like a mother sow with a litter."

"I know, Francis, but I just can't help but worry. I am usually not affected, but this thing is just too intense and must be as perfect as possible."

On midmorning of the anticipated day, the bugle call summoned the troops to assembly. The initial presentation would be the horse parade. All mounted troops had taken great care that the mounts were "flushed." It just would not do to have a horse make droppings on the parade field in front of this audience.

Henri and the other members of his peloton mounted and formed in columns of three with Lieutenant Roussell in the lead. They were the honor peloton and would lead the entire école. The bugle sounded again, and the drums began a tattoo of military cadence so familiar to all.

Lieutenant Roussell gave the command to draw sabres and present at the side. "Troop, forward at a walk" was the next command. The troop was a magnificent sight of precision, color, and perfection as they moved onto the parade ground. The lines were remarkably straight, and the troops seemed to move as one. The horses were exceptionally well behaved and almost seemed to be in step. Observers could sense the pride of the troop.

Napoleon was sitting on the right of the colonel and General de Chabot on his left. Madame de Chabot, Ange, and Jean were there as well as nearly a hundred other family members of the class.

Napoleon leaned over to the colonel and said, "Magnificent, monsieur. You and this entire école are to be congratulated. I have never before observed such perfection and horsemanship in a cadet corps."

"Indeed, Emile, and I would like to also add my congratulations," said the general.

"Your Excellency and General," said the colonel, "there is a reason for this, and leadership was the key. During this ceremony, I plan to single out the source of most of this perfection, and I am certain both of you will be pleased."

The honor peloton wheeled in perfect unison and formed a single line in front of the viewing stand and, at the command "Present salute," raised their sabres to the crowd.

"Momma, look at them," said Ange. "They are so perfect and proud. They all are."

The remainder of the troop formed in groups behind the honor peloton.

"Troop dismount! Grooms forward! Mounts to the rear!" came the next series of commands. The graduation and awards ceremony was about to begin. The commandant waited for the horses to be removed and addressed the troop.

"Your Excellency, honored guests, and family members. I take great pride in presenting before you this troop for graduation from this distinguished école. Each member here has earned the privilege of entering the officer corps in the Grande Armée of His Excellency with the rank of lieutenant. A document certifying completion and the insignia of his rank will be presented to each here. I offer my congratulations on their individual achievement. Every member of this class has graduated, and each is to be congratulated. I would, at this time, like to make a special award and presentation to the outstanding cadet of this corps for troop spirit and devotion to duty far beyond what is normally requested of a cadet. This cadet is partially responsible for the perfection seen in this troop here today. On his own initiative, he began a voluntary course of instruction whereby those strong in certain subject matter gave special and much-needed instructions to those struggling. As a result, all have graduated. This quality of leadership is what this école is created to promote. Cadet Henri Devreney, please step forward."

The general was amazed. No one could have ever expected this. Napoleon rose and started to applaud, and the rest of the audience followed his lead. Henri marched forward, trying not to blush too much. He had not expected this and was embarrassed. The emperor was given a special achievement award to present to Henri, and he did so with a kiss on each cheek.

"Very well done, Lieutenant. Welcome to my officer corps. I doubt either of us could have ever contemplated events as these when we first met."

"Oui, Your Excellency. I am at a loss for words. I do pledge my loyalty and life to you and France."

"Merci, my new lieutenant. Josephine sends her very best personal regards and best wishes. We are still the very best of friends and share much. She told me that you had invited her, and she had declined as it was politically correct."

"I understand, Excellency."

"Merci for friendship and loyalty. Take care of my old friend. You may return to your post."

Henri saluted sharply, did an about-face, and marched back to his position in the troop.

"Merde," whispered Francis, "what was that all about? You two seemed like old friends."

"I guess maybe we are, Francis, I will tell you all about it."

"Well, anyway, my friend," said Francis, "I am amazed, and try to stop blushing. It is unbecoming an officer."

The graduating troop was called one by one to the reviewing stand for their certificates and rank insignia. The commandant assisted Napoleon in making the presentations. As each received his promotion to officer, they smartly returned to the ranks. When the last award was presented, the colonel once again congratulated the new officers and gave permission for dismissal. A loud cheer went up from the troop, and the family members poured out of the viewing stand in search of their loved ones. Henri started toward the stand and was met nearly there by Ange and Jean.

"Oh, Henri, I am so proud of you I could almost burst," she whispered in his ear. "I do love you so much."

Jean shook his hand and slapped him on the back. "Henri, I can't believe what they say you have done. Congratulations. I am next to be here, and I hope I can do as well."

"You can, Jean. I know you can."

Madame gave Henri a hug. "Henri," she said, "we are so proud of you. This is a great accomplishment and to be recognized personally by the emperor. This is the second time for a personal recognition by His Excellency."

The general was talking to Napoleon and waved for the group to join them. As they went over, all bowed. Napoleon kissed the hands of Madame and Ange and shook hands with Jean.

"Henri," said the general, "as with our military custom, your emperor received your first salute as an officer. I would consider it my honor to receive your second one." The two exchanged salutes, and the general gave Henri one of his famous bear hugs.

Ange had not let loose of Henri's hand during almost all of this exchange and was clinging to it as though he might vanish at any second.

Napoleon noticed this and said, "Lieutenant, it would appear you have captured more than one heart this day. I wish you both a future filled with all things good and as you wish."

Ange and Henri smiled, and the general said, "Excellency, this has been developing for some time, and one would hope I can one day call Henri my son along with Jean. Jean will be eligible next fall for entry here and has been working hard on the requirements for entry."

Napoleon said, "I am certain he will do well, Andre, and join our officer corps with distinction. Pardon me, my friends, my aides are motioning for our return to Paris. There seems always to be problems, and there is no rest for the weary."

He whispered to the general, "As you know, Andre, there are unusual rumbles these days from the Russian Bear. Only this morning, we had reports of Russian troops starting to mass on the north of Austria. We think our old advisory is in complete agreement." He left hurrying to the awaiting carriage and mounted personal guard.

There was to be a luncheon for the honorees and guests with ample time to return to Paris before a late hour. Francis introduced Henri and his family to his family. Of course, the general and Francis's father knew each other.

Francis took Henri to one side and said, "My good friend, these days will live with me forever. I hope we will be friends for that long too. Don't forget me when you go wherever they send you."

"Francis, don't worry. I don't think any of us will ever forget what happened here. We need to stay in touch."

The graduating troop had packed in the days before and could return with their family if they wished. The others would report to their new duty stations and have leave from there, all of whom had talked about fine women, fine wine, and a fine time to be had by all.

At a brief gathering following the luncheon, the colonel, Lieutenant Roussell, and members of the troop gathered and wished the other good luck and Godspeed in their future endeavors.

"We shall never forget these days" was the general sentiment felt by all.

15

First Posting

It was a stirring and exciting ride home from the école. Henri experienced a sense of relief with twinges of sadness, leaving the friends and surroundings so familiar to him these many months. The buildings, grounds, staff officers, workers, and surrounding countryside would be emblazoned in his memory forever.

Ange was quietly sleeping with her head on his shoulder. They both were much more comfortable with being close now that it was an accepted fact that they were to be much more than just brother and sister. Madame quietly observed all of this and would watch the future developments much more closely. Young people sometimes just could not control the fires of passion, and careful and tactful methods may have to be put into action. The two were, to be sure, very proper and devout to family, religion, and moral obligation; but human nature, youth, and love often make decisions in haste or none at all. Family scandal was not even an option.

The general, Jean, and Henri were discussing events of the day, Henri's achievements, and his future posting to the general's command near Paris. He mentioned for both of them not to utter a word, but Napoleon had just confirmed to him that serious problems with Russia might be on the horizon. The senior staff and advisors had been aware of this for some time; and after brief studies, through deep concern, Napoleon was advised to be cautious. There were too many unknowns about the Russian lands and people. Russia was so vast and the winter months so brutal that any lengthy proposed campaign could bring disaster. Napoleon was advised to do all possible to maintain peace with this monster at all costs. The other allies could be dealt with, and now that Napoleon had married into the Austrian Empire, that could take away a large part of any allied threat.

The general took out a cigar, and Madame said, "Andre! Don't you dare light that smelly thing in this carriage! We can stop if you feel so compelled to smoke."

He laughed and said, "Ho, never fear, mon amour. I was not going to light it. I just wanted to tease you, and besides, many times when traveling, I just chew on them. I probably eat more cigars than I smoke."

"That is disgusting any way that you do it. For the life of me, I cannot understand men and that horrible habit."

"Well, mon amour, if you ever did dare to try one you would probably understand and like it as much as I do." And so it went with the teasing and chattering most of the rest of the way home. Henri had had a very long day and was dozing too, with his head leaning against Ange's.

"Look at those two," said the general. "How far does that sight take us both back in memory?"

"Wonderful and full years, Andre, wonderful years. They are so young, and now Henri is an officer. Do you seriously believe any of this Russian talk?"

"We in the staff dismiss most of it and know any campaign there could be very difficult. But come now, don't worry your pretty self about this." He patted her hand, and she snuggled closer. He whispered something in her ear, and she playfully slapped his hand. They would be home soon.

Henri was given a two-week leave before reporting to his first post as a *sous-lieutenant*. The general had requested that he be placed in his command, and the two discussed where he would be placed.

"Henri, I am going to throw you to the wolves. You will go directly to the ranks and earn your spurs. That is the best way to learn. Just jump in the water and go as deep as you dare without drowning. Some of the old crusty veteran sergeants will try to have you for a meal, but never show fear, and any respect must be earned."

"I understand, monsieur. All I can do is fall on my face."

"I know, and you probably will from time to time. Remember you are now considered the most worthless and dangerous thing in all of the Grande Armée. A very new sous-lieutenant who will attempt to give commands to seasoned veterans. They won't know that you are also a veteran and a decorated one at that. Take my advice and do not strut like the new rooster in the barnyard. Enlist the aid of your senior sergeant and tell him you will depend on his good judgment. Tell him you do not know merde from wild honey. See what will happen. I will ask you to report to me from time to time for a discreet talk and progress report." He clapped Henri on the back and left the room, roaring for Mimi to fix him some coffee.

Henri went out to the back garden and sat for a long time, pondering the general's words of wisdom. From past observations in the ranks, he knew the general was correct. He would have to mount the task or the task would mount him. He had seen similar things and several failures. He was determined he would succeed. Ange came outside looking for him and found him sitting alone under the open shed at the rear of the barn. The weather was damp, and a light mist was swirling in the late evening breeze.

"Henri, I have looked all over for you! What are you doing out here all by yourself? It's cold and damp this evening, and you will get a misery."

"Don't worry, Ange, I am too mean for a misery to catch me. I just wanted some time to think about my future as an officer and a leader of troops. Your father and I had a talk, and he gave me some very good advice. I will be going to my first command just after my leave, and I have got to do well. The entire future of so much I want will depend upon it. I have seen fools charge in before, and the wise old veterans have them for a meal. The foolish ones don't even suspect until it is too late. This will not happen to me. Forgive me, Ange, if I seem distant at times. This is something I seem destined to do. It has got to be right."

Ange grabbed his hands and looked directly in his eyes. Her dark brown eyes seemed to sparkle, and for a second, words were not necessary. "Henri, now you are an officer in the Grande Armée of France. Do not for one moment ever doubt any part of your ability either as a man or an officer. What you have already done should be proof to the entire world what you can do. Let me share in any worries you may have. I shouldn't tell you this, but I overheard Poppa telling Momma that she shouldn't worry either. You will be among the best, and he never says things like that unless they are the truth. He should know. He became an officer too at a very early age." She kissed him and pulled him by the hand. "Come on, Mimi is preparing some of her special hot tea."

The days passed rapidly as they always did when he was home. There just did not seem to be enough time to spend with each family member and especially Ange. They had had long and now very serious talks about their future. He would try to get firmly established as a career officer, and after several promotions, they could more realistically speak of marriage. Henri added several more things to their secret treasure for safekeeping. The little medal given to him by Josephine, the letter she had written him, and his certificates from the école.

"This is not fair," she complained, "I do not have anything to add, and you have these wonderful things."

"Add your beautiful self, Ange, and our treasure will be complete. It is ours and not just yours or mine," he said.

Henri reported for duty on the appointed day. He presented his orders to the officer in charge of personnel.

"So what have we here? A newly appointed sous-lieutenant and in the cavalry troop no less. I take it that you can successfully mount and stay a horse.

I do not have your personnel files as yet for proper evaluation and placement, but there is an immediate vacancy in the third brigade. Come with me, and I will introduce you to the capitaine in charge."

They went a short distance in an area with seemingly thousands of white tents all set into neat rows. There were fires burning between the rows, and the smoke hung over the area like a hazy, musty cloud. The entire area smelled of woodsmoke, and if the wind was just right, the smoke caused coughing and burning of the eyes. They approached a tent with the flag of the peloton set on a standard at the doorway. The officer raised the tent flap entranceway and motioned for Henri to enter. There were several men sitting inside on wooden bed affairs, talking and smoking.

"Capitaine LaBauve, I bring you a new target for the enemy cannon," said the officer.

The capitaine rose and shook his head. "Why, this is just a boy. Surely there must be some mistake. I need an officer to take command of the Second Section."

"I can certainly do that, monsieur," replied Henri. "I have just graduated from the école at Saint-Cyr. I am a combat veteran of two campaigns before that."

"Well, well, we shall see," mused the capitaine.

"Capitaine," said the personnel officer, "I do not have his personnel file yet. As soon as it shows up, I will bring it to you."

"*Très bien* then. Until I can review it, we will give credit where some credit may be due. Come with me, Lieutenant, and I will introduce you to the section sergeant. Maybe the two of you can discuss old war stories. He is an old veteran of many battles himself."

The capitaine put on his jacket and hat and winked at the others as Henri left the tent. They went a short distance to another tent with a standard and flag with a number 2 stitched on it.

"Sergeant Prejean, this is the new officer in charge of this section. Lieutenant Devreney. Please see that he receives quarters and whatever he requires."

"Oui, monsieur." Sergeant Prejean was a man of medium height and weight. He had dark hair and piercing dark eyes. His uniform was impeccable with boots and all metal objects polished and clothing neat and orderly. His area of the tent was equally as neat and well organized. One could readily see this was a career military man and also a man who would stand for no nonsense.

"Welcome to the Second Section, Lieutenant." Henri held out his hand and received a smart and firm handshake in return.

"Lieutenant, you are in the most capable hands in the brigade. I will call for you when your file arrives and I have an opportunity to review it."

"Oui, monsieur." The capitaine left, and an awkward silence ensued.

Finally Sergeant Prejean said, "We need to get you settled and a mount. The horse area is just behind this row of tents, but first let me show to your quarters."

They went to the end of the row and went into the first tent. There were three other men in the tent to whom Henri was introduced. These were all lieutenants as he and were assigned to the other surrounding sections.

"Hello, and welcome to the brigade. I am Adrien Richard of Section Three, and this is Elie Rabilais, Section One, and here is Basile Normand of Section Four. You can have that bed and locker box there in the corner. Make yourself a nest. We will show you around the area later."

Sergeant Prejean asked Henri to follow him and be introduced to his command. As they were walking back to the Second Section troop area, Henri asked if he could please have a private talk with the sergeant and, perhaps, better understand each other. They went out behind the area where the horses were stabled and stopped under a large grove of trees.

"Oui, monsieur, what would you like to discuss?"

"Sergeant, I am like a newborn sheep in this role as an officer. Even though I am a veteran of a few years and have seen combat, I know that I will have to depend heavily on you, your judgment, and your experience to make things work as they should. I ask your assistance and guidance and, short of beating me with a stick, lead me in the right direction. I will back your every order and not interfere with your duties as senior sergeant."

"Well, bite me on the ass. An honest officer for a welcome change. With all due respect of your rank, Lieutenant, I will run the troops if you will see to the proper administration of the command."

"A deal, Sergeant, and here is my hand on it." The two shook hands and started to return to the area.

"Lieutenant, it is my pleasure to know you and to have this understanding. You will have my best efforts."

"Merci, Sergeant."

"Come on, Lieutenant, we need to introduce you to your command."

The Second Section consisted of twenty-four cavalry troopers. All were seasoned veterans. Several were career soldiers and longtime veterans. Henri thought he recognized several. As they approached the area, the sergeant bellowed in his best command voice, "Second Section, fall out on the road. On the double." There was a scramble and bustling of tent flaps, and the troops lined up in whatever array of dress they happened to be in at the time. All had boots and trousers; but some were missing shirts, jackets, and head covers.

"Well, isn't this a pretty mess to meet your new commander. You look like a mob and not a troop. This is Lieutenant Devreney, your new commander."

"Merci, Sergeant," Henri said in his deepest possible officer voice. "It is my pleasure to meet you, gentlemen. Now I will give you exactly one minute to get back in this formation properly dressed as soldiers. Move out."

Another wild scramble; and the pushing, shoving, and clanking could be heard in the tents as they donned jackets, hats, and whatever else they had been lacking.

The sergeant said, "Très bien, Lieutenant. They needed that from you. I wondered how you would take this."

When the troop assembled again, it was a different scene. The rows were straight and the uniforms neat.

"Come to ease, gentlemen," said Henri. "I know things are a bit lax during this period when the Armée is idle. But we are soldiers, and we will always act and dress accordingly. I will meet with each of you during the next days, and we will get to know each other. I will expect each of you to be in complete uniform during training and drill periods. I should not have to tell you this. I also want to assure each of you that Sergeant Prejean has complete and total control of discipline with my complete backing. That will be all, gentlemen. I will turn the troop over to Sergeant Prejean for the morning drill."

One of the troops whispered to the other, "Damn, for a boy lieutenant, he has a bite. Maybe we have a leader."

Indeed they did have a conscientious and eager leader willing to work with them and be fair. Henri spent the rest of the day becoming familiar with the area and talking to Sergeant Prejean about certain of the troops and what he may expect. Late in the afternoon, Henri received a message to report to Capitaine LaBauve. The capitaine advised him that he was to go with the head groomsman and pick out his horse. Capitaine LaBauve and the groomsman looked at each other, but Henri caught the hint of a smirk between them. Something was up, and he would soon find out. As the three of them approached the horse stables, Henri noticed an unusual number of men in the area. All of the men in his command, Sergeant Prejean, and his three fellow lieutenants from the other sections were around. They were not in large groups but were trying to appear innocent and just meander here and there. What was this all about?

The head groomsman went into the large barn and returned with a large white stallion. He was saddled and ready to go. Henri noticed that while the horse appeared calm, his ears were laid back. Now he knew. This horse was like a cannon ready to fire, and he would be ready. He approached the horse, patted his neck, and quickly mounted. For a bare second, the horse stood still; and then he reared, screamed, and tried to throw this thing from his back. Henri stayed right with him through every move, and it was soon obvious that he would be there to stay. Then in a surprise move, Henri vaulted off the horse. The surprised horse stood still as Henri caught the reins. Henri hit the horse with all of his strength right across the nose, nearly knocking him down.

"Now, you son of Satan. You will know who is master or we will do this again." He mounted the horse again, and for some time, the horse stood still. Henri patted his neck and talked softly and gently to him. Finally Henri slapped the reins gently on the horse's neck, and he trotted around the fence area with Henri completely in control. No one in the crowd that had now assembled around the area said anything. They just looked at one another and wandered off. No words were necessary. They had just seen a horse mastered when they had expected to see the new one thrown on his ass. Henri dismounted and talked to the horse for some time all the while patting his neck and scratching his ears.

Finally he gave the reins to the groom and said, "He will do fine. He is very strong and seems intelligent. Does he have a name?"

"You called him Satan, and he was one. He has thrown many. Here. You are the first to really master and ride him. That hit on the nose was the thing that did it."

"Oh oui, it does get their attention. I know it does for me when I am in a fight. I was taught about horses before I could barely walk."

Henri walked back to the section area with a grinning Sergeant Prejean. "Lieutenant, you realize that was a test?"

"Oh oui, I sensed something was up when we were walking over there. I was waiting to see what evil had been dreamed up."

"Well, Lieutenant, you did prove yourself. I think our bunch was impressed as well as all of the others."

The week went by rapidly, and Henri was with the troop during all of the training exercises. As they had agreed, Sergeant Prejean gave most of the commands, and Henri followed suit. The capitaine and his fellow officers were, of course, very interested and followed the course of the Second Section's progress with interest. The general comment was that for his age, he was mature and serious and seemed to have his head on straight. He was not prone to get excited and seemed to maintain self-control. Combat would tell the tale. His control of his horse was done with a calm and very firm demeanor. The rest of his command seemed to take silent lessons from his actions, and it was recognized that he was no foolish young sprout.

For those residing in or near Paris, a one-day leave was granted after the normal duty week. However, if all was in order, they could leave at noon the day before. Every fourth week, Henri would be the duty officer and have to remain in camp. Henri rode into Paris with several others going to the same area. As was usual, he was beside himself with wanting to be with Ange. He was dropped off on the corner of the de Chabot Street and practically ran to the large iron gates. She was not waiting on the porch this time as no one could have guessed what time he might arrive. He opened the front door and crept toward the kitchen. He heard Mimi's voice and Ange's soft laughter. He stuck his head around the corner and saw Ange in an apron covered with flour and heaven knows what else. She saw him and emitted the usual squeal of delight. She ran to him and leaned over with pouty puckered lips.

"I am so glad you are here. We didn't know when to expect you. Mimi has been showing me how to bake a cake. The last time I tried, it fell in the middle and was a disaster. I will clean up in a little while and give you a proper greeting."

"Well, how about right now? A little flour never hurt anyone, and you and a hug is all I have been dreaming of for a week."

"My lord, you two just don't pay an old woman any attention. All of this talk of fiddle-faddle should be reserved for later in your lives, but that is all right. I can remember when I was young many years ago. I don't think I talked like that in front of peers though. I would have been whopped."

"Mimi, I'll bet you are still one to reckon with around gentlemen," said Henri. "I am going upstairs to change and be more comfortable than in this stiff heavy uniform."

The rest of the day was spent with Ange, Jean, and Madame, telling them all about life at the camp and the men of his command. The general came in later that afternoon just before the evening meal. He had been rousing with his fellow officers and was, as Madame said, "slightly pickled." He was in a very good mood, as was his usual, and laughing and teasing at everything.

"Lady of the house, when do we dine? I am famished. I have been living on camp food for a week."

Just then, Mimi, as if reading his mind, said the meal was ready. They ate silently for a while and then started conversations.

"Well, new officer, and how was the first week of the rest of your Armée career? Did the old sergeant and troops have you for a meal?"

"Quite the contrary, monsieur. I took your advice and had a confidential talk with the sergeant. All seems to be working out."

"I heard about the punch on the nose of your horse. The other officers were laughing about it, and I asked who had done this. When they told me, I had to laugh too. Did the family hear of this?"

"No, monsieur."

"Well, all, it seems a young new officer was given the meanest horse in the stable as a test of his horse skills. The officer promptly hits the horse on the nose with such force, the horse almost falls. After that establishment of who is master, there is no further problem. The others had never seen anything like this and thought it was quite amusing and appropriate. Damn, I wish I could have seen it. It appears you are making good first impressions, Henri. Keep it up."

The next day was Dimanche. It was a lovely day although cold during the French Novembre. The clear blue sky had only thin wisps of clouds moving rapidly in a seemingly endless river far above. The family walked to Notre

Dame for Mass. Ange had Henri's arm and snuggled as close as she could. The ever-watchful Madame nudged her and whispered not to create any scene. The general just smiled and whispered to Madame that he wished he were still young and could create scenes.

Madame hit his stomach with her elbow but smiled as she did so, whispering back, "You do very well, you old bear."

Henri's time in the afternoon after the noon meal was spent with Ange near the fireplace in the sitting room. Mimi's special tea and sweet cakes were always welcome, and there was plenty. He would have to leave just before dark and return to camp for the week ahead. They talked of many things and yet nothing of any specific significance. In later years, they would often reflect on these times and try to remember what the course of discussion was. They could never seem to remember, and just being together was satisfaction enough. The calm, quiet presence of the other and slight touch of the hands offered a part of their lives always remembered with a fondness never to be forgotten.

The time for return to duty was soon at hand, and they heard a call from the front of the house. Henri, with heavy heart, picked up his small leather bag, kissed Ange, and hurried down the front steps to the waiting carriage. He would be riding back with the general. The general boarded the carriage and looked back at Madame and Ange waving from the porch.

"Well now, lad, it would appear that we have more in common than just this damn Armée life. You and my Ange are both so young for any thought of a permanent situation. Or if I am wrong, please promise me as your father and her's that before any thoughts like that do arise, you will speak to us on the issue."

"On my honor, monsieur. I promise only the best thoughts regarding Ange."

"Merde, lad, I wasn't worrying about honor. I know both of you very well to suspect anything except infatuation at this point. What I meant was to talk to me if anything really serious ever does come about, or if you ever have need of a friend and father, I want you to always know that you can confide in me with complete trust."

"Merci, monsieur. And I appreciate it more than you know."

Oh, but I think I do, thought the general. They rode the rest of the way to camp in near silence, lost in thoughts of the coming week and what it might bring.

The shrill call of the bugle roused them the next morning. Basile Normand, the Section Four officer, said, "Merde, I was having a sweet lady-type dream, and now I am having a nightmare."

They were stirring and looking for their clothes and gear. Henri pulled his boots on and checked the rest of his uniform. Time for a new week and endless routines of training. It would appear all would be experts of charging and killing the enemy by this time. The next day, Henri's personnel file caught up with his assignment and was delivered to the personnel officer. The first entries were routine concerning his completion of drummer school, and then the officer noted the entry by the head of the school citing Henri for his activities of extra leadership abilities. It was impressive, and the officer read on about his duties in the Spanish campaign. So Henri was a combat veteran, but still only routine entries by his commanding officers. When he started to read about his involvement in the Austrian campaign and the personal citation by the emperor, he was astonished. This new lieutenant was the Bébé Tigre and the hero of that battle. He had been in that campaign, and the Tigre was the talk of the entire Armée. Mon dieu, and to have him here in this command. The capitaine must hear of this at once.

He nearly ran to the capitaine's tent with the file. "Capitaine, I have extraordinary news of our new sous-lieutenant of the Second Section."

"Oui, what is it? Did he crap his pants?"

"No, monsieur. Nothing like that. Read the entries where the marks are placed."

The capitaine read and had to sit down. "This young lad is the Bébé Tigre? I would never have thought it. We were in the Austrian campaign and not too far away from that action. Why, everyone was talking of what happened that day. Here is his personal citation from the emperor himself. I know of some who would give a ball for such an honor. And he is in my command. I will have to think on this. Please keep this to yourself and send the lieutenant to me as soon as you can locate him."

"Oui, Capitaine, I will."

Henri was with the troops going through some horse discipline maneuvers when he was told to report to the capitaine as soon as possible. He rode straight for the capitaine's tent, dismounted, tied his horse to the horse post, and asked permission to enter the tent.

"Come in, and please sit down. Lieutenant, your personnel records have just been received, and I am amazed at what I have seen. I was in the Austrian campaign and not too far from the action where you were. We all have heard of the Bébé Tigre and what happened."

"Capitaine, I'm afraid it was out of proportion with reality. I have heard these stories myself, and please, monsieur, could we keep this in confidence? I don't wish to flaunt this. Actually, I am embarrassed by the publicity of it all."

"As you wish, Lieutenant, but I must advise you your presence will have to be reported to General de Chabot. This is his command he demands to know all of his officers and especially those of notoriety."

"Monsieur, that is no problem. I was partially reared by the general and live with his family. Please keep this in confidence too. I have to make my own way in this Armée and would not want my future influenced."

"I understand, Lieutenant, and will do all possible to honor your request and keep your confidence. But first, and just between us this one time, I would like to shake the hand of a hero. What you did was not taken lightly and was an inspiration to all of us who heard the tale."

Henri smiled as they shook hands.

"That will be all, Lieutenant, you may return to duty. Your secret is safe with me."

"Merci, monsieur."

16

New Empress, New Napoleon

The winter months were more extreme than normal during the years of 1810 and 1811. France and the Grande Armée were at a near peace and mostly in a stand-down condition. Some troops were rotated to the occupation of Spain and other places of need, but Henri's group would remain in Paris. This was certainly all right with him. This year, the winter months in Paris were exceptionally bitter with cold, misty fog, and rain. On days when the weather was milder than others, only a slight training could be conducted. Officers were ordered to give the troops minimum duties and not to subject them to extreme weather unnecessarily. The sick bays were full anyway, with cases of colds to pneumonia. Several deaths resulted. Pray for spring was the general consensus.

There were still the nagging rumors of continual problems with Russia and that Napoleon was making attempts to maintain a stable peace. Most of his staff said this was only a delay tactic until he could be ready to mount a successful invasion with ample reasons. The empress Marie Louise was pregnant with Napoleon's first child, and the general said Napoleon was ecstatic for a true blood successor to his empire. Betting was rampant among the staff as to the sex of the child. Napoleon had stated he was positive the child would be a boy. The general said this should have been easy enough as the pattern for a boy was right there in front of him. He had worked exceptionally hard with conception, and a girl's pattern was easily mixed up. That pattern was there before him too. Best leave it to God.

The child was due sometime in the midspring of 1811, and to be certain, much lavishness and ceremony would be seen in Paris and France and especially among the loyal of His Excellency in Paris.

Almost before they realized how time had fled like a thief, the Christmas season was with them again. It was hard to realize this would be Henri's seventh year with the de Chabot family. The time had passed so quickly, and the events had been so vivid. He had almost successfully started the attempt of a mustache. He desperately wanted it to fill out and semihide the youthful face that went with his years.

Ange said, "That is silly, but with his troops and fellow officers, the boy must be replaced by manly actions and appearance in all ways. But it tickles and is stiff."

He assured her, "This is the first growth, and it will soften with age and time. At least that was what I have been told."

Mimi teasingly told him, "I can cut some hair from the tail of one of the cats in the barn and fix you a fine mustache in any array of colors you may want. Orange with stripes would be fitting. Tigre."

He told her, "I will pee in your flour barrel if you continue teasing me." Mimi whacked him on the arm with her large wooden stirring spoon as he ducked out of the kitchen laughing.

That evening at dinner with the general in his "rare" mood, Henri was jokingly asked about the growth under his nose. "Didn't they teach you lessons in philosophy at the école? A very famous philosopher once said that a wise man does not cultivate on his face what grows wild upon his ass."

With that, the general and Jean laughed so hard they nearly choked on Mimi's fine dish of chicken and potatoes. The rest at the table sat in silence, only smiling politely. Life was good these days, and all of the family seemed to be settling into the routines of the time and season.

Henri and the general were home nearly every weekend, much to the delight of Madame and Ange. The general confided in Henri during one of return trips to camp that while this was extremely good duty and rare, he did almost long for the excitement of a good campaign somewhere. Henri would understand this as time went along. A soldier's sole purpose in life is the waging of war. As the general said, an idle soldier is likened to trying to eat a piece of tough meat with a dull knife. He needed be honed to remain keen and sharp.

Jean was studying very hard at the école at Saint-Cyr. He would have one more year to go for graduation. His perpetual fault was his lack in physical condition and discipline. Henri helped him whenever he was home with sets of exercises that would trim off some of the flab, but Henri knew it was hopeless. Jean would sneak in Mimi's kitchen often in search of sweet cakes. Henri warned Jean about sneaking cakes. There just weren't any cakes to sneak at the école. His knowledge of military history and other subjects was above standard and would not present problems. Maybe Jean would be successful, graduate with officer rank, and have an uncomplicated assignment in planning or administration somewhere. After all, he was the general's son.

He had entered the école at the end of January after the Christmas season. Madame worried that he would miss his home life, and the general said it may also be the reverse. Madame would miss Jean. It is difficult as fledglings leave the nest. Jean had changed considerably since entering. Although still not a total team player, he was more considerate of others and readily followed orders. Armée life would certainly bring about the camaraderie part. It could be very lonely to be left out of things because of being an asshole. One needed to be trusted and basically liked.

The Christmas season came with the usual decorations in and around the house. Madame, Ange, Mimi, and all of the household workers had bustled around for days, making certain everything was perfect. They had the gardeners cut green sprigs from the shrubs and trees, and the sweet aroma of pine and evergreen was everywhere in the house. The decorations of delicate glass and crystal hanging ornaments were brought from the attic storage area and carefully unwrapped. These were placed in strategic places in the entrance hall, living and seating areas, and the dining room. The entire house took on an aura of beauty and change for the festival season. Mimi made her special candies and sweet cakes, and Ange was with her nearly every minute attempting to acquire her secrets.

"Angelette, I can hardly breathe with you this close. And, child, you can't possibly write all of this down. Most of what I know is locked up in my brains. I never try to remember all of it. I just do these things from habit. You know, a spec of this and a pinch of that. You will just have to watch, and I will try to explain, but Lord knows, you ask too many questions. Remember that brainless parrot the general brought home one time? He ranted all of the time. Well, take heed."

"Oh, Mimi, I don't want to be a bother, but I do want to learn your secrets of cooking. Henri will be so pleased one day. He does say you are the best cook in the whole world. If I could just come close to your methods, I know he would be happy."

"Child, you really do have your eyes set for him, don't you? I have never seen such young ones so involved in the old people things of this world. Why, it's almost scary to watch you two cooing like pigeons in the church square."

This year, the troops with families in or near Paris were given a one-week leave but advised to be alert for a recall at any time. The troops remaining on post were treated to short leaves into Paris, no duty except on urgent demand, and a feast for kings from the kitchens. The general said he would probably get more rest at the camp than at home, but home was where one's heart is during this season. Henri would rather be home than anywhere else in the world. This was his home now with a father, mother, brother, and sister. These people had accepted him as one of their own.

Michael and Henri met as often as they could. The Musique Corps was all the way on the other side of the huge encampment. Michael had to ask permission to visit Henri's area. Henri was, more or less, his own boss. As long as his duties were not neglected, he could steal over to Michael's area for a couple of hours. Henri invited Michael to the de Chabot's for Christmas, but Michael declined. He said that he couldn't possibly make it home and back in a week, and besides, some of the other fellows had planned a weeklong party complete with easy ladies lined up. He might drop by, but don't count on him. He asked Henri to try to make at least one of the festivities.

"Hell, old friend, maybe the ladies could teach you a few new 'procedures' to show Ange when you do ask the question. You aren't wise to the world with ladies that I know of, or are you?" He laughed.

Henri took a friendly poke at him and said he would have to think about it, but please come if he could.

At any rate, please save the detailed battle stories of the ladies for him. That should be "procedure" enough.

The emperor scheduled a special dinner for members of his court and staff. The general and the entire family were to attend. It promised to be a gala affair. The officers and men of the staff would be in their finest dress. Henri had to go to the tailor and be fitted with a new dress uniform. Madame went with him and advised the tailor that Henri's uniform must be modeled after the general's dress uniform with the same gold piping and braid and the same regimental insignia with the addition of a dragoon badge.

The smart uniform consisted of tight-fitting white pants, white shirt, with a black jacket with matching gold epaulettes on each shoulder. A smart black hat similar to the one worn by the emperor with an almost fernlike white feather completed the uniform. Henri went back for the first fitting two days later and was very pleasantly surprised at the fit and cut of the uniform. Ange went with him to his fitting, as she had to pick up her new dress, and gasped at him in his uniform.

"Henri!" she exclaimed. "I almost did not recognize you. You look like someone from a fairy tale."

"Ha, you must mean the ugly troll living under the bridge. Come on, let me see you in your new dress." Ange went into the fitting room and returned.

"Mon Petite Désordre, you take my breath away. It is perfect for you."

Ange had a deep scarlet full-bodice dress with a more than usual deep cleavage, revealing her ample budding young lady's figure. Around the bosom area was just a hint of fine white feathery lace with matching lace at each sleeve cuff and around the collar. She stood before the floor-length mirror and, turning, said, "Of course, it is plain for now, but with all of the accessories, it will do fine. I think if I ask really nice and say please, Momma might let me wear her rubies."

Henri said, "It is beautiful. I can't wait to see the completed you in it."

They took her dress in a large package and started for home. As they were passing Notre Dame, Ange asked if they could go in for a short time and offer a prayer. They did and knelt together slightly touching arms and were completely at peace with the world.

On the evening of the emperor's banquet, the entire house was a mayhem of activity. The banquet would start promptly at six. It was a total disgrace to arrive late. It would be better to offer some lame excuse and not go at all than to have everyone stare at a late arrival. The general was hurrying everyone, as usual.

When Henri came out in his uniform, everyone remarked about the welcome change from his old everyday one. With his medals, sabre, and rank, he looked the complete part as a young officer on the rise.

Madame had a deep blue velvet dress much the same cut as Ange's with the white lace at the same places as Ange's. With her diamond necklace, earrings, and matching diamonds in her carefully coiffured hair, she was a complete complement to the general.

Ange glided down the stairs, and Henri gasped in wonderment. Her scarlet dress, dark hair falling over her shoulders, dark exciting eyes, and now with the ensemble complete with the borrowed ruby accessories, she was indeed beautiful. All he could do was stare until the general hurrying everyone out of the door broke the magical spell.

Jean was on leave from the école and did not want to attend this evening. They mounted the carriage and drove the distance across Paris to the palace. The formal guard unit saluted as they entered the main drive and stepped out of the carriage. It was cold with a swirling fog this evening. As they entered the huge main entrance hall, servants took their great coats, capes, and shawls.

"What a dreadful evening for a party," remarked Madame.

"But, my sweet, it is not raining indoors," said the general. "Come, love, a little mist never hurts anyone." He whispered further in her ear, "Ha, merde floats, you know, but you are sugar and would melt."

She whispered back, "Andre, you need to watch your wine and tongue. I sense a scene coming."

The Tuileries Palace, joined to the Louvre on the southeast corner, was a blaze of lights. The soft strains of music drifted out to meet arriving guests. More were arriving by this time, and they entered the line to be announced to Napoleon and the new empress.

They were standing together greeting the guests. Marie Louise was a smallish blonde woman of slight build and very evidently large with child. Napoleon was, as usual, his charming self with his air of complete confidence. As they were announced, one by one, they bowed and offered greetings. Marie Louise replied to all with a warm smile and exact French with just a slight hint of Austrian accent. When Henri bowed before Napoleon, he was greeted with a warm smile and a hand on the shoulder.

"Well, my young friend, you look splendid this evening, and your lady is more charming than ever. My dear, please let me present my empress, Marie Louise, Princess of Austria. And this is Lieutenant Henri Devreney and his lady, Angelette de Chabot. With the permission of my general de Chabot, would you and Angelette join us at the head of the table this evening? I would like to show off one of my newest and most promising officers."

"Excellency, it would be our privilege and honor."

"We will be finished with this greeting line soon. Come then as dinner is announced. I am famished."

As they waited for the announcement of dinner, the general said, "Well now, we will be celebrities this evening. And at a personal invitation from His Excellency. Savor the moment, my children. This does not happen often in the lives of us commoners. You will both be the envy of Paris tonight."

With the announcement of dinner, Henri and Ange made their way to the head of the table. Napoleon and Marie Louise greeted them. As the royal couple was seated, the rest of the guests followed suit. Henri was seated at the right of Napoleon and Ange to the left of Marie Louise, and the small talk started immediately between the four. Napoleon inquired how Henri was becoming accustomed to life as a new officer and things of a military nature. Marie Louise and Ange talked mostly of lady things and, of course, the baby soon due in the spring. The talk grew less formal by the minute, and before long all were very comfortable and laughing at the witty jokes of Napoleon. They were not totally aware that all eyes at the long table were on them during the evening. There was much whispering and wonderment at this young officer and how well he carried himself in such royal company. Ange was a delight and a complete complement to this handsome pair. Her manner was flawless. Not too haughty and certainly not silly. Her sweet tinkling laugh was captivating.

Madame whispered to the general, "Oh, Andre, I wish I could capture this moment in a portrait forever. I am so proud. They look so wonderful and so completely at ease among royalty. I wonder when we shall have to make a 'special announcement'?"

The general whispered back, "Within the next year or so I am sure, chéri. Probably as soon as he gains another rank. I will look forward to that day and gain another fine son. I am more impressed with him each day. He is certain to have a brilliant future. He is so positive and never seems to play the fool. The recent reports I have seen show him respected among his troops and peers. Ah, I see we are having the famous roast duck tonight. I hope they give me an ample portion. I will probably raid Mimi's cupboard later anyway."

At the end of the long many-course formal dinner, Napoleon rose and asked the guests to please excuse him and the empress. The days getting closer to her birth were taxing and exhausting, and the doctors had advised for her to get as much rest as possible. There were further refreshments, cigars, and music in the great hall next to the dining room for those who chose to stay; and please do so.

Napoleon put his hand on Henri's shoulder and said, "Merci for such charming company this evening. It has been my pleasure to visit with you. Please do maintain a contact and let me know if I may ever do anything for you."

"You already have, Your Excellency. I owe you so much."

Marie Louise hugged Ange and said, "Oh please come visit me soon. We are nearly the same age and have much in common. I miss talking to those of my own age and one who can have excellent discussions without the drama of politics. This palace is filled with serious and old people in an ever-intense mood. My husband and I joke in private, but a ruler hardly ever has the privilege of appearing jolly or showing a sign of weakness. My parents are the same at home. Always so serious."

"I do promise to visit and soon. I have so enjoyed the evening and the delightful company."

As soon as Napoleon and the empress departed for their private chambers, the general said he was going to get several of the emperor's fine cigars and a glass of wine, maybe several; and then they could depart for an early trip home.

"Come, Sous-Lieutenant Celebrity, let us do our honorable duty and mingle with the common folk. And, Henri, I know you don't smoke, but please put several cigars in your pocket for me."

"Oui, monsieur."

As the two went into the great hall, Madame remarked to Ange, "I did not realize until this moment how those two are that much alike. It is almost like going back twenty years with Andre. Why, they even walk much alike. I wonder if they teach that swagger in military école. I must ask Jean."

"Momma, I have noticed certain things much alike in Poppa and Henri too," said Ange. "Maybe that is why I love him so."

The general and Henri soon returned; and as they were preparing to leave, they were greeted by Jean-Claude Ridoux, his parents, and Lydie.

"Henri, you *chien* (dog), you are the envy of us all this evening. How much did you have to pay to be seated in royal company? And, Ange, you have grown so much in these months, I barely recognized you. Please let me present my parents, Monsieur and Madame Ridoux, and I know you have already met my fiancée, Lydie."

"Oui, we know your parents," said the general. "Gaston, how have you been, and how are things with staff?"

"Fine, fine, Andre. Though I must admit the constant rumors concerning Russia do wrinkle brows."

"Oui, Gaston, to us all. I hope that huge bear sleeps forever and we do not rattle his cage. We were just about to depart for home and have an early evening. Would you care to visit for drinks?"

"Oh no, Andre, merci. We are about to do the same. The evening is so dreary."

Ange and Lydie were chatting away. Lydie said the wedding had been given a formal date of Avril 15, and the de Chabot family would be receiving a formal invitation. Lydie would contact Ange in the weeks just after the New Year about being a member of the wedding party.

As they waited for their carriage, Ange mentioned that Lydie was going to ask her to be a member of her wedding party and that she had replied oui. But Lydie would have to return the honor for her.

"Oh, and when might this be?" inquired the general.

"I wonder too. It would be good of her to let me in these things," remarked Henri. The general roared with laughter as they mounted the carriage. Madame made a feeble attempt to scold him, but she knew this would be impossible. Besides, he had had ample glasses of wine. Ange told him that they would ask permission in due time, and Henri just sat in embarrassed silence. The general made a comment about the size of the empress's midriff and her imposing birth.

"Le Patron has done himself proud this time. Why, with her size and at this time in her pregnancy, there must be an entire litter of tiny emperors in there."

"Andre! How can you say such a thing? The poor girl must be entirely miserable in her condition."

"I agree, Momma, she is miserable and very lonesome and homesick. I promised to visit her in the coming weeks. I hope I can," remarked Ange.

The general added, "There is a loneliness about her and yet a sadness too. She is constantly being compared to Josephine, and there is just no comparison. While Marie Louise may be a fine lady in her own right, she is certainly not a Josephine. Napoleon may have a successor to his throne, but there was still a tremendous void with an empress."

When they arrived home, the general and Madame went to their room and left Ange and Henri to enjoy the fire and quiet in the sitting room.

As they sat enjoying the quiet and a final glass of wine, Henri finally said, "With all of this talk of marriage, perhaps we do need to make a more serious approach to it. I guess we could never be more serious than we are now. I think I have always known from the first time I saw you. It still amazes me how such a tiny and cute little girl completely captured my heart. You know, maybe you are destined to be a great lady, and it is mine to provide for you. I do need to make more rank to care for a family though. And especially to care for you with what you have now. My pay now is so little we would have to rent your father's chicken house."

"Henri, you know I don't care about those things. All I want is to be with you, and as far as a great lady, great ladies always go with great men."

"Oh, I know, Ange, but all joking aside, the time would be very short when both of us would realize we cannot exist on love alone. And what about children? Who pays for them? It is so intimidating."

"We will talk more about this when you do get higher rank then, but please do all you can to rush things along. And another thing, no eyes for any other. I saw you looking at Lydie's bosom."

"One could not help but look. It almost fell out in front of me. And oui, oui, my impatient Petite Désordre, I will try harder, but rank is earned and given according to seniority. You know that being a general's daughter. He didn't get his overnight."

They did talk more that night, and as they sat holding hands, they both had the feeling that their world was nearly complete.

Christmas was much the same as the previous ones. The family attended Notre Dame and endured the long ceremonious Mass at midnight. They returned to Mimi's fine feast, and as usual, the men ate too much and groaned and complained the rest of the night. After the gift exchange, the general announced that this year, his and Madame's gift to Henri was a special appointment to the regimental arms depot to have his sabre properly named and engraved. Had he chosen, as tradition dictated, a name for his best military friend?

"Oui, monsieur, I have. I thought a long time for a proper name and have chosen 'Myosotis Gardien Ange' (Forget me not Guardian Angel)."

"How appropriate. Do I detect or sense the possibility that you may be using my daughter's name in your cause for protection?"

"Oui, monsieur, I believe you may, and could this request be with your blessing?"

"Consider it with my complete blessing, lad. Bring your sabre, and we will make a visit this week. First, however, I feel we need to share this moment."

The general roared for Ange. She came hurrying into the sitting room. Madame and Mimi came in too to see what the fuss was about this time.

"Ange, this sous-lieutenant in the Grande Armée of France has just requested my permission to name his sabre in your honor. You must accept this also as this honored sabre will one day be carried into battle. It will, no doubt, have to carve a throat or two. What say you, daughter of mine? Do you think a sous-lieutenant is worthy of this honor from the daughter of a general?"

"Oh, Poppa, you know very well this honor is very special for me. This will mean I will go into battle at his side and hopefully protect him. Monsieur Sous-Lieutenant, I am deeply honored and will always do as I can to protect you."

"Ange, I never could get the best of you. That was perfectly stated. Come, lad, let us go and plan this before I get into real trouble with the master of the house. She is glaring at me already." He reached over and gave Madame one of his famous bear hugs.

During the trip to the arms depot the next week, Henri asked the general if he might make a small request. "Monsieur, I am not in the habit of making requests and know I must go through official channels, but please guide me in the proper direction with this one."

"Oui, my boy, feel free to ask me anything. You know we share much in private that never leaves the two of us. What is it?"

"Monsieur, I have a personal friend who has been with me since drummer school and through two campaigns. He is also a gifted horseman. He is still in the Musique Corps, and I think he may be more valuable in the dragoons. He doesn't know about this and has never requested a favor of me, but if this may be considered, I am certain he will be an asset to our troop."

"If you will write his name for me when we return home, I will take the matter into consideration. The dragoons are the future of this Armée, highly mobile and the protectors of the infantry and artillery. If he is worth the flour in his bread, we can use him."

"Merci, monsieur, I don't think you will regret this."

Three weeks later, Michael reported for duty with the dragoons. He was assigned to the Third Section under Lieutenant Richard's command. As soon as he was settled, he immediately made a point of looking up Henri.

"You dog, did you have anything to do with my transfer from the Musique Corps to here? I was all settled in for a nice tour of walking and carrying that damn drum for the rest of my life when my world has come upset."

"Well, if you want to follow the drum, we can see to a transfer back."

"Not on either of our lives, my fine friend. I would have been here sooner, but I had to pass certain horse-qualifying tests first. I was the envy of all in the drum section when my orders came through. I had no idea. It was a complete and very pleasant surprise. How did you do it?"

"We are in need of good riders, and I thought it was a complete waste of talent for you to pound a drum. I know how it is to walk for miles when one can ride at least some of the time. And besides, pistols and sabres are much easier to maneuver than that damn drum."

"Henri, all joking aside, I am forever in your debt for this. I won't betray your trust."

"I have always known that, Michael, but enough of this girl talk. Come on, let's go over to the mess area and see if we can steal a sweet cake and mug of coffee."

Ange was true to her word and sent a note to Marie Louise during the next two weeks requesting for an appointment to visit. A reply messenger and note came the very next day stating a visit would be most welcome, and she couldn't wait for the company. A private carriage would be sent at ten in the morning, and if this was not convenient, please advise the bearer of the note. It was arranged, and at the appointed hour, the carriage arrived at the de Chabot gates. Ange noted the mounted guards and wondered what this was about. She wasn't that special to require a mounted escort. The footman opened the carriage door. Ange was very surprised when she entered the carriage and found Marie Louise inside.

"Oh, Marie Louise, I didn't expect you to personally come for me. This is a very pleasant surprise."

"I know this is a bit out of the normal manner of things, but it is a nice day. I just couldn't wait for our visit and to get out of that dreadful old pile of stones for a while. Why don't we take a short drive before we have to go back? I have not been able to get out very often these winter months, and I am feeling better today than recently. This child in me feels like a small horse and kicks like one too."

"That must be miserable and yet so joyful at the same time. I guess one day I will find out."

"Are you and Henri very serious about marriage soon? He seems like such a nice man and evidently is destined for great things to come. Napoleon seems very impressed with him and told me the story of his courage in battle. It seems he was in battle against my father's troops, but that is a man thing and not to worry us ladies. We always sit and wait for the men to play war before coming home."

"I was so worried about him when he first came home. He almost died or at least lost his leg. Napoleon gave him a special presentation and medal. Poppa was so proud and said he might give an arm for an honor like that. But again, those are man things."

"Oui, I agree. When we get to the palace, we can have a good look through my wardrobe and jewels. You just wouldn't believe the fine things that are there. I thought I had fine things in Austria as a princess, but as an empress, one just could not believe. I am so glad you came to visit. It is so lonely there with hardly anyone my age. I used to cry fairly often when I first arrived for home and friends in Austria. This place was and still is so strange. Now with me so huge with this child, the misery is compounded. All I can do now is waddle like an old goose. My mother and her lady will be arriving in the next few weeks for the birth. Ange, promise you will come to visit then and meet my mother."

The visit, the first of many over the next several months, went extremely well; and the two became very close friends. They shared much in common and chatted away for hours. During one such visit to the palace, Napoleon made a short appearance and inquired about Henri. Napoleon had, evidently, been reviewing personnel reports forwarded on his progress. He did not say as much, but having so many men under his command, it seemed he knew a lot of just this one. Ange promised herself not to reveal this to Henri, but she would secretly ask Poppa.

When Henri came home the following weekend, Ange was still bubbling with excitement about her first personal visit to the palace and the empress. During this first visit, Marie Louise said Napoleon was most often gone to one meeting or another.

"Well, he must have been available at least once. I agree with the general. There must be an entire litter in her belly."

"Oh, Henri, you men are dreadful. She has been very nice to me and thinks highly of you. I will share a very deep secret, but you must swear secrecy."

"All right, I swear, and now what is this deep secret?"

"Marie Louise confided in me that she has had several lovers before her marriage to Napoleon. She further told me that I should possibly test the waters too before I got married. I would never do it, of course. She said it makes one more experienced in lovemaking."

"Chéri, you know, she may have something there. We could gain a wealth of experience. Perhaps after the birth, I could call on her and maybe get some knowledge."

"Henri! That is just too dreadful and not in the very least funny. I will never understand you men."

"All right, all right. Don't get mad at me. I forgot my lady tiger has such sharp claws. I promise not to even think about it anymore. Give me a quick kiss before Madame or Mimi comes in here. Ange, with all of this talk of Marie Louise, perhaps we could arrange a visit to Josephine. She asked sometime back if we could visit and bring Madame."

"Henri, I know you are just changing the course of this conversation, but oui, I do agree. A visit to Josephine would be nice and long past due."

When the general arrived home for the weekend, Madame said, "Ange had proposed the idea of a visit to Josephine. With the politics of the court and the times, do you think such a visit would be wise?"

"Of course, my dear, and please do give Josephine my kindest regards. We are old friends, and to me, she will always be the first lady of France. No need, of course, to caution you to be very discreet about any relationship with our new empress. The tongues of her court and the gossips of Paris wag enough now with rumors and discontent. I am certain Josephine hears the latest news and gossip nearly before it is spoken, but any further additions should not come from the de Chabot house. Oh, and please advise Ange too. I know she is wise to politics, but sometimes the very slightest slip of the tongue can cause no end of gossip. She has been visiting the new empress and does not need to carry any tales of Marie Louise to Josephine."

Henri wrote a quick note to Josephine, and in the next two weeks, a messenger arrived at the de Chabot house. He had an invitation written personally in Josephine's fine hand. The appointed time for Henri, Madame, and Ange to visit Josephine was 11:00 on Samedi (Saturday) morning of the next week. Madame was requested if she could please bring some of Mimi's delightful special tea. Madame wrote a quick reply of acceptance and gave it to the messenger.

When Henri arrived home late on Vendredi evening, he was advised that he would not be able to sleep late in the morning. They would have to travel about 7:00 AM for the nearly two-hour travel time to Malmaison. Although Malmaison Château was only approximately sixteen kilometers from Paris, Madame never liked to travel fast and hated the bumpy ride of fast speed. The roads to that part of France were forever bumpy and rutty. The general came home later in the evening after his usual late "staff" meeting and was asked if he would care to attend.

"Oh, indeed not, mon amour. It is not in my suit to attend ladies' visits and drink tea and eat small patisseries. I do not envy poor Henri in this. Please give Josephine my love and regards, and make up some excuse for me. You know what to say. Besides, if any gossip to the contrary comes of this, we can always say I resisted your going and you had the servants tie me to the bed with ropes and hide my clothes."

"You old ogre, you always have a way of doing just what you want."

"Oui, chéri, that is my privilege of rank."

The next morning, there was the usual activity of everyone rushing around getting ready. Henri was examining his budding mustache in the hall mirror, and the general caught him.

"Well, I can see a little more now than just fuzz under your nose. Remember though, lad, hair on the upper lip does not make the man."

"I know, monsieur, and in all reality, I am thinking of just shaving the damn thing off. I get teased with or without one. And it does itch."

"Don't take affront, lad, I was only teasing. I was always naturally hairy and had no problem. You, on the other hand, are not hairy, and that is probably a blessing. Body hair does have disadvantages. Why, in the summer months in the field with the heat and dust, I nearly go mad with itching and scratching. And God forbid when I contact the damn little body bugs."

"I understand, monsieur, but I wish I could get this growth at least partially started."

The carriage came to the front of the house for departure, and as they climbed in, Madame remarked, "What a lovely day for this visit. It is as if God has planned this day for us."

Indeed, it was a lovely day. The early sun was still warming the earth, and only slight white cumulus clouds were like cotton balls on the horizon toward the sea. It was early spring, but already trees and flowers were showing signs of new growth. The god of spring was slowly winning the eternal battle over the god of winter. As they approached the outskirts of Paris, the odors of the fields were fresh and a pleasant change over the musty odors of the city. Freshly plowed fields have a fragrance like no other.

Henri breathed deeply, saying, "Oh, this morning brings very pleasant memories. I love the smells of the earth, fields, animals, and everything about the spring season. It has to be my favorite."

"Mine too," agreed Ange. "If only we could have spring forever and not the hot summer and cold winter."

"I guess God had all of these things in His master plan for us earthlings."

They arrived at the official residence of Josephine, the Château Malmaison. It was an imposing building three stories tall, with a lovely blue slate roof. It was painted in a light cream with blue accent on the walls and shutters to match the color of the roof. Madame said this château was very special to Josephine, and she had taken a badly dilapidated structure and created a jewel box over the years. It was a place of beauty with the well-kept lawns and gardens. A sparkling gem in the midst of a muddy pond, as Napoleon had once described it.

This had once been the official residence of both Napoleon and Josephine, and no expense had been spared in lavish redecorating. Napoleon hired Charles Percier and Pierre Fontaine, the two most fashionable architects of the day, for the task of complete redecoration. The result was an appealing blend of the classical and the warlike. The theme of ancient Rome was proposed and presented to Napoleon as reminiscent of a Caesar. Napoleon was wholeheartedly in approval, and the finished result won the approval of all. However, the distance from Paris and the size of Malmaison as compared to the Tuileries Palace demanded the move of Napoleon's official residence and business to Paris. Also, the Louvre, if required for large state functions, was just adjacent.

Both Napoleon and Josephine were enamored of the preromantic Troubadour Style of the building and further enhanced and graced by the gardens and greenhouses. The gardens became the passion of Josephine; and she scoured, requested, and often purchased seeds, seedlings, and exotics from all over the world. Some arrived on French naval ships as gifts, and some were even brought over from England, which Napoleon was hardly friendly. Josephine with her grace and charm was another story.

They rode through the grounds, which was said to be over four thousand five hundred acres of woods, ponds, wheat fields, and vineyards. Carefully placed pavilions and stone grottos were along the winding drive path to the main château. Ange said this was like going to another world. And it was. The driver parked the carriage on the large circular drive near the massive front doors. A male servant in the uniform of Josephine's personal guard opened the doors, said they were expected, and requested them to please follow him. They were escorted down a massive central hallway with mirrors, tapestries, and ornate furniture. At the entrance of large highly polished wooden doors, a bust of Napoleon on a white marble pedestal watched them as they entered a large sitting room. Even though the weather was relatively mild, a low fire glowed from the ornate white marble fireplace. Josephine rose as they entered the room.

"Oh, it is so good of you to come. It gets so lonely here with only my ladies and servants. Henri! You look so handsome in your new uniform of an officer. I do apologize I could not accept your invitation to the graduation, but I hope you understood the somewhat awkward circumstances."

"Oui, Your Majesty, and my apologies for any inconvenience of putting you in those circumstances."

"No apologies are necessary, and please do not call me Majesty. Those days are long since over. My name is Josephine, and you may address me as that."

Madame, Ange, and Henri were in the midst of a bow; and she corrected that too. "Please, we are all friends, and I am no longer in power. No bowing and groveling to this old has-been," she laughed. She hugged Madame and Ange and then Henri. "Ange, just look at you. How you have grown. I think the last time we met was possibly a carriage ride through Paris with a certain young hero."

"Oui, Maj . . . uh . . . Madame, uh . . . Josephine, I do remember. This is most difficult addressing you by your given name."

"And for me too," said Madame. "Here, Josephine, I have brought you some of Mimi's special tea."

"I gave the recipe to my chefs, and upon their lives, they cannot seem to duplicate this. I wonder what she does to it. I just may send my chef to your Mimi for special instructions."

"Henri said she spits in everything," said Ange, "but that is only a joke." They all laughed.

"Ange, you are so honest and full of life. Please come and have morning tea with me. I am not like Napoleon and have a heavy morning meal as soon as the sun rises. I much prefer a light meal in the midmorning." They talked for a short time and watched the fire die down considerably.

"Please excuse the fire on such a mild day. Remember I am from the islands, and the cold here seems to affect me more than most. The older I become, the worse the cold. It is like it settles in my very bones. I keep a shawl close by."

"Madame de Chabot, I know you have been here before; but for Ange and Henri, this is the first time. This château is known as one of the most magnificent in the world. Would you care to take a short personally guided tour? Please say oui. I adore showing off my home. I take great pride that most of the design and decorations were at my own personal request and consultation with the architects. A lot of 'just me' is in this place."

The first room had a large tent-shaped ceiling in yellow, off-white, and black. This had been Napoleon's main council room. A black and gold faux-bronze balustrade with lion's heads went around the lower part of the walls. The doors were flanked with mahogany and gilted bronze poles topped with eagles.

"This room was the showplace of Europe for Napoleon," said Josephine. The Roman theme continued throughout as they went into the salon, dining room, and library.

Josephine's bedroom was probably the most stunning of all. The mostly round room had the tentlike theme of the main council room. A circle of painted sky was at the top of the tent structure. Gilt wooden poles held up the lushly draped red silk tent structure with loops, spirals, and circles. The carpet was cream with red, gold, and blue decorations and had a pile seemingly as deep to one's knees.

"This is the softest carpet I have walked on," remarked Ange. "Would it be all right to take off my shoes and really feel it?"

Josephine laughed and said they all could try it if they wanted. Only Ange was bold enough to kick her shoes off.

"This is like walking in the clouds. I have never felt anything so soft to walk on."

The golden bed was a thing of wonder and almost too lavish to sleep on. It had been specially created with designs of swans and brimming cornucopias. The bed curtains were cream with gold border embroidery on the outside and lined with a curtain of cream with gold flowers. As in the other rooms, there was a white marble fireplace with an ornate mirror over it. A small writing desk in the corner had a lovely bouquet of roses. The visitors were stunned to silence at the magnificence.

"On such a lovely spring day, let's take a walk and tour the gardens and greenhouses.

"Are you up to the walk?"

"Oh oui," said Madame. "I have heard so much about the gardens here. We saw some of the grounds when we arrived."

"I am thrilled. Please let me get my shawl. I see you have yours, but do any of you require additional or heavier coverings?" They answered a collective no. Josephine pulled back the floor-length scarlet drapes and opened the large glass doors onto the veranda. Overlooking were the gardens below at the rear of the main château. The entire formal garden area included some three hundred acres of rolling small hills, ponds with swans, pavilions, and small grottos just as the main drive and entranceway.

"I know it is very early in spring now, but I have ordered the gardeners to plant new flowers from the hothouses. I hope the danger of a damaging frost is past. The master gardener has reported that most of the roses have survived the winter, and even so, he has an ample supply of replacements. Of all the flowers, roses are my favorite. They always remind one of the best and worst of this world. The blooms are so pleasant and not like any other in size, shape, and smell. But then they are so hardy and with thorns for protection."

They stood taking in the sight below. Tulips, hyacinths, carnations, and a wide variety of flowers were everywhere in splashes of color and coordinated completely with azaleas and flowering trees. Roses, her favorite, were in large beds. Other blooming roses were planted at intervals along the walkways. There appeared to be thousands of rose plants with blooms of every color.

"My gardeners experiment with the roses and have produced several new and variegated varieties. My passion for roses is well known, and I receive gifts of them as well as many other types from all over the world. There are many exotic plants in these gardens and hothouses."

The shrubs and bushes along the paved walkways were trimmed with exact precision.

"Oh, Madame Josephine," said Ange, "I have never seen anything so beautiful and breathtaking. Everything is so perfect. I could live here forever."

Josephine laughed and said, "I am certain you could, my dear. This place in heaven is my joy. I should not say, but Napoleon still visits here from time to time. We are still the closest of friends, and I am his confidant when he is troubled. It has always been that way. Madame de Chabot, I know that your Andre is probably the same with you. I wouldn't have it any other way. Ange, now I think it will be your turn."

"It already is my turn. Henri and I talk about almost everything."

Henri said, "Well, almost."

They strolled slowly talking among the flowers, trees, and around the small ponds. There were several geese among the flocks of swans, and they squawked loudly as they came closer. They sat for some time in Josephine's favorite pavilion overlooking a small lake and talked of a variety of lady things. Henri sat and was included, from time to time, in some small tidbits of the conversations. The general had been right in his wise overview of this visit. Evidently it was from some past experience. However, Henri was not entirely bored and was still so enthralled with Josephine and her charm. He secretly compared her to Ange at times and thought in silence how these two might compare at some future date. Henri and Ange took a small walk over to a bed of tulips to get a better look.

Josephine said to Madame, "I have watched those two since our carriage ride that day, and I cannot imagine a better match made by God. When do you think he do the serious thing and ask Andre's permission for your daughter's hand?"

"I think in another year or so when he gains more rank and pay. He is so independent and never asks for anything."

"Well, when he does and the date is set, I will certainly attend that ceremony and the devil take the gossip and stares of the political high and mighty."

After a small noon lunch, it was time to return to Paris and the real world. Their cordial hostess bade them goodbye and asked them to please visit again.

As she hugged Henri, she whispered in his ear, "Do not let this one escape you."

"I won't, Josephine, and I will never forget you."

She whispered about the same thing in Ange's ear. Ange hugged her tightly and thanked her for the visit and kind thoughts. They rode for a time in silence on the way home.

Finally Madame said, "I sense a great sadness in our Josephine. It is nearly like impending doom. She is so wise. It is no secret that what she said about Napoleon visiting is true. He still confides everything in her. She made a small mention of Russia when you were walking, and I sense a very great concern."

On Mercredi (Wednesday) Mars 20, 1811, the king of Rome, Napoleon II, was born to Napoleon and Marie Louise. A cannon signal was to be fired at the birth, twenty-one shots if a girl and one hundred if a boy. At the twenty-second shot, the populace of Paris poured into the streets with loud cheering and rejoicing. It seemed the one hundred cannon shots would resound forever. The general ordered Sections Two and Three of the dragoons for special duty at the palace.

Napoleon had notified him that his personal guard would be sufficient for the general duties around the palace, but just as an added precaution, it may be best to have additional troops nearby. Thousands of well-wishers were expected to gather around the palace hoping to get a glimpse of the child, and with certain feelings of discontent these days, one could not be too careful. The two sections of troops were advised they would be on this special assignment for at least several days and then be replaced by Sections One and Four. They immediately departed for the palace area.

When they arrived, Henri and Lieutenant Adrien Richard, the Third Section commander, reported to the commander of the Imperial Guard Unit. They were to patrol the area around the perimeter walls and surrounding neighborhoods and be on the alert for anything suspicious. The units would relieve each other for meals and rest periods, but one unit would be on duty at all times. The meals would be served in the Imperial Guard area just behind the large stables inside the palace walls. They could take their rest periods in the stables and be on ready alert should any problem arise. This was a very boring assignment, and

Henri had his troops patrol an area just to the south and along the Seine River. At least the weather was cooperating, and although some light rain fell during the second day, the rest of the assignment enjoyed the fair weather of spring.

Ange and Madame passed through Henri's area on the third day on their way to pay respects to the royal couple and the child. Henri asked Lieutenant Richard if he would assume command of both sections for an hour or so, he would escort them to pay his respects also. Henri climbed into the carriage, and they were allowed entrance through the main gates. They were announced, and the attendant went up the stairs to see if they could be received. They were immediately escorted up the huge circular stairs and taken into the chamber where Marie Louise and the child were.

The large bedchamber they entered was enormous and lavishly decorated with light blue and gold tapestry, ornate furniture with matching light blue upholstery. The carpets were of the same blue and gold and so plush they seemed nearly an ankle in depth. The large windows framed in floor-length blue drapes revealed a magnificent view of Paris and Notre Dame across the river.

"Oh, Ange, I am so glad you came. I have missed our visits, but as you can see, I have been busy. Please do come closer and sit on the bed with me. Madame de Chabot and Henri, it is so good of you to come. It is very nice to see you again. My husband is in a lengthy staff meeting and cannot receive you and extends his apologies. May I present my mother, Maria Theresa, Empress of Austria? My father could not attend, but we shall travel to Austria at midsummer when the weather is more stable and my son is a bit older."

"I am very pleased to meet you, Your Highness. Your daughter is a delight," said Madame, bowing with respect.

Henri also bowed and said, "Your Highness, our meeting is my honor."

"Mother, this is Henri, nearly betrothed to Ange and one whom I understand fought so gallantly against Father's troops some years ago." Henri blushed. Would he never live to see this tale go away?

"Indeed, but you appear so young to have been in battle," replied the empress in almost-flawless French.

"I was a boy in the drummer corps during those times, Your Highness."

"Let me show off my grandson. He has already been given the title of king of Rome. So tiny for such a large title. His father has given him the short name of l'Aiglon, the Eaglet. How he deduced that name, I shall never understand other than the eaglet you see perched on the child's cradle."

Napoleon Francis Joseph Charles Bonaparte, the two-day-old son and heir to the throne of France, was asleep in a magnificent and very ornate cradle specially created by personal artists to Napoleon. It was gold gilt with red velvet interior trim. An eaglet was cast on the foot overlooking the child below. The headpiece was a delicate angel holding a crown of stars from which draped gold-colored satin curtains for privacy. The child stirred slightly and moved his tiny hands as if waving at the visitors.

"Oh, he is so beautiful," said Ange, rushing back to hug Marie Louise. "I am so happy for you."

"Oui, and thank God the ordeal is over." She whispered to Ange, "One cannot have a concept of what it is to attempt to pass a small horse. I hope my destiny is fulfilled, and may I never go through this again. You can have the next one for me." The visit lasted nearly half an hour, and then the way was made for the next succession of visitors.

"Marie Louise, you appear tired, and you must rest," reminded her mother. "It is nearing the child's feeding time also."

Marie Louise took Ange's arm. "Ange, please, you must come back and visit. I have so much to tell you about all of this."

"Oui, I promise to return as soon as all of the festivities and visitors settle down."

They left and returned to the waiting carriage. As they left, Henri remarked, "I have never seen so much splendor lavished before."

Madame said, "Henri, that child is already a king and your future ruler. Of course, he deserves such things and ceremony considering his state."

"I realize that, madame. It is just that he will probably never know about all of this. I wonder if he will ever care later."

17

Celebrations

The entire remainder of Mars was filled with ceremonies centered around the birth of Napoleon II. Henri had been correct that this child would never be aware of any of this pomp in his honor. Maybe at a later date, but certainly not now. He slept through most of it. The ceremonies were for the adults and to satisfy egos and tradition. The entire dragoon troop was called upon several times to parade for this ceremony or that. Each event meant a complete new cleaning and polishing of everything. The troops grumbled at each event, saying over and over it would be easier to fight a major campaign than go through this. Finally in early Avril, the events slowed, and things seemed to settle to normal once more.

In early Avril, preparations were already under way for Jean-Claude and Lydie's wedding. Ange would be one of Lydie's ladies in attendance and would be escorted by Jean-Claude's cousin. Lydie told Ange they had to plan it this way because of family. Jean-Claude had a large family requiring more to honor while her family was relatively small. There were just too many boys for the small amount of girls. She had wanted Henri to escort Ange, but they were not certain if he would have the duty that weekend. This was not her doing, and she wanted Ange to know it.

"Oh, Lydie, it doesn't matter, and it is only for an hour or so. Besides, it may do Henri some good to see me walking on the arm of another."

"Or it may chase him away. Be careful, Ange."

"Henri is not jealous by nature, and I am certain he will not take this to heart."

When Ange told Henri of this arrangement, he said, "Never fear, chéri, I shall watch your every movement, and if this cousin does so much as even smile at you, I will carve out his heart and eat it."

"Henri! How horrible! Surely, you are joking! You know all of this will be very proper and in the holy church."

Henri laughed and said, "And other reasons to love you, chéri. You are always so honest with life. Of course I would never cause a scene and humiliate you and our family. This will be an adult event. Come a little closer, mon chéri. We could practice your father's famous bear hugs."

When Jean-Claude heard of the arrangements, he contacted Lydie and both mothers at once.

"Please let it be known that Henri is one of my close associates and a war hero. I insist he do us the honor of escorting Ange. Cousin Gerrard can go get guillotined! He has bad breath anyway, and he has never been close to our family." And so it was arranged.

Henri decided to have a bit of fun over this and told Ange when he found out about her and another man, he talked to Jean-Claude and told him about the heart-eating event that would surely happen. Then they both laughed so hard they had to sit down on the front steps of the house.

"I am glad that is settled," said Ange. "I would never kiss you again with someone else's blood on your lips."

On the morning of the wedding, a large group gathered in front of Lydie's house nearly two blocks from Notre Dame. It was customary for the groom to call on his bride at her residence and escort her to the place of the wedding. It was a lovely Avril day, balmy pleasant weather, new growth on the trees, flowers everywhere, and a perfect blue sky with not a dark cloud to be seen.

"Today will be perfect," Jean-Claude whispered to her.

Lydie was dressed in an elegant pale blue gown. Tiny white satin bows and pearls adorned the dress and train. She had gold and diamond accessories in her hair. Jean-Claude was dressed in his finest military uniform, complete with medals and sabre.

As these were people of station, the mayor of Paris held the first official ceremony on the large front porch. This was the civil ceremony, the only legal one, and the religious ceremony would follow at the church. The mayor read the article from the French Constitution that detailed the responsibilities and duties of the bride and groom, then he asked them individually if they accepted each other in marriage. The reply, of course, was oui. Bride, groom, both sets of parents, and four witnesses were asked to sign the document on a little table covered with white satin and covered with tiny bows of light blue. The colors chosen for the theme, white and blue, had significance, white symbolizing joy and blue purity. The entire civil ceremony had taken less than fifteen minutes. Now the procession to the church began to form. Musicians playing violins led followed by Lydie and her parents, and then Jean-Claude and his parents. The ladies and their escorts followed and finally the guests in number of approximately five hundred.

Henri, dressed in his uniform, presented a striking figure with his sabre and medals polished and flashing in the sunlight. Ange and all of the twelve attendants were dressed in powder blue dresses with soft white accessories and diamond necklace and earrings. The procession was one of splendor and hope for the future. Napoleon was the guest of honor and rode in the only open-top carriage in the procession with Empress Marie Louise. Along the way, children blocked the procession with white ribbons across their path. Lydie was handed a pair of scissors, and as she cut the ribbons, the children were offered small baskets of sweet cakes. This was custom symbolic of obstacles in life the couple would face and would have to overcome together. The emperor and empress would not attend the formal ceremony. They left the procession at the church after offering congratulations. Marie Louise hugged Lydie, Ange, and several of the attendants she knew.

Marie Louise whispered to Ange, "Ange, Henri is so striking, and you are so beautiful today. Don't ever let him get away, and please dance some for me. You still owe me a visit."

Notre Dame was decorated in such grandeur and rivaled even Easter and Christmas. Flowers and green tree branches were everywhere. White satin bows were on the forward pews. A white cloth stretched down the main aisle from the huge wooden doors to the main altar.

As they entered the church, Jean-Claude and Lydie clasped hands as they approached the altar. The priest, flanked by altar servers, was waiting. As Jean-Claude and Lydie knelt on a special padded bench covered in white satin, Henri slowly looked around at certain things and made mental notes for explanations later. A fragrant odor wafted in the immediate area around the altar. Finally Henri saw the source as blossoms from orange trees. Then he remembered that Lydie was carrying a small bouquet of the same blossoms. He had seen them many times in the gardens at home. Here the fragrant white blooms added a very special touch. The two were offered Holy Communion, and the entire congregation of attendants and guests followed suit.

As Henri and Ange stood side by side and took their communion and blessing, Ange squeezed Henri's arm in a silent communication that both instantly understood. Just before the final blessing, both mothers came forward and held a white silk veil over the heads of the newlyweds. This was a *carre* and, according to custom, is to prevent malice from descending on the couple.

The veil was to be saved and used for the same purpose at the baptism of their newborn child. And at last the final blessing by the priest. Jean-Claude kissed Lydie, and they started back down the aisle. Henri and Ange fell into the procession directly behind the newly married couple. The stress of formal ceremony was gone now, and all were laughing and teasing. As they went out of the doors and onto the main steps, they were showered with rice and wheat.

The wedding reception was to be held in a large hall just on the edge of the main church square. The hall too was decorated with flowers, branches, and orange blossoms. A huge *la piece monte* or wedding cake was on a special table covered in white cloth and surrounded by orange blossoms. Henri thought to himself, *There would be a precious small orange crop this year after this.*

Lydie stood on one side of the table and Jean-Claude on the other. The idea was to see if they could lean over the cake and kiss without touching the cake. This would symbolize a lifetime of prosperity. They did achieve the kiss without touching the cake, but did so with the assistance of several holding them. The cake was a masterpiece of small cream-filled pastry puffs piled in a pyramid and covered in a caramel glaze and spun sugar. Lydie's mother presented a beautiful crystal cup with two handles in the shape of hearts. This was the *la coup de mariage* and a treasured family heirloom. The couple filled it with wine and toasted each other several times under the watchful eye of her mother.

"Jean-Claude, Lydie, be very careful with this cup. It has been in our family for many years."

The attendants were allowed to toast each other and the newlyweds with the cup. Henri held the cup to Ange's lips and saw a look in her eyes he had not seen before. They were so full of love in this moment. It completely captivated him, and he quickly glanced away before anyone else saw him making a staring fool of himself. Almost everyone, that is!

Madame, standing just beside and behind him, silently smiled and tucked the moment with all of the rest in her heart. No doubt about these two. They were adults and more than ready to pledge vows. She quickly turned to Andre who was busy with wine and laughter. Men didn't notice much of these things anyway. Andre, although a love, had never been the romantic she was.

Toward the end of the reception when nearly everyone was laughing and filled with good wine, Jean-Claude whispered something to Lydie. She smiled and pulled her dress up just high enough to expose a white garter with tiny white and blue flowers. Jean-Claude took it off, and the two of them presented it to Henri and Ange. Everyone knew this meaning, and Madame and the general stood back with approval and smiles. With the garter off, a loud applause filled the hall. This signaled the end of the reception for the newly married couple. They left, and some of the other guests began to leave. Still, others began to dance and drink in earnest. It would be a long night for some. Henri asked Ange if she wanted to stay for a while, and Madame answered that it may be best if they all went home together.

The general said, "I agree. We had better keep a closer eye on them now. Angelette has that damn garter." Ange and Henri blushed and smiled. Why fight it?

The general said, "Come. We can walk home from here. It is such a short distance and much too beautiful an afternoon to ride in a stuffy old carriage.

A good walk will help digest some of the food and wine. I have eaten too much again."

Ange took off her shoes and stockings, and Madame said, "Angelette, that is so unlike a lady to bare her feet in public. Only peasant girls go about in their bare feet."

"Oh, Momma, we are so near home. No one will notice. My feet hurt in these new shoes."

Her long dress nearly hid her feet anyway as they walked the two blocks home. It had been a wonderful wedding and a fine day. Henri remarked that there had been many orange blossoms, and while the smell was very pleasant, there would be many oranges not made this year.

Madame said, "But, Henri, it was necessary and very traditional. The orange blossom represents fertility and prosperity." Henri blushed and said nothing.

He did whisper to Ange, "Poor Jean-Claude, if all of these blossoms did work, he would have his own little Armée."

When they arrived home, the general and Madame went directly to their room, leaving Henri and Ange in the sitting room.

"Ange, I am supposed to meet some fellows for *le charivari* (wedding night pranks). I won't be very late. Will you wait for me?"

"Oui, of course I will. What pranks will be for tonight?"

"We are going to hide behind the drapes in their bedchamber and watch a master lover at work and maybe learn a few new things."

"Henri! You wouldn't dare. That is not a prank. That is so immoral and so very vulgar."

He laughed and said there was not a prank scheduled for tonight as no one knew where the newlyweds were going. Jean-Claude had told him they were going to a very small and discreet inn just out of Paris. He had rented the entire inn for two days. Henri must remember this when his time came and obtain the name of this inn. He had seen the wedding night pranks before, and sometimes they did get out of hand especially with members of the Armée. After talking for a short time, they went to bed. It had been a long, tiring, and wine-filled day.

Avril, Mai, and on into Juin. The year was flying by and now with successions of intense training. The four groups of dragoons in Henri's battalion were training particularly hard. Capitaine LaBauve was particularly keen with long marches of twenty kilometers out and back in one day. Dragoons did not ride the entire way as Henri had thought when first entering the Armée. Most of the time, they walked at a fast pace, saving their horses for battle. They were expressly taught the methods and care of their animals with water, rations, checking the hooves, and the many other things they must know. A trooper who lost his animal was lost himself and no longer useful to the troop. Every trooper was expendable.

Napoleon and all of his staff recognized the extreme importance of preparedness, and all units of the Grande Armée toiled at perfection.

As Napoleon had been quoted many times, "The word 'impossible' is not in my vocabulary." They were all experienced believers that if the troops were well trained and cared for, the Armée would function like a fine tightly wound watch.

Various units from different regiments were assigned special details at times. Officers knew this also helped in keeping the troops active and alert. Henri's unit was attached to Napoleon's personal guard at the palace for a monthlong period. It was good duty and allowed the troopers to enjoy the good quarters and food of the personal guard. They could enjoy getting out of "tent city" and the better food than the field kitchens. They were to have passes into the city every weekend, and Henri could go home. Just after their second week of duty, Capitaine LaBauve made a special visit to the palace.

He told Henri this visit was to sample the food and see if it was adequate fare for his troopers. He laughed and said the true nature of his visit was to see Henri on a personal matter.

"Sous-Lieutenant, you have been promoted to full *chevalier* (lieutenant). Two of you, you and Basile Normand, have been brought up to your proper rank as section commanders. Congratulations, and I would like to personally commend you."

"Merci, merci, monsieur. I appreciate this." He couldn't wait to get home and share the news with Ange. He still could not afford a wife, but perhaps with the next rank to capitaine and careful management of funds, it could be a consideration if the chicken house was still for rent.

After duty on Friday, Henri hurried home. He left on foot as the de Chabot home was only about three kilometers from the palace, and he wouldn't be bothered with Satan over the weekend. Satan could stay in the stables with the personal guard horses. He must have hurried too much. When he arrived, he was drenched in sweat.

Ange met him in the hall and said after a push-back kiss, "Henri, you smell terrible. Please go wash before this goes any further."

"But I have news, excellent news," he tried to tell her. Madame came down the stairs and confirmed Ange's remarks about an offensive odor. So a deflated Henri went off to the trough in the back to make himself presentable.

"Wait, Henri. I will go with you," said Ange.

"No, you will not, young lady. He will have to at least partially disrobe. I will, with a bit of luck, see that you are a lady before my passing," said Madame.

"But, Momma, I have seen Henri without a shirt many times before."

"That is just my point. Please wait until he finishes his wash, and please put on shoes or at least stockings. You know about bare feet. You will be the death of me yet."

Ange reluctantly gave in and sat on the chair next to the back door as if to pout. Henri realized his unwashed body was not the only reason for this unpleasant odor and hurried upstairs to find fresh clothes. Strange how the offensive one was often the last to know of his own predicament. *Ha*, he thought, *just like passing gas among the men.* Everyone was innocent. He certainly knew better than to show up smelly like this, but he had been in such a hurry with his news. *That could wait for now*, he thought. He could use this as a means to make Ange feel sorry for him by causing a scene. Oh, he didn't blame her, but it would be fun to tease her. Everyone needed a little pity now and then. Mimi called this "ta-ta," and he loved his "ta-ta."

When a suitably fragranced Henri returned, Ange was in the sitting room waiting for him. "Well, Mr. Smelly, now please tell me this so important news."

"Oh, it really is nothing of great importance. It can wait until later. I am going to get a cup of tea. Would you like some?"

"Wait, Henri! Please tell me. You were so excited when you first arrived."

"I know, but now the importance is gone. Maybe it can wait until morning. I do want some tea."

"Now you are being cruel and teasing me. Please tell me."

"All right. It is nothing to shake the earth, but I have just been promoted to full lieutenant effective immediately."

Her excitement bubbled in a stream of chatter. "Henri, that is wonderful! I am so proud of you, and how could you keep this from me even for one minute. No more hugs for at least that one minute. You do know I love you very, very much. How much will the wages increase?" She was more excited than he had been.

Henri laughed. "Chéri, I knew that would be the next question. It will not be all that much. We will have to wait a little longer unless, of course, you would prefer the chicken house to all of this."

Ange kissed him quickly, jumped up, and ran upstairs to share the news with Madame. Henri went into the kitchen for his tea. He would share the news with Mimi.

The general came home in his usual Friday evening mood and said, "Oui, I know all about this. Who do you think signed the official orders for promotion? By god, I do know a few things that go on in my command. But all joking aside, my boy, congratulations. It was not given, it was earned."

The general went into dining room to refill his wineglass, and Ange followed him.

"Poppa, I need to ask you something. I know it is not my business, but I have been so curious. Is there a secret list of sorts that Napoleon and people of your rank keep to watch certain people? When Henri and I were dining with Napoleon and Marie Louise, he mentioned certain things about Henri he could not possibly have known without an informant."

"Well, my sweet baby daughter, you are correct that it is not your business; but swearing you to secrecy to the point of death, and it would be yours, I may tell you that very special and very promising members of the military are closely watched by Napoleon and certain senior staff, myself included. And oui, our Henri does have a place on that list. He has been placed there solely on his own merit. I have not pushed in the least. It would not be fair of me to do so. I will not push for Jean either. Both must make their own way. It turns out that our Henri is very high on Napoleon's list as showing tremendous promise and a brilliant future. And, my sweet baby daughter, please do not forget you are sworn to secrecy and are to share this with no one, especially our hero. Why, if he knew this, his hat would not fit in the future. I suspect, however, he knows he is being watched and will continue to do well."

"Merci, Poppa. I will never tell, not even a priest."

"And especially not a priest, baby daughter. Then God would know too."

On the next Mercredi evening, a massive bomb went off near the royal carriage on Rue Saint-Nicaise. The royal couple and guests were on their way to the opening night of the much-publicized opera *Creation* by Haydn. Royalist plotters had positioned a wagon with horses on the side of the street just near the probable path of the royal coach. The wagon held a large barrel filled with gunpowder and metal objects of chain pieces and other shrapnel. Just as the carriage turned onto the street, the fuse was lit. Napoleon had ordered his driver to go as fast as safely possible as they were late. The empress had delayed them over the choice of a scarf. Now with the speed of the carriage and the poor quality of the fuse and gunpowder, the bomb exploded just seconds after the carriage had passed and turned the corner.

The luck of Napoleon held as a tall brick building shielded the carriage and his troop. An estimated fifty-two people were killed or wounded by the bomb known later as the "infernal machine." One of the victims was a young girl who had been paid by the plotters to hold the reins of the horse and wagon. The power of the bomb destroyed several buildings, and the flying shrapnel broke windows and damaged things, some of it landing blocks away. The emperor's carriage continued to the theater some two blocks away. There he ordered the opera cancelled for the night and his driver to take them immediately back to the palace.

This was a plot not just to assassinate the emperor but to take command of the government as well. The bomb could be heard all over Paris; and simultaneously with the blast, and as a signal, a group of over one hundred armed conspirators rushed the palace gates and gained access to the yard and grounds. Henri and members of his troop along with some of the personal guard were just inside the main guardroom at the palace front doors. There were about ten men in the detail. At the sound of the blast, they hurried out to see the crowd rushing toward them. It was obvious this was an attack. The troops drew pistols and fired, dropping many, but still they came.

The troops drew sabres and met the onslaught at the bottom of the steps. The crowd was not comprised of experienced fighters and quickly lost heart after seeing many being cut down by these professionals. Other members of the guard and Henri's troopers were entering the melee, and soon it was just a chase. When it was over, Henri's group had four men killed and three wounded, but the conspirators had lost over forty and a considerable of their number wounded and captured. Henri had a cut on his shoulder and put his handkerchief over it to stop the bleeding. He was giving orders for the conspirators to lie facedown with arms spread and for his men to collect all arms and maintain strict order. The emperor's carriage rolled through the main gate. His mounted guard made swift work of the remaining conspirators trying to escape through the main gate and more surrounded the emperor. Napoleon dismounted and gave orders for several of the guard to escort the empress and the guests inside the palace and out of any potential danger. Henri saluted with his sabre and told Napoleon that all is well now. Napoleon could certainly tell by the bodies and the positions in which they fell what had happened here.

"Henri, is that you? In these shadows, I cannot be certain."

"Oui, Your Highness. It is me. We seem to have complete control now."

"Our country's thanks to you and these brave men this night. Well done. a very well done."

To his capitaine of the guard, he said, "Send a detachment to the scene of that explosion and investigate. There may be more dead and wounded there too. Do not rest tonight until I know the parties responsible for this. Henri, turn the duties over to the guard commander and see to your wound. I would never hear an end to the de Chabot ladies moaning if anything happened to you."

"It is only a scratch, Your Highness."

"Oui, I can see by the blood on your uniform the size of this scratch. Go!"

Henri went to the guard surgeon. His wound was cleaned and bound to stop any further bleeding.

"You will be all right in a week or so, Lieutenant. I have put in a few sutures and double bandages because of the bleeding. I am ordering you off duty. You can stay in the quarters here, or if you live in Paris, I will arrange a carriage to take you home. Come back for a clean dressing in a few days and if you need anything for pain. From initial reports, Lieutenant, you are the hero of tonight's events. Another of your men I attended stated that you were a master dealing with the intruders."

"Doctor, I am only fortunate to have been where I was."

Just then, Napoleon entered the infirmary. Henri tried to rise.

"Stay as you are," said the doctor.

"There you are, Henri. I wanted to see how you and the other wounded are and to, once again, merci for your excellent leadership tonight. I have had initial reports that you personally dispatched eight and wounded several more. How could this be in such a short time of a few seconds? Others told me you were like a shadow moving and slashing. This will certainly warrant special recognition. Is there anything I can do for you now before you go home?"

"No, Your Excellency. I am fine. Merci for your kind words. Are the empress and the others safe? I think that rabble came very close tonight. Thank God we were able to stop it."

"And once again thanks to you and those other brave troops. I will see you in a few days, but for now, go home and give Madame de Chabot and Ange my regards and best wishes."

"Oui, Excellency."

The hour was late when the capitaine of the guard knocked on the de Chabot door. The only light was in Madame's upper-floor room. She was often in the habit of reading late, but this night, she and Ange were having a lady's talk. They had been doing this more frequently these days, and Madame was very pleased that Ange was asking such personal and pertinent questions regarding private lady matters.

Her mother had not discussed these subjects with her. As a result, most of the lessons learned were often through blunder and embarrassment. Madame recalled her first time of the month session and how ignorant she was. She was terrified and thought she was dying. Her mean elder sister had laughed and said her guts were falling out. The loud knock on the door startled them.

Madame threw on her dressing gown and slippers, grabbed the lamp, and rushed down the stairs with Ange close behind. They unbolted the door to find the capitaine with two soldiers supporting Henri. The carriage and mounted troops were in the drive. Henri had his jacket covering most of the mass of bandages on his shoulder, and slight ooze of blood was seen seeping through.

"Henri! What has happened?" screamed Ange, rushing to him.

"It seems he was injured in putting down a revolt at the palace tonight, my lady. Do you want me to take him to his bed?"

"No, merci, Capitaine," said Madame. "We can put him in the sitting room until we can make him a comfortable place downstairs."

The capitaine gave Madame a small vial and said this was from the doctor to be mixed with tea if Henri's pain became too bad.

"He has already had one large dose tonight, and he should sleep."

Mimi came into the room and said, "My Henri, you are hurt! What happened! I thought I heard a clatter in here, but this old woman sleeps very soundly these days. Rest here, and I will fix your bed near the kitchen where you were before."

Henri awoke the next morning as if in a fog. His head was reeling. Where was he? What had happened? Then the events of the previous night started to come back to him. In the dim light, he could make out a figure in a chair next to his bed. It was Ange curled up with a blanket covering her slim figure. Her dark hair partially covered her face. Henri lay there a moment savoring the sight and trying to shake off the fuzziness. Then as he stirred, he called her name. She immediately rose and bent over him.

"Henri, are you all right? Are you in pain? Can I get you anything?"

"Oui, please, I am burning for a drink of water. My mouth feels like I have been chewing on a horse blanket."

She went into the kitchen and brought him a cup of water. "Well, I see you can still joke, but are you in pain?"

"No, just stiff and aching, but not pain. I guess I was luckier this time, and at least I can walk."

"What happened last night? We all heard a loud noise or explosion. We went on the front porch but could not see anything. Only a plume of smoke across the river. Then they brought you home with blood all over your jacket. I was so scared. The capitaine told Momma something about you killing a lot of people last night."

"Wait, chéri, not so many questions at one time. There was an attempt on the emperor's life and to take over the government last night. There was no harm to Napoleon or anyone of his group. A large group of conspirators rushed the palace, and that was their mistake. The explosion, I don't know about except it must have been a well-planned attempt. As far as me killing anyone, I guess maybe I did. They should not have been there. It is not a pleasant thing to hack someone, but I guess I did."

"Henri, mon amour, please try to rest now. You are getting excited."

"No, petite one, I am not excited, but I am starving. Do you suppose Mimi has any coffee or a sweet cake? I hear her in the kitchen."

Ange went into the kitchen and returned a short time later with a silver tray of coffee and sweet cakes.

"Ah, you are an angel. I thought I was going to starve. I need to sit up. I can't eat this way."

"Here let me help you sit up. I can prop you on these pillows."

"Oh, everything is turning. It must be that 'tea.' It does affect me that way. You should try it sometime. It chases pain and everything."

"Not right now, merci. You need to rest."

"Ange, I have rested all night. I really need to walk and not get stiff. After my tea, I will get up and walk. I will be all right."

"All right, Mr. Smartie, have it your way. I am going to make myself presentable for the day. Call us if you need anything. I will not be too long, and Mimi is just around the corner."

Alone, Henri reflected on the events of last evening. He had no doubts he had killed at least one. He had seen a neck nearly severed with his sabre. And the others he could remember had well-aimed slashes and hearing cries. He really didn't remember his own wound, but in the heat of conflict, one rarely does. What was to come of this? He had been at the right place and at the right time. If this had to happen, the timing could not have been more perfect. He was personally known to the emperor now and could have a recognition known to few at such an early age. The first time as Bébé Tigre could have been a tale, but not this time. He had been very deliberate in his actions and had lead troops in battle.

Ha! Maybe he would make an officer after all. With or without a mustache. It was growing a bit thicker now and starting to resemble a mustache. It was not just the growth under his nose that Mimi had teased him about. Had all of this really happened, or was this all part of a colorful youthful dream? Just then, Mimi came in and asked to check his wound and startled him back to reality. And now a bit of "ta-ta" from Mimi. He was going to delight in every second.

General de Chabot came home later that morning and stated that he would have to return to duty after only an hour or so. The entire Paris command was on high alert, and there were still many unanswered questions regarding last evening's events. Despite knowing the plot had been conceived by certain of the Royalists, Napoleon was using this to discredit the Jacobeans, his old nemesis. It seemed this radical group was always causing problems with something. They were never happy or satisfied.

There were arrest warrants out for "rogues of high places," as Napoleon had named them. The principal warrants were for Generals Jean Pichegru and Jean Moreau. The other main leader and chief planner of this episode was Georges Cadoudal. All were still believed to be in Paris, and the arrests would only be a matter of time. Many of those captured by Henri and his troops were well-known radicals and opponents of the emperor. Many already "interviewed" stated that the opposition to any pending preparations for war with Russia were the main motive behind this. However, Madame Guillotine would have a feast over this uprising, stated the general.

Napoleon had personally summoned General de Chabot and placed him in command of the Paris operation and hunt for the fugitives. Napoleon had briefed the general about Henri's involvement last evening.

"Merde, lad, what in hell happened? The emperor was almost dancing when he told me what you did. Did you know you have been officially credited with dispatching eight of the bastards and wounding seven more? Not to mention the sixty-three that your troops captured. The Little Master said it was all over by the time he arrived back at the palace, and you were in complete command of the situation. I interviewed the capitaine of the guard who rushed to the scene as it was ending, and he told me you were like a mad thing whirling and slashing. Knowing Napoleon, he will make an example of this and certain to have a special ceremony or function. Anything for publicity or a party. It seems as if you were at the right place at the right time again. I wonder what name you will be given over this, Madman perhaps."

He laughed and said, "Baby daughter, try never to make this man angry."

She stood there in wonderment. Could this person they were talking about be the same as her gentle, loving, and understanding Henri?

Later that day, Georges Cadoudal was captured. That evening, General Moreau was found hiding in his cousin's attic with weapons, food stores, and wine. His cousin was also taken into custody for harboring a fugitive. General Pichegru was captured attempting to leave Paris by a rarely used road through one of the slum areas. These rogues of high places plus some hundred fifty others of suspect had the prison nearly full.

The following days after court, Madame Guillotine did indeed have a feast. General Pichegru was found later strangled in his cell, a victim of suicide or, as rumors go, dispatched on orders. A kerchief was found around his neck twisted tightly with a piece of wood. Could this have been done by himself?

Henri's wound healed rapidly, and he enjoyed many moments of "ta-ta" from the ladies of the de Chabot household. The general said it made him nearly ill to see all of this "hovering about," but in reality, he was jealous of the attention. After two weeks, Henri begged the doctor to return him to duty. Enough was entirely enough. The doctor did agree, noting his wound had healed nicely from the inside to the outside, and no infection was present. Ange, Madame, and Mimi had worked another miracle.

Henri reported for duty to Capitaine LaBauve. The capitaine rose as he came into the tent. "Well, I see our errant hero has returned. Have you grown tired of being nursed and pampered?" He laughed. "It is good to see you up and about. Have they released you to full duty?"

"Oui, monsieur, the doctor said the wound may be a bit stiff, but it has healed nicely. I am ready to resume my normal duties."

"Be seated, Lieutenant. The coffee is over there in the flask. Help yourself. I will fill you in on certain events in your absence. The action at the palace is now very well known to not only our troop but the entire encampment here. The action also brought out your past history as the Tigre. I guess it had to come out, but maybe it is for the best. You are now a novelty probably known as an early riser in le Patron's eyes. There are some stronger rumors of war with Russia. Many fear the unknown lands of that vast country. We are ordered to prepare, but I feel we are already as prepared as we ever will be without some knowledge of the country and climate. As I hear more, I will share the information with you and the other commanders. I am pleased you are back. Is there anything I can add, or do you have any questions?"

"No, monsieur, but you will never know how good it is to be back. I was being smothered, and while it was good and I love them dearly, I was getting tired of it. I do appreciate your kind words. I was so lucky being there when I was. At least that is what General de Chabot has accused me of. With your permission, Capitaine, I will take my leave and join my troop now." Henri saluted and left the tent. *So*, he thought, *I am known as an early riser. Time will tell.*

He was punched and pounded with backslaps as he entered the tent shared with the other commanders.

"You pile of stinking horse shit! Why didn't you tell us you were the legendary Tigre of the Austrian campaign and had done those things," was the general comment. Over several cups of coffee, he had to relate the entire action at the palace to the others. And then the Bébé Tigre episode had to be told. He told it honestly and said the tales that resulted were, for the most part, greatly exaggerated; but it did make a good story to relate to his children and their children someday.

The following week, General de Chabot called Henri and Capitaine LaBauve to his quarters. Henri tied his horse in front of the long low building and entered. He was well known to the general's aide by now and told to go right in. The general and Capitaine LaBauve were waiting.

"Gentlemen, our emperor has planned a small party for the hero here tomorrow afternoon. The ceremony will be held here at the parade field. He also wants my family to attend. He has informed me it will only be a short ceremony as his father-in-law, the ruler of Austria, is visiting, and both are very busy. Due to the rather short ceremony, we will use the music corps from the regiment and not from the palace. Only our dragoons are to parade. Do either of you have any questions?"

"No, monsieur. We will make certain the troop is polished for the event," said the capitaine. "Are there any special orders or considerations for the event?"

"No, Capitaine. Just make certain they are ready for midday at the assembly point."

"Oui, monsieur."

As soon as they arrived back to the troop area, Capitaine LaBauve called all company commanders to his quarters. "Gentlemen, we have been invited to a special party in the honor of our local hero here. It will be a short ceremony at the parade field tomorrow afternoon. You know what that means, and I expect the troop to be the point of perfection without a single hair of a horse tail out of place. With the weather as it has been, I do not expect rain, but one never knows. Everyone turn to and make certain we have the best-looking troop in this Armée. Are there any questions?"

"No, monsieur." Everyone hurried off, but not before calling the Hero several unmentionable names for his part in this extra work.

The next afternoon, the troop assembled at the main gate leading into the parade field. They were standing at ease and making final critical checks of equipment, horses, and uniform. This was a moment not only for Henri's personal honor but for the entire troop. A trooper stationed at a vantage point notified the capitaine that carriages were approaching. The procession of the emperor's personal carriage, three others, and his personal mounted guard came into view. The capitaine shouted, "Troop attention! Mount!" The carriages passed the troops and into the parade field. Henri caught sight of Ange, Madame, and even Mimi in the second carriage with the empress.

The general, on his personal white stallion, rode up and said, "Well, Henri, this should be quite a party. Le Petit Tondu has brought our family, his family, and the visiting Austrian royalty as well."

The visitors climbed out of the carriages and made their way to the reviewing stand. Henri could just barely make out Ange. She wore a light blue dress and large white wide-brim hat. He felt his heart skip a beat as he caught sight of her. The emperor's personal guard dismounted and formed a line just to the side of the reviewing stand.

The signal was given, and the musique detachment began the stirring sounds of the march music of the republic. Henri would ride in the front of the troop with the general. "Troop, wheel right! Columns of four, forward at a walk" was the command. It was a magnificent sight as the mounted cavalry troop moved in precision almost as one. The columns and rows were straight, and the spacing was perfect. The horses seemed to step to the cadence of the drums and music.

The bright sunlight reflected in almost blinding glitters of the polished metal sabres, badges, bridles, and the many other components of the uniforms and horse adornments. The horses' coats had been brushed to a fine sheen, and as instructed, nearly every hair was in place.

The general and Henri rode side by side at the front of the column just in front of the flag bearers. As they approached the reviewing stand, Henri glanced out of the side of his eyes and saw the visitors standing to honor the flags. Ange was next to the empress, Madame, Mimi, and several other people he did not recognize. He did recognize the empress's mother, whom he had met at the birth of Napoleon II.

The general and Henri wheeled to the right and dismounted. Two grooms came running and took the mounts to the side of the guard detachment. The column continued on, formed a long straight line, and, then too, wheeled to the right, facing the reviewing stand. The music corps stopped playing, and Napoleon stood at a podium just at the foot of the reviewing stand.

"French people and patriots everywhere. Honored guests and allies. It is with the utmost pleasure and respect that this special ceremony is directed at a true hero of the Grande Armée of France. Lieutenant Devreney, while assigned guard duties at the palace on the night of the serious insurrection toward our empire, led and commanded his troops in such a brave and courageous manner that the situation was quickly put down. Although sustaining a serious wound, he continued to fight and lead his command. I am pleased to note that this is the second time in this man's life that I have had the privilege of bestowing special honors for bravery far above and beyond the call of normal duty. He is a proven leader, hero, and a major asset to his troop and the leadership of our Grande Armée. Lieutenant, please step forward."

An attendant came forward with a blue velvet box and gave it to Napoleon. Napoleon opened the box and took out a bright gold medal with a red-and-white striped ribbon. He reached up and placed the medal around Henri's neck and kissed him on each cheek.

He whispered, "You know, Henri, if these 'kiss' episodes continue, people may think we may be having an affair." He laughed and patted Henri on the shoulder. "Well done, again son of France."

Henri smiled and saluted, and Napoleon returned the salute. The band struck up the "La Marseillaise," the national anthem of France. After the anthem, Henri did a smart about-face and returned to his place beside the general.

Madame, looking on in awe, thought, *God has truly blessed me with my husband and my son standing there so proud at this moment in history.*

Henri glanced at the general and thought he saw a glint of slight moisture around his eyes. Ange was, once again, in complete awe of this latest moment in the short life of the man she loved with her entire being. What might the future bring? It was as if some uncontainable force was pulling him toward a final destiny.

With the presentation of the award, the ceremony was complete. The signal was given for the troops to withdraw. The band again played the favorite of the emperor; and the mounted troop moved forward, wheeled into the precise ranks of four abreast, and moved out of the parade field.

"Come, Hero mine, it is time for you to say hello to our family and the guests and show off your newest shiny medal," said the general.

Henri and the general went to the reviewing stand and mounted the steps. Ange was standing next to Empress Marie Louise, her mother, and Madame. As he approached, Ange grabbed his hand, and he detected a tear or two in her dark eyes. She didn't say anything and just stared at him for a second.

Marie Louise said, "Henri, what an honor. We are so proud of you and this achievement. Napoleon has been talking of this every day since it happened. He is so proud of you and calls you a true son of France."

"He just did call me that in private at the ceremony."

Napoleon motioned to the general to bring his group over to him. He was standing with a large heavyset man in a uniform Henri did not recognize. "Ladies, gentlemen, may I present His Highness, the emperor of Austria, Francis I, and the empress, Maria Theresa, father and mother of my wife, Marie Louise."

The group bowed, and the emperor of Austria spoke in almost-flawless French with a very slight hint of accent.

"Lieutenant, may I offer my congratulations on your achievement and honor. It is well to have men as you in our ranks."

Speaking to the general and Madame, the emperor of Austria said, "You must be very proud. He is young to have accomplished this so early in his career. Napoleon has told me about a Tiger's earlier achievement against my Austrian forces, and I am pleased to see him on our side now." He laughed and patted Henri on the shoulder.

Henri could only shyly smile.

Ange was clinging to his hand, and the empress said, "My dear, how have you been?"

Ange bowed. "Très bien, merci, Your Highness."

The empress turned to her husband and added, "We met after the birth of the baby. She and this young man were so kind to offer congratulations to my daughter."

"Oui, Highness, merci for remembering. Marie Louise is a good friend, and I enjoy her company."

Marie Louise grabbed Ange's hand and said, "And she has been a good friend to me. It was so lonely in that old pile of stones. She came to my rescue." They all laughed.

Napoleon said, "She is very busy now as a mother and with certain political duties, and still she calls it a pile of old stones."

He emphasized that they must leave shortly as there were affairs this afternoon that would demand his attention and a state dinner that night in honor of the visiting royalty. Henri held his breath that Napoleon wouldn't get the idea of a special invitation and show off the new hero. But nothing was mentioned. He was spared; and the royal troupe withdrew, mounted their carriages, and sped off surrounded with the mounted guard.

The general went over to the grooms and asked them to please take his and Henri's horse back to the regiment stable area as they would be going home with the family in the carriage. Henri went over to his troop and was greeted with the usual backslaps and joking. Capitaine LaBauve shook his hand and said he had the rest of the week off duty if he wished. Henri told him that he would prefer to return to duty in the morning if it was all right. There was still much to do with the training and preparations for a pending campaign in

Russia. Everyone had been ordered to keep the rumors at a minimum, but the knowledge was widespread.

Michael came up to Henri and did a slight bow. He grabbed Henri and hugged him. "So our hero receives another medal. Soon you will be so weighted down with those damn things you will not be able to walk. In all seriousness, mon ami, most sincere congratulations. This was well deserved and earned with blood again."

"Merci, Michael. Your words of friendship mean more than you know. I will have the rest of the day off and return to duty in the morning. I am sure the family will try to smother me."

"Oui, and I see one pretty lady over there watching us who can't wait to get her hands on you and start the smothering process."

Henri knew Michael was right in his assumption. He was eager to be smothered too. The ride home found Ange sitting so close the general said a feather could not be put between them. They both blushed and smiled back at him but did not make any move to separate. Madame didn't say anything and, as usual, kept all of these things in her heart.

For the evening meal, Mimi prepared a wonderful roast goose dinner complete with their favorite leek soup and vegetables. They all ate too much. The general was beside himself with toasts to the hero, his new medal, the emperor, France, his horse, and on and on. Madame asked him to please slow down a bit, saying these were just excuses for him to get another glass of wine. They had to skip dessert as the wine and the sweet cream-filled pastries would not blend well. A bout off the back porch or the chamber pot would be inevitable.

The general took Madame by the hand and said, "Come, mon amour. I think you need to put this old dog to bed, and I will need some assistance maneuvering the stairs."

"So be it, you old bear, come, let's see if both of us can maneuver the stairs. I think all of us can use a separation from celebrating and flowing wine."

Ange and Henri were left alone in the sitting room again. All of the candles and lamps were out; the flickering firelight from a slowly burning log cast shadows on the surrounding furniture and walls. Even though it was Août and summer in Paris, there was still just a slight chill after the sun went to sleep. Madame always seemed chilled and insisted on at least a low fire in the sitting room. Henri wondered if the visit to Josephine had anything to do with it. Maybe not.

As soon as the adults went upstairs, Ange moved over next to Henri, took his hand in hers, and laid her head on his shoulder.

"Henri, it is like we are caught in a wind and being pushed here and there. Events of these past several years have moved so fast, and sometimes I am completely at a loss and can't understand. Today, seeing you and Poppa standing there, and hearing all of the things the emperor said about you, my tiny heart was bursting with pride and yet wonder and confusion. I didn't know whether to cry, laugh, or just go mad. Most other friends of our family have boys who are still in school and play like children. You are their same age and are now a well-educated officer in the Armée, a decorated hero, and known personally to Napoleon. I am only fifteen years old and know that many girls my age are married with children, but I still cannot see myself as that yet. Darling, I know I am talking fast and foolishly. I hope you can understand a bit of what I am trying to say. Do you think I am foolish?"

"Chéri, I think I know exactly what you are saying. I wish I could say it that clearly. I am still shy and embarrassed with all of this publicity. I am confused by it all and know these things should happen to much older men. I try hard to be a man and a leader. I know I have been trained for this, but why? My sergeant and most of my men are older than I am, but I will have to cope with that. I admit with the knowledge out now about the Tigre stories and now this, I don't know what they will think. I feel, as you said, pushed by a strong wind of fate. Hold on tightly, mon amour, and we can be pushed together."

She tilted her head slightly. He looked deeply in her dark eyes and saw complete trust and love. Their lips met in a slight seeking kiss. The seeking kiss suddenly turned to a burst of passion, and their arms flew around each other. She pushed him back, slightly breathless, and he once again gazed deeply in her eyes.

"Henri, we can't tease each other this way. At times like this, I think I am completely mad. I feel the strongest urges to just go ahead and finish it," she said.

"Me too, chéri. I just need you to always stop us. I can't. When I am away from home and you, I am more miserable than you can ever know. Come, love, it is late. I will walk you upstairs."

He was gone in the morning before Ange arose. Henri and the general rode silently in the carriage back to the camp.

Finally the general said, "Well, my boy, I live in wonder at our future. Merde, I have got to stop calling you 'my boy.' 'My man' would be more proper, but everyone would think I was stupid. Correct me when I do this."

"No, monsieur, I could never correct a general. You have always called me that in private. I consider it a sign of belonging and respect."

"All right then, my whatever, I still wonder what the fates have in store for us. Most of the staff are very worried le Patron is getting a bit too bold with this Russia threat. That land is so vast, and no one really knows much about it. We do know the winters in the north can be very bitter but not too much else. There are many unanswered questions about everything there. Food, supplies, roads, and, most of all, the Russian army. We know nothing. Our spies have never returned. Bits of information gathered by paying certain others has gained almost nothing. Napoleon said last week not to worry. We can deal with it when the time comes. I hope it never does. How are the dragoons faring with training and the new issue of pistols?"

"Very well, monsieur. Most of us consider the pistols more of a bother as we only have one shot and then have to put the thing away. It is almost impossible to reload at a gallop. Maybe if we carried a bag full of pistols. Sabres and lances are much better."

"I understand, but those suggestions came from 'experts,' and we are compelled to at least try. Some seem to think it will give the mounted troops a little extra firepower when they come in range of the pistols. Let me know any comments on this as training does progress."

18

Faucon de la Nuit

The official announcement came through that clear afternoon in late March 1812. It rippled through the dragoon ranks like a fair breeze and soon reached the crescendo of a howling winter wind. Everyone was talking of the newly organized dragoon detachment with excitement and speculating of scouting and being far ahead of the main Armée.

Michael ran up to Henri and asked, "Did you hear about the new unit being formed? If it is true, this could be very good duty. I wonder if I could get in. Can you imagine scouting and being ahead of the main body? This group could have the pick of food and other things."

"Michael, you are just overly excited. I think you will have an equal chance. I just might go for it myself. It does sound like good duty. I think I would like to do scouting and foraging."

Even though the two were now considered men and soldiers, the boy was still there with the sense of adventure. Only the best were to be selected.

The selection process began the next morning. Capitaine LaBauve and four other senior officers sat at a table in the large armory building. Henri was among the first to be called. He was told the requirements, both physically and mentally, of the duties required for being a member of the group. Then he was asked if he wished to volunteer or if he needed more time to think about the assignment. He immediately volunteered in the affirmative, considering it an honor to be requested and to serve in such an elite unit. The process went on the remainder of that day and into the next. In all, two hundred fifty men were chosen, including Michael. There would be three officers, Capitaine LaBauve as commander, Henri, and one other yet to be named.

The detachment would be divided into two sections each under the command of an officer. Henri would have command of the first section and also be second in command to Capitaine LaBauve. Henri was delighted to see his old tentmate, Lieutenant Adrien Richard, as the other section leader. He was an excellent rider and was respected as a leader. Henri knew Adrien was excellent with the troops and held in high esteem. The staff and officers were now complete with the exception of the senior noncommissioned staff. Sergeant Prejean would be senior sergeant and report directly to Capitaine LaBauve. When this was announced, Sergeant Prejean winked at Henri and smiled slightly. This was an excellent selection of men and officers for the new detachment. Henri thought about promoting Michael to corporal and his second in command, but did not. First of all, it may have been considered favoritism, and second, Michael was still considered a prankster. Henri confronted Michael with his decision.

"Have you gone completely mad, mon ami? Me a corporal having to do the extra merde those in charge are always saddled with? Please do not do me the favor. I am happy with things as the way they are."

"Are you certain on this, Michael? No hard feelings or looking back?"

"We are still friends, shitbird, if that is what you are after. Maybe later, but please not now. All right?" Michael grinned and took a playful poke at Henri.

Training would now begin in earnest.

Capitaine LaBauve addressed the entire assembly on the third day, standing on a table at the parade ground. There was a silence as the group waited to hear every word. The separate sections were standing in orderly rows with the commander in front. Just behind him was the guidon who would carry the pennant of the section as they were issued. For the present, they carried an empty pennant staff.

"Men, please gather in as closely as you can so that I do not have to shout and lose my damn voice. You have been chosen to be among the elite of this division. Other divisions are choosing men like yourselves. I think we are the most fortunate and have the most experience to offer. Of course the others probably think the same." There was a rippling laughter. "Most of you here are combat veterans and no stranger to hardship. We have had scouts before, but not in the strength as this. These units will be the eyes and ears of the division and direct the foraging groups. As our emperor has stated many times, an Armée travels on its stomach. A simple truth is that if one cannot eat, one cannot fight. Your primary purpose will be to move in stealth and find and stalk the enemy.

"Today we will begin certain conditioning exercises for troopers and animals alike. I do not anticipate any movement of the Armée in the near future, but as soldiers, we must always be prepared. Condition of you men and your animals is paramount in the success of this venture. As always, should any of you have any questions, your officers and I will always be available. This special group will be known as 'Faucon de la Nuit' (Night Falcon). We will travel swiftly, silently, and in secrecy as if on wings. We will have the eyes and senses of the falcon and the ability to attack and withdraw as swiftly. This name was chosen by our commanding general, and I cannot think of any better description for this group. To achieve these objectives will take the efforts of every man present.

"We will have to rely on each other in all things and situations. I cannot emphasize enough the importance of working as a team. We will train as an entire unit for the next several weeks and then break into sections for specialized training with the individual commanders. For this first week, physical training for the men and animals will be emphasized. I am certain all here will hate my guts by the end of the first week. Now all troops turn to and get your mounts for a short twenty-mile stroll in the countryside. Return to this area in twenty minutes with full gear. Dismissed!"

The remaining days of the week saw the entire command on the "strolls." It was not only riding, for every trooper knows he walks with his mount more than he rides. There was no spare time as training between strolls was filled with things they already knew but would be drilled into them again and again. Map reading and making, compass reading, navigating by the stars, identifying edible things found in the field, learning proper personal hygiene, and on and on. They must be able to rely on each other as needed.

They would be granted half a day Samedi and Dimanche for leave and personal things. Every man was more than glad to see Saturday at noon. On Saturday morning, a dress inspection was held for men and mounts. They were developing into a very precise group. The rest of the troops in camp who could went to see the inspection. Every man of the new unit was proud of his presence and did his best not to let his fellow troopers down. The results were astounding. They looked every bit the part of one of the elite parade groups the emperor kept in Paris as part of his personal guard. Henri had not heard any grumbling over the rigorous training so far. He did hear complaints about how tired they were, but not about the schedule. He was more than ready for Saturday and then off for home and to see Ange.

He rode home with the general and was quizzed extensively about everything regarding the new detachment. Was morale high? What did the troopers think of this new group? Were they starting to form a team? How did the men take to their commanders? Henri answered the questions honestly as he was expected.

"Henri, I am most interested in the development of this unit. Foraging and reconnaissance have always been an important part of our army. We French have been noted for not taking a lot of rations and supplies and living from the lands we conquer. This will be the first attempt of an organized unit in strength with the prime purpose of such. The one or two scouts we generally send out cannot cope adequately with meeting the enemy. It often is a death sentence to send one or two, and we cannot rely on the reports. This was my idea, and having presented it to Napoleon, it must work. Please keep this to yourself and do keep me advised."

The general told him that he must take this very seriously as word was growing every day about the Russian Bear lurking in the woods. The entire Grande Armée staff were acutely aware of the complete lack of knowledge of Russia. No one knew what to expect. These new units may help observe and report accurate enemy troop movements and take and hold foodstuffs when found.

When they arrived home, no one was waiting to welcome them. This was most unusual.

They went inside, and the general shouted, "Where in the hell is everyone? These weary warriors are home, and no one is here to greet them!"

Madame shouted back, "We are in the dining room! Come and join us!"

As they went into the dining room, they were greeted with the entire household and a large cake and dishes of Mimi's special sweet cakes.

"So what is the celebration, mon amour? Did someone die and we inherit great wealth?"

"No, my husband and son. You have been so busy playing soldier, you have forgotten Henri's birthday. Ange reminded me earlier in the week. It was two days ago. We cannot have this. Our Henri is eighteen years of age and officially a man. Not that he isn't already, but this is a man's age of reckoning."

"Eighteen, damn lad, what do you make of all of this?"

"I am surprised. I didn't realize the day was here again."

Mimi fussed, "Hurry and cut your cake. The rest of us are starved and want to try this one. It is a new recipe filled with fruit. I hope you like it."

Ange was beaming as she handed Henri the knife to cut the cake.

"Careful with that thing, daughter. He can be very evil with a knife."

"Oh, Poppa, he is not evil."

"I hope not. Not around here anyway. He would have to cut me on the rear end. I would be going the other way." The general laughed and insisted on a toast, poured glasses of wine, and charged Henri to say words in his behalf for the occasion.

"I really don't know what to say except merci all for your kindness and love. I feel so blessed with my family. Whatever is my destiny, I will never forget."

"Bravo, Henri. No one could have said this better. It is from the heart and soul. I have had my fun at your expense knowing you are not one for making speeches. Now let's enjoy the cake and the company of family. Let's go into the sitting room and share the news of the week. I do have news. Henri, you need to tell Ange about the Faucon de la Nuit."

Ange and Henri decided to take their cake to the back porch so they could share some privacy. On the way, Henri hugged Mimi and thanked her for the special cake.

"Mimi, this cake is your best yet. It is so light and filled with fruit. If I could bake, I would be tempted to steal the recipe. Please give it to my best friend here and see if she can duplicate it."

"You are most welcome, my favorite young colt. It is good to have you home with us to celebrate your special day. Merci beaucoup for the kind words. They truly were from your heart. We all love you very much." Mimi nudged Ange as she said this and laughed.

They sat on a bench on the back porch and were quiet for a time while eating their cake.

"Henri, you are eating your cake as if you are starving. It was a huge piece. Haven't you eaten today?"

"Oh oui, I did eat, but with all of the additional exercise and training, it seems like we never have enough to eat. We eat like pigs, and still it is not enough."

"Henri, what is all of this additional exercise, and what did Poppa mean about night birds or whatever he was talking about?"

"A new detachment has been formed on orders of the emperor. Each division will have a special unit of dragoons. Their purpose will be reconnaissance in advance of the main body of the Armée. The name of our group will be Faucon de la Nuit. I have been selected to lead a unit of a hundred fifty men of the group. Michael will be one of them. This is a very good opportunity for advancement, and I may make capitaine within a year or so. You know what that could mean if you still want to wait."

"But isn't that dangerous going far out in front of the main Armée with just a few men? And, monsieur, what is all of this 'if I still want to wait' statement? At your insistence, I have waited all of this time, and I thought we made special plans. Are you thinking of another girl? How could you?"

"Oh, Ange, chéri, I was teasing you. You know there could never be anyone else. I apologize. You took that all wrong. I was trying to tease you."

She giggled, hugged him, and told him the tease was now turned around. "Now please tell me more of the dangers of this new assignment."

"This is no more dangerous than any other position in the Armée with the exception of the cooks and people who tend the things soldiers do not have to. Would you rather I try to be a cook? I could have Mimi teach me."

"Now you are making fun of this entire conversation. Sometimes I think there is not a serious thought in your wonderful head. But you do need to tell me all about your new assignment. It does sound exciting, and I do hope it is not dangerous. You wouldn't tell me anyway, would you? You are just like Poppa."

"I will, mon amour, let's walk in the back gardens. The spring is wonderful this year. The fruit trees are covered with blooms. I miss the stables and gardens here almost as much as I miss you."

Ange elbowed him in the ribs. He grabbed her hand as they slowly strolled through the newly planted vegetable gardens and flowering fruit trees, savoring the sweet odors of new plowed earth and nectars from the trees and blossoms.

Mimi was watching through the back window as Madame came up and looked out too.

"Madame, what a sight to warm this old heart. I think those two must have been put here for each other by God Himself."

"I almost agree, Mimi. They are adults now, and it will be only a matter of time before the inevitable happens. But this way, we will not lose a daughter or a son. We get to keep them both."

Later that night after the others had gone to bed, Ange opened Henri's door and shook him. "Henri, I know you are tired, but I couldn't sleep. I hoped you would be wanting some company."

"You know the answer to that. I wasn't really sleeping and hoping you might visit."

She left the door open. They moved the chairs over to the open window. They propped their feet up on the windowsill. Ange rubbed her bare toes on Henri's foot. There was still a bright sliver of moon hanging over the river. They could see the lights of the city, and the Seine washed in the moonlight. Only the slight sounds of the sleeping city could be heard. The real nightlife was over near the old marketplace where the night people always kept things going. An occasional dog barking or carriage wheels rattling on the next street broke the silence.

Once cats could be heard with loud yowling, and Henri remarked that Poppa Kitty was building another litter. Ange laughed and slapped his arm. They sat for a long time holding hands, enjoying and savoring the sights, sounds, odors, and each other. Both of them could be lost to the entire world and treasured these quiet times. So he was eighteen years old now. Ange would be seventeen that Décembre.

Where had the years gone? Only yesterday he had arrived here as a penniless waif. He was so blessed. Ange rested her head on his arm. He felt at complete peace with the entire world.

Henri awoke early the next morning as was his usual habit. He was starving and quickly pulled on his trousers and shirt. He was still in his socked feet and quietly padded down the hall and stairs. Mimi was just starting the fires for the coffee and morning meal.

"Bonjour, Mimi. How about some help with the fires or with the morning meal preparations?"

"And a bonjour to you, Henri. I could use just a few pieces of wood. I have enough for now in my kindling box, but later I will need more. And I guess this labor of yours will cost the usual arms and legs of this poor old woman."

"No cost, Mimi, but I could use a cup of coffee and a sweet cake if you have any to spare a starving soldier."

"Just as I thought. Nothing is free."

"I have never seen anything free. It all has a rope attached."

"Hurry with my wood and get your 'free' coffee and sweet cakes, Henri. You should be a poet and not a soldier. Here is your coffee, and the sweet cakes are in the cupboard just above your head. The honey is next to the sweet cakes. You had better save some for the old bear that will be in here later. He usually doesn't sleep late unless he and Madame stayed awake particularly late 'talking.'" Just then, Ange stumbled into the kitchen with her hair in tangles and sleepy eyes.

"Heavens, child, what brings you into the world this early? You are never out of bed at this hour."

"I know, Mimi, but today Henri will have to leave sooner than normal, and I want to spend more time with him. We can walk to an earlier Mass and have the day until early afternoon. I heard Poppa tell Momma last evening that they would be returning earlier today as there was much to do. Henri, is this to do with your new assignment, or can you tell me?"

"Oui, it probably does relate to the formation of the new units, but the entire division is starting to train more in earnest and prepare things for a campaign. It will be more intense as the weeks progress. Napoleon usually wages war in good weather. He says the winter is not a good time. Don't worry, I will let you know of anything I may hear, but your Poppa would be a much better source."

"He never tells us anything and says all we do is worry. He makes jokes of the situation just as you do. They must teach you that in the military school. Poppa says war is for the men, and besides, women have tongues wagging at both ends. That isn't fair."

Henri just laughed and did not reply. He had heard the general say this, and any comment from him now would certainly ruin the day. With Mimi and the fiery Ange present, this could become dangerous ground and an outnumbered situation. They drank their coffee and ate sweet cakes mostly in silence.

"Henri, let's get dressed and walk to Notre Dame for an earlier Mass, and then we can have a little time before you return to camp."

"That does sound good. I'll be back down shortly. All I have to do is wash and trim my mustache. Will you have enough time? Mass is in about an hour."

They both left in a hurry and nearly ran over the general as he was coming into the kitchen. "What in the hell is your big rush? Possibly a fire in the kitchen?"

"No, Poppa, we are going to an early Mass and have more time for the day," Ange said as they both rushed on.

It was a glorious day with the sky clear and the air still cool with only a slight breeze. The sun was starting its rise higher to obliterate the sinking moon in the western sky. Other people were hurrying to church. They crossed the bridge over the river and entered the large square in front of Notre Dame. The sight of the magnificent church never failed to instill a sense of awe in Henri.

The church was rapidly filling as they made their way to the de Chabot space in the large rows of pews. *This was a good idea of going to an early Mass,* thought Henri. They would have a bit more time together. It seemed there was never enough time to spend with Ange. The more life went on, the more he realized his love for her and the empty pangs when they were apart. Her life was his life. It seemed that it had always been so.

He remembered in readings somewhere the statement of "emptiness is the hollow heart of the soul." He would have to remember where he heard that. He was daydreaming and not paying the least attention to the Mass. Ange noticed this and nudged him back to reality. He sheepishly smiled at her and after a while went right back to his daydreaming. Finally Mass was over, and as they were leaving church, they met Jean-Claude's parents.

"Well, Henri and Ange, you are up and about early this beautiful morning. What brings you out so early? I'll bet Jean-Claude and Lydie will not be up before early evening. They announced two days ago that we may be grandparents. Of course, we are overjoyed."

"Congratulations to both of you," said Henri. "I know Jean-Claude must be proud and wishing for a boy. Please give them our congratulations."

"Oh oui," said Ange. "Please do and tell Lydie that I will schedule a visit in the near future."

"By the way, Henri, congratulations on your action at the palace. It was the talk of all of Paris."

"Merci, monsieur. As the general said, I was just in the right place at the right time."

They left the church and wandered along the many closed shops. Some were open this early, but only a scant few. They stopped at a small open-air café along the Seine and ordered coffee. They sat in silence for a time, sipping their coffee and enjoying the view.

Finally, Ange said, "*Je t'aime,* Henri. Not just for now or what you have done, but for always and always. Please be careful in this new assignment."

"Well, what has brought this on? Please try not to worry. We are being very well trained, and I never take any unnecessary risks. Hey, let's throw this doom and gloom in the river and enjoy the rest of the day. I love you too. If only you could ever know what you mean to me."

Her mood immediately changed, and a bright pretty smile beamed at Henri. They slowly walked along the river walk hand in hand and in their own world.

19

Survival Training

The next two weeks brought more physical training intensified to the point of near exhaustion. Capitaine LaBauve told his officers if any weak ones were to be found, now was the time. During missions in the future, it would be too late. A weak link in the chain could cause failure of the mission or, worse yet, danger and even death. Surprisingly enough, none had dropped out yet. All of the group knew the reasons for this rigorous training and knew what they were getting into at the outset. Most of those chosen were young with an average age of between eighteen and twenty-two. The older men such as Sergeant Prejean were the organizational arm of the group and would not be going on the extensive missions.

Capitaine LaBauve, at the grand old age of twenty-seven, drove himself as hard as he drove his command. He personally led many of the exercise classes. The general feeling was if he can do this, I can too. Very often the classes were so intense it was as if the men were trying to run the capitaine in the ground. He realized this and used it as a psychological tool.

Henri saw him several times in the woods at the edge of the camp on his knees throwing up after a particularly rough session. Others, including Henri and Michael, were throwing up too; but very few saw the capitaine. During this time, Henri and many of the others seemed to grow taller, and their frame was filled with muscles never there before. Ange saw him washing at the water trough at home and was amazed at the tanned, slim, hard, muscular man that he had become.

The horses were another matter. Satan was a disagreeable and surly animal. Henri often said he must be part donkey. The entire brain part! Actually, Satan was very intelligent, but if he could get out of certain duties, he would always give it his best. The two loved each other and had formed a bond unlike many of the others in the command.

Henri had broken an important rule of the dragoon corps. A trooper should never become sentimental about his animal. Many were lost in combat, and it was a known fact that wounded or otherwise crippled animals were the fare of the cook's fires. Henri knew this, but being his old farm self, he had a very sensitive nature toward animals and especially this one. Hell, maybe they would die together on some distant battlefield and solve the cook's problems.

Through the added exercise, both men and animals were starting to harden and gain strength. Along with the added routines, extra rations were ordered, so it wasn't really all bad.

Henri would go home on the weekends and nearly eat Mimi's kitchen out of everything. Mimi never fussed but did ask him several times if both his legs were hollow. All of that food had to be going somewhere. Henri told her he was stealing the food and selling it to the soldiers back at camp. If she could catch him, he would cut her in on the profits.

During the start of the fourth week, Capitaine LaBauve called the officer staff together and announced that the rigorous physical training would be reduced as another phase of training would start in the next week.

"Besides, gentlemen, aren't we all just a little tired of this chasing our tails? We are now in the best possible physical condition anyway. We can't kill the troops before we even get wherever we are going. For your information, a very special agent has been recruited to train this group in the arts of survival in the wilderness. This man is a relative of one of the senior staff officers. This officer approached General de Chabot with the idea, and the general interviewed the relative. All of this is with the general's complete blessing, so pay attention."

The next morning at assembly, a tall heavyset man was introduced to the command by the capitaine.

"Men, this is Monsieur Vitale Langlois from the Americas. He is considered an expert in the ways of the wilderness and has lived among the savages there. Pay close attention to his teachings. They may one day save your lives. Henceforth, classes with Monsieur Langlois will be with Section One in the morning and Section Two in the afternoon. The times you are not in his class, I am certain we can find nice things to keep you occupied and out of trouble. Section One, go into the armory with Monsieur Langlois. Section Two, see to your mounts and prepare for drill."

Monsieur Langlois was just over six feet tall with a heavy frame. One could see as he removed his coat and hat that he was not fat, but hard and muscular. He had a heavy mustache and large bushy eyebrows through which peered intense dark eyes. He took small square spectacles from his shirt pocket; and when he put them on, he resembled a banker, as someone whispered. He had lived with savages? This was hard to believe.

"Gentlemen, my name is Vitale Langlois, and I have just been introduced as monsieur. Please, for the sake of informality and learning, address me as Vitale. Or you may call me whatever is of your choosing, but please not late for mealtime."

There was a nervous laughter, and he continued, "As your capitaine has told you, I did live among the native people in the Americas. They are not savages. Most are a gentle people and only fight as needed. They have a lifestyle much different than any we could imagine. They are dedicated to their tribe, family, leaders, and religion. They are peaceful and yet warlike. During this course, I will try to relate to these people and their means of survival in a harsh environment. Actually it is not harsh at all if one is prepared and has the knowledge for survival.

"If I may at this time, I would like to enlighten you on my history and story. I love to talk and share my stories and sincerely hope I will not bore you. My father was in the French Armée with General Montcalm in the Canada wars with the British. As you may know, General Montcalm was killed near Quebec. My father was a young man then and was wounded in the same battle. While in hospital in Quebec, he met my mother who was tending wounded. They were married, and he never returned to France. I was born in 1763, the same year that ended the wars with the damn English. France gave up all rights in the Americas. As I became of age to work, there really wasn't much to do except maybe work on the riverboats or around the docks in Quebec. I went as far as the local schools would allow and knew I would have to leave.

"About age thirteen, I left home with three others near my age. We had heard about the wealth to be made trapping for furs along the rivers and lakes. It was early spring, and the snows were just starting to melt and fill the streams. We were warned about the strong currents. There were twelve of us in the party. Most were experienced trappers, and we were going along to help skin the animals and do whatever was asked to earn our keep and to learn the trade.

"We carried our entire lives in our packs. I had saved enough to buy a knife and fighting hatchet. The hatchet was called a tomahawk. This fine weapon I will describe later. The others, except for us newer ones, had muskets and pistols. I had never fired or held a gun in my life. The first time one of the others killed a small deer, the explosion scared me out of my wits.

"Leaving Quebec in three canoes with four men in each plus supplies, we paddled for several days until we reached a large lake one could not see across. We followed the shore until we came to a marsh area that seemed to have no end. Turning into a small river, we went another few miles and made our camp on a large hill covered with trees. A large dugout space was on the side of the hill.

"An entire day was spent cutting down small trees and making a cover over the cavelike affair. The older trappers said this would be ample cover during rain, and our fires would not be visible. They kept talking about the savages and, if possible, how they were to be avoided at all costs. We started setting traps the next day and by late afternoon already had twenty large beavers. It was important to learn how to skin the beaver without damage to the pelt. The first of many tasty beavers were eaten. We had them in stew, roasted, more stew, and more roasted. There was not much hunting as gunfire might alert the savages.

"We stayed there and trapped until just before the first snows. This was the first of many seasons for me. After that first season, I had enough to buy a musket and pistol and other supplies I would need. It gave my family enough to sustain us for the winter.

"Often the season was peaceful, but on several occasions, the savages did find us. At the worst of such, my party was wiped out other than three of us. We were going home at the end of a season, and just as we rounded a river bend, we were met with dozens of arrows from the trees along the bank. Some men were hit outright. All of the canoes overturned, and I was fortunate not to be hit and found myself under the overturned canoe, moving rapidly downstream. I went several kilometers, making certain the savages had not followed this far. I managed to get paddles and just a few meager things that floated by. I never did see any of my companions again. After hiding under the trees for several days and eating raw fish, roots, and berries, I ventured out in the canoe and finally made it home. All was lost for that season. The other two had survived somehow and had walked back.

"At one point, I lived with a tribe of friendly Indians and learned much about their culture and means of survival. These were the Moackh Tribe of the Iroquois Nation. I married a beautiful Indian girl and would probably be there with them yet. She and our child died during childbirth. I knew then that this life was not for me. My mother had told me many times that God does work in mysterious ways. I decided to go home to Quebec and try to make a new life. It was a harsh life in the wilderness and only for the young and hearty or, as my friends said, the dumb and ugly.

"While in Quebec, I was around the wharf and ship area one night visiting the taverns. As usual, I had a bit much of the firewater, as my Indian brethren called it. I woke up the next morning on a ship. We were on the St. Lawrence River just entering the Atlantic. The mate told me I could either swim back or work off my passage. Merde, hell of a choice! All I had was my clothes and the small bag with just a few spare clothes. My knife and purse were gone from the bag. But they had overlooked the small gold coins I had sewn in the waistband of my trousers. There were twenty in all, put there for emergencies.

"My father had died the previous year and my mother this year. My worthless brother was living in the house with his cow of a wife and their three snot-nosed brats. So I really had no reason to stay in Quebec.

"The ship, loaded with timbers, was sailing for England. The passage took nearly three weeks. The old scow of a ship wallowed and flopped about. Luckily I did not get sick with the pitching and rolling, but several other 'newly hired' fellows did. One cried that his wife and children needed him. I don't know whatever happened to him. He wailed all the time. I think they threw him over the side to shut him up."

Vitale told them all to take a short break. "Be back in fifteen minutes. We can't have anyone pissing in their pants and especially not me."

He resumed. "Late one afternoon, we landed at a shipyard down the river Thames from London. There were ships under construction everywhere, and we heard this was the main construction yard for armed merchant ships for the East India Trade. All I could think of was getting off that damnable scow. I wanted no more ships in my life. My chance came two days later when I was asked to go ashore with several others to fetch fresh supplies. When their back was turned, I slipped off in the direction of the lights I had seen the night before. Someone said it was London.

"I must have looked a sight with my scraggly beard and even worse clothes. I bought clothes, boots, a knife, and a few other things at a shop selling used things that were probably stolen. I went back to the dock area to seek any information about passage to France. There were relatives there I had never met, but at least they were my people. My father had told me their names long ago.

"Thank God for my gold coins. I could cut small portions off and buy much-needed articles and food. I would be very cautious this time and leave the firewater alone. I did get passage to France and made my way to Paris and the home of my cousin. After hearing my tales of survival and with the forming of this detachment, he asked if I thought sharing my experiences, as a part of your training, would be of value. We shall see. This is my tale, gentlemen, my history. It is not a proud one, but it is survival.

"We have developed a schedule of things that we consider most important to wilderness survival. Some you already know, but the application will be entirely different from anything you have seen until now. Possibly we can make you honorary savages. Not savages, gentlemen, Indians."

Henri was writing as fast as he could. This was one of the most incredible tales he had ever heard. He wanted to share every word with the family. He was certain they would be as fascinated as he was. Vitale noticed Henri writing as if not to miss a single word and paused several times to watch and let him catch up. *The fellow must have hand exhaustion by now*, he thought. As he concluded his introductory remarks, they were given another short recess. Henri went to Vitale and introduced himself.

"Monsieur, that was the most fascinating tale I have ever heard. This wilderness survival is very interesting to me. I hope to learn a lot and maybe pass it on to others."

"Merci. I saw you writing as fast as your crayon would go. There is much to learn about this, and lives can be saved or lost in an instant of battle or just walking down a wooded path."

"I know, monsieur. I have seen much of it in campaigns where I have been."

"Are you a combat veteran then?" inquired Vitale.

"Oui, monsieur, I have served in several."

Vitale thought, *How can this be? He is very young and an officer too. He must be one of those pampered kids they tend to stick in these positions.* Yet this was an elite unit with only the best and most qualified chosen.

During the meal period, he inquired of his cousin, "Just who is that impressionable young man? How was he given such responsibility at this age?"

His cousin laughed and told him, "Henri is a twice decorated hero and probably the best officer in the unit." When he related the story of the Bébé Tigre and the events during the revolt, Vitale was astounded. When he was told Henri was General de Chabot's adopted son, he was further astounded. He must get to know this man a bit better.

During the rest of the week, the schedule was reversed with Section Two in the morning and Section One in the afternoon. There seemed to be no end to the interesting things Vitale discussed. He approached the subject matter with interest and enthusiasm. He actually surprised himself with the way he was conducting the classes.

Henri was always there writing as fast as he could and asking questions. His questions were always correct and very sensible. On Saturday morning during the dress parade and their dismissal for the day of rest, Vitale made a point of watching Henri and the way he commanded his section. There was an air of confidence and sureness not found in many his age.

A day of rest! They were more than ready for this. As soon as they were dismissed, Henri took Satan to the stable area and noticed the general's carriage waiting in front of the headquarters building. If he hurried, maybe he could ride straight home and not with the others with the many stops. Luck was with him. As soon as he arrived, the general was coming out and asked if he wanted a ride. Henri got in, and the general told him they were going to have just a short "staff meeting," and it wouldn't take long.

They stopped at a tavern and found several other officers already cheerful with the fruit of the vine. Henri and the general had "several," and true to his word, they didn't stay more than an hour. Still, that was enough time for several toasts and mugs of wine. Henri, not used to this, was unsteady and wobbling a bit when they left.

The general laughed and said, "Now, my young officer, you are about to pay your dues and see what I have to go through when I go home with a belly full of giggle juice. No holding hands and sissy stuff for you this night. Not to worry, my boy. It is so much fun making amends. Tomorrow will be another day."

When they poured themselves out of the carriage, Ange and Madame were waiting and couldn't help but laugh at the two. They were greeted with hugs, some scolding, and comments as "birds of a feather."

Henri soon fell asleep in the sitting room, and Ange had to assist him up the stairs. She put him in his bed, pulled off his boots, took off his jacket, and covered him. He was partially awake when she kissed him and said, "No matter mon amour, welcome home. Just please do not make this a habit as Poppa does."

20

Weapon of War

The survival classes were scheduled to run for nearly three more weeks. Monsieur Vitale held their attention to the point of requests that he return after hours for more detailed instruction. His method of teaching was filled with the actual stories of real-life adventure and as much hands-on training as possible.

He instilled in them that the basic rule of survival was to never give up no matter the situation; always be aware of everything in the immediate surroundings; think smart, quick, and ahead; and above all improvise, improvise, improvise. There is always a way.

"Don't be afraid to shit in the forest. All other dumb creatures do it. Just don't get caught with your pants around your ankles."

The subject matter was so varied and so diverse that Henri often thought that this man could not have possibly done these things, and yet he had and proved it over and over again. They were instructed in great detail the improvising of just about everything: weapons, cooking, safe food, rope skills, direction finding, basic medical practices, and even hand-to-hand combat. Everyone agreed that they hoped never to get that close to the enemy.

A weapon could be just about anything. A rock tied to a rope or vine and swung around with force. A stick or pole could be sharpened by rubbing on a hard surface. They made slingshots with their belts and a piece of cloth torn from their uniform. Monsieur Vitale told them that David killed Goliath with one of these, so why not them. They made spears and learned to throw them. A straight sharpened pole could be thrown and hit a target at quite a distance if they practiced. That same pole is used to stop a charging horse and rider. Be on the alert for enemy on foot carrying sharpened poles.

Monsieur Vitale brought his fighting hatchet or tomahawk for demonstration. "I told you at the introduction that I would show you the fine art of this weapon. With the modern firearms, you may not think this useful. Believe me, it is deadly and silent. The savages use this with great accuracy. Other than the bow and arrow, it is their favorite in close quarters."

The razor-sharp axe blade was metal with a long wooden handle for balance. There were feathers tied to a thong in the bottom of the handle. He said this was for luck. The savages were a superstitious people but very realistic. Some of the tomahawks he had seen were of sharpened stone and the handle lashed on with leather strips. He showed them how to use the tomahawk in close combat, and it could also be thrown with great accuracy.

The most basic weapon was the knife. He preferred a knife with a long heavy blade for strength. His first knife was lost long ago when he was captured for his sea journey, but he had another made by a blacksmith near his cousin's house. It was encased in a heavy leather sheath and resembled a small short sword. He said this double edge one could cut in either direction and was much better than the normal single-edged version. The handle was made comfortable to the hand by wrapping it with leather, and it too had a thong for securing the knife to the wrist. This knife with the stout heavy blade could be thrown, as the tomahawk, with great accuracy if one practiced. He proved his point by marking a small circle on the side of the building. Monsieur Vitale stood with his back to the circle, a slow walk of about twenty paces, then a sudden movement and flash. All they heard was a *thunk* as the knife was imbedded deeply in the wood exactly in the middle of the circle. They were completely taken aback. Never had they seen such skill. Then he did the same thing with the tomahawk.

Capitaine LaBauve went to the general that evening with a request that the division blacksmiths make each man a knife and tomahawk. These were fighting tools that could be much needed in the stealth that they would be required to do. The general said it was most unusual, and he would look into it. When he called Monsieur Vitale and received a demonstration, he approved the request at once. It took the blacksmiths two weeks to complete the knives and tomahawks. When they were delivered, they were works of art. Each man was issued a knife and a tomahawk for individual training. Many hours were spent at the edge of the wooded area where the firewood was cut. With the many troopers throwing at stumps and logs, the noise resembled a herd of runaway horses. Each man did acquire a useful level of skill and accuracy.

Henri took his knife and tomahawk home and demonstrated his new skills to the family at the expense of the side of the stable. The general said this was the best investment yet to the fledgling unit of Faucon de la Nuit.

"Here, lad, let me try this infernal thing." He tried to throw the knife several times, but gave up, saying, "This is damn clumsy. I hope I never get that close to the bastards again anyway."

"It wasn't all that bad, monsieur. You did hit the side of the stable."

Ange laughed, and the general mumbled something about youth and respect and stalked back into the house.

Fires could be made with various means. Mostly they used flint and steel, but they were shown the small bow with the fast-twirling stick. They could use dry shavings or threads pulled from their clothes as tinder. Small shielded fires in holes in the earth provided warmth and means to cook yet were not visible at a distance. Never stare intently at a fire. When one looks back into the darkness, he cannot see an enemy.

Visibility and stealth were the means by which the small units penetrating far ahead of the main body of troops would survive. Noise, above all, was to be abated. Monsieur Vitale taught them not only how to cover or darken all shiny metal objects with soot or lampblack but also how to tie cloth strips around sabres, horse reins, and other things to stop the clanking and rattling. He said a body of savages in a war party could move through the forest with little or no detection. They would do well to learn and do likewise. Their fair white faces should be blackened with soot as well. A shining white face reflected like a lantern on a dark night. He proved this by having several men go several hundred paces and look back at the others in the reflecting sunlight. They looked like beacons. He suggested that possibly uniforms could be issued that would be drab and blend with the forest or surroundings. He said the bright colors and shining metal of the French uniforms were noticeable for miles.

It was not feasible to change all of this, but at least he did have each man issued a dark blanket to be used as cover during bright sunlight. This extra blanket was to be proven a godsend for man and beast alike during the piercing cold of Northern Europe and Russia. Monsieur Vitale showed them how to take the large blanket and cover the entire body, draping it over the horse. A hole was cut for vision, and the result was what resembled a detachment of ghost riders.

To prove the worth of this, they rode quietly through the entire encampment during a dark night, and no one knew of their presence. They rode up to a sentry and scared the poor fellow so badly he fired into the air, dropped his musket, and ran madly behind one of the buildings. He was yelling something about horrible, scary things in black with legs of a horse. Capitaine LaBauve had to give a report on the matter and merely stated a night falcon had scared the sentry. But the disguise was proven and its worth noted.

During the next week of instruction, Capitaine LaBauve called Henri into his office. "Lieutenant, I have just returned from staff headquarters, and not to be an alarmist, we have been ordered to intensify our training and to prepare for campaign departure near the first week of Mai. That is only two weeks away. Also, I have been promoted to major, and I will need you as capitaine and second in command of the group. You will still be required as leader of your section and also as my second in command. You are very young to have this responsibility, but you have proven yourself and your capabilities. There should be no problems. Do you have any questions?"

"No, monsieur. I am sure I can do this. The questions will come later when the shock wears off. Is there anything I need to do immediately?"

"Not immediately, my young capitaine, just be ready for anything at any time. I would like to present you with my old capitaine insignia. I like to think it has brought me good fortune a time or two. Possibly they will do the same for you. God knows, if we do go to the Russias, we will need all the good fortune we can gather."

"Merci, monsieur. I will be honored to wear your insignia. I hope I can do as well as you." *Damn, Henri thought to himself, I have just made capitaine and so fast. Usually this takes years. Things must be on the move. Capitaine (uh, Major) LaBauve did say to prepare for a campaign. I have to ask the general.*

Each trooper was issued a coil of small rope. They spent hours learning the various uses of the rope and knots.

"Merde, we are not in the navy, or are they thinking of sending us to sea with all of this?" they complained. Monsieur Vitale said this may be true, they were not sailors; but when the time came to tie oneself properly in a tree or lash together branches for shelter or any number of things, they would be doubly glad they had learned this skill.

They were taught direction finding without the compass. Once again they heard the fact that mosses always grow on the north side of trees, rocks, and things in the forest. One can key on the sun, moon, and stars for direction. They went over the skills with the compass again and again. It must always be read in the open without metal objects about. Every trooper was shown the compass and then the knife blade along the side to make the needle move, giving a false reading. Many already knew these skills; but this refresher, as it was presented, made everlasting impressions.

Each man was issued small rolls of cloth to be used as potential bandages or bindings. Very basic medical treatment in the field was taught by a field doctor. Medical personnel would not be assigned to these advance units. Each man would have to help himself or a fellow trooper in case of emergency.

Probably the most interesting classes were what is edible in the wild and what is not. A sick trooper is of no help to himself or his unit. Most things that do not reek of rot are edible. Bugs, worms, and grubs found under rocks and fallen trees, most any cleaned animal, or bird are edible. Always fish and even minnows and tadpoles. The bark of trees can be boiled into a tea of sorts. It may be bitter, but it is sustaining. Then one can eat the boiled bark. Some of the men said they would never eat anything as this.

Monsieur Vitale informed them, "You will eat these things and many others if you are hungry enough. The alternative is much worse. Just hold your nose, don't look, and swallow."

The final classes were of hand-to-hand combat. Here they were taught the fine art of death by bare hand and whatever else may be available. There is no gentlemanly honor in this. There are no rules except kill or be killed. Anything goes with knives, clubs, rifle butts, and anything one can find close by to strike with. Dirt thrown into an opponent's eyes, biting, scratching, kicking; all is fair and never forget this. In one demonstration, Monsieur Vitale threw a trooper to the ground, jumped on him, and in swift mocking succession said he had just broken both collarbones and both legs, kicked in his ribs, broken his neck, and torn his midsection open.

"Gentlemen, if this bastard gets up, run like the winds of hell."

Monsieur Vitale closed the sessions and the training with memorable words, "Men of Faucon de la Nuit, never fear the valley of the shadow of death as you are now the meanest bastards in the valley. With this training, I hope we have not created monsters, but survivors. I wish you all success and Godspeed."

21

Mon Capitaine

With the training classes at an end, the units went back on normal schedule of five and a half days per week and weekends of rest. The general sent word for Henri to be ready for home in midafternoon on Samedi. Henri hoped he would not have to endure another "staff meeting." Luck was with him as the general announced he needed to go straight home and spend as much time with Madame as possible. Henri would need to do the same with Ange. Orders had come to alert the entire Armée for movement within the next several weeks. This was the first week of May 1812. It was no surprise the objective was positively the Russias, and the campaign promised to be a lengthy one. It was evident things would happen soon as Henri had seen masses of supplies and provisions as never before. The general told Henri of certain recent plans and swore him to secrecy.

"Monsieur New Capitaine, I wouldn't be telling you any of this if you weren't trustworthy. Sometimes things just get imprisoned in my head and need to be shared. I can't share my true feelings to the staff as some of it may sound traitorous. This is an error of great magnitude my Napoleon is making. I have known him personally for many years, but he is as stubborn as our pack animals. We know nothing of these Russias except that the lands are vast, stark, bitter cold in winter, and seas of mud in the spring. This information is probably well known to the damn Russkies by now. Alexander has spies out everywhere. Our troop movements have been on the rise lately. They will know something is up.

"Napoleon has told us that the rains have passed for this spring and that we will be well established in Moscow by winter. He has told me in private not to worry. All of this has been researched in great detail. There should not be problems. Horse merde! Well, it is my duty to worry with being in command of so many lost souls who rely on my judgment. I still and will always feel this campaign is a mistake. I cannot share this with my wife, and be careful what you tell Ange. A soldier's news should always be optimistic, cheerful, and not full of gloom. Do I make sense, Henri? Sometimes I just tend to chatter like Mimi, but with you, I know I can be my true self and not worry about you blabbering."

"You can, monsieur. Anything you tell me never leaves. I feel the same bonding with you. You have become the father I never knew, and for that I am eternally grateful. There is just one thing I am shy about talking with you. Perhaps this is not the proper time."

"If you are about to request permission for my daughter's hand, son, for god's sake, spit it out. This may be the time before we have to leave for God only knows how long. I have never seen such a perfect match of young people in my life. Just do not blame me for her temper and what she may do to you later in life. She is, after all, her mother's daughter. I may be a general in the Grande Armée of France, but my wife can make me crawl and behave as no other ever has. You may be subject to the same fate. It is a common joke among men that if man had one of those 'things,' he could rule the world without equal or worry. That one 'thing' has been the nemesis of kings and nations alike since the beginning of time. Think about it, my boy."

"I have, monsieur, more than anything else in my life. Oh, I am so sorry! Please don't take it wrong, monsieur. I was not referring to the 'thing.' I was talking about Ange. Did I put my foot in my mouth?"

The general was laughing and said, "No disrespect taken, son. I will not divulge any secret thoughts of 'things.' This is men's talk. Hell, the ladies wouldn't catch on anyway."

"I did mean I do love Ange, monsieur, and will do everything to make her happy."

"Oui, I do believe you, son. I will speak to the keeper of my 'thing' about this when we arrive home. I am certain you have no worries on the matter."

When they arrived home, the general hurried into the dining room and busied himself at the wine cabinet. Madame joined him and knew at once something was in the wind.

"Andre, is something worrying you? You seem distant, and I do sense something."

"Ah, Vivien, mon amour, you read me like a book and sense my every thought. Oui, there is much on my mind, and I will share all of it after a staple of this fine relaxing juice of the vine. Here, my sweet, I will pour you a measure." After they had several glasses, they took their glasses into the sitting room.

"Great heavens, Vivien, it is hotter than probably Hades itself outdoors, and you have a fire in here. We will surely swelter, or is this maybe an excuse for us to shed our clothes."

"Andre, I will do no such in here without privacy. You know I am cold at times and do need a fire for relaxation. I love the comfort of a fire despite the time of the year. It is only a small fire anyway. Please don't keep me in suspense any longer. I fear you have news of the pending campaign, and you will have to leave again. Is this your news?"

"You have guessed my news as usual. I could never keep secrets from you. Oui, we will depart for the Russias in just a few weeks. I fear this will be a long and difficult campaign. Napoleon is determined to deal with Alexander and his Russian bear once and for all. I have spoken to Napoleon several times and expressed my fears and those of others in the staff. He will not move on his decision, and we must obey. He is our leader. However, this is not the extent of my news. It seems a certain capitaine in my command is very much in love with our daughter and has approached me concerning her hand in marriage."

"What! A capitaine you say! Pray tell me, what is his name? Do I know him?"

"Wait, Vivien, I thought you would not be surprised, but we have known the day would come someday for these two."

"But, Andre, you said a capitaine in your command. Henri is a lieutenant. Oh! Unless he has been rapidly promoted and now thinks he can support a wife. Is that it? I know they are both of age, but they are still my babies. Oh, hold me, Andre. I suddenly feel so old. My baby daughter and the other young man of our lives." She put her head on his shoulder and started to cry.

"These are tears of joy, sadness, and relief, Andre. I have known in my heart this day would come for a long time. This was known to God for a long time and since they were small children. Am I to understand that our Henri is now a capitaine?"

"Oui, love, he has been promoted and is second in command in the new unit. Please don't tell him, but I am so proud of him. Everything this young man has done has been of his own merit. He is destined for a brilliant future if he maintains this course. And my baby daughter is to be the wife of such a fine man. I must tell you, my dear Vivien, I am elated. I know she will be safe in his care and trust him with my life as well as that of my daughter. If you are in agreement, I will make the announcement at dinner tonight. I would like to have Mimi at the table with us. Our children are hers as well as ours."

Madame had a confidential talk with Ange and told her that Henri had informally asked the general if he could have Ange's hand in marriage. Ange was not surprised and told her mother that Henri and she had spoken of this many times in the past year. It would be her dream come true if she could become the wife of Henri. Madame said the general would like to make the betrothal announcement at dinner that evening, and would she please ask Mimi if she could dine with them for this special occasion. Ange ran to Henri's room and softly knocked on the door.

"Oui, please come in."

"Henri, Mother has just told me that Father would like to formally announce our betrothal tonight. Did you know anything of this? I am involved too, I think."

"I did speak about it in the carriage coming home this afternoon, but I did not know he planned a scene of it so soon. Do you agree, or is this too sudden?"

"Henri, I am overjoyed, and you know it. I have dreamed of this and being your wife for what seems like all of my life. You know all that we have talked about. It is just that this was so sudden and surprising. I was startled, I must admit; but oui, the sooner the better."

"Oui, I know, and I am happy that these people could agree to let me marry the girl of my dreams."

Ange came over to him and kissed him as almost never before. The kiss weakened his knees and nearly took his breath away. He felt the intense tingling as never before. "Mon dieu, I am dying or have died and gone to heaven."

"Just think, Henri, we can kiss like that every day for the rest of our lives."

"Then I know I will die," he stammered.

She left him saying that she must get ready for this special dinner and announcement that would change the course of their lives.

Mimi served the meal and then served herself and sat at the table next to Madame. There was silence for a time with only a slight tinkling of utensils on the plates or a glass of wine being refilled, or perhaps a slight cough or chewing sounds. Finally Madame could stand it no longer.

"Andre, you are deliberately causing this silence to make us anxious. We all know why we are here and what is going to happen. Please don't amuse yourself and toy with us any longer."

The general laughed to break the tension and looked around the table at all staring at him. "I apologize, my dear family. I have been thinking about this announcement I will make for some time. Not just for tonight, but as we all have come to realize, this event has been inevitable for some time. In honest truth, I am somewhat at a loss of perfect words for this occasion. I know all of you must find that hard to believe, but it is true. The matter before me and us all is very precious to my heart just as the ones I must speak about.

"As my dear wife so aptly put it this afternoon, we are not giving up a daughter or a son. We are, in essence, gaining or losing no one. The ones gaining in this instance are only the dear people directly involved. You are both very young, but in this rapidly moving world of war and conquest, it is the proper time. I must ask you both formally here and in front of the rest of your family if you are ready to accept this responsibility and to commit and pledge to one another your love and allegiance."

Henri stood, pulled Ange to her feet, and faced her. They faced each other as Henri looked directly into her eyes. He held both of her hands. Madame and Mimi were trying their best to hold their composure and fight back the tears.

"Monsieur, and my family, I am no great speaker as all of you know. I have known and believed with all my heart that this moment would come. I have tried to think of perfect words, but somehow any words I choose do not seem adequate. I only know that Ange has been and will always be the love of my life. I will do everything within my power to assure her well-being and happiness. Monsieur, I ask you and the rest of the family to please accept my request for Ange's hand in marriage."

"And now, baby daughter, what do you say to this request?"

"I can only say oui with all of my heart and being. I have loved Henri, I think, from the first time we met. I will pledge my life to his happiness and strive to be a perfect wife."

That brought Madame and Mimi rushing around them, crying and hugging each of them. The general entered the hugging and finally said the occasion warranted a toast and just one of many. Ange stood on her toes and kissed Henri who was grinning and the epitome of relief. The general had poured generous glasses of wine for all. They were standing facing one another except Ange who was clinging to Henri's arm.

"Baby daughter, you may let him loose now. He is yours to keep, and please don't break his arm. I am certain I will need him in my Armée in the future. Henri, welcome, the second time, to our family. I sincerely wish the two of you all eternal and God-blessed happiness. Damn, I feel so old with the youth of our house officially betrothed. Drink up, drink up, we have several more toasts pending. Henri, you are grinning as I have never seen you before. You resemble one of the packhorses after eating a bitter weed."

Everyone laughed and agreed but knew it must be the relief of all reliefs for Henri. Madame and Mimi were chattering away with Ange about future plans. Madame said they could certainly stay here and could just take over the entire third floor or at least until children were expected. Henri and Ange blushed a deep crimson. Madame said it was the way of life and no need to be embarrassed. She was looking forward to grandchildren. Henri was astounded at her frankness and looked at Ange. She was still blushing. Mimi told them after the fourth toast that she wasn't used to this and needed to get back to her duties.

The general said, "Vivien, I thought you said they could have the entire third floor. I thought we all knew about them renting the chicken house. That would be good enough." Madame glared at him as he laughed pouring another glass of wine.

Before leaving, Mimi held the general's and Madame's arms and said, "I can never merci enough for your kindness over the years and accepting me as family. You will never know what this means to this old woman. My two babies now getting married. I agree, Andre, I too feel so very old. But it's a good 'old.' Such happiness I don't think I have ever felt."

She went over to Henri and Ange, similarly grabbed each by the arm, and said, "I am happier at this moment than you shall ever know. God's blessing to you both." She turned quickly and walked very fast to the kitchen. Everyone knew she was going to have a good cry of happiness.

After a time and more toasts, Henri and Ange started gathering the dishes and food from the table and taking the things into the kitchen. They would help Mimi tonight. The general and Madame said their good nights and went up the stairs holding hands.

"Look at the lovebirds, Henri. Do you suppose we will ever be that way after years of marriage?"

"Well, I hope so, and I never get too old to tease or want you. It is hard enough now to keep your modesty in the right perspective."

"You can get away with that statement now that we are betrothed; and to tell the truth, I am having problems too, thinking of what will be." She blushed and turned to the kitchen with an armload of dishes.

22

The Russias Loom

The next Jeudi, the general sent for Henri. "Henri, do not breathe a word of this, but we march next *semaine*. Those of us who can will be on leave this coming Samedi and until the following Mercredi. Then we will report back on Jeudi and move out the next day. Your unit will have special orders being among the first troops deployed and leading the advance. This is the life of a soldier, and we must live it to the fullest when we can. It is a life of constant greetings and departures to our loved ones. It can sometimes be a good life or the total reverse of things. Hell, I don't know why I am telling you all of this. These are things you already know, but you are just so recently betrothed, and I know you feel the pangs of loneliness even now just as I do. It just never seems to be any easier given the frequency over the years. One sees much through the adventure but does miss so much of home."

"I know how you feel, monsieur. I have felt it many times. Already, as a soldier, I have seen these going-and-coming things. I agree it is not easy to say goodbye. Maybe one day when we have conquered the world, we can stay home."

"Ha, do not count those chickens before they hatch from little square eggs. I wonder if our Small Master will ever have sufficient lands in his basket. He seems driven with it and drives us without mercy. But please be ready for this last leave. I will see you at the carriage for home on Samedi morning. We can, at least, have several days to contemplate our fate. I plan to make the most of my leave."

The official word was relayed through the ranks later that morning. The shock was realized as final. All were hastening in last-minute preparations before the last leave home. Many were just too far from home and could not do anything except try to rest and relax their minds as best they could. Many fitful naps would be taken.

To counter this and relieve the minds of the troops, many things of last-minute preparations were conceived by the officers. Everyone realized the reasoning behind this and accepted the orders as inconsequential and yet just a part of being soldiers far away from home. They were not supposed to think, just follow the orders. Idleness and slack time gives one time to think, and strange things often happen when large groups of mostly uneducated troops think and conceive rumors of every magnitude. So they polished everything in sight, carried this there or that somewhere else, brushed their horses, checked and rechecked everything for the seemingly thousandth time.

Michael teased, "Well, Monsieur Almost Married One, what are you going to do with your time?"

"I really don't have any plans, Michael. I just want to spend as much time with Ange as I can. What are you going to do?"

"I am going to the inn, find me the biggest jug of wine I can. Then the most willing girl and spend the entire time guzzling and fornicating. It will give me something to remember and maybe something to come back to."

"I know what you mean about something and someone to come back to."

On Samedi morning, Henri made his way to the general's waiting carriage. He had lain awake on his cot that night, listening to the rain *plop, plop, plop* on the canvas tent and thought about leaving. He knew that Ange would be prepared for the news of the Armée marching to the Russias but would be upset with the final news. The knowledge of leaving, while always present, was not as evident and vivid as now.

Everything seemed so final now like a monstrous ocean wave crashing onward sweeping everything in its path. No opposing force on this earth could stop it now, and one either accepts this fate or goes mad with trying to devise a method to change it. He would have to busy himself with dedication and duties to his command to take his thoughts from Ange, home, and all he held dear. It would be impossible at times, and he knew he would have many more fitful and restless nights notwithstanding the exhaustion of forced march through strange country.

He had heard it over and over a wise soldier does not dwell on his fate and keeps those precious thoughts of home and loved ones in a small corner of his heart. He draws them out in private times to cherish and to give him courage and determination for returning to his home. He was certain all soldiers did this and knew it to be true when he observed someone smiling silently and privately to himself.

It was misting rain on that dreary morning, and Henri was very anxious with the waiting. The driver told him to go ahead and get in the carriage as the general had notified him that he would be a bit more tending to some last-minute things before departing for home. Henri was glad to get in the carriage and out of the rain. The carriage was musty and damp even though the driver kept it swept out, cleaned, and aired as much as possible. The general said it was the leather seats that were several years old and the many cigars he had burned in it. In a few minutes, the general came rushing out and ordered the driver to make haste for home.

"Damn all of this merde anyway. There are always last-minute things everyone forgets. Then it becomes an emergency to get it done. This always happens when I am about to leave for something important like going home. This time, it is very important to get home and spend as much time as possible. Henri, are you prepared for this debacle that will take us away again?"

"Oui, monsieur, as ready as I shall ever be. Everything is in order. We have checked everything several times and hope we have not forgotten anything. The horses have been exercised and appear to be in very good shape. The pack animals have been tested with over heavy loads. I think we are ready. The only major task will be today and telling the news."

"Oh, I agree to that. I always dread telling my wife of leaving. She knows this is our life, but it still is not easy. It is the loneliness and unknowing that really bothers her. There are precious few communications during these campaigns, and those left at home are subject to rumors very often unfounded. During the Egyptian campaign, one of my fellow officers was reported among the dead. His poor family was distraught for several months until word came he was not. While he was missing and lost for a time, he certainly was alive and well."

The remainder of the ride home was mostly in silence with each to his own thoughts about what to say and how the news would be received. It was never easy, and Henri was trying to think of kind and encouraging words not only to ease the pain of Ange but also to relieve him of the guilt he felt.

They arrived much earlier than usual this Samedi, and they didn't have to say anything about the impending departure. The ladies somehow knew due to their early arrival and the looks on their faces. Madame grabbed Andre by the arm, and they silently went into the sitting room. Henri took Ange by the hand, and they went out onto the back porch and sat watching the rain. The rain was coming down more steadily now and promised to be an all-afternoon affair. *Just as well*, thought Henri. The weather matched the mood.

"Henri, when are you leaving, and do you have any idea for how long? I have dreaded this moment from the first I knew of it."

"I will be home with you until next Mercredi. Jeudi is final preparations and the Armée marches on Vendredi. I wish I could make this easy for both of us, but we both knew this life from the beginning. What can I say or do? I feel so helpless, Ange. The other times I left were not nearly as bad as this time. We just cannot tell when we will return. Before, we had to sneak around for affections, but no more. We can hold hands and even hug with short kisses, and no one will care that much. Oh, I am sorry, chéri, for blabbering on. Nothing I can say or do make this easier."

"I know what you mean and how you feel, mon amour. I felt the same every time you have left. There are just no words, but please let's not dwell it. It is going to happen no matter what. Let's enjoy the time we have and think about happier times and those to come."

"I guess with you watching your mother all of your life in these same circumstances, you do understand more than most would. You are so wise. As we would say, you are a true trooper. Merci for your understanding. I am just feeling sorry for myself. Come, chéri, let's go bother Mimi for a cup of tea and maybe some sweet cakes. I need to tell her the news too. I'll wager she will be happy that she will not have to fix any of that hash stuff for a time."

The time went by faster than anticipated, and with the virtual twinkle of an eye, it was next Mercredi afternoon. Ange and Henri had gone to the marketplace and the large square at Notre Dame. They had stopped at their favorite small café overlooking the river and enjoyed tea and cakes. Henri did not wear his uniform and preferred it that way. He said when he was in uniform, it seemed everyone stared at him and considered him too young to have such rank and decorations. She chided him at these times, saying he was too self-conscious. He should be proud of who and what he was. He would answer that he was, but he was not a braggart either and preferred to remain more anonymous.

That night at the evening meal, Mimi did indeed serve the hash, saying, "The general's cook would have to perform the duties of it from now on." She gave him a bag of fresh peppers and several bottles of the sauce from hell. She gave Henri a bottle too, but he said to keep his with the general. He doubted he would be eating any hash for a while.

With the meal over, Ange and Henri went on the back porch to sit and talk. Both of them remarked that they spent so much time just sitting, talking, and sharing and remembering back to their earlier years, they really couldn't remember what the conversations were all about.

"But that is all right. We know each another as few couples do before marriage," observed Henri.

"Henri, mon amour, have you given thought to children we may have?"

They agreed on at least four or as many as God may bestow. They would like to make their future home in Paris and not too far from their family. They both wished they could find another Mimi but knew she was incomparable with any other. She had been with Madame's family before joining the general and Madame at their marriage. She was friend and family. They went up the stairs to their bedrooms, and Ange kissed Henri and whispered to stay awake if he could, and they could talk more into the night. It would be their last chance for probably many months.

Henri lay on his bed with just his trousers on, watching the half-moon rising over Paris. The weather had cleared, but the air was still heavy with moisture holding the heat of the day. He could hear the birds nesting in the trees surrounding the house and a few night insects singing that the birds were not wary to their presence. He heard the latch click as the door quietly opened.

Ange softly whispered, "Henri, are you awake? Did you give up on me?"

"No, sweet one, I am awake. I don't think I could sleep anyway. I can barely see you in this dim moonlight. I wish there were a brighter moon to see you better. I still carry the small portrait you gave me, but you have changed so much that I will need a new one. I don't really need an image for your memory anyway. I could never forget your beautiful face."

She came over to him and put her arms around his waist, drawing him to her. He put his arms around her waist. She raised her face to his, and their lips met. They kissed for a long time until both of them were nearly breathless. Their two bodies were melted as one. The passion was raging when they pushed apart and slumped in the chairs near the window. They sat holding hands, and no words were spoken for some time with each in their own thoughts of tomorrow. The only sounds were heavy breathing and the night sounds outside.

Finally Henri spoke, "Oh, my very special little Petite Désordre, you will never know how close I was not being able to stop just now. I love you so much. Please forgive any wrong behavior. I will carry these moments with you in my heart wherever this thing takes me. I have carried your memory with me before, and it gives me courage. I do love you and promise to return."

"I know, mon amour, I know. Oh how I know. I wanted so much to give you more to take with you." She squeezed his hand and put her head on his shoulder.

He could feel the moist warm tears as they silently trickled down his chest and mingled with his own.

The carriage left for camp early the next morning, and secretly the two occupants may have been relieved to finally be onward to the latest adventure. The waiting, frustration, and preparations were over. Now they must busy themselves with the emperor's business of war.

Napoleon had devised the Continental System that banned all trade with England from continental Europe. He was determined to choke his hated enemy. Russia had enjoyed extensive trade in prior times, and this system was certainly hurting the Russian economy. Czar Alexander was forced, by internal pressure, to turn a blind eye to those traders who broke the rules. Napoleon decided to bring the Russians back into the fold with the gathering of a massive army to enforce his rules. The initial intent was to frighten the Russians, but the threat failed. The czar ordered deployment of two large Russian armies to protect the motherland.

The result of Napoleon's Grande Armée was units from Poland, Saxony, Italy, Hesse, Bavaria, Holland, Spain, Portugal, Westphalia, Württemberg, Baden, Switzerland, Naples, and even Austria and Prussia. In all, this Grande Armée amassed over six hundred fifty thousand men and was the largest army ever seen in Europe. The preparations and supplies had been amazingly well organized to support such a massive force. There were more than one thousand five hundred supply wagons of every size to carry some twenty million rations of rice and bread, which were pulled by fifty thousand draft horses. The total horses involved in the campaign would be over one hundred fifty thousand.

The general had told Henri that this Grande Armée would be much worse than a plague of locusts swarming over the countryside devouring everything in its path. Locusts at least just ate the vegetation. This mob would devour everything except rocks and probably try to violate every female over the age of five. The destruction would be complete for friend and foe alike.

As the carriage entered the campsite, everything was a bustle of activity. There were several hundred men tending the final packing and tying down of supplies in a line of wagons as far as the eye could see. Other men were checking again the wheels of a long line of cannons and caissons. There were more cannons than Henri had ever seen in one column. And again the immense use of draft animals. Henri heard later that this was only part of the total assemblage of cannons for this campaign. There would be over one thousand cannons when all of their allies' cannons were added. He couldn't conceive the thunder of over a thousand cannons. The din of two or three hundred was deafening enough. To find oneself on the receiving end of such bombardment must be terrifying beyond belief. He felt a sense of relief to know he would be behind and not before this conflagration.

There were thousands of foot soldiers starting to assemble and line the roads each with their heavy loads of muskets, ammunition, and personal supplies. They would sleep in place as assembled this night and move out at first light. Each soldier had to carry his 4.5 kg musket, thirty musket shots and powder, one brush bag, two to three pairs of boots, 1 kg dried biscuits, two shirts, one pair thick liner trousers, one packet of bandage and lint, spare hobnails and boot soles, and 5 kg of flour or rice. The flour and rice would be given to the cooks as required, and each man was eager to be among the first relieved of his burden. The other things would be shared among his comrades as needed on the march. Officers were ordered to notice any soldier trying to "share" with the bushes and ditches along the route.

Major LaBauve called a last-minute staff meeting. He had a large map held in place with several rocks on a table. He explained that this map had been printed from large copper plates of the original map of Russia. The plates had been "borrowed" and handsomely paid for by French conspirators. The war office had these maps printed and the Russian characters changed to French. Napoleon ordered maps issued to each general and commander of special detachments.

Pointing with his small baton to a specific line marked on the map, he said, "Gentlemen, tomorrow at first light, we have the honor to lead. Please note the markings on this map. This will be the route to the Russias as chosen by our emperor. Notice that there should be ample water and forage along the route. It will be our duties to observe the choice forage areas and send a messenger back to the trailing forage units. We will have to note all accessible bridges or means of crossing rivers considering the enormous amount of men and supplies.

"We are to rendezvous with many units of allies along the way. Thus, I need every man in our command to be doubly alert and not to mistake them for an enemy. I do not think this will happen, but be alert. These troops will be in many different uniforms, and it may be confusing. Please bear in mind that the Russian army is far yet to the north, and we should not meet them for some time. I am sure our leader would find it most embarrassing if we blundered and stuck a brother in the ass with a French sword. So be alert, gentlemen.

"We will be approximately fifteen to twenty kilometers in advance of the main group during this phase of noncombat advance. The distance will vary depending on the situation during combat operations. I will leave it up to the individual unit commanders to choose his individual dispatch riders. Without fail, these riders must report exact facts and conditions. Stress this! I do not want to be embarrassed with wrong and faulty information being returned. Get as much rest as you can before dawn. I will always be available to you for any questions. We will sleep in place tonight. See to your animals and any last-minute details. Bonne chance and Godspeed to us all."

Caissons to the front. Move up.

After a fitful and restless night next to Satan, the camp was roused to the sound of bugles and drums. This was it. Everyone in the surrounding areas was stirring and rising. The cooks already had the fires started, and the kitchen helpers came with more wood and water for the morning coffee and tea.

Henri took Satan to the large pile of hay, tied him to the stake there, and went to the cook area. He filled his flask with coffee, took several of the hard biscuits, and stuffed them in his coat pocket. They were like eating rocks, but they did sustain one. Actually when softened in the mouth or with water or coffee, it wasn't all that bad. Tasteless things though. In lieu of his bottle of peppers, Mimi had given him a small cloth bag of peppers. A bite of biscuit, a pinch of pepper, and a mouthful of coffee made a sad but filling morning meal.

He went back to Satan and pulled him away from the hay. "Not too much this morning, you old hog. We have long way to go. We can't have you traveling on a full belly. You will get ample good grass during the next several days. Much better than this old smelly hay."

He saddled Satan and tied down all of his gear. All of his command was finished about the same time. All of this was so well rehearsed, they could almost do it in their sleep. A faint rose color was appearing in the eastern sky when the order to stand ready to mount was given. The order given was to mount from the front ranks and relayed through the troops. He swung on Satan and heard the familiar sound of saddle leather creaking. The next command of "forward" came within the next minute, and the column of Faucon de la Nuit moved at a steady walk to the north and on to the Russias.

May God's hand rest on every man's shoulder, thought Henri.

Henri's group of men was second in the column. Henri thought this would be ideal, and they would not have to eat as much dust as the troops in the rear. However, it had been raining a bit lately, and the dust wouldn't be much of a problem. Farther on, who knows? Michael was riding just behind Henri and moved his horse up next to Henri.

"Well, now what do you suppose we are in for? I hope we are not old men with gray beards by the time we return if we ever do."

"I know how you feel, my friend. This time, leaving was very hard. I know she understood, but I am not sure I do. I guess life is like that at times. There is just so much uncertainty. You may be right about the gray hair. I think we are about to find out."

"Henri, my leave was the best I have ever had. I did find a lovely, very willing girl who would not quit her loving. It went on and on until I finally had to ask her to slow down. I never thought I would do that."

The column passed the general's command center. The general was outside watching the first units moving out. Henri saluted; and the general returned the salute, waved, and yelled something about good luck.

"Bonne chance indeed," said Michael. "It makes one wonder what he knows that we do not."

"A whole helluva lot, Michael. You can bet your last pair of clean boot socks on that. Even with me being so close and almost his son, he won't tell me all that much. He told me one time that it is very lonely at the top, but it does let one taste the best wine."

They rode in silence for some time. Henri swung around in the saddle to see if he could see the last sights of Paris, home, and Ange. In the lightening sky to the east, he could just barely see the outline of the spires of Notre Dame above the tree line. He thought Ange would be there today with Madame to light candles. Suddenly he felt very empty and lonely. He turned his head as the spires fell behind the tree line. The empty feeling passed only partially.

He knew it would never go completely away as long as he had a breath of life.

23

Lithuanians

The long columns of military might snaked their way northward across France. The plan was to follow the river network of Europe as much as possible to afford adequate water for the vast amount of men and animals. Not only were the sources of water important, but the grasslands along the banks would provide much-needed food for the horses and pack animals.

Henri and the men of the Faucon de la Nuit were in the main group of four columns approaching the Russian frontier. The Grande Armée would converge on fronts from the Baltic Sea to the Vistula River in Poland. The main and center group was composed of all French under the direct command of Napoleon. The two hundred thousand men of this group was the largest and would merge with Duke Andoche Junot of Westphalia advancing from Warsaw with seventy-nine thousand Westphalians, Saxons, and Poles. Another group under Prince Karl Philipp Schwarzenberg was marching from Galicia in southeastern Poland with thirty thousand Austrians. Viceroy Eugene de Beauharnais of Italy was routed from Konigsberg with some seventy-nine thousand five hundred Bavarians, Italians, and more French. Other units from Hesse, Holland, Spain, Portugal, Württemberg, Baden, Switzerland, Naples, and other smaller units were arriving daily and adding to the massive army. The total array for the invasion would represent twenty European nations amounting to over six hundred fifty thousand men.

The men of the Faucon de la Nuit did not see the immense army following at their rear and flanks and could not have comprehended the size of such a force anyway. They were far in front of the main body scouting for forage and any military intelligence that could be relayed to Napoleon and the staff officers following. Michael stayed right with Henri most of the time.

"I need to stay close just in case we run into enemy troops and I possibly need to save your worthless ass. Maybe the Boss would give me a medal over that. Or I might just let you get carved up, and I could take your place with a certain pretty girl I know."

"And you would try too, you bag of horse shit. She wouldn't have you anyway. I am so much more handsome and more well endowed. No one could ever replace me."

"Well, you just get carved on somewhere and we will see."

And the small talk and joking went on and passed the boredom of being in the saddle and walking from dawn until dusk and even longer if they could see to travel. Their training of stealth was not needed during the first several weeks of this march. They were in French-controlled territory, and there was no need.

They marched east to the Moselle River and followed the river to Trier. Trier was an ancient city said to be founded one thousand three hundred years before Rome. The native settlements along the river were structured by Rome, and the city of Augusta Treverorum was founded by the Romans in 16 BC. Henri's group crossed the river at Trier over a huge Roman bridge. He leaned over in the saddle and studied the huge pillars of black basalt supporting the main wooden trusses and timbers. How had the Romans accomplished such a feat? They passed through the main city gates, a huge Roman amphitheater, and field after field of grape arbors.

There was definitely wine in abundance here. There were signs of Roman ascendancy everywhere from the main city buildings, city walls, and to the stone farmhouses and outbuildings. They camped for the night in a large grove of trees near the river. There was a large sandy area in the bend of the river here that afforded a place for the horses to safely acquire water. Troopers were gathering wood for fires. Some of the men had "found" chickens and several geese at local farms as they passed. Roasted meat and good hot tea and coffee would be tasty with the infernal hard biscuits. Henri and Michael took their horses to the sandbar. Both stripped to the waist and washed in the stream.

"Well, mon ami, I guess we will have to bathe as the prostitutes do from here on. It is so good to get the dust out of my hair, off my face and body, and feel the cleanliness again. Merde, I even have the damn stuff caked in my ears."

"You do not smell any better though, Michael. I think both of us smell like the north end of the horse going south, as the general so adequately put it. It is good to get the dust off though. I was starting to itch as if I had fleas or lice. I need to check a little closer. I probably do have the little bastards by now."

"You know, Henri, I have been wondering since we started just how far this campaign will take us. You say you saw the capitaine's map. Oh, I forgot! He is major now, and you are a capitaine. Anyway, how far do you think we will have to travel to see any Russians?"

"Oh, they are probably weeks away. I am sure we will see them soon enough, and we will be told when to start this fight."

They finished their wash, filled their canteens, dressed, and took the horses back to the bivouac area. They joined a small group who had fires and were starting to roast several chickens. After eating, they slept near the fires, sleeping like they had never slept before and might never sleep again.

So on and on it went, relentlessly, day by day. Major LaBauve held a short meeting each morning just before moving out. Each section commander was made aware of any news of the following army and any important instructions. Each day, it was their duty to send messengers to the rear and report progress and any scouting information. Major LaBauve always made certain each messenger was counseled on the correct information. The messengers were sent in pairs and usually returned in two days.

Three days later, they approached Koblenz. The Moselle and Rhine rivers merged here, and all marveled at the merging currents of the two mighty rivers. The torrents swirled like some mad thing trying to devour everything within reach. The men were warned not to wade deeper than their ankles and to make certain their horses did not get into the currents. There was a large stone bridge that crossed the Rhine and illustrated the same architecture as other bridges in the region, all basically Roman. This was the region of the old Frankish kings and had been since 9 BC. They all marveled at the huge and ancient fortress of Ehrenbreitstein situated high on a cliff over the Rhine. There seemed no possible way this fortress could be conquered.

Two days later, they arrived at Dresden and crossed the Elbe River. They were moving faster now and becoming more acclimated to the routine of travel. The next day, the messengers arriving from the main group advised Major LaBauve to slow his pace and maintain his present distance. The main body being affected by the heat and the vast size of the column was experiencing difficulty keeping pace. Indeed, the column was many miles long and included the slow-moving wagons of supplies and the artillery. The slower pace and more frequent rest stops were beneficial to all except Napoleon who always wanted to increase the pace. This time, he could not drive the columns any faster and was irritated. The general told Henri on one of their visits later that the Short Corporal sometimes appeared like a child having a fit of temper.

The next major stop was Wroclaw, another ancient city with many Gothic-style buildings. Here they crossed the Odra River, skirted the foothills of the massive Sudety Mountains. Even at this time of year and in all this heat, there was snow on the distant peaks. They made their way farther northward toward Warsaw, the capital city of the area. The main column of Napoleon and that of Duke Andoche Junot would merge here and advance on northward toward Lithuania.

The Faucons approached the city of Warsaw and camped just out of town in a grove of trees near the Vistula River. Major LaBauve summoned Henri.

"Capitaine, I will go into the city and advise the duke of our arrival and the arrival of Napoleon and his main column. See to the troops here. You will be in command until my return. I should return within several hours."

"Oui, monsieur. This will be a good area to camp for the night. I will see to it. Do you have any early word how long we are to stay here?"

"No, Henri, not as yet, but I may have news when I return. I can assume it may be several days as Napoleon will want to rest the troops here, meet with the duke, and assume proper command of both armies. I will send our messenger on my return. No foraging other than explicitly necessary for food and certainly not the female population of the area. There are several who would, and you know the ones who bear watching. They have the sexual characteristics of male goats. I do not want any problems with the local populace or with the Short Corporal arriving in a short time."

"Oui, monsieur. There will be no problems." Henri warned the section leaders that offenders to orders to leave the local ladies alone may be subject to castration with a dull bayonet.

Napoleon arrived early the following afternoon and went directly into the city to meet the duke. With the main body so close, Henri asked permission to see the general. It was granted as they would be here for another day or so while the two columns merged and command changed. Henri rode to the staff area and found the general's tent. His aide was checking the workers and making certain the tent was secure for the stay here. The general was returning from a wash in the Vistula River a short walk away.

"Henri, good to see you! I feel near human again with this damn dust washed away. We heard from the messengers of the progress of your group. Well done with the foraging. We have had some fair amounts of good beef, goat, and mutton and have been advised not to strip the farms of fowl as the farmers would find it harder to replace them this time of year.

"Le Patron has been driving us hard, and I fear we will lose many animals, and we are hearing of some desertions. Not many, but we are probably just losing the weak ones as usual. Good riddance. They wouldn't fight anyway. Napoleon is beside himself with this slower pace, but with this sizable force, we cannot go faster. He is very frustrated, and when he is in this mood, it is best to distance one from his wrath.

"The heat is unusual, so I hear, for this time of year. I have requested Napoleon to slow down a bit to conserve horses and men, but he is determined to get to Lithuania as soon as possible. He said we can rest there for a time, but he needs this show of strength for the czar. Are you and the group adjusting to the rigorous pace in this damnable heat?"

"Oui, monsieur, we are doing fine although probably not as bad as you riding in that damn coach. I much prefer the saddle. It is more tiring, but at least I am out in the open air. I hate being locked away in that bouncing box with wheels."

"Ah, oui, I know sometimes those of us in the carriage get the sickness of seafarers with all of the bouncing and swaying. The sickness along the heat and the dust and those who seem to let their mouths of a horse be carried around on tiny bird legs. I get so tired of the same old jokes and prattle of old war stories over and over again. It will be good to rest in my tent in solace for a day or so, but I am sure the Boss will have several meetings. No rest for the wicked. Can you stay for dinner with me this evening? I would enjoy pleasant company and not speak of military things for a change."

"I would be pleased to join you, monsieur. First let me report back to my major that I will be here until later in the evening. Then I will go to the river, tend Satan, and wash a bit. I think I have the dust to make several gardens on us. I will return in an hour or so."

The meal had been prepared especially for Henri's presence or so the general stated. Indeed, possibly it had been as Henri recognized the smell as soon as the cook brought the meal to the table.

"I hope you are hungry, Henri. I have instructed the cook to prepare a hash, and I have a bag of the peppers from home. We can wash the whole mess down with two bottles of special wine I have been saving just in case you did get an opportunity to visit."

The meal of hash seasoned with the peppers was the best Henri had dined on in the weeks since they left Paris. They talked of home, Madame, Ange, Mimi, and Jean. Henri could tell that the general was missing home as much as he was. He said reports from École de Saint-Cyr indicated Jean was doing well. Jean had another year in the academy and then would have to prove himself as an officer. The general said he would approach that the same way he had with Henri. Swim or sink. He hoped he would swim.

"Henri, maybe I should not share this with you so early in this campaign, but I have a very ominous feeling about the future. I have not shared this with anyone else and would not. Le Patron is very touchy about subjects he regards as superstitious or full of omens. He calls those who discuss these things bearers of evil. All of us at staff always try to speak of supportive and optimistic things, but this time, there is an aura of gloom and premonition. No one speaks openly of it, but the feeling is there. I can sense I am not the only one to feel this, but no one will speak of it. It is an uneasy feeling and causes me concern. I have never had this feeling before. Please do not speak of this to anyone else. But now, let's change the subject and not become depressed.

"Oh, before my memory fails me again, I have a map for you. I know your commander has one, but with your group so far out in front of the main body, another map will prove useful."

"Merci, monsieur. I will advise Major LaBauve that there are now two maps in our group. This map will be very useful."

Henri shared some of his feelings about Ange with the general, stating that he felt truly blessed that he had been accepted into the family and now was betrothed to such a lovely lady. Henri drank several glasses of the wine, and the general finished the last bottle. Both were now starting to relax and get sleepy. It had been a long day of many. Henri excused himself, shook hands with the general, and walked back to his area. He would sleep very well this night.

The stop in Warsaw lasted two days and was a welcome relief to the entire command. Word came in the evening of the second day that the Armée would begin the final push to the Lithuanian border in the morning. The groaning was widespread, but all knew it was inevitable. Henri's unit crossed the Vistula River at Warsaw on two huge very old stone bridges. Later that morning, they crossed the Bug River flowing out of the east. The two rivers would merge further downstream and flow toward the Baltic Sea. Another day and the Grande Armée of Napoleon would be at the gates of the Russian provinces and the czar.

One final night camped on the march and then midday they reached the banks of the Niemen River. This was the Russian frontier, and beyond this river was a Russian army of some reported four hundred thousand strong. The men of the Faucon de la Nuit followed the river about ten kilometers to the north and camped just outside the town of Alytus and would wait here for Napoleon. All columns would wait and organize along the river and await Napoleon's orders.

Within several days, the mightiest mass of military strength ever seen on the continent of Europe was poised for invasion. Napoleon waited for several days and had hoped, up to this point, that Czar Alexander would sense the futility of defense against this mighty force and sue for peace. So far, there was no such word. The czar was in Vilna, the capital of Lithuania, attending a series of balls and parties, evidently unconcerned. During one of the parties, the floor gave way under the czar's chair and nearly cost him his life. Many said this was a bad omen for the Russians.

The French were busy constructing several temporary bridges along the river to rapidly move troops across. Napoleon arrived and immediately started plans for the crossing. On the late evening of Juin 23, 1812, he was seen with a small group of his staff in the very forward area wearing the cap and cloak of a Polish officer. He stayed a long time and moved farther to the south, closely examining the far riverbanks with his field glass. He came close to the area of the Faucon de la Nuit, and Henri recognized him. Henri approached the group now on foot, standing in a wooded area near the bank.

"Monsieur, good evening. It is me, Henri. Please forgive me, but am I supposed to not recognize you without your usual uniform?"

"Henri, I haven't seen you in some time. Oui, you may recognize me, but I am wary of Russian marksmen who may also want to recognize me with a musket ball. I often use a disguise when this close to the front lines. I was assured that the Russians had withdrawn, but I must be sure. I see nothing beyond the far banks. Even a small force in hiding could not inflict any serious damage as we cross. Are you ready for the invasion which I assure you will occur in a very short time?"

"Oui, monsieur. We have all been ready for some time."

"Bonne chance then, my faithful friend. Indeed, bonne chance to us all."

Napoleon and his small group mounted and rode off. Within the hour, in the darkness, troops started crossing the temporary bridges and the large wooden bridge at Alytus. Henri's group, along with a major portion of the troops under Napoleon's command, would remain until dawn and proceed north to the city of Kaunas. It would be a two-pronged advance to Vilna, the capital city, but first they had to be assured the Russians could not attack their left flank. The taking of Kaunas to the north would assure this, and Vilna would be theirs.

The Faucon de la Nuit unit would lead a fast-moving regiment of chasseurs to scout Kaunas and, if there were no Russian troops, to secure the city. Napoleon would arrive within the day. As the dawn was breaking on Juin 24, they saw an awe-inspiring sight. On the highest point on the left bank were the tents of Napoleon and his entourage. Around that hill, and on every slope and valley that could be seen, was teeming with tents, fires, men, and horses. The reflective flashing of polished metal in the early morning light would surely incite fear in any enemy watching. The spectacle resembled millions of fireflies that would have been seen on the darkest night. The major stopped the troop for just a moment, and they all looked back. Henri etched this sight in his memory for all time. The great mass of troops was still crossing the bridges. Some were headed to the east in the direction of Vilna, and some were starting to follow Henri's group. Messengers were arranged to return to Napoleon and report the progress every hour.

The rapidly moving force arrived on the edge of the city of Kaunas at midafternoon. The Faucon de la Nuit was split into two groups and would forge a wide circle around the city to ascertain no Russians were present before entering the city proper. The chasseurs would wait to protect the advance scout troops if necessary. Henri's group would circle to the west, cross the Niemen River, and proceed north. The other group under Major LaBauve would cross the river just south of Kaunas and circle to the east and then north. The two groups would meet to the north of Kaunas just as darkness was falling. If all went well, messengers would report to the chasseurs, and they would enter the city from the south and the Faucon de la Nuit from the north.

Henri's group crossed the river on a stone bridge just at a point downriver from where the Niemen and Neris rivers merged. As they crossed the bridge, they could see the tumultuous waters swirling as if fighting for the rights to be first downstream. The Neris flowing through Vilna would end here, and the Niemen would surge on to the Baltic Sea.

As they crossed the bridge, they were met by a small mounted troop of cavalry in strange uniforms. Henri, thinking they may be Russian, advanced and asked who was in command. A tall slim officer replied in halting French.

"I am in command of this troop. Lieutenant Jonas Zuyev at your service, monsieur. We are Lithuanians and mean to join the army of Napoleon and assist in ridding our country of the damn Russians."

Henri extended his hand. "Welcome, monsieur. I am Capitaine Henri Devreney of the French Grande Armée. We are the lead reconnaissance unit looking for any Russian troops that may be in the area."

"There are none, Capitaine. The Russians withdrew completely toward Vilna several days ago. And a good riddance, I might add."

Henri immediately sent a messenger to the major with the news and started his entry from the western side of the city. This would save a long ride for both groups.

As they entered Kaunas, they wondered at the old part of town with the ancient stone castle, churches, and buildings. People came out from homes and shops to stare at the troops. When the other group of Faucons came from the east and the regiment of chasseurs approached from the south, many went back inside to hide. The people were very wary of troops no matter how friendly they may seem as this region had been plagued for centuries with many armies marching back and forth over their lands. The major sent a messenger to Napoleon, and all knew he would be there in the morning.

Napoleon did arrive the next morning and decided rather than subject the populace of Kaunas to such a force, he would center his command about a league to the north at the village of Zagariskes. There were many fields here and a small lake, much more adequate for this sizable force than the confines of the city. This would be an ideal place to initiate the invasion of Vilna. While barely there through midmorning, he received word from Vilna that Czar Alexander had fled that city and was rapidly retiring to Russia. With his flanks covered, Napoleon decided to advance at once to Vilna. His master plan was to establish his presence in Lithuania, and perhaps the czar would sue for peace.

Without sufficient rest, Napoleon turned his Armée toward Vilna. This was an extremely hot summer in the region; and the heat, drought, and rough terrain took an appalling toll of the horses. The general told Henri later that some fifteen thousand horses died on the march and were added to the cook's pots. The Armée would eat well; but soon, he feared, the horses would be in the soldier's bellies leaving nothing to pull wagons and artillery. Along with that, an estimated fifty thousand troops from the support nations deserted and just went home. On Juin 27, the Faucon de la Nuit saw the first spires of Vilna churches. They halted at the main Neris River bridge to wait for the main body with Napoleon. Messengers from within the city confirmed the Russians were gone. Later that day, Napoleon entered Vilna and was warmly greeted as a liberating hero.

Then, as an omen, as the superstitious ones grumbled, Lithuania had a sudden and very violent summer thunderstorm that lasted for five days. The drenching rain made any existing road an impassable quagmire. All movement of supply trains following the Grande Armée became disorganized and nearly brought to a standstill. The sea of deep, thick mud caused more strain on the already weary horses and men. The group of Lithuanians with Jonas was now merged with Henri's, and the two were rapidly becoming close friends.

"Jonas, is this weather normal for this time of year? I think we should all go home and come back next year when your country is friendlier."

"This is unusual, and I would believe the damn Russians have cursed us with this storm and mud. Frenchy, if you go home now, you will never get back, so it is best you stay and be miserable with the rest of us."

"You called me Frenchy! Suppose I call you Russkie or horse shit or something? My name is Henri."

Jonas laughed. "All right, all right, your message is conveyed. No dishonor intended. No more Frenchy and certainly no Russkie or horse shit. How about brothers in arms?"

The two were nearly the same age. Jonas was taller than Henri, but both had the same medium build and dark hair and eyes, and both certainly enjoyed humor and jokes. Michael fit right in with his humor. The three spent a lot of time together and shared their life stories. Jonas was the son of a wealthy landowner near Mazeiki in one of the northern provinces. He had been attending the university at Vilna and was home on vacation when this threat of invasion came.

Jonas had a smattering of previous military experience and offered his services to the Lithuanian regiment near his father's estate. He was made a lieutenant on the spot and in a few days was sent south to Kaunas. After the Russians were driven out, Lithuania would be a free nation, and he was destined to be one of the political leaders from his region. At least that is what his father had planned. Jonas felt there were still many girls to meet and beer to be consumed. He had his own ideas, but his father maintained control of the purse strings and generally all of his surroundings.

It was evident Napoleon would stay in Vilna for a time, and that would give the troops and animals a much-needed rest. The supply situation was critical and must be resolved. The general sent for Henri and requested him to visit.

"I apologize for taking you away from any pressing duties, but I did want to see how you were and if I could assist with anything. The truth of the matter is that I am lonesome for family, and you are the closest one about. Can you stay for a meal, and we can visit?"

"Oui, monsieur, I would enjoy a good visit, and possibly you have more of that good wine, and the cook can make a pot of the hash again."

"Consider it a pact then. You furnish the good company, and I will see to the rest."

"Monsieur, I would like to bring a guest and have you meet him. He is my Lithuanian counterpart, and his command is attached to mine."

"Oh oui, by all means, Henri. I would like to meet one of our Lithuanian allies."

As soon as Henri returned to his area, he told Jonas that he would like to invite him for the evening meal and meet his future father-in-law.

"General de Chabot, may I present my good friend and comrade in arms from Lithuania, Lieutenant Jonas Zuyev." The two shook hands.

The general greeted him, saying, "Welcome to my table, Lieutenant. I hope you came hungry and like the special stuff that only Henri and I will eat. The rest of our family will not touch it. I fell in love with this dish while on a campaign in Austria. Complemented with special peppers from another campaign in Egypt, it is special, but very hot. Do you eat spicy foods?"

"At times, monsieur. Traditionally, we do not eat other than mild seasoning. I cannot class what you may say as hot."

They sat down and were served the hash, hard biscuits, wine, and a flask of freshwater. The general brought out his little bag of peppers and put it on the table. Henri warned Jonas that these were very hot and to take just a tiny taste initially. Jonas did so and immediately downed nearly the entire flask of water.

"*Mano dievas* (my god)! That is the hottest thing I ever put in my mouth. Even just the small taste is like embers from the fire. Please, messieurs, do not take offense if I do not eat any more of your peppers. I would surely die if I ate more. The hash is good, but not the peppers."

The general and Henri laughed and said they certainly understood. Henri admitted that even after eating certain spicy foods all of his life, the peppers from hell did have their revenge the next morning. Michael had laughed at him the last time he dined with the general. The revenge was particularly bad that morning, and he had to soak his posterior in the river for a time. That day in the saddle was a time remembered and a lesson learned. The general admitted to the same thing and swore Henri to secrecy with the rest of the family.

They visited until well after dark. The general told of his adventures and campaigns with Napoleon and talked of things Henri had not heard before.

Jonas told of his home, life at the university, and the political situation now in Lithuania. Henri, for the most part, listened intently to the stories, absorbing the information like a sponge. It was a very relaxing evening and took their minds off the rigors they knew would come.

During the next several days, Jonas became a guide for Henri and Michael. His mother was originally from Vilna and often returned for visits during the spring and summer months. Winter, of course, would be impossible. He had attended the university here and knew Vilna well. He showed them the old castle of Geddimus on the highest hill overlooking the city. The buildings of the old town area were quaint and charming. Most houses were painted shades of blue, yellow, and green. Jonas said in winter months, the colors took away much of the otherwise drab surroundings.

There were many churches in the city. It seemed there was one on every major street corner, but the one that captivated Henri was St. Anne's Cathedral. The ornate and delicate designs and spires made it a work of art. There were many types of bricks used in the construction, and the various reddish shades and blending colors in a lovely sunset were awe inspiring.

Napoleon must have been captivated with the church too, for he had announced that possibly he would have the church moved back to France. Whether joking or not, the city fathers took the remark very seriously and responded that no such thing would occur with one of their irreplaceable treasures.

The cafés with their excellent dishes of pork and fowl were a welcome relief from the kitchens of the Armée cooks. This food was prepared with artistry and not just thrown in the pot. The wine was plentiful, but the beer was the best Henri had ever tasted. He was not a beer drinker, but this beer was so easy to acquire a taste for. Some of the best was blended with honey, making it very smooth and palatable. As smooth as it was, one could drink excess amounts quickly and suffer later as they all found out.

A favorite place where Jonas and his friends gathered was named Old Paradise and had the elegant charm of the medieval world with huge wooden beams and various weaponry and tapestries on the walls. There was a newly added Russia Cossack's bearskin hat. Rumor had it that one of the patrons had been in a group chasing the last Russians from Vilna, and the Cossack had dropped his hat in his haste to flee.

On Sunday morning, Jonas asked Henri and Michael if they would have the noon meal at the home of his uncle and his family. After Mass at St. Anne's, they walked near the Neris River toward the center of town and approached a high stone wall with a huge wooden gate. Jonas opened the gate and rang the small brass bell hanging on the inside of the stone archway to announce their arrival.

They entered a charming courtyard with a large central fountain and flowering plants everywhere. There was a single tree with ivy clinging to the trunk, shading the courtyard. In the center of a large bed of yellow tulips just at the front door of the house, there was a dainty statue of the Virgin Mary. This statue would ward off any evil from entering the house, explained Jonas. One could never have imagined this tranquil and passive place behind the wall.

The large wooden door with multicolored design of a flower window opened. They were greeted by a portly, semibald gentleman of medium height sporting a large mustache and a lady, a bit portly too, with a white dress. Designs of multicolored thread were sewn in her large apron. She appeared about the same age as her husband. A beautiful dark-haired girl that closely resembled Ange followed them out of the door.

"Gentlemen, this is my uncle Martynas, my aunt Agne, and my cousin Jurgita. My cousin Tomas is nearly my same age and has left the university as have I and is in the military somewhere. We are all trying to get in our blows while we can. Uncle Martynas, Aunt Agne, Jurgita, this is Henri and Michael from the Grande Armée of Napoleon. Henri is a unit commander, and I, and my command, have been placed with his."

Uncle Martynas smiled and shook hands with Henri and Michael, and Aunt Agne gave each a broad smile and a welcome hug. Uncle Martynas said something to Jonas. He laughed and translated that he apologized that his French was very bad, but he did welcome them to his humble home and to please make his home their home. Henri told Jonas to thank his uncle for the welcome and if he did understand any French at all to please try to converse. Any of his French would certainly be better than Henri's Lithuanian. They all understood Henri and laughed. Jurgita, while not fluent in French, did understand and was not shy about trying to communicate. Jurgita must have noticed Henri staring at her. She smiled and held out her hand. Her voice was very pleasant, but it was her deep dark eyes that captivated him the most.

"I am very pleased to meet you, Capitaine. Welcome to our home and our country. I hope your stay here is pleasant. Do you think you will be here long?"

Henri was almost tongue-tied but did manage to gain control and replied evenly, "I really do not know how long we will be here. Napoleon is very impatient and wants to push on as soon as possible. We may be here for only several days."

"But enough of the talk, gentlemen," said Uncle Martynas. "Come, let us eat. I have been smelling the food since early morning and can stand it no longer."

The interior of the house was well furnished with highly polished wooden tables and plush embroidered cushioned chairs. The house definitely had the touch of the wife. In the main room of the living area, there were elegant embroidered table runners and doilies, figurines, and fresh flowers. Paintings, tapestries, and other works of art adorned the rich dark wood walls. A large stone fireplace dominated nearly the whole of one wall. Henri stopped to admire a lovely white table runner, and Jurgita told him it was of woven flax. She and her mother had woven it and made many of the things in the house. She had been taught the arts of weaving and homemaking as a very young girl.

They entered the large dining room with a highly polished table that would seat sixteen people. The outer wall was entirely of windows. The same décor as the living room prevailed here. The matching buffet along the wall opposite the windows was completely covered with dishes of steaming food whose odors were maddening. Henri knew what Uncle Martynas had meant about the wait for such enticing food.

According to Lithuanian dining etiquette, all were assigned places at the table. The men were seated opposite the ladies, and Henri had the good fortune to be seated just opposite Jurgita. They sat on finely carved wooden chairs with cushions embroidered in different scenes of animals and art. Henri admired his cushion, and Jurgita told him that she and her mother had made them.

The meal began with Uncle Martynas slicing the bread that was his sacred duty. The bread was a white loaf for this special occasion. Normally they ate a black rye bread. He broke off one corner and gave a piece to Henri and Michael. They were the honored guests, and this gesture wished them good fortune and many sons. He then sliced most of the loaf and placed the cut face toward the windows and the sunlight. Jonas was explaining things as the events took place. This was to be a traditional and customary Lithuanian meal. The open face of the loaf toward the sunlight was to show the bread respect so it would not take revenge and cause harm to the household.

Uncle Martynas poured each person a glass of honey beer from a large pitcher and then placed the pitcher in the center of the table. He raised his glass, urged the others to do likewise, and offered a toast to eternal health. The other dishes were served. They had *skilandis*, a delicious sausage, and *kuldunai*, a dumpling with meat inside served with a tasty bacon-and-mushroom gravy.

Henri made mention that he had eaten a lot of mushrooms in Lithuania and was told they were plentiful and a traditional food. Many varieties were available in the forests and woods. Aunt Agne kept urging that the guests take more and more. Jonas quietly whispered to Henri that this was tradition and the sign of a generous host. Henri and Michael were stuffed. They had arrived hungry, and the quality and quantity of food were more than adequate. During the meal, Henri noticed Jurgita taking short glances at him, and she caught him returning the glances. He could not help but look at this lovely girl who in so many ways reminded him of Ange.

After the meal, when everyone was excused, the men retired to the courtyard for a cigar while the women cleaned the table. Jonas explained that in good weather, it was better to smoke outdoors and not stink up the house with cigar smoke. Aunt Agne hated the cigars, and Uncle Martynas usually smoked outdoors or in one of the sheds during bad weather. Henri stated that it was the same with the general and his wife back in Paris. Outdoors or not at all!

They were sitting on the benches in the courtyard when Aunt Agne and Jurgita came out to join them. Henri was sitting on one end of a long bench, and Jurgita sat next to him. Jurgita had her pet dog, Grantas, with her. She introduced Grantas, and he offered Henri his paw to shake. Grantas was a very friendly large brown dog and instantly took to Henri. Henri explained he had been around animals all of his life and seemed to have a way with them.

Henri and Jurgita talked and exchanged many questions and compared life here, in France, and the Armée. He told her about Ange back in Paris and how Jurgita reminded him of her. They were about the same size and dark hair and eyes and had the same pleasing manner. He showed her the small picture he carried and explained it was an old picture made when she was very young. They left the courtyard and walked behind the house to a small garden area with barns and sheds on one side. This further reminded him of home. They picked fresh apples and nibbled on them as they walked. They were not far from the river and went down to the bank, sat on the grass under a tree, and watched the water as they talked. Both realized that an instant bond had formed. Grantas was fast asleep next to Jurgita and softly snoring. The lazy afternoon went all too fast, and soon Jonas and Michael came looking for them.

"What is this, you two? Are the rest of us being rejected just so you can have private conversations? We have watched you making cow eyes at each other."

"Jonas! No such thing," said Jurgita. "I have been explaining to Henri the fine quality of life here, and he has told me much of France and the Armée. And what do you mean cow eyes? He has been a perfect gentleman and explained at the outset that he is engaged to be married on his return to France."

Jonas laughed and grabbed Jurgita in a bear hug. "Cease, my favorite and fiery cousin. I meant nothing except a little joke. I have never seen you with a man before and found your reaction unusual."

"Not unusual, you *bulius* (ox)! I consider myself very normal and friendly with gentlemen, and Henri is certainly one of the highest order."

Henri and Michael went back to the house and thanked their host and hostess for a very memorable time they would not soon forget. Henri shook hands very delicately with Jurgita and noticed a lingering for both as if not wanting to let go. They looked into each other's eyes, and sparks and unasked questions were evident.

When Henri returned to camp, he went down to the river and sat for a long time, looking at Ange's picture and contemplating this test. Oui, it was a test, he realized. He was so lonesome for Ange, and Jurgita resembled her so much.

If it had not been so unmasculine to do so, he would have cried with loneliness. And possibly he did.

Several days later, word came that they would be leaving with the dawn. Henri asked the major if he could have an hour to finish some personal business. He rode to Jurgita's house and told her that they would be leaving at dawn. He thanked her for her friendship and said he would remember the Sunday afternoon as long as he lived. She told him to wait just a moment and that she would be right back. She returned with a sash she said could be used as a neck scarf. He wouldn't need it now but surely would during winter months in Russia. It was a handcrafted scarf with symbols and patterns in blue and red she said were for luck and long life. She had made it sometime back for someone special, and here he was. She looked deeply into his eyes, kissed him quickly on the cheek, and ran back into the house. She was crying, and he knew it. He knew also that he would probably never see her again.

After the eighteen-day stay in Vilna, the French Armée pushed on into Russia. The men of Faucon de la Nuit and the detachment of Lithuanian cavalry were in front as advance scouts, but this time, they would be very wary as the Russian Bear was closer at hand now and could bite very hard if cornered or provoked.

24

Flights of the Faucon

The thunderstorm curse evoked by the Russians proved a calamity for the Grande Armée as it moved farther across Lithuania and on to the Russian plains. There was a breakdown in discipline from the shortages of food and water. The saviors of the land now became the plunderers. Friendly peasants were mistreated, looted, and even killed, owing to some of the foraging techniques. The general had been quite correct in his description of a plague of locusts or worse.

The retreating Russians had contemplated the supply situation of such a vast force and destroyed and burned much of the food sources. They drove enormous herds of horses and animals through creeks, small streams, and other water sources to muddy and contaminate them. They had forced the peasant farmers to clean the animal barns and sheds of any filth and throw it into the water sources.

It would have been very wise at this stage to halt the advance and wait for the supply lines to catch up. But "wait" was not in Napoleon's vocabulary either, and onward they were pushed. The Faucon de la Nuit was much more fortunate than most. They had the lion's share of initial foodstuffs. The limited sources of freshwater for the first sections of advancing troops were good, but after that, the rest had to deal with the mess and contamination. Now with the shortage of food and the contaminated water, diarrhea, dysentery, and typhus plagued the troops in ever-frightening numbers. There was little that could be done, and the sick were left behind in temporary hospital camps.

Thousands died from filth, starvation, and just generally deplorable conditions. The desertions continued as troops saw what they classed as a death march to nowhere. The general told Henri that they were losing an estimated one of every ten men every day. It was evident to many of the staff that the Russians were retiring in such a manner as to drain strength of the Armée, and it was working because the Russians were destroying the available supplies before they left a region, and the supplies being shipped to the Armée could not keep up. Still they pushed on with Napoleon telling them that the situation would improve with the arrival of fresh supplies.

Henri's group was using the stealth they had learned from the old Indian fighter, and it was proving valuable. They had their special dark cloaks to cover their much brighter uniforms and had advised the Lithuanians to obtain some for themselves. They kept their polished metal either covered or used the black ball or coal dust from the fires. Bits of cloth were wrapped on metal equipment to prevent rattling. Most of the group had dark-colored horses, and the few white or light colored ones were smeared with mud during times of close encounter. Henri found it a real mess to smear Satan with mud and then wash him off in a stream as they camped for the night. But he realized Satan was worth the effort. He had been a good, strong, and intelligent animal. No cook's pot for his steed. At a distance in the dark forests, they could not be detected. A few days later, in darkening evening, Henri's group was moving through a heavily wooded forest area just adjacent to a main roadway. Major LaBauve had the follow-up group a kilometer or so to the rear. The advance scout gave the hand signal for the column to halt. Henri, Jonas, and Michael rode forward.

"What is it, Corporal? Did you see something?"

"I'm not sure what it is, monsieur, but there was something over there. There were reflections in those far trees on the other side of the road just beyond that small clearing. There! See? They are more visible."

"Oui, I do see them. The setting sun is reflecting on whatever it is. And they seem to be on a wide front. It looks as though maybe we have caught up with our Russian friends."

"Good job, Corporal. Stay here and out of sight. We will watch for a while, and if they do not move on soon, I will send a messenger back to the main body. Jonas, what do you make of it?"

"I think you are correct, my friend. Either we have caught up to them or they are positioning in wait for us. Either way, our men could use a rest."

"I agree. Michael, give the order for the group to move one hundred meters farther back in the trees, be quiet, and stay out of sight. Send another two men to the front with the corporal here." Henri took his map case and unrolled his map. Jonas and Henri studied the map. "We are here just off the main road near the small town of Wilkomir. This place would be perfect for an ambush if they were going to attempt it. Jonas, I don't like this. Send a messenger back and tell the major we are halting and observing."

Henri, Jonas, and Michael rode in a wide circle through the dense forest. There they observed from about a cannon shot away the church spire and buildings of the town of Wilkomir situated along a small river. On the hillside that dissected the road they had approached on from the other direction, they could see a force of approximately thirty thousand infantry accompanied by artillery and cavalry. They would have walked right into the Russian trap. That was the Russian method of defense for a strong position. They would hide as well as possible and let the enemy approach as near as they could without detection. When the enemy is within easy range of muskets and artillery, a sudden and massive barrage of rolling fire is laid down to confuse and bewilder the enemy soldiers. Often it is successful, but this time, the reception was foiled. The three made haste for the others still well hidden and waiting. Just as the major was preparing another messenger, the general and several staff officers rode up.

"Why the delay, Major? Your messenger said something of a possible deployment of enemy troops."

"Oui, General, we have detected a force waiting with the usual Russian reception as soon as we advance down this road and approach the river. The officers here have just returned from the far left flank and observed their strength and what we may expect."

"General," said Henri, referring to his map, "we approached the town from the woods near this point. We couldn't cross the river as the only bridge is in enemy hands, but we did observe a sizable force of nearly thirty thousand infantry with artillery and about four squadrons of cavalry. The initial ranks are here in the deep woods along both sides of the road on this side of the river. There is one bridge crossing the river here. I believe the Russians plan to let our troops get as near as possible here, lay down a tremendous fire, and then retreat across the river. Then they could either destroy or defend the bridge with ease and halt our advance until we eventually outflank them. By then, they could continue their withdrawal with much less losses."

"Well, it certainly looks like you have seen through their scheme, Capitaine. Russians always like an ambush. I want you to send scouts out immediately and see if we can ford the river at any point on their extreme left flank. They may be the ones in for the surprise if we act quickly. I will report back to Napoleon and halt the advance until I hear from this group. Are they aware of our presence as yet?"

"We can't say for certain, monsieur, but they do not have any pickets or scouts out. I think they were relying on the Armée just blindly marching down the road with all of the usual bright colors and noise. We approached in the woods with our dark cloaks."

"Possibly the fates are with us still. Get the scouts out quickly and report back within the next several hours. Merde, you men resemble a band of thieves in that garb."

"Oui, monsieur." The general mounted, winked at Henri, and rode off through the trees in the gathering darkness.

"Major LaBauve," said Henri, "with your permission, I would like to lead this scouting party. I was there before and will know what to expect in the darkness."

"And we would like to attend his party too," said Jonas. "We were there also."

"Go then and be careful. Remember this is a matter of most urgency."

The five men rode at a soft gallop to gain as much ground as possible in the waning light. They approached the river and tested a few spots before they found a solid and shallow enough crossing place. It was very dark now, and they chanced to approach the town through a dense forest section. Stopping about one hundred meters from the town proper, they observed low campfires and the Russians settling in for the night. Evidently they knew nothing would happen tonight, and the battle would commence with the dawn.

They silently made their way back to the ford area and within an hour were back with Major LaBauve. Henri reported, and the major asked if the three would report to the general. Indeed, they would, and off they rode at a steady but spirited gait.

As they approached the staff area, Henri was challenged by the sentry and allowed to pass. General de Chabot was in his hastily assembled tent with two other officers and Napoleon. "You didn't waste any time getting back, Capitaine. Did you obtain useful information? I have advised His Excellency of the situation."

"Oui, monsieur," Henri reported as he unrolled his map. "We found a decent ford approximately here, about three kilometers from the town. We did cross and approached the town to a distance of about one hundred meters. We dared not approach closer for fear of sentries, but there were none evident. I don't think the Russians are expecting anything from their rear and flank. The current of the stream is flowing away from the town so that muddy water at our crossing will not be noticed. There is heavy forest cover all around the town on this side. We could see the Russians getting ready for the night, probably suspecting nothing until the dawn."

"Excellent observations and report, Capitaine. Ha! And what a surprise they shall have with the rising sun," said Napoleon. "I know you men must be tired, but you are needed to guide two squadrons of chasseurs across that crossing tonight. After a decent meal and a short rest, of course. I think we have time and luck on our side this night."

Turning to his staff officers, he said, "Gentlemen, look at this map. With the dawn, the infantry will advance down the main road. Not with the usual lackluster of just troops on the march, but wary and battle ready. This will be a battle group advance. That in itself should be a surprise to our friends, but with the first cannon shot, the chasseurs will charge from the rear. The trap will snap shut, and the Russians will be ambushed and not us. That is the plan, and General de Chabot will finalize the details. Henri, this is very good work tonight. Are you medal hungry again, or will just a kiss suffice this time?" He laughed, and that was the signal for all to laugh. "Who might these gentlemen with you be?"

"Monsieur, this is Lieutenant Jonas Zuyev of the Lithuanian troops attached to our Faucon de la Nuit, and this is Trooper Michael Pasar of our troop. He has been with us since the conception of the troop."

"Well done, gentlemen, and I am pleased to meet an officer of our allies pledged to our cause. Trooper, I think I recall you from past meetings. Henri, once again, a very well done. You know, I am not certain I approve of my troops having the appearance of beggars, but it does seem to serve the purpose of this scouting. I think I remember from somewhere that Hannibal employed some of the same methods." Napoleon shook hands with each of the three and wished all good luck. He abruptly left as he always did, in a hurry. He seemed never to slow his pace and expected no less of all in his commands.

"Well, son," said the general as he grabbed Henri by the back of the neck, "let us go and present you fellows to our officer's cooks and get some decent food down you. I could use a bite myself. I will send for the chasseurs, and that should take an hour or so for them to make ready. To their commanding officer's great dismay, I will tell them that Napoleon has placed you and the lieutenant here in charge of this mission. You will give them advice on how to advance, as you do, through the woods with none of the noise and clanking those damn chasseurs usually do."

They ate a meal of horse stew with potatoes and the inevitable hard biscuits soaked in the stew gravy. It was the first hot food since Vilna, and horse or no horse, it was wonderful. The general said they ate horse at nearly every meal, and his aide said the general was starting to whinny in his sleep. The horses were dying at a fast rate, and the supply in the pots was much more plentiful than the supply as beasts of burden. They returned to the staff area and found two majors and two lieutenants waiting.

"Gentlemen, please look at this map. There is no time for formal introductions tonight, but this capitaine and these gentlemen will guide you through the forest to a position here behind and to the side of the town of Wilkomir just to our front here. They will give you instructions on silent movement, and this is extremely important as the enemy must not know of your presence. You are to remain hidden and silent until the dawn. Your signal to attack in force will be the first cannon shots just after dawn, hopefully while the Russians are at their morning meal and duties. Create as much hell, havoc, and confusion as possible. Our infantry will attack from the front here on the main road. Two more squadrons of cavalry will follow your path across the ford and reinforce you. Your main objective is to capture the one bridge on the main road intact. Are there any questions? Good! Have a good night's 'rest,' gentlemen, and bonne chance."

The general slapped Henri on the shoulder and said, "I still could use you back here on my staff one day. Think about it. Bonne chance, son. Be safe or your mother and my daughter will have my balls nailed to the stable door again."

Faucon de la Nuit or,
as Napoleon describes,
"resembling a band of bandits and beggars"

Within two hours, the two squadrons of chasseurs and the Faucon de la Nuit had forded the river and were quietly dispersed in the woods about a thousand meters from the town. They were resting in place and keeping their horses quiet. The dawn was still a few hours away, and they would need to get some rest before the big event at dawn.

"Michael, are you asleep?" whispered Jonas.

"No, I really don't think I could with the merde that has happened tonight and what the dawn will bring. What is it?"

"Does Napoleon really know Henri that well to joke with him as he did? And what is this thing about him kissing him again? I knew he had lived with the general and was betrothed to his daughter, but I had no idea about him and Napoleon."

"Jonas, you are right about having no idea about Henri. I will tell you, but please do not relate any of this to Henri. He is very shy on the subjects of his accomplishments, but they are well-known facts. Henri has been a good and close friend since our first days in the military together, and I know he can be deadly to an enemy as well."

Then Michael related the tale of Bébé Tigre and the events at the uprising and that Henri was twice personally decorated by Napoleon. Jonas was astounded.

"Little wonder he has such rank at such an early age then. I did notice he has the absolute respect of his men. He seems to quietly command that respect without even noticing he is doing so."

There were only slight hints of pink and yellow as the dawn approached in the east. Already the chasseurs had tended their horses and had a swift and silent breakfast of the hard biscuits or river stones as they called them. No fires to heat water for tea or coffee; they had settled for plain water from their canteens. The coffee and tea would come later after the business at hand was finished.

They watched as the gathering light revealed the Russians starting to stir and build up their fires for breakfast. From across the river, the faint sounds of drums could be heard. The advance was on and their signal to mount and be ready. They walked their mounts in the heavy dark forest to within one hundred meters of the unsuspecting Russians. The Russians continued their unconcern and eating when a massive cannonade sounded from the French lines across the river. Now the Russians were starting to show concern, and a few groups were running toward the bridge.

The mounted troops charged out of the forest with screams, yells, and sabres flashing. They were upon the Russians before they realized what was happening, and the rout was on. One squadron of chasseurs went to the left and cut off the running Russians. The other group and the Faucon de la Nuit went straight through the fleeing ranks and made for the bridge. Major LaBauve, Henri, and Jonas were side by side in the charge, leading their section of troops. They had to be careful so as not to interfere with the chasseurs in their charge.

Henri remembered hitting several Russians with his sabre, but in particular, one with his bearded face twisted in a snarl. It was indeed a hateful sight. It was mostly over in a matter of minutes. The Russian troops on the other side of the river were trapped, and many were swimming the river and easy targets for the infantry now on the banks. Like shooting fish in a tub as the general described the scene later. There seemed to be hundreds of bodies floating down the river in the semiswift crimson current. The field where the initial charge by the chasseurs had taken place was littered with bodies. What remained of the Russian force on the town side of the river was still running down the road and through the forest. French infantry were starting to gather the Russians who had surrendered. Others were swarming over the bridge. It was a complete and resounding victory for Napoleon.

By midmorning, the French were well established in the town and had set up a field hospital, and the cooks were starting fires for the usual horse stew. At least it would be a hot meal and not cold biscuits and water this time. French troops had suffered nearly one thousand dead and wounded, but the Russians had fared much worse. The surprise of the sudden assault from both directions had caught the Russians completely by surprise.

Now the way to the prize, Moscow seemed open unless the Russians tried more stalling and ambush tactics. Already troops replacing the ones involved in the initial engagement were passing through the town and on their way eastward. Napoleon did not want to waste any time and kept the fleeing Russians on their heels. This delay could have been a blessing as much of the desperately needed supplies were starting to catch up.

The Faucon de la Nuit had lost eight men, three killed and five wounded. Two of the wounded were doubtful as their maiming wounds were serious. One poor fellow would lose an arm at the elbow. He was from Henri's section, and when Henri went to visit him, the trooper said he was elated. To lose an arm was bad, but he would survive that, but now he would heal and be able to return home to his village and farm. No more war for him. Henri knew he was putting on a front and was sorry he could no longer ride with the men he had trained so hard with. The Lithuanians had lost only two, and both were killed in the first charge on the bridge. Jonas said at least they could be buried on Lithuanian soil and not somewhere in Russia.

Major LaBauve sent for Henri late that afternoon. "Capitaine, I have orders to move out again at dawn. Tell the men to prepare and get as much rest as they can for now. I know it is soon after battle, but we are in a race for Moscow before the winter. At least that is what I am told."

Henri did see the general in the late evening. "Henri, I am glad you came when you did. There was a dispatch pouch that caught up with us this morning. Both of us have letters, and I will let you guess who from. I started to read yours first but didn't want to hear your whining or possibly stick me in the ass with your sabre." He laughed and dug a small package wrapped in heavy brown paper out of his coat pocket.

There were red wax seals at every fold in the paper. There had been several months now since any word from home and his Ange. The package was addressed to General de Chabot to the personal attention of Capitaine Henri Devreney in the fine and small penmanship of Ange. He could never mistake her handwriting. He tore at the package and found tightly wrapped in oilcloth a small portrait of Ange and a letter neatly folded. He showed the portrait in the small oval silver frame to the general.

"Oh, a very lovely likeness. She is much like her mother with her delicate beauty. We are both very fortunate men."

Henri could not agree more. He hastily read the letter, folded it, and put it and the small portrait in his coat pocket over his heart. He would read it over and over and study every word and every feature of the portrait later in private. The general noticed this, smiled silently to himself, and said nothing. He would do the same.

"Henri, Napoleon had all praise for the way things went this morning. He was very explicit about you and the way the Faucon de la Nuit have developed into a scout and reconnaissance unit without equal. We have always had scouts and pickets, but not a highly trained unit as this. I have sent for Major LaBauve to relay Napoleon's words, but I wanted you to hear this from me too. What happened this morning could not have been accomplished without this special troop and the manner in which it operates. Any other time and we would have walked right into that trap.

"My Vivien tells me that nothing much has changed at home except it is an unusually hot summer in Paris. Mimi has had an exceptional crop of apples and pears this spring, and they will probably be eating the damn things at every meal for a time. The usual chatter about the house except for our private things that I am sure are in your letter too."

They sat and talked for a time and drank a few cups of wine while the general smoked his cigar. He was still teasing Henri about not liking cigars. This man was truly the father Henri had longed for all of his life. Henri kept taking the portrait of Ange out of his pocket and studying it over and over. Then they shook hands, and Henri went back to his area to prepare for the inevitable march tomorrow.

"My Dearest Henri," the letter began, "I hope this finds you well and in good health and spirit. We have not had much news from the *campaign except the few articles in the newspapers here. We know that is only the political things that Napoleon sends back by courier and has nothing relating to you and Poppa except that you are there. The articles say that the Armee is going to Moscow. I went into Poppa's study and found a book with a map. I did find Lithuania and then Vilna. I found Paris and Moscow, too, and they are so very far apart. I showed it to Momma and Mimi. I held the map to my heart somehow hoping it would make me feel closer to you. But of course, that was silly and you would be the first to tell me so. You are there in my heart and nothing will ever change that.*

"I am sending the new portrait I had painted for you and hope you like it. You know when I was sitting for it I realized I did not have one of you. We must take care of that as soon as you return. The thoughts of your return seem to consume me. I think about it most of the time and even dream of it a night. I go into your room often at night and sit in our favorite place. I see the moon and stars over the river and wonder if you are looking at the same moon and stars. The next time you look at the moon, know that I am looking at it, too and thinking of you. I wear your betrothal ring and kiss it often. I never take it off.

"Jean came home from school and says he is doing well. He is the leader of one his classes and says he will do everything to make you and Poppa proud of him. He is so different now and a nice man and good brother.

"Mimi and all of the servants are the same. Mimi is taking more time with me now and teaching me her methods of cooking. I hope I learn well and please you when we are married. Momma has been spending a lot of time with me, too, and telling me things she says will make me a better wife. Some are very private things that I will not tell you here. You will just have to wait and find out for yourself.

"There is so much more I want to say to you, but I will wait until you come home. I love you with all of my heart, my Henri. Please hurry home and please be careful. I remember two other times you came home hurt. I love you, I love you, I love you, I love you.

Ange

Henri studied every detail of her portrait. Her lovely dark hair with the blue ribbon, her dazzling dark eyes, her delicate features of nose, cheeks, chin, and those lovely, full, almost pouty lips he knew so well. No portrait could ever do her justice. He could only imagine the lovely and petite body and longed to hold her tight and never let go for all of eternity. He folded the letter, placed it back in the oilcloth with the portrait, and safely buttoned it away in the pocket over his heart. He looked up at the nearly full moon and smiled to himself. Could he really see Ange's smiling face there? Henri sat next to a small tree and covered himself with his dark cape.

Capitaines and leaders in the Grande Armée of France and Napoleon do not shed tears over trivial matters of the heart. The hell they don't!

25

No Rest for the Weary

Problems continued for the Grande Armée as they penetrated deeper and deeper into Russia. The swift victory at Wilkomir had been only a delaying action to cover the retreat of the main Russian forces. This fact was even more evident in that the French had only captured twenty-eight pieces of artillery, and old ones at that. The Russians reportedly had some one thousand one hundred guns. The force that had been so swiftly defeated had been a sacrificial lamb for the retreat. The question now among the French staff officers was would the Russians do this again? Surely they would not surrender their lands so easily.

The Faucon de la Nuit advanced along the main road to Moscow and mostly out of the heavily forested areas. The plains were massive and flat, often with only sparse woods near the scattered villages and along the small rivers. They still practiced stealth in their advance, but the now-open fields and flat plains afforded little cover. They would often stop for long periods to observe for enemy scouts. Often they could detect mounted figures far in the distance and were aware they too were being watched.

Occasionally, but not often, they would happen on peasants at a small village or farm. These were generally very old and sick people who could not escape. Most people had fled either to the extreme north or south of the retreating Russian army and the advancing Grande Armée. The villagers were just as wary of the Russians as they were of the French. The Russians left nothing for the enemy and had burned and destroyed everything of any food or shelter source. Every well was contaminated with dead animals and filth from the barns. The small streams were essentially the same, and often the Faucons had to scout far off the main roads and path of the Russian retreat to find decent water.

"Food sources are just nonexistent. Everything is gone. Foraging is like vultures picking the bare bones of a year-old dead horse," commented Major

LaBauve. "The horses are starting to suffer from lack of sufficient grasslands. You are to closely examine each mount at every rest period and report back to me if you see a significant problem."

They took turns going to the north and south for several kilometers along each stream. Usually at this time of year, fresh grass and sufficient water could be found. They would be all right, but for the advancing troops behind them, there would be nothing. The heat was most repressing during this particular summer and only added to the misery of this march. If the Russians were suffering more than the Grande Armée, it certainly was not very apparent.

Michael had requested to accompany the messengers to the rear and was just now returning. The men usually alternated the messenger duties in hopes of at least a hot meal of horse stew. Anything palatable except those damn river rocks washed down with canteen or stream water. Michael related stories of extreme hardship for the troops following. Hospital areas had been erected at intervals along the advance for the many with dysentery, diarrhea, and other inflictions brought on by the exposure, food, water, and sanitary problems. Each day brought more and more cases of sick and dying to the hospital areas. The medical staffs there were overwhelmed and often just left the men to fend for themselves and continued with the advance.

"I have seen a huge pile of fresh bodies at the most recent hospital site awaiting burial. The quick meal of hot horse stew wasn't worth the trip to the rear area." He implored, "Henri, please do not let me go again. I will never knowingly eat horse stew again. I have seen a huge pile of horse carcasses that the cook's helpers were cutting for the next meals. Others were constantly dragging new additions for the pile. It was repulsive, and the smells are locked in my nose."

He and the others returning with him brought back as many sacks of the hard biscuits as their packhorses could carry. Rather the damn river rocks any day now than go back and see the plight following.

It was a wondrous event when some of the men rummaging through the smoldering remains of a farmhouse happened upon an intact root cellar. Evidently the retreating Russians had overlooked it or were just too hurried in leaving. Whatever the facts, the results were a feast for the first men who found it. There were potatoes, turnips, carrots, apples, a few barrels of salt meat, and, wonders of all wonders, many bottles of homemade fruit wines. It wasn't the usual wine, but wine is wine, and at this point, source and kind was not an option or to be questioned. Henri, Jonas, and Michael made certain they had their share and also a share for Major LaBauve. The four were sitting under a small tree enjoying a fine meal of raw vegetables, pieces of salt meat, and the inevitable biscuits; and each had a bottle of wine.

"This wine does have a bite," declared Michael. "It tastes like a blend of apples and, possibly, wild berries. It's unusual, but the best I have had today."

"I will not ever complain again about anything," said Jonas.

"I agree, my friend. This wine does have the tart taste of those little green apples we found nearby, but there is the sweetness of some kind of berries. I could really learn to love this stuff but would need at least another ten bottles to make certain."

"When you gentlemen have been on the more severe campaigns I have served on, you will not complain at all," said Major LaBauve. "We are so fortunate now to be far in front of the horde following. At least we are not subjected to the sickness and can, at times like this, find a few decent things. I think I shall name the three of you Les Trois Mousquetaires after the characters an acquaintance of mine is preparing a novel about. Ah, I do miss him and the comradeship. He is such a character. His name is Alexandre Dumas, and I first met him in Paris a few years ago. He frequents the same very elite brothels and taverns that several of my other friends attend. He is a ladies' man of little equal in Paris. He is a very astute and suave fellow who works in the office of the duc d'Orléans in the Palais Royal. The tales he tells of the old days of the king's elite guardsmen and the Mousquetaires' confrontations with the king are very vivid and hilarious. He was working on notes for his novel, and I had the privilege of reading some of them and commenting on true military life. The main characters are very close rascals called Mousquetaires that are reminiscent of the three of you."

"But, monsieur, I am Lithuanian and not French."

"That is no problem, Jonas. We shall make you an honorary Frenchman," said Henri.

"I am not so certain how to take this, my friend."

"As I would, should you choose to make me an honorary Lithuanian, an honor."

"Well then, let us do this honor matter, brother in arms."

The two stood and shook hands. Not to be outdone, Major LaBauve and Michael stood and also shook hands all around. And now they were all brothers in arms, French and Lithuanian. How does the saying go, one for all and all for one? Major LaBauve thought to himself that he had never before had such a close relationship with his subordinates as he had with these men. He had always been afraid of losing discipline when befriending underlings. This was a different set of circumstances. The Faucon de la Nuit was an elite and unique group often on their own and relying totally on each other for survival. They had formed a bond of brotherhood, as they just had stated. These men would not lose respect for his rank or his commands. It was a pleasure and a relief to know this and to be associated with them and this group. Command is often very lonely.

On the march, Napoleon kept up the relentless pace and seemed unmindful to the sufferings around him. He seemed driven to catch the entire retiring Russian army or at least make it difficult for them to destroy so much. Thus far, this advance march had claimed another eight thousand horses. Broken carriages and wagons had to be abandoned and hopefully could be repaired by the troops bringing up the rear and could be returned useful. Most of the captured cattle herds were having a very hard time keeping pace. They too were dying and could not be driven faster. Napoleon was being severely criticized by his staff of maintaining the ambitious assumptions of the Armée's ability to continue without proper rest, food, and necessities.

If the Russians were experiencing any of the hardships of the French, it was not evident. There were not significant amounts of dead horses or abandoned wagons or equipment in the line of retreat, and they certainly had sufficient food as they were taking all they could carry and destroying the rest. This scorched earth in retreat policy was taking its toll. The next main point in the French march to Moscow would be Vitebsk, and Napoleon had promised a stop and rest here.

The Faucons approached Vitebsk late in the afternoon of Juillet 29, 1812, and immediately sent scouts to encircle the small city. There were still no indications of the Russian army. Not even any detachments left for a delaying action. Evidently the Russians were moving more rapidly now and constantly retreating deeper into the interior of Russia toward Moscow.

Major LaBauve led his unit into the city and was appalled at the sights. Although the city had not been burned or demolished, it was evident that everything of value and foodstuffs had been destroyed or taken in the retreat. In the large central square, there was a tremendous heap of foodstuff, furniture, all manner of household items, and slaughtered sheep, goats, and horses that had been burned. It was a sickening and horrific sight and not one that the Grande Armée would have any intention of cleaning.

Among the few people still in the town were elderly and sick and an old priest found hiding in the church. They were brought to Major LaBauve for questioning. They related that the Russians had passed through Vitebsk several days ago and looted or destroyed everything of value. The people, who could leave, did so, to the north and south to other villages where they could seek refuge from the marauding Russians. This was Russia, and how could the retreating army be so brutal and apathetic to their own people?

This would never happen in France or other countries where they had campaigned. Perhaps the czar was desperate in his measures to curtail the oncoming tide of the Grande Armée. Major LaBauve sent a messenger back to Napoleon that there was nothing left in Vitebsk but a revolting mess and to give the town proper a wide berth. The only bridge at Vitebsk had been burned, but there was an alternate bridge sufficient for use some three kilometers to the south. The only blessing about this place was the very good water fed by three rivers so fast flowing that the Russians could not have possibly polluted them for very long.

The weary troops did spend several days here, and Henri's unit spent their time at a small village about seven kilometers downriver. The village was untouched and afforded shelter and food from the houses, gardens, root cellars, and barns. They prowled the nearby woods and found several pigs and several dozen chickens. Now this was a change of diet and a very welcome one. Pity the poor souls in the main body of troops who were at the mercy of the masses and were probably still surviving on horse stew. Messengers sent to the rear were carefully chosen and ordered not to tell anyone of this sanctuary. Even rumors of such could have caused panic and a mad dash to get here.

After three days of rest and pillaging the small village, the Faucons left in the direction of Smolensk, another obstacle on the path to Moscow. Smolensk was an ancient city built on high bluffs on each side of the Dnieper River. High brick and rock walls erected in the seventeenth century encircled the city. The walls were thirty feet high and fifteen feet thick at the base, a perfect fortress for the Russians to stage a defense. Smolensk was a special place to the Russians and considered their holy city. The churches and main cathedral were considered the most beautiful in the region. The cathedral housed one of the most venerated icons attributed to Saint Luke. At a point some thirty kilometers from Vitebsk, the advance scouts noticed large evidence of troop movements split in three directions. One track led to the north, one to the south, and the largest of the three pointed straight to Smolensk.

Major LaBauve ordered the scouts, "Follow each of the three tracks, move fast, and do not be observed. You should try to get as far to the flanks of each column as possible and obtain information of troop strength and guns. Report back to this place at dusk tomorrow. The remainder of the troops will camp on the banks of a small stream and wait for your return."

Within hours of the next dusk, the scouts reported back. Major LaBauve hastily assembled his reports and sent messengers to the rear. There were sizable troop formations to the north and south. The main group had gone to Smolensk. Was this a trap? If Napoleon made a direct frontal assault on the city, would the troops to the north and south converge in a pincer movement? The Faucons advanced to nearly fifteen kilometers from the city and camped on the banks of a small stream. Scouts were sent out under cover of darkness to observe and report back before dawn. It was confirmed the Russians were in Smolensk in great strength. Napoleon's attack on the city would have to be done by frontal assault.

The main body of French troops arrived on August 16, 1812, and the next day just before noon, the battle commenced. The Russians behind the enormous city walls had the advantage. By the well-placed Russian cannon, the French troops, in a direct frontal assault, were cut down by the hundreds. By dusk, the battle started to die down with the French in control of the outlying areas. The Russians still controlled the city but could no longer utilize their cannons effectively. The losses had been tremendous on both sides with the Russians losing nearly four thousand and the French nearly nine thousand.

Then the Russian troops started a retreat eastward, abandoning the city. Napoleon was delighted at the news while the news of further retreat and choice to avoid contact was received in dismay in Moscow. Why had the Russian army chosen to retreat and abandon the holy city and a prize after the loss of so many men? Napoleon entered Smolensk and reported in a letter back to Paris that the city was in ruins, the streets were littered with dead and burned bodies. The heat was intense, and there was a lot of dust that was rather trying.

"The whole of the Russian army was here." It was ordered to fight but dared not. "We have killed three to four thousand of the enemy, wounded thrice as many, and found plenty of guns here. According to accounts from captured Russians, a number of their divisional generals were killed. The Russian army is marching toward Moscow in a very discouraged and discontented state." Napoleon did not state that he had lost overall nearly one hundred thousand men, not to mention horses and equipment, since leaving Vilna.

No rest for the weary or the wicked. Just after the battle was decided, Napoleon ordered the Faucon de la Nuit to get as close to the retreating Russian army as possible and try to obtain information. During the battles, Napoleon ordered his special reconnaissance group out of harm's way and not to engage in the fighting. They had proven much too valuable to be utilized as cannon fodder.

Four days later, they approached Viasma and saw large columns of smoke rising from the city. Thus far, they had not encountered any rear guards, and it was as if the Russians were in a hurry to devastate as much as possible to deny the French anything of value as foodstuffs and shelter. Napoleon had all intentions to attempt to save the town by rushing to get there before the Russians could destroy it.

Although there was not much left of Viasma for the advancing French, Napoleon wrote a glowing report back to Paris. "I am in a rather handsome city. There are thirty churches, fifteen thousand inhabitants, and many shops with vodka and other useful objects for the troops."

Napoleon failed to mention that the deeper they penetrated into the depths of Russia, they were met with utterly terrified local people and devastation. The retreating army continued to destroy everything, leaving nothing for the French. Not only the towns but entire villages were wiped off the face of the earth and the inhabitants sent fleeing to survive as best they could. Napoleon noted in his personal diary, "Nothing is more dangerous to us than a prolonged war."

Henri, Jonas, and Michael were riding in the advance scouts as they approached the outskirts of Gzhatsk. They could already see more of the same desolation, but it did not appear as bad this time. The Russians had not had the time to carry out their usual techniques. Still, there was not much left, and as they scoured the town the rest of the day, they found meat, but the salt supply was ruined. There was a large warehouse with flour, and the sacks had been cut open, and horses and cattle marched over it. Dead animals were in nearly every well. They did, however, find several wells untouched.

"Damn, what manner of animals would do such?" asked Michael.

"It is working though," said Henri. "Our troops have nothing left except that damned horse stew, the river rocks, and whatever they can forage. We are the fortunate ones and can, at least, be the first with whatever is left."

Jonas said, "Henri, I haven't said anything to Major LaBauve as yet, but several of my men have deserted. One, a good friend, came to me two days ago and told me he was going home. He said this was a death march and that most of the rest of our troops agreed. He and four others left in the middle of the night. All I could do was wish them well. To be honest, I have had some of the same thoughts, but I will certainly talk with you if I should resolve such a ridiculous thing."

"Jonas, I understand a large amount of your troops are volunteers and possibly needed at home with other obligations. Napoleon and the others on the staff would certainly not understand and possibly have them shot if caught. Please be careful whomever you tell. Sometimes desertion can be the fault of the commander if not reported and stopped. I would hate to have to shoot you. On second thought, I do not think they would waste shot and powder. We would probably just see how far a lance would go up your ass. It would be less expensive."

He laughed and slapped Jonas on the shoulder. "Your secret is safe with me, my friend. Let's keep this among friends. On my last visit to the general, he told me many others, mostly among our allied troops, were doing the same."

The retreating Russians passing through Gzatsk had absorbed the local reserves totaling some fifteen thousand five hundred men, all of their military supplies, and one hundred twenty-five guns. The heat was the worst burden on the French troops. This was an unusually hot summer, and the temperatures were hovering in the 90s F most of the time. This far inland, there were precious few breezes of any kind. The men of the Faucons soaked in the small streams with their horses at every opportunity. Thus far, Satan was holding up as well as most of the horses in this advance unit. The horses following were not so fortunate. Napoleon decided to rest here for several days, and Henri had the opportunity to visit the general.

Henri rode to the staff area and saw the general's carriage and tent with his personal flag. Henri dismounted and stuck his head inside the tent flap. The general was sitting at his small table writing.

"Oh, hello, my boy. Do come in. I will be finished here in just a minute. It is so good to see you. I have been wondering how you and our advance scouts were faring."

Henri entered the tent, took off his sabre, and sat on the chair next to the table. The general's aide came in with a tray of hot fresh coffee and some sweet cakes he had "found" in the officers' mess area.

"Henri, good to see you again. I will be right back with another cup and more cakes. I didn't expect you. I gather you have heard the good news that Napoleon has decided to rest here for a few days. We think he has given up on catching the Russians before they reach Moscow. Surely they will not burn their prize city. A Frenchman would never burn Paris and defend it unto death."

26

Advance to Moscow

The last obstacle before the grand prize of the entire campaign, Moscow, lay some seventy kilometers to the west of the great city. Borodino was a small village and of no great military advantage other than the retreating Russian army had chosen this place to finally make a stand. The Russian commanders well knew that any failure here would bring about the capture of Moscow and humiliation to the motherland.

Napoleon knew this also and in every staff meeting hammered home that this battle must be won. Failure on the Grande Armée's part would bring about defeat of the entire campaign. Victory here would mean supplies and shelter for the pending winter. It was already starting to turn a bit cold during evening hours, and Napoleon had studied the harshness of the cruel Siberian winters.

"Henri, hurry and make ready," commanded Major LaBauve. "We have been summoned to the general's staff meeting. We are certain to have some word on the pending advance." Henri was writing in his personal journal and noted the date as Septembre 3, 1812, in the late evening. He hurriedly put on his blouse, boots, and sabre before joining the major. The general's tent area was only a short walk, and it would not be necessary to bother with horses.

"Major, there is a chill in the air during the late evening and night hours. Winter cannot be far away. Jonas is worried and tells wild tales of snow and ice lasting until next Mars or Avril. Provisions are scarce or none at all. He said it is imperative that we find adequate shelter and supplies for the winter or we cannot survive. He has secretly told me that many of his men are thinking seriously of going home before it is too late and they are trapped here. Do you suppose that our leaders are aware of this situation?"

"Oh, Henri, I am certain they are and know we must take Moscow quickly to avoid the things Jonas is telling you. Having lived it all of his life, he is probably very correct about the winter in these northern regions. I have heard it can be very trying for anyone not properly prepared, not to mention an entire army of thousands."

They were sent right in to the general. He shook hands with Henri and the major and offered them a cup of red wine. He unrolled a large map on the table.

"Gentlemen, I have summoned you here in advance of the meeting for special operations orders from the Short Corporal himself. The Faucons are to approach the Russian front at night and cautiously divide into two groups. Use the special cloaks and use the darkness. You will travel parallel to the Russian front, staying out of sight as much as possible. Do all possible to avoid contact or being observed. This is strictly a mission to verify what we will encounter. I would be almost certain they will know of your presence and hopefully not try to engage you. Gentlemen, please study this map with me. There is not much on this map regarding our area. It is evident there will be a battle of much magnitude here as Russian peasants interviewed thus far have told of many troops scattered between here and Moscow.

"We must gather as much information as possible about the troop concentrations, terrain, and especially this stream here that flows like a barrier along the entire front. Any crossings for troop concentrations will be most valuable. You will have two days for your mission, but please report earlier if the information is gathered. Haste is of foremost importance, but accuracy will be the key to success. Do either of you have any questions?"

"No, monsieur," said Major LaBauve. "We will leave within the hour. Darkness is falling fast now. We will report complete findings as soon as possible."

"Merci, gentlemen. Henri, a letter arrived in the dispatch. It may keep you company on this dark night. Go with God, gentlemen."

The general clapped Henri on the back and hurried off to the staff meeting. Henri put the letter in his jacket pocket and hurried back to the Faucon's area with Major LaBauve. As they arrived, they hastily assembled the officers. The troops were advised to ready for immediate departure and to make certain all metallic objects were rattle proof, canteens were filled, and their cloaks were ready. Henri pulled Jonas and Michael to one side.

"This will probably be our most serious mission to date. It may be quite dangerous as there is reported to be many of the enemy in the area. Please ask all to make special considerations for quiet and discreet movement. Thank God we do not have a full moon, and the moon that does show is partially covered by clouds. Our dark cloaks may take care of the rest. The entire troop will move forward to a point where the forward scouts advise we are closest to the enemy and not yet observed. We will move slowly and divide into two groups, one to the left and one to the right. We will move to the left. We will depart as soon as everyone is ready."

Henri, remembering his letter, went to the adjacent cook area to scrounge a final mug of tea and read his letter in privacy. The script was in the fine, tiny hand of Ange, and he could smell a fragrance and almost sense her presence on the paper. He held the letter to his nose for some time, taking in the very essence of the love of his life. So near in his memory and yet so far away. A virtual lifetime away.

My Dearest Henri,

> *The last letter I received from you was just when you were leaving Vilnius. Is everything all right? Please try to write as often as you can, or maybe you have found a lovely Russian girl by now. If you do not write, I will ask Poppa to spy on you for me. Only joking, mon amour, but I do miss you so. I beg a small word when you can.*
>
> *We are still following the progress of the Grande Armee on the map on Poppa's study wall. I hope we are accurate and we now have you very near to Moscow. People here tell us that the Armee must find suitable quarters in Moscow, or nearby, before the winter sets in. They say the winters are very fierce and brutal, lasting well into the next late spring. All of this saddens me more knowing that you will be gone for many more months. If you are safe, that is all that matters. That, and the knowledge that you will be coming home to these arms that ache to hold you and the body that aches for your touch. One would think that the pain of absence might lessen in a period of months, but mine seems to grow each day. I don't know how Momma has done it all of these years. She calls it putting on her happy face. I will try for I know that you will be a soldier just like Poppa.*
>
> *It has been very hot the past month. It has rained the past two days and the moist air rises in clouds. Mimi says it would be like taking a hot bath in steam from her water kettle. At night, and please do not tell anyone, I have started sleeping without night clothes. Momma would have a fit, but it is much more comfortable. Maybe we can try it when you come home and we are married. I await that day and again and again pledge my everlasting and eternal love to you.*
>
> *Je t'aime,*
> *Ange*

Henri took out his small picture and stared for some time, thinking of the words he had just read. He could picture the image of Ange lying naked on the bed and silently sleeping. His loneliness and deep thoughts were broken by Michael calling for him. He hurriedly wrapped the letter with his others in the oilskin packet. Time to put all of this in the corner of his heart with all of the rest he carried there and return to the present world of war.

Fallen trooper

Henri made a short inspection of his men but knew this was just a formality. They were ready, and all seemed in order. All had their cloaks, and as the general had said, they resembled a command of ghosts. Well, they would have to move with the stealth of a ghost regiment this night. The Russians were close at their front and would probably shoot at anything. Two advance scouts were sent out early to detect just how close they were. They knew the Russians were in the forests, but in what strength? After a short talk with Major LaBauve, the command to mount and move out was whispered. Once again as they passed the staff command area, the general and others were watching them. They waved as the column silently passed into the darkness. There was a very narrow sliver of moon, but high clouds drifted over, giving the entire scene one of eerie suspense. With the wolves howling in the distance, a sinister and foreboding scene was present. Jonas commented that the entire set of things made his hair bristle. *Indeed, it did*, thought Henri.

They moved in two columns across the newly cut cornfields toward a distant tree line of forest. They were in the wide open with no cover at all. The scouts rode up and advised Major LaBauve that the columns should divide in about five hundred meters and to be very wary of the forest area to the right. They had seen many fires in the forest and as far as they could see on either side of the trees. It was evident the enemy was present in great strength. A silent "good luck" and the columns divided one to the right with Major LaBauve and the other to the left with Henri.

Henri's group filed silently through the fields and approached the river. The tree line of the forest was just on the other side of the stream. Henri ordered a dismount and advance on foot. Each man held his horse's bridle short to prevent any noise from the horses. Some of the randy rascals just might catch an odor of a lovely Russian mare and sound an alarm. Luck seemed with them as they approached the steep banks. No fires were evident in the trees, but they did smell woodsmoke. The slight breeze was carrying the smoke odor from the Russian troop concentrations near where the columns had split. Just then, the heavy sounds of cannon fire and the sharp report of muskets split the distant night air.

"My god," whispered Jonas, "the major's group must have been sighted and is under attack. Do we dare to go to their aid?"

"No," said Henri. "We couldn't do anything at this stage anyway, and we have our own mission. Let's get this over with and leave this place before we find some Russians too. Everyone mount and let's see how far the stream goes and if there are any shallow crossing places."

The stream was fast moving, had steep high banks, and seemed deep in spots. This was the one indicated on the general's map, and it coursed its way along the entire front just behind the large cut fields and near the forest tree lines. It was a perfect barrier for the Russians if crossing places could not be found. The distant sounds of gunfire were slowly ceasing. The cannons had stopped altogether, and the musket fire was only sporadic. Finally it stopped altogether. Henri hoped this was a good sign and the major and his group had escaped without serious injury. At least they now knew where the Russians were.

They went downstream several kilometers and finally came to a fairly wide spot of maybe a half kilometer where the water eddied into more shallow pools. Henri and the first of twenty men crossed with ease and, after surveying the far side, motioned for the others to follow. One of the men rode up to Henri and advised him there was a small bridge just wide enough for a single wagon on the other side of the shallow area. Perfect for cannon and supply wagons but one at a time over the weak structure. They went to the road, meandering from the bridge into the trees of the forest. Henri sent two scouts and had the rest stay with him until any sightings of the enemy could be confirmed. There was none, and the entire troop advanced at a soft gallop. They soon came upon a small sleeping village. A barking dog alerted someone in a small house near the road. A rough voice shouted at the dog to shut up. Henri rode up to the house and dismounted.

"Jonas, see if you can communicate with these people and see if there are any troops about and how close we might be to the main force."

Jonas took several men and went up to the house and dragged a terrified man out. He spoke to him in a language Henri only guessed was Russian. The man replied and during the conversation made many gestures toward the right where the columns had split. In the faint light, the man drew lines in the dirt. Jonas added the stream and marked the village.

"Monsieur, he says this is the village Yel'nya; and there is another village, Utitsa, a bit farther along this road. He hasn't seen Russian troops in several days, but before that, large numbers came along this road. This river is called the Kolocha, and the bridge here is the only one until Utitsa. That bridge is small and only for farm wagon traffic just like this one."

"Très bien, Jonas. Thank him and warn him not to tell anyone of our passing. We will come back and cut off his head and feed him to the dogs if I find out otherwise."

"Oui, monsieur."

There was still no evidence of the enemy. Could this be so? Could they have left this entire section of their flank exposed, or did they know that the stream was crossable at this point? Well, for whatever reason, if a sizable force could cross, they could create havoc with this exposed left flank. Henri decided to go on to the next village and see how far the Russians were and size of the force.

The two scouts left at a fast gallop and the main body not far behind at a slower pace. Utitsa was nearly the same size as Yel'nya and much nearer the stream. It was still in the very early morning hours, and a heavy ground fog hid most of their movements. Henri looked back and noted that this was truly a ghostly scene. Horsemen with only an upper part visible covered with dark cloaks seemingly moved on a cloud. It was indeed an eerie sight. The two scouts returned and stopped the main body just out of the village.

"Monsieur, there are signs of the enemy just on the other side of the village. We rode around the village and sighted several fires in the forest on the other side. We also sighted a small bridge similar to the other at the other village. There did appear to be several soldiers sitting near the bridge. No one saw or heard us."

"Excellent, men. Jonas, Michael, let's get into the deep forest and make camp before the dawn catches us here in the open. It will give us a chance to rest the men and horses. This will be a dry camp. For tea and coffee, use only the small fires well banked and with very dry sticks as we were taught. Post the watch to be rotated every two hours. Send a group of ten men to the river for filling everyone's canteens. Inform the sentries to be doubly alert. We still don't know if the enemy will converge in this area or not."

They arrived at an area very thick with pine and fir trees just as the first signs of dawn were approaching. There was a small creek near. That would save the canteen detachment and also assure the horses plenty of water. This would be an ideal spot to camp for the day. Henri, Jonas, and Michael stopped in a very small clearing between two huge pine trees. Michael gathered some small dry sticks, dug a hole in the soft earth next to one of the trees, and started a fire. Only a soft glow emitted from the hole as Michael took a small teakettle he had "rescued" from a previously encountered farmhouse and started to fill it with water from his canteen.

"Ah, good, hot water for a morning coffee. I can't wait after all of the adventure this morning. Henri, Jonas, do you have your mugs?"

"Oui, mon ami, I can't wait either," said Henri. "In the early afternoon, after we rest, I will ask you fine gentlemen to accompany me and three others on a short trip through this area and see what things look like in the daylight."

"I will be honored," said Michael. "Maybe we could happen on some fine village, some ladies, or a few chickens for an evening meal before we depart. Either or both would make my day."

"Michael, that is just like you always thinking of your sex life and your belly. I'll bet if we cut your head open, we would find hundreds of tiny naked ladies screaming for sexual favors and another leg of chicken."

"I wouldn't ever doubt otherwise, mon ami, and I hope things never change. I still volunteer to take your place with Ange when you get your ass shot."

"She wouldn't have you anyway. Once I have met one, they are ruined for others."

They made coffee and drank in pleasured silence. The hot liquid felt good as it warmed their throats and stomachs. The river rocks were something else and lived up to their name. They were filling though, and most of the men were ravenous by now. Henri checked on the men and found most already asleep under their capes. The horses were staked close in the scattered grassy areas. He cautioned the sentries to be doubly alert and to use the field glasses often especially in the direction of the road and two villages. This was no place to be caught unawares. Henri went back to his place and was soon in a restless sleep.

Henri woke with a start. Then realization came as he became aware of where he was. He checked the sun and gauged the time nearing noon. Some of the men were awake, quietly talking and drinking coffee and tea. He rubbed his eyes and pulled on his boots. He woke Michael and Jonas.

"Wake up, sleeping lovelies. You promised to take a ride in the countryside with me. We can leave when you gain your senses and have some coffee. There is no hurry. We will leave this area just at dusk, cross the bridge near the shallow crossing, and make the Armée camp well after darkness."

Henri, Michael, Jonas, and three of Jonas's men tracked farther back into the forest in order to reach a point well behind the village of Utitsa where they knew the enemy was in wait. They crossed a small stream flowing toward the village and came upon a large field freshly cut. Henri decided it would be safer to skirt the edge of the field and stay in the trees. That would put them farther than anticipated on the other side of the village. They would have to be cautious. After a time, they did see the village through the trees. They dismounted and studied the village for a long time with field glasses, noting a small enemy force scattered and not at all wary of any danger. Six men were near the small bridge, and a few were lounging under some trees near a house. Other than that, none were seen. There were no horses, so they must all be infantry. It would be relatively easy to cross the bridge at Yel'nya and quickly capture this one, thus giving a fairly large force rapid access to the left flank of the enemy.

Henri started to think of the action at Wilkomir with essentially this same situation. Could the Russians have possibly left this flank open on purpose with the intention of setting a trap? It would be a fine time and place. Any force advancing here toward the main Russian forces could easily be cut off and trapped. Then they could cross the stream and have a run at Napoleon's flank. It could be Wilkomir in reverse. Henri told Jonas and Michael his thoughts, and they agreed it was conceivable.

"Well, I know how we can step on that mouse. We will leave two men in the forest on the side of the bridge opposite the village Utitsa. The villagers and others will think we have left. Then the Russians will start to move into the area if they are going to do so. Our men can easily spot them and return with the warning."

"Excellent idea, Henri," said Jonas. "We can leave the two advance scouts. They are a little more adept at hiding tactics."

"Come, gentlemen, it is nearing midafternoon. By the time we get back to the others and rest a bit, have some coffee, it should be nearing time to leave."

The troop rode through the Yel'nya and crossed the bridge. Henri took note of the condition of the bridge and estimated a weight capacity. The two scouts quickly broke off and hid in the trees. Henri was certain no one had observed the scouts, and the others rode at a light gallop toward the Grande Armée. They did not go back the way they came but made for a more direct line. No need to go back to the area where the two columns had split.

Henri and the others had discussed the concerns of the firefight the major's column had encountered and hoped nothing serious had happened. They hesitated at the edge of the forest while Henri and others scoured the distant fields with their field glasses. Satisfied danger was not imminent, they proceeded across the freshly cut cornfields. They were careful to go down the long rows and cross them at opportune times. The stiff corn stubble could play havoc with the horse's legs and hooves. They arrived at the camp well after dark, and Henri reported at once to the general. They went to the area designated to the Faucons.

Henri asked Michael, "Please take Satan to the horse area. I must report as soon as possible."

He did notice in his haste that many of the Faucons appeared to be missing but thought little of it at that moment. He hurriedly walked to the general's tent and requested to see him. The general came out in his undershirt and without boots.

"Henri, good to see you back. With what happened to Major LaBauve and part of the command, we feared the worst for you. There is an urgent staff meeting in a few minutes, and I want you to come and make your report directly to the Short One. I don't have time to plow through it, and you know him and can speak direct. Get yourself a mug of coffee and a sweet cake from the table over there. I will finish dressing while I tell you about Major LaBauve."

The general sat on his cot and strained to pull his boots on. Henri poured his coffee and quickly ate a sweet cake and then another. He picked up the third, and the general commented that Henri must be starving. How true.

"Henri, I have very bad news. Major LaBauve was killed when his unit encountered the enemy. Only thirty-nine men of the hundred returned, and twelve of those were wounded. We do not expect several to live the night. They were caught point-blank by the Russian cannon, and an entire infantry regiment did the rest. They didn't have a chance. Reports from the survivors said the major and his horse were blown completely apart. I guess it was merciful as he probably didn't know a thing. You will assume command of the Faucons, and I will explain the details when we return. Come, let us hurry. Our Short Friend is not one to be kept waiting as you already know."

They hurried to Napoleon's area and entered a large tent ablaze with lanterns. There were large tables set up with maps and papers. More tables held refreshments of coffee, tea, and several types of cakes. *What luxury*, thought Henri. Even here in the middle of nowhere, an emperor must have his tea and cakes. Napoleon and other staff officers entered the tent. Napoleon went directly to Henri and put his hands on both shoulders.

"Well, my faithful comrade, I see you have returned safely to us once more. We were worried when a portion of your scout's troop was hit by the Russians. I haven't much time as of now, but do wish a personal visit in the near future. I hope you have good things to report. They have been few and far between as of late."

"I hope so, Your Excellency. My group was far luckier than poor Major LaBauve's. We went to the left and the other troop to the right of the Russian front. The large fields at our front are, for the most part, freshly cut corn fields. The stubble and rows will make any advance hard for infantry and cavalry, not to mention cannon. I see a map of this area on the table and can explain our findings better if indicated on a map reference."

Moving to the map, Henri continued, "We entered the forest here, and the stream called the Kolocha flows along the entire front. It is a fast-moving stream with high banks and quite deep in places. We proceeded farther to the left to a point about here and found not only a suitable crossing but a small bridge used for farm wagons. It will hold the weight of horses, cannons, and supply wagons if they are spaced. We proceeded back along the stream toward the known Russian positions and came to a village, Yel'nya, about here. While questioning a villager, we obtained basic information about the area and that the Russians had been through there only two days prior.

"We went to the next village, Utitsa, here. There is a very small infantry detachment at the village that appears to be guarding another small bridge similar to the first one. It appeared to be in good condition as far as we could observe from a distance. We retreated and hid in the forest until dusk and came back for this report. Monsieur, I remember a similar situation prior to the battle at Wilkomir. We were lucky there and did catch them by surprise. Something just did not seem right about this situation. If we did cross a sizable force, the Russians could set a trap, devastate the group, and hurriedly cross the stream and hit our flank. I left two men in hiding for the entire day tomorrow to confirm this will not be the case. They should be back tomorrow night with their report."

Napoleon gripped Henri on the shoulder. "Excellent report and observations. This is the information I was hoping to obtain. I will hit the entire Russian front a hard blow with the dawn of first light tomorrow. Henri, I will be very busy tomorrow, but I will not forget the two men you have positioned to return. If they have positive reports and the Russians have blundered again, report this to me at once. They will have another surprise on their left flank, and Moscow will be in our grasp."

27

Faucon Commander

"Henri," said the general, "return to my tent and await my return. I will be there just after this briefing on tomorrow's battle. I hope not to be long, but make yourself comfortable and help yourself to my wine stock and stash of cheese and bread. I need to confirm the orders for your troop."

Henri went to the general's tent and did as he was instructed with the wine, cheese, and bread. It seemed he never could get enough to eat these days. The orderly was sitting with him when the general came in.

"Well, it seems our corporal is very pleased with your report and the professional manner it was presented. He said you have never disappointed him from your first meeting. Beware, mon ami, if you ever do disappoint him, he will forget the good times. He can be a good friend and a deadly enemy. Now to the matter at hand.

"I realize you are still young to assume complete command of a troop, but you have proven yourself, and there is simply no time to appoint another replacement for Major LaBauve. You will retain your present rank for now and immediately assume command of the Faucons. You may tell your other officers and let me know if there appears to be any problems. You are to stay in place during tomorrow's battle and report at once with the arrival of the two scouts. I am certain there will be considerable guide duties for a flanking movement if the reports are in the affirmative.

"And now to the most important matter of all. Major battles be damned. I have been chastised, again, regarding not writing home. This time, you were included in my criticism. My Vivien accuses me of training you in my methods of ignoring ladies' requests for letters, sweet words of nothing, and all that dallypoo. She says I am the worst ever about writing, and now you are second worst with not writing to Ange. Please put pen to paper and get us both back in good graces. I will try to write, but tonight and in the next several days, I expect we will both be too busy and not even think of home. I'll let you get back to your troop, Henri. I know you are tired."

"Oui, monsieur, I am tired, but never too tired to talk of home. Merci for the sharing. I am terrible about writing. One more little mug of the wine and I will take my leave. I know I will sleep well tonight."

Henri walked slowly back to the Faucon area and thought hard about what to say to the other officers. He knew Jonas would be all right with this and wondered if some of the others may think he was too close to the general and this was the reason for this move. Well, to hell with it. He would just do his best, and if that wasn't good enough, that would be all right too. With the allies in the troop on his side, he shouldn't have to worry about any animosity.

As soon as he arrived at the area, he called all officers to a meeting. Actually there were only two more lieutenants including Jonas. Several had been killed with Major LaBauve. The Faucon troop now consisted of one hundred eleven hearty souls and another twelve wounded. Eight of those were not expected to recover, and the other four would require considerable hospital care. There would not be much hope for any of the wounded to return. There would not be replacements as their duties in scouting required the type of training that was extensive, and there was no time for such here in the field.

"Messieurs, I will be very brief with this. I have been appointed commander of the Faucons and know you will join me in loyalty to our nations and this command. I feel very badly about Major LaBauve, and I am sure we shall never forget him. In coming days, I will meet with each of you individually and share any thoughts we all may have on any issues of the troop. I promise to always be available for anything that may require my input. Here is my hand to each of you, in friendship, loyalty, and to the best troop in the Grande Armée."

Henri shook hands with the beaming lieutenants. They answered almost in unison that they were so relieved that he was the new commander. They had worried that some officer not educated in their ways of this special group might be appointed.

Jonas slapped him on the shoulder and said, "This indeed calls for a celebration, and I promise the next time I find a fine vintage wine, we will all toast to your new appointment. Joking aside, Henri, and I am certain I speak for all here, we are pleased that you are our leader. I too pledge my loyalty as well as my friendship. This is a unique group and much different than the other units I see around us. We are comrades as well as soldiers. I am proud to serve here. My men feel the same."

Henri could have melted with relief. He had promised himself not to worry, and he really was not about his abilities, but the awesome responsibility was just now being realized. He would be father, mother, big brother, nurse, comrade, and whatever else was required to all of these men. Major LaBauve had told him one time that the commander must even wipe asses and blow noses if that is what it took. He had essentially done the same before, but he had always had another in command as a buffer. Now he was the final judge, jury, and hangman if needed.

Henri explained to the officers, "The battle will commence at dawn, and the Faucons will stand down and await the return of our scouts. Then, with a positive report, a fast action will be required to guide a flanking movement. Until then, get all the rest you can."

Just before dawn that clear and cool Septembre 6, 1812, morning, the earth trembled, and the night air reverberated with the sounds of five hundred ninety cannons of various calibers firing almost simultaneously. All they could do was cover their ears and watch as the flames leaped from the muzzles.

Napoleon had briefed his senior staff and advised them in parting, "After a victory, there are no enemies, only men. We will, this day, see the end of enemies and count the men whether they be alive or dead."

The battlefield was open farmland and mostly freshly harvested cornfields. The very dense forest behind the Russian lines hid the mass concentrations of the main troops. After the initial barrage of cannon fire and during the first lull, the Russians ran to strengthen the front lines. The stream would be only a minor barrier in certain places and could be utilized as a funnel effect to concentrate repulsing fire on advancing troops. Other than that, the Russian positions were not very strong since the main battlefield would be mostly flatlands with no major obstacles to the Grande Armée. The Russians, under the command of Marshall Kutuzov, had seventy-two thousand regular infantry, ten thousand semitrained militia, seventeen thousand cavalry, seven thousand Cossacks, and six hundred forty cannons. Napoleon had one hundred thousand infantry, twenty-eight thousand cavalry, and five hundred ninety cannons. Napoleon, in later years, called this the "battle of the giants." Both leaders were determined in the victory of this battle.

Marshall Kutuzov proclaimed to his army, "Trusting in God, we shall either win or die here. Napoleon is God's enemy. He will desecrate His churches. Think of your wives and children who rely on your protection. Think of your emperor who is watching you. Before the sun has set on this battle, you will have written on this field the record of your faith and patriotism in the blood of your enemy."

Napoleon had proclaimed to his Grande Armée, "This is the battle you have so long desired! Now victory depends on you. We have need of it. Victory will give us abundance of supplies, good winter quarters, and a prompt return to our motherland. Conduct yourselves as you did at Austerlitz, Friedland, Vitebsk, and Smolensk. Let distant posterity say to each of you, 'He was present at the great battle beneath the walls of Moscow.'"

The massive cannon fire lasted for nearly a half hour. Henri, Michael, Jonas, and the others watched with fingers in their ears and with the usual awe at the spectacle. The cannons were firing as fast as the crews could reload them. They watched as some in the gun crews poured water on the heated barrels, causing steam to rise in clouds. The smoke was overwhelming and drifted around the area in choking clouds. Finally a soft breeze carried the wretched stuff over the fields to partially cover the areas of advance. Well, at least, that may afford some manner of cover for the advance.

Henri knew, however, that the Russians had the entire line of advance zeroed in at some point. All of them had made many advances through the years, and he could sense the terror of the troops as they gathered. Many would die this day. The signal for advance was given, and the cannons continued to fire. They would do so until the advance troops were in danger of being hit by their own guns. He saw the drummers line up just behind the main assault group and start to sound the cadence. Oh the memories of this. He recalled his first battle and how terrified he was. The units and battalions were aligned and stepped out smartly. The different regimental colors were a spectacle in themselves. There were greens, reds, blues, many units with the tall black shakoes.

Reflections of metallic flashes were everywhere with the polished brass and silver of the uniforms. Bayonets and swords flashed in the ever-brightening sky as they were carried at high port. When the advancing troops were nearing midfield, the French cannons were elevated to their maximum. Now shell bursts could be seen just on the other side of the stream and nearing the tree line of the forest. This was as close as their range would permit without moving them forward. Orders were given for some of the guns to move up and cover the advance. The move would be too late, for as the troops neared the stream, the tree line erupted in a wall of flame and smoke. The Russian cannons were firing point-blank into the French ranks. The carnage was horrific as shots tore through the ranks. The French troops were running forward now and approaching the stream. Many carried hastily constructed ladders to throw across the stream as bridges.

The high banks of the stream afforded some measure of protection as the shots went over the heads of those fortunate enough to slide down into the mud. The ladders were sufficient, but now a bottleneck was forming with the many men trying to hang on and cross. Some were swept downstream and swam for the far bank while others were jumping in the water to fight the current and eventually reached the opposite side. Once on the opposite side, they would have to advance to the forest now seemingly alive with Russians.

The Grande Armée was now swarming up out of the stream banks and reaching the first trees of the forest. They were met there by hundreds of Russians, and fierce hand-to-hand fighting was seen on a wide front. The fighting went to and fro like a mad beast. Shouts, screams, and curses were heard in many languages, adding to the horrific noise of musket and pistol fire and hacking of hundreds of swords, rifle butts, lances, and virtually anything that could be picked up and used as a weapon.

The exhausted French halted just inside the forest to regroup and reform the lines of advance. The Russians hurled themselves at the French over and over, taking severe losses. Indeed, both sides were taking brutal casualties. The carnage went on all day with periodic lulls in between. At dusk, both sides stayed at their present position. The fields and stream had been crossed. Now it would be a matter of reinforcing the weary first lines of assault and pushing the Russians back.

The quiet was overpowering. Only the moans and cries of the wounded could be heard. Medical teams from both sides were picking their way through the battlefields, taking only those wounded that could potentially be saved. In most cases, the choices were not difficult. These were cruel times with the bludgeons of war and the lack of proper care at the front. The wounded, whether severe or not, usually died of infection and exposure.

The two scouts returned just at dusk and reported directly to Henri. They had waited hidden all day in the thick forest near the bridge at Yel'nya. Nothing was seen and, just before leaving, to make absolutely certain, they had crossed the bridge, widely skirted the village, and scouted the road on the far side. No sign of any enemy troops. Henri ran to tell the general. The general was with Napoleon and several other officers just returning from the front.

"Monsieur, the two scouts have returned, and nothing was observed of the enemy. To be certain, the scouts did a brief reconnoiter of the first village and the road beyond nearly to the second village. They are certain the area is clear."

Napoleon said, "That is what I have been waiting to hear. Henri, be ready to depart at once and guide the four brigades of dragoons I have set aside for this. Cross as we have discussed at the ford and bridge and take two of them all the way to the second village and capture the bridge there. This is the dragoon commander, and he has instructions to contact the other two brigades and have them cross at the second bridge. All four brigades will group and hit the Russian flank as hard as possible. At night and in all of the confusion, the exhausted Russians will not know what is hitting them. Other cavalry and dragoons will follow as reinforcements. If we are fortunate, this battle is over. We have suffered enough this day. Keep me and General Dubois here informed of the progress by courier."

"Oui, monsieur, we leave at once."

"Henri," said the general, "the emperor and I will be in the staff tent for the remainder of the night. Have the couriers report to us there."

"Oui, Your Highness." And Henri rushed away to gather his command.

The Faucons guided the four brigades to a point just below the village of Utitsa. Here Henri told the commander to wait, and in about fifteen minutes or less, the scouts would contact them and lead them to the bridge at the village.

The rest of the Faucons and the other two brigades hurried for the bridge at Yel'nya. They crossed with no problems, some taking the bridge and some fording at the shallow place. A part of the Faucons made a wide sweep of Utitsa and came up on the road on the far side of the village, cutting off any Russians who could run and sound the alarm. The village was rapidly taken, and the second group of dragoons started crossing the bridge.

Now with four full brigades at the Russian flank, they poised to attack. Henri conferred with the dragoon commanders, and it was agreed to let the Faucons creep as close as possible to the Russians before any attack was made. The campfires were visible through the trees as they eased closer and closer.

At a point nearly thirty meters from a large group of fires and tents, the dragoons and Faucons mounted and prepared for the assault. With screams and yells, the French horsemen hit the Russian encampment, decimating it, and went on to the next and the next large concentrations of Russians. The darkness and swiftness of the attack had the Russians running in confusion. Many had no weapons and boots and were only half clothed. Unmanned horses were running among the troops, adding to the chaos.

Marshall Kutuzov was awakened at once and ordered a hasty general retreat toward Moscow. He must save what was left of his army for defense of the capital city, having so stated in a general staff meeting some hour earlier.

"French attacks have been successfully repulsed everywhere, and tomorrow I shall put myself at the head of the army and drive the enemy from the sacred soil of Russia."

It was then that he was advised that they had lost their entire front line. He refused to believe it. In all, the Russians had lost around forty-four thousand men and the French thirty-five thousand including forty-three ranking officers and generals. Now with the French rolling up his left flank and apparently in great strength, his army must flee to save itself.

The four brigades and Faucons had made tremendous havoc in the Russian rear area, and now was the time to fall back and regroup for possible reinforcements. They were afraid the Russians might come to know their limited strength and counterattack. As it was, the field was theirs this night. Some hours later nearing dawn, Napoleon and his staff officers rode up to the scene of the entire Russian army fleeing, taking only what they could. The guns were being swiftly moved with large teams of horses pulling them as fast as possible. Napoleon would let them go. Any further efforts would just prove to be exhausting and possibly futile. They would rest here for as long as it would take and lick their wounds. He realized then that Moscow was his.

The general asked for his aides to locate the Faucon troop area, find Henri, and have him report to Napoleon and him at once. The Faucons were near the river soaking in a shallow area and washing themselves and the horses. Henri was sitting with Jonas, Michael, and several others, drinking a mug of coffee.

"Capitaine, come with us at once. The emperor and the general request your presence as soon as possible. Hurry! These are not people to be kept waiting."

"Well, merde! I can't even have a mug of coffee. I'll be back later, *mez amis*. You may pleasure yourself with my share of the coffee."

Henri dismounted and went over to Napoleon and the general. Napoleon was beaming and grabbed Henri's arm.

"I hope you realize what has transpired during this battle, my fine capitaine. With the efforts of your troop and the dragoons, we are on the door stoop of Moscow, and nothing can stop us now. There may be some semblance of shallow resistance, but we will be in Moscow within days. Please help yourself to the refreshments on the tables over there and come back. We need to talk about the night's events."

Henri swiftly ate three small cakes and washed them down with a mug of dark black coffee. He was ravenous, and this was much better than river rocks and the foul liquid called coffee Michael had made. He went back over to the officers, and the general gave him one of his famous bear hugs.

"Ha! I can do that now whether you are a capitaine or not. You are almost my son and my son-in-law as well. From the destruction we have observed, the actions here last night may have been the driving force in winning this battle. The master here has so rightly pointed out that Moscow will be our next objective, and the prize is evidently ours. I owe our ladies a letter, and this time, I will have a lot to write about."

"Monsieur, please do not tell too much. Madame will tell Ange, and she worries about these things. I am trying to be careful and not get hurt."

"Oui, I know all of that, but I will relate some of your latest exploits. Come, the emperor wants to talk to you, and he hasn't much time."

Napoleon raised his head from the maps on the table before him and smiled. He, again, grabbed Henri by the arm.

"Henri, here you are, my boy. I wanted to offer the thanks of a grateful emperor and nation for your excellent work with the Faucons. And of course, there will be another piece of tin or so to add to your collection when we return to Paris. I hesitate to kiss you again though. I am certain now there will be those who will think we are having an affair of the heart. I really just wanted to see and merci briefly. I am very busy now with the final assault on Moscow. Merci for coming." Napoleon laughed, slapped Henri on the shoulder, and went right back conferring with several officers over map points.

Henri went back to his troops soaking in the stream and pondered the next actions. His personal history in this Armée and with the emperor had seemed like a dream. He seemed destined to be at the right place for recognition. He was known personally to one of the most powerful men in the world, and yet all of this made him feel very humble. He would have to return to his men and check on the wounded. The Faucons had lost three killed and seven more wounded in the fighting last night. And now on to Moscow. How many more to be sacrificed?

28

Moscow

The orders were to rest in place until further instructions. That suited the Faucons just fine, and they found a place near the stream and far enough away from the battlefield. There were literally thousands of bodies in the cornfields and all the way to the forest tree lines and beyond. Troops were picking up the French dead and laying them in long trenches along the edge of the fields. Weapons of every sort were being collected and placed in huge heaps. Wagons were coursing their way among the rows picking up the weapons for return to the rear area.

The people digging the trenches had gone to the villages close by and commandeered labor and plows. Almost as fast as the trenches could be dug, they were filled with the dead. Over thirty-five thousand French and other allies would have eternal sleep here. The bodies were handled gently at first, but now it became an urgent matter to get them buried. Even though the days were cloudy, enough sun and heat was causing the bodies to emit the usual offending rotting odor. They would tend only to the allied dead.

The Russian bodies would just rot where they lay, and there were over forty-four thousand of these. They must move on very soon. Already the carrion-eating birds were starting to gather. They were feasting even now and would in the coming days after the Grande Armée had moved on. Luckily, Henri had moved the Faucons to a distance farther in the trees upwind if there was such a thing. It seemed the smell followed everywhere. They were not noticed or summoned for any of the duties of digging or collecting the dead. Out of sight, out of mind.

During this rest period, Henri knew he must write to Ange or suffer the same fate of a tongue-lashing as the general. He borrowed paper and a waxed waterproof envelope from the general's company clerk and went off under the trees near the stream.

Septembre 8, 1812

My Dearest Ange,

I am somewhere near Moscow at a place called Borodino. A major battle was fought here yesterday and has been won by Napoleon and the Grande Armee. I am sitting in a lovely spot untouched by the battle. There are nice trees and a stream sings to me nearby. I am perfectly content and very safe. The only thing lacking is your beautiful presence. I have your picture resting on a large rock, and you are smiling at me as I write this.

You are so correct complaining that I do not write often. With the lack of written word, please do not think I have run off with a Russian lady as you thought. There is not a Russian or any other lady that could ever compare with you. You have captivated me from nearly the first moment we met. I sometimes think it was our destiny evolved by God that someday we would be as one. That is all that I think about most days and, indeed, is what keeps me going. I do love you, my Little Angel. Please help me bear this burden of loneliness and being apart from each other. I pray it will end soon.

I have seen your father several times during the past weeks and he is well. Please tell your mother that he has been extremely busy day and night with the Emperor and this steady advance toward Moscow. He has promised to write more often and as he can. The Emperor keeps a very fast pace and expects all others in his world to do the same. Little wonder he is the military master of his time. His energy seems boundless.

I will close for now, mon amour. Remember to look at the moon and know that I am looking at the same moon and thinking of you.

Je t'aime,
Henri

On the second afternoon after the battle, Henri was summoned to the general.

"Are you and your den of thieves tired of lying around on your asses while others do the dirty work? I saw your troop hiding in the trees. I don't blame you, but now we have need of your expertise. Come, Henri, look at the maps with me. Your troop is to follow the retreating Russians all the way to Moscow. We are certain that will be their next stop for an engagement. Remain at a distance and estimate their strength and mark positions of heavy concentrations on your map.

We took a very heavy loss here and really can't afford further drastic losses. Of course, the Russians have suffered worse than us; but if we are to winter here, we must remain as much as possible at full strength. As usual, report to me each day with couriers. If your troop is rested enough, you can leave tonight or early in the morning. I will leave that up to you. Do you have any questions?"

"No, monsieur. I have written a letter to Ange and would appreciate your including it with the next dispatches to Paris. I really didn't know what to write except small talk and dallypoo as you call it. I didn't know whether to tell the things I have seen, but thought it best I did not. I don't think she would understand, and just make her worry."

"I know what you mean. I never write anything to my wife that could give her alarm. We have discussed some of what I have seen, but I have never written about it. I think you are doing correct and never putting anything in writing that could worry or upset them. And also, one can never be certain who opens and reads these things. Our master has his ways and spies everywhere. Can I do anything for you or see that your troops have everything before you depart?"

"No, monsieur. We are fine. Actually, several of my 'thieves' found some supplies in an abandoned Russian field kitchen, and they have divided the spoils. We are well supplied. I have a box with some bottles of Russian vodka to be delivered to you later. Of course some of it was sampled by your friendly Faucons to see if it was poisoned. It isn't too bad, but it does have a bite. I hope you enjoy it."

"Merci, Henri. I will share it with some of the other officers and will certainly let them know where it came from."

"Oui, monsieur, and after thinking of our departure, it may be better to leave just after dark and travel at night until we catch up with the Russians. They may have a far rear guard out, and I certainly don't want to run into them. We can camp and hide during the daylight hours and observe their movements better."

"So be it, Henri. As usual, go with God."

The Faucons slowly mounted and quietly departed just after dusk. It was good to get away from this place of death. Very soon, the fresh pungent odor of the deep pine forest erased that of death. There was almost no moon, and that was good. They must hide their presence at all costs. Jonas had warned of the fierce Cossacks who often served as roving units and rear guards. Even with the darkness, they had their capes on. They were comfortable in the crisp coolness of the night air. The Lithuanians knew this was the first sign of winter. Word came from some of the older men that the signs of winter were early this year. They could well do to prepare for the worst in the next month or so. After about ten kilometers, Henri sent out the scouts. They disappeared into the night almost as ghosts. One minute they were there, and the next, they were gone.

All was done in near silence. Henri heard night birds calling and thought if they might be welcoming his Faucons. No, not these damn Russian night birds.

He would much prefer the birds near Paris. He looked up at the tiny sliver of moon smiling at him through the intervals in the trees as they passed through the forest. He thought of his words to Ange and smiled knowingly to himself.

Michael, as usual, was riding next to him. Jonas was a rank back with his men. "Boss man, I have been thinking."

"That is a dangerous thing, Michael. What about?"

"Oh, don't ridicule, you idiot. This is a serious moment. I was thinking of how fortunate our unit has been all during this entire advance. We have lost our share of men, but we have been out in front of the main parties. We have had the pick of what was left of the Russian supplies and, for the most part, have fared very well. As I looked at those dead lying in the fields yesterday, I thought that could have been us if we still had to pound those damn drums. Do you remember in Spain when we went on the battlefield and collected the wounded? I thought that was bad, but this! Henri, I will always be eternally grateful to you for getting me here with you. Now I am getting sentimental, and that is not like me."

"No, it isn't, my friend. What is truly on your mind? Pour it out. That is what friendship is all about. I will certainly climb in your ears if I need."

"If something should happen to me, I ask that you bury me in a single grave in pleasant surroundings. Please do not let them throw me in a trench with all of the other stinking bodies. Plant a small tree over me so I can fertilize it. And finally don't ever forget me. I have never had a brother other than you."

"Michael, this is truly not you. I will do all that you ask, but nothing is going to happen to either of us. Try to put all of these thoughts out of your mind. I am depressed too after seeing thousands of dead, but this is war and our business. I can only imagine about poor Major LaBauve and wonder if he had any last-moment thoughts."

"I don't think so. One of the men that survived told me that they were riding parallel to the Russian front trying to find their flank. The major thought maybe they could have skirted the flank and obtained some information about strength and emplacements. They evidently got too close to the Russians and were seen. All of a sudden, the woods erupted with flames of firing cannons. He said there were at least a hundred fired in the first volley. Most of the men leaped from their horses at once but not before the first volley tore them apart.

"The major was mounted yelling for them to get low and stay that way. A cannon shot of the second volley hit him and his horse right at the saddle. He said bits of the major and the horse went everywhere and showered him and several others nearby with blood, bone, and other grisly things. One poor soul had his head taken right off and sat in his saddle for some time without his head. Others were smashed to pulp as the major and others were lying everywhere.

"The survivors saved themselves by running back across the fields. As they ran, they could see the flashes of the Russian infantry firing as they came on. He figured the wounded didn't have a chance and were probably shot or bayoneted. The fellow telling me all of this kept making the sign of the cross as he spoke. I guess that spooked me too. That and seeing more dead than I have in some time. It makes one think of his own destiny and just how short this life really is. I'm sorry for being a burden. You have your own problems."

"Since when is a brother a burden? Without shedding tears all over Satan here, I feel the same way. Let's stop this talk and think of happier times in the past and to come. Maybe Moscow is full of beautiful Russian girls, fine wine, and food."

A scout came out of the darkness and reported a small village about two kilometers ahead. Did Henri want to advance through the village or be discreet and skirt it?

"Skirt it by the easiest passage, by all means. There are still several hours of good darkness and no need to sound an alarm before we really know where the Russians are. Remember the Cossacks. They may be in the village."

The other scout returned and advised a wide route to the north. He had seen more forest with widely spaced fields. There would be ample cover. The same two scouts were sent out, and the advance continued.

Nearing dawn, they observed another sizable village. Henri decided to wait here until there was light enough to confirm there were no Russians in the area. Then they would approach the village and see what they could "find" in the way of fresh food, chickens, and hopefully wine or vodka. He knew, however, that the damned Russians probably had taken it all and ruined what they could not carry.

This time it was different. This village had not been pillaged. Henri ordered the men to take only what they would need for today and make camp in the woods on the far side of the village. The couriers would ride in pairs and report to the general. Henri had spotted a villager's ducks near a small pond and had several picked up and put in a sack.

"Deliver these ducks to the general personally and be certain to tell him it is payment for his wine, cheese, and crackers. He will know the meaning."

Two scouts were sent out in the direction of where Henri thought the retreating Russians might be. They would camp here until the scouts returned. Most of the men were building small fires for coffee and tea. Others were in the village interviewing the people and gathering a few chickens, ducks, and other foodstuff. Jonas came over to Henri.

"Henri, the villagers tell us that no Russians have been through here for some time and are surprised at our presence. Many heard the sounds of battle yesterday and have wondered about it. We have told them that we will not take everything, but do need fresh food for today and light provisions for the next several days. I have instructed my men not to enter the personal homes and disturb the inhabitants. Only take food. Several of the village women have offered to make bread if we will not take from them. A fair trade. We haven't had fresh bread in some time. And miracle of all miracles, we have found many bottles of this year's wine ageing under the hay in a barn. All is in safe hands now, and of course, your share will be coming. I promised you a toast to your promotion as our leader at the next instance of a find."

"Merci, Jonas. I will look forward to the toasting. Be certain to keep guards watching. Until our scouts return, we do not know how far the Russians are from us."

Michael came over with a mug of coffee for Henri, and Jonas asked where his might be. He was duly informed, with a wide grin, that Michael was not a servant or a slave; and furthermore, Jonas was not in the fair shape of a woman to have the right to ask such a thing. If so, they would certainly trade a mug of coffee for "something." Jonas asked if Michael would be willing to trade a mug of coffee for a bottle of wine. The trade was sealed.

The two scouts returned in three hours, reporting that the Russians were about ten kilometers away in two long columns. The first of the columns must surely be nearing Moscow by now. A rear guard composed mostly of Cossacks was seen at both columns.

"Good, send two more couriers at once to the general with this news. Napoleon may want to send mounted troops to hurry the Russians along and unsettle them before they can devise defensive positions."

The Faucons had done all that had been asked, and short of engaging Cossacks, there was nothing else to do except follow the retreating columns at a distance and report as required. The smell of roasting chickens and ducks was everywhere, and the Faucons were about to feast for the first time in days. They would rest here for the next day and await any word from the general and gather further information about the Russians.

The chickens and ducks, while plentiful at first, were soon depleted; and it was evident the villagers had taken the vast majority of their stock into the woods. So be it, there were several pigs and a pen full of chickens that had been singled out and were under guard. Michael, Jonas, and the men of the Faucons did have the toast to Henri's first full command.

And now to follow the Russians and report any movements and any possible defensive stands between here and Moscow. This would be a, hopefully, peaceful operation; and all the Faucons had to do was stay out of the way. Henri would spend a lot of time with the field glass. Indeed, they all would. Michael was among the advance group on the left flank. Late that evening, he observed the Russians setting up approximately one hundred cannons just inside the perimeter of a small tree line. But this would not be the most exciting part of his report. In the evening twilight, he could barely make out tall spires of churches. Moscow!

At long last, they were at the gates of the capital of Russia. This had been a long and torturous journey and very costly to both armies, and now the end was near. Michael and his small band rode back to Henri as fast as they could. Two couriers were immediately dispatched to the general with the position of the rear guard cannon and the news that Moscow was in sight. The Grande Armée was advancing, but at a slow, cautious pace. They had camped for the night as the couriers arrived and gave the news to the general. Napoleon, with this news, ordered the advance at a rapid pace with morning's first light. Moscow would be his tomorrow. He noted the Russian cannon emplacement on his map and ordered the advance troops to divide and encircle the Russians. They could be taken without firing a shot if things went properly. The couriers returned to Henri with orders to avoid contact but advance as far as they could during the night, all the way into Moscow if possible.

The Faucons quickly ate, tended their mounts, and proceeded at a slow pace toward Moscow. At first daylight, there it was. In the eastern sky against the hues of pink, blue, and purple, they could clearly see the church spires and cupolas of the onion-top buildings for which Moscow was noted. At the first buildings in the suburbs, Henri ordered a halt and sent two more couriers to the rear with the question, should they hold here and wait for the emperor to advance first into Moscow, or should they advance and test the safety of the city before his entrance? The Grande Armée was moving up rapidly now, and the couriers returned within the hour with orders to advance cautiously as far as they could.

The Faucons moved into the city through the huge gates of the fortress for the main city itself very cautiously and halted at a large square. The city seemed deserted. No one was in sight. The only life about were several stray dogs and cats.

"This place is devoid even of birds," Jonas remarked to Henri in a whisper.

Around the square were shuttered shops and houses. The men dismounted and were starting to inspect the shops for things to eat or drink. Others were trying to peer into the dark recesses of the houses. A rear guard of the Faucons rode up with word that Napoleon was only less than an hour away. Henri decided to let the emperor claim his prize now that all seemed safe. A courier had reported earlier that the rapidly advancing Armée had bypassed and surrounded the Russian cannon emplacement, and the Russians gave up without firing a single shot. Napoleon had surmised correctly.

Napoleon, riding in his carriage, clasped his hands over his crossed knees and repeated over and over, "Moscow, Moscow. I am here at last."

He was not comforted by the triumph at Borodino. He had been unable to sleep, seemed very irritated, and was suffering with a cold. His personal valet had reported that he was very upset when a horse from his entourage had stepped on a wounded Russian officer on the battlefield, and the soldier had cried out a curse to be on Napoleon personally and the entire Grande Armée. He considered this a very bad omen and had shared it with the general.

Napoleon's personal secretary, Baron Claude-Francois de Meneval, wrote in his personal journal of the entrance to the city, "A curious and impressive sight was the sudden appearance of this great city, Asiatic rather than European, spreading out at the end of a great naked plain, topped with its 1,200 spires and sky blue cupolas, strewn with golden stars and linked to one another with golden chains. No noise disturbed the solitude of the city streets, save only the rumbling of the cannon and of the artillery caissons. Moscow seemed asleep in a deep sleep."

Napoleon saw the Faucons in formation in the square. Henri was at the head and saluting with his sabre. He bade the group of carriages to halt and commanded the presence of Henri. Henri galloped over and smartly dismounted. Napoleon got out of his carriage, and the general did likewise from his carriage just behind Napoleon's.

"Well, mon young capitaine, I see you have beat me to my prize. Do you claim it for your men here?" He chuckled and was joined by the general and several other officers.

"No, monsieur. We advanced as far as we dared to confirm safety for you and the entering troops. We have saved the grand entrance for you. May we escort you and your guard in a tour of this magnificent city? It does seem totally deserted although one would wonder what lurks behind the closed doors and shutters."

"No, Henri, you and your men have done enough and deserve a time of rest. We have gone far enough for today. The hour is growing late, and I am sick with this damn cold. I just want to find a decent bed for the night, drink some good wine, and sleep this sickness away. We will see to further explorations in the morning."

The group of carriages turned around and started for a small group of houses just outside the city gates.

"Henri," called the general, "have your troops follow us and camp in the area just next to that group of houses or in the houses not taken by the staff, *s'il vous plaît*. I wish your company at a duck dinner complete with Russian vodka this evening."

"Oui, monsieur, and it will be my pleasure. Should I bring the duck?"

"You know very well what I am talking about. I vow, sometimes you are worse than my impertinent daughter. You will make an excellent match. Now be off with you."

Henri made certain his men were bivouacked and secure and then made his way to the house the general and several other officers had commandeered. The general's carriage was outside. Henri saw Napoleon's carriage at a house next to this one. Napoleon's guards were everywhere, and Henri was challenged as he approached. This was as it should be. No chances were being taken with the emperor's safety. He advanced into the light, was recognized, and allowed to proceed into the general's house.

"Now isn't this a pigsty. There are the bare basics of tables, chairs, and beds; but all are at the point of collapse. I was going to try the bed, but it appears to be working alive with several sorts of pestilence. How do these people live like this? I am even afraid to sleep on the floor and have my nose and ears nibbled by the mice and Lord only knows what. I will sleep in my carriage for the night. Henri, I hope your people have fared a bit better. At least we can eat at the table as civilized people, but after that, I will vacate this place. Come in, my boy, and sit. We must talk."

"To be truthful, monsieur, I did not have time to check the several houses we are in, but I will certainly do so when I return. I want no part of strange things crawling on me. I think there are several species there now. Ah, I do smell something very tantalizing. Is it really roast duck?"

"Oui, and I hope it is as good as it smells. It isn't the duck you sent, however. Those did not last very long. Our cooks managed to find a few more on the way here. I still have some of the vodka you sent though. Foul stuff it is too. How in hell do you boys drink that swill?"

"If at first you take a large mouthful, it seems to deaden all other senses, and it will go down smoothly. My Lithuanian friends taught me that. Give it a try sometime. It isn't really all that bad."

"The hell I will. I have survived this long without that poison. Come let us eat, the cooks are calling."

There were the general and several other officers at the table, and the duck was delicious and plentiful. The cooks had managed to find potatoes and a few fresh vegetables from gardens. Henri had not eaten civilized, as the general had stated, for some time and remarked it seemed strange to sit at a table. He said he was lacking on proper etiquette. The general laughed and remarked Henri's future bride would take care of any manners problems. She was always so proper and often reminded him on the use of knife, fork, and spoon.

They were aroused in the wee hours of the morning by sentries sounding an alarm. Fires were seen in various parts of the city. The damn Russians were starting to burn the city rather than surrender it. Bands of convicts newly released for this purpose, and other dregs of the earth, including a few organized military units, were roaming the streets setting fires. Napoleon ordered all troops to advance in the city at once and shoot to kill any and all people on the streets or hiding under bridges, in cellars, or in the churches. They must try to find any equipment to fight the fires already burning. No firefighting equipment was available. It had been taken or broken into uselessness. Most of the fires would just have to burn themselves out.

Napoleon was beside himself and livid at the burning city.

"Merde! I have been awakened from the first decent slumber in days to this. Send the entire Armée into the city at once. Shoot anyone seen running about.

Anyone out at this ungodly hour is up to no good and deserves to be shot. Go now and quickly. Before these damn fools burn the entire city."

Thousands of troops poured into the city, but already many buildings were blazing. Some of the troops did the best they could to combat the fires, but without proper equipment, most efforts were hopeless. The fires spread rapidly in the stiff breeze, and in some areas, the intense uprising heat was creating its own draft. Well, at least the royal palaces, buildings, and most of the fine churches were not blazing. The fires had been concentrated in the business areas and shopping districts.

They were, again, leaving nothing for the invaders. Already the chill of winter was taking hold. Most may be able to find decent shelter in the churches and buildings left intact. Supplies would be another matter for these thousands. The Faucons were among the first to enter a portion of the city not yet ablaze. Several men were seen running back under bridges and down alleyways. Henri ordered his men to shoot on-site. Others were breaking down the doors of apparent shops, stores, and potential warehouses. They must save anything they could.

The scene was described in the memoirs of Baron de Meneval: "Each moment one saw smoke followed by flames breaking out of the houses which had remained intact and in the end fire broke out in every house in the city. Moscow was one mighty furnace from which sheaves of fire burst heavenwards lighting up the horizon. From which, too, masses of flame, mingling together were rapidly caught up in a strong wind that spread them in every direction. From which, in addition, came explosions, roaring, and whistling noises, as well as the cries and yells of the wretched people left to fend for themselves. There were looters, too, who when caught in a suddenly flaming house, ran outside, only to perish in the streets which formed a blazing labyrinth."

Napoleon with his personal guard had made his way to the Kremlin. He had found the vast halls and rooms of golden, rich blues, and many shades of red completely empty. The hundreds with him explored the empty palace with wonder and awe. They were the victors, and yet it was an empty victory. They had again been cheated by the Russians. There was precious little to claim in this hollow victory. Napoleon and the general stood by one of the upper windows and gazed on the destruction unfolding around them. Oh, they would be safe here, but the city was being totally devastated.

Napoleon told the general, "I cannot believe this. I have never in my life felt so completely frustrated at a victory. I cannot ever imagine our Paris as this. I would gladly give that beautiful city to the Mongol hordes rather than commit this terrible crime. Even as the conquering hordes approached Rome, this was never considered. Whatever shall we do, Andre? I fear this will be an extension of the suffering from supplies we endured at our coming to this wretched place.

The final retreat—the flower is lost

"The only decent thing I have seen here is the river, and the damn Russians would probably do something to that too if they could. Andre, I feel so badly about leading my thousands here and seemingly all for naught. Stay with me, old friend. I fear I have made a grave error in judgment of the czar and his rabble."

"We have been together many years now, Napoleon. Never fear, I will never abandon you. I have always felt honored that with all of the power you have gained, you have considered me a friend, and we can speak in confidence as this."

Both of them fell silent and watched the fires of Moscow rage. Both noticed large glowing embers, and sparks were reaching the Kremlin itself. Someone yelled that there were several loaded caissons just inside the Kremlin gates, and sparks were falling around them. They were hurriedly moved to cover, but this was only one immediate concern to be addressed. The raging fires were almost completely surrounding the Kremlin and threatened to destroy even it.

The general said to Napoleon, "Monsieur, we must leave for your safety. The heat will soon be overwhelming. Look, all here are sweating, and it is becoming difficult to breathe. Feel the windowpanes on all sides of the building. They are hot to the touch."

Then shouts came from below that fires had actually started in the rear of the Kremlin itself. As they were descending the stairs, a captured military policeman was being dragged into the large entrance hall. The man admitted that he had set the fire in the Kremlin. Napoleon gave the signal, and the unfortunate loyalist to the czar had his head removed by a sudden sword swipe from the rear. Now with the fires everywhere outside and now in the Kremlin, it was time to leave. They rushed to the outer gates of the complex to find nearly every route of escape blocked by the fires and intense heat. At that point, a group of the Faucons led by Henri came down a narrow alleyway leading to the river.

"Monsieur, General, this way to the river. Hurry, all else is a blazing trap."

The some hundred men of the trapped band ran down the alleyway to safety. The victor of Moscow could have very nearly died with his prize.

Finally safely away, Napoleon and his staff waited for the fires to die down. They were quartered in the Petroffsky Palace on the edge of Moscow and untouched by the ravage. Two-thirds of Moscow had been destroyed.

Napoleon wrote a letter to Czar Alexander, suing for peace: "My Lord Brother. Beautiful, magical Moscow exists no longer. How could you consign to destruction the loveliest city in the world, a city it has taken hundreds of years to build?"

The cold, never-ending bitter cold

29

Jurgita

The wind howled from the north with the ferocity of fork-tailed demons that early morning of October 19, 1812. Napoleon had decided there was nothing left for him in Moscow. Fearing spending the winter months without supplies and adequate shelter for his Armée, he decided to leave the conquered and mostly burned city. He told the general he was tempted to burn the rest of the city, but it was just too beautiful. The palaces and Kremlin were indeed ornate and finished with fine materials. Napoleon, at least, did have a heart where Alexander had proven his feelings.

Henri and the Faucons were the first to leave, as usual. They were the Corps d' Observation, the eyes and ears for the Armée. The Faucons had dwindled from the initial nearly two hundred to a mere fifty-three. Most of the Lithuanians had gone home, leaving in twos and threes. They had talked to Jonas as they did so and were not scoffed at or admonished. Indeed, those that knew of their departure were envious and wished they could have gone also. There was just nothing left in Moscow or the surrounding countryside to support such a mass of humanity. There would not even be sufficient firewood by winter's end. And there would be nothing left on the return march as Napoleon had decided to take the same route to Vilna as the advance. His staff, knowing the supply situation, had begged him to take another route, possibly through St. Petersburg or farther to the south; but he was determined, saying he knew this route, and it was shorter.

Henri, Michael, and Jonas were riding at the head of the Faucons. "Merde, it's cold this morning," said Henri.

"I know. Even my damn bones are frozen. I tried to pee this morning and couldn't find it. He was so shriveled up and hiding in the bushes," retorted Michael.

Henri laughed, "It isn't all that big anyway, Michael. You had better tie a string on it so you can locate it."

Jonas observed, "Winter is very early this year, my friends. If it were not for orders of maintaining a pace with the rest of the Armée, we could be in my country and safe within a week or so."

They rode in silence for a time, knowing that they must find food and shelter for the pending night. The temperature was getting increasingly colder, and the wind now was mixed with snow and sleet.

"Pity the poor fellows on foot this day. It is difficult enough on a horse," said Henri. "I only wonder how many kilometers I have slept in my saddle. I know we are being watched by the enemy but do not anticipate any attacks. I hope they only want their country back destroyed as it is."

How wrong he was. As the troop made its way toward Borodino that first day, the Russians could be seen riding in the distance, attempting to get ahead of them.

"Look over there! There must be several hundred of the bastards. By the time we go much farther, they will surely be to our front waiting for us. Jonas, Michael, make certain all are alert and have all weapons ready. Send a messenger to the rear and inform the general we are seeing what appears to be Cossacks and mounted troops in large numbers trying to cut us off."

But the Russians did not want this group. It was Napoleon and his group they were after. For safety's sake, Napoleon and the staff must remain in the center of the retreating Armée. Now the hunter was the hunted. As they approached the plain near Borodino, they could still see the bodies of thousands lying as they had fallen. Most of the French had been buried; but the Russian troops, horses, and equipment littered the ground partially covered with snow.

"God, I am glad it is cold now and the wind is blowing. With all of the dead, there must have been a terrible stench. Let's move quickly through here. This graveyard makes me nervous."

"And us too, oh, Great Leader."

"Michael, is there no end to your teasing? Have you no reverence for the dead?" Henri laughed and slapped Michael on the back. They quickly cleared the area and made for the main road near a tree line.

It was growing darker with the heavy clouds by now, and they decided to rejoin the main group several kilometers to the rear. This would not be a place for the Russians to find them. They eventually found an abandoned farmhouse with a barn attached well off the main road. It had not been burned, just looted of all furniture worth carrying off or used for firewood. In the garden next to the house, there were a few sparse vegetables, and that was all. The men pulled all of the carrots and dug in what appeared to be a potato patch. It was indeed a potato patch and included a few onions. Soon a massive potato, onion, and carrot stew was brewing in a large battered pot found near the house. The pot had evidently been used for laundry purposes at one time, but it would have to do. There was still a pile of hay in the barn for the horses and shelter for some of them. The others were tied on the downwind side of the dwellings. They would be safe here for the night.

The snow and sleet was blowing harder by morning; and the Armée prepared, once more, to move out to safety. Henri and his troop moved out quickly with orders to return in all haste if attacked. These were orders not to be taken lightly, and haste would mean just that. An attacking Cossack horde was nothing to be reckoned with. The Armée was moving very slow now. With the weather, plus being weakened with hardly any supplies, a toll was being taken. Any horse showing as lame was immediately destined for the stew pot. Attacks on the stragglers, usually by Cossacks, were frequent.

Cossacks were fast-moving mounted troops, and often they could hit and run, killing scores before the rest could form a defense. These small skirmishes were often during the day and at one point grew into a battle involving thousands. Napoleon had turned the Armée in hopes he could drive the infuriating Russians away. Napoleon narrowly escaped being captured at Malojaroslavetz when a group of several hundred Russian cavalry swept through the encampment near dusk.

Henri gathered the Faucons and spoke to them, "Men, I have just spoken to the general, and the situation is desperate. He has ordered us to try to get to the twin bridges at Borisov over the Beresina River and to hold them. We are to take a brigade of dragoons and move fast. If we are successful, Vilna can be within our reach next. This will be the last major river to cross on the way back. We are to leave at dawn. Everyone, please make certain your horses are in good order, and please do not take anything you do not absolutely need."

The weather worsened, and the snow and ice storm enveloped them. This was no light snowfall as before. The snow came at them in clumps, swirling and dancing in the ever-driving wind.

"The damn stuff is coming at us almost horizontal!" Henri screamed over the wind to Michael. Thank God for the heavy cloaks. They at least could have some place to hide under as they rode.

Troops in the rear column began to experience buttons falling apart on their greatcoats. The buttons were of pewter, and pewter disintegrates in extreme cold. This was not anticipated at the time of their manufacture. It was just not known. The troops started to tear at anything available to make sashes in order to keep the coat together at the front. Some just took the coat off and reversed it, putting the solid part to the front. It looked odd, but it worked. The temperature continued to fall, and at one point, twenty degrees below zero was recorded by one of Napoleon's staff. And they were still a long, long journey to safety and even farther to France.

The Faucons and the dragoon troops moved out with the dawn. They would have to move fast, and any potential stragglers were warned they would be left.

"Well, at least this movement will help keep us warm," said Michael. "It is good to be out in front with some protection this time."

"Oui, it is," said Henri, "I don't like going back to the rear every night and see the Grande Armée completely falling apart. The general told me that we are down to some fifty thousand of good fighting men. Oh, there are many more with the stragglers, but they are being picked off like fleas on a dog's back. And to think, we started this campaign with six hundred thousand. Jonas said we will be lucky to get back to Lithuania at all with this weather. It doesn't seem to bother these bastard Cossacks."

"Oh, I am certain it does, my friend," Jonas responded. "It is just that they are much better with supplies than we are and much more used to this climate. They seem to thrive on it."

The next day approaching midafternoon, they arrived at Borisov. The bridges were burned with the charred timbers lying in the freezing water. One bridge was completely gone, but the other was repairable if they could get to it. The Russians would have to be driven back for any repairs. Henri took out his field glass and observed the far bank.

"Merde! They are over there and waiting for us. With the enemy behind us and now this to our front, we will be trapped like rats. This is the main road, however, and possibly there are alternate means to cross this river. You know the drill. It has worked before. Michael, take three men and go to the north. Jonas, do the same to the south. Perhaps you can find other bridges. Don't let the enemy see you doing this. Go out for as long as you dare and report back as soon as you can."

A messenger was sent back to the general to inform him of this most recent calamity of the bridges being destroyed. Michael and Jonas each took three men, retreated for several hundred meters, and in the cover of the tree line would follow the river in each direction. They hoped they had not been spotted. Henri took the rest of the troop into the village to wait for the return of Jonas and Michael. Most huddled in small groups and began to search for firewood. What the hell? The enemy knew they were there, and no attempt to hide was made. One of the Faucons made an obscene gesture toward the far bank, and the response was several musket shots. Too far away, though, as the shots fell short into the river. But at least it made the French aware of their presence. Cannon could be another story.

In the early afternoon, Jonas returned with word there were two very small farm bridges several kilometers downstream, but they couldn't cross many troops at the same time. One of the bridges was at the point of collapse, and the other wasn't much better. Michael and his group returned soon after and reported there were three small farm bridges upstream and that the bridges were in, essentially, the same condition as the ones Jonas had found. Henri immediately went to the rear to see the general. All bridges must be taken and held. If enough troops could cross in the several positions, maybe they all could get across. This would take swift action involving mounted troops crossing the bridges and holding in place for the remainder of the Armée.

Henri rode into the camp at dusk. The general was still in his carriage just preparing to stop for the night. When Henri explained the situation and pointed out the map references, the general said to come with him. They must communicate this to Napoleon at once. They found Napoleon in his carriage. Henri noticed the gold emblem on the door had been removed. This led to further belief the situation was growing more desperate. The rear of the oversized carriage had been fitted with a small stove. Napoleon spent much of his time in the carriage and often slept in there. The general knocked on the door, and Napoleon raised the curtain.

"Napoleon, Henri has brought disturbing and yet hopeful news." He quickly outlined the situation to Napoleon and the thoughts to move quickly.

"By all means, Andre, take what you need and hold those bridges. This could be our salvation after all. I had hoped the bridges at Borisov would be crossable, but the several smaller ones could be a welcome alternate. Henri, your scouting has proven valuable once more." Napoleon laughed nervously. "This will not constitute another medal and kissing episode for us, will it?"

"No, monsieur, I just want to go home and not turn into a piece of ice."

"Indeed we all do, indeed I wish we all could."

A dragoon brigade would be assigned to each bridge with orders to cross at once and hold the bridge. All of the five brigades left within the hour and followed Henri back to Borisov and the area of the destroyed bridges. They arrived in the night, and Henri told the troop commanders they should get as much rest as possible that night. They would be guided to the bridges at first light. Henri tended to Satan and made him lie down. He wrapped himself in his blanket and fell fitfully asleep snuggled up next to Satan.

Still in the dark and with very little light showing to the east, Henri woke and told Jonas and Michael to rouse the troops and make ready to guide the other units to the bridges. They were not to venture out on the main road, but cut into the tree lines along the banks. He certainly did not want the Russians to see any parallel movement along the banks and suspect anything. Another smaller group would appear at the foot of the destroyed bridges, build fires, and appear confused. Henri hoped this would further draw any attention from the other groups going to the bridges. He told those guiding to report back as soon as each bridge was secure. Within several hours, all scouts were back with word all five bridges were secure.

And now to get the main bodies of troops across the bridges. Henri and Michael rode back to the general. It was good to be on the move. *Idle hands were the devil's workshop, but ha, he thought, this was a helluva workshop.* If the mass of the dragoons could cross at all five bridge locations, the enemy would be forced to fall back to avoid being caught in a pincer movement. Then the Armée could cross in safety. The plan was to have a smaller group approach the destroyed bridgeheads, set up cannons, and fire at the enemy. This would look like preparations for a crossing here, and they were trying to drive the Russians back so they could attempt a repair of the bridges. In the meantime, the others would cross the five bridges in strength. After that, they could turn and catch the Russians in a trap.

"Good news, Henri," said the general. "Now maybe we can cross in earnest. I will send all available mounted units. We must have the horses across. Your idea of having cannon firing at the Russians is a good one. We can use that as a signal to announce to the troops to hit the Russians hard and drive them back from the bridges. We need to make certain, however, that both sides of the pincer are in place. Would you gentlemen like to dine with me tonight? I am afraid I can't offer much, probably that revolting horse stew, but it a can be cut with excellent company and good wine."

"Oui, monsieur, we would be honored. Perhaps you have a few of the small peppers to kill the taste. Michael, what say you?"

"A lot of peppers, Henri. You know how I detest horse stew. I can nibble on the potatoes, but that damn horsemeat, ugh! What a waste of fine horse flesh. One would think they could find another method of preparation than stew and that foul gravy with potatoes. God only knows what is swimming in it."

After the meal, Henri and Michael decided to ride back to Borisov, which was only approximately ten kilometers. They rode in silence for a time, each in his own thoughts. The only sounds were the eerie cry of wolves, the crunching of horse hooves on the fresh fallen snow, and the creaking of saddle leather. It was a clear and very cold night. Henri could see the clouds of steam coming from the breath of the horses. Henri looked up at the moon and some of the most brilliant stars seen in some time. He envisioned Ange at his room window maybe looking at the same moon. Ange, his Ange. What was she doing at this moment? Was she thinking of him, and if so, what about him? His thoughts rambled on to the steady canter of the hoof beats of the horses.

Finally Michael said, "My fortune for your thoughts, Henri, but I'll bet it is about home and Ange. You are so fortunate to have found someone as her this early in life."

"Oui, I know, Michael, and how in hell could you guess what my thoughts were? I thought I was being more discreet."

"I guess I know you as you know me, mon ami. You can always guess what I am thinking of or at least pretty close. We have been through much together, and I hope there are many years of the same."

"And I, mon ami, and I."

They arrived late, and Henri advised his scouts to take the house on the far side of the village and be ready to guide the mounted troops to the bridges. They found Jonas, and he told Henri that several more of his men had decided to go home and had taken several of the French with them. Well, so be it. They could not be blamed for not wanting to die in a strange frozen foreign land. Henri would go too if it were not for honor, Ange, the general, and Napoleon. The next morning before dawn, more mounted troops began to arrive. They divided with some going north and others going south. Messengers would be sent back when all had crossed safely. Other troops started to arrive and mingle around the destroyed bridges. They built fires, set up cannons, and presented a sight of general confusion.

By late afternoon, all five scouts had returned with news the mounted troops were safely across and holding in place. Henri told the commander of the artillery that all scouts had reported readiness. He could give the signal when ready. The roar of the cannon split the quiet of the evening, and soon the melee of battle across the river could be heard. Henri tried to see the events with his field glass, but the swirling snow made everything almost a white cloud. The sounds on the far bank did not last long; and soon, mostly, it was quiet again except for sporadic musket fire.

Had they succeeded? Soon messengers arrived with news that victory was theirs. They had chased the surprised Russians for kilometers, killing as many as possible. They had captured considerable horses, stores, ammunition, and nearly one hundred cannons. They had in their possession several leading officers along with maps and other things important to the general and Napoleon. The ruse had worked again, but how lucky would they be in the future? Lithuania and France were still many, many kilometers away, and the weather seemed to be getting worse.

Crossing the river was a minor problem as compared to events to come. The weather was taking a fearful toll, and the lines of stragglers went back for many kilometers. Like the tail of a self-destructing comet, one officer was heard to say. It was snowing almost constantly now. The infernal and maddening wind continued to sing the hapless troops to eternal sleep. The Cossacks and even many of the local peasants were preying heavily on the stragglers. This was a prize with boots, muskets, clothing, and any number of items to be had. The dead were stripped and the dying killed. Many naked troops were in this tail of the comet. One knew if he fell behind, it was almost a death sentence.

Within the Faucons, there were Henri, Michael, Jonas, and sixteen others. All of the rest had either been killed, been deserted, or been forced into the straggler column. Henri saw many friends lose their mounts and have to stagger forward on foot. These men would eventually join the stragglers. The small band crossed the river early in the morning.

Henri remarked, "I can't believe this. Only nineteen men out of our original over two hundred. We have been sacrificed for a Moscow that does not exist. Now the enemy will surely kill us all. There does not seem to be any escape."

"Henri, may I make a suggestion?" requested Jonas. "We are closer to my country now, and if we strike out on our own, we can possibly make it. The Russians are hounding the main units like the devils they are, but a small band going more to the north then bear to the west can have a better chance. What say you?"

"Jonas, I have truly thought on this, but I must speak to the general. Our Faucons are no more and probably of little use as scouts. This was probably our final mission. You are right. I will go to the general now and return with the answer. If it may be a no, then you take what is left of us on. I will stay with the general."

"Monsieur, our situation is grave, and I ask your permission to cut our few men from the main column and make a wider course to the north. We are no longer of any use for observation, and some of us may survive. Otherwise, we shall all surely die."

"Who put you up to this, my boy? I am joking, and I know this is urgent. It is an excellent idea, and with your wilderness training, you will stand a much better chance of making it to safety. By all means, do so. Our situation grows more desperate here by the hour it seems. Napoleon knows he has made a grave mistake, and his Grande Armée is no more. Would you believe, he cried like a baby with me last evening, saying the death of all of these brave souls now falls upon his shoulders. He brought them to this. I wanted so to console him but knew in my heart he was right.

"Go, Henri, I will not speak of this to him, but if one of us can be saved and care for our family, then all the better. I will not leave him. We have endured just too much. He really needs me now. Go with God, my son." They hugged, and with tears in his eyes, Henri rode back to the others.

As he arrived, he could see the engineers working lantern light trying to pull the timbers out of the frozen river to repair the one bridge. *How futile*, he thought. The one bridge would not make that much difference.

"We must travel light and fast, men. This could be our salvation. Each of you cut an extra horse from the captured ones. If any of your horses are weak or drawing up lame, change them. I know it sounds ghoulish, but prowl through some of the dead and dying and try to find anything of use, pistols, powder, shot, a warmer coat, anything light that you think you may need. Keep your sabres, but not the rifles. They are much too heavy to get just one shot off. On second thought, do bring two muskets in case we find small game. We leave in maybe an hour. Off with you now, and please keep this among only us."

They did leave in the hour, crossed at the far bridge, and slipped off through the forest headed north by Henri's compass. They would ride this way most of the night and then seek shelter for the day tomorrow. They could only hope the Cossacks would not be in the vicinity. Their band was so small. It was still snowing, and any tracks would be covered quickly.

The never-ending wind continued, and Michael said, "I will never complain if I never hear the damn wind howling again."

They stopped well before dawn in an abandoned farmhouse. This place had been empty for some time, and the roof had fallen in places. Drifts of snow filled the open rooms, but there were several places covered well enough to afford shelter. The barn attached to the house was nearly down but would afford some shelter for the horses. They built a fire in the center of the main room of the house, careful to use the driest wood they could find. Damp wood always makes smoke. The woodsmoke odor they could do nothing about. They would take turns watching, but Henri was sure most of the Cossacks were farther to the south plaguing the main body of troops. They were hungry, but mostly just exhausted. Henri and Michael ate a river rock and were soon asleep. Henri woke with a start. What had he been dreaming to startle him so? It was probably just the events of the past day. He felt so badly asking the general about leaving, but these were very serious circumstances.

The rest were rousing now, and the inevitable hunt for food would begin soon. Some of the men went to try to find food for the horses. There were a few sparse patches of dying grass under the snow, but to the horses, it was like new mown hay. There was just nothing here to eat. No vegetable garden or anything else to dig or hunt. Not even small game. Short of the sparse grass for the horses, there was nothing. Better luck at the next stop. At least they had sufficient river rocks and, praise the Lord, plenty of snow to melt for water.

They rode north for half that day and then turned toward the west at the next small farm road. Jonas said they should not run into any enemy troops this far north. He estimated they would need to travel for nearly a week, maybe more, to reach Lithuania and safety. They traveled the road nearly to dusk and approached a small village. Now what to do? Seek shelter in the village or travel on in hopes of finding a farmhouse? They decided it was safer to do the latter.

They approached the farmhouse, and Henri and Jonas knocked on the door. They could hear much movement behind the door, and finally a voice came from the side of the house. The farmer had slipped out of the back way. He asked in Russian "What do you want?" Was he armed? They hoped not.

Jonas replied in Russian, "Only shelter for the night and anything you could spare to eat. We do not mean to harm you and will be on our way tomorrow."

The farmer did not want trouble and knew these men would take what they wanted anyway. "You could put the horses in the barn with my animals and help yourselves to the hay."

This would help the poor horses immensely. Most were showing ribs. Satan had never looked like this. Henri decided to alternate his spare horse with Satan. He suggested the others do the same. The farmer said there would not be room for them in his small house, but they were welcome to use the barn. There were plenty of potatoes, onions, and some dried meat. They were so hungry, they ate it raw. They must have appeared as animals to the farmer and his family. A little girl kept staring at Henri eating a raw onion. Finally he just smiled and turned away. The barn, with all of the body heat from the animals and men plus the small fires, soon became cozy and warm. Henri slept better than he had in some time. They rotated the watch through the night, wary that the farmer may try to contact someone from the village. No one came or went.

They slept in until midmorning, making sure the animals were full and ready to travel. Each man was given several potatoes, onions, and some of the dried meat. They just might make it after all. They traveled the small farm road until it just ended at the edge of the forest. Evidently this road had been used to haul trees from the forest. Henri asked Jonas if he thought they might be far enough in front of the enemy and try for the main road to Vilna. It would be much better traveling than plowing through the forest. They agreed it was worth a try, and if the enemy was about, they would just move farther north and try again.

Just approaching darkness, they came upon the main road. They would travel parallel for a time and confirm the enemy was to their rear. After several kilometers, the lead scout stopped and froze. There was something on the other side of the road. Something had flickered. Henri took out his field glass and could barely make out what appeared to be a fire with figures moving about. Was it Russians? It must be. Here on a night like this.

The lead scout went farther on and crossed the road to circle back. They must confirm if this was just a small party or a larger force. The scout came back with word that this was a band of Cossacks, but a small one. He had counted only about five, maybe six. They had a fire and were cooking something.

Jonas boasted, "Hell, Henri, as small as the group is, we could run over them and take what they are cooking. Let us give it a go. I'm starving."

They followed the scout and tied the horses to small trees some distance away. As they crept closer, each man had two pistols at the ready. Suddenly one of the men stumbled over a fallen tree in the snow and fell, breaking several dry limbs. The Cossacks jumped up at the noise. The Faucons rushed the Cossacks, firing as they ran the final fifteen meters. The skirmish was over in seconds with all of the Cossacks down. Henri approached one who was wounded and feigning death. As he got closer, the Cossack lunged with his sword. The blade entered Henri's leg almost at the same place as the previous wound from years back. Henri shot the Cossack in the head.

"Merde, Henri, he got you, but how bad is it?" asked Michael.

"I do not know, mon ami, but it hurts like all hell itself." The others, not taking any chances, were confirming the deaths of the other Cossacks. Henri sat on a small log moaning and holding his leg as he rocked back and forth.

Michael came up to him and said, "Let's have a look and see just how bad he did get you. Out here where we are, this could be serious." Henri threw his coat to one side, and Michael slit his trousers leg with his knife to reveal a small but deep stab wound. It was bleeding but not too heavily. He started to tear up an old shirt for bindings, saying, "First we will pack it with some fresh snow and see more about it in the morning. Really it doesn't look too bad, only deep."

They feasted on three rabbits the Cossacks were roasting over the fire.

By the next morning, Henri's leg was hurting and very stiff. He had hardly slept that night and was miserable. The Faucons had relieved the Cossacks of their very heavy fur coats and hats.

"Little wonder they can fight like they do with gear as this. Henri, there are coats for nearly all of us, and you have earned this bastard's coat and hat," said Michael.

The heavy fur coat was much warmer, and the hat kept the cold entirely out. Flaps came down over the ears, and that was a blessing. Many of the troops tied anything they could find over their ears in vain attempts to stave off the cold.

They mounted to move out, and Henri was helped up on Satan. "Do not slow down. If I fall back, keep going."

"Oh, shut up, hero," said Michael. "You know we would never leave you. I might, though, and go see Ange when I get back to Paris."

"You just would too, you *merder*."

Every step that Satan took was agonizing at first, then the hurt began to settle and become just a constant dull ache. Damn, of all things. He would have gladly given back this wonderful coat and hat not to have had this wound. If only he had some of the magic tea. He would do all in his power not to slow the others. On the bright side, he was mounted and not on foot as many thousands of others at their rear.

A day later, he was aware of infection starting to set in. The wound was deep and not wide enough to allow for much drainage. He found a tree with moss and packed his wound with it as he remembered in his wilderness training. It would be a long passage to Lithuania.

For over a week, they traveled the main road of their previous advance, avoiding the villages and towns. The danger of the Cossacks was behind them, but still they hid at night in the forest and kept their fires low and in holes in the frozen earth. Several times they had the advantages of abandoned farms or buildings partially destroyed by the Russians during their retreat. They did find some food, but it seemed they were always hungry. As they neared the border of Lithuania, they were bolder with the local populace and, as a consequence, ate better.

Henri's leg had grown swollen and was feverish. The bleeding had long since stopped and was replaced with an oozing of infection. Even with the cold, he was sweating, and that made him feel all the more cold. At night when they stopped, he would be helped from Satan and just collapse. He was trying to keep his strength but really had no appetite.

"Michael, I am worried," Henri said. "I can feel myself getting weaker. How much longer to Vilna does Jonas think we are? If it comes down to me or the group, promise me you will shoot me rather than let me linger a horrible death. I am so glad we are here and not back there with the rest."

"Oh merde, Henri. Think positive. We are going to get through this. All of us. Don't worry, I will shoot you rather than let you suffer, but you have a long way to go with the suffering. Remember you promised to do the same for me."

Jonas encouraged them, saying, "It is only two or three days at the most to Vilna now. We are near the Lithuanian border now, and Vilna is about a one-day ride from there. One of the men has found a farmhouse, and we will stay the night here. The farmer has given us several chickens and some potatoes, and a stew is in the making. Henri, you have to eat and maintain your strength."

Henri did eat, but not all that much. He was wracked with fever at times, and his leg had swollen more. He was delirious at times and could picture Ange and home. The next morning as Michael helped Henri on Satan, he nearly fell over the other side. He just did not have the strength to hold on.

"Jonas! Help me with Henri. He is so weak, he cannot hold on. I have several pieces of rope here. Come, we need to tie him on the horse. Wait, I need to check the wound first. Mon dieu, look at this! Not to scare you, mon ami, but we must get you to a doctor quickly or you will be in danger of losing your leg or your life."

Indeed, the wound was very red, swollen, and feverish. The ooze had turned to a greenish and was beginning to smell. Michael gathered some fresh moss from a tree and repacked and bandaged the wound.

Jonas said, "We will ride faster and longer today and see how much closer to Vilna we can get. I know doctors there, and you are right, Michael, we must get him to one."

They tied Henri in the saddle and made off at a fairly fast pace. Henri passed in and out of consciousness, swaying in the saddle as if dancing at times. When he was conscious, he felt for the small picture of his Ange and tried to think of only her and not the agonizing ache in his leg. They were moving at a faster pace now and not trying to spare the weak horses at all. The several farms they had visited over the last several days had sufficient hay, and the horses were not nearly as bad off as the men. One man had a severe cold with fever and was hanging on as best he could. Finally they had to tie him in the saddle too to keep pace. One of the men had ridden on ahead to see if anything could be seen of Vilna.

They were in Lithuania now, and Jonas said he could almost smell home. The scout returned at midafternoon with news that Vilna was within sight, and they would make it before dark or soon thereafter. The pace was increased, and Henri swayed and moaned. Finally to the position of just leaning over on Satan's neck. When he was conscious, it seemed every step Satan made was directly on his leg. Then he was off again in the blessed relief of sleep. Just after dark, they reached the outlying areas of Vilna. Jonas said all must make it to the house of his uncle and aunt where they would be welcome and safe.

They rode up to the gate, and Jonas rang the bell nearly off the wall. After a time, Uncle Martynas yelled from the other side, "Who is it? What do you want?"

"It is Jonas with sick and weary travelers, Uncle Martynas. Please open the gate."

The gate was opened, and Aunt Agne and Jurgita rushed out. Jurgita went directly to Henri. He was unconscious and hanging over in the saddle. "Oh, he is very ill. Please help me get him in the house. Poppa, please go for the doctor at once."

Henri was taken into the house and placed on the large sofa in the sitting room. Jurgita and Aunt Agne started to remove his clothes. "My lord, he smells worse than Poppa's barn. I'll bet he hasn't bathed in weeks." And he had not. There was just no time for such where he had been. They quickly rinsed him off, and when they saw the wound, they gasped.

Aunt Agne said, "If this boy doesn't lose this leg, it will be a miracle. Why, he is burning with a fever too. Look, there is another large scar right next to this wound. I guess he got that in the wars too. Cover him, Jurgita. I hope the doctor comes soon."

Jurgita pulled a chair up next to Henri. He was moaning and calling what sounded like "Ange, Ange."

The doctor did arrive soon after, examined the leg wound, and pronounced the leg would have to be removed. It appeared gangrene was starting, and if it went any further, it could kill him.

Jurgita pleaded with the doctor to give her several days with Henri and see if she could not quell some of the infection.

"Very well, child, but you must keep the wound open and let it drain. Keep it clean and bathed often with a warm salt water solution. Press around the area and make it drain. I know it will smell badly, but it must be done. We could take him to the hospital, but he will be better off here. I would hate to move him in his condition. Is there a bed where we can place him?"

"*Taip* (yes), mine," said Jurgita. "I will pull up a chair and stay with him. He may need something, and I will be there."

The doctor said, "Very well, child. He is your patient. Try to get something down him, some warm broth and plenty of hot tea. I will return in the morning, but I will not give you false hope about this leg. If it has to come off, we will have to do it quickly. Even so, in his state, he may die. I need to examine these others. They must have had a horrible journey."

The man with the severe cold died during the night. He would never see his France again. The others were recovering with the hot tea and care. Two hundred had started this journey to Moscow, and now only six had survived with Henri in serious contention of joining the dead. Michael stayed with Jurgita, lying on a pallet next Henri's bed. He explained to Jurgita that Henri was his dearest friend, and wild horses could not drag him from Henri's side. Jurgita stayed with Henri during the night, rousing every hour or so to check the wound and press around the area as she was instructed. Remarkably, by noon the next day, he did appear to be a bit better.

The doctor came later that day and, after a thorough inspection of Henri's leg, said, "Well now, the pressing of the wound seems to be helping the draining and, with it, the infection. Keep it up, girl."

Henri was awake, and the doctor told him the seriousness of his infected wound. Henri responded with he would not be a cripple and would go to his grave with all of his body parts.

"I would rather be dead," he retorted. "Michael, please, for the love of God, do not let them take my leg. Jurgita, help me." And he fell back into unconsciousness.

Jurgita continued to press and bathe the wound almost every hour on the hour. By the next day, there was a remarkable difference. The doctor said he had seen next to a miracle. Possibly with his youth and care he was getting, the leg may be able to be saved.

Henri's fever had broken, and the infection was being arrested. He was more alert now and taking food. Jurgita may have saved his leg and probably his life.

"I can never thank you enough, Jurgita," he said. "My life for me without my leg would have been over. You know, that is the second time in my life this leg has been saved. It must be a very special leg. I think I'll keep it. By the way, sweet lady, what else did you happen to observe while I was nearly dying?"

"Nothing of any great consequence, brave warrior. We will talk of that later when you fully regain your strength. You did call for Ange quite a bit. I found her picture in your uniform pocket. She is quite lovely. Did she nurse you before in your previous time with this leg?"

"Oui, she did. Almost the same as you have done here except she had the best doctors in Paris to help her and give instructions. She is very special in my life. I don't want to mislead you. You are a dear friend and probably the closest one to me other than Ange. Merci, Jurgita, from all of my heart."

Jurgita started to cry and put her head on Henri's chest. He smelled her cleanliness and a faint odor of some sort of sweetness or body oil. She cried for some time whether from relief of her ordeal or what he had just told her. She was deeply in love with this man and had been since nearly their first meeting. She had shared things with him as no other.

She rose up and apologized for her outburst, saying, "Henri, I am so sorry. I am usually stronger than this. I guess it's just the accumulation of recent events that have touched me so. I am so happy about your leg and your life. I promise we will talk of many things in the days to come. It is such a joy to my heart to have you here."

"And me too. Please don't stray too far. I feel we have a lot to talk about."

Henri was up and about the next week and could stump around with the aid of a walking stick. He had moved from Jurgita's room to one of the spare rooms with Michael and Jonas.

"Henri," asked Jonas, "did you know you snore like a horse giving birth? I will help you move back into Jurgita's room if you want."

"I do not snore, Jonas. I was told that one time, and I stayed awake all night just to see, and I do not."

"Well, I will stand by Jonas," said Michael. "You do snore and worse than a horse giving birth. It is more like those braying donkeys back home in Paris."

Henri clumped out of the room and went to the large back window to watch it snow. He was better. They all were better. They had survived. Just barely.

30

Goodbyes

"Henri, we need to go to the area around St. Anne's Cathedral. I have talked to one of Napoleon's personal guard. The Armée is starting to come in, and he tells me it is a horrible sight," cried Michael. "They are just staggering in and falling in the parks and streets or wherever they can. The local people can't take them. There are just too many. Most are sick and starving. There are reports of just stacking the dead in the area near the foot of the bridge. Napoleon did make it back and is staying near St. Anne's in a lodging house. The general is there too and has been wounded."

Henri hurriedly dressed and, although still very weak, hobbled along with the help of Michael and Jonas. They passed the ornate red brick structure, and soldiers were everywhere. As Michael had heard, there were so many the local populace could not contend with them. It was cruel, but they just locked the doors and gates. They looked inside the church as they passed and saw the interior teeming with soldiers.

In every street and protected place, soldiers were everywhere, mostly in small groups huddled around fires. Any heat of which was at a premium now. They had started to tear down anything they could to obtain firewood—sheds, barns, fences, even shutters from houses. The three were in the coats and hats of the Cossacks, but no one seemed to take note. They had to stop often and wait for Henri. He was in a very weakened state and could not move fast. They went around the corner from St. Anne's and down a narrow cobblestone street. Henri looked in the gates of a courtyard and saw the carriages of the general and Napoleon.

"They must be here," he said hopefully.

Just inside the gate, they were challenged by several sentries. Henri identified himself as an officer, stating they needed to see the general. They were told to wait and be identified.

The general's orderly came out and exclaimed, "Henri! My god, man, we all thought you and your group were annihilated. No one has seen or heard from you in weeks. I am glad you are here. The general is badly wounded and has been asking for you or any information about you. Come, I will take you to him. He comes and goes of consciousness, but he was awake when I just left him."

They entered the small inn; and again, there were Napoleon's guard and staff officers everywhere, lying in the hall and every available space. Anything to be away from the cold and obtain some manner of heat. The general was in a small room near the back of the inn. There was sparse furniture and only one small bed. Henri bade the others to wait for him and asked them to try to find some hot tea if they could.

The general was awake as he entered and mumbled in a very weak, raspy voice, "Who is there? Pierre, is that you?"

"No, monsieur, it is me, Henri."

"Oh, thank God, thank God. We thought you were dead. I never did hear anything more after you left."

"Monsieur, are you all right?"

"Hell no, I am not all right. I am dying and know it. That son of a bitch Cossack nearly ran me through with his damn lance. My guts are on fire when I am awake, and then they give me the stuff to put me out. Come closer, son, I can't talk very loud and do want to talk with you." Henri sat in the chair next to the general's bed.

"My son, I am so glad you are all right and that you did come before I leave this world. I so wish it was in my bed at home with my Vivien by my side, but thus is the life of a soldier. I charge you with the safety of my family. I know how you feel about my Ange, but please include the rest in your love and caring. I have on the table, there, my watch with the gold chain and my angel coin. It was given to me by my father, and now I want you to have it. By rights, I guess it should go to Jean, but you have earned it and much more." He hesitated and grimaced in pain.

"Damn that Cossack anyway. It was my fault for being in the open. I was running for the carriage when he hit me. It was a hit-and-run thing, and they very nearly got Napoleon. Back to the watch, though, please tell my Vivien that you have it and the significance. The angel coin on the chain was given to me by Vivien at the birth of Angelette. I have always treasured the watch and coin. I remember the time you were accused of stealing it.

"I have written letters to those I love at home, and they are next to the watch. There is even one for you and Angelette, and one for Mimi. I wrote them nearly a week ago when I realized my time was near. There are many things unsaid as there always will be, but know that I loved each one. I was going to have Napoleon deliver them, but now that you have come back to life, I will give you the honors."

They talked for some time of years past and the happier events of their lives. At intervals, the general would grimace again and have to stop, but he wanted to talk. It was as if it was a cleansing of the soul, and with it, he could rest at last. He said this was a very important time for him, and he was so glad Henri was here to share.

Finally, Henri said, "Monsieur, please let me see the orderly and get you something for your pain. I will be here anytime you need me. I promise not to leave."

"Henri, I know that, and merci. There is just one more thing I must ask of you, and please do not tell me no."

"Anything, monsieur. Just let me know."

"I hesitate to ask. I have already charged you with the safety of my family and am not worried about that any longer. Do you, perchance, have a sidearm?"

"Why, oui, monsieur, I do. Why do you ask?"

In a raspy and weakened voice as he tightened his grip on Henri's hand, he said, "Please just put it in my hand as you leave, and do not shed tears for this old soldier. I am dying and cannot stand this pain. This will never be known to anyone except us. I do love you, my son."

"Papa! This is much you ask. Your blood will be on my hands. I cannot do this."

"You must, and I will consider it the greatest of favors. I am suffering and cannot last another day anyway at this pace. No blame will come of this."

Shaking and trembling, Henri took out his pistol, checked it, cocked it, and placed it in the general's hand. He stood for some time with the general holding his hand, tears streaming down his face. He untangled his fingers from the general's and put the letters, the angel coin, and the watch in his coat pocket.

"Papa, I love you," he choked and left the room. Henri met the orderly and the others outside the room. They were all drinking tea and quietly chatting.

"Henri, what is the matter? You are paler than ever, and I can tell you have been crying. Was the walk over here too much?" said Michael.

At that, there was a loud report from toward the general's room.

"Mon dieu!" exclaimed the orderly and rushed through the door.

Henri started to collapse, and Michael caught him. People seemed to come from everywhere, Napoleon among them.

Napoleon went directly to Henri. "Lad, I am so glad you are among the living. We had given up hope for you. What was that noise? It sounded loud and like a shot."

"I am afraid it was, monsieur. I would like to tell you all about it before my firing squad commences."

"Henri, what in hell are you talking about? Oh, mon dieu! Did you give in to Andre's request and shoot him? He asked that of me several days ago."

"No, monsieur, I did not, but just as well have. I placed my cocked pistol in his hand. He was suffering so and was near death. I know I would have wanted him to do it for me if the situation was reversed."

"Oui, I do agree, lad." Napoleon put his hand on Henri's shoulder. "Come with me and rest. We can talk of Andre and many things past and yet to come."

"Monsieur, may I please return tomorrow? I promise to do so. I have been wounded again and am still very weak. This has been a very trying day for me. I feel like I have committed murder."

"Oui, of course, Henri. I am very sorry about Andre. He was a dear friend, and I will miss him. I do understand you and this. Do not feel regret, Henri. It was his wish. Come tomorrow if you can."

Henri and the others watched as a litter covered with the general's coat was carried out of his room and out the side door.

Henri did not sleep that night. How could he tell those at home he had helped their father to his death? He could never forget it. He told Jurgita what had happened and cried more. She held his head in her arms and let him cry it out. What torture all of this must be to this man she loved with all of her heart. What would happen now with more and more of the French gathering in Vilna? Would they be going back to France as soon as they could? Henri was much too weak to travel, and she hoped to keep him around as long as she could.

The next day, Henri returned to Napoleon. He was ushered in to the room, and Napoleon was sitting by the fire in his sock feet. Napoleon rose as Henri entered and came over to him and put his hand on Henri's shoulder.

"Oh, Henri, I must tell you again how terribly sad I am about Andre. I have thought of ways to prepare his burial. I thought of letting him freeze outdoors and taking him back to France, but that would not be logical for his wife and family. No, I think we should bury him here with his men. There are so many here now to keep him company. I have lost the flower of my Grande Armée. It is no more, and I can partially blame my own vanity on this terrible tragedy. The blood of thousands is now staining my hands. I can never wash them clean." He sat down again and hung his head.

"Monsieur, no one feels worse about this venture to Moscow more than I, but please do not take the personal blame. It was just a military campaign went wrong. True, the Grande Armée is gone, but we did survive and can rebuild for the sake of our France."

"Henri, merci for your kind words and trying to cheer me. Andre did the same. I just cannot help this feeling. So, so many are gone. The Russians are hard at our heels and will come here this spring if not before. I had no idea the winter would be this bad, and vanity would not let me listen to my staff. I must go back to France as soon as possible. There is certain to be an uprising among those who do not support me at home, and I must be there. Already there are rumors in Paris. When can you travel?"

"As you wish, monsieur. I am weak and cannot mount, but I can ride in a carriage if there will be room."

"Very good, my boy. There will always be room for you. I will give you Andre's carriage. It always served him well. I will want to leave within a week or ten days as soon as everyone going can regain strength and make ready. I will give you Andre's personal things for his family, and one more thing, Henri."

"Oui, monsieur."

"I will want you to join my personal guard. There are a precious few I can trust with my life, and you have certainly proven just that. Would you give it consideration?"

"Monsieur, I will be honored to be in the guard. Please consider me one of your chosen. I will be in contact about the leaving date. I can scarcely contain myself at the prospect of going home. May I please take my best friend, Michael, who has been with me since the beginning of our military life?"

"Oh oui, I have met this Michael. You might approach him about the personal guard issue and see if he too may be interested. The guard has been seriously depleted and in need of being brought back to strength. You are a capitaine now, and I think I know just the place for you."

"Oui, monsieur. I will certainly ask him."

With all of the recent grief in his life, Henri walked on clouds all the way back to Jurgita's. How would he explain leaving so soon? He had expected to be here for several months. There was some innate thing within him attempting to hold him here. He loved his Ange with all of his heart, but there was something about Jurgita that drew him like a moth to a flame. Was it possible to love two so completely at the same time? Was there nothing in this damn life that was not complicated?

Henri arrived at Jurgita's and quietly told Michael of the recent events. "Merde! Would I? That is a position to be fought over. Do you realize the ladies' affections those guards command, the special uniforms, special food, lodging, and on and on? Henri, you have got to be joking; and if you are not, if you were not so damn ugly, I would kiss you. Hell, I just might anyway." And he did right on Henri's forehead.

And now how to approach Jurgita with the news of his leaving in a short time. He would put it off until tomorrow. After a wonderful dinner of roast pork and potatoes, Henri was sitting by the fire with Jurgita drinking the good Lithuanian beer and quietly talking. They talked of the general and many past events. Jurgita brought up the conversations they had before he left for Russia. Did he ever think of those again? Indeed, he did. He considered Jurgita a wonderful person and one he could share so much with. They talked until the fire started to die down, and Henri got up to go in his room. All the rest were asleep. It seemed they could not get enough rest these days. He was slowly regaining his strength, and the others were too.

Jurgita took his hand to pull herself up, and their eyes met. They gazed at each other for a moment, and then Jurgita kissed him ever so slightly, just a brush of her lips on his. His arm twined around her waist as he drew her to him, pressing his lips to hers, feeling her slim body pressed to his. They remained that way for seemingly an eternity, lips rubbing and working against the others. Henri touched his tongue to Jurgita's lips, and she answered with her tongue.

Finally, she pushed back and took Henri by the hand and quietly led him to her room. She closed and bolted the door and came into his arms once more. He did not fully realize the shedding of clothes and Jurgita lying back on the bed. Her beautiful slim figure lying there before him. Her pulling his head and lips to hers and him into her. Nor did he realize the fullness of this passionate moment until all the bells and lights in heaven went off at once. Jurgita gasped, as did he, and it was over. They lay naked, crumpled and exhausted in each other's arms.

"Jurgita, I am so sorry," he finally whispered. "You have been the best friend in the world to me, and now I have taken advantage of you. Please forgive me."

"Henri, nothing that happened here this night was anything that I did not want to happen. I think I could have stopped, but I will never know. I love you so much, and I will carry this memory to my grave. It was my first time with any man. You were my first." She cuddled up to his naked body and pulled the quilt over them.

"And you were my first. Were you hurt? I have heard it does the first time."

"Never, mon amour. A bit at first, I guess, but, mon amour, for you absorbed all pain."

And they commenced to explore and play nearly the entire night. There seemed no end to the wonder of their enjoyment and exploring of each other. There was no talk of any tomorrows or a future. The night was theirs and theirs alone. Toward dawn, Henri quietly partially dressed and crept into the room where the others lay. They were all in deep sleep and never knew of his absence.

The next day, Henri and Jurgita went to church at St. Anne's. The ornate red brick structure was even more beautiful brushed with snow. Little wonder Napoleon had wanted to take it to France. They went inside the main chapel with usual soldiers lying all over. Jurgita took Henri to the back altar where the priests had their private times at prayer. It was empty, and they knelt side by side before the small altar. He asked forgiveness, and he assumed Jurgita did the same. He never asked, and she never told him. He was sorry, and again he was not. He had never experienced this phase of love in his life. He had planned for Ange to be the first, but fate would have it otherwise. How would he ever explain this to her, if indeed he ever would? They left the small chapel after a time and went to a small restaurant for tea in the old part of town near the river.

It wasn't a far walk, but just enough for Henri to gain his courage about the coming trip home. Jurgita beat him to the subject.

"Well, my favorite lover, now with the gathering of more French troops every day, when do you expect to be going home?"

"Jurgita, there are so many things I want to tell you. I think I need to tell you, but I can't seem to get the courage. The words are just not there. Going home is one of them. These things we have shared are so intense and unlike anything in my life. I am torn between staying here forever and going home. Napoleon has asked for me in his personal guard. That in itself is an honor as I know this man personally. He has been my mentor of sorts and always there for me. I will have a very bright future with him if I behave and know I can do that. I owe him this allegiance. And I owe you an allegiance too. I owe you so, so much. My leg, possibly my life, but I do know that if I do not return home with him, I will never be anything again. Can you understand what I am trying and fumbling to say?"

"Oui, I can, mon amour. While I can capture your body briefly, I really don't think I can capture your entire being and heart. I would rather see you go than be here and the shell of a man. You will always be in my heart and dreams. I will and could never forget my Frenchman. I know I will cry and miss you terribly, but this is something you and I must do. Just tell me that you love me and will try to return someday, even if you do not mean it." They sat silently, sipping tea and holding hands for a while, and then left for home.

The French soldiers were piled like stacks of wood in an area near the foot of the bridge. The ground was frozen, and graves could not be dug. More were dying every day, adding to the piles. There were thousands already. The human river of tragedy continued to flow into the city. Not only the soldiers but the camp followers, the wounded, lame, men, women, and even children. One account told was of a canteen keeper and a young mother and camp follower. She had kept her young baby alive by feeding it horse's blood on the long march. Napoleon had indeed lost the flower of his Armée. By all that his staff could estimate, only some five thousand to thirteen thousand men of the original six hundred thousand that went to Russia could be called upon to fight. And they probably would not.

Jurgita and Henri met in her room each night for the duration of his stay. It seemed they were consumed with the passion of each other. Henri was so torn between leaving and staying. Jurgita knew this and never said a word, trying to keep him here. The choice would be his and his alone. Henri had never known such passion and love in his life and seemed never to want the sessions to end. Lying in each other's arms after and quietly talking gave him peace as no other time.

Aunt Agne knew of these quiet meetings and had a talk with Jurgita. "Child, he will go away, and your heart will be broken. You will, in all probability, never see or hear of him again."

"I know, Momma, but I love him so. I want all happiness while he is still here. When he leaves, I shall never forget him, and my life will go on, as shall his."

"I hope you are right, my daughter, just please be very careful. You know what I mean."

"Oui, Momma, I do, and I will. Merci for your understanding."

Jurgita knew an artist in the town who did portraits and talked Henri into a sitting. It was only a small portrait, but she said she must have it as a remembrance of her first and only true love. He agreed only if she would have one done for him. They sat giggling at each other while the frustrated artist was trying to make them be still. Henri's portrait of Jurgita was in a small oval frame much like that of Ange he always carried. Henri's was in a larger frame. "Oh, Henri, the likeness is perfect. I will treasure this always. Merci."

The artist had captured both of them in every respect. The one of Jurgita was especially good. He had captured her delicate features, the slim nose, full almost-pouting lips, sparkling dark eyes, and dark hair with the green ribbon that brought out the green sparkles in her eyes. Henri's was of his usual serious nature with only the hint of a smile, but it truly reflected the dark hair and eyes much as Jurgita's.

"Jonas, please, I need to speak to you in private," said Henri. "We will be leaving shortly for home. God only knows what is to come. Before I leave, I want you to know I will always treasure our friendship. If I may, I would like to leave you something that means a lot to me, Satan. He has been a loyal and good horse, but I cannot take him back to France. Please take him or try to find a decent home for him."

"Why, of course, I will take him. I will be going home in the spring, and by then, he should be back to his old frisky self. I have always admired Satan and will do all I can to make him the pride of our stables at home. Merci immensely, my friend. I haven't had a chance to really talk to you these days. You and Jurgita seem engrossed with each other. Have you had thoughts of staying?"

"Oui, I have. Jurgita is very special. She not only saved my life and leg, she is my best friend, present company not mentioned."

"I know, my friend, I have watched the 'closeness' since before our departure for the Russias. Jurgita is very special. You would do well to stay here and marry her. We could go to my home in the north and have you run the estates or some such. You would never want or worry other than the Russians coming back. By that time, you would be one of us."

"Jonas, merci. Napoleon has asked me to join his personal guard, and this is something I must do. I don't know where life will take me; but I will always hold you, Jurgita, and our Lithuanians in my heart. Please, let's exchange contact information. I promise to write when I can and if you will respond."

Decembre 6, 1812, Napoleon decided to leave for France and home. He, those that were going, and the horses were now strong enough to make the journey. They would only take three carriages as they were safe for now and would be on the journey. They would not stop in any large places where they would be recognized. This was to be a swift journey only involving several days across Poland and Germany and on into France. They reckoned it would only take four days, five at the most, pending weather. The personal guard would follow with whatever troops that could be salvaged from the tragedy of the Russias. Most of the rest of the survivors would winter here and travel when the weather became better.

Henri and Jurgita had their final farewell that night, and she cried as he held her cradled helplessly in his arms. "Jurgita, I am so torn about leaving. I do love you and promise to try to return at some point in the future. I cannot and never will forget you."

Henri went out to the stable to bid a final adieu to his old friend Satan. *This is the final thing I can ever do to repay him, somehow,* he thought. *He has been my faithful friend and carried me through hell.* No one would ever understand how his heart was breaking over so many recent losses and now this. He was leaving so much in this frozen land, so much. He could not begin to calculate and comprehend the losses.

Yet there was life yet to come in his losses. There was home, Ange, and his promising career. What gypsy might foretell his future. As he entered the stable and called Satan's name, he heard an excited whinny in reply. Satan stood in a separate stall with a blanket over his back. He was snorting and stamping his feet as Henri walked up smiling. His ears were standing straight up, anticipating the usual rub. And, possibly, a piece of apple.

Henri entered the stall and did rub Satan's ears and his neck, and then he hugged his neck, whispering, *"Mon vieux fidèle ami,* where I am going soon, it will not be possible to take you; but you will be safe now. I hope you understand. I wonder if I understand though. Life is so confusing these days. No more fighting for you, mon ami, no more danger. I want you to find a lovely mare and have many more just like you. You deserve this and much more. I will always remember you, and merci for everything you have done for me. Merci, *vieux ami,* more than you will ever know. The gods of the horses go with you."

Satan nodded his head up and down and snorted as if understanding. Henri had several apples and was cutting and feeding them to Satan in pieces as he spoke. Satan gently took each piece, chewing it as if savoring every bite. No more words were spoken. There was no need. Henri's eyes misted over, and only by all that he could do did he keep from openly shedding tears.

It just wouldn't do, however, to have Satan see him cry. Imagine, a grown, experienced, decorated combat officer in the Grande Armée of France crying in the sight of his mount. He hugged Satan's neck a final time, took his knife, and cut a small cluster of white hair from Satan's mane. He tied them together with a green satin ribbon he had "borrowed" from Jurgita. He slowly walked away and, not looking back, closed the stable door.

There was a soft sniffing, of sort, at the back of the stable, however. Unbeknown to Henri, Uncle Martynas was in a stall near the back and had heard every word. He knew enough French to understand this emotional moment. Never had he heard such a touching exchange between man and his horse. A bond existed between the two that no one could comprehend. He thought he might relate this to Jurgita after Henri had departed, but not before. There was enough grief and emotion about without adding more.

The carriages would leave from the inn where Napoleon was staying. Henri asked of Jurgita not accompany him there. He wanted to remember her always as she was right now, here in his arms and at home. Jurgita and Aunt Agne had packed Henri and Michael a basket of meat, bread, cheese, sweet cakes, two flasks of water, and other incidentals for their journey. He kissed her goodbye, turned at the gate, and looked back. He saw her waving to him, head erect and smiling with tears running down her face. He was tempted to run back. Michael tugged at his sleeve. And then he was gone.

He was very quiet, and Michael knew to leave him in his thoughts. His heart bled for his friend, but only he could make this decision. Much, much had happened during the last several weeks. They approached the inn gates and found them open and the carriages nearly ready.

Each carriage would have a relief driver and a spare string of horses. The horses would be changed at intervals. Inside the general's carriage, Henri found the personal effects of the general. There wasn't much. His sword, his uniform with medals, and his personal papers. All else had been lost in the fury to get this far. As careful as the general was, Henri was certain there was nothing in the papers to embarrass the family. Napoleon and others came out of the inn and started to mount the carriages.

Napoleon came over to Henri. "I have instructed that Andre's personal effects be put in his carriage and in your care. We could not bury him as the ground is completely frozen, but he is with his comrades. And, Henri, he will never be alone. There are thousands more to keep him company."

"I did find his things, monsieur, and I thank you."

"Well, goodbye to Lithuania, Andre, my old faithful friend and the greatest tragedy of my life. I hope better things are in our future," said Napoleon. "My heart is so heavy."

Henri thought to himself, *And mine as well. I leave more here than anyone can know. My very soul itself it seems. All of my heart, and now my soul too.*

31

Home Is the Soldier

Henri sat staring out of the carriage window deep in thought. The events of the past several weeks were overwhelming. All he could seem to think about was Jurgita. He felt so guilty as he was going home to Ange. He knew he would probably never see Jurgita again, but he could not get her out of his mind. They had discussed this, and both felt the same but accepted his leaving. With every rolling slosh of the carriage wheels, it was Jurgita, Jurgita, Jurgita, Jurgita. He subconsciously slapped his cheek as if to rouse himself back to reality. The sound made Michael look over to him.

Michael whispered, "Well, welcome back to the world. You have been lost somewhere since we left. Do you want to talk, or can I help?"

"No, merci, mon ami. What I have, I must work out for myself. You know which tiger I am fighting right now, and there seems to be no relief."

"I understand, Henri. Let me know if I can help."

The day was as miserable as was Henri. Winter months in the northern countries were usually dreary and cold. Today was no exception. It was heavily overcast with the wind blowing fresh snow over the road and surrounding countryside. They passed over small streams, and if no bridge, shallow crossing places were iced over, making it treacherous for the horses to cross. Even the bridges were iced, and the teams had to be led across so as not to slip. At times, the carriage would sway unduly as the winds hit the side. The poor drivers were bundled in heavy Russian fur coats and caps, but still they were in the elements.

And yet it was a winter wonderland with the heavy conifer forests of southern Lithuania dusted with the white of the snow and ice. The open fields were like white carpets in the finest palaces. They would not make much speed for some time. All hoped the pace would increase more to the south through Poland and beyond as the roads and weather improved a bit. They passed small villages, but no signs of life could be seen. People and animals just did not venture out in this weather. The livestock and basis of this remote and rural life were all in the barns and would be until better days. Most barns were attached to the houses or very nearby so people and animals did not have to venture out much in the weather. Henri wondered how these hardy people survived at all and why would they want to live in such. It was much better in warmer regions. But then, he did know the difference. Most here probably did not.

At dusk, they reached the border of Poland and stopped at a small inn for an evening meal and to change horses. The worn-out horses were left here as fresh ones were available to replace them. They would be more plentiful in Poland and closer to home. Napoleon had decided to travel the night too. He was aware that any fast-moving Cossacks could have known of his departure through spies and enemies in Vilna. They sat at a fine meal of roast pork and potatoes with plenty of wine. Henri was really not that hungry, passing it off on his leg wound hurting from the bouncing of the carriage. He did take some to add to his basket just in case. They were on the road again within the hour. There was little moon that night, but the snow had stopped. Clouds could be seen scudding over what little moon there was, the slim crescent hanging in the sky like the golden scythe of the harvester of souls. Several times the drivers had to slow to nearly a walk to keep on the narrow road.

Henri, Michael, and the two others in the carriage had a fitful and mostly sleepless night. Henri was thankful for his Cossack coat and the warmth. It brought back memories of his being stuck with the sword and all that followed. He wondered what Jurgita was doing at this moment. And as he gazed out upon the light increasing in the east, he took out the two pictures and held them up side by side. Angelette and Jurgita. He slowly put Jurgita back into his coat and continued to stare at Ange. His Ange. Something seemed to stir within him as he looked into her eyes, and he knew then what his destiny would be. He would put Jurgita in a tiny corner in his heart as Aunt Mags had told him to do with such memories and draw her out from time to time in fantasy. With Ange, it would be different. She was the real and only one. It was as if God had lifted a mighty blanket from his heart. He looked over at Michael and watched his head bob about at times. He seemed so peaceful. Nothing seemed to bother him. He wondered if any girl could truly steal this man's heart. He smiled silently to himself.

By the next afternoon, they were nearly across Poland and nearing Germany. They would spend the night at the next inn. All had been complaining of the bouncing and swaying and in need of a proper rest for a few hours. Henri, with his wound, was more miserable than most as it ached all of the time. He had been given some of the tail of the tiger to add to his tea, but it was only temporary relief. At times he could change positions and get a little relief. The damn thing just ached constantly. Other times more than usual, but always aching. It was healing nicely but was stiff and in a place where he could not readily exercise and move to work it out. It seemed he was constantly wriggling his toes trying to relieve the ache or increase circulation. He was miserable, and proper sleep was impossible.

Henri was out of some of his despondency and talked to Michael more. He explained the situation with Jurgita and swore him to secrecy.

Michael responded, "I know about Jurgita. A blind man could see what was going on with you two." Michael teased and said, "This is the time to steal Ange for myself."

Henri retorted, "You just might try it if you don't fear I will shoot you or stick you in the ass."

At the inn that night, they all had a good meal, and Henri spent the night in a real bed where he could rest and stretch out his leg.

The next morning as they were crossing the German border, Henri felt for the slight bulge of the general's watch and letters in his jacket pocket. He had nearly forgotten them with all of his other clothes and the weight of the Cossack coat. He took the watch out. It had stopped. He asked one of the others for the time then wound and set the watch. It was a lovely gold pocket watch with matching heavy gold chain. The "Angelette coin" was attached near the watch. He held it to his ear. *This ticking of the movement is like a heartbeat,* he thought to himself. *This is why he gave it to me. He will always be with me. This is not just a watch. This is the general speaking to me. Ticktock,* I love you, Vivien. *Ticktock,* I love you, Ange. *Ticktock,* I love you, Henri, and on and on.

He took the letters out; and there was one for Madame, Jean, Mimi, and another addressed to both Ange and him. He decided to read the letter before Ange in an attempt to sift out any further heartache. He tore open the envelope.

November 11, 1812

My Dearest Children, Angelette and Henri,

One may think it odd that I am penning this to you both, but that is how I now think of you, always together and as one. You were close as children, always together, and now the same. If Henri does get through this, he may be able to explain to my beautiful daughter what happened to her Poppa. If my Henri does not appear, then the task shall belong to Napoleon. I shall never again see home or my wonderful family. Such is the life of a soldier. Do not shed tears for me. This has been my life. I have never shirked my duties and of that you may be proud. I will be known in the annals of history as one who totally supported his Emperor and our country, France.

My Angelette, you were so precious and beautiful when you came into our lives. I have watched my beautiful baby daughter grow into a beautiful, wonderful, and wise woman. One who has stolen the heart of my adopted son. I would be proud to see your marriage and your family to come. I will be with you as you walk down the aisle at Notre Dame when your special day arrives. Poppa will always be there for you, my Angelette.

My Henri, you have grown in wisdom and stature since coming to us and have proven yourself a leader in all ways of the military and of life. Of that, I am proud. Not just of your accomplishments, but the way they came about. I have never heard of your attempting personal gain at the expense of others. What you have done in your accomplishments was on your own merits. If you are reading this letter, I will know my daughter and my family will be safe and cared for. I love you as my son, equally to my Jean, and yet individually. My Ange, if you are reading this alone, then you will want to know these things about Henri from me. He is a unique individual and one of whom I am proud to call son.

And to you both, I pray, soon to be joined as one, praise God. God, in all of his wisdom, could never have found a more perfect union in his kingdom. The both of you have seemed perfect for the other since the time Henri came to us. Please know that I love you both as companions for life, and should life take you along other paths as individuals, my love forever, with all of my heart.

Go and grow with God, my children.

Poppa

Henri read the letter several times, absorbing every word. This man had written this to him and his bride-to-be. What wisdom. Henri was so sad he was gone and still had the tremendous guilt of helping him on his way. Oh, Napoleon had absolved him, but still the guilt was there and always would be. He might tell only Ange, but for Madame's sake, he would not relate to any suffering of the general. This was a burden he would carry forever, and best it be shared with one he could truly share it with. He held the watch to his ear and listened for a long time. *Ticktock,* I love you, *ticktock, ticktock.*

The trip across Germany was boring and yet excitable too. He wanted to get home so badly, and yet he dreaded the arrival. He was coming home, and the general was not. He would forever be with his last command. Henri tried to sleep as he could, but it was fitful and not a resting one. There was just too much on his mind. What would he say to Ange? How would he ever explain about the general? Would he tell her about Jurgita? *In all fairness and for future peace,* he thought he had better not. Some things in his single and private life were best unsaid. Married, well that would be a different circumstance.

As they neared the border of France, the weather seemed to clear a bit. It was still cold, but now and then, one could see patches of blue in the sky. It had long since stopped snowing, and now it was just wet. The wetness and rain had been almost constant. Mud was over everything, the horses, carriages, and occupants too, when they dismounted. The entire world seemed mud.

Henri listened to the slosh of the wheels in the muddy ruts of the road; and now they sang Ange, Ange, Ange, Ange. He could feel himself getting jittery and edgy about the prospect of coming home after such calamitous experiences. As he thought back, there had been many months with so much death and anxiety since leaving. So much, so very, very much. He had heard Father Etty say that God never gave man a burden that he could not cope with. Well, this was as close as it was meant to be. He would have to tell Father Etty about this burden. He looked at the other letters and wondered what words may be inside. Whatever it was, he hoped it may bring some sort of peace and closure to each one. Death is so certain and so final. He had been close to death before, but this time it was too close. There would have been no possibly going home had it not been for Jurgita.

He started to think of her again—the coy smile; the sharp, cute little nose; the very closeness of her; the smell of her hair, her clothes, her lovely slim figure lying before him; the sweet odors of sex. He was driving himself mad again. He was sorely tempted to take her picture out but did not. Instead, he took Ange's picture out, and Jurgita went back into her little corner of his heart. He would never forget her and knew it would get easier over time to keep Jurgita in her place. She would probably meet someone and have a large family. She may even forget him completely. Jonas and he had promised to correspond, and possibly he could keep up with her over the years. Would he ever go back? Would he ever even consider it?

They crossed the border of France at Strasbourg but did not stop. Henri looked out of the carriage window and saw the Rhine River and the old part of the ancient city flash by. They turned due west and made for Nancy where they would see how things were going. Napoleon would decide if to go on or spend the night if the hour was too late. They arrived at Nancy near dark and stopped at a small inn to eat and change horses. Napoleon had decided to go on and just as well. The excitement was paramount in all of them so near home.

Henri was beside himself and could scarcely eat. He did manage a bite or two of the beef stew and potatoes and two cups of wine. Real beef meat and not a damn horse. Ah, French wine again. Much better than the stuff they had been subject to. Lithuanian wine was tolerable, their beer better than good, but that damn vodka in the field was really abominable. Little wonder the Russians fought so. Anyone that could call that swill their national drink would be naturally despicable. A quick meal, a change of horses, and on again. Napoleon had said with these good roads and the better weather, they could be in Paris by midnight or the early hours. Henri hoped so as he was exhausted, and the aching in his leg had been constant. Even the anticipation of home and Ange could not keep him awake in the early evening, and he fell asleep under his Cossack coat.

The next he knew, Michael was shaking him. "Henri, Henri, the drivers are yelling we are nearing Paris. Wake up." As they lowered the windows and peered out of the side curtains, indeed they were entering small villages on the outskirts of Paris. Even the air smelled of home.

"Michael, I want you to stay with us until you get a way home if you are going. With the Faucons no more and Lord only knows where we will be or for how long, best you stay with us. No cow eyes at my Ange though." Henri laughed and poked at Michael.

Henri had realized with his recent deep thoughts on this journey, with the retreat from Russia, and the events that followed just what Michael meant to him. He had taken Michael for granted some of the time, but both had been busy in other things. Michael in his world and Henri in his. Yet the two worlds were deeply associated. Michael was his brother and not just in arms either. They whispered at some length of this, and Michael felt the same about Henri. The two had developed a bond through their wars together that could never be broken. Henri recalled the times at drummer school, in Spain, the Faucons, and on and on. It all seemed an eternity from the present.

In the early hours of the morning of Decembre 12, 1812, the carriage stopped at the general's residence. Napoleon came to Henri. "I need to speak to Vivien and express my personal sympathy for my old and faithful friend. There will be no other like him. I owe this man so much."

They entered the unlocked side door off the side porch. A dim light from the fireplace was shining from the sitting room. The Christmas decorations were already in place, and the house smelled of the freshly cut pine branches. A slight figure was visible sitting on the sofa, reading by the firelight.

"Bonjour, madame, is that you? Are you awake?"

She jumped up, startled. "Mon dieu! Henri, it is you!" She jumped up and ran to him, flinging her arms around him, starting to cry. Napoleon was in the shadows. "Where is my Andre? We have heard horrible tales here about the situation there. Is he all right?"

Henri silently held her for a moment, and she pushed back with her hands to her face. "Please tell me the truth. I have not been able to sleep for some time. I have had a terrible empty feeling that something was wrong."

Napoleon stepped forward and reached for Vivien. He took her in his arms. "Our Andre is in eternal rest with his command, Vivien. I would give anything in this world to bring him home to you, but I cannot. Is there anything I can do? I know it is early with this news, and you need to gain your wits, but please let me know anything you need."

She was crying uncontrollably with her head on Napoleon's shoulder. Ange and Mimi had heard the commotion and came into the room.

"Henri!" Ange screamed and ran to him. "Mon dieu, mon dieu." She was crying too and holding him so tight, he thought he would be crushed. "The emperor is here," Ange finally said, "I see and Michael too. Where is Poppa? Where is my Poppa?"

Henri was shaking his head silently.

"Oh, mon dieu! You can't mean?"

"Oui, mon amour. Our Poppa will not be coming home. I will explain later." Henri spoke softly. He was crying too and holding Ange.

Napoleon stayed for a short time and then excused himself, telling Vivien, once more, to call on him at any time day or night. "Henri, you and Michael are home for as long as you need. I will call you when the time comes to join the guard. Please let me know if I can do anything."

"Oui, mon emperor, and merci for everything."

Vivien was sitting on the sofa still crying, but not as before at the first realization of her Andre not coming home. Ange was sitting on the sofa trying to console her mother and herself at the same time.

Mimi pulled Henri and Michael by the hand into the kitchen for some of her coffee that Henri said there was no equal. "Henri, you and Michael are thin as fence posts. They must have starved you in those Russias places. We will soon put some meat on your bones."

Ange came into the kitchen. "There you are. I don't want to let you out of my sight. Henri, I noticed you limping on the leg you injured before. Did you get it hurt again?"

"Oui, Ange, you might say I did, but it is much better now. It is just sore and aches from the anguish of the carriage ride home. You know how I hate long carriage rides. I will tell you all about it later."

Ange pulled him into the little room near the kitchen where he had been during the first episode with the leg. She came into his arms, raised her lovely face, and lifted her lips to his. Nothing was said. Nothing need be. He was home and safe in the arms of one who could never be replaced. Light was starting to show in the east. Henri could almost make out the spires of Notre Dame, and suddenly he was so drained.

Ange took him upstairs to his room and stopped at the door. "I will be here when you need me. I love you very much. I am so glad you came home to me."

She started to cry again, and Henri said, "I am so tired, mon amour, but please stay with me. Neither of us needs to be alone right now. Leave the door open, but I really do not think anyone will mind anyway."

They both climbed on the bed and fell asleep in each other's arms.

32

Recovery and Remembrance

Henri awoke with a start. He lurched up and then realized something was snuggled next to him. As his eyes focused, he saw Ange next to him. Was he dreaming? Then as his senses slowly returned, he started to recollect the tumultuous events of past weeks. He lay there not wanting to move and disturb this miracle next to him. He watched her for some time in the peace of her slumber. She moved ever so slightly and rubbed her pert nose with the back of her hand and sighed slightly. She was beautiful and the very essence of peace.

Finally his bladder got the best of the situation, and he had to move and get up. Very careful not to disturb Ange, he moved carefully away from her and got out of bed. His leg was throbbing again, and he wondered if it would ever stop. The general's watch was on the table and indicated the time was nearing noon. He wound the watch to stop, laid it back on the table, and padded down the hall to the water closet.

On the way back, he checked Michael's room. He was fast asleep and snoring like wagons rumbling on cobbled streets. Madame's room door was partially open, and he looked in. There was no one there and little wonder. It would be a long time, if ever, if she would want to sleep there again. His leg was still aching and stiff as he hobbled down the stairs and toward the kitchen. Madame was asleep on the sofa next to the fire. She looked peaceful and would need her rest for the days to come. He knew she would have to receive those who were really concerned about the general and her feelings and the curiosity seekers. He hoped she would be strong.

Mimi was in the kitchen, and the odors of her cooking were overpowering. "Mimi, what are you cooking? It smells like heaven in a pot."

"Well, seat yourself, and I will serve you a dish of heaven," she said.

Henri was starving and tore at the plate of roast chicken and potatoes as a starving wolf. "I haven't had food like that in so long, Mimi. You wouldn't believe what we ate and had to eat to stay alive. I will never eat horsemeat again."

He got up and helped himself to another plate of heaven. They sat for a while; and he told Mimi of the advance into Russia, the trials there, and his wound trying to get to safety. He left out the parts of his healing process and the general dying, only telling her that he had died peacefully.

Mimi cried, holding her head in her apron, and said, "Oh, that poor dear man. And to be left there in that cold and miserable place. This is the saddest day of my life, Henri. I have been with Andre and Vivien since they were married. He was like a son."

He let Mimi have her cry and said, "We must all be strong now for Madame. Christmas season is nearing, and it has always been a very special time of the year for us all and especially for Madame."

"Oui, I know that, Henri, but I am just so sad for us all. We have lost a great man."

"I agree, and Napoleon knows it as well. This is a very great loss to our armies and to him personally."

Ange came into the kitchen, her hair all disheveled and sleepy eyed. "Where did you go, Henri? I woke up searching for you. I thought at first all of this was some mad dream." She ran into his arms. "But it is not," she said as she snuggled into his shoulder.

The household started to wake by then. Madame came in the kitchen. Her hair was in tangles and her eyes red and puffy as Ange's.

She calmly stated, "My Andre, he was so full of life. I shall miss him, but we must all go on. I think I will plan to be here with you for the Christmas season. Then I will go spend some time with my sister in Orléans. I have wanted to do so anyway, and I do need to be away for a time. Ange, would you want to go with me? But from what I saw when I peeked in Henri's room during the night, you will be busy on your own."

"Momma! We weren't doing anything wrong."

"No implications, child. I know that."

"Momma, I want to stay here and be with Henri as much as possible in case he has to go again."

Henri said, "I think I will be here or very close. Napoleon has requested Michael and I to join his personal guard, and one would assume most duties will be here in Paris for a time."

"In his personal guard! Henri, that is wonderful," said Madame. "You can be close by when Napoleon is here. It is an honor to be chosen. He is very particular of those close to him."

"Oui, madame, I know. To change the subject, The general wrote personal letters to us all. I have yours upstairs. Would you like for me to get yours now or wait awhile?"

Madame said, "Oui, I would like to read it now, if you please. Don't worry about me in this, Henri. Andre and I spoke many times of this event, and it has come to pass."

He brought her the letter, and she went to her private place on the sofa.

Novembre 11, 1812

My Dearest Vivien,

As you read these penned words, realize they do come from the heart and very soul of one who loves you beyond all things. I have not lied to you in life and will not in death. I am hurting as I write this, but it is not that bad. The pill rollers are keeping me from too much pain with their special tea. To my great misfortune a Cossack lancer has found my great midsection. How could he miss me? I know that I shall never again see home or the one I treasure most in this world. Thus is the life of a soldier, mon amour. We have discussed these dangers and my possible event many times. I know you are as prepared as one can be for such.

I can never relate enough to you the presence you have meant in my life. You, Vivien, were my stabilizing force. I always knew that you would be there and save me from the ravages of maddening war. If only I could truly state the words that my heart cries out to say to you. You have given me love as no other in my life, a wonderful family, and a solid foundation for all of our lives. I was the one that had to wander with our short Corporal and conquer the world, and through it all, there was always you, you, you. I go to my eternal rest knowing peace through the knowledge of you and your love for me.

I will not make a long issue of this, but know that I loved you with every fiber of my being and lived only for you. Hug and kiss all for me.

Forever in my heart,
Your Andre

She sat for some time and read the letter again and again. This was so like Andre. Short and direct to the point. He knew she would be all right with this.

They both knew his time could come at any moment. Possibly it was best this way. Things would not be complicated and drawn out. This letter would be her closure. At least she had that. She only hoped she would have the courage to go on and live the rest of her life without Andre. There could be no other. She would indeed plan to have a talk with Ange on this subject. Life was so fragile in the military of Napoleon and especially during these times. Earlier it was much less a danger, but now with the allies and the enemies of Napoleon getting bolder, how much longer?

With the charm, grace, and attitude of Madame, the days that followed were much easier than Henri had expected. The well-wishers and allies of Napoleon flowed to the house the first week as news of Andre's loss was circulated around Paris. Father Etty was with them all of the time during the first week. He had taken leave from his church, knowing he was needed here. Mimi was kept busy with cakes, tea, coffee, and other refreshments. Jean came home from school the second week. He was completely changed and so caring and loving to Madame, Ange, Mimi, and all. He, Henri, and Michael had long talks of tales of the advance to Moscow and the disastrous retreat. Jean was like a sponge, soaking up the things of military and the wars.

The end of the second week, the visitors slowed to a trickle with only a few each day. Everyone seemed relieved. Henri, Michael, and Jean were forever in their uniforms; and it was a relief to shed them. Ange loved Henri in his uniform and said he was most handsome. Michael could and did go hide at times, but Henri was family and had to be around. Ange and Michael teased and played. Michael told the ever-serious Henri that Ange was the sister he never had and please do not read anything into his teasing. There was no worry. Henri laughed and hugged them both.

The second week after their return, there was a special ceremony at the palace to honor the general. The palace was filled to capacity with dignitaries and political figures. A fragile yet strong Madame dressed in black, head held high and proud, accepted a medal from Napoleon and word that the general's wages would be paid to her for the remainder of her life. He whispered to her again that she could call him friend and come to him at any time should she ever need.

Jean was at the ceremony and sat next to his mother with Henri on the other side. Both were holding Madame's hands, Ange sat next to Henri with her arm wrapped in his. They must have all been a pretty sight sitting there like that, but who would really notice and care? Andre had been a very popular "people's" general and a hero of the republic. This was for him. After the ceremony, a very silent group mounted the carriage for a very empty house. For Madame, it would never be a home again; it would just be another house, a place to exist, and an empty shell of former life.

When they settled for a bit and had glasses of wine, Henri went to his room and found the letter for Jean from his father. Jean went into the study and sat at his father's desk to read it in private.

Novembre 11, 1812

Dear Jean, my son,

>*As you read this letter, I hope you will realize the vast responsibility I ask of you. I know I do not have to ask it, but I feel I must. You are now the man of our house with all of the responsibilities bestowed. Carry the responsibilities well, my son. They are great and yet very rewarding. There is much love, understanding, and patience to give and to receive in return. You have grown much in both stature and honor these last years, and please know that I am so proud to call you son. Many times fathers and sons do not show affection due to some misconception of masculinity or a show of foolish pride. If I have done this, I most profoundly apologize to you. I was missing for many of your formative years, and for that I apologize, also. I pray that in your adult years, you will understand and accept it as I do now with my fate.*

>*To both of our misfortunes, I cannot be there to teach and guide you. A Cossack lancer has found my sizable midriff and duly stuck it. I am in pain, but not unbearably so. The doctors are keeping me pumped full of stuff to relieve the pain, but I know my fate. I pray God will always be with you, my son. Do well in all things and trust in God.*

>*I Love You,*
>*Poppa*

Jean read the letter several times, digesting every word and pondering it. He stared blankly into space for many more minutes. Then he replaced the letter in its envelope and returned to the sitting room.

Madame did have a talk with Ange in the next several days over the prospects of Henri one day not coming home. Ange said she knew these things, but she and Henri had never discussed it. Life was becoming less complex now as they prepared for Christmas. The holiday had come so fast upon them. Henri and Michael scurried to the market to find something suitable for Ange.

As they walked along, Michael asked, "Any ideas for a gift, mon ami? You should have no trouble with your choice. Why don't you just tie a red ribbon around your private part and see what she would do."

"Ha, she would probably scream and run at the size of it," said Henri. "You know how I am endowed."

"Oui, boss, not the largeness, but the smallness. She wouldn't scream. She would laugh."

"You *merder*!"

He did find a small gold ring with her birthstone. Michael bought her a matching gold necklace. They both bought things for Madame and Mimi. Jean was another situation. Henri had no idea what to get him and would take Ange and let her help.

That afternoon, Henri caught Mimi in a private moment and gave her the letter.

Novembre 11, 1812

Our Mimi,

I know at this moment you must be in your kitchen fussing about with the things you always do so well. I could not in good conscience go to my maker without telling you what you have meant to Vivien and me. When we were first married and you came to us from Vivien's family, I had thoughts that you were just too good to be true. My thoughts then are now reality. You are to us as family itself. Your presence in our lives has added that lustre of probably the best cook and housekeeper in Paris if not all of France. Not only those skills, Mimi, but your manner, your love, and just being our Mimi. We all love you very much and each time you cook that awful hash stuff, as you call it, think of me. I will always be watching through your kitchen window. Take care of my Vivien and all who call you family.

Love,
Andre

Henri sought out Jean, and the two went into the sitting room. "Jean, I want you to know that I am most profoundly sorry about our father. I was with him when he died, and although he had been in much pain, he died peacefully. Napoleon has been a good friend through all of this, and I do owe him much. He has requested me to enter his personal guard, a duty I much look forward to."

"Henri, that is wonderful. Do you realize what this appointment could mean?"

"Oui, Jean, I do, and I am looking forward to it. It could also mean the end of my combat career unless we get into a situation where it would warrant."

"Would you want that?"

"At this moment, oui. I think I have seen enough war and the death that goes with it. I would like to stay home for a time and settle down."

"Ha! Marry my sister, you mean. I don't blame you for that. She is lovely, and you two have been at this for most of our lives. I would be proud to call you brother for real."

"And myself, Jean. One more thing though. The general gave me his watch on his deathbed and asked that I take it. With your permission, I would like to keep it. It is a precious thing to me."

"I know you have it, mon ami, and please do keep it." Jean laughed and slapped Henri on the back. "After all, you did steal it sometime ago. I am heartily sorry for that. I guess I was just so desperate for our father's affection and attention, but I am sorry. I did read my father's letter. He said he loved me and was proud to call me son. I will try to uphold his honor."

Henri reached to embrace Jean. "C'est la guerre. C'est la vie."

The Christmas season came, but the spirit and heart of the household lay frozen far to the north with the thousands of his last command. It was on no consequence that there were thousands like him who would never return. He was the very spirit of this holiday, and it would just not be the same without his presence. They all went through the rituals and motions of attending Midnight Mass at Notre Dame and eating the feast Mimi had prepared, but they all felt that this holiday would never again be complete. It had been his favorite of all holidays.

Mid-Janvier 1813, a messenger came from Napoleon requesting that Henri and Michael report to the Imperial Guard headquarters and after to Napoleon personally. The messenger would wait and escort them to the palace. Henri's leg was much better now, and he and Michael had felt the boredom of being off duty. Henri thought he could never get used to doing nothing and needed to be occupied. Ange was another story and seemed completely happy to just sit and converse the day away. They did have a lot to catch up on. Several times he thought of bringing up the subject of the general's last day and Jurgita, but he never seemed to get the courage. Maybe someday, but not now.

He did explain about the wound and nearly losing his leg and maybe his life, but he could not mention Jurgita. Ange looked at him with puzzlement as he was explaining but never said anything. He told her about Jonas, Uncle Martynas, and Aunt Agne and very passingly about Jurgita. In the manner she looked at him, it was as if she was expecting more. He soon shut up before she started to ask questions. His feeling of guilt made him certain she knew something had gone on he wasn't telling. She certainly was not a fool and had a woman's strong intuition so talked about. He often teased her that she knew things before God did.

They arrived at the palace midmorning and were told to wait for the commander of the guards. He would be with them shortly. The commander colonel, Raymonde Arnot, greeted them warmly, shook their hands, and said he was very glad to meet them and to welcome them to the most elite group in the Armée. The group had been severely depleted during the retreat from Moscow. Many had given their lives in defense of the emperor. He said that Napoleon said that Henri had been wounded and asked if he was fit for duty.

"Oui, merci, monsieur. It will be my pleasure to return to duty. An extended leave is nice, but boredom does set in."

"I can certainly understand that, Capitaine. I just returned to duty myself."

He gave them a short orientation about the history of the guard and the honor it was to be recommended to join these ranks. Then he sent them off to the quartermaster to draw their new uniforms and to have them fitted. These were not to be just any uniforms but the dress uniforms of the personal Imperial Guard of Napoleon.

"After your fitting, return to me," he instructed. "Napoleon wishes to greet you to his guard. He does this with each member."

They were escorted to the quartermaster, and it was evident that this man took great pride in his creations. He issued each man a pair of black boots with a gold tassel at the front. He instructed them to work on the boots with the kit for such he gave them and make them as glass. A complete new wardrobe was issued, complete with undergarments. They were fitted for the traditional white trousers, a bottle green waistcoat with red-and-gold trim, a red cape with white trim, a black fur hat with a tassel of green and red with gold trim, and several pairs of white gloves issued for state occasions. He asked about any medals they may have. They must be worn on the uniform and to bring them back for the final fit. He would place them on the uniform. The uniforms would be ready in three days, and they could return then. The uniforms were stunning and very impressive.

Michael said as they left, "Henri, can you imagine the ladies I am going to impress with this? And then there is you, stuck with only one."

"Oui, but the pick of the litter, mon ami. Those others could never compare, and you know it."

"Henri and Michael, welcome to the palace and my personal guard," said Napoleon. "I will not have very much time. Already this early in the year, I have to put to rest rumors and intrigue. It seems while we were away, certain ones here were making their presence known. The world of politics never seems to stop. Has everything been to your satisfaction?"

They replied almost in unison, "Oui, Your Excellency." Henri again added his gratitude for Napoleon's kindness and consideration to the family. Napoleon smiled warmly and offered each his hand and asked if Michael would excuse them for just a moment.

"Henri, as you know, I am rebuilding the Armée. This appointment is but a stopping place in my plans for you. As you gain in years and wisdom, I plan to put you on my staff of officers. Andre was a dear friend and one of absolute trust. I would hope one day to have you in the same capacity. Please stay in touch, and let me know how our Vivien is faring."

In the next month, Fevrier 1813, trouble started to brew again with Prussia backing out of ties with France and going to Russia. Both of them declared war on France. In August, Austria joined against France. One by one, others began to ally against not just France but Napoleon.

Henri had been installed as commander in the Chasseur à Cheval of the Imperial Guard or horse cavalry. For his youth, he proved to be an excellent choice in discipline and character. He was one of the most popular commanders in the guard, always firm yet fair. Michael was now his sergeant and also doing an excellent job.

Henri had planned to marry Ange that spring, but the fortunes of war dragged him away again. Napoleon had many meetings trying to save his Confederation of the Rhine. It seemed he was always being called for escort here or there. Ange said she understood, but really, she was frustrated too. Madame left in Mars when the weather was better and traveled to her sister in Orléans. For the first time in their adult lives, Henri and Ange were alone other than the servants.

They were in his room sitting in their usual place near the window, looking out at the moonlit river and the peace below. The night sounds of the crickets and soft sounds of distant dogs barking were as a melody. It was early spring, and the scents of blossoms and new life wafted through the window. A light evening rain seemed to enhance the freshness of the newly cleansed earth.

"Henri, I know we meant to wed this spring, and I am trying to be patient and understand, but honestly, I can't seem to plan with you being called away so often."

"I know, Ange. It seems as if I am forever being called to escort the emperor to one place or another. These are dire times for him. It seems all of the countries of Europe are lining up against France and Napoleon. He has shared some of his personal feelings and fears, and I am bound on my honor to assist in any way possible."

"Oh, Henri, I know that. It is just I want our times so badly. You will never know how much I missed you when you went to the Russias."

He stood up and pulled her up into his arms. She reached up and ran her fingers through his hair and pulled her lips to his. They kissed for a long time, and his body ached for more. At last, he pushed her back slightly and kicked the door shut. He took her in his arms again and kissed her, brushing his tongue over her lips. She responded. He ran his hand under the back of her blouse and felt her bare skin. He started to unbutton her blouse, and she held his hand to stop him.

"Please, my darling, I am so vulnerable right now and want you so badly, but we promised."

He was breathing so hard, he thought he might faint. They did need to cool off a bit. "I know, I know. It is just that I love you so much and so completely. I am sorry, Ange. I did not mean to take advantage. I would never hurt you." He opened the door, and they sat down again holding hands.

"I have wondered what it will be like, our first time," he finally said.

"Henri, tell me. Have you ever had another? During all of your soldier travels, you must have been tempted."

"I have been tempted but never had the courage," he lied. "There were girls in Spain, but we were all just boy drummers. Michael was there, and I guess he was tempted too." The subject of Lithuania did not arise. She knew he had been wounded while there.

"Mon amour, there is something I must share with you though. Something that you must know and has been troubling me for some time. I told you that I was with the general when he died, but I have never related to anyone how he died."

"Henri, you do not have to tell me this if you do not want to."

"Oui, I do, and please let this be between us. I never want Madame or Jean to know. Please."

"I promise, Henri. It will be ours to keep."

"The general had been run nearly through in his midsection by a Cossack lance, and infection had set in. I have heard the Cossacks put things on their lance and sword tips to bring on infections if only a slight hit was involved. The general was in severe pain, and the only relief was with the special tea from the doctors. He was dying and knew it. He begged me for my pistol, and I could not refuse. I would hope someone could do the same for me someday. I placed my cocked pistol in his hand and walked out. We were in the hall when the shot rang out. I will never forget that shot. I am so sorry, Ange. I loved him with my whole heart. Can you forgive me?"

She hesitated for a time and let his words sink in. "Oh, Henri, you have been carrying this burden. You should have told me sooner. Of course, I forgive you if that is what you ask, but there is nothing to forgive. Poppa was suffering and dying. You probably gave him peace." She jumped up, started to cry, sat on Henri's lap, and put her head on his shoulder.

Napoleon was furiously rebuilding his Armée, and the allies were steadily gaining strength against him. Indeed, Russia and Prussia had formed the

Kalisz alliance against France. In March 1813, the Russians fighting against Napoleon reached Berlin. The French garrison there evacuated the city without a fight. In June, Napoleon met with the ruler of Austria and was informed he must sue for peace if he wanted the continued support of Austria. However, as Napoleon's representatives were meeting in Prague to discuss peace, the Prussians attacked. At the Battle of Großbeeren, the French were repulsed. It was evident the allies wanted to rid Europe of Napoleon and considered him their worst nightmare.

At the Battle of Dresden in August 1813, the allies once again defeated Napoleon, and the chase was on. In October, the French faced Russia, Austria, and Prussia at the Battle of Leipzig and was soundly defeated. In December, with the Christmas season approaching, approximately eighty-three thousand Prussian and Russian troops chased Napoleon back across the Rhine at Pfalzgrafenstein Castle. They held in place at the Rhine for the duration of the winter months. That spring, with the Russian, Prussian, and Austrian troops on one side, the duke of Wellington approached from the other side and defeated Napoleon at Toulouse. Napoleon had no choice but abdicate the throne of France.

In one short year, Napoleon had gone from the most powerful ruler in Europe to being captured and held by the allies. Alexander I of Russia entered Paris as the head of the anti-Napoleon coalition. The allies were now in total control. At Fontainebleau, Napoleon and the allies signed a treaty. Napoleon was allowed to keep his title as emperor, given a pension by the French government, and banished to the island of Elba.

Henri was devastated. He had gone from a member of Napoleon's personal guard to now being held in "area" arrest. He would still have his freedoms but within the city only.

"How can this be, Michael? It seems as if the time we came home, things have totally reversed. We are like old men tied up, and now with the military gone, what will become of us?"

"I really can't imagine, mon ami. The military is all I know and have. I can't imagine farming or working in a shop. The very thought makes me shudder."

Henri had a long and serious talk with Ange about their future. She told him that just as long as they were together, nothing else mattered. Henri was more realistic and worried about their financial well-being. Suppose he would have to go to prison or worse, but what could be worse than that?

Then in a week, Henri and Michael were summoned to the palace. There was quite a group of Napoleon's personal guard standing and sitting around in small groups. The commander made the announcement that Napoleon would be allowed his personal guard in exile, and they were to go if they were willing. The decision would be theirs.

"Michael," Henri said, "I am torn between my loyalties to Napoleon and to Ange. I love both and owe so much. I must speak to the emperor personally before I make my decision."

"I am going, Henri. I have no urge to join the ranks of farmers or go back home and possibly work in the warehouses or join a ship's crew."

Henri did request to see Napoleon and was ushered into his presence.

"Henri, how good of you to come. Please be seated, and I will order a carafe of wine for us while we sit."

"Merci, monsieur. I am pleased to hear you are to keep your title. What I need to know is how long will the troops at your command be stationed with you. Will there be rotational duty so one can return home now and then? As you know, Ange and I plan to wed, and she will surely need to know."

Napoleon laughed as he poured the wine. "My boy, what I am about to reveal to you is not to leave you. I will accept your oath of silence. They are bringing that bastard king back from England. Louis XVIII is to restore Bourbon rule back into my France. We guillotined his brother, and if I were he, I would be afraid of the same thing. This galls me terribly. I go into my exile, but there are powers here in France that will keep me apprised of all here. One day soon I will return, Henri, rebuild my Armée and return France to her former glory. This exile period will not last that long. In the interim, however, I perfectly understand your feelings and will see to it that troops are rotated home as we can. I might have to ask that you carry messages to and fro, but that is only for those in whom I have complete trust. Does this ease your burden?"

"Oui, Excellency. I am greatly relieved, and I know Ange will be too. I am yours for as long as you require. I will relate only that I will be free to come home."

"Merci, Henri. When we finally do get to Elba, I will call on you from time to time just for a chat if you do not mind. I get so lonesome for Andre. I will blame myself for his death and that of my Armée for as long as I live. Please do give my fondest regards to Vivien and Ange."

Ange was upset, to say the least. "Henri, I am so frustrated. I know you are to leave in two days, but where is this Elba place, and how long do you think it will be until I can see you again? I don't want to worry you, but I love you so much and want to be with you. Is there a remote chance we could be married right away and I go with you? Oh, I know that is foolish, and I should not have said that. I will wait until eternity if I must." She put her head on his shoulder and cried.

He patted her head, but nothing could console either of them at this point. He was a soldier, and he knew he must do his duty. "Sweetheart, I do not know how long this will go on. I only know that I love you beyond all things. Your welfare and safety is ultimate. It is bad enough being the daughter of a general in the Grande Armée, but married to a member of Napoleon's personal guard.

The allies would have a grand time with that and possibly think of terrible harm for you. I could never forgive myself."

"I understand, Henri, it is just that I love and want you so badly."

That night they sat in their usual place talking and holding hands. It was another peaceful night except they knew the allies were in Paris, Napoleon was a captive, and Henri must leave tomorrow. They were trying their best to remain calm, and the nervous chatter was but a cover-up to the morning dawn and what the day would bring.

Suddenly Ange stood up, took both of Henri's hands, and said, "I love you, man of my life." She released his hands, took a step back, closed the door, and started to unfasten the buttons on her dress. The dress slid to the floor at her feet. There was nothing underneath, and she stood before him like a naked goddess. Henri gasped and rose. He took her in his arms without a word. They kissed, their lips parted, as tongues sought tongues and danced over lips.

"No fair," she said as she tugged at his belt. His pants dropped to the floor, and she helped him out of his shirt. They embraced again. Ange pulled him toward the bed. They lay against each other kissing in labored gasps, feeling each other's bodies, exploring. Henri kissed her neck, throat, and down to the nipples of her bare breasts. Ange was moaning slightly. As he started to pull her to him, a barking dog, a squealing cat in the yard below, and a loudly shouting neighbor jolted them back to reality. They parted ever so slowly. Henri rolled onto his back trying to catch his breath. Ange did the same with an arm over his chest.

"Oh, mon amour," he said, "I will never forget this night. This is the first time I have seen you like this. I will never forget. Your lovely image is burned in my memory."

"And your image in mine," she said. "I think we both needed this moment. I would have gladly let you take me. I know we both promised, but I wanted you so." She started to cry through the frustration of the moment and knowledge of his leaving again.

Henri pulled her to his nakedness, and they embraced. "Don't cry, mon amour. I am yours forever. I know we are both embarrassed, but this will be our secret. I love you so much, and I can't live without you, Ange. Please don't cry. I feel so helpless."

Her hot wet tears fell on his chest as she pulled the light blanket over them and snuggled closer.

33

Elba and Exile

With the dawn, Henri and Michael saddled their horses and rode in silence for the palace. "This is another very difficult parting for me, Michael. It seems the past two years have all been adieu and very little *saluant*. God only knows when we will get back. Exile seems so permanent." Henri remembered what Napoleon had told him, that this would not last that long. Mon dieu, he hoped so.

It was just after Avril 11, 1814, and the Treaty of Fontainebleau. There was a contingency of troops both French and members of the allies at the palace as they arrived. The allies were under the personal command of Colonel Monsieur Neil Campbell, the British allied commissioner detailed to arrest Napoleon and who had done so at Fontainebleau Palace. Henri was told the rumor that Napoleon had tried to commit suicide by drinking a potion of opium, belladonna, and hellebore; but the poison only made him retch. Henri had heard too that the official report of Napoleon's arrest found him to be frustrated, despondent, and pacing the length of his apartment like some wild animal. Knowing the energy of Napoleon, Henri could only imagine the frustration of falling from the most powerful man in Europe, or indeed the entire world, to one of captivity and exile.

As they arrived at the palace, they were made to dismount, surrender their horses, and join the group of French troops. Thank God Satan was safe in Lithuania, thought Henri. There were British troops everywhere and probably numbered several hundred. Henri counted the French troops at only thirty-five. An officer took the roster of the French. Carriages and wagons loaded with Napoleon's personal belongings began to assemble just outside the palace walls. The emperor and several senior staff officers, including his loyal generals Bertrand and Drouot, came out and quickly entered one of the carriages. Other

French troops got in the other carriages. They would not even be able to ride and were to be herded in the carriages like so many pigs. Henri had heard the isle of Elba was near Tuscany off the coast of Italy. With the mass of their allied escort, one would fear this could be a last journey to nowhere. Michael said as much as the French were allowed no arms other than personal sabres. Henri and Michael were lucky and had a carriage with only two others. They could imagine if they would have had to ride in the wagons. Some were covered, and some were not. The other carriages were crowded with weary souls at nearly twice the normal capacity. It grew warmer as the sun rose in the sky that April day. There was a fairly stiff breeze, thank God, from the west and the distant ocean. That afternoon, they were blessed with a drenching thunderstorm. The long snake of wagons and carriages slowly made their way southward toward the coast of France. The word was that their destination would be Marseille and then by ship to the island of Elba. Merde! At this rate, it may take a week to get there.

Actually it was four days; and for three of the days, they went straight through, only stopping for meals, stretch the legs and limbs, and the necessaries of nature. During the late afternoon of the fourth day, the caravan reached Marseille and made straight for the waterfront. No stopping in the city. The weather was clear, and only scant clouds were evident. With the sun starting to settle on the western horizon, the French were told they could bed down for the night as best they could but were not allowed to leave the group. A British warship, the *Undaunted*, was in the harbor and would take them to Elba Island, a short day's sail.

"Mon dieu, it is good to get out of that damn bouncing box on wheels. I hate carriage rides," complained Henri.

"I agree, mon ami. My legs are in knots. I will have to learn to walk all over again if you will pull them straight for me," agreed Michael.

They were served hardtack and water. It was all they would be served to eat. Later, a wagon came around with wine. Henri snatched two bottles when the fellow handing out the wine was distracted by Michael and looked away for a moment.

"Ha," said Michael, "this will improve the sleeping this evening."

"And will enhance a good headache in the morning too. What is this stuff? It smells like the bottom of the wine vat after stomping."

"Hold your nose and guzzle, mon ami. Take big gulps," laughed Michael.

And they did. And they slept well. And the predicted headache pounced on them the next morning. The wagons came by again and served hardtack, water, and wine.

"Merde, is this all they have? This hardtack is almost worse than those damn river rocks. It tastes as if we are chewing on rotten logs or worse."

Shortly after sunrise, two smaller British ships arrived and lowered their sails, and the sailors were busy with ropes at the dockside. This would be their total escort. The allies were taking no chances. Gangplanks were put over to the dock, and the troops lined up to load the contents of the supply wagons. They were a sorry-looking lot and knew it. Their uniforms were wrinkled and dirty. They had not bathed in days, and the hot, sweaty carriage ride did not help with the foul body odors. Most were miserable and could not wait to get to wherever they were going and some semblance of a wash and rest. This Elba Island must be a rathole of a place to have been picked by the allies.

What should have been a pleasant day's sail turned into an all-day-and-into-the-late-evening episode due to winds and the ships having to tack into it. Most of the nonseafaring French became seasick. Henri and Michael were no exception. Many were lining the rails, and the lower deck was awash with the foul results. They were made to haul buckets of seawater and throw over it.

"Oh, Henri, I am so sick. I have been on boats before, but not like this. I know I have thrown up my guts and toenails too."

Finally late that afternoon, Elba Island rose on the horizon. Napoleon was heard to say to his staff and those close by, "My god, my god! Able was I ere I saw Elba." They steered into the harbor of Portoferraio, and the ships neared a small wharf area. From what Henri could see from the ship, Elba Island was not a rathole. Indeed, it looked like paradise.

The weather had cleared, and the sky was a solid blue with no clouds visible against the setting sun. The rising hills were lush with vegetation and dotted with the red tile roofs of houses and buildings. The climate was very pleasant, a bit warm, but pleasant. They soon went down the gangplanks loading the supplies and personal effects in more wagons for a trip to somewhere. There was a mass of fishing boats near the wharf. Henri could see numerous fishermen going about their tasks of readying their boats for the night, repairing nets and other boats, and the thousand and one things fishermen do.

On the other side of the wharfs were large buildings with chimneys. Smoke was rising from several. Henri asked a nearby curious bystander about them and was told that this was the ironworks and had been in existence since the days of the Romans here. There were quite a few deposits of iron ore on the island, and the smelters were involved in manufacturing everything from weapons to everyday household items.

There was an enthusiastic large crowd of local officials and what appeared to be the entire town to greet them at the large main square. Napoleon's title as emperor of Elba made this a sovereign state under his jurisdiction.

They formed ranks to march through the town and toward the hills. The ever-present watchdog British troops were escorting them. The hills rose in a slow incline from the town proper to a large palace overlooking the entire scene below. Evidently this is where they were going. Maybe there was a bathing area nearby. Henri itched and was by now, in this heat, getting a rash in the areas of his private parts. They marched through the center of town and the large central square with a large ornate Romanesque church on one side. The houses were mostly small, and all had the predominant red tile roofs. Henri could see other farmhouses nestled in the hills as they made their climb.

Their destination was the large palace high on the hill. The view was spectacular and had an excellent overlook of the harbor and town with the clear blue of the ocean as a backdrop. The mountains, some nearing one thousand meters, seemed to drop directly into the ocean. Napoleon and his staff officers went to the main palace building while the guard unit was shown their quarters just behind. There were three imposing stone buildings in the group. Two large two-story stone buildings and one a bit smaller. The smaller was the stable, and the other two would be the quarters. The kitchen area and dining hall comprised the bottom floor of one of the larger ones.

The smells wafting from the kitchen reminded Henri that he was hungry. The excitement of the journey had taken away some of the hunger pangs. Oh to have Mimi here! They were assigned rooms with officers having personal rooms on the upper floor over the kitchen. This would be handy for forays to the kitchen in the wee hours if needed. The second larger building was in dormitory settings with each soldier having only a footlocker for personal things. The cooks and servants would be housed here too. So this was to be home for the time being. It really wasn't that bad.

After the meal, the officers were told to go to the stable and choose a mount. So they were going to have mounts after all. Henri chose a medium-sized black. Michael came in later and chose a black with a large white spot on the nose.

"I think I will call him Spot," he said.

The saddles and other riding gear were in terrible shape, and sufficient effort would be required to get them back into the semblance of military order. The entire mounted troop would consist of only ten men led by Henri. Michael was his sergeant. They were the escort in the event Napoleon had to journey to town. But that was all, only escort duties, and just for show. There were several more infantry to serve the same purpose.

"Ha! Mon ami, this is a far cry from our Faucons, but it will have to do," said Henri. Of all of the two hundred plus of the Faucons, Henri and Michael were the only two left. A couple of others had stayed in Lithuania, but that was all of the living ones. The remainder were resting in the snows of Russia or died on the march to get there.

That afternoon, they were given permission to go to the bay and bathe. The bathing facilities were very primitive at the quarters, consisting only of wooden tubs and no one to fill them. The bay would be much better. They would go in sections, and Henri's group was lucky and in the first section. There were no provisions for drying, of course, and they would just have to drip-dry. One of the men was heard to say, "Do they expect us to just shake like dogs?"

If the troops were bitching, they were happy, Henri remembered from some of the general's words of wit and wisdom. They went to a private beach area with sparse vegetation and white sand. But the water was very pleasant, warm, and soothing for the soul. As they were splashing in the waves, Henri noticed how white their bodies were. The entire group was nearly snow white. One of the men said they were as white as a fish belly. After about an hour, they were the color of the tile roofs.

As they started to don clothes for the trip back to the quarters, Henri remarked to some of the others, "My skin feels as though someone has boiled it. What a stupid thing to do."

They were not used to the hot Tuscan sun and the clarity of the atmosphere. It did not take long to cook a fair skin in these regions. They would learn. The medical orderly, laughing at the episode, gave them olive oil from the kitchen. That helped some of the burning, as he told them that it would take a few days, but they would survive. Michael and several others had been lying on their backs nude and were very concerned with their semicooked private part. Henri's was too, but not nearly as bad. Michael swore he saw his starting to cook with the oil. They all laughed. As time would progress over the months, they would become a golden brown.

Henri's small room was furnished with a single bed, a small table, a chair, and a wall locker for clothes. The furniture was rustic and very old, but adequate for the stay here. He attempted to polish the desk and chair but finally gave up and accepted the age of the furniture. A window provided scenery of the mountainside below all the way to the sea. Several trees obscured the view some, but it was still spectacular.

Henri had Ange's picture on the desk along with a small vase that he put a fresh flower in every day. Today seemed special in that he had a red flower which accented the gold frame and Ange's dark hair. He could almost sense her presence as he stared at the picture and the scene below for some time. He was lonesome and homesick and wondered how long this exile would go on. It sounded so permanent and long lasting. One year, two years? Would they be old and gray before they left? And what of Ange and the marriage plans? Thinking of these things only made him more miserable, but he could not help himself.

As was Henri's curious nature, and to pass the boring time, he studied the area of his posting for local history and culture of the people. Elba Island was excellent for such. He had ample time to question the cooks, local shopkeepers, local priests, and certain people of influence and even spend time visiting at the fishing boat docks.

Elba Island had been inhabited long before Roman times, and the principal industry was the mining of iron ore and the subsequent ironworks. A particular high quality of iron weapons was much sought after by the Romans and others. And of course, there was the usual wine, olive oil, and fruits. The island had seen many rulers over the years and was now a part of the French Empire. Elba consisted of some 223 square kilometers and was about 10 kilometers from the Italian mainland and Tuscan coast. The weather was pleasant for most of the year with only occasional storms during the winter months. Had the circumstances been different, this would have been paradise. Henri wished for Ange. If she could only come here, the picture would be complete.

Napoleon busied himself with any project to occupy his time and involved all around him. Henri was no exception. Often he and his men were detailed to supervise one project or another. Napoleon's energy seemed to know no bounds, and he directed changes here as he had directed the change of an entire continent. He had his staff draw up plans for a road system, courts of law, a theater, and various other projects. The allies were very generous with payments in gold coins and hoped Napoleon was on Elba to stay.

That Aout, Napoleon's mother, the foreboding Letizia, known as Madame Mère, moved to the island. Napoleon sent message after message pleading with his wife, Marie Louise, to visit and bring their young son. There was never any reply. Napoleon knew that the situation was controlled by his mother-in-law, the empress of Austria.

Letizia was of medium size with the dark hair and eyes of their Corsican lineage. Her eyes appeared to pierce the depths of the soul as she spoke. Her hair was always drawn back in a severe bun at the back of her head and held in place with combs. She must have had a large variety of combs for she was never seen with the same one in several weeks wearing. Some said she was strange and could read thoughts of others.

Whether or not, she was a commanding person and demanded respect even from her son, the emperor. She had borne thirteen children, five of whom had died at early ages. She dressed mostly in blacks, reds, and greens; and always her gowns were ankle length. She did wear some jewelry, but it was never in the gaudy styles worn by many at court. She was a very religious and devout woman and expected all about her to be the same. Henri had met her before in Paris but had never talked to her at length, only in passing courtesy. He felt this was one to be wary of and kept at length.

In due time, the palace was finished to Napoleon's satisfaction. The projects of roads and the courts of law were under way, and Napoleon seemed bored again with this confined life. He went riding every afternoon; and often Henri, or several of the troop, would accompany him. On one of the excursions through the hills farther than they had been before, Napoleon observed an abandoned farm that was falling into ruin and decay. It had evidently been very lavish in its day, but now time was taking its toll. Napoleon rode up to the main house and went inside. It was huge with very large formal rooms and what appeared to be large living quarters all along one side. To Henri, the place was a ruin, but Napoleon kept on and on with changes that could be made. The more he looked, the more excited he became.

"Henri, look at this beautiful fountain in the central courtyard. Very little needs to be done with it. And look at the size of the great hall and rooms. This could be magnificent."

The basic stucco walls of the house and buildings were in fairly good shape and would need only patching and painting. The interior did consist of huge rooms, one being a grand ballroom of sorts. The terrace went completely around the house and had access to many of the interior rooms by large glass doors. The huge yard could become a park, and he went on and on. They stayed nearly two hours with Napoleon making mental notes of this or that.

"Henri, this will become a hideaway for me. I have always wanted to do this, and now is the time. Look at the view all the way to the ocean. It is magnificent. I must have it."

And he did. His sister sold an overvalued pearl necklace to an Italian noble and gave him the money. He had given it to her in the first place after "finding" it on one of his conquests somewhere. In addition, she sent her personal gardener to transform the surrounding grounds. Work began immediately, and Napoleon and Henri made the ride every day to check the results. Things never went as Napoleon wished, and when rants and raves proved to no avail to the local laborers, promises of handsome bonus for extra effort did. The results were amazing to Henri. At one point, nearly one hundred fifty workmen and artists worked at their tasks.

All of the walls of the main house were painted with frescoes of different scenes directed by Napoleon. In one room, the ceiling was painted as pearls to honor his sister who had sold the necklace. The ceiling in the dining room was painted with love knots held up by doves. He said this was in honor of his wife, Marie Louise, whom he was trying to entice to visit him here. In the largest room, the one he called his Egyptian Room, the walls were painted with Egyptian columns, hieroglyphics, and symbols. The large area surrounding the house was transformed into a thing of beauty. The grounds were now a park with flowers and gardens everywhere. Small buildings had been erected at strategic places for one to sit discreetly and watch the sunrise or sunset. Henri thought the place was magic and said so to Napoleon many times. Henri was not fooled though and knew this place was to replace his greatly missed Malmaison.

Often Henri would sit in one of the private places and contemplate the future and how he missed his Ange. One day, some four months after their arrival, Henri was sitting in his usual spot watching the sun set over the western horizon. The colors and hues of reds, yellows, purples with the clouds drifting over it was a spectacular sight. He never tired of the sunrise or sunset. It was his private time to think. Napoleon rode up and dismounted.

"Well, my friend, you seem at peace with the world. May I join you?"

"Of course, Your Excellency. I would enjoy the good company. We haven't had much time for a visit since our arrival."

"Oui, I know, my young friend. We each have been busy trying to stay busy. But, Henri, please do not be fooled with all of my busy days. I am like a horse tied to a post with wanting to return to France and save it from the mad king and his cronies. All of this activity is but a farce to fool the allies into complacency. When the time is right, I will make my move. Meanwhile, I do need your services in the form of a messenger to Paris. If you cannot go, let me know, and I will find someone else."

Henri jumped up, exclaiming, "Majesty, will I go! I will swim at once if you say the word."

Napoleon laughed and said, "I know you want to go. I know how you must miss Ange as I miss my wife and child. I fear I shall never see them again. That old bitch, her mother, controls everything around her. She will never let her visit me here. Come see me early in the morning, Henri. I have messages written for you to memorize. I have cleared your departure with the allies, stating only that your leave period is at this time. You should leave on the weekly supply ship tomorrow afternoon."

"Your Majesty, you have made me alive again. I cannot tell you how much this means."

"Oh, but I do know, Henri, and I do need the messages. Come tomorrow." He laughed at Henri's enthusiasm and excitement, mounted his horse, and rode back along the trail.

Henri was going home. Thank God! Henri literally floated back to the barracks on clouds of anticipation. Henri slept fitfully that night with the excitement of travel home and to Ange. He rose very early and was sitting on the large porch with a cup of coffee when Michael came out, rubbing his eyes. He had his mug of coffee too.

"My, aren't you the early bird this morning. Careful you don't catch a worm. What in hell would you do with one if you did catch it?"

"Michael, don't tell a soul. I am going to Paris on this afternoon's supply ship. It will only be for a short leave, but this means all the world to me. Is there anything you need from home, or can I do anything for you while there?"

"Henri, I am so glad for you. I don't need anything that I can think of at the moment. Please do try to see Ange, though, and tell her how much I miss her and love her."

"I will be most happy, my worthy brother and partner in crime. Someday I'll stick you in the ass with my sabre."

Henri reported to Napoleon in the next few hours and was given instructions of whom to see, a password, and the messages. He would be given return messages for memorization and return to Napoleon. He was cautioned this was a highly secret mission, and he must tell no one. Napoleon had trusted him with much and was aware of his complete loyalty.

Henri was given a letter by the allied commander of the island. The letter would be his passage on the ship and while in France. He was informed he would catch the mail carriage on arrival in Marseille and be in Paris in less than two days. This was the official mail and message carriage and went straight through with only limited stops to change horses and food and to do the necessaries of nature. Merde! Another damn long carriage ride, but this would be a good one.

In Paris, Ange had been busy fighting with herself, her conscience, and her future as the wife of Henri. She had not a reason of doubt as to her love for this man and had lived for his love and to be his wife. It was her destiny since a young girl. However, the last scene of their lovemaking and the fact of almost losing all self-control troubled this girl with a strict Catholic upbringing. She tried to consider all things and consequences. If only Henri were here. He would understand more than anyone. After only partially confiding in Mimi, she decided to visit Father Etty. She could trust him for sage advice as only a relative in religion could. But how to tell this man all their problems and what had actually transpired? She knew the only way was honesty.

Ange left the next morning for the nearly half hour's walk to Father Etty's church. The day was a bright one, and the heat had not become an issue this early in the year. As she walked along the Seine and over into the city, she carefully reflected on what she would say. It had to come out right, and she did not need any further confusion added to her mind.

Madame's cousin, Father Etty, had visited their home often when in need of a good meal, get away from his duties, or just to enjoy pleasant company. He had been one of the general's favorites. The two had often shared stories together accompanied by too much wine and laughter. She started several times to turn around and go back home but knew this must be done for her own peace of mind. Arriving at the back of the church where she knew the livings quarters were, she rang the bell on the wall next to the huge wooden doors. After a time, an aged man in the cloak of a priest opened one of the doors. She asked to see Father Guillot and was admitted.

"Angelette, what a pleasant surprise! Come in, please. Would you like coffee or some sweet cakes? What brings you all the way over here? I hope it isn't bad news."

"No, Father. No ill news, but I do need advice as only I feel you will understand." She told him the events of her and Henri sleeping together nude and their almost losing control with sex. She burst into tears, telling him of her love for Henri and wanting him so much. Of course, Father Etty knew Henri well and what a fine man he had become.

"My child, I am not at all surprised at what you are telling me. The fact that you did not indulge in the flesh other than what you have told me is commendable. Let's have some coffee and go on the terrace where we will be comfortable and can talk. I need a little time to think of the proper answers for you. Now stop crying, child. All will be well, I promise."

They took their coffee in large mugs and a small plate of sweet cakes and went on the terrace overlooking the small central square at the rear of the priest's quarters. It was now nearing midmorning, and the square was buzzing with activity. Several fruit and vegetable carts were doing a thriving business. The smell of fresh bread wafted over the area as if to advertise the bakery on one side of the square. They sat for a time chatting about small things, family, and local gossip. Ange was getting anxious about her reason for being here.

Finally, Father Etty approached the subject. "Angelette, what I have to say is probably not what you would like to hear. I have known you and Henri since you were children, and you are correct that I know and understand more than most what is happening. Henri has been called to duty more than his share of times, and this does not help with the problem. I understand your love and the frustration of not fulfilling that love. What the two of you have done is certainly not entirely wrong and not a mortal sin. I would consider this a borderline venial and mortal sin. This sin will lead to a mortal sin if future actions are consummated. Both of you are only mortals with instincts driven by a powerful love.

"You can have absolution only if you will try to avoid these situations in the future. I know Henri is a man of honor and will honor your request. He is probably troubled by the same things and would do nothing in his power to bring dishonor to either of you. Your secret is safe with me as I consider this conversation a confession of sorts. I will not mention this visit. As a matter of fact, Vivien and I discussed these same things sometime ago. I know how troubled you are with this. So please come back anytime if you need. Does this seem to ease you at all?"

"Oui, Father. It does, and you can't imagine how it is to share this burden. Merci so much for understanding and being here for Henri and me. I must go now. I know how busy you are with things in the church, and it is a long walk back home." She rose to leave, and Father Etty gave her a hug.

"Go with God, my child. Please come again. But you know, this visit has made me realize I have been hungry for some of Mimi's fine cuisine. I will try to come over in a week or two."

The supply ship docked in Marseille late in the evening just before dark. Henri was met by an allied officer inquiring who he was and why he was on the ship. The officer did not speak French very well, but when Henri presented the letter, all seemed well. The mail carriage was waiting for the ship, and he would have to ride with the mail pouch and some things for Paris. They would leave within the hour. Henri was the only passenger and had the coach to himself.

Midway through the late evening, the relief driver came in for a nap. He would be driving through most of the night. He immediately went to sleep, and Henri could smell the stench of wine on him. Little wonder he needed a nap. Henri fell asleep soon after the relief driver, rocked to sleep by the sway of the carriage. Nearing morning, they stopped at a small inn to eat and change horses. Henri wolfed his sausage and hard bread washed down with several mugs of coffee. He was hungrier than he realized. He took several small loaves with him and refilled his flask with water.

The carriage swayed and bounced its way all through the day, rumbling through small villages and the wide-open farmland of southern France. They thundered over small bridges and larger ones, over streams with no names. It was hot, dry, and dusty this time of the year. It evidently had not rained for some time.

Henri reflected on another hot and dusty afternoon so far back in his past. He pondered on his mother, Marcel, Aunt Mags, and the rest in his early years. He must return to investigate one day. It seemed at times he could almost smell Paris, the Seine, and Ange's fragrant perfume. She had changed several times over the years but always returned to her favorite. To Henri, the scent was like no other. It was like fresh morning blossoms drenched with dew, so clean and fresh.

They stopped at noon for another hasty meal, another change of horses, and on again. This was indeed a fast ride home. Late that evening at the next stop, Henri was informed due to the excellent weather they were making more than usual time and would arrive the next afternoon.

Henri again slept through most of the night, waking at times when they hit a deep rut in the road or thundered over a bridge. The villages were becoming more frequent as they neared Paris. The noon stop was at a fairly large inn filled with soldiers of France also eating there. One of the officers came over to Henri and asked about his uniform.

"What is your unit, mon capitaine? I haven't seen the uniform or insignia before."

"I am with Napoleon on the isle of Elba. I am assigned to his personal guard."

"Our emperor! Is he well? We get so little news of him these days. In all honesty, most in the military long for the old days and his leadership. This new army is not an army at all. It is only a dictated thing by the allies and their puppet king. Have you been with him long?"

"For most of my military career, through officer école, and his wars after. I was very fortunate to make it back from Russia."

"And I, mon ami, and I. I left so many friends there. Please wish His Majesty well and God bless."

It was good for Henri to hear these things. It only stabilized his belief that Napoleon would escape this exile and return France to its former glory. True to their word, the drivers steered the carriage through the outskirts of Paris late that afternoon. Henri was beside himself. He went from windows on each side of the carriage and finally saw the spires of Notre Dame glowing in the sunset. He could almost visualize where the house was in relation.

The carriage made a final stop at the large building housing the allied headquarters in Paris. Henri would have to walk the last blocks home, but that was good. His legs were cramped, and his wounded one seemed to have a deep ache. Not a bad ache, but just a slight presence to let him know the leg was still there. He wondered how long the leg would give him problems. He gathered his shoulder bag, checked out with the duty officer, and walked along the Seine. It was dark now, and the street lamps were just being lit. A few people were out, but most were home and enjoying an evening meal. There were a few ladies of the night out trying to get an early start to the area where they plied their wares. Small cafés along his route were at near capacity, and he could hear the revelry.

Henri entered the de Chabot Street and opened the large iron gate. The front door was never locked. After all, who in their right mind would try to enter the house of a general? It had always been so. With the way things were these days, Henri felt he must caution them to bolt, at least, the doors. There were all sorts of derelicts, mostly of the past Armée, prowling the streets. Not as much in this area, but still the danger was present. He peeked in the kitchen, and Mimi squealed and ran to hug him. Ange was sitting on the back porch drinking a cup of tea. She looked around and saw Henri. The tea went up in the air along with a saucer of sweet cakes as she ran squealing into his arms.

"Henri! You are here! I can't believe it. I wish I would have known. I am a disaster."

"You are the most beautiful creature I ever saw. I love you so much."

They hugged for a long time. Each other feeling the close presence of the other. Ange was crying with joy and Henri almost so. Mimi finally asked if the lovebird was hungry, and he realized he was. Madame had left for another visit to Orléans nearly a month now, and Ange was mistress of the house.

"Oui, Mimi, I think I could eat a whole chicken and wash it down with several liters of wine. I am starving. Come, Ange, please sit with me."

As he ate, he related that it was his time for a two-week leave at home. He would get one every six months. He told her all of the news of Elba Island and what a paradise it was. During the conversation, Ange related that she had some bad news for him.

Evidently he had not heard Josephine had died. He was startled. Ange said Madame and she had attended the small ceremony at Saint-Pierre-Saint-Paul in Rueil several kilometers from Malmaison, her palatial home. There was only a sparse crowd, some of her friends, some curiosity seekers, and none of the new ruling clan of snobs. Ange was surprised Henri had not heard of Josephine's death. She further mentioned there were spies everywhere, and she was certain both Madame and she were on some sort of watch list somewhere at the palace. Well, so be it.

After eating, he was much more tired than he realized and begged off to go to bed. He went to the backwater trough for a quick wash and to get the dust off. Ange was right there with him every step of the way. She stated he was home, was hers for two weeks, and she wasn't about to let him out of her sight. They went upstairs, and Henri stripped off his boots and pants.

"Henri, look how brown you are. Why, you look like one of the servants they bring in from Africa and the islands at times."

"I know, beautiful white one. I am brown all over too. Do you want to see?"

She blushed and hugged him tightly.

"Go to sleep, mon amour. We can talk tomorrow."

A quick kiss of her luscious lips and she was gone. Henri did not remember getting into bed and going to sleep.

34

The Mission

Henri awoke early the next morning, so stiff he realized he must have died in place and not moved much during the night. Feeling drained physically and emotionally with being home, he silently promised himself to do nothing that required any stress other than his mission. He must get on that this day and donned shirt, pants, and old slop shoes. Ha! No boots today, and it was a welcome relief. When he peeked in Ange's room, he saw her sleeping peacefully. She truly was an angel. He watched her for a few minutes and marveled at how fortunate he was to be here with her. Meeting Mimi in the kitchen, he enjoyed his usual mug of coffee and cakes.

"Henri, it is so good to have you here with us. It has been unusually lonely with just knowing poor Andre is gone and now Madame off to Orléans. She just hasn't the courage to stay here much anymore, and I can't say I blame her. Friends come as often as they can, but with the new rulers of our land and the spies all over, everyone seems afraid to go as they once did. Madame still receives the general's wages or whatever they call it.

"The école is still open, and Jean is there, but there is no place for him in the present military with him being the general's son. Did you know that just after you left, men came here and wanted to know about the general, Madame, Jean, Ange, and even me and the other servants? They inquired about you and seemed very interested that you were with Napoleon. I am sure we are all watched. We heard later that they had been doing this all over Paris and possibly France itself. It is a sad time for us all. But now tell me how you have been and about this place where you are now."

He told her all about Elba and life there. It wasn't so bad, but he couldn't be home. At this time of his life and wanting to be married, he was very lonely at times. He was told that Ange was lonely too. Mimi had seen her many evenings sitting on the large back porch drinking her tea and watching the sun set. Often she spent the night in Henri's room hugging his pillow. Henri felt very badly about this and wondered if he could marry Ange and take her to Elba. He would approach the subject with Napoleon on his return.

Ange came into the room with her hair already combed and just a hint of lip rouge. She really did not need any more than that with her fair skin and enhancing eyes.

"Well, Mr. Early Bird, I am ready for whatever you have planned for the day. I was surprised you were up this early. You were snoring before your head hit the pillow last evening."

"Mon amour, I want to do nothing today, and it would be my extreme pleasure for you to join me. We can walk the Seine, go to Notre Dame, visit shops and restaurants, and just generally enjoy life. Care to go?"

"Will I! Let's go now."

Henri laughed. Mimi giggled, saying, "Nothing will be awake this early except a few pigeons near the church. Besides, you need to get something for the morning meal."

After midmorning, they did leave. Henri was dressed in his old sloppy civilian clothes and in no way resembled the position he held. Ange was dressed in one of her favorite blue dresses and was careful to wear her "wandering" shoes as she called them.

They walked down to the river and along the bank to the bridge that led to the church and the large square with the shops and cafés. Henri made a silent note of the café he must visit for his contact. They stopped at several shops where Ange bought ribbon and a few sewing things. She explained that in addition to teaching her to cook, Mimi had been teaching the fine arts of a seamstress. Henri never had realized Mimi was multitalented and thought of her only as a cook. These were things a good wife must know, she said.

That brought up the subject of their marriage again, and as they sat in a small sidewalk café, Henri told her what he had thought of about taking her to Elba. Ange said she had mixed emotions about that. What kind of life would they and she have? And for how long? She said they would discuss it further and at great length, but asked to be given a chance to think on it. They had a small lunch of a bowl of leek-and-onion soup, bread, sweet cakes, and tea. They sat for some time, each catching up on the other's lives and just enjoying the day.

"Oh, Henri, please forgive me. I visited Lydie last week. With all of the recent whirlwind of events, I totally have forgotten. She had the baby, a little boy. Jean-Claude was there with both her and his parents. They were all so proud. Jean-Claude is working in some sort of capacity with his father. Of course, all military things are out for them now, but his father does own a trading company. They only vaguely mentioned Napoleon, until I told them where you were. They opened up some but were still secretive. Jean-Claude said for you to please come and see them when you returned. He knew you had gone to the Russias, but not much more. I shared some of your news. I hope that was all right. I am so sorry to tell you that your friend from Saint-Cyr, Francis, was also in the Russias. They have never heard what happened and have never heard from him."

"Of course, Ange. I hold no secrets from anyone especially you. You can tell whomever and whatever to our friends. Poor Francis. I have not seen him since Saint-Cyr, but he was a good friend. I wish him peace. I saw thousands go, and I hope he went without pain. I will try to see Jean-Claude, but I do not want to take time away from you. It is just too precious to me."

After the leisurely lunch, Henri suggested they visit shops nearer the center of town. He secretly knew this was where the café Or Oie (gold goose) was located, and he must make contact today to set up a meeting. They visited several shops, and Henri saw the sign of the café across the way on the corner. *How appropriate*, he thought, *the goose that laid the golden eggs*. Henri said he was tired, and he really was and knew Ange also needed a rest. It had been quite a day already, and they still had a fairly long walk back home. They decided to sit on the small terrace on the far corner out of the sun and where there was a slight breeze. The waiter came over. Henri inquired if Monsieur Cheval was there. There was no Monsieur Horse there, of course, but the inquiry started a chain of events.

"Monsieur," the waiter laughed, "but if you will follow me, I will show you to the men's accommodations. Would the lady like to seek similar?"

Ange replied, "Oui, please."

They followed the waiter to a small set of stairs leading to the second floor. Ladies to the left and men to the right, announced the waiter. A man of slight build wearing the apron of a cook entered with Henri.

"Monsieur, may I assist you? You have given the word of one of us."

"Oui, please. I am Capitaine Henri Devreney with Napoleon on Elba. I have reasons to contact a Monsieur Dronet for an exchange of messages. I am living at the residence of General de Chabot on the other side of the Seine."

"Ah, oui, we know the residence well. You will be contacted later this evening for a rendezvous with Monsieur Dronet. We have been expecting a communication."

Henri met Ange in the hallway, and they returned to their table. Henri realized that he should share this secret messenger business with her. He would think on it, but he certainly did not want any harm to come to her on his account. But she did have the right to know the true nature of his visit and any impending events on their future and marriage. They left the restaurant after another leisurely cup of tea and a small plate of hard biscuits and pate.

Later that evening, the front doorbell clanged as it was twisted back and forth. Henri said he would see who that might be and went to the door. "Oui, monsieur, may I be of assistance?" inquired Henri to the same man he had met in the upstairs of the restaurant.

"I have been assigned as your contact since we use visual recognition for the very important messages. Can you meet with Monsieur Dronet this evening? If so, a carriage will be here in precisely one hour."

Henri replied to the affirmative and knew he would need to share this with Ange now. Henri briefly told Ange of his mission. She was very curious but knew these were men things. The general's daughter had had an upbringing of such matters. Almost precisely to the hour, the carriage arrived, and the driver rang the bell for Henri. Monsieur Dronet was in the carriage, the driver announced. Dronet was mostly in darkness and said he preferred it that way. There was numbing silence until they departed the de Chabot Street.

"So, Henri, you are the fabled Bébé Tigre I remember hearing so much about you a few years ago. You have come far since. I was in the cabinet of Napoleon here in Paris and was present at your medal ceremony. But of course, you would not have remembered as I was but a spectator. I remember Andre well, and he was a loyal and dear friend. Please remember me, and if you ever need anything, please let me know. What message do you have from my emperor?"

Henri told him the memorized messages of really nothing except the frustration of being on Elba Island, being a mock emperor, and wanting to come back at the first opportunity.

"Well, I do have some news, and I hope our Short One can be patient just a bit longer. There is much unrest in France these days. That stupid plaything-king of the allies and his cronies are trying to establish royal rule again and having little success other than with the Royalists. There is a huge middle class now that they are trying to suppress as before the revolution. Everything we can do to speed the unhappiness, believe me, we are doing. The movement to bring Napoleon back is growing by great leaps. However, we cannot hasten things too fast as the allies will get suspicious and try countermeasures. There are spies everywhere being well paid by the allies. We know of many and feed false information now and then to discredit them.

"At any rate, we have planned the rental of a small frigate and will get it to Elba on February 26 of next year in the wee hours. I wish this could occur sooner, but there are many underlying circumstances preventing an earlier date. We must not be hasty about this. This will be the target date for him to plan against, and if anything changes, we will see that he gets the information readily. Please tell the emperor that this is the very best we can do. These will be in the winter months, and the weather may just be of assistance. Otherwise, all is as before.

"The emperor has many loyal to him here, and we anxiously await his return. Please convey to him that we have contacted many of his military associates, and they are ready and willing to rejoin him. I hope this helps, mon ami. Are you and the general's daughter still planning to marry?"

"Oui, monsieur, and this information helps more than you can realize. I was actually planning to ask His Excellency if I could bring Ange to Elba. Now I shall wait until we return and settle again. It will be so much better, and we can have a proper marriage in Notre Dame as we want. May I do anything for you while I am here?"

"Nothing other than prayers of a swift resolution to all of this madness. Our carriage must be nearing the de Chabot Street again, and I will bid you well. Go with God."

"And you, mon ami."

Henri was overjoyed at the news. It would be another few months, and all would be back as it should.

He went into the house, and Ange inquired, "What was that all about, Henri? Why should you be called out in the darkness like some spy or something?"

"Come, my sweet. Let us have tea on the back porch. There are things you must know." They went into the kitchen and made cups of tea from the hot water kettle that was always on Mimi's stove. Ange delicately balanced the cup on her saucer as they went onto the back porch.

"Henri, honestly, I wish you would use a saucer. It is so much more mannered."

They went on the back porch. Ange kicked off her shoes and propped her pretty bare feet up on a small table.

"Ange, you have the prettiest feet in all of Paris, if not France."

"Don't try to change the subject about the saucer, and since when have you been looking at ladies' feet?"

"I always am aware of pretty feet, and I never could get used to a saucer. Besides, no one uses them where I am. Anyway, Ange, there are many things that I must share with you. I trust you with my life, but promise me you will never reveal any of this to a living soul. It is all extremely secret and has to do with our very future. I am here on a special mission for His Excellency, to take a message to those loyal to him and receive news and messages from here.

"What I have been told this evening concerns me greatly. I had planned to talk to you about going to Elba with me. It is a lovely place, and we could be happy there. Now I understand there is an escape planned for next February, and of course, I will be among those leaving. I do not know what to expect from there. Maybe more war. I just don't know."

"Henri, what you have told me I have been suspecting for some time. Several of mother's friends talk of the return of Napoleon, but I did not conceive it would be this soon. To be honest, I am overjoyed and can certainly wait for another few more months. God knows, it has been forever and a week now. And I have something to tell you too. What happened the last time you were home greatly troubled me. I made a special trip to Father Etty for advice and for my own peace of mind.

"I told him everything that happened between you and me. Well, he listened and said he understood having known both of us since we were children. He said we were destined to be husband and wife, but for our soul's sake, we must wait for the sex part. He advised not to get into situations where we would be tempted and get carried away. Can you understand any of this, mon amour? I want to be with you completely with all of my heart, but cannot damn us to hell for it."

"Oh, Ange, how could I hurt you? I have thought of this many times. I knew it was wrong to tempt both of us, but I just could not help myself. I never could keep my hands off you since we were children. But I always wanted to do it with honor and respect."

"I know, and Father Etty said the same. He considers you a man of honor, but did say we were only human and both involved in a powerful love. We will still visit in your room, and I do plan to sleep in your bed with you, but there will be no tempting to the point of having sex before we are married. That would hurt you and me, and I would never forgive myself. Merci for being my very special Henri and understanding."

She got up, sat on his lap, put her head on his shoulder, and cried softly. He patted her soft curls and cradled her in his arms. Tears were in his eyes too. Nothing was said. Mere words could never be sufficient. A sense of relief and peace overcame both of them. Henri had not known such peace in a long time.

The next week, Henri and Ange visited Jean-Claude and Lydie. They were staying in the house of her parents for the care of the baby and would move home as she became stronger. She had had a difficult birth but was getting stronger and better by the day. Jean-Claude was there taking time off from duties he described as clerical with his father in their business. Jean-Claude pulled at his sleeve after some minutes and motioned with his head. They went downstairs and sat in large chairs in the salon. Jean-Claude poured two large goblets of wine.

"Henri, my friend, I hear you are with 'him' on the island. Forgive the secrecy, but it is just part of life these days. The damn king and allies have spies all over. Even certain household servants are paid to inform. One never knows. I think we are safe enough here. Is there any encouraging news of his returning and relieving us all of this mess, or do you know? We hear rumors all of the time."

"Jean-Claude, I never hear anything except the rumors brewed by the solitude of those with us. I think they stir the merde just to have things to talk about. Ange told me about my old friend Francis. Did you know him?"

"His father worked with mine, and I only knew him in passing. He seemed like a nice fellow. His father was devastated as many were. There was much concern with no news for months. We only heard the horror stories from the retreat, but no real news of loved ones."

"There were just too many. Our poor Armée, for the most part, froze or starved to their deaths. There were many thousands that I saw. I very nearly was a casualty myself."

"Oui, I know. Ange did tell us about your wound and survival. I hear you are a capitaine now. Your incident with the revolt at the palace was the talk of all Paris at the time. How the hell do you manage to grab all of the glory for yourself and leave us poor vagabonds with none?" Jean-Claude laughed.

And the talk continued. "I am secretly thinking about the prospects of trying to book passage to the Americas, but we would have to wait until Lydie and the baby are stronger. My father and I have been stashing away hidden funds for just such a move. Indeed, many here are doing the same. There is a huge population of French people in New Orleans."

Henri had never heard of New Orleans. With his happy times at the convent in Orléans, a new one could not be that bad. He must remember this.

Jean-Claude reiterated over again things were going from bad to even worse here, and if Napoleon did not return, things could really get bad. "We are all trying to find some ray of hope," he said.

The time seemed to fly by, and with the twitch of his head, Father Time motioned it was time to return to Elba. True to her word, Ange and Henri had slept every night together. Other than the usual kissing and hugging, nothing had transpired. Several times, Henri would have been a guilty partner, but Ange always was the stronger and kept things as they should. They had spent nearly every waking minute and every sleeping minute together. Henri rose early the morning of leaving, and Ange was right there with him as he dressed and went downstairs to get coffee and something to eat.

"Henri, mon amour, no more goodbyes. Starting this morning I will say 'till you come home.' I really don't ever want to tell you 'adieu' again. It sounds so lasting and forever. I want to tell you 'until we meet again.'"

"It will be our agreement then, Ange. No more 'adieu,' not ever. I love you too much for any adieu. It shall be, as you say, 'until we meet again.' This time, both of us know it may well be in a few short months."

The carriage ride back to Marseille was routine, and all the way, Henri thought of how to tell Napoleon about Josephine. He knew Napoleon still loved her and would be deeply upset and hurt. The fact that the allies and his enemies had kept this from him would upset him even further. The date of February 26 could give him strength and possibly fortify him in his grief. The supply ship docked in the early afternoon, and Henri reported to Napoleon at once.

"Monsieur, I bring news both good and bad. I am very sorry to bear this to you, but the empress passed away in Mai."

"Mon dieu! And why was I not informed? That was several months ago. I should have been there. What is the news of her passing, Henri?"

"Only that she had a malady for some time and passed peacefully in her sleep. She is buried at a small church very near to Malmaison. She would have wanted that. To be near the place she so dearly loved. Monsieur, I am so sorry to be the one to bear this news. Please accept my deepest sympathy and prayers for her soul. She was very special to me too."

"Oui, you are right, of course. However, I shall never forgive those who withheld the information from me. You said bad and good news. Pray tell me the good now."

"I spoke to Monsieur Dronet at length. He reports there is much unrest and said you were aware of that. They are doing everything possible to stir more unrest. He said a small frigate had been chartered very secretly and would dock here at Elba on the night of Fevrier 26 next year. He said it had to be that long as many details are to be made that the particular night, and you will want to be fully prepared. He said you would understand."

Napoleon put his hand on Henri's shoulder and smiled. "Oui, I do, of course. There are many details to work out here for that night. Do not relate this to a soul, Henri. It means our going home, and I can be emperor again and not this plaything. I will start making plans at once. Go and get some rest, my boy, and merci with all of my being for the manner of which you bring me this news. Mon dieu, mon dieu. My lady, my lady. I should have been there. I will surely visit you when I return."

The next morning, Napoleon went to one of his favorite places of solitude. Everyone knew it was to mourn Josephine, and this had to be. He had loved her as no other. The monastery of the Sanctuary of the Madonna was high in the forest above the tiny village of Marciana. Henri and Napoleon had stumbled across the monastery while riding some months ago; and Napoleon had mentioned then this was a perfect place for solitude, peace, and reflections. The twelve monks had made them welcome and shared a tiny meal with them. Napoleon could be at peace here.

Three days later, he was back at his residence and once more his old self. His energy seemed boundless, and more projects were planned. He had several more secret conversations with Henri, telling him that most of this activity was a diversion to keep the allies thinking he was happy and doing well. He did write a passionate letter to the allies' commander in Paris, reflecting his extreme disappointment of not receiving word on the death of Josephine. There never was a reply.

In late November, Napoleon summoned Henri to his office at the palace. When he arrived, Napoleon was at an area where a new road was being constructed. However, the personal secretary said that Henri had a letter from Paris, and he was certain this was the reason for Napoleon to summon Henri. The letter was from Ange. Henri thanked the secretary and went to a private place to read his letter. *Why the privacy though*, he thought. It is evident from the repaired seal this letter has been opened and thoroughly read. There were no secrets in it anyway. Ange was too cautious.

6 Octobre 1814

My Dearest Henri,

It has only been over a month since you left and already it seems an eternity. I have tried to keep busy with the household things and staying more in the kitchen with Mimi.

Can you believe it? She says I am doing very well in my cooking. I can even bake cakes and pastries now. Who would have believed it? I still sleep in your room at night, and have not washed the bedclothes. Your pillow still has the faint scent of the one I love.

It is raining today and starting to turn cold. From what you told me of where you are, it must be paradise. Does the weather ever get cold there?

The major reason I am writing is that a week after you left, two men came to our house and asked for you. It was so strange and I could tell they knew exactly where you were and all about you. Thanks to God, Momma was here and they didn't quiz very much. You know how she can be at times. I really think they were from the royalists and just poking around. I hope this letter is not read, and if you see Poppa's seal broken, you will know.

I miss you more and more each day. Father Etty said to tell you hello and that we were foolish. Do you agree? I think your next leave will be early next year, so that will give you ample time to write me.

I love you with all of my heart and soul,

Ange

Henri was not really that surprised that he had been watched and fully believed his meeting with Dronet was not observed. He would advise Napoleon of the matter this afternoon. Everything, even the smallest details, was so important these days. They could leave nothing to chance. He returned in an hour, and Napoleon had returned.

"Monsieur, I have had a letter from Ange, and she informs me that two men were at the de Chabot house inquiring about me. Would you like to read the letter?"

"No, Henri, and I am not surprised. They watch everyone and especially one of my officers. It is good that you are wary though. I received a coded message in the form of a recipe to another member of my staff. Fevrier 26 is still the date of our departure. Why this date, I will never know, but believe me when I say it will be a famous date in history."

"I can't wait, monsieur, as I am certain you cannot."

The months flew through the holiday seasons of Christmas and the New Year. No one except a well-chosen few knew of Fevrier 26. On February 1, Napoleon summoned Henri to the palace. Adjacent to Napoleon's office was a small private study, and Henri was told to go right in. There were several others there including Generals Bertrand and Dronet. Napoleon was sitting at the head of the table and invited each to a glass of wine.

"Gentlemen, the reason for this meeting is to lay final plans for our escape from this prison paradise. Each of you will be given certain duties coordinated down to the last possible second. The ship will arrive at near midnight on the twenty-sixth of Fevrier. We will plan not to be in the harbor more than long enough to board the ship and sail at once. To do that, we must be ready. I have drawn a map of the harbor, the wharfs, and the roads leading there. Note that the new road takes a more direct route than the old one.

"I and the staff will take the new road and leave about nine. Thirty minutes later, the rest of the troops, under the command of Capitaine Devreney, will leave the barracks in small sections of two to four and meet on the road here. Capitaine, you are not to release any word of this until about an hour before leaving. We cannot take any chances of a leak of information no matter how innocent the remark may seem." He was pointing to each place in progression of the events.

"We will all meet in this warehouse where the doors will be left open to the seaside only. Everyone is to bring only his uniform and a small kit bag. Nothing large and nothing that one cannot move fast without. All sabres and objects that rattle must be secured. Capitaine, you well know the methods of stealth. Use them. The ship should put into the harbor and stay at the pier for about three to four minutes. That should be sufficient time for all to board. I am certain there will be some changes, and any questions that arise will be answered. Do any of you have any questions for me now?"

"Only one, monsieur," said Henri. "May I confide this to my faithful companion, Michael? He could be instrumental in assisting with passing the word and getting the troops ready on time."

"Oui, you may, I think Michael would be an excellent choice to assist you in a rapid spread of the word and preparedness of the men. Swear him to secrecy, though, and if word of this does get out, I will find the culprit and roast his balls over a slow fire."

"Oui, monsieur."

Napoleon laughed, and everyone followed suit as protocol dictated. Henri thought to himself, *He means it as no joke.*

Fevrier 1, 1815

Dearest Ange,

> *I want you to know that I missed you terribly during the Christmas Season. The church here was decorated in the finest they have. Most of the houses were decorated with colored ribbons. We had a fine feast at our quarters of roast mutton, potatoes, and several other vegetables. And, of course, there was plenty of wine. We had three days of no duty so headaches were many. I haven't had the chance to buy much here for you, but I will make up for it when I return. Tell Father Etty I heed his words, but some things even he cannot change. My leave will start on time this month as far as I know and I can't wait to see and hold you. This will be a short letter as I have to get this letter cleared for the supply boat leaving this afternoon.*
> *I love you and miss you,*

Henri

Fevrier 26, 1815, seemed forever arriving; and when it did, the time raced past. It seemed a normal day except for the fateful few with the knowledge of what was about to transpire. Early that afternoon, Henri and Michael went behind the stables for a last-minute survey of details. They agreed that all should appear normal until the word was given, which should happen just after the evening meal. Henri would call a short meeting in the stable, citing something to do with the horses. Henri went to the palace and had a short last-minute audience with Napoleon to see if there were any final details and to let him know that all was in readiness. Napoleon was very edgy but confident about what was about to take place.

At the evening meal, Henri asked if everyone would please come to the stable. He did want to offer some strong suggestions about the horses. He said the men had been neglecting certain duties, and he wanted to make sure they understood. The meeting would be in fifteen minutes. When all of the men were assembled, Henri stood before them.

"Men, happy faces all around. Tonight we leave Elba for France and home. I know this is a surprise, but it had to be so for security reasons. Listen carefully to my instructions. They have been very carefully calculated to the last possible minute. Each of you remain dressed in your uniform and pack one small kit shoulder bag of personal things. Nothing large. Your sabres are to be secured so that it will not rattle. Cloth tie strips have been prepared and are over there in that box. Use them. You are to leave the horses. Others will be provided in France. Even Napoleon walks tonight. It is dark tonight, but still, each of you rub lampblack on your shiny things. I will meet you back here in thirty minutes. We are going home. You are not to tell any of the cooks or anyone else. Do not hurry and please do be relaxed. Nothing suspicious now and no undue noise. Appear as normal as possible. Go now. Questions later, *s'il vous plaît*."

There were looks of surprise and shock on all the men's faces. There was the usual mumbling among them as they went back to their area. Henri hurried off to get his things.

Michael said, "Merde, I can't wait. The ladies here are nice, but not like Paris. There is one little lady at a café in town that I wish I could have just a bit more time with though."

Henri was waiting, and all of the men were earlier than the thirty minutes. He directed them in groups of three to the large trees just out of the main gate. They would take the road down to the warehouse area. The night was overcast, and a fine mist was in the air. The weather was perfect for such an adventure. The men gathered under the trees, and Henri motioned to follow him. He had been over this route many times in the past month and could almost do the course in his sleep.

They arrived at the warehouse area and went into the one with the open doors to the seaside. This was perfect as they could see the bay and no one could see them. Napoleon and the staff were there. General Bertrand had stationed himself near the door and was watching seaward for a mast or sail.

At long last, he gave the word that a shadow of ship was barely in sight through the mist. She had no running lights. Another member of the staff lit a small lantern and waved it in the doorway. The ship must have seen it, for they steered directly for the light and the warehouse. The ship had only one small sail on the main mast and lowered it as they got nearer the dock. Ropes came over the side, and the ship settled alongside.

A gangplank came onto the dock, and it took all of two minutes for the total contingent of troop to board. Men in the rigging raised the sails, and the small ship was under way. Next stop Marseille, and, God be praised, home.

35

One Hundred Days and Waterloo

It was a fast passage with a brisk southerly breeze blowing most of the night. Henri and the others were advised to try to get some sleep as the morning would bring a rapid set of events. No one really knew what to expect. Would the troops in the area be receptive to Napoleon or not? Napoleon stood alone on the high deck near the wheel most of the night, staring out toward the imminent French shoreline. He wanted to be alone and was given his peace. He reflected on what he had done with his life, the extreme events of life and doom, and most of all the words prophesied to him by Madame Mère, his mother. "Fulfill your destiny, my son. You were not created to die on this island."

The ship docked in Marseille, was met by several men, and immediately escorted into a large warehouse. In the darkness broken only by a few lanterns, Henri could see another one hundred or so uniformed men in the huge building. Saddled horses were waiting for them. There was a sparse few minutes of greetings all around. Then Napoleon said they must ride for Paris as soon as possible. They still did not know what to expect.

They moved rapidly forward as the sun was starting to appear in the eastern sky. It was a cool, clear, and crisp morning and very comfortable in the heavy uniforms. Henri could recognize the uniforms of the others now, and there were some from many regiments of his past. He recognized some, and others not. But they were all French and riding with a single purpose. They must reach Paris with all haste. All went well until about noon when they encountered a large force of about another one thousand men coming toward them.

Everyone halted, and a rider approached from the other group. Greetings were offered, and the troops asked permission to join Napoleon. Now there was a small army of approximately one thousand one hundred men. During the day, smaller groups appeared and joined the growing ranks. They stopped for the night, and Henri and others moved about through the small camps, seeing old acquaintances and reliving past experiences. All were veterans of Napoleon's wars and eager for his return to power.

The next day around noon, as they were approaching the village of Laffray, they were met by a battalion of Napoleon's old Fifth Regiment of the Line. These were the first hostile troops encountered. The troops formed up in ranks, having been given orders to stop Napoleon at all costs. The king had ordered Napoleon brought to him dead or alive, preferably in a cage like a wild beast. Napoleon told the others to halt. He rode forward to within a pistol shot of the hostile troops, dismounted, and walked forward. Everyone held their breath. Here it would end or begin anew.

Napoleon brazenly stood before them with his coat held open and shouted, "Let him that has the heart kill his emperor!"

The opposing troops withdrew their arms and cried, "Vive l'Empereur!" They formed up with the others and continued the march to Paris. Napoleon and his group, who continued to grow and look more like an army each day, were greeted at every small village and town with hospitality and welcome. At the city of Lyons, the people greeted him as their emperor and dismissed the local governor appointed by the allies. By now, the army had grown to over one hundred thousand men and included many of Napoleon's old and trusted commanders. The march slowed down now as more and more joined the ranks. Henri was amazed, and this was much more than he had expected. He saw Napoleon only once during the march to Paris, and he told Henri that he too was surprised at this unexpected allegiance. He seemed so proud to be back in his element. On Mars 20, 1815, they reclaimed Paris. The king had fled to Belgium after the allies had failed to mount any sort of opposing force.

The allied powers were not happy with Napoleon on the prowl again. They had always considered him the plague of Europe and only had consented to peace with him so as not to be invaded and occupied. Napoleon sent emissaries to each of the allied powers at once, making it vividly clear that if they accepted peace, so would he. The allies met in Vienna and declared Napoleon a brigand, further stating they did not want to give him any time to regroup and build an army.

Henri was home again and this time for good except for what plans Napoleon may have in mind. He asked Napoleon during the first week of being home about the wedding. Napoleon said to please go ahead and make plans and please do not leave him off the guest list. All the time, Napoleon was suing for peace with the allies and said he hoped to become a very old man here in Paris as the head of his country.

Henri couldn't wait to tell Ange the news that she could begin her planning at once. They studied the calendar and decided on June 24, 1815. Madame was home and was excited too. They would go to the dressmaker and have the seamstress start on Ange's wedding dress. Ange would have to pick her attendants. There was no doubt as to who Henri's best man would be. Michael said weddings made him nervous as that was just too damn close to losing his freedom, but he would agree if he could accompany the two on their wedding night. He was certain Henri may need advice.

Jean would escort Ange to Henri in the place of the general. Mimi was starting to plan the menu and said she would need help for such a large crowd. Madame informed Mimi that she only had to arrange plans with an agency who did prepare large amounts of different foods. The large hall next to Notre Dame was reserved for the wedding day. Father Etty would perform the ceremony in Notre Dame, saying there could be no other to join these two he had seen grow into such wonderful adults. The plans grew. Ange and Madame were busy most nights with lists of guests and the frightful amount of things that go into planning such an event.

Still Ange and Henri found the time for their private moments, and they spent many hours quietly talking of children and their future. These were some of the most relaxing moments of Henri's recent life. Through all of the mayhem he had endured, he was finally going to be with the one he loved most in this world. They talked about that too, and Ange agreed to the same feelings. It was a resolve, and both were at peace. Henri still had his duties every day but was home in the evenings.

But the ugly monster of separation was rearing its head once more. No time was being wasted by the allies in preparing to eliminate Napoleon once and for all. Napoleon realized this and was busy working day and night to organize his army. He hastily took measures to increase the strength and size of his army. Reserve units and local militia were activated. Old friends were requested to do whatever they could. A free France was in question. He did not reinstate conscription because he did not want the public against him.

In all, he had managed to bring three hundred thousand men to arms. This was to oppose the allies over one million strong. Word passed among the ranks that another conflict was inevitable. Henri made Ange aware of this, but she said damn to another war, she was getting married this time. The war could just wait.

Napoleon called a staff meeting on Juin 1, 1815, and told the men gathered that he would have two strategies available to him. He could mass his troops in a defensive ring around Paris and Lyons. This would leave major portions of France to be taken without resistance, and the public outcry would be immense. This would not look good in the eyes of those who now supported him. The defensive tactic may wear down the allies, but they would control the majority of France.

The second option was to attack a vastly superior force and hope to catch them by surprise. If this could happen, the French could roll over the allies and scatter their forces before they could organize a repulse. He had decided to attack and gave his plans. The allies were massed on the northern borders of France in Holland. His deadly enemy, Lord Wellington, was there and would no doubt try to coordinate a defense and then organize the eventual counterattack.

Henri, as commander of Napoleon's personal chasseur guard, was present at the meeting. He could see his wedding plans begin to slip away again as Napoleon needed to attack in the next week or so. Those at the meeting were sworn to secrecy. All present knew there were spies everywhere just thirsting for this news.

Henri hurried home that evening, wondering how in the world to tell Ange this latest in their tumultuous lives. To say she would be upset would only be a matter of words. Damn, they had waited so long; but duty, country, and emperor were calling once more.

"Mon amour, I have news that you will not like, but I must tell you. My short boss has decided to go after the allies before they invade. They will surely invade later, and then all will be lost. He is wise to do it. Whatever happens, it should not be that long."

"Oh, damn, damn, damn, and when does he plan to do this crazy thing and run off with my man again?" She started to cry. Henri reached for her and cradled her in his arms. He felt so helpless.

On the misty and overcast early morning of Juin 15, the French troops secretly massed on the northern borders and rushed at the allies with screams and yells. The objective was Charleroi, and the schedule was taking the town by that afternoon. The attack was a complete surprise, and the Prussian troops in the area were routed and fleeing from the oncoming French. Due to mud and road conditions, the French were not able to take the town, but the situation was more than satisfactory to Napoleon. The next day, the French pushed further with Napoleon ordering several brigades of cavalry and chasseurs cut off the Prussians from the main body of Wellington's army. Wellington was camped just north of Waterloo near Brussels. This was to have been the final objective in this area.

The rest of the French army marched on Quatre Bras in hopes of splitting the allied army. Communications were not good. In fact, many orders were lost or arrived late. Henri saw Napoleon twice during the day, and he was livid both times. He overheard him say that if things did not improve, the allies would regroup and attack with no mercy. The muddy conditions continued to give problems, and the artillery and troops could not move as expected. Word came that the majority of the Prussians had escaped and made it to Wellington.

In spite of all of the problems, the French scored a victory at Quatre Bras, but many of the allied troops there escaped and also joined Wellington. Henri and his chasseurs were next to Napoleon and charged with his personal safety. He could see the allied troops in the distance fleeing. They would fight another day and should not have been allowed to escape. Napoleon knew he must end it here with a quick and decisive crushing blow. His plan given to his generals was simple, hit hard and spare nothing. Henri thought, *If only Andre were here.* This would not be happening. It just would not.

There were still communication problems, and several critical orders did not arrive on time to units in the field. Henri watched from the vantage point high over the hills at Waterloo as the entire French army wheeled to the left and struck directly at the entire front lines of Wellington's troops. For a time, the allies were driven back; and then the Prussians, having reorganized, joined the skirmish to the French right flank. The entire assault ground to a halt, and then the French began to give ground, having to fight on two fronts. Henri could see in the distance more allied troops starting to join and push the French back. Then the ranks broke as cavalry units raced through and began to separate the French. Napoleon sat alone on Marengo, one of his favorite mounts, and watched in dismay as the battle began to fall apart. He motioned to Henri.

"I fear all is lost this time. We had a chance and could have won here, but for this damn mud and the lack of courage of some of my leaders. Henri, some of the damned allies are blocking our way back to France. Take your chasseurs and mount a charge to cut through. My staff and I will be right with you."

Henri drew his sabre and signaled the bugler to sound a charge. The troop wheeled and rode at a slight gallop down the hillside, through a small tree line, and struck the surprised enemy. They rode right through and were gone before many shots could be fired. Henri saw several of his men go down, but the majority got through. They regrouped and rode through the night, approaching Paris just before dawn.

"Henri, my gratitude again. This time for saving me from a sure capture on the battlefield. Go home and await my call tomorrow. There is one more mission you must do for me, my faithful friend. I know I have lost my France this time, but we will talk tomorrow."

Just as the dawn was breaking over Paris, Henri and Michael rode to the de Chabot house and put their weary animals in the stable. They stripped off their uniform jackets and washed in the trough.

"My uniform is a complete muddy mess, but I don't think I will need it much longer," said Michael.

"I agree, mon ami. I don't think either of us will need them. Now what? I wonder. We may have some of Jean's things here that could fit you. If not, we can certainly buy some. Napoleon told me to see him later, and he had another mission. What the hell now. All is lost, and he knows it, but he is always scheming."

"Oh, he probably wants us to slip through the allied lines and murder Wellington," said Michael.

"Don't joke, mon ami, he just might want that."

They went into the house, ate, and drank coffee. After a short visit with the family and the news of defeat, they collapsed and slept for the first time in several days.

36

Escape

Henri dozed, but as tired as he was, he really could not sleep soundly. In one of his moments of partial awakening, he realized something was across his chest and snuggled up to his back. The something was Ange. She had come into bed without his realizing it. He turned to face her and, as was one of his passions, looked into her peaceful and beautiful sleeping face. He remembered long ago when he first saw her napping on the sofa and she had awakened to find him staring at her. She still teased him about that. He was so embarrassed. There was so much of their sharing over the years, growing together, and now what was to happen?

Ange stirred and opened her eyes. "Henri, you are home," she said sleepily. "Is the fighting all over and you can stay home for a while?"

"The fighting is over all right, but now what happens may be known only to God. We were defeated and escaped to Paris riding through the night. I am to see Napoleon today for God knows what this time. I am sure the allies will be here within the week, and all those loyal to Napoleon will be subjected to prison or worse. I don't know what to do and will wait and see what Napoleon has in mind. Let's go downstairs and get something to eat. I am famished."

Henri dressed in his civilian clothes and looked in on Michael before going downstairs. Ange dressed and went down with him. He informed Mimi and Madame what had happened at Waterloo, their escape back to Paris, and Napoleon wanting to see him later. Mimi had sweet cakes and coffee, but of course, Ange preferred her tea.

In the early afternoon, Henri saddled his horse and rode to the palace. Napoleon's secretary announced that Henri was there. Napoleon was alone in his study and shook hands with him.

"Henri, the time is not right for you to meet the men I planned. They have been delayed until tomorrow, but that could be to our advantage. These men are from the Americas, and I hope to gain passage there. There is a strong French influence in Louisiana that would welcome us and perhaps give me a chance to reorganize. I want you and several others to go with me."

"Monsieur," Henri interrupted, "what about Ange and our plans to marry very soon? I cannot leave her again."

"I have thought of that, and could you possibly be married in the next day or so? We will be hunted men and possibly go to prison when the allies arrive."

"I must hurry off at once and see what I can do, Your Excellency."

"One more thing, Henri. I am having the carpenters prepare two 'special' chests for packing your and Ange's personal things. I cannot use them as it would be too conspicuous. They will be delivered to your home this afternoon. They will be heavier than most as the bottoms will be false and lined with gold bars. I have, on the table there, a special belt of gold coins for Ange and one for you to carry. You shall be my treasurer of sorts. Please go and see about the marriage, and, my capitaine, God bless."

Henri took the belts with the gold coins, mounted his horse, and galloped home at a fast pace. He had heard it from Napoleon that he would be hunted by the allies and possibly imprisoned. He ran into the house and explained everything to Ange, Madame, Michael, and Mimi. Madame called for one of the servants to have the carriage prepared at once. With Ange's and Henri's permission, they would go to Father Etty and inquire what could be done about their marriage. Things were moving just too fast, but they had to react before the allies arrived.

The carriage ride to St. Joseph, Father Etty's church, was full of apprehension. Madame cried and sent Ange to tears. Henri and Michael just sat and stared. Ange was clinging to Henri's hand with a tight grip of mixed emotions. They were to have been married anyway, but not like this. They deserved a formal wedding blessed by a multitude of guests, but if this was to be, maybe God had His reasons. They arrived at the church and requested to be announced to Father Etty. The old cleric said he was about somewhere, and he would have to find him.

As Father Etty entered the room, he said, "Well, this is pleasant surprise, or is it? From the looks on your faces, I see something is unsettling you all. Henri, I thought you had gone off with the Short Corporal."

Henri explained what had happened over the last several days and, in particular, their present circumstances. Madame asked if Henri and Ange might be married right away. Father would have to speak to the bishop at Notre Dame, but oui, he could not foresee any problems given the present circumstances. He would be back very soon as soon as he could locate and speak to the bishop.

He was back within an hour and asked for all to please follow him to Notre Dame. He led them into the main church and to the huge ornate altar. The bishop was there with several more priests, explaining that they all wanted to be present at such a special ceremony and to honor the daughter of a famous general and a son of France. It would be their honor.

Michael stood next to Henri, and Madame stood next to Ange as the ceremony began. Mimi stood aside as a witness. Madame and Michael stepped back. Father Etty had Henri and Ange kneel at the altar. He conducted the ceremony with emotion and appeared to nearly cry at times. This was an emotional time for them all. When he said that they were now man and wife and let no man put asunder to the joining of these two, he did break. Tears were running down his face as he gave them the final blessing. Everyone, including the bishop and the other priests, hugged the two who were crying by this time. The bishop gave them a special blessing.

"I am so sorry, my children," said Father Etty. "I had never planned for your marriage to happen in this manner. And then for the two of you to have to run for your lives. May God go with you wherever He takes you. Please stay in touch as you can."

Husband and wife rode in mostly silence back to the house. They were one now as it should have been since long ago. It was nearing darkness when they arrived; and Mimi prepared a feast of roast duck, potatoes, leek soup, and carrots. The table was set with candles and the finest china and silver.

Madame had Mimi sit with them, saying that she was family and should share this moment. She did have an announcement to make that would affect all present. She was going to move to Orléans in a small house just down from her sister and wanted Mimi to go with her. They would close this house but keep all of the servants for security reasons. Madame had not the heart to sell it nor live in it either. Jean could have it as his inheritance if that was all right with Ange. Ange responded that the house was to be Jean's and that she would have her own someday. The small talk was filled with anxiety, and no one seemed to have the appetite for the wonderful food. Their lives had changed forever in just one short afternoon.

Mimi said that workmen had delivered two trunks that afternoon and that they were upstairs in the hall. The workmen complained about the weight of an empty trunk and getting them up the stairs. As Henri and Ange went upstairs, there were the trunks. They weren't very large and just right to pack their belongings. The trunks brought reality to the fact that they would be leaving in a day or so. A great sadness came over Ange as she looked around at things familiar since her birth. Would she ever see them again?

She turned to Henri, and the two stood for some time, holding and hugging, not saying a word. Finally he said, "Mon amour, I had wanted this night to be so very special and not the hurried thing it was. I am so sorry for involving you in this."

She raised her face to his. "This is something devised by God, and who are we to question His reasons? I am so proud to be your wife no matter the circumstances. Think what tales we will have to tell our children and grandchildren."

"I agree, but you know we are talking too much, and besides, they don't need to know this night's events."

To which Ange responded, "Come, mon amour, *je veux faire l'amour avec toi.*"

She raised her lips to his and slowly parted them, and their tongues touched. He reached around her and unfastened her dress, and it slid to the floor. She stood before him in only her underclothes and said, "No fair." She tugged at his shirt. He took off his shirt, and his pants slid to the floor to join her dress.

Ange came to him and put her arms tightly around his waist. She said, "No stopping this night, mon amour, you are mine totally and completely." She took a step back and slipped off her underclothes. As she stood naked before him in the candlelight, he was nearly breathless at her beauty. She blew out the candle as he came to her. She almost glowed in the moonlight filtering in the room through the trees and window.

Their world stood still as they nestled into bed, Henri cradling her in his arms. She kissed him with a fiery passion that she had not shown before. Her tongue was like a wild thing dancing on his lips and searching for his tongue. His hands went to her breasts, and he felt her stiffen and moan slightly. Her nipples rose and hardened like berries as he took one and then the other in his mouth.

"Slow down, mon amour. We have all night and then the rest of our lives," she said in a raspy voice.

Finally she rolled on her back and pulled him to her. He entered her very slowly, heard her gasp, and felt her stiffen. He was afraid he had hurt her and drew back slightly. Then her legs moved around his waist and over his back. She pulled him to her deeper and deeper, uttering a small cry as she did so. They hesitated a moment and lay in each other's arms. Then their passion reached for the tallest mountains, the stars, and beyond to the end of the universe. The ultimate explosion seemed to melt their very brains with a searing white heat as it happened to both almost simultaneously. Henri collapsed on top of her as she went completely limp.

"Mon dieu, Henri, I never dreamed of this. I knew, but never like this. I love you. I love you. I love you." She gasped between breaths.

"Nor I, nor I," was all he could manage to gasp out.

The night slipped away, but not before several other bouts of exploration and passion. They awoke the next morning with Ange snuggled next to him. This time, both were naked and unashamed. They kissed and hugged. Ange said she could not possibly go again, and Henri said neither could he. They both laughed and got out of bed.

"If I would have but known, Henri, this may have happened much sooner." She giggled. "Never mind about Father Etty or the entire world with our lovemaking."

"Ange, did I hurt you in any way? I would never want to."

"Only for a slight moment when a girl became a woman. It was the loveliest moment of my life, Henri. I think I loved you more at that moment than ever before."

They dressed and went downstairs to a beaming Mimi. "Well, have you two worked up an appetite, or did you manage to survive on the fruits of love?" She giggled. They both turned several shades of red, and Mimi laughed all the harder.

"Don't either of you be ashamed of life, love, being happy. I am so happy for both of you. Henri, a messenger left this note for you a few minutes ago. He insisted on seeing you, but I told him you were totally indisposed with your new bride. He understood but asked that you read it early this morning."

The note had the special red wax and seal of Napoleon.

Henri,

The two men I spoke of yesterday will be at the palace just after noon. Please make this very important appointment.

Napoleon Bonaparte

"Ange, I have an appointment with Napoleon just after the noon hour. I will let you know about everything when I return."

"I will have the servants start to help pack the trunks this morning. Is there anything special that I need to consider? I will not be extravagant in my packing and take only what I will need. I do have a savings and can buy new things wherever we go."

"Please make certain you have our special box with you. There are things in there that cannot ever be replaced."

Henri rode to the palace just at noon. Napoleon was waiting in his study. This time, there were two men with him.

"Henri, I want you to meet Monsieur Jean Laffite and his brother Pierre Laffite from Louisiana in the Americas. Messieurs, this is Capitaine Henri Devreney of my personal guard. These men bear letters from supporters in the Americas. We will be most welcome, but we must depart as soon as possible to avoid the allies who will be searching for us very shortly. From last reports, they are advancing on our northern borders without any resistance. I have tried to form a resistance here, but to no avail. The local supporters will not hear of it again, fearing a frightful reprisal. And so I must run like a donkey or risk being captured again. This time, there will be no escape."

They talked for a while over glasses of wine and a plate of cakes. Jean Laffite was not a large man but seemed fit and athletic. He had a sharply pointed nose and was, evidently, not of Louisiana birth. In fact, as he did relate, his father was French, and his mother was Spanish, hence his darker-than-normal complexion. He had been partially raised on the island of Española and fled during a revolution to the Louisiana Territory. He commented that he was a privateer operating in the Gulf of Mexico and adjacent waters. Pierre was equally slim, athletic, and of darker complexion and the less outspoken of the two. He was older than Jean. One could see a definite family relationship. He explained their ship was docked at Biarritz on the Atlantic coast of France near Bayonne. They planned to sail immediately on the arrival of their guests. Napoleon explained it would be best that they go in small groups to Biarritz several days apart. Napoleon had several things to complete in Paris and would be among the last to leave.

"Monsieur," Henri said, "should not you be among the first? We can hold the allies here until you make your escape."

"No, Henri, I want you to leave as early as possible. Do you have your packing done?" Henri knew what he meant and wanted to get his treasure out as soon as possible.

"Oui, monsieur. We can leave early in the morning. How long will the ride be?"

Jean Laffite replied, "It will take all of two days. You will come with me, and I'll show you the way to the ship." It was agreed.

"By the way, messieurs, the capitaine is newly married and will be taking his new bride. I trust there will be no problems," said Napoleon.

"She will be the only lady among my scoundrels, messieurs, but I assure you not a hair of her head will be harmed lest I chop off the head of the offender," assured Laffite.

"And I as well," retorted Henri.

"Just to mention it, messieurs, Henri is the Bébé Tigre from years back in my military. He has been with me since a boy and is like a son."

Laffite was surprised. "Indeed, the real Bébé Tigre! Even in Louisiana we heard of the fable. It is a pleasure to meet a true hero of France. Little wonder you will be accompanying the emperor."

Napoleon asked the Laffites to please excuse them. He came over to Henri, put his hand on his shoulder, and said, "My son, I offer you and Ange my most sincere congratulations. I know I have challenged you with a difficult past and will probably do so again in the future. To have one as you that I can totally rely upon is the world to me. You have replaced my old friend Andre. I thank you with all of my being. Should things go afoul, do what you must to survive. Go with God."

Henri rushed home to tell the others the news. Ange had the trunks packed with clothes, personal toiletries, and a set of Madame's china and silver. Madame had insisted she take it to start her new life. Jean came home from school later that afternoon, saying they had closed the school until things finally settled down. He was surprised to hear that Ange and Henri were married and leaving so soon.

"Tomorrow! That is just too damn early. Come, you two, into the living room. You must tell me everything. Momma has told me about the house and her leaving for Orléans. This old house will never be the same. Everything and everyone I have known here will be gone. It takes people and love to make a house a home. Now it will be just a house. I am thinking seriously of selling it. If I do, Ange, rest assured I will send your part."

"Please you keep it or give part of the sales to Momma. I won't need it, and if I do, I will write. I will try to write as soon as we are settled and let you know where to find us. This is sort of scary, but I will have my Henri to protect me. It does sound like fun of sorts."

They talked into the night and devoured more wine than they should have. But what the hell. Who would ever know when they could be together again? Madame was tipsy and went to bed first, then Michael, saying tomorrow would be a challenge. He was to ride about a quarter mile to the rear of the carriage with another ten men. They would all be well armed and in civilian clothes. Ange, Henri, and Jean stayed up the longest. Jean apologized over and over in his stupor of overindulgence about his actions in their younger days. He cried and asked his new brother to please take care of his sister, saying that he loved them both.

Finally he went to sleep on the sofa, and Henri could not rouse him. Ange covered him with a shawl, and the two went to bed. They finally gave up after several fumbled attempts at lovemaking. They both laughed at the fools they were making of themselves and hoped no one was listening.

The carriage arrived just after midmorning with Jean and Pierre Laffite. There were many tearful goodbyes. The entire house staff was there with Mimi, Jean, and Madame to see them off. Ange promised to write and tell them all about their new world. Jean hugged Henri and Ange and again charged Henri with the safety of his sister. The carriage was loaded, and the driver slapped the reins on the horses. Ange looked back at her home until they rounded the corner, and it disappeared from view. Would she ever see it again?

Jean Laffite was the epitome of a gentleman. When he discovered who Ange was and knowing of Henri, he said he was among royalty. As they talked, he related to his trade. When Ange inquired what a privateer meant, he explained. She replied, "Why, that is almost like a pirate." Jean laughed and said maybe so, but the pay was excellent. Pierre dozed most of the first day. Jean explained there had been considerable wine, women, and song the previous night; and Pierre was a fool for each or all at one time as would suit his fancy. Henri and Ange were a hive of questions about the Americas and Louisiana and kept up a constant stream of questions to Laffite. He patiently answered each one and seemed to enjoy sharing his world with these two eager listeners. He explained they would put into port at Barataria, which was where his headquarters were in the vast marshes of southern Louisiana. From there they would go to New Orleans upriver. He commented on the weather, living conditions, and many other items of interest in the area.

They stopped at a small inn and had a hasty lunch with mugs of coffee and tea. The horses would not be changed here but would be in the morning. While there, Michael and the others rode up. Henri had a few brief words with Michael. It was confirmed they were not being followed, and Michael had seen no signs or concern. Still they would have to be very careful and take no chances.

Napoleon had warned Henri not to tell anyone about the gold, and he meant no one other than Ange. If anyone suspected they were conveying such a treasure, they were certain to be relieved of it. It was expected that Napoleon would carry such with him in a few days. Ange asked Henri if she could maybe relieve herself of this damn belt of gold coins. It was uncomfortable and heavy. She giggled and said that it made her feel pregnant. Henri's belt bothered him too but knew they must bear this until they arrived at the ship.

After a short stop for an evening meal and a brief chat again with Michael, they rode through the night. Henri slept fitfully with Ange in his arms. She seemed at peace, and Henri thought she could probably sleep standing up. He could hear her deep breathing and knew she was sleeping soundly. Just after midnight, they stopped at another inn just on the other side of a sleeping town. There was a lit lantern on the front gate, and they could hear noises in the small courtyard. There was a semblance of a late night party going on, but the driver did manage to have the horses changed. Michael said they would not change horses here as theirs did not seem that tired. They were still safe as far as he could see to their rear.

The Laffites slept soundly through most of the night and only started to stir with the dawn breaking in the east. Henri watched the lovely French sunrise and wondered at the colors of pink, yellow, purple, and blue giving way to the eternal sun. *How many times in history had this occurred,* he thought to himself. *Probably millions upon millions.* Ange stirred in his arms, lifted her face, and smiled up at him in a way as only she could. He thought again how fortunate he was and hoped to keep her from all harm and distress. And what of this? They soon stopped for a welcome morning meal and several mugs of steaming coffee. They walked for a few minutes, relieved themselves, and were gone again in a short time.

Toward noon, Henri thought he could smell the ocean carried on the breeze from the west. Jean said it was indeed the ocean, and he could not wait to get back on his ship. Late evening saw the lights of Bayonne and knew they would be at Biarritz in another hour. A very weary group finally crawled out of the damnable carriage at the dock.

Henri noted that the low black-hulled ship had three masts and lights on in the rear cabin area. She looked like some dark wild beast straining at her tethers for freedom. The watchman greeted the Laffites. Jean told him to roust some of the crew and help with the baggage of his guests. There was a tiny private cabin near the rear of the vessel for Henri and Ange. Two men put the trunks in the cabin. Jean said this would be their home for several weeks. He would have their meals served in here or in his cabin as they desired. They would wait here for Napoleon. Henri bolted the door and guided a worn-out Ange to the small bed. They did not remember going to sleep aided by the rocking of the boat.

Morning found the sleeping Michael and the remainder of his group sprawled on the deck covered by their greatcoats. They would stay until Napoleon arrived and then go back to a very strange France. During the day, Michael asked Henri if he could make the journey to the Americas with him. Without Napoleon and the military, there was nothing left here for him. It was all he had ever known, and he certainly did not want to go home to a peasant lifestyle.

Henri asked Laffite about the possibility of Michael going with them. He was told that passage was paid only for Napoleon and those chosen by him. There was precious little room, but he would take it into consideration. Maybe Michael could work off his passage. Henri told Laffite that he had a small savings and would be happy to pay Michael's way. A deal was struck with Henri and Laffite agreeing that no one else should know. Hell, they all would probably want to go.

They waited for another five days. Henri stayed with Ange most of the time during the day, talking of what to possibly expect, their future children, and the multitude of things those in love and first married find to talk about. Most topics were dreams, but what else is life except hope and dreams. They were so perfect for each other. Henri knew he would never tire of this lovely God-given creature. In the evenings after dark, they could go on deck to fresh air and enjoy the smell of the sea and cool night breezes. During the day, they may be seen and recognized by spies who watched everywhere. France was certain to be evacuated by those who could afford passage as the news of Waterloo spread throughout France.

On the fifth day in the late evening, a messenger came and asked for Henri. He was informed that Napoleon had waited until it was too late and had been captured by the allies. This messenger had been sent by Jean to warn Henri and Ange that allied agents had been to the house inquiring about Henri and where he might be found. It was dangerous to return. They must sail at once and without Napoleon. Henri informed Laffite of Napoleon's capture and the news that he was a hunted man.

"Ha! Welcome to the association of the hunted," said Laffite. "I have looked down that gun barrel as well." He agreed they must sail at once and avoid any British patrol ships that may sail in at any time. He yelled an order to the first mate, and men began crawling in the rigging and loosening the sails. Michael could go free of charges now. Napoleon and several others would not be coming. Henri went below and informed Ange the news. They could sense movements of the vessel as she came alive.

They went up on deck just in time to see the last ropes slip over the side and fall back to the dock. The ship started to move like a live thing set free of its snare. Michael came over and without a word slipped his arm around Henri's waist. The three stood in arm-locked silence and watched as the lights of the city and their France disappeared bit by agonizing bit into the darkness of the vast sea.